BLACK AS HE'S PAINTED
LAST DITCH
GRAVE MISTAKE

Dame Ngaio Marsh was born in New Zealand in 1895 and died in February 1982. She wrote over 30 detective novels and many of her stories have theatrical settings, for Ngaio Marsh's real passion was the theatre. Both actress and producer, she almost single-handedly revived the New Zealand public's interest in the theatre. It was for this work that she received what she called her 'damery' in 1966.

'The finest writer in the English language of the pure, classical puzzle whodunit. Among the crime queens, Ngaio Marsh stands out as an Empress.'   *The Sun*

'Ngaio Marsh transforms the detective story from a mere puzzle into a novel.'   *Daily Express*

'Her work is as nearly flawless as makes no odds. Character, plot, wit, good writing, and sound technique.'   *Sunday Times*

'She writes better than Christie!'   *New York Times*

'Brilliantly readable . . . first class detection.'   *Observer*

'Still, quite simply, the greatest exponent of the classical English detective story.'   *Daily Telegraph*

'Read just one of Ngaio Marsh's novels and you've got to read them all...'   *Daily Mail*

NGAIO MARSH

Black As He's Painted

Last Ditch

Grave Mistake

AND

Evil Liver

HARPER

HARPER

an Imprint of HarperCollins*Publishers*
77-85 Fulham Palace Road
Hammersmith, London W6 8JB
www.harpercollins.co.uk

This omnibus edition 2009
1

Black As He's Painted first published in Great Britain by Collins 1974
Last Ditch first published in Great Britain by Collins 1977
Grave Mistake first published in Great Britain by Collins 1978
Evil Liver first published in Great Britain in *Death on the Air
and Other Stories* by HarperCollins*Publishers* 1995

Ngaio Marsh asserts the moral right to
be identified as the author of these works

ISBN 978 0 00 732878 9
Printed and bound in Great Britain by
Clays Ltd, St Ives plc

Mixed Sources
Product group from well-managed
forests and other controlled sources
www.fsc.org Cert no. SW-COC-1806
© 1996 Forest Stewardship Council

FSC is a non-profit international organisation established to promote the
responsible management of the world's forests. Products carrying the FSC
label are independently certified to assure consumers that they come
from forests that are managed to meet the social, economic and
ecological needs of present and future generations.

Find out more about HarperCollins and the environment at
www.harpercollins.co.uk/green

CONTENTS

Black As He's Painted

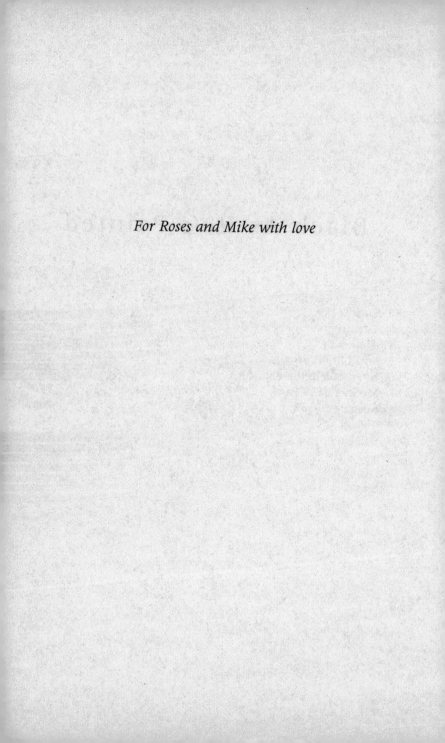

For Roses and Mike with love

Contents

Cast of Characters

Mr Samuel Whipplestone	*Foreign Office (retired)*
Lucy Lockett	*A cat*
The Ambassador in London for Ng'ombwana	
A Lady	
A Young Gentleman	*Of Messrs Able & Virtue*
A Youth	*Land & Estate Agents*
Chubb	*House Servant*
Mrs Chubb	*His wife*
A Veterinary Surgeon	
Mr Sheridan	*No.1a Capricorn Walk (basement flat)*
His Excellency	*The Boomer, President of Ng'ombwana*
Bartholomew Opala, CBE	
An ADC	
Mr and Mrs Pirelli	*Of the Napoli, shop-keepers*
Colonel Cockburn-Montfort	*Late of the Ng'ombwanan Army (retired)*
Mrs Cockburn-Montfort	*His wife*
Kenneth Sanskrit	*Late of Ng'ombwana. Merchant*
Xenoclea Sanskrit	*His sister. Of the Piggie Pottery, Capricorn Mews, SW3*
A mlinzi	*Spear Carrier to The Boomer*
Sir George Alleyn, KCMG, etc. etc.	
Superintendent Roderick Alleyn	*CID*
Troy Alleyn	*Painter. His wife*
Inspector Fox	*CID*
Superintendent Gibson	*Special Branch, CID*
Jacks	*A talented sergeant*
Detective-Sergeant Bailey	*A finger-print expert*
Detective-Sergeant Thompson	*A photographer*
Sundry police, Ng'ombwanan servants and frequenters of the Capricorns, SW3	

The author's warmest thanks are due to
Sir Alister McIntosh, KCMG and
P. J. Humphries, Esq., for their very kind advice
on matters ambassadorial and linguistic.

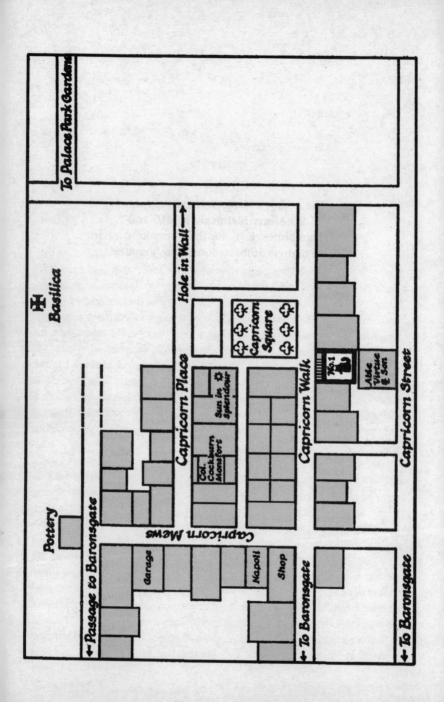

CHAPTER 1

Mr Whipplestone

The year was at the spring and the day at the morn and God may have been in his Heaven but as far as Mr Samuel Whipplestone was concerned the evidence was negligible. He was, in a dull, muddled sort of way, miserable. He had become possessed, with valedictory accompaniments, of two solid silver Georgian gravy-boats. He had taken his leave of Her Majesty's Foreign Service in the manner to which his colleagues were accustomed. He had even prepared himself for the non-necessity of getting up at 7.30, bathing, shaving, breakfasting at 8.00 – but there is no need to prolong the Podsnappian recital. In a word he had fancied himself tuned in to retirement and now realized that he was in no such condition. He was a man without propulsion. He had no object in life. He was finished.

By ten o'clock he found himself unable to endure the complacent familiarity of his 'service' flat. It was in fact at that hour being 'serviced', a ritual which normally he avoided and now hindered by his presence.

He was astounded to find that for twenty years he had inhabited dull, oppressive, dark and uncomely premises. Deeply shaken by this abrupt discovery, he went out into the London spring.

A ten-minute walk across the Park hardly raised his spirits. He avoided the great water-shed of traffic under the quadriga, saw some inappropriately attired equestrians, passed a concourse of scarlet and yellow tulips, left the Park under the expanded nostrils of Epstein's liberated elementals and made his way into Baronsgate.

As he entered that flowing cacophony of changing gears and revving engines, it occurred to him that he himself must now get

into bottom gear and stay there, until he was parked in some sub-
fuse lay-by to await – and here the simile became insufferable – a
final to wing-off. His predicament was none the better for being
commonplace. He walked for a quarter of an hour.

From Baronsgate the western entry into the Capricorns is by an
arched passage too low overhead to admit any but pedestrian traffic.
It leads into Capricorn Mews and, further along at right angles to the
Mews, Capricorn Place. He had passed by it over and over again and
would have done so now if it hadn't been for a small, thin cat.

This animal flashed out from under the traffic and shot past him
into the passageway. It disappeared at the far end. He heard a scream
of tyres and of a living creature.

This sort of thing upset Mr Whipplestone. He disliked this sort of
thing intensely. He would have greatly preferred to remove himself
as quickly as possible from the scene and put it out of his mind.
What he did, however, was to hurry through the passageway into
Capricorn Mews.

The vehicle, a delivery van of sorts, was disappearing into
Capricorn Place. A group of three youths outside a garage stared at
the cat which lay like a blot of ink on the pavement.

One of them walked over to it.

'Had it,' he said.

'Poor pussy!' said one of the others and they laughed objection-
ably.

The first youth moved his foot as if to turn the cat over.
Astonishingly and dreadfully it scrabbled with its hind legs. He
exclaimed, stooped down and extended his hand.

It was on its feet. It staggered and then bolted. Towards Mr
Whipplestone who had come to a halt. He supposed it to be con-
cussed, or driven frantic by pain or fear. In a flash it gave a great
spring and was on Mr Whipplestone's chest, clinging with its small
claws and – incredibly – purring. He had been told that a dying cat
will sometimes purr. It had blue eyes. The tip of its tail for about two
inches was snow white but the rest of its person was perfectly black.
He had no particular antipathy to cats.

He carried an umbrella in his right hand but with his left arm he
performed a startled reflex gesture. He sheltered the cat. It was
shockingly thin, but warm and tremulous.

'One of 'er nine lives gawn for a burton,' said the youth. He and his friends guffawed themselves into the garage.

'Drat,' said Mr Whipplestone, who long ago had thought it amusing to use spinsterish expletives.

With some difficulty he hooked his umbrella over his left arm and with his right hand inserted his eyeglass and then explord the cat's person. It increased its purrs, interrupting them with a faint mew when he touched its shoulder. What was to be done with it?

Obviously, nothing in particular. It was not badly injured, presumably it lived in the neighbourhood and one had always understood its species to have a phenomenal homing instinct. It thrust its nut-like head under Mr Whipplestone's jacket and into his waistcoat. It palpated his chest with its paws. He had quite a business detaching it.

He set it down on the pavement. 'Go home,' he said. It stared up at him and went through the motion of mewing, opening its mouth and showing its pink tongue but giving no sound. 'No,' he said, 'go home!' It was making little preparatory movements of its haunches as if it was about to spring again.

He turned his back on it and walked quickly down Capricorn Mews. He almost ran.

It is a quiet little street, cobbled and very secluded. It accommodates three garages, a packing agency, two dozen or so small mid-Victorian houses, a minute bistro and four shops. As he approached one of these, a flower shop, he could see reflected in its side windows Capricorn Mews with himself walking towards him. And behind him, trotting in a determined manner, the little cat. It was mewing.

He was extremely put out and had begun to entertain a confused notion of telephoning the RSPCA when a van erupted from a garage immediately behind him. It passed him and when it had gone the cat had disappeared: frightened, Mr Whipplestone supposed, by the noise.

Beyond the flower shop and on the opposite side of the Mews was the corner of Capricorn Place, leading off to the left. Mr Whipplestone, deeply ruffled, turned into it.

A pleasing street: narrow, orderly, sunny, with a view, to the left, of tree-tops and the dome of the Baronsgate Basilica. Iron railings and behind them small well-kept Georgian and Victorian houses.

Spring flowers in window-boxes. From somewhere or another the smell of freshly brewed coffee.

Cleaning ladies attacked steps and door-knockers. Household ladies were abroad with shopping baskets. A man of Mr Whipplestone's own age who reeked of the army and was of an empurpled complexion emerged from one of the houses. A perambulator with a self-important baby and an escort of a pedestrian six-year-old, a female propellant and a large dog, headed with a purposeful air towards the Park. The postman was going his rounds.

In London there are still, however precarious their state, many little streets of the character of the Capricorns. They are upper-middle-class streets and therefore, Mr Whipplestone had been given to understand, despicable. Being of that class himself, he did not take this view. He found the Capricorns uneventful, certainly, but neither tiresomely quaint nor picturesque nor smug: pleasing rather, and possessed of a quality which he could only think of as 'sparkling'. Ahead of him was a pub, the Sun in Splendour. It had an honest untarted-look about it and stood at the point where the Place leads into Capricorn Square: the usual railed enclosure of plane trees, grass and a bench or two, well-kept. He turned to the right down one side of it, making for Capricorn Walk.

Moving towards him at a stately pace came a stout, superbly dressed coal-black gentleman leading a white Afghan hound with a scarlet collar and leash.

'My dear Ambassador!' Mr Whipplestone exclaimed. 'How very pleasant!'

'Mr Whipplestone!' resonated the Ambassador for Ng'ombwana. 'I am delighted to see you. You live in these parts?'

'No, no: a morning stroll. I'm – I'm a free man now, your Excellency.'

'Of course. I had heard. You will be greatly missed.'

'I doubt it. Your Embassy – I had forgotten for the moment – is quite close by, isn't it?'

'In Palace Park Gardens. I too enjoy a morning stroll with Ahman. We are not, alas, unattended.' He waved his gold-mounted stick in the direction of a large person looking anonymously at a plane tree.

'Alas!' Mr Whipplestone agreed. 'The penalty of distinction,' he added neatly, and patted the Afghan.

'You are kind enough to say so.'

Mr Whipplestone's highly specialized work in the Foreign Service had been advanced by a happy manner with Foreign, and particularly with African, plenipotentiaries. 'I hope I may congratulate your Excellency,' he said and broke into his professional style of verbless exclamation. 'The increased rapprochement! The new Treaty! Masterly achievements!'

'Achievements – entirely – of our great President, Mr Whipplestone.'

'Indeed, yes. Everyone is delighted about the forthcoming visit. An auspicious occasion.'

'As you say. Immensely significant.' The Ambassador waited for a moment and then slightly reduced the volume of his superb voice. 'Not,' he said, 'without its anxieties, however. As you know, our great President does not welcome – ' he again waved his stick at his bodyguard – 'that sort of attention.' A sigh escaped him. 'He is to stay with us,' he said.

'Quite.'

'The responsibility!' sighed the Ambassador. He broke off and offered his hand. 'You will be at the reception, of course,' he said. 'We must meet more often! I shall see that something is arranged. Au revoir, Mr Whipplestone.'

They parted. Mr Whipplestone walked on, passing and tactfully ignoring the escort.

Facing him at the point where the Walk becomes the north-east border of the Square was a small house between two large ones. It was painted white with a glossy black front door and consisted of an attic, two floors and a basement. The first-floor windows opened on a pair of miniature balconies, the ground-floor ones were bowed. He was struck by the arrangement of the window-boxes. Instead of the predictable daffodil one saw formal green swags that might have enriched a della Robbia relief. They were growing vines of some sort which swung between the pots where they rooted and were cunningly trimmed so that they swelled at the lowest point of the arc and symmetrically tapered to either end.

Some workmen with ladders were putting up a sign.

He had begun to feel less depressed. Persons who do not live there will talk about 'the London feeling'. They will tell you that as they walk down a London street they can be abruptly made happy, up-lifted in spirit, exhilarated. Mr Whipplestone had always taken a somewhat incredulous view of these transports but he had to admit that on this occasion he was undoubtedly visited by a liberated sen-sation. He had a singular notion that the little house had induced this reaction. No. 1, as he now saw, Capricorn Walk.

He approached the house. It was touched on its chimneys and the eastern slope of its roof by sunshine. 'Facing the right way,' thought Mr Whipplestone. 'In the winter it'll get all the sun there is, I dare say.' His own flat faced north.

A postman came whistling down the Walk as Mr Whipplestone crossed it. He mounted the steps of No. 1, clapped something through the brass flap and came down so briskly that they nearly collided.

'Whoops-a-daisy,' said the postman. 'Too eager, that's my trouble. Lovely morning, though, innit?'

'Yes,' said Mr Whipplestone, judiciously conceding the point. 'It is. Are the present occupants – ' he hesitated.

'Gawn. Out last week,' said the postman. 'But I'm not to know, am I? People ought to make arrangements, din' they, sir?' He went off, whistling.

The workmen came down their ladders and prepared to make off. They had erected a sign.

FOR SALE

All enquiries to

Able, Virtue & Sons

17 Capricorn Street, SW7

II

The Street is the most 'important' of the Capricorns. It is wider and busier than the rest. It runs parallel to the Walk and in fact Messrs Able and Virtue's premises lie exactly back to back with the little house at No. 1.

'*Good* morning,' said the roundabout lady at the desk on the left-hand side. '*Can* I help you?' she pleaded brightly.

Mr Whipplestone pulled out the most non-committal stop in his FO organ and tempered its chill with a touch of whimsy.

'You may satisfy my idle curiosity if you will be so good,' he said. 'Ah – concerning No. 1, Capricorn Walk.'

'No. 1, the Walk?' repeated the lady. 'Yes. Our notice, ackshally, has only just gone up. For Sale with stipulations regarding the basement. I'm not quite sure – ' she looked across at the young man with a pre-Raphaelite hair-do behind the right-hand desk. He was contemplating his fingernails and listening to his telephone. 'What *is* it about the basement, of No. 1,' he rattled into it, 'is at present occupied as a pied – '

He clapped a languid hand over the receiver: 'Ay'm coping,' he said and unstopped the receiver. 'The basement of No. 1,' he rattled into it, 'is at present occupied as a pied-à-terre by the owner. He wishes to retain occupancy. The Suggested Arrangement is that total ownership pass to the purchaser and that he, the vendor, become the tenant of the basement at an agreed rent for a specified period.' He listened for a considerable interval. 'No,' he said, 'ay'm afraid it's a firm stipulation. Quate. Quate. Theng you, madam. Good morning.'

'That,' said the lady, offering it to Mr Whipplestone, 'is the situation.'

Mr Whipplestone, conscious of a lightness in his head, said: 'And the price?' He used the voice in which he had been wont to say: 'This should have been dealt with at a lower level.'

'Was it thirty-nine?' the lady asked her colleague. 'Thirty-eight.'

'Thirty-eight thousand,' she relayed to Mr Whipplestone, who caught back his breath in a civilized little hiss.

'Indeed?' he said. 'You amaze me,'

'It's a Desirable District,' she replied indifferently. 'Properties are at a premium in the Capricorns.' She picked up a document and glanced at it. Mr Whipplestone was nettled.

'And the rooms?' he asked sharply. 'How many? Excluding, for the moment, the basement.'

The lady and the pre-Raphaelite young gentleman became more attentive. They began to speak in unison and begged each other's pardon.

'Six,' gabbled the lady, 'in all. Excluding kitchen and Usual Offices. Floor-to-floor carpets and drapes included in purchase price. *And* the Usual Fitments: fridge, range, etcetera. Large recep' with adjacent dining-room, ground floor. Master bedroom and bathroom with toilet, first floor. Two rooms with shower and toilet, second floor. Late tenant used these as flat for married couple.'

'Oh?' said Mr Whipplestone, concealing the emotional disturbance that seemed to be lodged under his diaphragm. 'A married couple? You mean?'

'Did for him,' said the lady.

'I beg your pardon?'

'Serviced him. Cook and houseman. There was an Arrangement by which they also cleaned the basement flat.'

The young man threw in: 'Which it is hoped will continue. They are Strongly Recommended to purchaser with Arrangement to be arrived at for continued weekly servicing of basement. No obligation, of course.'

'Of course not.' Mr Whipplestone gave a small dry cough. 'I should like to see it,' he said.

'Certainly,' said the lady crisply. 'When would you – ?'

'Now, if you please.

'I *think* that would suit. If you'll just wait while I – ' She used her telephone. Mr Whipplestone bumped into a sudden qualm of near-panic. 'I am beside myself,' he thought. 'It's that wretched cat.' He pulled himself together. After all he was committed to nothing. An impulse, a mere whim induced, he dared say, by unaccustomed idleness. What of it?'

The lady was looking at him. Perhaps she had spoken to him.

'I beg your pardon,' said Mr Whipplestone.

She decided he was hard-of-hearing. 'The house,' she articulated pedantically, 'is open to view. The late tenants have vacated the premises. The married couple leave at the end of the week. The owner is at home in the basement flat. Mr Sheridan,' she shouted. 'That's the vendor's name: Sheridan.'

'Thank you.'

'Mervyn!' cried the lady, summoning up a wan and uncertain youth from the back office. 'No. 1, the Walk. Gentleman to view.' She produced keys and smiled definitively upon Mr Whipplestone. 'It's a Quality Residence,' she said. 'I'm sure you'll think so.'

The youth attended him with a defeated air round the corner to No. 1, Capricorn Walk.

'Thirty-eight thousand pounds!' Mr Whipplestone inwardly expostulated. 'Good God, it's outrageous!'

The Walk had turned further into the sun, which now sparkled on No. 1's brass door-knocker and letter-box, Mr Whipplestone, waiting on the recently scrubbed steps, looked down into the area. It had been really very ingeniously converted, he was obliged to concede, into a ridiculous little garden with everything on a modest scale.

'Pseudo-Japanese,' he thought in a panic-stricken attempt to discredit it.

'Who looks after *that*?' he tossed at the youth. 'The basement?'

'Yar,' said the youth.

('He hadn't the faintest idea,' thought Mr Whipplestone.)

The youth had opened the front door and now stood back for Mr Whipplestone to enter.

The little hall and stairway were carpeted in cherry red, the glossy walls were an agreeable oyster-white. This scheme was continued in a quite sizeable drawing-room. The two bow windows curtained in red and white stripes were large and the whole interior remarkably light for a London room. For some twenty years he had vaguely regretted the murkiness of his service flat.

Without warning he was overtaken by an experience that a less sophisticated man might have been tempted to call hallucinatory. He saw, with the utmost clarity, his own possessions occupying this light-hearted room. The Chippendale wall-desk, the crimson sofa with its companion table, the big red glass goblet, the Agatha Troy landscape, the late Georgian bookcase: all were harmoniously accommodated. When the youth opened double-doors into a small dining-room, Mr Whipplestone saw at a glance that his chairs were of precisely the right size and character.

He dismissed these visions. 'The partition folds back,' he said with a brave show of indifference, 'to form one room, I suppose?'

'Yar,' said the youth and folded it back. He opened red and white striped curtains in the rear wall and revealed a courtyard and tub-garden.

'Lose the sun,' Mr Whipplestone sneered, keeping his head, 'Get none in the winter.'

It was, however, receiving its full quota now.

'Damp,' persisted Mr Whipplestone defiantly. 'Extra expense. Have to be kept up.' And he thought: 'I'd do better to hold my tongue.'

The kitchen was on the left of the dining-room. It was a modernized affair with a service hatch. 'Cramped!' Mr Whipplestone thought of saying but his heart was not in it.

The stairs were steep which ought to have been a comfort. Awkward for trays and luggage and suppose one died how would they get one out of it? He said nothing.

The view from the master-bedroom through the french windows embraced in its middle distance the Square with the Sun in Splendour on the left and – more distantly on the right – the dome of the Basilica. In the foreground was the Walk with foreshortened views of pedestrians, parked cars and an intermittent passage of traffic. He opened a french window. They were ringing the bells in the Basilica. Twelve o'clock. Some service or another, he supposed. But you couldn't say the house was noisy.

The bells stopped. Somewhere, out of sight, a voice was raised in a reiterated, rhythmical shout. He couldn't distinguish the sense of it but it came nearer. He went out on one of the two little balconies.

'Air-eye-awf,' shouted the voice, and round the far corner of the Square came a horse-drawn cart, nodding with tulips and led by a red-faced man. He passed No. 1 and looked up.

'Any time. All fresh,' he bawled directly at Mr Whipplestone who hastily withdrew.

(His big red glass goblet in the bow window, filled with tulips.)

Mr Whipplestone was a man who did not indulge in histrionics but under the lash of whatever madness now possessed him he did, as he made to leave the window, flap the air with two dismissive palms. The gesture brought him face to face with a couple, man and woman.

'I beg your pardon,' they all said and the small man added. 'Sorry, sir. We just heard the window open and thought we'd better see.' He glanced at the youth. 'Order to view?' he asked.

'Yar.'

'You,' said Mr Whipplestone, dead against his will, 'must be the – the upstairs – ah – the – '

'That's right, sir,' said the man. His wife smiled and made a slight bob. They were rather alike, being round-faced, apple-cheeked and blue-eyed and were aged, he thought, about forty-five.

'You are – I understand – ah – still – ah – '

'We've stayed on to set things to rights, sir, Mr Sheridan's kindly letting us remain until the end of the week. Gives us a chance to find another place, sir, if we're not wanted here.'

'I understand you would be – ah – '

'Available, sir?' they both said quickly and the man added, 'We'd be glad to stay on if the conditions suited. We've been here with the outgoing tenant six years, sir, and very happy with it. Name of Chubb, sir, references on request and the owner, Mr Sheridan, below, would speak for us.'

'Quite, quite quite!' said Mr Whipplestone in a tearing hurry. 'I – ah – I've come to no conclusion. On the contrary. Idle curiosity, really. However. In the event – the remote event of my – be very glad – but so far – nothing decided.'

'Yes, sir, of course. If you'd care to see upstairs, sir?'

'What!' shouted Mr Whipplestone as if they'd fired a gun at him. 'Oh. Thank you. Might as well, perhaps. Yes.'

'Excuse me, sir. I'll just close the window.'

Mr Whipplestone stood aside. The man laid his hand on the french window. It was a brisk movement but it stopped as abruptly as if a moving film had turned into a still. The hand was motionless, the gaze was fixed, the mouth shut like a trap.

Mr Whipplestone was startled. He looked down into the street and there, returning from his constitutional and attended by his dog and his bodyguard, was the Ambassador for Ng'ombwana. It was at him that the man, Chubb, stared. Something impelled Mr Whipplestone to look at the woman. She had come close and she too, over her husband's shoulder, stared at the Ambassador.

The next moment the figures animated. The window was shut and fastened and Chubb turned to Mr Whipplestone with a serviceable smile.

'Shall I show the way, sir?' asked Chubb.

The upstairs flat was neat, clean and decent. The little parlour was a perfectly respectable and rather colourless room, except perhaps for an enlarged photograph of a round-faced girl of about sixteen which attracted attention on account of its being festooned in black ribbon and flanked on the table beneath it by two vases of dyed *immortelles*. Some kind of china medallion hung from the bottom

edge of the frame. Another enlarged photograph of Chubb in uniform and Mrs Chubb in bridal array, hung on the wall.

All the appointments on this floor, it transpired, were the property of the Chubbs. Mr Whipplestone was conscious that they watched
him anxiously. Mrs Chubb said: 'It's home to us. We're settled like.
It's such a nice part, the Capricorns.' For an unnerving moment he
thought she was going to cry.

He left the Chubbs precipitately, followed by the youth. It was a
struggle not to re-enter the drawing-room but he triumphed and
shot out of the front door to be immediately involved in another
confrontation.

'Good morning,' said a man on the area steps. 'You've been looking at my house, I think? My name is Sheridan.'

There was nothing remarkable about him at first sight, unless it
was his almost total baldness and his extreme pallor. He was of middle height, unexceptionally dressed and well-spoken. His hair, when
he had had it, must have been dark since his eyes and brows and the
wires on the backs of his pale hands were black. Mr Whipplestone
had a faint, fleeting and oddly uneasy impression of having seen him
before. He came up the area steps and through the gate and faced
Mr Whipplestone who, in politeness, couldn't do anything but stop
where he was.

'Good morning,' Mr Whipplestone said. 'I just happened to be
passing. An impulse.'

'One gets them,' said Mr Sheridan, 'in the spring.' He spoke with
a slight lisp.

'So I understand,' said Mr Whipplestone, not stuffily but in a
definitive tone. He made a slight move.

'Did you approve?' asked Mr Sheridan casually.

'Oh, charming, charming,' Mr Whipplestone said, lightly dismissing it.

'Good. So glad. Good morning, Chubb, can I have a word with
you?' said Sheridan.

Mr Whipplestone escaped. The wan youth followed him to the
corner. Mr Whipplestone was about to dismiss him and continue
alone towards Baronsgate. He turned back to thank the youth and
there was the house, in full sunlight now, with its evergreen swags
and its absurd garden. Without a word he wheeled left and left again

and reached Able, Virtue & Sons three yards in advance of his escort. He walked straight in and laid his card before the plump lady.

'I should like the first refusal,' he said.

From that moment it was a foregone conclusion. He didn't lose his head. He made sensible enquiries and took proper steps about the lease and the plumbing and the state of repair. He consulted his man of business, his bank manager and his solicitor. It is questionable whether, if any of these experts had advised against the move, he would have paid the smallest attention but they did not and, to his own continuing astonishment, at the end of a fortnight Mr Whipplestone moved in.

He wrote cosily to his married sister in Devonshire: ' – you may be surprised to hear of the change. Don't expect anything spectacular, it's a quiet little backwater full of old fogies like me. Nothing in the way of excitement or "happenings" or violence or beastly demonstrations. It suits me. At my age one prefers the uneventful life and that,' he ended, 'is what I expect to enjoy at No. 1, Capricorn Walk.'

Prophecy was not Mr Whipplestone's strong point.

III

'That's all jolly fine,' said Superintendent Alleyn. 'What's the Special Branch think it's doing? Sitting on its fat bottom waving Ng'ombwanan flags?'

'What did he *say*, exactly?' asked Mr Fox. He referred to their Assistant Commissioner.

'Oh, *you* know!' said Alleyn. 'Charm and sweet reason were the wastewords of his ween.'

'What's a ween, Mr Alleyn?'

'I've not the remotest idea. It's a quotation. And don't ask me from where.'

'I only wondered,' said Mr Fox mildly.

'I don't even know,' Alleyn continued moodily, 'how it's spelt. Or what it means, if it comes to that.'

'If it's Scotch it'll be with an h, won't it? Meaning: "few". Wheen.'

'Which doesn't make sense. Or does it? Perhaps it should be "weird" but that's something one drees. Now *you're* upsetting me, Br'er Fox.'

'To get back to the AC, then?'

'However reluctantly: to get back to him. It's all about this visit, of course.'

'The Ng'ombwanan President?'

'He. The thing is, Br'er Fox, I know him. And the AC knows I know him. We were at school together in the same house: Davidson's. Same study, for a year. Nice creature, he was. Not everybody's cup of tea but I liked him. We got on like houses on fire.'

'Don't tell me,' said Fox. 'The AC wants you to recall old times?'

'I do tell you precisely that. He's dreamed up the idea of a meeting – casual-cum-official. He wants me to put it to the President that unless he conforms to whatever procedure the Special Branch sees fit to lay on, he may very well get himself bumped off and in any case will cause acute anxiety, embarrassment and trouble at all levels from the Monarch down. And I'm to put this, if you please, tactfully. They don't want umbrage to be taken, followed by a highly publicized flounce-out. He's as touchy as a sea-anemone.'

'Is he jibbing, then? About routine precautions?'

'He was always a pig-headed ass. We used to say that if you wanted the old Boomer to do anything you only had to tell him not to. And he's one of those sickening people without fear. And hellish haughty with it. Yes, he's jibbing. He doesn't want protection. He wants to do a Haroun el Raschid and bum round London on his own looking as inconspicuous as a coal box in paradise.'

'Well,' said Mr Fox judiciously, 'that's a very silly way to go on. He's a number one assassination risk, that gentleman.'

'He's a bloody nuisance. You're right, of course. Ever since he pushed his new industrial legislation through he's been a sitting target for the lunatic fringe. Damn it all, Br'er Fox, only the other day, when he elected to make a highly publicized call at Martinique, somebody took a pot shot at him. Missed and shot himself. No arrest. And off goes the Boomer on his merry way, six foot five of him, standing on the seat of his car, all eyes and teeth, with his escort having kittens every inch of the route.'

'He sounds a right daisy.'

'I believe you.'

'I get muddled,' Mr Fox confessed, 'over these emergent nations.'

'You're not alone, there.'

'I mean to say – this Ng'ombwana. What is it? A republic, obviously, but is it a member of the Commonwealth and if it is, why does it have an Ambassador instead of a High Commissioner?'

'You may well ask. Largely through the manoeuvrings of my old chum, The Boomer. They're still a Commonwealth country. More or less. They're having it both ways. All the trappings and complete independence. All the ha'pence and none of the kicks. That's why they insist on calling their man in London an Ambassador and setting him up in premises that wouldn't disgrace one of the great powers. Basically it's The Boomer's doing.'

'What about his own people? Here? At this Embassy? His Ambassador and all?'

'They're as worried as hell but say that what the President lays down is *it:* the general idea being that they might as well speak to the wind. He's got this notion in his head – it derives from his schooldays and his practising as a barrister in London – that because Great Britain, relatively, has had a non-history of political assassination there won't be any in the present or future. In its maddening way it's rather touching.'

'He can't stop the SB doing its stuff, though. Not outside the Embassy.'

'He can make it hellish awkward for them.'

'What's the procedure, then? Do you wait till he comes, Mr Alleyn, and plead with him at the airport?'

'I do not. I fly to his blasted republic at the crack of dawn tomorrow and you carry on with the Dagenham job on your own.'

'Thanks very much. What a treat,' said Fox. 'So I'd better go and pack.'

'Don't forget the old school tie.'

'I do not deign,' said Alleyn, 'to reply to that silly crack.'

He got as far as the door and stopped.

'I meant to ask you,' he said. 'Did you ever come across a man called Samuel Whipplestone? At the FO?'

'I don't move in those circles. Why?'

'He was a bit of a specialist on Ng'ombwana. I see he's lately retired. Nice chap. When I get back I might ask him to dinner.'

'Are you wondering if he'd have any influence?'

'We can hardly expect him to crash down on his knees and plead with the old Boomer to use his loaf if he wants to keep it. But I did vaguely wonder. 'Bye, Br'er Fox.'

Forty-eight hours later Alleyn, in a tropical suit, got out of a Presidential Rolls that had met him at the main Ng'ombwana airport. He passed in a sweltering heat up a grandiose flight of steps through a Ruritanian guard turned black, and into the air-conditioned reception hall of the Presidential Palace.

Communication at the top level had taken place and he got the full, instant VIP treatment.

'Mr Alleyn?' said a young Ng'ombwanan wearing an ADC's gold knot and tassel. 'The President is so happy at your visit. He will see you at once. You had a pleasant flight?'

Alleyn followed the sky-blue tunic down a splendid corridor that gave on an exotic garden.

'Tell me,' he asked on the way, 'what form of address is the correct one for the President?'

'His Excellency, the President,' the ADC rolled out, 'prefers that form of address.'

'Thank you,' said Alleyn, and followed his guide into an anteroom of impressive proportions. An extremely personable and widely smiling secretary said something in Ng'ombwanan. The ADC translated: 'We are to go straight in, if you please.' Two dashingly uniformed guards opened double-doors and Alleyn was ushered into an enormous room at the far end of which, behind a vast desk, sat his old school chum: Bartholomew Opala.

'Superintendent Alleyn, your Excellency, Mr President, sir,' said the ADC redundantly and withdrew.

The enormous presence was already on its feet and coming, light-footed as a prizefighter, at Alleyn. The huge voice was bellowing: 'Rory Alleyn, but all that's glorious!' Alleyn's hand was engulfed and his shoulder-blade rhythmically beaten. It was impossible to stand to attention and bow from the neck in what he had supposed to be the required form.

'Mr President – ' he began.

'What? Oh, nonsense, nonsense, nonsense! Balls, my dear man (as we used to say in Davidson's).' Davidson's had been their house at the illustrious school they both attended. The Boomer was being too establishment for words. Alleyn noticed that he wore the old school tie and that behind him on the wall hung a framed photograph of Davidson's with The Boomer and himself standing together in the back row. He found this oddly, even painfully, touching.

'Come and sit down,' The Boomer fussed. 'Where, now? Over here! Sit! Sit! I couldn't be more delighted.'

The steel-wool mat of hair was grey now and stood up high on his head like a toque. The huge frame was richly endowed with flesh and the eyes were very slightly bloodshot but, as if in double-exposure, Alleyn saw beyond this figure that of an ebony youth eating anchovy toast by a coal fire and saying: 'You are my friend: I have had none, here, until now.'

'How well you look,' the President was saying. 'And how little you have changed! You smoke? No? A cigar? A pipe? Yes? Presently, then. You are lunching with us of course. They have told you?'

'This is overwhelming,' Alleyn said when he could get a word in. 'In a minute I shall be forgetting my protocol.'

'Now! Forget it now. We are alone. There is no need.'

'My dear – '

'"Boomer." Say it. How many years since I heard it!'

'I'm afraid I very nearly said it when I came in. My dear Boomer.'

The sudden brilliance of a prodigal smile made its old impression. 'That's nice,' said the President quietly and after rather a long silence: 'I suppose I must ask you if this is a visit with an object. They were very non-committal at your end, you know. Just a message that you were arriving and would like to see me. Of course I was overjoyed.'

Alleyn thought: this is going to be tricky. One word in the wrong place and I not only boob my mission but very likely destroy a friendship and even set up a politically damaging mistrust. He said –

'I've come to ask you for something and I wish I hadn't got to bother you with it. I won't pretend that my chief didn't know of our past friendship – to me a most valued one. I won't pretend that he didn't imagine this friendship might have some influence. Of course he did. But it's because I think his request is reasonable and because I am very greatly concerned for your safety, that I didn't jib at coming.'

He had to wait a long time for the reaction. It was as if a blind had been pulled down. For the first time, seeing the slackened jaw and now the hooded, lacklustre eyes he thought, specifically: 'I am speaking to a Negro.'

'Ah!' said the President at last, 'I had forgotten. You are a police-man.'

'They say, don't they, if you want to keep a friend, never lend him money. I don't believe a word of it, but if you change the last four words into "never use your friendship to further your business" I wouldn't quarrel with it. But I'm not doing exactly that. This is more complicated. My end object, believe it or not, sir, is the preservation of your most valuable life.'

Another hazardous wait. Alleyn thought: 'Yes, and that's exactly how you used to look when you thought somebody had been rude to you. Glazed.'

But the glaze melted and The Boomer's nicest look – one of quiet amusement – supervened.

'Now, I understand,' he said. 'It is your watch-dogs, your Special Branch. "Please make him see reason, this black man. Please ask him to let us disguise ourselves as waiters and pressmen and men-in-the-street and unimportant guests and be indistinguishable all over the shop." I am right? That is the big request?'

'I'm afraid, you know, they'll do their thing in that respect, as well as they can, however difficult it's made for them.'

'Then why all this fuss-pottery? How stupid!'

'They would all be much happier if you didn't do what you did, for instance, in Martinique.'

'And what did I do in Martinique?'

'With the deepest respect: insisted on an extensive reduction of the safety precautions and escaped assassination by the skin of your teeth.'

'I am a fatalist,' The Boomer suddenly announced, and when Alleyn didn't answer: 'My dear Rory, I see I must make myself understood. Myself. What I am. My philosophy. My code. You will listen?'

'Here we go,' Alleyn thought. 'He's changed less than one would have thought possible.' And with profound misgivings he said: 'But of course, sir. With all my ears.'

As the exposition got under way it turned out to be an extension of The Boomer's schoolboy bloody-mindedness seasoned with, and in part justified by, his undoubted genius for winning the trust and understanding of his own people. He enlarged, with intermittent gusts of Homeric laughter, upon the machinations of the Ng'ombwanan extreme right and left who had upon several occasions made determined efforts to secure his death and were, through some mysterious process of reason, thwarted by The Boomer's practice of exposing himself as an easy target. 'They see,' he explained, 'that I am not (as we used to say at Davidson's) standing for their tedious codswallop.'

'*Did* we say that at Davidson's?'

'Of course. You must remember. Constantly.'

'So be it.'

'It was a favourite expression of your own. *Yes*,' shouted The Boomer as Alleyn seemed inclined to demur, 'always. We all picked it up from you.'

'To return, if we may, to the matter in hand.'

'*All* of us,' The Boomer continued nostalgically. 'You set the tone (at Davidson's),' and noticing perhaps a fleeting expression of horror on Alleyn's face, he leant forward and patted his knees. 'But I digress,' he said accurately, 'Shall we return to our muttons?'

'Yes,' Alleyn agreed with heartfelt relief. 'Yes. Let's.'

'Your turn,' The Boomer generously conceded. 'You were saying?'

'Have you thought – but of course you have – what would follow if you *were* knocked off?'

'As you say: of course I have. To quote your favourite dramatist (you see, I remember), "the filthy clouds of heady murder, spoil and villainy" would follow,' said The Boomer with relish. 'To say the least of it,' he added.

'Yes. Well now: the threat doesn't lie, as the Martinique show must have told you, solely within the boundaries of Ng'ombwana. In the Special Branch they know, and I mean they really *do* know, that there are lunatic fringes in London ready to go to all lengths. Some of them are composed of hangovers from certain disreputable back-waters of colonialism, others have a devouring hatred of your colour. Occasionally they are peope with a real and bitter grievance that has grown monstrous in stagnation. You name it. But they're there, in considerable numbers, organized and ready to go.'

'I am not alarmed,' said The Boomer with maddening compla-cency. 'No, but I mean it. In all truth I do not experience the least sensation of physical fear.'

'I don't share your sense of immunity,' Alleyn said. 'In your boots I'd be in a muck sweat.' It occurred to him that he had indeed aban-doned the slightest nod in the direction of protocol. 'But, all right. Accepting your fearlessness, may we return to the disastrous effect your death would have upon your country? "The filthy clouds of heady murder" bit. Doesn't that thought at all predispose you to pre-caution?'

'But, my dear fellow, you don't understand. I shall not be killed. I know it. Within myself, I know it. Assassination is not my destiny: it is as simple as that.'

Alleyn opened his mouth and shut it again.

'As simple as that,' The Boomer repeated. He opened his arms. 'You see!' he cried triumphantly.

'Do you mean,' Alleyn said very carefully, 'that the bullet in Martinique and the spear in a remote village in Ng'ombwana and the one or two other pot-shots that have been loosed off at you from time to time were all predestined to miss?'

'Not only do I believe it but my people – *my people* – know it in their souls. It is one of the reasons why I am reelected unanimously to lead my country.'

Alleyn did not ask if it was also one of his reasons why nobody, so far, had had the temerity to oppose him.

The Boomer reached out his great shapely hand and laid it on Alleyn's knee. 'You were and you are my good friend,' he said. 'We were close at Davidson's. We remained close while I read my law and ate my dinners at the Temple. And we are close still. But this thing we discuss now belongs to my colour and my race. My blackness. Please, do not try to understand: try only, my dear Rory, to accept.'

To this large demand Alleyn could only reply: 'It's *not* as simple as that.'

'No? But why?'

'If I talk about my personal anxiety for you I'll be saying in effect that I *don't* understand and *can't* accept, which is precisely what you do not want me to say. So I must fall back on my argument as an unwilling policeman with a difficult job. I'm not a member of the Special Branch but my colleagues in that Department have asked me to do what I can, which looks a bit like damn-all. I do put it to you that their job, a highly specialized and immensely difficult one, is going to be a hundred per cent more tricky if you decline to co-operate. If, for instance, on an impulse you change your route to some reception or walk out of your embassy without telling anybody and take a constitutional in Kensington Gardens all by yourself. To put it badly and brutally, if you are killed somebody in the Special Branch is going to be axed, the Department's going to fall into general disrepute at the highest and lowest levels, and a centuries-old reputation of immunity from political assassination in England is gone for good. You see, I'm speaking not only for the police.'

'The police, as servants of the people,' The Boomer began and then, Alleyn thought, very probably blushed.

'Were you going to say we ought to be kept in our place?' he mildly asked.

The Boomer began to walk about the room. Alleyn stood up.

'You have a talent,' The Boomer suddenly complained, 'for putting one in the wrong. I remember it of old at Davidson's.'

'What an insufferable boy I must have been,' Alleyn remarked. He was getting very bored with Davidson's and really there seemed to be nothing more to say. 'I have taken up too much of your Excellency's time,' he said. 'Forgive me,' and waited to be dismissed.

The Boomer looked mournfully upon him. 'But you are lunching,' he said. 'We have agreed. It is arranged that you shall lunch.'

'That's very kind, your Excellency, but it's only eleven o'clock. Should I make myself scarce in the meantime?'

To his intense dismay he saw that the bloodshot eyes had filled with tears. The Boomer said, with immense dignity: 'You have distressed me.'

'I'm sorry.'

'I was overjoyed at your coming. And now it is all spoilt and you call me Excellency.'

Alleyn felt the corners of his mouth twitch and at the same time was moved by a contradictory sense of compassion. This emotion, he realized, was entirely inappropriate. He reminded himself that the President of Ng'ombwana was far from being a sort of inspired innocent. He was an astute, devoted and at times ruthless dictator with, it had to be added, a warm capacity for friendship. He was also extremely observant. 'And funny,' Alleyn thought, controlling himself. 'It's quite maddening of him to be funny as well.'

'Ah!' the President suddenly roared out, 'you are laughing! My dear Rory, you are laughing,' and himself broke into that Homeric gale of mirth. 'No, it is too much! Admit! It is too ridiculous! What is it all about? Nothing! Listen, I will be a good boy. I will behave. Tell your solemn friends in your Special Branch that I will not run away when they hide themselves behind inadequate floral decorations and dress themselves up as nonentities with enormous boots. There now! You are pleased? Yes?'

'I'm enchanted,' Alleyn said, 'if you really mean it.'

'But I do. I do. You shall see. I will be decorum itself. Within,' he added, 'the field of their naive responsibilities. Within the UK in fact. OK? Yes?'

'Yes.'

'And no more Excellencies. No? Not,' The Boomer added without turning a hair, 'when we are *tête-à-tête*. As at present.'

'As at present,' Alleyn agreed and was instantly re-involved in an exuberance of hand-shaking.

It was arranged that he would be driven round the city for an hour before joining the President for luncheon. The elegant ADC reappeared. When they walked back along the corridor, Alleyn looked through its french windows into the acid-green garden. It was daubed superbly with flamboyants and veiled by a concourse of fountains. Through the iridescent rise and fall of water there could be perceived, at intervals, motionless figures in uniform.

Alleyn paused. 'What a lovely garden,' he said.

'Oh yes?' said the ADC, smiling. Reflected colour and reflected lights from the garden glanced across his polished charcoal jaw and cheekbones. 'You like it? The President likes it very much.'

He made as if to move. 'Shall we?' he suggested.

A file of soldiers, armed, and splendidly uniformed, crossed the garden left, right, left, right, on the far side of the fountains. Distorted by prismatic cascades, they could dimly be seen to perform a correct routine with the men they had come to replace.

'The changing of the guard,' Alleyn said lightly.

'Exactly. They are purely ceremonial troops.'

'Yes?'

'As at your Buckingham Palace,' explained the ADC.

'Quite,' said Alleyn.

They passed through the grandiloquent hall and the picturesque guard at the entrance.

'Again,' Alleyn ventured, 'purely ceremonial?'

'Of course,' said the ADC.

They were armed, Alleyn noticed, if not to the teeth, at least to the hips, with a useful-looking issue of sophisticated weapons. 'Very smartly turned out,' he said politely.

'The President will be pleased to know you think so,' said the ADC and they walked into a standing bath of heat and dazzlement.

The Presidential Rolls heavily garnished with the Ng'ombwanan arms and flying, incorrectly since he was not using it, the Presidential standard, waited at the foot of the steps. Alleyn was ushered into the back seat while the ADC sat in front. The car was air-conditioned and the windows shut and, thought Alleyn, 'If ever I rode in a bullet-proof job – and today wouldn't be the first time – this is it.' He wondered if, somewhere in Ng'ombwana security circles there was an influence a great deal more potent than that engendered by the industrious evocation of Davidson's.

They drove under the escort of two ultra-smart, lavishly accoutred motor-cyclists. 'Skinheads, bikies, traffic cops, armed escorts,' he speculated, 'wherever they belch and rev and bound, what gives the species its peculiar air of menacing vulgarity?'

The car swept through crowded, mercilessly glaring streets. Alleyn found something to say about huge white monstrosities – a Palace of Culture, a Palace of Justice, a Hall of Civic Authority, a Free Library. The ADC received his civilities with perfect complacency.

'Yes,' he agreed. 'They are very fine. All new. All since The Presidency. It is very remarkable.'

The traffic was heavy but it was noticeable that it opened before their escort as the Red Sea before Moses. They were stared at, but from a distance. Once, as they made a right hand turn and were momentarily checked by an oncoming car, their chauffeur, without turning his head, said something to the driver that made him wince.

When Alleyn, who was married to a painter, looked at the current scene, wherever it might be, he did so with double vision. As a stringently trained policeman he watched, automatically, for idiosyncrasies. As a man very sensitively tuned to his wife's way of seeing, he searched for consonancies. Now, when confronted by a concourse of round, black heads that bobbed, shifted, clustered and dispersed against that inexorable glare, he saw this scene as his wife might like to paint it. He noticed that, in common with many of the older buildings, one in particular was in process of being newly painted. The ghost of a former legend showed faintly through the mask – SANS RIT IMPO T NG TR DI G CO. He saw a shifting, colourful group on the steps of this building and thought how, with simplification, re-arrangement and selection Troy would endow them with rhythmic significance. She would find, he thought, a focal point, some figure to which the others were subservient, a figure of the first importance.

And then, even as this notion visited him, the arrangement occurred. The figures reformed like fragments in a kaleidoscope and there was the focal point, a solitary man, inescapable because quite still, a grotesquely fat man, with long blond hair, wearing white clothes. A white man.

The white man stared into the car. He was at least fifty yards away but for Alleyn it might have been so many feet. They looked into each other's faces and the policeman said to himself: 'That chap's worth watching. That chap's a villain.'

Click, went the kaleidoscope. The fragments slid apart and together. A stream of figures erupted from the interior, poured down the steps and dispersed. When the gap was uncovered the white man had gone.

IV

'It's like this, sir,' Chubb had said rapidly. 'Seeing that No. 1 isn't a full-time place being there's two of us, we been in the habit of helping out on a part-time basis elsewhere in the vicinity. Like, Mrs Chubb does an hour every other day for Mr Sheridan in the basement and I go to the Colonel's – that's Colonel and Mrs Cockburn-Montfort in the Place – for two hours of a Friday afternoon, and every other Sunday evening we baby-sit at 17 The Walk. And – '

'Yes. I see,' said Mr Whipplestone, stemming the tide.

'You won't find anything scamped or overlooked, sir,' Mrs Chubb intervened. 'We give satisfaction, sir, in all quarters, really we do. It's just An Arrangement, like.'

'And naturally, sir, the wages are adjusted. We wouldn't expect anything else, sir, would we?'

They had stood side by side with round anxious faces, wide-open eyes and gabbling mouths. Mr Whipplestone had listened with his built-in air of attentive detachment and had finally agreed to the proposal that the Chubbs were all his for six mornings, breakfast, luncheon and dinner: that provided the house was well kept up they might attend upon Mr Sheridan or anybody else at their own and his convenience, that on Fridays Mr Whipplestone would lunch and dine at his club or elsewhere and that, as the Chubbs put it, the wages 'was adjusted accordingly'.

'Most of the residents,' explained Chubb when they had completed these arrangements and got down to details, 'has accounts at the Napoli, sir. You may prefer to deal elsewhere.'

'And for the butchery,' said Mrs Chubb, 'there's – '

They expounded upon the amenities in the Capricorns.

Mr Whipplestone said: 'That all sounds quite satisfactory. Do you know, I think I'll make a tour of inspection.' And he did so.

The Napoli is one of the four little shops in Capricorn Mews. It is 'shop' reduced to its absolute minimum; a slit of a place where the customers stand in single file and then only eight at a squeeze. The proprietors are an Italian couple, he dark and anxious, she dark and buxom and jolly. Their assistant is a large and facetious cockney.

It is a nice shop. They cure their own bacon and hams. Mr Pirelli makes his own pâté and a particularly good terrine. The cheeses are excellent. Bottles of dry Orvieto are slung overhead and other Italian wines crowd together inside the door. There are numerous exotics in line on the shelves. The Capricornians like to tell each other that the Napoli is 'a pocket Fortnum's'. Dogs are not allowed but a row of hooks has been thoughtfully provided in the outside wall and on most mornings there is a convocation of mixed dogs attached to them.

Mr Whipplestone skirted the dogs, entered the shop and bought a promising piece of Camembert. The empurpled army man, always immaculately dressed and gloved, whom he had seen in the street was in the shop and was addressed by Mr Pirelli as 'Colonel'. (Montfort? wondered Mr Whipplestone.) The Colonel's lady was with him. An alarming lady, the fastidious Mr Whipplestone thought, with the face of a dissolute clown and wildly overdressed. They both wore an air of overdone circumspection that Mr Whipplestone associated with the hazards of a formidable hangover. The lady stood stock still and bolt-upright behind her husband but as Mr Whipplestone approached the counter, she side-stepped and barged into him, driving her pin heel into his instep.

'I beg your pardon,' he cried in pain and lifted his hat.

'Not a bit,' she said thickly and gave him what could only be described as a half-awakened leer.

Her husband turned and seemed to sense a need for conversation. 'Not much room for manoeuvrin',' he shouted. 'What?'

'Quite,' said Mr Whipplestone.

He opened an account, left the shop and continued his explorations.

He arrived at the scene of his encounter with the little black cat. A large van was backing into the garage. Out of the tail of his eye he thought he saw briefly a darting shadow and when the van stopped he could have fancied, almost, that he heard a faint, plaintive cry. But there was nothing to support these impressions and he hurried on, oddly perturbed.

At the far end of the Mews, by the entrance to the passageway is a strange little cavern, once a stable, which has been converted into a shop. Here, at this period, a baleful fat lady made images of pigs either as doorstops or with roses and daises on their sides and a hole in their backs for cream or flowers as the fancy might take you. They varied in size but never in design. The kiln was at the back of the cavern and as Mr Whipplestone looked in the fat lady stared at him out of her shadows. Above the entrance was a notice: 'X. & K. Sanskrit. Pigs.'

'Commercial candour!' thought Mr Whipplestone, cracking a little joke for himself. To what nationality he wondered could someone called Sanskrit possibly belong? Indian, he supposed, And 'X'? Xavier perhaps. 'To make a living,' he wondered, 'out of the endless reduplication of pottery pigs? And why on earth does this extraordinary name seem to ring a bell?'

Conscious that the fat lady in the shadows still looked at him, he moved on into Capricorn Place and made his way to a rosy brick wall at the far end. Through an opening in this wall one leaves the Capricorns and arrives at a narrow lane passing behind the Basilica precincts and an alleyway ending in the full grandeur of Palace Park Gardens. Here the Ng'ombwana Embassy rears its important front.

Mr Whipplestone contemplated the pink flag with its insignia of green spear and sun and mentally apostrophized it. 'Yes,' he thought, 'there you are and for my part, long may you stay there.' And he remembered that at some as yet unspecified time but, unless something awful intervened, in the near future, the Ambassador and all his minions would be in no end of a tig getting ready for the state visit of their dynamic President and spotting assassins behind every plane tree. The Special Branch would be raising their punctual plaint and at the FO, he thought, they'll be dusting down their imperturbability. 'I'm out of it all and (I'd better make up my mind to it) delighted to be so. I suppose,' he added. Conscious of a slight pang, he made his way home.

CHAPTER 2

Lucy Lockett

Mr Whipplestone had been in residence for over a month. He was thoroughly settled, comfortable and contented and yet by no means lethargically so. On the contrary, he had been stimulated by his change of scene and felt lively. Already he was tuned in to life in the Capricorns. 'Really,' he wrote in his diary, 'it's like a little village set down in the middle of London. One runs repeatedly into the same people in the shops. On warm evenings the inhabitants stroll about the streets. One may drop in at the Sun in Splendour where one finds, I'm happy to say, a very respectable, nay, quite a distinguished, white port.'

He had been in the habit of keeping a diary for some years. Until now it had confined itself to the dry relation of facts with occasionally a touch of the irony for which he had been slightly famous at the FO. Now, under the stimulus of his new environment, the journal expanded and became, at times, almost skittish.

The evening was very warm. His window was open and the curtains, too. An afterglow had suffused the plane trees and kindled the dome of the Basilica but now was faded. There was a smell of freshly-watered gardens in the air and the pleasant sound of footfalls mingling with quiet voices drifted in at the open window. The muted roar of Baronsgate seemed distant, a mere background to quietude.

After a time he laid down his pen, let fall his eyeglass and looked with pleasure at his room. Everything had fitted to a miracle. Under the care of the Chubbs his nice old bits and pieces positively sparkled. The crimson goblet glowed in the window and his Agatha Troy seemed to generate a light of its own.

'How nice everything is,' thought Mr Whipplestone.

It was very quiet in his house. The Chubbs, he fancied, were out for the evening but they were habitually so unobtrusive in their comings and goings that one was unaware of them. While he was writing, Mr Whipplestone had been aware of visitors descending the iron steps into the area. Mr Sheridan was at home and receiving in the basement flat.

He switched off his desk lamp, got up to stretch his legs and moved over to the bow window. The only people who were about were a man and a woman coming towards him in the darkening Square. They moved into a pool of light from the open doorway of the Sun in Splendour and momentarily he got a clearer look at them. They were both fat and there was something about the woman that was familiar.

They came on towards him into and out from the shadow of the plane trees. On a ridiculous impulse, as if he had been caught spying, Mr Whipplestone backed away from his window. The woman seemed to stare into his eyes: an absurd notion since she couldn't possibly see him.

Now he knew who she was: Mrs or Miss X. Sanskrit. And her companion? Brother or spouse? Brother, almost certainly. The pig-potters.

Now they were out of the shadow and crossed the Walk in full light straight at him. And he saw they were truly awful.

It wasn't that they were lard-fat, both of them, so fat that they might have sat to each other as models for their wares, or that they were outrageously got up. No clothes, it might be argued in these permissive days, could achieve outrageousness. It wasn't that the man wore a bracelet and an anklet and a necklace and earrings or that what hair he had fell like pond-weed from an embroidered headband. It wasn't even that she (fifty if a day, thought Mr Whipplestone) wore vast black leather hotpants, a black fringed tunic and black boots. Monstrous though these grotesqueries undoubtedly were, they were as nothing compared with the eyes and mouths of the Sanskrits which were, Mr Whipplestone now saw with something like panic, equally heavily made-up.

'They shouldn't be here,' he thought, confusedly protecting the normality of the Capricorns. 'People like that. They ought to be in Chelsea. Or somewhere.'

They had crossed the Walk. They had approached his house. He backed further away. The area gate clicked and clanged, they descended the iron steps. He heard the basement flat bell. He heard Mr Sheridan's voice. They had been admitted.

'No, really!' Mr Whipplestone thought in the language of his youth. 'Too much! And he seemed perfectly respectable.' He was thinking of his brief encounter with Mr Sheridan.

He settled down to a book. At least it was not a noisy party down there. One could hear little or nothing. Perhaps, he speculated, the Sanskrits were mediums. Perhaps Mr Sheridan dabbled in spiritism and belonged to a 'circle'. They looked like that. Or worse. He dismissed the whole thing and returned to the autobiography of a former chief of his Department. It was not absorbing. The blurb made a great fuss about a ten-year interval imposed between the author's death and publication. Why, God knew, thought Mr Whipplestone, since the crashing old bore could have nothing to disclose that would unsettle the composure of the most susceptible of vestal virgins.

His attention wandered. He became conscious of an uneasiness at the back of his mind: an uneasiness occasioned by sound, by something he would rather not hear, by something that was connected with anxiety and perturbation. By a cat mewing in the street.

Pah! he thought, as far as one can think 'pah'. Cats abounded in London streets. He had seen any number of them in the Capricorns: pampered pet cats. There was an enormous tortoiseshell at the Sun in Splendour and a supercilious white affair at the Napoli. Cats.

It had come a great deal nearer. It was now very close indeed. Just outside, one would suppose, and not moving on. Sitting on the pavement, he dared say, and staring at his house. At him, even. And mewing. Persistently. He made a determined effort to ignore it. He returned to his book. He thought of turning on his radio, loudly, to drown it. The cries intensified. From being distant and intermittent they were now immediate and persistent.

'I shall not look out of the window,' he decided in a fluster. 'It would only see me.'

'Damnation!' he cried three minutes later. 'How dare people lock out their cats! I'll complain to someone.'

Another three minutes and he did, against every fibre of disinclination in his body, look out of the window. He saw nothing. The feline lamentations were close enough to drive him dotty. On the steps: that's where they were. On the flight of steps leading up to his front door. 'No!' he thought. 'No, really this is not good enough. This must be stopped. Before we know where we are – '

Before he knew where he was, he was in his little hall and manipulating his double lock. The chain was disconnected on account of the Chubbs but he opened the door a mere crack and no sooner had he done so than something – a shadow, a meagre atomy – darted across his instep.

Mr Whipplestone became dramatic. He slammed his door to, leant against it and faced his intruder.

He had known it all along. History, if you could call an incident of not much more than a month ago history, was repeating itself. In the wretched shape of a small black cat: the same cat but now quite dreadfully emaciated, its eyes clouded, its fur staring. It sat before him and again opened its pink mouth in now soundless mews. Mr Whipplestone could only gaze at it in horror. Its haunches quivered and, as it had done when they last met, it leapt up to his chest.

As his hand closed round it he wondered that it had had the strength to jump. It purred and its heart knocked at his fingers.

'This is too much,' he repeated and carried it into his drawing-room. 'It will die, I dare say,' he said, 'and how perfectly beastly that will be.'

After some agitated thought he carried it into the kitchen and, still holding it, took milk from the refrigerator, poured some into a saucer, added hot water from the tap and set it on the floor and the little cat sat beside it. At first he thought she would pay no attention – he was persuaded the creature was a female – her eyes being half-closed and her chin on the floor. He edged the saucer nearer. Her whiskers trembled. So suddenly that he quite jumped, she was lapping, avidly, frantically as if driven by some desperate little engine. Once she looked up at him.

Twice he replenished the saucer. The second time she did not finish the offering. She raised her milky chin, stared at him, made

one or two shaky attempts to wash her face and suddenly collapsed
on his foot and went to sleep.

Some time later there were sounds of departure from the basement flat. Soon after this, the Chubbs affected their usual discreet
entry. Mr Whipplestone heard them put up the chain on the front
door. The notion came to him that perhaps they had been 'doing for'
Mr Sheridan at his party.

'Er – is that you, Chubb?' he called out.

Chubb opened the door and presented himself, apple-cheeked,
on the threshold with his wife behind him. It struck Mr
Whipplestone that they seemed uncomfortable.

'Look,' he invited, 'at this.'

Chubb had done so, already. The cat lay like a shadow across
Mr Whipplestone's knees.

'A cat, sir,' said Chubb tentatively.

'A stray. I've seen it before.'

From behind her husband, Mrs Chubb said: 'Nothing of it, sir, is
there? It don't look healthy, do it?'

'It was starving.'

Mrs Chubb clicked her tongue.

Chubb said: 'Very quiet, sir, isn't it? It hasn't passed away, has it?'

'It's asleep. It's had half a bottle of milk.'

'Well, excuse me, sir,' Mrs Chubb said, 'but I don't think you
ought to handle it. You don't know where it's been, do you, sir?'

'No,' said Mr Whipplestone, and added with a curious inflection
in his voice. 'I only know where it is.'

'Would you like Chubb to dispose of it, sir?'

This suggestion he found perfectly hateful but he threw out as airily as he could: 'Oh, I don't think so. I'll do something about it myself
in the morning. Ring up the RSPCA.'

'I dare say if you was to put it out, sir, it'd wander off where it
come from.'

'Or,' suggested Chubb. 'I could put it in the garden at the back, sir.
For the night, like.'

'Yes,' Mr Whipplestone gabbled, 'thank you. Never mind. I'll
think of something. Thank you.'

'Thank you, sir,' they said, meaninglessly.

Because they didn't immediately make a move and because he was in a tizzy, Mr Whipplestone, to his own surprise said, 'Pleasant evening?'

They didn't answer. He glanced up and found they stared at him.

'Yes, thank you, sir,' they said.

'Good!' he cried with a phoney heartiness that horrified him. 'Good! Good night, Chubb. Good night, Mrs Chubb.'

When they had gone into the kitchen, he felt sure they opened the refrigerator and he distinctly heard them turn on a tap. Washing the saucer, he thought guiltily.

He waited until they had retired upstairs and then himself sneaked into the kitchen with the cat. He had remembered that he had not eaten all the poached scallop Mrs Chubb gave him for dinner.

The cat woke up and ate quite a lot of scallop.

Entry into his back garden was effected by a door at the end of the passage and down a precipitous flight of steps. It was difficult, holding the cat, and he made rather a noisy descent but was aided by a glow of light from behind the blinds that masked Mr Sheridan's basement windows. This enabled him to find a patch of unplanted earth against the brick wall at the rear of the garden. He placed the cat upon it.

He had thought she might bolt into the shadows and somehow escape, but no: after a considerable wait she became industrious. Mr Whipplestone tactfully turned his back.

He was being watched from the basement through an opening between the blind and the window frame.

The shadowy form was almost certainly that of Mr Sheridan and almost certainly he had hooked himself a peephole and had released it as Mr Whipplestone turned. The shadowy form retreated.

At the same time a slight noise above his head caused Mr Whipplestone to look up to the top storey of his house. He was just in time to see the Chubbs' bedroom window being closed.

There was, of course, no reason to suppose they, also, had been watching him.

'I must be getting fanciful,' he thought.

A faint rhythmic scuffling redirected his attention to the cat. With her ears laid back and with a zealous concentration that spoke volumes for her recuperative powers, she was tidying up. This exercise was

followed by a scrupulous personal toilette, which done, she blinked at
Mr Whipplestone and pushed her nut-like head against his ankle.

He picked her up and returned indoors.

II

The fashionable and grossly expensive pet-shop round the corner in
Baronsgate had a consulting-room, visited on Wednesday mornings
by a veterinary surgeon. Mr Whipplestone had observed their notice
to this effect and the next morning, being a Wednesday, he took the
cat to be vetted. His manner of conveying his intention to the
Chubbs was as guarded and non-committal as forty years' experience in diplomacy could make it. Indeed, in a less rarefied atmosphere it might almost have been described as furtive.

He gave it out that he was 'taking that animal to be attended to'.
When the Chubbs jumped to the conclusion that this was a euphemism for 'put down' he did not correct them. Nor did he think it
necessary to mention that the animal had spent the night on his bed.
She had roused him at daybreak by touching his face with her paw.
When he opened his eyes she had flirted with him, rolling on her
side and looking at him from under her arm. And when Chubb came
in with his early morning tray, Mr Whipplestone had contrived to
throw his eiderdown over her and later on had treated her to a
saucer of milk. He came downstairs with her under *The Times*, chose
his moment to let her out by the back door into the garden, and
presently called Mrs Chubb's attention to her. She was demanding
vigorously to be let in.

So now he sat on a padded bench in a minute waiting-room,
cheek by jowl with several Baronsgate ladies, each of whom had a
dog in tow. One of them, the one next to Mr Whipplestone, was the
lady who trod on his foot in the Napoli, Mrs Montfort as he subsequently discovered, the Colonel's lady. They said good morning to
each other when they encountered, and did so now. By and large
Mr Whipplestone thought her pretty awful, though not as awful as
the pig-pottery lady of last night. Mrs Montfort carried on her over-
dressed lap a Pekinese, which, after a single contemptuous look,
turned its back on Mr Whipplestone's cat who stared through it.

He was acutely conscious that he presented a farcical appearance. The only container that could be found by the Chubbs was a disused birdcage, the home of their parrot, lately deceased. The little cat looked outraged sitting in it, and Mr Whipplestone looked silly nursing it and wearing his eye-glass. Several of the ladies exchanged amused glances.

'What,' asked the ultra-smart surgery attendant, notebook in hand, 'is pussy's name?'

He felt that if he said 'I don't know,' or 'It hasn't got one,' he would put himself at a disadvantage with these women. 'Lucy,' he said loudly and added as an afterthought: 'Lockett.'

'I see!' she said brightly and noted it down. 'You haven't an appointment, have you?'

'I'm afraid not.'

'Lucy won't have long to wait,' she smiled, and passed on.

A woman with a huge, angry, short-haired tabby in her arms came through from the surgery.

The newly-named Lucy's fur rose. She made a noise that suggested she had come to the boil. The tabby suddenly let out a yell. Dogs made ambiguous comments in their throats.

'Oh lor!' said the newcomer. She grinned at Mr Whipplestone. 'Better make ourselves scarce,' she said, and to her indignant cat: 'Shut up, Bardolph, don't be an ass.'

When they had gone Lucy went to sleep and Mrs Montfort said: 'Is your cat very ill?'

'No!' Mr Whipplestone quite shouted and then explained that Lucy was a stray starveling.

'Sweet of you,' she said, 'to care. People are so awful about animals. It makes me quite ill. I'm like that.' She turned her gaze upon him. 'Kitty Montfort. My husband's the warrior with the purple face. He's called Colonel Montfort.'

Cornered, Mr Whipplestone murmured his own name.

Mrs Montfort smelt of very heavy scent and gin.

'I know,' she said archly, 'you're our new boy, aren't you? At No. 1, The Walk? We have a piece of your Chubb on Fridays.'

Mr Whipplestone, whose manners were impeccable, bowed as far as the birdcage would permit.

Mrs Montfort was smiling into his face. She had laid her gloved hand on the cage. The door behind him had opened. Her smile became fixed as if pinned up at the corners. She withdrew her hand, and looked straight in front of her.

From the street there had entered a totally black man in livery with a white Afghan hound on a scarlet leash. The man paused and glanced round. There was an empty place on the other side of Mrs Montfort. Still looking straight in front of her, she moved far enough along the seat to leave insufficient room on either side of her. Mr Whipplestone instantly widened the distance between them and with a gesture, invited the man to sit down. The man said, 'Thank you, sir,' and remained where he was, not looking at Mrs Montfort. The hound advanced his nose towards the cage. Lucy did not wake.

'I wouldn't come too close if I were you, old boy,' Mr Whipplestone said. The Afghan wagged his tail and Mr Whipplestone patted him. 'I know you,' he said, 'you're the Embassy dog, aren't you? You're Ahman.' He gave the man a pleasant look and the man made a slight bow.

'Lucy Lockett:?' said the attendant, brightly emerging. 'We're all ready for her.'

The consultation was brief but conclusive. Lucy Lockett was about seven months old and her temperature was normal, she was innocent of mange, ringworm or parasites, she was extremely undernourished and therefore in shocking condition. Here the vet hesitated. 'There are scars,' he said, 'and there's been a fractured rib that has looked after itself. She's been badly neglected – I think she may have been actively ill-treated.' And catching sight of Mr Whipplestone's horrified face he added cheerfully: 'Nothing that pills and good food won't put right.' He said she had been spayed. She was half-Siamese and half God knew what, the vet said, turning back her fur and handling her this way and that. He laughed at the white end to her tail and gave her an injection.

She submitted to these indignities with utter detachment, but when at liberty, leapt into her protector's embrace and performed her now familiar act of jamming her head under his jacket and lying next his heart.

'Taken to you,' said the vet. 'They've got a sense of gratitude, cats have. Especially the females.'

'I don't know anything about them,' said Mr Whipplestone in a hurry.

Motivated by sales-talk and embarrassment, he bought on his way out a cat bed-basket, a china dish labelled 'Kit-bits', a comb and brush and a collar for which he ordered a metal tab with a legend: 'Lucy Lockett. 1 Capricorn Walk' and his telephone number. The shop assistant showed him a little red cat-harness for walking out and told him that with patience, cats could be induced to co-operate. She put Lucy into it and the result was fetching enough for Mr Whipplestone to keep it.

He left the parrot cage behind to be called for and heavily laden, with Lucy again in retreat under his coat, walked quickly home to deploy his diplomatic resources upon the Chubbs, little knowing that he carried his destiny under his jacket.

III

'This is perfectly delightful,' said Mr Whipplestone, turning from his host to his hostess with the slight inclinations of his head and shoulders that had long been occupational mannerisms. 'I *am* so enjoying myself.'

'Fill up your glass,' Alleyn said. 'I did warn you that it was an invitation with an ulterior motive, didn't I?'

'I am fully prepared: charmingly so. A superb port.'

'I'll leave you with it,' Troy suggested.

'No, don't,' Alleyn said. 'We'll send you packing if anything v.s. and c crops up. Otherwise it's nice to have you. Isn't it, Whipplestone?'

Mr Whipplestone embarked upon a speech about his good fortune in being able to contemplate a 'Troy' above his fireplace every evening and now having the pleasure of contemplating the artist herself at her own fireside. He got a little bogged down but fetched up bravely.

'And when,' he asked, coming to his own rescue, 'are we to embark upon the ulterior motive?'

Alleyn said, 'Let's make a move. This is liable to take time.'

At Troy's suggestion they carried their port from the house into her detached studio and settled themselves in front of long windows overlooking a twilit London garden.

'I want,' Alleyn said, 'to pick your brains a little. Aren't you by way of being an expert on Ng'ombwana?'

'Ng'ombwana? I! That's putting it much too high, my dear man. I was there for three years in my youth.'

'I thought that quite recently when it was getting its independence – ?'

'They sent me out there, yes. During the exploratory period: mainly because I speak the language, I suppose. Having rather made it my thing in a mild way.'

'And you have kept it up?'

'Again, in a mild way: oh, yes. Yes.' He looked across the top of his glass at Alleyn. 'You haven't gone over to the Special Branch, surely?'

'That's a very crisp bit of instant deduction. No, I haven't. But you may say they've unofficially roped me in for the occasion.'

'Of the forthcoming visit?'

'Yes, blast them. Security.'

'I see. Difficult. By the way, you must have been the President's contemporary at – ' Mr Whipplestone stopped short. 'Is it hoped that you may introduce the personal note?'

'You are quick!' Troy said and he gave a gratified little cackle.

Alleyn said: 'I saw him three weeks ago.'

'In Ng'ombwana?'

'Yes. Coming the old-boy network like nobody's business.'

'Get anywhere?'

'Not so that you'd notice: no, that's not fair. He did undertake not to cut up rough about our precautions but exactly what he meant by that is his secret. I dare say that in the upshot he'll be a bloody nuisance.'

'Well?' asked Mr Whipplestone, leaning back and swinging his eyeglass in what Alleyn felt had been his cross-diplomatic-desk gesture for half a lifetime. 'Well, my dear Roderick?'

'Where do you come in?'

'Quite.'

'I'd be grateful if you'd – what's the current jargon? – fill me in on the general Ng'ombwana background. From your own point of view. For instance, how many people would you say have cause to wish The Boomer dead?'

'The Boomer?'

'As he incessantly reminded me, that was His Excellency's schoolboy nickname.'

'An appropriate one. In general terms, I should say some two hundred thousand persons, at least.'

'Good Lord!' Troy exclaimed.

'Could you,' asked her husband, 'do a bit of name-dropping?'

'Not really. Not specifically. But again in general terms – well, it's the usual pattern throughout the new African independencies. First of all there are those Ng'ombwanan political opponents whom the President succeeded in breaking, the survivors of whom are either in prison or in this country waiting for his overthrow or assassination.'

'The Special Branch flatters itself it's got a pretty comprehensive list in that category.'

'I dare say,' said Mr Whipplestone drily. 'So did we, until one fine day in Martinique a hitherto completely unknown person with a phoney British passport fired a revolver at the President, missed, and was more successful with a second shot at himself. He had no record and his true identity was never established.'

'I reminded The Boomer of that incident.'

Mr Whipplestone said archly to Troy: 'Y'ou know, he's much more fully informed than I am. What's he up to?'

'I can't imagine, but do go on. I, at least, know nothing.'

'Well. Among these African enemies, of course, are the extremists who disliked his early moderation and especially his refusal at the out-set to sack all his European advisers and officials in one fell swoop. So you get pockets of anti-white terrorists who campaigned for inde-pendence but are now prepared to face about and destroy the govern-ment they helped to create. Their followers are an unknown quantity but undoubtedly numerous. But you know all this, my dear fellow.'

'He's sacking more and more whites now, though, isn't he? However unwillingly?'

'He's been forced to do so by the extreme elements.'

'So,' Alleyn said, 'the familiar, perhaps the inevitable, pattern emerges. The nationalization of all foreign enterprise and the appro-priation of properties held by European and Asian colonists. Among whom we find the bitterest possible resentment.'

'Indeed. And with some reason. Many of them have been ruined. Among the older groups the effect has been completely disastrous. Their entire way of life has disintegrated and they are totally unfit-ted for any other.' Mr Whipplestone rubbed his nose. 'I must say,' he added, 'however improperly, that some of them are *not* likeable individuals.'

Troy asked: 'Why's he coming here? The Boomer, I mean?'

'Ostensibly, to discuss with Whitehall his country's needs for development.'

'And Whitehall,' Alleyn said, 'professes its high delight while the Special Branch turns green with forebodings.'

"Mr Whipplestone, you said "ostensibly",' Troy pointed out.

'Did I, Mrs Rory? – Yes. Yes, well it has been rumoured through tolerably reliable sources that the President hopes to negotiate with rival groups to take over the oil and copper resources from the dispossessed who have, of course, developed them at enormous cost.'

'Here we go again!' said Alleyn.

'I don't suggest,' Mr Whipplestone mildly added, 'that Lord Karnley or Sir Julian Raphael or any of their associates are likely to instigate a lethal assault upon the President.'

'Good!'

'But of course behind those august personages is a host of embittered shareholders, executives and employees.'

'Among whom might be found the odd cloak-and-dagger merchant. And apart from all these more or less motivated persons,' Alleyn said, 'there are the ones policemen like least: the fanatics. The haters of black pigmentation, the lonely woman who dreams about a black rapist, the man who builds Anti-Christ in a black image or who reads a threat to his livelihood in every black neighbour. Or for whom the commonplace phrases – "black outlook, black record, as black as it's painted, black villainy, the black man will get you" and all the rest of them, have an absolute reference. Black is bad. Finish.'

'And the Black Power lot,' Troy said, 'are doing as much for "white", aren't they? The war of the images.'

Mr Whipplestone made a not too uncomfortable little groaning noise and returned to his port.

'I wonder,' Alleyn said, 'I do wonder, how much of that absolute antagonism the old Boomer nurses in his sooty bosom.'

'None for you, anyway,' Troy said, and when he didn't answer, 'surely?'

'My dear Alleyn, I understood he professes the utmost *camaraderie*.'

'Oh, yes! Yes, he does. He lays it on with a trowel. Do you know, I'd be awfully sorry to think the trowel-work overlaid an inimical understructure. Silly, isn't it?'

'It is the greatest mistake,' Mr Whipplestone pronounced, to make assumptions about relationships that are not clearly defined.'

'And what relationship is ever that?'

'Well! Perhaps not. We do what we can with treaties and agreements, but perhaps not.'

'He did try,' Alleyn said. 'He did in the first instance try to set up some kind of multi-racial community. He thought it would work.'

'Did you discuss that?' Troy asked.

'Not a word. It wouldn't have done. My job was too tricky. Do you know, I got the impression that at least part of his exuberant welcome was inspired by a – well, by a wish to compensate for the ongoings of the new regime.'

'It might be so,' Mr Whipplestone conceded. 'Who can say?'

Alleyn took a folded paper from his breast pocket.

'The Special Branch has given me a list of commercial and professional firms and individuals to be kicked out of Ng'ombwana, with notes on anything in their history that might look at all suspicious.' He glanced at the paper.

'Does the same Sanskrit mean anything at all to you?' he asked. 'X. and K. Sanskrit to be exact. My dear man, what *is* the matter?'

Mr Whipplestone had shouted inarticulately, laid down his glass, clapped his hands and slapped his forehead.

'Eureka!' he cried stylishly. 'I have it! At last. At last!'

'Jolly for you,' said Alleyn, 'I'm delighted to hear it. What had escaped you?'

' "*Sanskrit, Importing and Trading Company, Ng'ombwana*".'

'That's it. Or was it.'

'In Edward VIIth Avenue.'

'Certainly, I saw it there: only they call it something else now. And Sanskrit has been kicked out. Why are you so excited?'

'Because I saw him last night.'

'You *did*!'

'Well, it must have been. They are as alike as two disgusting pins.'

'They?' Alleyn repeated, gazing at his wife who briefly crossed her eyes at him.

'How could I have forgotten!' exclaimed Mr Whipplestone rhetorically. 'I passed those premises every day of my time in Ng'ombwana.'

'I clearly see that I mustn't interrupt you.'

'My dear Mrs Roderick, my dear Roderick, do please forgive me,' begged Mr Whipplestone, turning pink. 'I must explain myself: too gauche and peculiar. But you see – '

And explain himself he did, pig-pottery and all, with the precision that had eluded him at the first disclosure. 'Admit,' he cried when he had finished, 'it *is* a singular coincidence, now isn't it?'

'It's all of that,' Alleyn said. 'Would you like to hear what the Special Branch have got to say about the man – K. Sanskrit?'

'Indeed I would.'

'Here goes, then. This information, by the way, is a digest one of Fred Gibson's chaps got from the Criminal Record Office. "Sanskrit. Kenneth, for Heaven's sake. Age – approx 58. Height 5 foot 10. Weight: 16 stone 4. Very obese. Blond. Long hair. Dress: eccentric: Ultra modern. Bracelets. Anklet. Necklace. Wears make-up. Probably homosexual. One ring through pierced lobe. Origin: uncertain. Said to be Dutch. Name possibly assumed or corruption of a foreign name. Convicted of fraudulent practices involving the occult, London 1940. Served three months' sentence. Sus. connection with drug traffic, 1942. Since 1950 importer of ceramics, jewellery and fancy goods into Ng'ombwana. Large, profitable concern. Owned blocks of flats and offices now possessed by Ng'ombwanan interests. Strong supporter of apartheid. Known to associate with Anti-Black and African extremists. Only traceable relative: Sister, with whom he is now in partnership, pottery business 'The piggery', Capricorn Mews, SW3."'

'There you are!' said Mr Whipplestone, spreading out his hands.

'Yes. There we are and not very far on. There's no specific reason to suppose Sanskrit constitutes a threat to the safety of the President. And that goes for any of the other names on the list. Have a look at it. Does it ring any more bells? Any more coincidences?'

Mr Whipplestone screwed in his eyeglass and had a look.

'Yes, yes, yes,' he said drily. 'One recognizes the disillusioned African element. *And* the dispossessed. I can add nothing. I'm afraid, my dear fellow, that apart from the odd circumstance of one of your remote possibilities being a neighbour of mine, I am of no use to you. And none in that respect, either, if one comes to think of it. A broken reed,' sighed Mr Whipplestone, 'I fear, a broken reed.'

'Oh,' Alleyn said lightly, 'you never know, do you? By the way, the Ng'ombwanan Embassy is in your part of the world, isn't it?'

'Yes, indeed. I run into old Karumba sometimes. Their Ambassador. We take our constitutional at the same hour. Nice old boy.'

'Worried?'

'Hideously, I should have thought.'

'You'd have been right. He's in a flat spin and treating the SB to a hell of a work-out. And what's more he's switched over to me. Never mind about security not being my proper pigeon. He should worry! I know The Boomer and that's enough. He wants me to teach the SB its own business. Imagine! If he had his wish there'd be total alarm devices in every ornamental urn and a security man under The Boomer's bed. I must say I don't blame him. He's giving a reception. I suppose you've been invited?'

'I have, yes. And you?'

'In my reluctant role as The Boomer's old school chum. And Troy, of course,' Alleyn said, putting his hand briefly on hers.

Then followed rather a long pause.

'Of course,' Mr Whipplestone said, at last, 'these things don't happen in England. At receptions and so on. Madmen at large in kitchens or wherever it was.'

'Or at upstairs windows in warehouses?'

'Quite.'

The telephone rang and Troy went out of the room to answer it.

'I ought to forbear,' Alleyn said, 'from offering the maddening observation that there's always a first time.'

'Oh, nonsense!' flustered Mr Whipplestone. 'Nonsense, my dear fellow! Really! Nonsense! Well,' he added uneasily, 'one *says* that.'

'Let's hope one's right.'

Troy came back. 'The Ng'ombwanan Ambassador,' she said, 'would like a word with you, darling.'

'God bless his woolly grey head,' Alleyn muttered and cast up his eyes. He went to the door but checked. 'Another Sanskrit coincidence for you, Sam. I rather think I saw him, too, three weeks ago in Ng'ombwana, outside his erstwhile emporium, complete with anklet and earring. The one and only Sanskrit, or I'm a displaced Dutchman with beads and blond curls.'

IV

The Chubbs raised no particular objection to Lucy: 'So long as it's not unhealthy, sir,' Mrs Chubb said, 'I don't mind. Keep the mice out, I dare say.'

In a week's time Lucy improved enormously. Her coat became glossy, her eyes bright and her person plumpish. Her attachment to Mr Whipplestone grew more marked and he, as he confided in his diary, was in some danger of making an old fool of himself over her. 'She is a beguiling little animal,' he wrote, 'I confess I find myself flattered by her attentions. She has nice ways.' The nice ways consisted of keeping a close watch on him, of greeting him on his reappearance after an hour's absence as if he had returned from the North Pole, of tearing about the house with her tail up, affecting astonishment when she encountered him and of sudden onsets of attachment when she would grip his arm in her forelegs, kick it with her hind legs, pretend to bite him and then fall into a little frenzy of purrs and licks.

She refused utterly to accommodate to her red harness but when Mr Whipplestone took his evening stroll, she accompanied him: at first to his consternation. But although she darted ahead and pranced out of hiding places at him, she kept off the street and their joint expeditions became a habit.

Only one circumstance upset them and that was a curious one. Lucy would trot contentedly down Capricorn Mews until they had passed the garage and were within thirty yards of the pottery-pigs establishment. At that point she would go no further. She either bolted home under her own steam or performed her familiar trick of leaping into Mr Whipplestone's arms. On these occasions he was distressed to feel her trembling. He concluded that she remembered her accident and yet he was not altogether satisfied with this explanation.

She fought shy of the Napoli because of the dogs tied up outside but on one visit when there happened to be no customers and no dogs she walked in. Mr Whipplestone apologized and picked her up. He had become quite friendly with Mr and Mrs Pirelli and told them about her. Their response was a little strange. There were ejaculations of *'poverina'* and the sorts of noises Italians make to cats. Mrs Pirelli advanced a finger and crooned. She then noticed the white tip of Lucy's tail and looked very hard at her. She spoke in Italian to her husband, who nodded portentously and said *'Si'* some ten times in succession.

'Have you recognized the cat?' asked Mr Whipplestone in alarm. They said they thought they had. Mrs Pirelli had very little English. She was a very large lady and she now made herself a great deal larger in eloquent mime, curving both arms in front of her and blowing out her cheeks. She also jerked her head in the direction of Capricorn Passage. 'You mean the pottery person,' cried Mr Whipplestone. 'You mean she was that person's cat!'

He realized bemusedly that Mrs Pirelli had made another gesture, an ancient one. She had crossed herself. She laid her hand on Mr Whipplestone's arm. 'No, no, no. Do not give back. No. *Cattivo. Cattivo,'* said Mrs Pirelli.

'Cat?'

'No, signor,' said Mr Pirelli. 'My wife is saying "bad". They are bad, cruel people. Do not return to them your little cat.'

'No,' said Mr Whipplestone confusedly. 'No, I won't. Thank you. I won't.'

And from that day he never took Lucy into the Mews.

Mrs Chubb, Lucy accepted as a source of food and accordingly performed the obligatory ritual of brushing round her ankles. Chubb, she completely ignored.

She spent a good deal of time in the tub garden at the back of the house making wild balletic passes at imaginary butterflies.

At 9.30 one morning, a week after his dinner with the Alleyns, Mr Whipplestone sat in his drawing-room doing *The Times* crossword. Chubb was out shopping and Mrs Chubb, having finished her housework, was 'doing for' Mr Sheridan in the basement. Mr Sheridan, who was something in the City, Mr Whipplestone gathered, was never at home on weekday mornings. At 11 o'clock Mrs Chubb would return to see about Mr Whipplestone's luncheon. The arrangement worked admirably.

Held up over a particularly cryptic clue, Mr Whipplestone's attention was caught by a singular noise, a kind of stifled complaint as if

Lucy was mewing with her mouth full. This proved to be the case. She entered the room backwards with sunken head, approached crab-wise and dropped something heavy on his foot. She then sat back and gazed at him with her head on one side and made the inquiring trill that he found particularly fetching.

'What on earth have you got there?' he asked.

He picked it up. It was a ceramic no bigger than a medallion but it was heavy and must have grievously taxed her delicate little jaws. A pottery fish, painted white on one side and biting its own tail. It was pierced by a hole at the top.

'Where did you get this?' he asked severely.

Lucy lifted a paw, lay down, looked archly at him from under her arm and then incontinently jumped up and left the room.

'Extraordinary little creature,' he muttered. 'It must belong to the Chubbs.'

And when Mrs Chubb returned from below he called her in and showed it to her. 'Is this yours, Mrs Chubb?' he asked.

She had a technique of not replying immediately to anything that was said to her and she used it now. He held the thing out to her but she didn't take it.

'The cat brought it in,' explained Mr Whipplestone, who always introduced a tone of indifference in mentioning Lucy Lockett to the Chubbs. 'Do you know where it came from?'

'I think – it must be – I think it's Mr Sheridan's, sir,' Mrs Chubb said at last. 'One of his ornaments, like. The cat gets through his back window, sir, when it's open for airing. Like when I done it just now. But I never noticed.'

'Does she? Dear me! Most reprehensible! You might put it back, Mrs Chubb, could you? Too awkward if he should miss it!'

Mrs Chubb's fingers closed over it. Mr Whipplestone looking up at her, saw with surprise that her apple-pink cheeks had blanched. He thought of asking her if she was unwell but her colour began to reappear unevenly.

'All right, Mrs Chubb?' he asked.

She seemed to hover on the brink of some reply. Her lips moved and she brushed them with her fingers. At last she said: 'I haven't liked to ask, sir, but I hope we give satisfaction, Chubb and me.'

'Indeed you do,' he said warmly. 'Everything goes very smoothly.'

'Thank you, sir,' she said and went out. He thought: 'That wasn't what she was about to say.'

He heard her go upstairs and thought: 'I wish she'd return that damn'd object.' But almost immediately she came back.

He went through to the dining-room window and watched her descend the outside steps into the back garden and disappear into Mr Sheridan's flat. Within seconds he heard the door slam and saw her return.

A white pottery fish. Like a medallion. He really must not get into the habit of thinking things had happened before or been heard of or seen before. There were scientific explanations, he believed, for such experiences. One lobe of one's brain working a billionth of a second before the other or something to do with Time Spirals. He wouldn't know. But of course, in the case of the Sanskrit person it was all perfectly straightforward: he *had* in the past seen the name written up. He had merely forgotten.

Lucy made one of her excitable entrances. She tore into the room as if the devil was after her, stopped short with her ears laid back and affected to see Mr Whipplestone for the first time: 'Heavens! You!'

'Come here,' he said sharply.

She pretended not to hear him, strolled absently nearer and suddenly leapt into his lap and began to knead.

'You are *not*,' he said, checking this painful exercise, 'to sneak into other people's flats and steal pottery fish.'

And there for the moment the matter rested.

Until five days later when, on a very warm evening, she once more stole the medallion and dumped it at her owner's feet.

Mr Whipplestone scarcely knew whether he was exasperated or diverted by this repeated misdemeanour. He admonished his cat, who seemed merely to be thinking of something else. He wondered if he could again leave it to Mrs Chubb to restore the object to its rightful place in the morning and then told himself that really this wouldn't do.

He turned the medallion over in his hand. There was some sort of inscription fired on the reverse side: a wavy X. There was a hole at the top through which, no doubt, a cord could be passed. It was a common little object, entirely without distinction. A keepsake of some sort, he supposed.

Mr Sheridan was at home. Light from his open kitchen window illuminated the back regions and streaked through gaps in his sitting-room curtains.

'You're an unconscionable nuisance,' Mr Whipplestone said to Lucy Lockett.

He put the medallion in his jacket pocket, let himself out at his front door, took some six paces along the pavement and passed through the iron gate and down the short flight of steps to Mr Sheridan's door. Lucy, anticipating an evening stroll, was too quick for him. She shot over his feet, and down the steps and hid behind a dwarfed yew tree.

He rang the door bell.

It was answered by Mr Sheridan. The light in his little entrance lobby was behind him so that his face was in shadow. He had left the door into his sitting-room open and Mr Whipplestone saw that he had company. Two armchairs in view had their backs towards him but the tops of their occupants' heads showed above them.

'I do apologize,' said Mr Whipplestone, 'not only for disturbing you but for – ' he dipped into his pocket and then held out the medallion – 'this,' he said.

Mr Sheridan's behaviour oddly repeated that of Mrs Chubb. He stook stock still. Perhaps no more than a couple of seconds passed in absolute silence but it seemed much longer before he said:

'I don't understand. Are you – ?'

'I must explain,' Mr Whipplestone said: and did.

While he was explaining the occupant of one of the chairs turned and looked over the back. He could see only the top of the head, the forehead and the eyes but there was no mistaking Mrs Montfort. Their eyes met and she ducked out of sight.

Sheridan remained perfectly silent until the end of the recital and even then said nothing. He had made no move to recover his property but on Mr Whipplestone again offering it, extended his hand.

'I'm afraid the wretched little beast has taken to following Mrs Chubb into your flat. Through your kitchen window, I imagine. I am so very sorry,' said Mr Whipplestone.

Sheridan suddenly became effusive. 'Not another syllable,' he lisped. 'Don't give it another thought. It's of no value, as you can see. I shall put it out of reach. Thank you so much. Yes.'

'Good night,' said Mr Whipplestone.

'Good night, good night. Warm for the time of year, isn't it? Good night. Yes.'

Certainly, the door was not shut in his face but the moment he turned his back it was shut very quickly.

As he reached the top of the iron steps he was treated to yet another repetitive occurrence. The Sanskrits, brother and sister, were crossing the street towards him. At the same moment his cat who had come out of hiding barged against his leg and bolted like black lightning down the street.

The second or two that elapsed while he let himself out by the area gate brought the Sanskrits quite close. Obviously they were again visiting down below. They waited for him to come out. He smelt them and was instantly back in Ng'ombwana. What was it? Sandarac? They made incense of it and burnt it in the markets. The man was as outlandish as ever. Even fatter. And painted. Bedizened. And as Mr Whipplestone turned quickly away, what *had* he seen, dangling from that unspeakable neck? A medallion? A white fish? He was further disturbed by the disappearance so precipitately of Lucy, and greatly dismayed by the notion that she might get lost. He was in two minds whether to go after her to call to her and make a fool of himself in so doing.

While he still hesitated he saw a small shadow moving towards him. He did call and suddenly she came tearing back and, in her familiar fashion, launched herself at him. He carried her up his own steps.

'That's right,' he said. 'You come indoors. Come straight indoors. Where we both belong.'

But when they had reached their haven, Mr Whipplestone gave himself a drink. He had been disturbed by too many almost simultaneous occurrences, the most troublesome of which was his brief exchange with Mr Sheridan. 'I've seen him before,' he said to himself, 'and I don't mean here, when I took the house. I mean in the past. Somewhere. Somewhere. And the impression is not agreeable.'

But his memory was disobliging and after teasing himself with unprofitable speculation, he finished his drink and in a state of well-disciplined excitement, telephoned his friend Superintendent Alleyn.

CHAPTER 3

Catastrophe

The Ng'ombwanan Embassy had been built for a Georgian merchant prince and was really far too grand, Alleyn saw, for an emergent African republic. It had come upon the market at the expiration of a long lease and had been snatched up by The Boomer's representatives in London. It would not have ill-become a major power.

He saw a splendid house, beautifully proportioned and conveying, by its very moderation, a sense of calm and spaciousness. The reception rooms, covering almost the whole of the ground floor, gave at the rear on to an extensive garden with, among other felicities, a small lake. The garden had fallen into disrepair but had been most elegantly restored by Vistas of Baronsgate. Their associated firm, Decor and Design, also of Baronsgate, had been responsible for the interior.

'They must have got more than they bargained for,' Alleyn said, 'when the occupants brought in their bits and pieces.'

He was casing the premises in the company, and at the invitation, of his opposite number in the Special Branch, Superintendent Fred Gibson, a vast, pale, muted man who was careful to point out that they were there at the express invitation of the Ng'ombwanan Ambassador and were, virtually, on Ng'ombwanan soil.

'We're here on sufferance if you like,' Gibson said in his paddy voice. 'Of course they're still a Commonwealth nation, of sorts, but I reckon they could say "thanks a lot, goodbye for now" any time they fancied.'

'I believe they could, Fred.'

'Not that I want the job. Gawd, no! But as soon as His Nibs pokes his nose out of doors he's our bit of trouble and no mistake.'

'Tricky for you,' said Alleyn. He and Gibson had been associates in their early days and knew each other pretty well.

They were at one end of a reception saloon or ballroom to which they had been shown by an enormous African flunkey, who had then withdrawn to the opposite end where he waited, motionless.

Alleyn was looking at a shallow recess which occupied almost the whole of their end. It was lined with a crimson and gold paper on which had been hung Ng'ombwanan artifacts – shields, masks, cloaks, spears – so assembled as to form a sort of giant African Trophy flanked with Heraldic Achievements. At the base of this display was a ceremonial drum. A spotlight had been set to cover the area. It was an impressive arrangement and in effect harked back to the days when the house was built and Nubian statues and little black turbaned pages were the rage in London. The Boomer, Alleyn thought, would not be displeased.

A minstrels' gallery ran round three sides of the saloon and Gibson explained that four of his men as well as the orchestra would be stationed up there.

Six pairs of french windows opened on the garden. Vistas had achieved a false perspective by planting on either side of the long pond yew trees – tall in the foreground, diminishing in size until they ended in miniatures. The pond itself had been correspondingly shaped. It was wide where the trees were tall and narrowed throughout its length. The *trompe l'oeil* was startling. Alleyn had read somewhere or another of Henry Irving's production of *The Corsican Brothers* with six-foot guardsmen nearest the audience and midgets in the background. The effect here, he thought, would be the reverse of Irving's, for at the far end of the little lake a pavilion had been set up where The Boomer, the Ambassador and a small assortment of distinguished guests would assemble for an *al fresco* entertainment. From the saloon, they would look like Gullivers in Lilliput. Which again, Alleyn reflected, would not displease The Boomer.

He and Gibson spoke in undertones on account of the flunkey.

'You see how the land lies,' said Gibson. 'I'll show you the plan in a sec. The whole show – this evening party – takes place on the ground floor. And later in the bloody garden. Nobody goes upstairs except the regular house-staff and we look after that one. Someone at every stair-head, don't you worry. Now. As you see, the entrance hall's behind us at a lower level and the garden through the windows in front. On your left are the other reception rooms: a smaller drawing-room, the dining-room – you could call it a banqueting hall without going too far – and the kitchens and offices. On our right, opening off the entrance hall behind us, is a sort of ladies' sitting-room and off that, on the other side of the alcove with all the hardware,' said Gibson indicating the Ng'ombwanan trophies, 'is the ladies cloakroom. Very choice. You know. Ankle-deep carpets. Armchairs, dressing-tables. Face-stuff pro-vided and two attendants. The WCs themselves, four of them, have louvre windows opening on the garden. You could barely get a fair shot at the pavilion through any of them because of intervening trees. Still. We're putting in a reliable female sergeant.'

'Tarted up as an attendant?'

'Naturally.'

'Fair enough. Where's the men's cloakroom?'

'On the other side of the entrance hall. It opens off a sort of smoking-room or what-have-you that's going to be set up with a bar. The lavatory windows in their case would give a better line on the pavilion and we're making arrangements accordingly.'

'What about the grounds?'

'The grounds are one hell of a problem. Greenery all over the shop,' grumbled Mr Gibson.

'High brick wall, though?'

'Oh, yes. And iron spikes, but what of that? We'll do a complete final search – number one job – at the last moment. House, garden, the lot. And a complete muster of personnel. The catering's being handled by Costard et Cie of Mayfair. Very high class. Hand-picked staff. All their people are what they call maximum-trusted, long-service employees.'

'They take on extra labour for these sort of jobs though, don't they?'

'I know, but they say nobody they can't vouch for.'

'What about – ' Alleyn moved his head very slightly in the direc-tion of the man in livery who was gazing out of the window.

'The Ng'ombwanan lot? Well. The household's run by one of them. Educated in England and trained at a first-class hotel in Paris.

Top credentials. The Embassy staff was hand-picked in Ng'ombwana, they tell me. I don't know what that's worth, the way things are in those countries. All told, there are thirty of them but some of the President's household are coming over for the event. The Ng'ombwanans, far as I can make out, will more or less stand round looking pretty. That chap, there,' Mr Gibson continued, slurring his words and talking out of the corner of his mouth, 'is sort of special: you might say a ceremonial bodyguard to the President. He hangs round on formal occasions dressed up like a cannibal and carrying a dirty big symbolic spear. Like a mace-bearer, sort of, or a sword-of-state. You name it. He came in advance with several of the President's personal staff. The Presidential plane, as you probably know, touches down at eleven tomorrow morning.'

'How's the Ambassador shaping up?'

'Having kittens.'

'Poor man.'

'One moment all worked up about the party and the next in a muck sweat over security. It was at his urgent invitation we came in.'

'He rings me up incessantly on the strength of my knowing the great panjandrum.'

'Well,' Gibson said, 'that's why *I've* roped you in, isn't it? And seeing you're going to be here as a guest – excuse me if my manner's too familiar – the situation becomes what you might call provocative. Don't misunderstand me.'

'What do you want me to do, for pity's sake? Fling myself in a protective frenzy on The Boomer's bosom every time down in the shrubbery something stirs?'

'Not,' said Gibson, pursuing his own line of thought, 'that I think we're going to have real trouble. Not really. Not at this reception affair. It's his comings and goings that are the real headache. D'you reckon he's going to co-operate? You know. Keep to his undertaking with you and not go drifting off on unscheduled jaunts?'

'One can but hope. What's the order of events? At the reception?'

'For a kick-off, he stands in the entrance hall on the short flight of steps leading up to his room, with this spear-carrying character behind him and the Ambassador on his right. His aides will be back a few paces on his left. His personal bodyguard will form a lane from the entrance right up to him. They carry sidearms as part of their full-dress issue. I've got eight chaps outside, covering the walk from the cars to the entrance and a dozen more in and about the hall. They're in livery. Good men. I've fixed it with the Costard people that they'll give them enough to do, handing champagne round and that, to keep them in the picture.'

'What's the drill, then?'

'As the guests arrive from 9.30 onwards, they get their names bawled out by the major-domo at the entrance. They walk up the lane between the guards, the Ambassador presents them to the President and they shake hands and pass in here. There's a band (Louis Francini's lot. I've checked them) up in the minstrels' gallery and chairs for the official party on the dais in front of the hardware. Other chairs round the walls.'

'And we all mill about in here for a spell, do we?'

'That's right. Quaffing your bubbly,' said Gibson tonelessly. 'Until 10 o'clock when the french windows will all be opened and the staff, including my lot, will set about asking you to move into the garden.'

'And that's when your headache really sets in, is it, Fred?'

'My oath! Well, take a look at it.'

They moved out through the french windows into the garden. A narrow terrace separated the house from the wide end of the pond which was flanked on each converging side by paved walks. And there, at the narrow end, was the pavilion: an elegant affair of striped material caught up by giant spears topped with plumes. Chairs for the guests were set out on each side of that end of the lake and the whole assembly was backed by Mr Gibson's hated trees.

'Of course,' he said gloomily, 'there will be all these perishing fairy-lights. You notice even they get smaller as they go back. To carry out the effect, like. You've got to hand it to them, they've been thorough.'

'At least they'll shed a bit of light on the scene.'

'Not for long, don't you worry. There are going to be musical items and a film. Screen wheeled out against the house, here, and the projector on a perch at the far end. And while that's on, out go the lights except in the pavilion, if you please, where they're putting an ornamental god-almighty lamp which will show His Nibs up like a sitting duck.'

'How long does that last?'

'Twenty minutes all told. There's some kind of dance. Followed by a native turn-out with drums and one or two other items including a singer. The whole thing covers about an hour. At the expiration of which you all come back for supper in the banqueting room. And then, please God, you all go home.'

'You couldn't persuade them to modify their plans at all?'

'Not a chance. It's been laid on by headquarters.'

'Do you mean in Ng'ombwana, Fred?'

'That's right. Two chaps from Vistas and Decor and Design were flown out with plans and photographs of this pad at which the President took a long hard look and then dreamt up the whole treatment. He sent one of his henchmen over to see it was laid on according to specification. I reckon it's as much as the Ambassador's job's worth to change it. And how do you like this?' Gibson asked with a poignant note of outrage in his normally colourless voice. 'The Ambassador's given us definite instructions to keep well away from this bloody pavilion. President's orders and no excuse-me's about it.'

'He's a darling man is The Boomer.'

'He's making a monkey out of us. I set up a security measure only to be told the President won't stand for it. Look – I'd turn the whole exercise in if I could get someone to listen to me. Pavilion and all.'

'What if it rains?'

'The whole shooting-match moves indoors and why the hell do I say "shooting-match"?' asked Mr Gibson moodily.

'So we pray for a wet night?'

'Say that again.'

'Let's take a look indoors.'

They explored the magnificence of the upper floors, still attended by the Ng'ombwanan spear-carrier who always removed himself to the greatest possible distance, but never left them completely alone. Alleyn tried a remark or two but the man seemed to have little or no English. His manner was stately and utterly inexpressive.

Gibson re-rehearsed his plan of action for the morrow and Alleyn could find no fault in it. The Special Branch is a bit of a loner in the Service. It does not gossip about its proceedings and except when they overlap those of another arm, nobody asks it anything. Alleyn, however, was on such terms with Gibson and the circumstances were so unusual as to allow them to relax these austerities. They retired to their car and lit their pipes. Gibson began to talk about subversive elements from emergent independencies, known to be based on London and with what he called 'violence in their CRO'.

'Some are all on their own,' he said, 'and some kind of coagulate like blood. Small-time secret societies. Mostly they don't get anywhere but there are what you might call malignant areas. And of course you can't discount the pro.'

'The professional gun?'

'They're still available. There's Hinny Packmann. He's out after doing bird in a Swedish stir. He'd be available if the money was right. He doesn't operate under three thousand.'

'Hinny's in Denmark.'

'That's right, according to Interpol. But he could be imported. I don't know anything about the political angle,' Gibson said. 'Not my scene. Who'd take over if this man was knocked off?'

'I'm told there'd be a revolution of sorts, that mercenaries would be sent in, a puppet government set up and that in the upshot the big interests would return and take over.'

'Yes, well, there's that aspect and then again you might get the solitary fanatic. He's the type I really do *not* like,' Gibson said, indignantly drawing a nice distinction between potential assassins. 'No record, as likely as not. You don't know where to look for him.'

'You've got the guest list of course.'

'Of course. I'll show it to you. Wait a sec'

He fished it out of an inner pocket and they conned it over. Gibson had put a tick beside some five dozen names.

'They've all been on the Ng'ombwanan scene in one capacity or another,' he said. 'From the oil barons at the top to ex-businessmen at the bottom and nearly all of them have been, or are in the process of being, kicked out. The big idea behind this reception seems to be a sort of "nothing personal intended" slant. "Everybody loves everybody" and please come to my party!'

'It hurts me more than it does you?'

'That's right. And they've all accepted, what's more.'

'Hullo!' Alleyn exclaimed, pointing to the list. 'They've asked *him!*'

'Which is that? Ah. Yes. Him. Now, he *has* got a record.'

'See the list your people kindly supplied to me,' Alleyn said and produced it.

'That's right. Not for violence, of course, but a murky background and no error. Nasty bit of work. I don't much fancy *him.*'

'His sister makes pottery pigs about one minute away from the Embassy,' said Alleyn.

'I know that. Very umpty little dump. You'd wonder why, wouldn't you, with all the money he must have made in Ng'ombwana.'

'Has he still got it, though? Mightn't he be broke?'

'Hard to say. Question of whether he laid off his bets before the troubles began.'

'Do you know about this one?' Alleyn asked, pointing to the name Whipplestone on the guest list.

Gibson instantly reeled off a thumbnail sketch of Mr Whipplestone.

'That's the man,' Alleyn said. 'Well now, Fred, this may be a matter of no importance but you may as well lay back your ears and listen.' And he related Mr Whipplestone's story of his cat and the pottery fish. 'Whipplestone's a bit perturbed about it,' he said in the end, 'but it may be entirely beside the point as far as we're concerned. This man in the basement, Sheridan, and the odious Sanskrit may simply meet to play bridge. Or they might belong to some potty little esoteric circle: fortune-telling or spiritism or what have you.'

'That's the type of thing Sanskrit first got borrowed for. Fortune-telling and false pretences. He's a sus for drugs. It was after he came out of stir that he set himself up as a merchant in Ng'ombwana. He's one of the dispossessed,' said Gibson.

'I know.'

'You do?'

'I think I saw him outside his erstwhile premises when I was there three weeks ago.'

'Fancy that.'

'About the ones that get together to bellyache in exile: you don't, I suppose, know of a fish medallion lot?'

'Hah!' said Gibson disgustedly.

'And Mr Sheridan doesn't appear on the guest list. What about a Colonel and Mrs Montfort? They were in Sheridan's flat that evening.'

'Here. Let's see.'

'No,' Alleyn said, consulting the list. 'No Montforts under the M's.'

'Wait a sec. I knew there was something. Look here. Under C. "Lt-Col. Cockburn-Montfort, Barset Light Infantry (retd)." What a name. Cockburn.'

'Isn't it usually pronounced Coburn?' Alleyn mildly suggested. 'Anything about him?'

'Info. Here we are. "Organized Ng'ombwanan army. Stationed there from 1960 until Independence in 1971 when present government assumed complete control!"'

'Well,' Alleyn said after a longish pause, 'it still doesn't have to amount to anything. No doubt ex-Ng'ombwanan colonials tend to flock together like ex-Anglo-Indians. There may be a little clutch of them in the Capricorns all belly-aching cosily together. What about the staff? The non-Ng'ombwanans, I mean.'

'We're nothing if not thorough. Every last one's been accounted for. Want to look?'

He produced a second list. 'It shows the Costard employees together. Regulars first, extras afterwards. Clean as whistles, the lot of them.'

'This one?'

Gibson followed Alleyn's long index finger and read under his breath, '"Employed by Costards as extra waiter over period of ten years. In regular employment as domestic servant. Recent position: eight years. Excellent references. Present employment – " Hullo, 'ullo.'

'Yes?'

' "Present employment at 1 Capricorn Walk, SW3." '

'We seem,' Alleyn said, 'to be amassing quite a little clutch of coincidences, don't we?'

II

'It's not often,' Alleyn said to his wife, 'that we set ourselves up in this rig, is it?'

'You look as if you did it as a matter of course every night. Like the jokes about Empire builders in the jungle. When there was an Empire. Orders and decorations to boot.'

'What does one mean exactly, by "to boot"?'

'You tell me, darling, you're the purist.'

'I was when I courted my wife.'

Troy, in her green gown, sat on her bed and pulled on her long gloves. 'It's worked out all right,' she said. 'Us. Wouldn't you say?'

'I would say.'

'What a bit of luck for us.'

'All of that.'

He buttoned up her gloves for her. 'You look lovely,' he said. 'Shall we go?'

'Is our svelte hired limousine at the door?'

'It is.'

'Whoops, then, hark chivvy away.'

Palace Park Gardens had been closed to general traffic by the police so the usual crowd of onlookers was not outside the Ng'ombwanan Embassy. The steps were red-carpeted, a flood of light and strains of blameless and dated melodies, streamed through the great open doorway. A galaxy of liveried men, black and white, opened car doors and slammed them again.

'Oh, Lord. I've forgotten the damn card!' Troy exclaimed.

'I've got it. Here we go.'

The cards, Alleyn saw, were being given a pretty hard look by the men who received them and were handed on to other men seated unobtrusively at tables. He was amused to see, hovering in the background, Superintendent Gibson in tails and a white tie, looking a little as if he might be an Old Dominion Plenipotentiary.

Those guests wishing for the cloakrooms turned off to the right and left and on re-entering the hall were martialled back to the end of the double file of Ng'ombwanan guards where they gave their names to a superb black major-domo who roared them out with all the resonant assurance of a war drum.

Troy and Alleyn had no trappings to shed and passed directly into the channel of approach.

And there, at the far end of the flight of steps leading to the great saloon, was The Boomer himself, in great state, backed by his spearcarrier and wearing a uniform that might have been inspired by the Napoleonic Old Guard upon whom had been lightly laid the restraining hand of Sandhurst.

Troy muttered: 'He's wonderful. Gosh, he's glorious!'

She'd like to paint him, thought Alleyn.

The patiently anxious Ambassador, similarly if less gorgeously uniformed, was stationed on The Boomer's right. Their personal staff stood about in magnificent attitudes behind them.

'Mis-tar and Mrs Roderick Alleyn.'

That huge and beguiling smile opened and illuminated The Boomer's face. He said loudly: 'No need for an introduction here,' and took Alleyn's hands in both his gloved paws.

'And this is the famous wife!' he resonantly proclaimed. 'I am so glad. We meet later. I have a favour to ask. Yes?'

The Alleyns moved on, conscious of being the object of a certain amount of covert attention.

'Rory?'

'Yes, I know. Extra special, isn't he?'

'Whew!'

'What?'

' "Whew." Incredulous whistle.'

'Difficult, in competition with Gilbert and Sullivan.'

They had passed into the great saloon. In the minstrels' gallery instrumentalists, inconspicuously augmented by a clutch of Gibson's silent henchmen, were discussing *The Gondoliers*.

'*When everyone is somebodee*

Then no one's anybody,'

they brightly and almost inaudibly chirped.

Trays with champagne were circulated. Jokes about constabular boots and ill-fitting liveries were not appropriate. Among the white servants it was impossible to single out Fred Gibson's men.

How to diagnose the smell of a grand assembly? Beyond the luxurious complexity of cosmetics, scent, flowers, hairdressers' lotions, remote foods and alcohol, was there something else, something peculiar to this particular occasion? Somewhere in these rooms were they burning that stuff-what was it? – sandarac? That was it. Alleyn had last smelt it in the Presidential palace in Ng'ombwana. That and the indefinably alien scent of persons of a different colour. The curtains were drawn across the french windows but the great room was not overheated as yet. People moved about it like well-directed extras in the central scene of some feature film.

They encountered acquaintances: the subject of a portrait Troy had painted some years ago for the Royal Commonwealth Society; Alleyn's great white chief and his wife; someone he knew in the Foreign Office and, unexpectedly, his brother, Sir George Alleyn: tall, handsome, ambassadorial and entirely predictable. Troy didn't really mind her brother-in-law but Alleyn always found him a bit of an ass.

'Good Lord!' said Sir George. 'Rory!'

'George.'

'And Troy, my dear. Looking too lovely. Charming! Charming! And what, may one ask, are you doing, Rory, in this *galère?*'

'They got me in to watch the teaspoons, George.'

'Jolly good, ha-ha. Matter of fact,' said Sir George, bending archly down to Troy, 'between you and me and the gatepost I've no idea why I'm here myself. Except that we've all been asked.'

'Do you mean your entire family, George?' inquired his brother. 'Twins and all?'

'So amusing. I mean,' he told Troy, 'the *corps diplomatique* or at least those of us who've had the honour to represent Her Majesty's Government in "furrin parts",' said Sir George, again becoming playful. 'Here we all are!' *Why,* we don't quite know!' he gaily concluded.

'To raise the general tone, I expect,' said Alleyn gravely. 'Look, Troy, there's Sam Whipplestone. Shall we have a word with him?'

'Do let's.'

'See you later, perhaps, George.'

'I understand there's to be some sort of *fête champêtre.'*

'That's right. Mind you don't fall in the pond.'

Troy said when they were at a safe remove, 'If I were George I'd thump you.'

Mr Whipplestone was standing near the dais in front of the Ng'ombwanan display of arms. His faded hair was beautifully groomed and his rather withdrawn face wore a gently attentive air. His eyeglass was at the alert. When he caught sight of the Alleyns he smiled delightedly, made a little bow, and edged towards them.

'What a *very* grand party,' he said.

'Disproportionate, would you say?' Alleyn hinted.

'Well, coming it rather strong, perhaps. I keep thinking of Martin Chuzzlewit.'

' "Todgers were going it"?'

'Yes.' Mr Whipplestone looked very directly at Alleyn. 'All going well in your part of the picture?' he asked.

'Not *mine*, you know.'

'But you've been consulted.'

'Oh,' said Alleyn, 'that! Vaguely. Quite unofficial. I was invited to view. Brother Gibson's laid on a maximum job.'

'Good.'

'By the way, did you know your man was on the strength tonight? Chubb?'

'Oh, yes. He and Mrs Chubb have been on the caterer's supplementary list for many years, he tells me. They're often called upon.'

'Yes.'

'Another of our coincidences, did you think?'

'Well – hardly that, perhaps.'

'How's Lucy Lockett?' Troy asked.

Mr Whipplestone made the little grimace that allowed his glass to dangle. 'Behaving herself with decorum,' he said primly.

'No more thieving stories?'

'Thank God, no,' he said with some fervour. 'You must meet her, both of you,' he added, 'and try Mrs Chubb's cooking. Do say you will.'

'We'd like that very much,' said Troy warmly.

'I'll telephone tomorrow and we'll arrange a time.'

'By the way,' Alleyn said, 'talking of Lucy Lockett reminds me of your Mr Sheridan. Have you any idea what he does?'

'Something in the City, I think. Why?'

'It's just that the link with the Sanskrit couple gives him a certain interest. There's no connection with Ng'ombwana?'

'Not that I know.'

'He's not here tonight,' Alleyn said.

One of the ADCs was making his way through the thickening crowd. Alleyn recognized him as his escort in Ng'ombwana. He saw Alleyn and came straight to him, all eyes and teeth.

'Mr Alleyn, His Excellency the Ambassador wishes me to say that the President will be very pleased if you and Mrs Alleyn will join the official party for the entertainment in the garden. I will escort you when the time comes. Perhaps we could meet here.'

'That's very kind,' Alleyn said. 'We shall be honoured.'

'Dear me,' said Mr Whipplestone when the ADC had gone, 'Todgers *are* going it an' no mistake.'

'It's The Boomer at it again. I wish he wouldn't.'

Troy said: 'What do you suppose he meant when he said he had a favour to ask?'

'He said it to you, darling. Not me.'

'I've got one I'd like to ask him, all right.'

'No prize offered for guessing the answer. She wants,' Alleyn explained to Mr Whipplestone, 'to paint him.'

'Surely,' he rejoined with his little bow, 'that wish has only to be made known – Good God!'

He had broken off to stare at the entrance into the saloon where the last arrivals were coming in. Among them, larger, taller, immeasurably more conspicuous than anyone else in their neighbourhood, were Mr Whipplestone's bugbears: the Sanskrits, brother and sister.

They were, by and large, appropriately attired. That is to say, they wore full evening dress. The man's shirt, to Mr Whipplestone's utterly conventional taste, was unspeakable, being heavily frilled and lacy, with a sequin or two winking in its depths. He wore many rings on his dimpled fingers. His fair hair was cut in a fringe and concealed his ears. He was skilfully but unmistakably *en maquillage*, as Mr Whipplestone shudderingly put it to himself. The sister, vast in green, fringed satin, also wore her hair, which was purple, in a fringe and side-pieces. These in effect squared her enormous face. They moved slowly like two huge vessels, shoved from behind by tugs.

'I thought you'd be surprised,' Alleyn said. He bent his head and shoulders, being so tall, in order that he and Mr Whipplestone could converse without shouting. The conglomerate roar of voices now almost drowned the orchestra which, pursuing its course through the century, had now reached the heyday of Cochran's Revues.

'You knew they were invited?' Mr Whipplestone said, referring to the Sanskrits. 'Well, *really*!'

'Not very delicious, I agree. By the way, somewhere here there's another brace of birds from your Capricorn preserves.'

'Not – '

'The Montforts.'

'That is less upsetting.'

'The Colonel had a big hand, it appears, in setting up their army.'

Mr Whipplestone looked steadily at him. 'Are you talking about Cockburn-Montfort?' he said at last.

'That's right.'

'Then why the devil couldn't his wife say so,' he crossly exclaimed. 'Silly creature! Why leave out the Cockburn? Too tiresome. Yes, well, naturally, *he'd* be asked. I never met him. He hadn't appeared on the scene in my early days and he'd gone when I returned.' He thought for a moment. 'Sadly run to seed,' he said. 'And his wife, too, I'm afraid.'

'The bottle?'

'I should imagine, the bottle. I did tell you, didn't I, that they were in Sheridan's basement, that evening when I called? And that she dodged down?'

'You did, indeed.'

'And that she had – um – ?'

'Accosted you in the pet-shop? Yes.'

'Quite so.'

'Well, I dare say she'll have another fling if she spots you tonight. You might introduce us, if she does.'

'Really?'

'Yes, really.'

After about ten minutes, Mr Whipplestone said that there the Cockburn-Montforts, in fact, were, some thirty feet away and drifting in their direction. Alleyn suggested that they move casually towards them.

'Well, my dear fellow, if you insist.'

So it was done. Mrs Cockburn-Montfort spotted Mr Whipplestone and bowed. They saw her speak to her husband, obviously suggesting they should effect an encounter.

'Good evening!' she cried as they approached. 'What odd places we meet in, don't we? Animal shops and Embassies.' And when they were actually face to face: 'I've told my husband about you and your piteous little pusscat. Darling, this is Mr Whipplestone, our new boy at No. 1, The Walk. Remember?'

'Hiyar,' said Colonel Cockburn-Montfort.

Mr Whipplestone, following what he conceived to be Alleyn's wishes, modestly deployed his social expertise. 'How do you do,' he said, and to the lady: 'Do you know, I feel quite ashamed of myself. I didn't realize, when we encountered, that your husband was *the* Cockburn-Montfort. Of Ng'ombwana,' he added, seeing that she looked nonplussed.

'Oh. Didn't you? We rather tend to let people forget the Cockburn half. So often and so shy-makingly mispronounced,' said Mrs Cockburn-Montfort, gazing up first at Alleyn and then at Mr Whipplestone, who thought: At least they both seem to be sober; and he reflected that very likely they were never entirely drunk. He introduced Alleyn and at once she switched all her attention to him, occasionally throwing a haggard, comradely glance at Troy upon whom, after a long, glazed look, the Colonel settled his attention.

In comparison with the Sanskrits they were, Mr Whipplestone thought, really not so awful or perhaps, more accurately, they were awful in a more acceptable way. The Colonel, whose voice was hoarse, told Troy that he and his wife had been hard on the Alleyns' heels when they were greeted by the President. He was evidently curious about the cordiality of their reception and began, without much subtlety, to fish. Had she been to Ng'ombwana? If so, why had they never met? He would certainly not have forgotten if they had, he added, and performed the gesture of brushing up his moustache at the corners while allowing his eyes to goggle slightly. He became quite persistent in his gallantries and Troy thought the best way to cut them short was to say that her husband had been at school with the President.

'Ah!' said the Colonel. 'Really? That explains it.' It would have been hard to say why she found the remark offensive.

A hush fell on the assembly and the band in the gallery became audible. It had approached the contemporary period and was discussing *My Fair Lady* when the President and his entourage entered the salon. They made a scarcely less than royal progress to the dais under the trophies. At the same time, Alleyn noticed, Fred Gibson turned up in the darkest part of the gallery and stood, looking down at the crowd. 'With a Little Bit of Luck,' played the band, and really, Alleyn thought, it might have been Fred's signature-tune. The players faded out obsequiously as The Boomer reached the dais.

The ceremonial spear-carrier had arrived and stood, motionless and magnificent, in a panoply of feathers, armlets, anklets, necklets and lion-skins against the central barbaric trophy. The Boomer seated himself. The Ambassador advanced to the edge of the dais. The conductor drew an admonitory flourish from his players.

'Your Excellency, Mr President, Sir. My Lords, Ladies and Gentlemen,' said the Ambassador and went on to welcome his President, his guests and, in general terms, the excellent rapprochement that obtained between his government and that of the United Kingdom, a rapprochement that encouraged the promotion of an ever-developing – his theme became a little foggy round the edges but he brought it to a sonorous conclusion and evoked a round of discreet applause.

The Boomer then rose. Troy thought to herself: I'm going to remember this. Sharply. Accurately. Everything. That great hussar's busby of grey hair. Those reflected lights in the hollows of temple and cheek. The swelling blue tunic, white paws and glittering hardware. And the background, for Heaven's sake! No, but I've got to. I've got to.

She looked at her husband who raised one eyebrow and muttered: 'I'll ask.'

She squeezed his hand violently.

The Boomer spoke briefly. Such was the magnificence of his voice that the effect was less than that of a human instrument than of some enormous double-bass. He spoke predictably of enduring bonds of fellowship in the Commonwealth and less formally of the joys of revisiting the haunts of his youth. Pursuing this theme, to Alleyn's deep misgiving, he dwelt on his schooldays and of strongly cemented, never to be broken, friendships. At which point, having obviously searched the audience and spotted his quarry, he flashed one of his startling grins straight at the Alleyns. A general murmur was induced and Mr Whipplestone, highly diverted, muttered something about 'the cynosure of all eyes'. A few sonorous generalities rounded off the little speech. When the applause had subsided, the Ambassador announced a removal to the gardens and simultaneously the curtains were drawn back and the six pairs of french windows flung open. An enchanting prospect was revealed. Golden lights, star-shaped and diminishing in size, receded into the distance and were reflected in the small lake, itself subscribing to the false perspective that culminated, at the far end, in the brilliantly lit scarlet and white pavilion. Vistas of Baronsgate had done themselves proud.

'The stage-management, as one feels inclined to call it,' said Mr Whipplestone, 'is superb. I look forward excitedly to seeing you both in the pavilion.'

'You've had too much champagne,' Alleyn said and Mr Whipplestone made a little crowing noise.

The official party passed into the garden and the guests followed in their wake. Alleyn and Troy were duly collected by the ADC and led to the pavilion. Here, they were enthusiastically greeted by The Boomer and introduced to ten distinguished guests, among whom Alleyn was amused to find his brother George, whose progress as a career-diplomat had hoisted him into more than one Ambassadorial post. The other guests consisted of the last of the British governors in Ng'ombwana and representatives of associated African independencies.

It would be incorrect to say that The Boomer was enthroned in his pavilion. His chair was not raised above the others but it was isolated and behind it stood the ceremonial spear-bearer. The guests in arrow formation flanked the President. From the house and to the guests seated on their side of the lake they must present, Alleyn thought, a remarkable picture.

The musicians had descended from their gallery into the garden and were grouped, modestly, near the house among trees that partly concealed the lavatorial louvre windows Gibson had pointed out to Alleyn.

When the company was settled, a large screen was wheeled in front of the french windows, facing down the lake towards the pavilion. A scene in the Ng'ombwanan wild-lands was now projected on this screen. A group of live Ng'ombwanan drummers then appeared before it, the garden lights were dimmed and the drummer performed. The drums throbbed and swelled, pulsed and thudded, disturbing in their monotony, unseemly in their context: a most unsettling noise. It grew to a climax. A company of warriors, painted and armed, erupted from the dark and danced. Their feet thumped down on the mown turf. From the shadow, people, Ng'ombwanans presumably, began to clap the rhythm. More and more of the guests, encouraged perhaps by champagne and the anonymity of the shadows, joined in this somewhat inelegant response. The performance crashed to a formidable conclusion.

The Boomer threw out a few explanatory observations. Champagne was again in circulation.

Apart from the President himself, Ng'ombwana had produced one other celebrity: a singer, by definition a bass but with the astonishing vocal range of just over four octaves, an attribute that he exploited without the least suggestion of break or transition. His native name, being unpronounceable by Europeans, had been simplified as Karbo and he was world-famous.

He was now to appear.

He came from the darkened ballroom and was picked up in front of the screen by a strong spotlight: a black man in conventional evening dress, with a quite extraordinary air of distinction.

All the golden stars and all the lights in the house were out. The orchestra lamps were masked. Only the single lamp by the President, complained of by Gibson, remained alight, so that he – the President – and the singer, at opposite ends of the lake, were the only persons to be seen in the benighted garden.

The orchestra played an introductory phrase.

A single deep sustained note of extraordinary strength and beauty floated from the singer.

While it still hung on the air a sound like that of a whiplash cracked out and somewhere in the house a woman screamed and screamed and screamed.

The light in the pavilion went out.

What followed was like the outbreak of a violent storm: a confusion of voices, of isolated screams, less insistent than the continuous one, of shouted orders, of chairs overturned, of something or someone falling into water. Of Alleyn's hand on Troy's shoulder. Then of his voice: 'Don't move, Troy. Stay there.' And then, unmistakably, The Boomer's great voice roaring out something in his own tongue and Alleyn saying: 'No, you don't. No!' Of a short guttural cry near at hand and a thud. And then from many voices like the king and courtiers in the play: 'Lights! Lights! Lights!'

They came up, first in the ballroom and then overhead in the garden. They revealed some of the guests still seated on either side of the lake but many on their feet talking confusedly. They revealed also the great singer, motionless, still in his spotlight and a number of men who emerged purposefully from sev-

eral directions, some striding up to the pavilion and some into the
house.

And in the pavilion itself men with their backs to Troy shutting
her in, crowding together and hiding her husband from her. Women
making intermittent exclamations in the background.

She heard her brother-in-law's voice raised in conventional
admonition: 'Don't panic, anybody. Keep calm. No need to panic,'
and even in her confusion thought that however admirable the
advice, he did unfortunately sound ridiculous.

His instructions were in effect repeated, not at all ridiculously, by
a large powerful man who appeared beside the singer.

'Keep quiet, and stay where you are, ladies and gentlemen, if you
please,' said this person, and Troy at once recognized The Yard manner.

The screaming woman had moved away somewhere inside the
house. Her cries had broken down into hysterical and incomprehensible speech. They became more distant and were finally subdued.

And now, the large purposeful man came into the pavilion. The
men who had blocked Troy's view backed away and she saw that
they had all been looking at it.

A prone figure, face down, arms spread, dressed in a flamboyant
uniform, split down the back by a plumed spear. The sky blue tunic
had a glistening patch round the place of entry. The plume, where it
touched the split, was red.

Alleyn was kneeling by the figure.

The large purposeful man moved in front of her and shut off this
picture. She heard Alleyn's voice: 'Better clear the place.' After a
moment he was beside her, holding her arm and turning her away.
'All right?' he said. 'Yes,' she nodded and found herself being shepherded out of the pavilion with the other guests.

When they had gone Alleyn returned to the spiked figure and
again knelt beside it.

He looked up at his colleague and slightly shook his head.

Superintendent Gibson muttered, 'They've done it!'

'Not precisely,' Alleyn said. He stood up and at once the group of
men moved further back. And there was The Boomer, bolt upright
in the chair that was not quite a throne, breathing deeply and looking straight before him.

'It's the Ambassador,' Alleyn said.

CHAPTER 4

Aftermath

The handling of the affair at the Ng'ombwanan Embassy was to become a classic in the annals of police procedure. Gibson, under the hard drive of a muffled fury, and with Alleyn's co-operation, had, within minutes, transformed the scene into one that resembled a sort of high-toned drafting-yard. The speed with which this was accomplished was remarkable.

The guests, marshalled into the ballroom, were, as Gibson afterwards put it, 'processed' through the dining-room. There they were shepherded up to a trestle table upon which the elaborate confections of Costard et Cie had been shoved aside to make room for six officers, summoned from Scotland Yard. These men sat with copies of the guest-list before them and with regulation tact checked off names and addresses.

Most of the guests were then encouraged to leave by a side door, a general signal having been sent out for their transport. A small group were asked, very civilly, to remain.

As Troy approached the table she saw that among the Yard officers Inspector Fox, Alleyn's constant associate, sat at the end of the row, his left ear intermittently tickled by the tail of an elaborately presented cold pheasant. When he looked over the top of his elderly spectacles and saw her, he was momentarily transfixed. She leant down. 'Yes, Br'er Fox, me,' she murmured, 'Mrs R. Alleyn, 48 Regency Close, SW3.'

'Fancy!' said Mr Fox to his list. 'What about getting home?' he mumbled. 'All right?'

'Perfectly. Hired car. Someone's ringing them. Rory's fixed it.'

Mr Fox ticked off the name, 'Thank you, madam,' he said aloud. 'We won't keep you,' and so Troy went home, and not until she got there was she to realize how very churned up she had become.

The curtained pavilion had been closed and police constables posted outside. It was lit inside and glowed like some scarlet and white striped bauble in the dark garden. Distorted shadows moved, swelled and vanished across its walls. Specialists were busy within.

In a small room normally used by the controller of the household as an office, Alleyn and Gibson attempted to get some sort of sense out of Mrs Cockburn-Montfort.

She had left off screaming but had the air of being liable to start up again at the least provocation. Her face was streaked with mascara, her mouth hung open and she pulled incessantly at her lower lip. Beside her stood her husband, the Colonel, holding, incongruously, a bottle of smelling salts.

Three women in lavender dresses with caps and stylish aprons sat in a row against the wall as if waiting to make an entrance in unison for some soubrettish turn. The largest of them was a police sergeant.

Behind the desk a male uniformed sergeant took notes and upon it sat Alleyn, facing Mrs Cockburn-Montfort. Gibson stood to one side, holding on to the lower half of his face as if it was his temper and had to be stifled.

Alleyn said: 'Mrs Cockburn-Montfort, we are all very sorry indeed to badger you like this but it really is a most urgent matter. Now. I'm going to repeat, as well as I can, what I *think* you have been telling us and if I go wrong please, *please* stop me and say so. Will you?'

'Come on, Chrissy old girl,' urged her husband. 'Stiff upper lip. It's all over now. Here!' He offered the smelling salts but was flapped away.

'You,' Alleyn said, 'were in the ladies' cloakroom. You had gone there during the general exodus of the guests from the ballroom and were to rejoin your husband for the concert in the garden. There were no other guests in the cloakroom but these ladies, the cloakroom attendants, were there? Right? Good. Now. You had had occasion to use one of the four lavatories, the second from the left. You were still there when the lights went out. So far, then, have we got it right?'

She nodded rolling her gaze from Alleyn to her husband.

'Now the next bit. As clearly as you can, won't you? What happened immediately after the lights went out?'

'I couldn't think what had happened. I mean *why*? I've told you. I really do think,' said Mrs Cockburn-Montfort squeezing out her voice like toothpaste, 'that I might be let off. I've been *hideously* shocked, I thought I was going to be killed. Truly. Hughie – ?'

'Pull yourself together, Chrissy, for God's sake. Nobody's killed you. Get on with it. Sooner said, sooner we'll be shot of it.'

'You're so *hard*,' she whimpered. And to Alleyn: 'Isn't he? Isn't he *hard*?'

But after a little further persuasion she did get on with it.

'I was still *there*,' she said. 'In the loo. Honestly! – Too awkward. And all the lights had gone out but there was a kind of glow outside those slatted sort of windows. And I suppose it was something to do with the performance. You know. That drumming and some sort of dance. I knew you'd be cross, Hughie, waiting for me out there and the concert started and all that but one can't help these things, can one?'

'All right. We all know something had upset you.'

'Yes, well, they finished – the dancing and drums had finished – and – and so had I and I was nearly going when the door burst open and hit me. Hard. On – on the back. And he took hold of me. By the arm. Brutally. And threw me out. I'm bruised and shaken and suffering from shock and you keep me here. He threw me so violently that I fell. In the cloakroom. It was much darker there than in the loo. Almost pitch dark. And I lay there. And outside, I could hear clapping and after that there was music and a voice. I suppose it was wonderful but to me, lying there, hurt and shocked, it was like a lost soul.'

'Go on, please.'

'And then there was that ghastly shot. Close. Shattering, in the loo. And the next thing – straight after that – he burst out and kicked me.'

'Kicked you! You mean deliberately – ?'

'He fell over me,' said Mrs Cockburn-Montfort. 'Almost fell, and in so doing kicked me. And I thought now he's going to shoot me. So of course I screamed. And screamed.'

'Yes?'

'And he bolted.'

'And then?'

'Well, then there were those three.' She indicated the attendants. 'Milling about in the dark and kicking me too. By accident, of course.'

The three ladies stirred in their seats.

'Where had they come from?'

'How should I know! Well, anyway, I *do* know because I heard the doors bang. They'd been in the other three loos.'

'All of them?'

Alleyn looked at his sergeant. She stood up. 'Well?' he asked.

'To try and see Karbo, sir,' she said, scarlet-faced. 'He was just outside. Singing.'

'Standing on the seats, I suppose, the lot of you.'

'Sir.'

'I'll see you later. Sit down.'

'Sir.'

'Now, Mrs Cockburn-Montfort, what happened next?'

Someone, it appeared, had had a torch, and by its light they had hauled Mrs Cockburn-Montfort to her feet.

'Was this you?' Alleyn asked the sergeant, who said it was. Mrs Cockburn-Montfort had continued to yell. There was a great commotion going on in the garden and other parts of the house. And then all the lights went on. 'And that girl,' she said, pointing at the sergeant, 'that one. There. Do *you know what she did?*'

'Slapped your face, perhaps, to stop you screaming?'

'How she *dared*! After all that. And shouting questions at me. And then she had the impertinence to say she couldn't hang round there and left me to the other two. I must say, they had the decency to give me aspirins.'

'I'm so glad,' said Alleyn politely. 'Now, will you please answer the next one very carefully. Did you get an impression at all of what this man was like? There was a certain amount of reflected light from the louvres. Did you get anything like a look at him, however momentary?'

'Oh, yes,' she said quite calmly. 'Yes, indeed I did. He was black.'

An appreciable silence followed this statement. Gibson cleared his throat.

'Are you sure of that? Really sure?' Alleyn asked.

'Oh perfectly. I saw his head against the window.'

'It couldn't, for instance, have been a white person with a black stocking over his head?'

'Oh, no. I think he *had* a stocking over his head but I could tell.' She glanced at her husband and lowered her voice. 'Besides,' she said, 'I smelt him. If you've lived out there as we did, you can't mistake it.'

Her husband made a sort of corroborative noise.

'Yes?' Alleyn said, 'I understand they notice the same phenomenon in us. An African friend of mine told me that it took him almost a year before he left off feeling faint in lifts during the London rush hours.'

And before anyone could remark upon this, he said: 'Well, and then one of our people took over and I think from this point we can depend upon his report.' He looked at Gibson. 'Unless you – ?'

'No,' Gibson said, 'Thanks. Nothing. We'll have a typewritten transcript of this little chat, madam, and we'll ask you to look over it and sign it if it seems OK. Sorry to have troubled you.' And he added the predictable coda. 'You've been very helpful,' he said. Alleyn wondered how much these routine civilities cost him.

The Colonel, ignoring Mr Gibson, barked at Alleyn. 'I take it I may remove my wife? She ought to see her doctor.'

'Of course. Do. Who is your doctor, Mrs Cockburn-Montfort? Can we ring him up and ask him to meet you at your house?'

She opened her mouth and shut it again when the Colonel said: 'We won't trouble you, thank you. Good evening to you.'

They had got as far as the door before Alleyn said: 'Oh, by the way! Did you by any chance get the impression that the man was in some kind of uniform? Or livery?'

There was a long pause before Mrs Cockburn-Montfort said: 'I'm afraid not. No. I've no idea.'

'No? By the way, Colonel, are those your smelling-salts?'

The Colonel stared at him as if he was mad and then, vacantly, at the bottle in his hand.

'Mine!' he said. 'Why the devil should they be mine?'

'They are mine,' said his wife grandly. 'Anyone would suppose we'd been shop-lifting. Honestly!'

She put her arm in her husband's and, clinging to him, gazed resentfully at Alleyn.

'When that peculiar little Whipples-whatever-it-is introduced you, he might have told us you were a policeman. Come on, Hughie darling,' said Mrs Cockburn-Montfort and achieved quite a magnificent exit.

II

It had taken all of Alleyn's tact, patience and sheer authority to get The Boomer stowed away in the library, a smallish room on the first floor. When he had recovered from the effects of shock which must surely, Alleyn thought, have been more severe than he permitted himself to show, he developed a strong inclination to conduct inquiries on his own account.

This was extremely tricky. At the Embassy they were, technically, on Ng'ombwanan soil. Gibson and his Special Branch were there specifically at the invitation of the Ng'ombwanan Ambassador, and how far their authority extended in the somewhat rococo circumstances of that Ambassador having been murdered on the premises was a bit of a poser.

So, in a different key, Alleyn felt, was his own presence on the scene. The Special Branch very much likes to keep itself to itself. Fred Gibson's frame of mind, at the moment, was one of rigidly suppressed professional chagrin and personal mortification. His initial approach would never have been made under ordinary circumstances and now, Alleyn's presence on, as it were, the SB's pitch, gave an almost grotesque twist to an already extremely delicate situation. Particularly since, with the occurrence of a homicide, the focus of responsibility might now be said to have shifted to Alleyn in whose division the crime had taken place.

Gibson had cut through this dilemma by ringing up his principals and getting authority for himself and Alleyn with the consent of the Embassy to handle the case together. But Alleyn knew the situation could well become a very tricky one.

'Apparently,' Gibson said, 'we carry on until somebody stops us. Those are my instructions, anyway. Yours too, on three counts: your AC, your division, and the personal request of the President.'

'Who at the moment wants to summon the entire household including the spear-carrier and harangue them in their own language.'

'Bloody farce,' Gibson mumbled.

'Yes, but if he insists – Look,' Alleyn said, 'it mightn't be such a bad idea for them to go ahead if we could understand what they were talking about.'

'Well – '

'Fred, suppose we put out a personal call for Mr Samuel Whipplestone to come at once – you know: "be kind enough" and all that. Not sound as if we're breathing down his neck.'

'What about it – ?' asked Gibson unenthusiastically.

'He speaks Ng'ombwanan. He lives five minutes away and will be at home by now. No. 1, Capricorn Walk. We can ring up. Not in the book yet, I dare say, but get through,' said Alleyn to an attendant sergeant, and as he went to the telephone, 'Samuel Whipplestone. Send a car round. I'll speak to him.'

'The idea being?' Mr Gibson asked woodenly.

'We let the President address the troops – indeed, come to that, we can't stop him, but at least we'll know what's being said.'

'Where is he, for God's sake? *You* put him somewhere,' Mr Gibson said as if the President was a mislaid household utensil.

'In the library. He's undertaken to stay there until I go back. We've got coppers keeping obbo in the passage.'

'I should hope so. If this was a case of the wrong victim, chummy may well be gunning for the right one.'

The sergeant was speaking on the telephone.

'Superintendent Alleyn would like a word with you, sir.'

Alleyn detected in Mr Whipplestone's voice an overtone of occupational cool. 'My dear Alleyn,' he said, 'this is a most disturbing occurrence. I understand the Ambassador has been – assassinated.'

'Yes.'

'How very dreadful. Nothing could have been worse.'

'Except the intended target taking the knock.'

'Oh . . . I see. The President.'

'Listen,' Alleyn said and made his request.

'Dear me,' said Mr Whipplestone.

'I know it's asking a lot. Damn cheek in fact. But it would take us some time to raise a neutral interpreter. It wouldn't do for one of the Ng'ombwanans . . .'

'No, no, no, no, quite. Be quiet, cat. Yes. Very well, I'll come.'

'I'm uncommonly grateful. You'll find a car at your door. 'Bye.'

'Coming?' Gibson said.

'Yes. Sergeant, go and ask Mr Fox to meet him and bring him here, will you? Pale. About sixty. Eyeglass. VIP treatment.'

'Sir.'

And in a few minutes Mr Whipplestone, stepping discreetly and having exchanged his tailcoat for a well-used smoking jacket, was shown into the room by Inspector Fox, whom Alleyn motioned to stay.

Gibson made a morose fuss of Mr Whipplestone.

'You'll appreciate how it is, sir. The President insists on addressing his household staff and – '

'Yes, yes, I quite understand, Mr Gibson. Difficult for you. I wonder, could I know what happened? It doesn't really affect the interpreter's role, of course, but – briefly?'

'Of course you could,' Alleyn said. 'Briefly then: Somebody fired a shot that you must have heard, apparently taking aim from the ladies' loo. It hit nobody but when the lights went up the Ambassador was lying dead in the Pavilion, spitted by the ceremonial Ng'ombwanan spear that was borne behind the President. The spear-carrier was crouched a few paces back and as far as we can make out – he speaks no English – maintains that in the dark, when everybody was milling about in a hell of a stink over the shot, he was given a chop on the neck and his spear snatched from him.'

'Do you believe this?'

'I don't know. I was there, in the pavilion, with Troy. She was sitting next to the President and I was beside her. When the shot rang out I told her to stay put and at the same time saw the shape of The Boomer half rise and make as if to go. His figure was momentarily silhouetted against Karbo's spotlight on the screen at the other end of the lake. I shoved him back in his chair, told him to pipe down and moved in front of him. A split second later something crashed down at my feet. Some ass called out that the President had been shot. The Boomer and a number of others yelled for lights. They came up and – there was the Ambassador – literally pinned to the ground.'

'A mistake then?'

'That seems to be the general idea – a mistake. They were of almost equal height and similar build. Their uniforms, in silhouette, would look alike. He was speared from behind and, from behind, would show up against the spotlit screen. There's one other point. My colleague here tells me he had two security men posted near the rear entrance to the pavilion. After the shot they say the black wait-er came plunging out. They grabbed him but say he appeared to be just plain scared. That's right, isn't it, Fred?'

'That's the case,' Gibson said. The point being that while they were finding out what they'd caught, you've got to admit that it's just possible in that bloody blackout, if you'll excuse me, sir, some-body might have slipped into the pavilion.'

'Somebody?' said Mr Whipplestone.

'Well, anybody,' Alleyn said. 'Guest, waiter, what have you. It's unlikely but it's just possible.'

'And got away again? After the – event?'

'Again – just remotely possible. And now, Whipplestone, if you don't mind – '

'Of course.'

'Where do they hold this tribal gathering, Fred? The President said the ballroom. OK?'

'OK.'

'Could you check with him and lay that on, I'll see how things are going in the pavilion and then join you. All right? Would that suit you?'

'Fair enough.'

'Fox, will you come with me?'

On the way he gave Fox a succinct account of Mrs Cockburn-Montfort's story and of the pistol shot, if pistol shot it was, in its rela-tion to the climactic scene in the garden.

'Quite a little puzzle,' said Fox cosily.

In the pavilion they found two uniformed policemen, a photo-graphic and fingerprint expert – Detective-Sergeants Bailey and Thompson – together with Sir James Curtis, never mentioned by the press without the additional gloss of 'the celebrated pathologist'. Sir

James had completed his superficial examination. The spear, horridly incongruous, still stuck up at an angle from its quarry and was being photographed in close-up by Thompson. Not far from the body lay an over-turned chair.

'This is a pretty kettle of fish you've got here, Rory,' said Sir James.

'Is it through the heart?'

'Plumb through and well into the turf underneath, I think we'll find. Otherwise it wouldn't be so rigid. It looks as though the assailant followed through the initial thrust and, with a forward lunge, literally pinned him down.'

'Ferocious.'

'Very.'

'Finished?' Alleyn asked Thompson as he straightened up. 'Complete coverage? All angles? the lot?'

'Yes, Mr Alleyn.'

'Bailey? What about dabs?'

Bailey, a mulishly inclined officer, said he'd gone over the spear and could find evidence of only one set of prints and that they were smeared. He added that the camera might bring up something latent but he didn't hold out many hopes. The angle of the spear to the body had been measured. Sir James said it had been a downward thrust. 'Which would indicate a tall man,' he said.

'Or a middle-sized man on a chair?' Alleyn suggested.

'Yes. A possibility.'

'All right,' Alleyn said. 'We'd better withdraw that thing.'

'You'll have a job,' Sir James offered.

They did have a job and the process was unpleasant. In the end the body had to be held down and the spear extracted by a violent jerk, producing a sickening noise and an extrusion of blood.

'Turn him over,' Alleyn said.

The eyes were open and the jaw collapsed, turning the Ambassador's face into a grotesque mask of astonishment. The wound of entry was larger than that of exit. The closely cropped turf was wet.

'Horrible,' Alleyn said shortly.

'I suppose we can take him away?' Sir James suggested. 'I'll do the PM at once.'

'I'm not so sure about that. We're on Ng'ombwanan ground. We're on sufferance. The mortuary van's outside all right but I don't think we can do anything about the body unless they say so.'

'Good Lord!'

'There may be all sorts of taboos, observances and what have you.'

'Well,' said Sir James, not best pleased, 'in that case I'll take myself off. You might let me know if I'm wanted.'

'Of course. We're all walking about like a gaggle of Agags, it's so tricky. Here's Fred Gibson.'

He had come to say that the President wished the body to be conveyed to the ballroom.

'What for?' Alleyn demanded.

'This assembly or what-have-you. Then it's to be put upstairs. He wants it flown back to Ng'ombwana.'

'Good evening to you,' said Sir James and left.

Alleyn nodded to one of the constables, who fetched two men, a stretcher and a canvas. And so his country's representative re-entered his Embassy, finally relieved of the responsibility that had lain so heavily on his mind.

Alleyn said to the constables: 'We'll keep this tent exactly as it is. One of you remains on guard.' And to Fox. 'D'you get the picture, Br'er Fox? Here we all were, a round dozen of us including, you'll be surprised to hear, my brother.'

'Is that so, Mr Alleyn? Quite a coincidence.'

'If you don't mind, Br'er Fox, we won't use that word. It's cropped up with monotonous regularity ever since I took my jaunt to Ng'ombwana.'

'Sorry, I'm sure.'

'Not at all. To continue. Here we were, in arrowhead formation with the President's chair at the apex. There's his chair and that's Troy's beside it. On his other side was the Ambassador. The spear-carrier, who is at present under surveillance in the gents' cloaks, stood behind his master's chair. At the rear are those trestle tables used for drinks and a bit further forward an overturned, pretty solid wooden chair, the purpose of which escapes me. The entrance into the tent at the back was used by the servants. There were two of them, the larger being one of the household henchmen and the other a fresh-faced, chunky specimen in Costard's livery. Both of them were in evidence when the lights went out.'

'And so,' said Fox, who liked to sort things out, 'as soon as this Karbo artist appears, his spotlight picks him up and makes a splash on the screen behind him. And from the back of the tent where this spear expert is stationed anybody who stands up between him and light shows up like somebody coming in late at the cinema.'

'That's it.'

'And after the shot was fired you stopped the President from standing up but the Ambassador *did* stand up and Bob, in a manner of speaking, was your uncle.'

'In a manner of speaking, he was.'

'Now then,' Fox continued in his stately manner. 'Yes. This shot. Fired, we're told by the lady you mentioned, from the window of the female conveniences. No weapon's been recovered, I take it?'

'Give us a chance.'

'And nobody's corroborated the lady's story about this dirty big black man who kicked her?'

'No.'

'And this chap hasn't been picked up?'

'He's like an insubstantial pageant faded.'

'Just so. And do we assume, then, that having fired his shot and missed his man, an accomplice, spear-carrier or what have you, did the job for him?'

'That may be what we're supposed to think. To my mind it stinks. Not to high Heaven, but slightly.'

'Then what – ?'

'Don't ask me, Br'er Fox. But designedly or not, the shot created a diversion.'

'And when the lights came on?'

'The President was in his chair where I'd shoved him and Troy was in hers. The other two ladies were in theirs. The body was three feet to the President's left. The guests were milling about all over the shop. My big brother was ordering them in a shaky voice not to panic. The spear-carrier was on his knees nursing his carotid artery. The chair was overturned. No servants.'

'I get the picture.'

'Good, come on, then. The corroboree, pow-wow, conventicle or coven, call it what you will, is now in congress and we are stayed for.' He turned to Bailey and Thompson. 'Not much joy for you chaps at present but if you can pick up something that looks too big for a female print in the second on the left of the ladies' loo it will be as balm in Gilead. Away we go, Fox.'

But as they approached the house they were met by Gibson looking perturbed, with Mr Whipplestone in polite attendance.

'What's up, Fred?' Alleyn asked. 'Have your race relations fractured?'

'You could put it like that,' Mr Gibson conceded, 'He's making things difficult.'

'The President?'

'That's right. He won't collaborate with anyone but you.'

'Silly old chump.'

'He won't come out of his library until you've gone in.'

'What's bitten him, for the love of Mike?'

'I doubt if he knows.'

'Perhaps,' Mr Whipplestone ventured, 'he doesn't like the introduction of me into the proceedings?'

'I wouldn't say that, sir,' said Gibson unhappily.

'What a nuisance he contrives to be,' Alleyn said, 'I'll talk to him. Are the hosts of Ng'ombwana mustered in the ballroom?'

'Yes. Waiting for Master,' said Gibson.

'Any developments, Fred?'

'Nothing to rave about. I've had a piece of that sergeant in the cloakroom. It seems she acted promptly enough after she left her grandstand seat and attended to Mrs C-M. She located the nearest of my men and gave him the info. A search for chummy was set up with no results and I was informed. The men on duty outside the house say nobody left it. If they say so, nobody did,' said Gibson sticking his jaw out, 'We've begun to search for the gun or whatever it was.'

'It sounded to me like a pistol,' said Alleyn. 'I'd better beard the lion in his library, I suppose. We'll meet here. I'm damned sorry to victimize you like this, Sam.'

'My dear fellow, you needn't be. I'm afraid I'm rather enjoying myself,' said Mr Whipplestone.

III

Alleyn scarcely knew what sort of reception he expected to get from The Boomer or what sort of tactics he himself should deploy to meet it.

In the event, The Boomer behaved pretty much according to pattern. He strode down upon Alleyn and seized his hands.

'Ah!' he roared. 'You are here at last. I am glad. Now we shall get this affair settled.'

'I'm afraid it's far from being settled at the moment.'

'Because of all these pettifogging coppers. And believe me, I do not include you in that category, my dear Rory.'

'Very good of you, sir.'

' "Sir, Sir. Sir" – what tommy-rot! Never mind. We shall not waste time over details. I have come to a decision and you shall be the first to hear what it is.'

'Thank you, I'll be glad to know.'

'Good. Then listen. I understand perfectly that your funny colleague: what is his name?'

'Gibson?' Alleyn ventured.

'Gibson, Gibson. I understand perfectly that the well-meaning Gibson and his band of bodyguards and so on were here at the invitation of my Ambassador. I am correct?'

'Yes.'

'Again, good. But my Ambassador has, as we used to say at Davidson's, kicked over the bucket and in any case the supreme authority is mine. Yes?'

'Of course it is.'

'Of course it is,' the Boomer repeated with immense satisfaction, 'It is mine and I propose to exercise it. An attempt has been made upon my life. It has failed as all such attempts are bound to fail. That I made clear to you on the happy occasion of your visit.'

'So you did.'

'Nevertheless, an attempt has been made.' The Boomer repeated. 'My Ambassador has been killed and the matter must be cleared up.'

'I couldn't agree more.'

'I therefore have called together the people of his household and will question them in accordance with our historically established democratic practice. In Ng'ombwana.'

As Alleyn was by no means certain what this practice might turn out to be, he said cautiously, 'Do you feel that somebody in the household may be responsible?'

'One may find that this is not so. In which case – ' The great voice rumbled into silence.

'In which case?' Alleyn hinted.

'My dear man, in which case I hope for your and the well-meaning Gibson's collaboration.'

So he'd got it all tidied up, Alleyn thought. The Boomer would handle the black elements and he and the CID could make what they liked of the white. Really it began to look like a sort of inverted form of apartheid.

'I don't have to tell you,' he said, 'that authorities at every level will be most deeply concerned that this should have happened. The Special Branch, in particular, is in a great taking-on about it.'

'Hah! So much,' said The Boomer with relish, 'for all the large men in the shrubberies. What?'

'All right. *Touché.*'

'All the same, my dear Rory, if it was true that I was the intended victim, it might well be said that I owe my life to you.'

'Rot.'

'Not rot. It would follow logically. You pushed me down in my chair and there was this unhappy Ambassador waving his arms about and looking like me. So – blam! Yes, yes, yes. In that case, I would owe you my life. It is a debt I would not willingly incur with anyone but you – with you I would willingly acknowledge it.'

'Not a bit,' Alleyn said, in acute embarrassment, 'It may turn out that my intervention was merely a piece of unnecessary bloody cheek.' He hesitated and was inspired to add, 'as we used to say at Davidson's.' And since this did the trick, he hurried on:

'Following that line of thought,' he said, 'you might equally say that I was responsible for the Ambassador's death.'

'That,' said The Boomer grandly, 'is another pair of boots.'

'Tell me,' Alleyn asked, 'have you any theories about the pistol shot?'

'Ah!' he said quickly. 'Pistol! So you have found the weapon?'

'No. I call it a pistol-shot, provisionally. Gun. Revolver. Automatic. What you will. With your permission we'll search.'

'Where?'

'Well – in the garden. And the pond, for instance.'

'The pond?'

Alleyn gave him a digest of Mrs Cockburn-Montfort's narrative. The Boomer, it appeared, knew the Cockburn-Montforts quite well and indeed had actually been associated with the Colonel during the period when he helped organize the modern Ng'ombwanan army. 'He was efficient,' said The Boomer, 'but unfortunately he took to the bottle. His wife is, as we used to say, hairy round the hocks.'

'She says the man in the lavatory was black.'

There followed a longish pause, 'If that is correct, I shall find him.' he said at last.

'He certainly didn't leave these premises. All the exits have been closely watched.'

If The Boomer was tempted to be rude once more about Mr Gibson's methods he restrained himself.

'What is the truth,' he asked, 'about this marksman? Did he in fact fire at me and miss me? Is that proved?'

'Nothing is proved. Tell me, do you trust – absolutely – the spear-carrier?'

'Absolutely. But I shall question him as if I do not.'

'Will you – and I'm diffident about asking this – will you allow me to be there? At the assembly?'

For a moment he fancied he saw signs of withdrawal but if so they vanished at once. The Boomer waved his paw.

'Of course. Of course. But, my dear Rory, you will not understand a word of it.'

'Do you know Sam Whipplestone? Of the FO and lately retired?'

'I know *of him*. Of course. He has had many connections with my country. We have not met until tonight. He was a guest. And he is present now with your Gibson. I couldn't understand why.'

'I asked him to come. He speaks your language fluently and he's my personal friend. Would you allow him to sit in with me? I'd be very grateful'

And now, Alleyn thought, he really was in for a rebuff – but no, after a disconcerting interval The Boomer said: 'This is a little difficult. An enquiry of this nature is never open to persons who have no official standing. Our proceedings are never made public.'

'I give you my firm undertaking that they wouldn't be in this instance. Whipplestone is the soul of discretion, I can vouch for him.'

'You can?'

'I can and I do.'

'Very well,' said The Boomer. 'But no Gibsons.'

'All right. But why have you taken against poor Gibson?'

'Why? I cannot say why. Perhaps because he is too large.' The enormous Boomer pondered for a moment. 'And so pale,' he finally brought out. 'He is very, very pale.'

Alleyn said he believed the entire household was now assembled in the ballroom and The Boomer said that he would go there. Something in his manner made Alleyn think of a star actor preparing for his entrance.

'It is perhaps a little awkward,' The Boomer reflected. 'On such an occasion I should be attended by my Ambassador and my personal *mlinzi* – my guard. But since the one is dead and the other possibly his murderer, it is not feasible.'

'Tiresome for you.'

'Shall we go?'

They left, passing one of Gibson's men in Costard's livery. In the hall they found Mr Whipplestone, patient in a high-backed chair. The Boomer, evidently minded to do his thing properly, was extremely gracious. Mr Whipplestone offered perfectly phrased regrets for the Ambassador's demise and The Boomer told him that the Ambassador had spoken warmly of him and had talked of asking him to tea.

Gibson was nowhere to be seen but another of his men quietly passed Alleyn a folded paper. While Mr Whipplestone and The Boomer were still exchanging compliments, he had a quick look at it.

'Found the gun,' it read. 'See you after.'

IV

The ballroom was shut up. Heavy curtains were drawn across the french windows. The chandeliers sparkled, the flowers were brilliant. Only a faint reek of champagne, sandarac and cigarette smoke suggested the aftermath of festivities.

The ballroom had become Ng'ombwana.

A crowd of Ng'ombwanans waited at the end of the great saloon where the red alcove displayed its warlike trophies.

It was a larger assembly than Alleyn had expected: men in full evening dress whom he supposed to be authoritative persons in the household, a controller, a secretary, undersecretaries. There were some dozen men in livery and as many women with white headscarves and dresses, and there was a knot of under-servants in white jackets clustered at the rear of the assembly. Clearly they were all grouped in conformance with the domestic hierarchy. The President's aides-de-camp waited at the back of the dais. And ranked on each side of it, armed and immovable, was his guard in full ceremonial kit: scarlet tunics, white kilts, immaculate leggings, glistening accoutrements.

And on the floor in front of the dais, was a massive table bearing under a lion's hide the unmistakable shape of the shrouded dead.

Alleyn and Mr Whipplestone entered in the wake of The Boomer. The guard came to attention, the crowd became very still. The Boomer walked slowly and superbly to his dais. He gave an order and two chairs were placed on the floor not far from the bier. He motioned Alleyn and Mr Whipplestone to take them. Alleyn would have greatly preferred an inconspicuous stand at the rear but there was no help for it and they took their places.

'I daren't write, dare I?' Mr Whipplestone muttered. 'And nor dare I talk.'

'You'll have to remember.'

'All jolly fine.'

The Boomer, seated in his great chair, his hands on the arms, his body upright, his chin raised, his knees and feet planted together, looked like an effigy of himself. His eyes, as always a little bloodshot, rolled and flashed, his teeth gleamed and he spoke in a language which seemed to be composed entirely of vowels, gutturals and clicks. His voice was so huge that Mr Whipplestone, trying to speak like a ventriloquist, ventured two words.

'Describing incident,' he said.

The speech seemed to grow in urgency. He brought both palms down sharply on the arms of his chair. Alleyn wondered if he only imagined that a heightened tension invested the audience. A pause and then, unmistakably, an order.

'Spear chap,' ventriloquized Mr Whipplestone. 'Fetch.'

Two of the guards came smartly to attention, marched to meet each other, faced front, saluted, about-turned and marched out. Absolute stillness followed this proceeding. Sounds from outside could be heard. Gibson's men in the garden, no doubt, and once, almost certainly, Gibson's voice.

When the silence had become very trying indeed, the soldiers returned with the spear-carrier between them.

He was still dressed in his ceremonial garments. His anklets and armbands shone in the lamplight and so did his burnished body and limbs. But he's not really *black*, Alleyn thought, 'If Troy painted him he would be anything but black – blue, mole, purple, even red where his body reflects the carpet and walls.' He was glossy. His close-cropped head sat above its tier of throat-rings like a huge ebony marble. He wore his lion's skin like a lion. Alleyn noticed that his right arm was hooked under it as if in a sling.

He walked between his guards to the bier. They left him there, isolated before his late Ambassador and his President and close enough to Alleyn and Mr Whipplestone for them to smell the sweet oil with which he had polished himself.

The examination began. It was impossible most of the time for Alleyn to guess what was being said. Both men kept very still. Their teeth and eyes flashed from time to time but their big voices were level and they used no gesture until suddenly the spearman slapped the base of his own neck.

'Chop,' breathed Mr Whipplestone. 'Karate. Sort of.'

Soon after this there was a break and neither man spoke for perhaps eight seconds and then, to Alleyn's surprise and discomfiture, The Boomer began to talk, still in the Ng'ombwanan tongue, to him. It was a shortish observation. At the end of it, The Boomer nodded to Mr Whipplestone who cleared his throat.

'The President,' he said, 'directs me to ask you if you will give an account of what you yourself witnessed in the pavilion. He also directs me to translate what you say as he wishes the proceedings to be conducted throughout in the Ng'ombwanan language.'

They stood up. Alleyn gave his account, to which The Boomer reacted as if he hadn't understood a word of it. Mr Whipplestone translated.

Maintaining this laborious procedure, Alleyn was asked if, after the death had been discovered, he had formed any opinions as to whether the spearman was, in fact, injured.

Looking at the superb being standing there like a rock, it was difficult to imagine that a blow on the carotid nerve or anywhere else for that matter could cause him the smallest discomfiture. Alleyn said: 'He was kneeling with his right hand in the position he has just shown. His head was bent, his left hand clenched and his shoulders hunched. He appeared to be in pain.'

'And then,' translated Mr Whipplestone, 'what happened?'

Alleyn repressed an insane desire to remind The Boomer that he was there at the time and invite him to come off it and talk English.

He said: 'There was a certain amount of confusion. This was checked by – ' he looked straight at The Boomer – 'the President, who spoke in Ng'ombwanan to the spearsman who appeared to offer some kind of statement or denial. Subsequently five men on duty from the Special Branch of the CID arrived with two of the President's guard who had been stationed outside the pavilion. The spearsman was removed to the house.'

Away went Mr Whipplestone again.

The Boomer next wished to know if the police had obtained any evidence from the spear itself. Alleyn replied that no report had been released under that heading.

This, apparently, ended his examination, if such it could be called. He sat down.

After a further silence, and it occurred to Alleyn that the Ng'ombwanans were adepts in non-communication, The Boomer rose.

It would have been impossible to say why the atmosphere, already far from relaxed, now became taut to twanging point. What happened was that the President pointed, with enormous authority, at the improvised bier and unmistakably pronounced a command.

The spearsman, giving no sign of agitation, at once extended his left hand – the right was still concealed in his bosom – and drew down the covering. And here was the Ambassador, open-mouthed, goggle-eyed, making some sort of indecipherable declaration.

The spearsman, laying his hand upon the body, spoke boldly and briefly. The President replied even more briefly. The lionskin mantle was replaced, and the ceremony – assembly – trial – whatever it might be, was at an end. At no time during the final proceedings had The Boomer so much as glanced at Alleyn.

He now briefly harangued his hearers. Mr Whipplestone muttered that he ordered any of them who had any information, however trivial, bearing however slightly on the case, to speak immediately. This met with an absolute silence. His peroration was to the effect that he himself was in command of affairs at the Embassy. He then left. His ADCs followed and the one with whom Alleyn was acquainted paused by him to say the President requested his presence in the library.

'I will come,' Alleyn said, 'in ten minutes. My compliments to the President, if you please.'

The ADC rolled his eyes, said, 'But – ', changed his mind and followed his Master.

'That,' said Mr Whipplestone, 'was remarkably crisp.'

'If he doesn't like it he can lump it. I want a word with Gibson. Come on.'

Gibson, looking sulky, and Fox, were waiting for them at their temporary quarters in the controller's office. On the desk, lying on a damp unfolded handkerchief, was a gun. Thompson and Bailey stood nearby with their tools of trade.

'Where?' said Alleyn.

'In the pond. We picked it up with a search lamp. Lying on the blue tiled bottom at the corner opposite the conveniences and three feet in from the margin.'

'Easy chucking distance from the loo window.'

'That's correct.'

'Anything?' Alleyn asked Bailey.

'No joy, Mr Alleyn. Gloves, I reckon.'

'It's a Luger,' Alleyn said.

'They are not hard to come by,' Mr Whipplestone said, 'in Ng'ombwana.'

'You know,' Alleyn said, 'almost immediately after the shot, I heard something fall into the pond. It was in the split second before the rumpus broke out,'

'Well, well,' said Fox. 'Not,' he reasoned, 'a very sensible way for him to carry on. However you look at it. Still,' he said heavily, 'that's how they do tend to behave.'

'Who do, Br'er Fox?'

'Political assassins, the non-professionals. They're a funny mob, by all accounts.'

'You're dead right there, Teddy,' said Mr Gibson, 'I suppose,' he added, appealing to Alleyn, 'we retain possession of this Luger, do we?'

'Under the circumstances we'll be lucky if we retain possession of our wits. I'm damned if I know. The whole thing gets more and more like a revival of the Goon Show.'

'The AC, your department, rang.'

'What's *he* want?'

'To say the Deputy Commissioner will be calling in to offer condolences or what have you to the President. And no doubt,' said Gibson savagely, 'to offer me his advice and congratulations on a successful operation. *Christ!*' he said and turned his back on his colleagues.

Alleyn and Fox exchanged a look.

'You couldn't have done more,' Alleyn said after a moment. 'Take the whole lay-out, you couldn't have given any better coverage.'

'That bloody sergeant in the bog.'

'All right. But if Mrs Cockburn-Montfort's got it straight the sergeant wouldn't have stopped him in the dark, wherever she was.'

'I told them. I told these bastards they shouldn't have the blackout.'

'But,' said Fox, in his reasonable way, 'the gun-man didn't do the job anyway. There's that aspect, Mr Gibson, isn't there?'

Gibson didn't answer this. He turned round and said to Alleyn: 'We've to find out if the President's available to see the DC.'

'When?'

'He's on his way in from Kent. Within the hour.'

'I'll find out.' Alleyn turned to Mr Whipplestone. 'I can't tell you, Sam, how much obliged to you I am,' he said, 'If it's not asking too much, could you bear to write out an account of that black – in both senses – charade in there, while it's still fresh in your mind? I'm having another go at the great panjandrum in the library.'

'Yes, of course,' said Mr Whipplestone. 'I'd like to.'

So he was settled down with writing materials and immediately took on the air of being at his own desk in his own rather rarefied office with a secretary in deferential attendance.

'What's horrible for us, Fred?' Alleyn asked. It was a regulation
inquiry for which he was known at the Yard.

'We've got that lot from the tent party still waiting. Except the
ones who obviously hadn't a clue about anything. And,' Gibson
added a little awkwardly, 'Mrs Alleyn. She's gone, of course.'

'I can always put her through the hoops at home.'

'And – er, and er,' said Gibson still more awkwardly, 'there is –
er – your brother.'

'What!' Alleyn shouted, 'George! You don't tell me you've got
George sitting on his fat bottom waiting for the brutal police bit?'

'Well – '

'Mrs Alleyn and Sir George,' said Fox demurely. 'And we're not
allowed to mention coincidence.'

'Old George,' Alleyn pondered, 'what a lark! Fox, you might press
on with statements from that little lot. Including George. While I
have another go at The Boomer. What about you, Fred?'

'Get on with the bloody routine, I suppose. Could you lend me
these two – ' he indicated Bailey and Thompson – 'for the ladies'
conveniences? Not that there's much chance of anything turning up
there. Still, we've got this Luger-merchant roaming round somewhere in the establishment. We're searching for the bullet, of
course, and that's no piece of cake. Seeing you,' he said morosely
and walked out.

'You'd better get on with the loo,' Alleyn said to Bailey and
Thompson and himself returned to the library.

V

'Look,' Alleyn said, 'it's this way. You – Your Excellency – can, as of
course you know, order us off whenever you feel like it. As far as
inquiries inside the Embassy are concerned, we can become *persona
non grata* at the drop of a hat and as such would have to limit our
activities, of which you've no doubt formed an extremely poor opinion, to looking after your security whenever you leave these premises.
We will also follow up any lines of enquiry that present themselves
outside the Embassy. Quite simply, it's a matter of whether or not
you wish us to carry on as we are or make ourselves scarce. Colonel

Sinclaire, the Deputy Commissioner of the Metropolitan Police, is on his way. He hopes he may be allowed to wait upon you. No doubt he will express his deep regrets and put the situation before you in more or less the same terms as I have used.'

For the first time since they had renewed their acquaintance Alleyn found a kind of hesitancy in The Boomer's manner. He made as if to speak, checked himself, looked hard at Alleyn for a moment and then began to pace up and down the library with the magnificent action that really did recall clichés about caged panthers.

At last he stopped in front of Alleyn and abruptly took him by the arms. 'What,' he demanded, 'did you think of our enquiry? Tell me?'

'It was immensely impressive,' Alleyn said at once.

'Yes? You found it so? But you think it strange, don't you, that I who have eaten my dinners and practised my profession as a barrister, should subscribe to such a performance. After all, it was not much like the proceedings of the British Coroner's Inquest?'

'Not conspicuously like. No.'

'No. And yet, my dear Rory, it told me a great deal more than would have been elicited by that highly respectable court'

'Yes?' Alleyn said politely. And with a half-smile: 'Am I to know what it told Your Excellency?'

'It told My Excellency that my *nkuki mtu mwenye* – my *mlinzi* – my man with the spear, spoke the truth.'

'I see.'

'You are non-committal. You want to know how I know?'

'If it suits you to tell me.'

'I am,' announced The Boomer, 'the son of a paramount chief. My father and his and his, back into the dawn, were paramount chiefs. If this man, under oath to protect me, had been guilty of murdering an innocent and loyal servant he could not have uncovered the body before me and declared his innocence. Which is what he did. It would not be possible.'

'I see.'

'And you would reply that such evidence is not admissible in a British court-of-law.'

'It would be *admissible*, I dare say. It could be eloquently pleaded by able counsel. It wouldn't be accepted, *ipso facto*, as proof of innocence. But you know that as well as I do.'

'Tell me this. It is important for me. Do you believe what I have said?'

'I think I do,' Alleyn said slowly. 'You know your people. You tell me it is so. Yes. I'm not sure, but I am inclined to believe you are right.'

'Ah!' said The Boomer. 'So now we are upon our old footing. That is good.'

'But I must make it clear to you. Whatever I may or may not think has no bearing on the way I'll conduct this investigation: either inside the Embassy, if you'll have us here, or outside it. If there turns out to be cogent evidence, in our book, against this man, we'll follow it up.'

'In any case, the event having taken place in this Embassy, on his own soil, he could not be tried in England,' said The Boomer.

'No. Whatever we find, in that sense, is academic. He would be repatriated.'

'And this person who fires off German weapons in ladies' lavatories. You say he also is black.'

'Mrs Cockburn-Montfort says so.'

'A stupid woman.'

'Tolerably so, I'd have thought.'

'It would be better if her husband beat her occasionally and left her at home,' said The Boomer with one of his gusts of laughter.

'I should like to know, if it isn't too distressing for you to speak of him, something of the Ambassador himself. Did you like him very much? Was he close to you? Those sorts of questions?'

The Boomer dragged his great hand across his mouth, made a long rumbling sound in his chest and sat down.

'I find it difficult,' he said at last, 'to answer your question. What sort of man was he? A fuddy-duddy, as we used to say. He has come up, in the English sense, through the ranks. The peasant class. At one time he was a nuisance. He saw himself staging some kind of *coup*. It was all rather ridiculous. He had certain administrative abilities but no real authority. That sort of person.'

Disregarding this example of Ng'ombwanan snob-thinking, Alleyn remarked that the Ambassador must have been possessed of considerable ability to have got where he did. The Boomer waved a concessionary hand and said that the trend of development had favoured his advancement.

'Had he enemies?'

'My dear Rory, in an emergent nation like my own every man of authority has or has had enemies. I know of no specific persons.'

'He was in a considerable taking-on about security during your visit,' Alleyn ventured, to which The Boomer vaguely replied: 'Oh. Did you think so?'

'He telephoned Gibson and me on an average twice a day.'

'Boring for you,' said The Boomer in his best public school manner.

'He was particularly agitated about the concert in the garden and the blackout. So were we for that matter.'

'He was a fuss-pot,' said The Boomer.

'Well, damn it all, he had some cause, as it turns out.'

The Boomer pursed his generous mouth into a double mulberry and raised his brows, 'If you put it like that.'

'After all, he is dead.'

'True,' The Boomer admitted.

Nobody can look quite so eloquently bored as a Negro. The eyes are almost closed, showing a lower rim of white, the mouth droops, the head tilts. The whole man suddenly seems to wilt. The Boomer now exhibited all these signals of ennui and Alleyn, remembering them of old, said: 'Never mind. I mustn't keep you any longer. Could we, do you think, just settle these two points: First, will you receive the Deputy Commissioner when he comes?'

'Of course,' drawled The Boomer without opening his eyes.

'Second. Do you now wish the CID to carry on inside the Embassy or would you prefer us to clear out? The decision is your Excellency's, of course, but we would be grateful for a definite ruling.'

The Boomer opened his slightly bloodshot eyes. He looked full at Alleyn. 'Stay,' he said.

There was a tap at the door and Gibson, large, pale and apologetic, came in.

'I'm sure I beg your pardon, sir,' he said to the President. 'Colonel Sinclaire, the Deputy Commissioner, has arrived and hopes to see you.'

The Boomer, without looking at Gibson, said: 'Ask my equerry to bring him in.'

Alleyn walked to the door. He had caught a signal of urgency from his colleague.

'Don't you go, Rory,' said The Boomer.

'I'm afraid I must,' said Alleyn.

Outside, in the passage, he found Mr Whipplestone fingering his tie and looking deeply perturbed. Alleyn said: 'What's up?'

'It may not be anything,' Gibson answered, 'It's just that we've been talking to the Costard man who was detailed to serve in the tent.'

'Stocky, well-set up, fair-haired?'

'That's him. Name of Chubb,' said Gibson.

'Alas,' said Mr Whipplestone.

CHAPTER 5

Small Hours

Chubb stood more-or-less to attention, looking straight before him with his arms to his sides. He cut quite a pleasing figure in Costard et Cie's discreet livery: midnight blue shell-jacket and trousers with gold endorsements. His faded blond hair was short and well-brushed, his fresh West Country complexion and blue eyes deceptively gave him the air of an outdoor man. He still wore his white gloves.

Alleyn had agreed with Mr Whipplestone that it would be best if the latter were not present at the interview. 'Though,' Alleyn said, 'there's no reason at all to suppose that Chubb, any more than my silly old brother George, had anything to do with the event.'

'I know, I know,' Mr Whipplestone had returned. 'Of course. It's just that, however illogically and stupidly, I would prefer Chubb *not* to have been on duty in that wretched pavilion. Just as I would prefer him *not* to have odd-time jobs with Sheridan and those beastly Montforts. And it *would* be rather odd for me to be there, wouldn't it? Very foolish of me no doubt. Let it go at that.'

So Alleyn and an anonymous sergeant had Chubb to themselves in the Controller's office.

Alleyn said: 'I want to be quite sure I've got this right. You were in and out of the pavilion with champagne which you fetched from an ice box that had been set up outside the pavilion. You did this in conjunction with one of the Embassy servants. He waited on the President and the people immediately surrounding him, didn't he? I remember that he came to my wife and me soon after we had settled there.'

'Sir,' said Chubb.

'And you looked after the rest of the party.'

'Sir.'

'Yes. Well now, Chubb, we've kept you hanging about all this time in the hope that you can give us some help about what happened in the pavilion.'

'Not much chance of that, sir. I never noticed anything, sir.'

'That makes two of us, I'm afraid,' Alleyn said, 'It happened like a bolt from the blue, didn't it? Were you actually in the pavilion? When the lights went out?'

Yes, it appeared. At the back. He had put his tray down on a trestle table, in preparation for the near blackout about which the servants had all been warned. He had remained there through the first item.

'And were you still there when the singer, Karbo, appeared?' Yes, he said. Still there. He had had an uninterrupted view of Karbo, standing in his spotlight with his shadow thrown up behind him on the white screen.

'Did you notice where the guard with the spear was standing?' Yes. At the rear. Behind the President's chair.

'On your left, would that be?'

'Yes, sir.'

'And your fellow-waiter?'

'The nigger?' said Chubb, and after a glance at Alleyn, 'Beg pardon, sir. The native.'

'The African, yes.'

'He was somewhere there. At the rear, I never took no notice,' said Chubb stonily.

'You didn't speak to either of them, at all?'

'No, thanks. I wouldn't think they knew how.'

'You don't like black people?' Alleyn said lightly.

'No, sir.'

'Well. To come to the moment when the shot was fired. I'm getting as many accounts as possible from the people who were in the pavilion and I'd like yours too, if you will. You remember that the performer had given out one note, if that's the way to put it. A long-drawn-out sound. And then – as you recall it – what?'

'The shot, sir.'

'Did you get an impression about where the sound came from?'

'The house, sir.'

'Yes. Well, now, Chubb. Could you just, as best as you are able, tell me your own impression of what followed the shot. In the pavilion, I mean.'

Nothing clear-cut emerged. People had stood up. A lady had screamed. A gentleman had shouted out not to panic. (George, Alleyn thought.)

'Yes. But as to what you actually *saw* from where you were, at the back of the pavilion?'

Hard to say, exactly Chubb said in his wooden voice. People moving about a bit but not much. Alleyn said that they had appeared, hadn't they? 'Like black silhouettes against the spotlight screen.' Chubb agreed.

'The guard – the man with the spear? He was on your left. Quite close to you. Wasn't he?'

'At the start, sir, he was. Before the pavilion lights went out.'

'And afterwards?'

There was a considerable pause: 'I couldn't say, exactly, sir. Not straightaway, like.'

'How do you mean?'

Chubb suddenly erupted, 'I was grabbed,' he said. 'He sprung on me. *Me!* From behind. *Me!*'

'Grabbed? Do you mean by the spearsman?'

'Not him. The other black bastard.'

'The waiter?'

'Yes. Sprung it on me. From behind. *Me!*'

'What did he spring on you? A half-Nelson?'

'Head-lock! I couldn't speak. *And* he put in the knee.'

'How did you know it was the waiter?'

'I knew all right. I knew and no error.'

'But *how?*'

'Bare arm for one thing. And the smell: like salad oil or something. I knew.'

'How long did this last?'

'Long enough,' said Chubb, fingering his neck. 'Long enough for his mate to put in the spear, I reckon.'

'Did he hold you until the lights went up?'

'No, sir. Only while it was being done. So I couldn't see it. The stabbing. I was doubled up. *Me!*' Chubb reiterated with, if possible, an access of venom. 'But I heard. The sound. You can't miss it. And the fall.'

The sergeant cleared his throat.

Alleyn said: 'This is enormously important, Chubb. I'm sure you realize that, don't you? You're saying that the Ng'ombwanan waiter attacked and restrained you while the guard speared the Ambassador.'

'Sir.'

'All right. Why, do you suppose? I mean, why you, in particular?'

'I was nearest, sir, wasn't I? I might of got in the way or done something quick, mightn't I?'

'Was the small, hard chair overturned during this attack?'

'It might of been,' Chubb said after a pause.

'How old are you, Chubb?'

'Me, sir? Fifty-two, sir.'

'What did you do in World War II?'

'Commando, sir.'

'Ah!' Alleyn said, quietly, 'I see.'

'They wouldn't of sprung it across me in those days, sir.'

'I'm sure they wouldn't. One more thing. After the shot and before you were attacked and doubled up, you saw the Ambassador, did you, on his feet? Silhouetted against the screen?'

'Sir.'

'Did you recognize him?'

Chubb was silent.

'Well – did you?'

'I – can't say I did. Not exactly.'

'How do you mean – not exactly?'

'It all happened so quick, didn't it? I – I reckon I thought he was the other one. The President.'

'Why?'

'Well. Because. Well, because, you know, he was near where the President sat, like. He must of moved away from his own chair, sir, mustn't he? And standing up like he was in command, as you might say. And the President had roared out something in their lingo, hadn't he?'

'So, you'd say, would you, Chubb, that the Ambassador was killed in mistake for the President?'

'I couldn't say that, sir, could I? Not for certain. But I'd say he might of been. He might easy of been.'

'You didn't see anybody attack the spearsman?'

'*Him!* He couldn't of been attacked, could he? I was the one that got clobbered, sir, wasn't I? Not him: he did the big job, didn't he?'

'He maintains that he was given a chop and his spear was snatched out of his grasp by the man who attacked him. He says that he didn't see who this man was. You may remember that when the lights came up and the Ambassador's body was seen, the spearsman was crouched on the ground up near the back of the pavilion.'

Through this speech of Alleyn's such animation as Chubb had displayed, deserted him. He reverted to his former manner, staring straight in front of him with such a wooden air that the ebb of colour from his face and its dark, uneven return, seemed to bear no relation to any emotional experience.

When he spoke it was to revert to his favourite observation.

'I wouldn't know about any of that,' he said, 'I never took any notice of that.'

'Didn't you? But you were quite close to the spearsman. You were standing by him. I happen to remember seeing you there.'

'I was a bit shook up. After what the other one done to me.'

'So it would seem. When the lights came on, was the waiter who attacked you, as you maintain, still there?'

'Him? He'd scarpered.'

'Have you seen him since then?'

Chubb said he hadn't but added that he couldn't tell one of the black bastards from another. The conventional mannerisms of the servant together with his careful grammar had almost disappeared. He sounded venomous. Alleyn then asked him why he hadn't reported the attack on himself immediately to the police and Chubb became injured and exasperated. What chance had there been for that, he complained, with them all being shoved about into queues and drafted into groups and told to behave quiet and act cooperative and stay put and questions and statements would come later.

He began to sweat and put his hands behind his back. He said he didn't feel too good. Alleyn told him that the sergeant would make a typescript of his statement and he would be asked to read and sign it if he found it correct.

'In the meantime,' he said, 'we'll let you go home to Mr Whipplestone.'

Chubb reverting to his earlier style said anxiously: 'Beg pardon, sir, but I didn't know you knew – '

'I know Mr Whipplestone very well. He told me about you.'

'Yes, sir. Will that be all, then, sir?'

'I think so, for the present. Good night to you, Chubb.'

'Thank you, sir. Good night, sir.'

He left the room with his hands clenched.

'Commando, eh?' said the sergeant to his notes.

II

Mr Fox was doing his competent best with the group of five persons who sat wearily about the apartment that had been used as a sort of bar-cum-smoking-room for male guests at the party. It smelt of stale smoke, the dregs of alcohol, heavy upholstery and, persistently, of the all-pervading sandarac. It wore an air of exhausted raffishness.

The party of five being interviewed by Mr Fox and noted down by a sergeant consisted of a black plenipotentiary and his wife, the last of the governors of British Ng'ombwana and *his* wife, and Sir George Alleyn, Bart. They were the only members of the original party of twelve guests who had remembered anything that might conceivably have a bearing upon events in the pavilion and they remained after a painstaking winnowing had disposed of their companions.

The ex-governor, who was called Sir John Smythe, remembered that immediately after the shot was fired, everybody moved to the front of the pavilion. He was contradicted by Lady Smythe who said that for her part she had remained riveted in her chair. The plenipotentiary's wife, whose understanding of English appeared to be rudimentary, conveyed through her husband that she, also, had remained seated. Mr Fox reminded himself that Mrs Alleyn, instructed by her husband, had not risen. The plenipotentiary recalled that the chairs had been set out in an inverted V shape with

the President and his Ambassador at the apex and the guests forming the two wide-angled wings.

'Is that the case, sir?' said Fox comfortably, 'I see. So that when
you gentlemen stood up you'd all automatically be forward of the
President? Nearer to the opening of the pavilion than he was?
Would that be correct?'

'Quite right, Mr Fox. Quite right,' said Sir George, who had
adopted a sort of uneasy reciprocal attitude towards Fox and had, at
the outset, assured him jovially that he'd heard a great deal about
him to which Fox replied: 'Is that the case, sir? If I might just have
your name?'

It was Sir George who remembered the actual order in which the
guests had sat and although Fox had already obtained this information from Alleyn, he gravely noted it down. On the President's left
had been the Ambassador, Sir John and Lady Smythe, the plenipotentiary's wife, the plenipotentiary, a guest who had now gone home
and Sir George himself, 'In starvation corner, what?' said Sir George
lightly to the Smythes, who made little deprecatory noises.

'Yes, I see, thank you, sir,' said Fox. 'And on the President's right
hand, sir?'

'Oh!' said Sir George waving his hand. 'My brother. My brother
and his wife. Yes. 'Strordinary coincidence.' Apparently feeling the
need for some sort of endorsement he turned to his fellow guests.
'My brother, the bobby,' he explained. 'Ridiculous, what?'

'A very distinguished bobby,' Sir John Smythe murmured, to
which Sir George returned: 'Oh, quite! Quite! Not for me to say
but – he'll do.' He laughed and made a jovial little grimace.

'Yes,' said Fox to his notes. 'And four other guests who have now
left. Thank you, sir.' He looked over the top of his spectacles at his
hearers. 'We come to the incident itself. There's this report: pistol shot
or whatever it was. The lights in the pavilion are out. Everybody
except the ladies and the President gets to his feet. Doing what?'

'How d'you mean, doing what?' Sir John Smythe asked.

'Well, sir, did everybody face out into the garden, trying to see
what was going on – apart from the concert item which, I understand, stopped short when the report was heard.'

'Speaking for myself,' said Sir George, 'I stayed where I was.
There were signs of – ah – agitation and – ah – movement. Sort of

thing that needs to be nipped in the bud if you don't want a panic on your hands.'

'And you nipped it, sir?' Fox asked.

'Well – I wouldn't go so far – one does one's best. I mean to say – I said something. Quietly.'

'If there had been any signs of panic,' said Sir John Smythe drily, 'they did not develop.'

' – "did not develop",' Mr Fox repeated. 'And in issuing your warning, sir, did you face inwards? With your back to the garden?'

'Yes. Yes, I did,' said Sir George.

'And did you notice anything at all out of the way, sir?'

'I couldn't see anything, my dear man. One was blinded by having looked at the brilliant light on the screen and the performer.'

'There wasn't any reflected light in the pavilion?'

'No,' said Sir George crossly. 'There wasn't. Nothing of the kind. It was too far away.'

'I see, sir,' said Fox placidly.

Lady Smythe suddenly remarked that the light on the screen was reflected in the lake. 'The whole thing,' she said, 'was dazzling and rather confusing.' There was a general murmur of agreement.

Mr Fox asked if during the dark interval anybody else had turned his or her back on the garden and peered into the interior. This produced a confused and doubtful response from which it emerged that the piercing screams of Mrs Cockburn-Montfort within the house had had a more marked effect than the actual report. The Smythes had both heard Alleyn telling the President to sit down. After the report everybody had heard the President shout out something in his own language. The plenipotentiary said it was an order. He shouted for lights. And immediately before or after that, Sir John Smythe said, he had been aware of something falling at his feet.

And then the light had gone up.

'And I can only add, Inspector,' said Sir John, 'that I really have nothing else to say that can have the slightest bearing on this tragic business. The ladies have been greatly shocked and I must beg you to release them from any further ordeal.'

There was a general and heartfelt chorus of agreement. Sir George said, 'Hear, hear,' very loudly.

Fox said this request was very reasonable he was sure, and he was sorry to have put them all to so much trouble and he could assure the ladies that he wouldn't be keeping them much longer. There were no two ways about it, he added, this was quite a serious affair, wasn't it?

'Well, then – ' said Sir John and there was a general stir.

At this juncture Alleyn came in.

In some curious and indefinable fashion he brought a feeling of refreshment with him rather like that achieved by a star whose delayed entry, however quietly executed, lifts the scene and quickens the attention of his audience.

'We are so sorry,' he said, 'to have kept you waiting like this. I'm sure Mr Fox will have explained. This is a very muddling, tragic and strange affair and it isn't made any simpler for me, at any rate, by finding myself an unsatisfactory witness and an investigating copper at one and the same time.'

He gave Lady Smythe an apologetic grin and she said – and may have been astonished to hear herself – 'You poor man.'

'Well, there it is and I can only hope one of you has come up with something more useful than anything I've been able to produce.'

His brother said: 'Done our best. What!'

'Good for you,' Alleyn said. He was reading the sergeant's notes.

'We're hoping,' said Sir John, 'to be released. The ladies – '

'Yes, of course. It's been a beastly experience and you must all be exhausted.'

'What about yourself?' asked Lady Smythe. She appeared to be a lady of spirit.

Alleyn looked up from the notes. 'Oh,' he said, 'you can't slap me back. These notes seem splendidly exhaustive and there's only one question I'd like to put to you. I know the whole incident was extremely confused, but I would like to learn if you all, for whatever reason or for no reason, are persuaded of the identity of the killer?'

'Good God!' Sir George shouted. 'Really, my dear Rory! Who else could it be but the man your fellows marched off. And I must compliment you on their promptitude, by the way.'

'You mean – ?'

'Good God, I mean the great hulking brute with the spear. I beg your pardon,' he said to the black plenipotentiary and himself turned scarlet. 'Afraid I spoke out of turn. Sure you understand.'

'George,' said his brother with exquisite courtesy, 'would you like to go home?'

'I? We all would. Mustn't desert the post, though. No preferential treatment.'

'Not a morsel, I assure you. I take it, then,' Alleyn said, turning to the others, 'that you all believe the spear-carrier was the assailant?'

'Well – yes,' said Sir John Smythe. 'I mean – there he was. Who else? And, my God, there was the spear!'

The black plenipotentiary's wife said something rather loudly in their native tongue.

Alleyn looked a question at her husband, who cleared his throat, 'My wife,' he said, 'has made an observation.'

'Yes?'

'My wife has said that because the body was lying beside her, she heard.'

'Yes? She heard?'

'The sound of the strike and the death noise.' He held a brief consultation with his wife. 'Also a word. In Ng'ombwanan. Spoken very low by a man. By the Ambassador himself, she thinks.'

'And the word – in English?'

' "Traitor",' said the plenipotentiary. After a brief pause he added: 'My wife would like to go now. There is blood on her dress.'

III

The Boomer had changed into a dressing-gown and looked like Othello in the last act. It was a black and gold gown and underneath it crimson pyjamas could be detected. He had left orders that if Alleyn wished to see him he was to be roused and he now received Alleyn, Fox and an attenuated but still alert Mr Whipplestone, in the library. For a moment or two Alleyn thought he was going to jib at Mr Whipplestone's presence. He fetched up short when he saw him, seemed about to say something but instead decided to be gracious. Mr Whipplestone, after all, managed well with The Boomer. His diplomacy was of an acceptable tinge: deferential without being fulsome, composed but not consequential.

When Alleyn said he would like to talk to the Ng'ombwanan servant who waited on them in the pavilion The Boomer made no comment but spoke briefly on the house telephone.

'I wouldn't have troubled you with this,' Alleyn said, 'but I could-
n't find anybody who was prepared to accept the responsibility of
producing the man without your authority.'

'They are all in a silly state,' generalized The Boomer. 'Why do
you want this fellow?'

'The English waiter in the pavilion will have it that the man
attacked him.'

The Boomer lowered his eyelids. 'How very rococo,' he said and
there was no need for him to add: 'as we used to say at Davidson's.'
It had been a catchphrase in their last term and worn to death in the
usage. With startling precision, it again returned Alleyn to that dark
room smelling of anchovy toast and a coal-fire and to the group
mannerisms of his and The Boomer's circle so many years ago.

When the man appeared he cut an unimpressive figure, being
attired in white trousers, a singlet and a wrongly buttoned tunic. He
appeared to be in a state of perturbation and in deep awe of his
President.

'I will speak to him,' The Boomer announced.

He did so, and judging by the tone of his voice, pretty sharply. The
man, fixing his white-eyeballed gaze on the far wall of the library,
answered with, or so it seemed to Alleyn, the clockwork precision of
a soldier on parade.

'He says no,' said The Boomer.

'Could you press a little?'

'It will make no difference. But I will press.'

This time the reply was lengthier. 'He says he ran into someone
in the dark and stumbled and for a moment clung to this person. It
is ridiculous, he says, to speak of it as an attack. He had forgotten the
incident. Perhaps it was this servant.'

'Where did he go after this encounter?'

Out of the pavilion, it appeared, finding himself near the rear
door, and frightened by the general rumpus. He had been rounded
up by security men and drafted with the rest of the household staff
to one end of the ballroom.

'Do you believe him?'

'He would not dare to lie,' said The Boomer calmly,

'In that case I suppose we let him go back to bed, don't we?'

This move having been effected, The Boomer rose and so, of course, did Alleyn, Mr Whipplestone and Fox.

'My dear Rory,' said The Boomer, 'there is a matter which should be settled at once. The body. It will be returned to our country and buried according to our custom.'

'I can promise you that every assistance will be offered. Perhaps the Deputy Commissioner has already given you that assurance.'

'Oh, yes. He was very forthcoming. A nice chap. I hear your pathologist spoke of an autopsy. There can be no autopsy.'

'I see.'

'A thorough enquiry will be held in Ng'ombwana.'

'Good.'

'And I think, since you have completed your investigations, have you not, it would be as well to find out if the good Gibson is in a similar case. If so I would suggest that the police, after leaving and at their convenience, kindly let me have a comprehensive report of their findings. In the meantime, I shall set my house in order.'

As this was in effect an order to quit, Alleyn gave his assurance that there would be a complete withdrawal of the Yard forces. The Boomer expressed his appreciation of the trouble that had been taken and said, very blandly, that if the guilty person was discovered to be a member of his own household, Alleyn, as a matter of courtesy, would be informed. On the other hand the police would no doubt pursue their security precautions outside the Embassy. These pronouncements made such sweeping assumptions that there was nothing more to be said. Alleyn had begun to take his leave when The Boomer interrupted him.

He said: 'There is one other matter I would like to settle.'

'Yes?'

'About the remainder of my stay in England. It is a little difficult to decide.'

Does he, Alleyn asked himself, does The Boomer, by any blissful chance, consider taking himself back to Ng'ombwana? Almost at once? With the corpse, perhaps? What paeans of thanksgiving would spring from Gibson's lips if it were so.

' – the Buck House dinner party, of course, stands,' The Boomer continued. 'Perhaps a quieter affair will be envisaged. It is not for me to say,' he conceded.

'When is that?'

'Tomorrow night. No. Tonight. Dear me, it is almost two in the morning!'

'Your other engagements?' Alleyn hinted.

'I shall cancel the tree-planting affair and of course I shall not attend the race-meeting. That would not look at all the thing,' he said rather wistfully, 'would it?'

'Certainly not.'

'And then there's the Chequers visit. I hardly know what to say.' And with his very best top-drawer manner to the fore The Boomer turned graciously to Mr Whipplestone. 'So difficult,' he said, 'isn't it? Now, tell me. What would you advise?'

This, Alleyn felt, was a question to try Mr Whipplestone's diplomatic resources to their limit. He rose splendidly to his ordeal.

'I'm quite sure,' he said, 'that the Prime Minister and, indeed, all the organizations and hosts who had hoped to entertain your Excellency will perfectly understand that this appalling affair puts anything of the sort out of the question.'

'Oh,' said The Boomer.

'Your Excellency need have no misgiving under that heading, at least,' Mr Whipplestone gracefully concluded.

'Good,' said The Boomer, a trifle dismally Alleyn thought.

'We mustn't keep you up any longer,' Alleyn said, 'but before we take ourselves off, I would like, if I may, to ask one final rather unorthodox question.'

'What is that?'

'You are, I know, persuaded that neither the Ng'ombwanan waiter nor the guard – the *mlinzi*, is it? – is a guilty man.'

'I am sure of it.'

'And you believe, don't you, that Mrs Cockburn-Montfort was mistaken in thinking her assailant was an African?'

'She is a very stupid, hysterical woman. I place no value on anything she says.'

'Have they – the Cockburn-Montforts – any reason to harbour resentment against you or the Ambassador?'

'Oh, yes,' he said promptly. 'They had reason and I've no doubt they still do. It is well known that the Colonel, having had a hand in the formation of our armed forces, expected to be retained and promoted. I believe he actually saw himself in a very exalted role. But, as you know, my policy has been to place my own people in all key positions. I believe the Colonel went into unwilling retirement, breathing fire. In any case,' The Boomer added as an afterthought, 'he had become alcoholic and no longer responsible.'

'But they were asked to the reception?'

'Oh yes! It was a suitable gesture. One could not ignore him. And now – what is this unorthodox question, my dear Rory?'

'Simply this. Do you suspect anyone – specifically – of the murder of your Ambassador?'

Again that well-remembered, hooded look with the half-closed eyes. After a very long pause The Boomer said: 'I have no idea, beyond my absolute certainty of the innocence of the *mlinzi*.'

'One of your guests in the pavilion?'

'Certainly not.'

'I'm glad about that, at least,' said Alleyn drily.

'My dear boy!' For a moment Alleyn thought they were to be treated to one of those bursts of Homeric laughter, but instead his friend touched him gently on the shoulder and gave him a look of such anxiety and affection that he found himself oddly moved.

'Of course it was not a guest. Beyond that,' The Boomer said, 'I have nothing to say.'

'Well, then – ' Alleyn glanced at Fox and Mr Whipplestone who once more made appropriate motions for departure.

'I too have a question,' said The Boomer and they checked. 'My government wishes for a portrait to be hung in our Assembly. I would like, formally, to ask if your wife will accept this commission.'

'I'll deliver the message,' said Alleyn, concealing his astonishment.

At the door he muttered to the others: 'I'll join you in a moment,' and when they had gone he said: 'I've got to say this. You will look after yourself, won't you?'

'Of course,'

'After all – '

'You need have no qualms. I shall sleep very soundly with my *mlinzi* outside my door.'

'You don't mean – ?'

'Certainly. It is his treasured privilege.'

'For God's sake!'

'I shall also lock my door.'

Alleyn left on a gale of laughter.

They went in silence to their extemporized office. When they got there Mr Whipplestone passed his thin hand over his thinner hair, dropped into a chair and said, 'He was lying.'

'The President, sir?' asked Fox in his best scandalized voice. 'About the spearsman?'

'No, no, no, no! It was when he said he didn't suspect anybody – specifically – of the crime.'

'Come on,' Alleyn said. 'Tell us. Why?'

'For a reason that you will find perfectly inadmissible. His manner. I did, at one time, know these people as well, perhaps, as a white person can. I like them. They are not ready liars. But, my dear Alleyn, you yourself know the President very well indeed. Did you have the same reaction?'

Alleyn said: 'He is an honourable person and a very loyal friend. I believe it'd go deeply against the grain for him to lie to me. Yes, I did think he was uncomfortable. I think he may suspect somebody. I think he is withholding something.'

'Have you any idea what?'

Alleyn shoved his hands down in his trouser pockets and walked about the room. In his white tie and tails with miniatures on his coat and with his general air of uncontrived elegance he presented an odd contrast to Mr Fox in his workaday suit, to the sergeant in uniform and even to Mr Whipplestone in his elderly smoking-jacket and scarf.

'I've nothing,' he said at last, 'that will bear the light of day. Let's leave it for the moment and stick to facts, shall we? Sam, could you, before we go, give us a résumé of what was said at that showdown in the ballroom? I know you've written a report and I'm damn grateful and will go over every word of it very carefully indeed. But just to go on with? And also exactly what the waiter said, which sounds like a sequel to what the butler saw, doesn't it? When he came into the library?'

'I'll try,' said Mr Whipplestone. 'Very well. The waiter. At the outset the President told him to give an account of himself during the crucial minutes before and after the murder took place. His reply as far as I can translate it literally was, "I will say what I must say."'

'Meaning, in effect, "I must speak the truth"?'

'Precisely, but he could equally have meant: "I will say what I am forced to say."'

'Suggesting that he had been intimidated?'

'Perhaps. I don't know. He then said that he'd collided with the other waiter in the dark.'

'Chubb?'

'Quite so,' said Mr Whipplestone uneasily.

'And Chubb says the man attacked him.'

'Exactly. So you have told me.'

'Do you think the man was lying?'

'I think he might have merely left out mention of the attack.'

'Yes, I see. And the man himself: the spearsman – *mlinzi* or whatever? Was he at all equivocal?'

Mr Whipplestone hesitated. 'No,' he said at last. 'No, with him it was different. He said – and I think I remember it exactly – that he had taken a terrible – in the sense of awe-inspiring – terrifying, if you like – oath of loyalty to the President and therefore could never, if he were guilty, declare his innocence to the President on the body of his victim.'

'That's almost exactly how the President translated him to me.'

'Yes. And I think it is a true statement. But – well, my dear Alleyn, I hope you won't think I've got an awful cheek if I suggest to you that the President is on the whole a naïve person and that he is not going to heed, not even perhaps notice, any vague ambiguities that might cast doubt upon his men. But of course you know him very well and I don't.'

'Do I?' said Alleyn. 'Perhaps. There are times when I wonder. It's not a simple story: I can assure you of that.'

'There's something very likeable about him. You were quite close friends, I think you said, at school.'

'He's always roaring out that I was his best friend. He was certainly one of mine. He's got a very good brain, you know. He sailed through his law like nobody's business. But you're right,' Alleyn said thoughtfully, 'he cuts dead anything he doesn't want to believe.'

'And of course he doesn't want to believe that one of his own people committed a crime?' Mr Whipplestone urged. Fox made a noise of agreement.

Alleyn said: 'No. Perhaps he doesn't – *want* to,' and vexedly rubbed his nose. 'All the same,' he said, 'I think we may be fishing in the wrong pond. In very muddy waters, at all events.'

'Do you mind,' Mr Whipplestone asked, 'if I put a very direct question to you?'

'How can I tell, till I hear it?'

'Quite. Here goes then. Do you think an attempt was made upon the President?'

'Yes.'

'And do you think it will be repeated?'

'I think it's only too likely that something else may be tried. Only too likely,' said Alleyn.

There was a long silence.

'What happens now, Mr Alleyn?' asked Fox at last.

'I'm damned if I know. Call it a night, I suppose. We've been given our marching orders and no mistake. Come on. We'd better tell Fred Gibson, hadn't we?'

Mr Gibson was not sorry to get the sack from the Embassy. It relieved him of an untenable and undefinable task and left him free to supervise the orthodox business of mounting security measures outside the premises and wherever the President might take it into his head to go during the remainder of his visit. He expressed muffled but profound satisfaction when Alleyn pointed out that the public appearances would probably be curtailed when not cancelled.

'You could say,' he mumbled presently, 'that after a fashion we've picked up a bit of joy in this show.' And he divulged that they had found the shell of the shot fired from the Luger. It was on the ground outside the lavatory window. They'd had no luck with a bullet.

'But,' said Gibson with a kind of huffy satisfaction, 'I don't reckon we need to shed tears over that one. Take a look at this.'

He opened his large pale hand. Alleyn and Fox bent over it.

'Wad?' Fox said. 'Here! Wait a sec. I wonder now.'

'Yes,' Alleyn said, 'Fred. I wonder if you've drawn a blank.' They left the Embassy.

Troy was awake when Alleyn got home. She called out to him to save him the trouble of trying not to disturb her. When he came in she was sitting up in bed with her arms round her knees.

'Not a nice party, after all,' he said, 'I'm sorry, my darling.'

'Have you – ?'

'No. Troy. I had to let you go off without a word. I couldn't look after you. Were you very much shocked?'

'I didn't really see. Well – yes – I did see but in a funny sort of way it didn't look – real. And it was only for a flash – not more than a second or two. In a way, I didn't believe it.'

'Good.'

'Everybody sort of milling round.'

'That's right.'

'And you got us all out of the way so very expeditiously.'

'Did I?'

'Yes. But – ' she bit her lip and said very quickly – 'it was the spear, wasn't it? He was speared?'

He nodded and put her irregular dark locks of hair out of her eyes.

'Then,' Troy said, 'haven't you arrested that superb-looking being?'

'The Boomer says the superb-looking being didn't do it. And anyway we haven't the authority inside the Embassy. It's a rum go and no mistake. Do you want to hear?'

'Not now. You'd better get some sleep.'

'Same to you. I shall have a bath. Good morning, my love. Oh – I forgot. I have a present for you from The Boomer!'

'For me? What can you mean?'

'He wants you to paint him. His suggestion, not mine.'

Troy was immovable for several seconds. She then gave Alleyn a quick exultant look and suddenly burrowed into her pillow.

He stared down at her and reflected on things one was supposed to remember about the artistic temperament. He touched her hair and went off to his bath with the dawn light paling the window.

CHAPTER 6

Afternoon in the Capricorns

When, in response to a telephone call taken by Troy, Alleyn called on the following afternoon at No. 1, Capricorn Walk, he was received on the front steps by Lucy Lockett, the cat.

She sat, with a proprietory air on the top step and had a good look at him.

'I know who *you* are,' said Alleyn. 'Good afternoon, my dear.' He extended his forefinger. Lucy rose, stretched elaborately, yawned and advanced her whiskers to within an inch of the fingertip. Mr Whipplestone looked out of his open bow window.

'There you are,' he said. 'I won't be a second.'

Lucy sprang adroitly from the steps to the window-sill and thence into the bosom of her master, who presently opened the front door, still carrying her.

'Come in, do, do,' he said. 'We've been expecting you.'

'What a nice house you've got.'

'Do you think so? I must say I like it.'

'You hadn't far to walk last night – or this morning.'

'No. Do you know, Alleyn, when I was coming home at whatever eldritch hour, I caught myself wondering – well, *almost* wondering – if the whole affair could have been some sort of hallucination. Rather like that dodging-about-in-time nonsense they do in science fiction plays: as if it had happened off the normal temporal plane. The whole thing – so very – ah – off beat. Wasn't it?'

'Was and is,' Alleyn agreed.

He found Mr Whipplestone himself rather off-beat as he sat primly on his desk chair in his perfectly tailored suit, with his Trumper-style hair-cut, his discreet necktie, his elegant cuff-links, his eyeglass and, pounding away at his impeccable waistcoat, his little black cat.

'About Chubb,' he said anxiously, 'I'm awfully *bothered* about Chubb. You see, I don't know – and he hasn't said anything – and I must say Mrs Chubb looks too ghastly for words.'

'He hasn't told you the black waiter attacked him?'

'He hasn't told me anything. I felt it was not advisable for me to make any approach.'

'What's your opinion of Chubb? What sort of impression have you formed, by and large, since the Chubbs have been looking after you?'

Mr Whipplestone had some difficulty in expressing himself but it emerged that from his point of view the Chubbs were as near perfection as made no difference. In fact, Mr Whipplestone said wistfully, one had thought they no longer existed except perhaps in the employment of millionaires.

'I've sometime wondered if they were too good to be true. Ominous foreboding!' he said.

'Didn't you say Chubb seemed to have taken a scunner on blacks.'

'Well, yes. I rather fancied so. It was when I looked over this house. We were in the room upstairs and – Oh, Lord, it was the poor old boy himself – the Ambassador – walked down the street. The Chubbs were near the window and saw him. It was nothing, really. They stared. My dear Alleyn, you won't take from this any grotesque suggestion that Chubb – well, no, of course you won't.'

'I only thought a prejudice of that sort might colour any statement he offered. He certainly made no bones about his dislike when we talked to him.'

'Not surprising when you tell me one of them had half-strangled him!'

'*He* told me that.'

'Don't you believe him?'

'I don't know,' Alleyn said with an odd twist in his voice. 'Perhaps. But with misgivings.'

'Surely,' Mr Whipplestone said, 'it can be a very straight-forward affair, after all. For whatever motive, the Ng'ombwanan guard and the waiter conspire to murder either the Ambassador or the President. At the crucial moment, the servant finds Chubb in the way and doubles him up, leaving the guard free to commit the crime. The guard kills the Ambassador. To the President he confesses himself to be what my poor Chubb calls clobbered.'

'Yes,' Alleyn said. 'As neat as a new pin – almost.'

'So you see – you see!' cried Mr Whipplestone, stroking the cat.

'And the pistol shot?'

'Part of the conspiracy – I don't know – yes. That awful lady says it was a black person, doesn't she? Well, then!'

'Whoever it was probably fired a blank.'

'Indeed? There you are, then. A diversion. A red-herring calculated to attract the attention of all of you away from the pavilion and to bring the President to his feet.'

'As I said,' Alleyn conceded. 'New pins aren't in it.'

'Then – why – ?'

'My dear man, I don't know. I promise you, I don't know. It's by the pricking of my thumbs or some other intimation not admissible in the police manuals. It just all seems to me to be a bit too much of a good thing. Like those fish in aspic that ocean-going cruisers display in the tropics and never serve.'

'Oh, come!'

'Still, there are more tenable queries to be raised. Item. Mrs C-M's black thug with a stocking over his head. Seen dimly against the loo window, unseen during the assault in the dressing-room. Rushed out of the "Ladies" into the entrance hall – there's no other exit – where there were four of Gibson's men, one of them hard by the door. They all had torches. None of them got any impression of anybody emerging precipitately into the hall. Incidentally there was another SB man near the master-switch in the rear passage, who killed the blackout about ten seconds after he heard the pistol shot. In those ten seconds the murder was done.'

'Well?'

'Well, our girl-friend has it that after the shot her assailant, having chucked her out of the loo, emerged still in the blackout, kicked her about a bit and then bolted, leaving her prone and still in the dark. And then, she says, the loo-ladies, including our blushing sergeant, emerged and fell about all over her. Still in the dark. The loo-ladies, on the other hand, maintain they erupted into the anteroom immediately after the shot.'

'They were confused, no doubt.'

'The sergeant wasn't.'

'Drat!' said Mr Whipplestone. 'What's all this got to do with my wretched Chubb?'

'I've not the remotest idea. But it tempts me to suspect that when it comes to equivocation your black candidates have nothing on Mrs Cockburn-Montfort.'

Mr Whipplestone thought this over. Lucy tapped his chin with her paw and then fell asleep.

'Do I take it,' he asked at last, 'that you think Mrs C-M lied extensively about the black man with the stocking over his head?'

'I think she invented him.'

'Then who the devil fired the shot?'

'Oh,' Alleyn said. 'No difficulty with that one, I fancy. She did.'

II

Mr Whipplestone was much taken aback by this pronouncement. He gave himself time to digest its implications. He detached his cat and placed her on the floor where, with an affronted and ostentatious air, she set about cleaning herself. He brushed his waistcoat, crossed his legs, joined his finger-tips and finally said: 'How very intriguing.' After a further pause he asked Alleyn if he had any more specific material to support his startling view of Mrs Cockburn-Montfort's activities.

Not specific, perhaps, Alleyn conceded. But he pointed out that a black male person planning to fire the pistol, whether or not it was loaded with a blank, would have been much better advised to do so from the men's lavatory, where his presence would not be noticed, than from the women's where it extravagantly would. In the men's he would be taken for an attendant if he was in livery and for a guest if he was not.

'Really,' Alleyn said, 'it would be the height of dottiness for him to muscle-in to the female offices where he might – as indeed according to Mrs C-M he *did* – disturb a lady already *in situ.*'

'True,' said Mr Whipplestone moodily. 'True. True. True.'

'Moreover,' Alleyn continued, 'the sergeant, who, however naughty her lapse, displayed a certain expertise in the sequel, is persuaded that no rumpus, beyond the shot and subsequent screams of Mrs C-M, disturbed the seclusion of those premises.'

'I see.'

'As for the weapon, an examination of the barrel, made by an expert this morning, confirms that the solitary round was probably a blank. There are no finger-prints. This is negative evidence except that the sergeant, supported by the two orthodox attendants, says that Mrs C-M was wearing shoulder length gloves. The normal practice under these circumstances is for such gloves to be peeled off the hand from the wrist. The glove is then tucked back into the arm-piece which remains undisturbed. But the lady was fully gloved and buttoned and according to her own account certainly had no chance to effect this readjustment. She would hardly sit on the floor putting on gloves and yelling pen and ink.'

'All very plausible,' said Mr Whipplestone. Alleyn thought that he was hurriedly re-arranging his thoughts to accommodate this new development.

'I fancy,' Alleyn said, 'it's better than that. I can't for the life of me think of any other explanation that will accommodate all the discrepancies in the lady's tarra-diddle. And what's more she was taking dirty great sniffs at her own smelling-salts to make herself cry. At any rate I'm going to call upon her.'

'When!' quite shouted Mr Whipplestone.

'When I leave you. Why? What's up?'

'Nothing.' he said in a hurry, 'nothing really. Except that you'll probably be admitted by Chubb.'

'By *Chubb*!'

'He, ah, he "does for" the Cockburn-Montforts on Friday afternoons. There's nothing in that, you know, Alleyn. The Chubbs have one or two, as it were, casual jobs about the neighbourhood. They baby-sit every other Sunday at No. 17 for instance. It's an arrangement.'

'And Mrs Chubb obliges your tenant in the basement, doesn't she?'

'An hour, every other day. She will give us tea, by the way.' He glanced at the clock. 'Any second now. I asked for it very early, hoping you would join me. Mrs Alleyn said something about you not having had time for luncheon.'

'How very kind, I shall enjoy it.'

Lucy, after some preparatory clawing at the foot of the door, succeeded in opening it widely enough to make an exit which she effected with her tail up and an ambiguous remark.

'Sometimes,' said Mr Whipplestone, 'I've felt almost inclined to pump the Chubbs.'

'About Sheridan and the Cockburn-Montforts?'

'Discreetly. Yes. But of course, one doesn't do that sort of thing. Or,' Mr Whipplestone said with a self-deprecatory lift of his hand, 'I don't.'

'No,' Alleyn said, 'I don't suppose you do. Do you mind, though, if I have a word with Mrs Chubb?'

'Here? Now?' he said, evidently dismayed by the suggestion.

'Well – later if you'd rather.'

'She's awfully upset. About Chubb being man-handled by that black waiter and interviewed afterwards.'

'I'll try not to add to her woes. It really is just routine, Sam as far as I know.'

'Well, I do hope it doesn't turn out to be – anything else. Sh!'

He held up his finger. From somewhere outside the room came a series of intermittent bumps or taps. They grew louder.

Alleyn went to the door into the hall, left ajar by Lucy Lockett, and looked out.

To see Lucy herself backing down the stairs crab-wise and dragging some small object by a chain. It bumped from step to wooden step. When she arrived at the bottom she contrived with some difficulty to take the object up in her mouth. Giving out distorted mews she passed Alleyn, reentered the drawing-room and dropped her trophy at Mr Whipplestone's feet.

'Oh no, oh no!' he cried out. 'Not again. For pity's sake, not again!'

But it was, in fact, a white pottery fish.

While he still gazed at it with the liveliest dismay a clink of china sounded in the passage. With extraordinary swiftness Alleyn scooped up the fish and dropped it in his pocket.

'Not a word,' he said.

Mrs Chubb came in with a tea-tray.

Alleyn gave her good afternoon and brought forward a small table to Mr Whipplestone's chair, 'Is this the right drill?' he asked and she thanked him nervously and set down her tray. When she had left and he had heard her go upstairs he said: 'It's not Sheridan's fish. She brought it from above.'

Mr Whipplestone's jaw dropped. He stared at Alleyn as if he had never seen him before. 'Show me,' he said at last.

Alleyn produced the object and dangled it by its chain in front of Mr Whipplestone who said: 'Yes. It is. I've remembered.'

'What have you remembered?'

'I think I told you. The first time she stole it. Or rather one like it. From down below. I had the curious feeling I'd seen it before. And then again, that evening when I returned it to Sheridan. Round that ghastly fellow Sanskrit's fat neck. The same feeling. Now I've remembered: it was on the day I inspected the premises. The fish was in the Chubbs' room upstairs. Hanging from a photograph of a girl with black ribbon attached to the frame. Rather morbid. And this,' said Mr Whipplestone, ramming home his point, 'is it.' He actually covered his face with his hands. 'And that,' he said, 'is *very* uncomfortable news.'

'It may turn out to be of no great matter, after all. I wouldn't get too uptight about it, if I were you. This may simply be the outward and visible sign of some harmlessly potty little cult they all belong to.'

'Yes, but *Chubb?* And those dubious – those more than dubious Cockburn-Montforts and those frankly appalling Sanskrits. No, I don't like it,' said Mr Whipplestone. 'I don't like it at all.' His distracted gaze fell upon Lucy who was posed tidily *couchant* with her paws tucked under her chest. 'And the cat!' he remembered. 'The cat, of whose reprehensible habits I say nothing, took fright at the very sight of that ghastly pair. She bolted. And the Pirellis at the Napoli think she belonged to the Sanskrit woman. And they seem to think she was ill-treated.'

'I don't quite see . . .'

'Very well. Very well. Let it pass. Have some tea.' Mr Whipplestone distractedly invited, 'and tell me what you propose to do about that thing: that medallion, that – fish.'

Alleyn took it from his pocket and turned it over in his hand. A trade-mark like a wavy X had been fired into the reverse side.

'Roughish little job,' he said. 'Lucky she didn't break it. If you don't mind, I think I'll go upstairs and return it to its owner. It gives me the entrée, doesn't it?'

'I suppose so. Yes. Well. If you must.'

'It'll save you a rather tricky confrontation, Sam.'

'Yes. Thank you. Very good. Yes.'

'I'll nip up before she has time to return to her kitchen. Which is their sitting-room?'

'First door on the landing.'

'Right.'

He left Mr Whipplestone moodily pouring tea, climbed the stairs and tapped at the door.

After a pause it was opened by Mrs Chubb who stared at him with something like terror in her eyes. He asked her if he might come in for a moment and for a split second wondered if she was going to say no and shut the door in his face. But she stood aside with her fingers at her lips and he went in.

He saw, at once, the photograph on the wall. A girl of about sixteen with a nice, round, fresh-looking face very like Mrs Chubb's. The black ribbons had been made into rosettes and fastened to the top corners of the frame. On the photograph itself, neatly written, was a legend: 'April 4, 1953-May 1st, 1969.'

Alleyn took the medallion from his pocket. Mrs Chubb made a strange little falsetto noise in her throat.

He said: 'I'm afraid Lucy has been up to her tricks again. Mr Whipplestone tells me she's done this sort of thing before. Extraordinary animals, cats, aren't they? Once they get a notion into their heads, there's no stopping them. It belongs here, doesn't it?'

She made no move to take it. A drawing-pin lay on the table under the photograph. Alleyn pushed it back into its hole and looped the chain over it. 'The cat must have pulled it out,' he said: and then: 'Mrs Chubb, you're feeling poorly, aren't you? I'm so sorry. Sit down, won't you, and let me see if I can do something about it? Would you like a drink of water? No. Then, do sit down.'

He put his hand under her arm. She was standing in front of a chair and dropped into it as if she couldn't help herself. She was as white as a sheet and trembling.

Alleyn drew up another chair for himself.

'Mr Whipplestone told me you'd been very much upset by what happened last night and now I'm afraid I've gone and made matters worse,' he said.

Still she didn't speak and he went on: 'I don't expect you know who I am. It was I who interviewed your husband last night. I'm an old friend of Mr Whipplestone's and I know how greatly he values your service.'

Mrs Chubb whispered: 'The police?'

'Yes, but there's no need to worry about that. Really.'

'He set on 'im,' she said. 'That – ' she shut her eyes for a second – '*black* man. Set on 'im.'

'I know. He told me.'

'It's the truth.' And with a startling force she repeated this, loudly, 'It's the truth. Sir. Do you believe that, sir? Do you believe it's the truth?'

Alleyn waited for a moment.

He thought: 'Do I believe this, do I believe the other thing? Everybody asking what one believes. The word becomes meaningless. It's what one knows that matters in this muddle.' He waited for a moment and then said: 'A policeman may only believe what he finds out for himself, without any possible doubt, to be true. If your husband was attacked, as he says he was, we shall find out.'

'Thank Gawd,' she whispered. And then: 'I'm sorry, I'm sure, to give way like this. I can't think what's come over me.'

'Never mind.'

He got up and moved towards the photograph. Mrs Chubb blew her nose.

'That's an attractive face,' Alleyn said, 'Is it your daughter?'

'That's right,' she said. 'Was.'

'I'm sorry. Long ago?'

'Six years.'

'An illness?'

'An accident.' She made as if to speak, pressed her lips together and then shot out, as if defiantly: 'She was the only one, our Glenys was.'

'I can see the likeness.'

'That's right.'

'Was the medallion special to her, perhaps?'

She didn't answer. He turned round and found her staring at the photograph and wetting her lips. Her hands were clasped.

'If it was,' he said, 'of course you'd be very upset when you thought you'd lost it.'

'It wasn't hers.'

'No?'

'I hadn't noticed it wasn't there. It gave me a turn, like. When you – you held it out.'

'I'm sorry,' Alleyn repeated.

'It doesn't matter.'

'Was it in London – the accident?'

'Yes,' she said and shut her mouth like a trap.

Alleyn said lightly: 'It's a rather unusual-looking medallion, isn't it? An order or a badge or something of that sort, perhaps?'

She pulled her hands apart as if the gesture needed force to accomplish it.

'It's my husband's,' she said, 'It's Chubb's.'

'A club badge, perhaps?'

'You could call it that, I suppose.'

She had her back to the door. It opened and her husband stood on the threshold.

'I don't know anything about it,' she said loudly. 'It's got nothing to do with anything. Nothing.'

Chubb said: 'You're wanted downstairs.'

She got up and left the room without a glance at Alleyn or at her husband.

'Were you wanting to see me, sir?' Chubb asked woodenly. 'I've just come in.'

Alleyn explained about the cat and the medallion. Chubb listened impassively, 'I was curious,' Alleyn ended, 'about the medallion itself and wondered if it was a badge.'

Chubb said at once and without hesitation, 'That's correct, sir. It's a little social circle with an interest in ESP and so forth. Survival and that.'

'Mr and Miss Sanskrit are members, aren't they?'

'That's correct, sir.'

'And Mr Sheridap?'

'Yes, sir.'

'And you?' Alleyn said lightly.

'They was kind enough to make me an honorary member, like. Seeing I go in and do the servicing for some of their meetings, sir. And seeing I was interested.'

'In survival after death, do you mean?'

'That kind of thing.'

'Your wife doesn't share your interest?'

He said flatly: 'She doesn't come into it, does she? It's kind of complementary to my services, isn't it? Like wearing a livery button used to be.'

'I see. You must find a different place for it, mustn't you?' Alleyn said easily. 'Out of reach of Lucy Lockett. Good afternoon to you, Chubb.'

Chubb mouthed rather than sounded his response to this and Alleyn left him, almost as bleached as his wife had been five minutes earlier.

Mr Whipplestone was still sipping tea. Lucy was discussing a saucer of milk on the hearthrug.

'You must have some tea *at once?*' Mr Whipplestone said, pouring it out. 'And some anchovy toast. I hope you like anchovy toast. It's still quite eatable, I think.' He tipped back the lid of the hot-server and up floated the smell that of all others recalled Alleyn to his boyhood days with The Boomer. He took a piece of toast and his tea.

'I can't stay long,' he said. 'I oughtn't to stay at all, in fact, but here goes.'

'About the Chubbs?' Mr Whipplestone ventured. Alleyn gave him a concise account of his visit upstairs. On the whole it seemed to comfort him. 'As you suggested,' he said, 'the emblem of some insignificant little coterie and Chubb has been made a sort of non-commissioned officer in recognition of his serving them sandwiches and drinks. Perhaps they think he's psychic. That makes perfectly good sense. Well, doesn't it?'

'Yes, of course. It's not without interest, do you agree,' Alleyn asked, 'that Sanskrit is on the police records for fraudulent practice as a fortune-teller and a phoney medium? *And* he's suspected of the odd spot of drug trafficking'

'I am not in the least surprised,' Mr Whipplestone energetically declared. 'In the realms of criminal deception he is, I feel sure, *capable de tout*. From that point of view, if from no other, I do of course deplore the Chubb connection.'

'And there's Mrs Cockburn-Montfort, who seems to be a likely candidate for the attempt-on-the-President stakes. Not a nice influence either, would you say?'

'Oh *drat*!' said Mr Whipplestone. 'Very well, my dear fellow. I'm a selfish, square old bachelor and I don't want anything beastly to happen to my Chubbs because they make life pleasant for me.' His exasperated gaze fell upon his cat. 'As for *you*,' he scolded. 'If you'd be good enough to keep your paws to yourself this sort of thing wouldn't happen. Mind that!'

Alleyn finished his tea and toast and stood up.

'Are you going, my dear chap?' Mr Whipplestone asked rather wistfully.

'Needs must. Thank you for my lovely cuppa. Goodbye, my dear,' he said to Lucy Lockett. 'Unlike your boss, I'm much obliged to you. I'm off.'

'To see Mrs C-M?'

'On the contrary. To see Miss Sanskrit. She now takes precedence over the C-M.'

III

Alleyn had not come face to face with the Sanskrits at the Embassy. Like all the guests who had not been in or near the pavilion, they had been asked for their names and addresses by Inspector Fox, ticked off on the guest list and allowed to go home. He didn't think, therefore, that Miss Sanskrit would recall his face or, if she did, would attach more importance to it than to any that she had seen among a hundred others at the reception.

He walked down Capricorn Mews, past the Napoli grocery shop, the flower shop and the garages. The late afternoon was warm, scents of coffee, provender, carnations and red roses drifted on the air and, for some reason, the bells in the Basilica were ringing.

At the far end of the Mews, at its junction with the passageway into Baronsgate, was the converted stable now devoted to the sale of pottery pigs. It faced up the Mews and was, therefore, in full view for their entire length. Alleyn, advancing towards it, entertained somewhere in the back of his thoughts a prospect of stamping and sweating horses, industrious stablemen, ammoniacal fumes and the rumble of Dickensian wheels. Pigeons, wheeling overhead, and intermittently flapping down to the cobbled passage, lent a kind of authenticity to his fancies.

But there, as he approached, was the nonedescript signboard 'K. & X. Sanskrit. Pigs.' And there, deep in the interior and in a sort of alcove at the far end, was a faint red glow indicating the presence of a kiln and, looming over it, the dim bulk of Miss Sanskrit.

He made as if to turn off into the passageway, checked, and stopped to peer through the window at the exhibits ranked on shelves nearest to it. A particularly malevolent pig with forget-me-nots on its flanks glowered at him rather in the manner of Miss Sanskrit herself, who had turned her head in the shadows and seemed to stare at him. He opened the door and walked in.

'Good afternoon,' he said.

She rose heavily and lumbered towards him, emerging from the alcove, he thought, like some dinosaur from its lair.

'I wonder,' Alleyn said, as if suddenly inspired, 'if you can help me by any chance. I'm looking for someone who could make castings of a small ceramic emblem. It's to be the badge for a newly-formed club.'

'We don't,' rumbled an astonishingly deep voice inside Miss Sanskrit, 'accept commissions.'

'Oh. Pity. In that case,' Alleyn said, 'I shall do what I came to do and buy one of your pigs. The doorstop kind. You don't have pottery cats, I suppose? With or without flowers?'

'There's one doorstop cat. Bottom shelf. I've discontinued the line.'

It was indeed the only cat: a baleful, lean, black, upright cat with blue eyes and buttercups on its haunches. Alleyn bought it. It was very heavy and cost five pounds.

'This is perfectly splendid!' he prattled while Miss Sanskrit busied her fat, pale hands in making a clumsy parcel. 'Actually it's a present for a cat. She lives at No. 1, Capricorn Walk and is positively the double of this one. Except that she's got a white tip to her tail. I wonder what she'll make of it.'

Miss Sanskrit had paused for a second in her wrapping. She said nothing.

He rambled chattily on. 'She's quite a character, this cat. behaves more like a dog, really. Retrieves things. Not above indulging in the odd theft, either.'

She turned her back on him. The paper crackled. Alleyn waited. Presently she faced round with the parcel in her hands. Her embedded eyes beneath the preposterous beetroot-coloured fringe were fixed on him.

'Thank you,' she growled and he took the parcel.

'I suppose,' he said apologetically, 'you couldn't recommend anybody for this casting job? It's quite small. Just a white fish with its tail in its mouth. About that size.'

There was something in the way she looked at him that recalled, however grotesquely, the interview with Mrs Chubb. It was a feral look: that of a creature suddenly alarmed and on guard and he was very familiar with it. It would scarcely be too fanciful to imagine she had given out a self-defensive smell.

'I'm afraid,' she said, 'I can't help you. Good afternoon.' She had turned her back and begun to waddle away when he said:

'Miss Sanskrit.'

She stopped.

'I believe we were both at the same party last night. At the Ng'ombwana Embassy.'

'Oh,' she said, without turning.

'You were with your brother, I think. And I believe I saw your brother a few weeks ago when I was in Ng'ombwana.'

No reply.

'Quite a coincidence,' said Alleyn. 'Good afternoon.'

As he walked away and turned the corner into Capricorn Place he thought: Now, I wonder if that *was* a good idea. She's undoubtedly rattled, as far as one can think of blubber rattling. She'll tell Big Brother and what will they cook up between them? That I'm fishing after membership? In which case, will they get in touch with the other fish to see what *they* know? Or will she suspect the worst of me and start at once, on her own account, ringing round the circle to warn them all? In which case she'll hear I'm a cop in as short a time as it takes Mrs Cockburn-Montfort to throw a temperament. And in *that* case we'll have to take damn good care she and Big Brother don't shoot the moon. I don't mind betting, he thought as he approached No. 19, The Place, that those dubious premises accommodate more than pottery pigs. Has Brother *quite* given up the drug connection? A nice point. Here we go again.

No. 19, Capricorn Place, although larger, was built in much the same style as Mr Whipplestone's little house. The window-boxes, however, were more commonplace, being given over to geraniums. As Alleyn crossed the street he saw, behind the geraniums, Mrs Cockburn-Montfort's bizarre face looking much the worse for wear and regarding him with an expression of horror. It dodged away.

He had to ring three times before the Colonel opened the door on a wave of gin. For a moment Alleyn thought, as he had with Chubb, that it might be slammed in his face. Inside the house someone was speaking on the telephone.

The Colonel said: 'Yes?'

'If it's not inconvenient I'd like to have two words with Mrs Cockburn-Montfort,' Alleyn said.

'Out of the question I'm 'fraid. She's unwell. She's in bed.'

'I'm sorry. In that case, with you, if you'll be so good as to put up with me.'

'It doesn't suit at the moment. I'm sorry. Any case we've nothing to add to what we said last night.'

'Perhaps, Colonel, you'd rather come down to the Yard. We won't keep you long.'

He glared, red-eyed, at nothing in particular and then said. 'Damn! All right. You'd better come in.'

'Thank you so much,' said Alleyn and did so, pretty smartly, passing the Colonel into a hall with a flight of stairs and two doors, the first of which stood ajar.

Inside the room a voice, hushed but unmistakably Mrs Cockburn-Montfort's was speaking. 'Xenny,' she was saying, 'It's true. Here! Now! I'm ringing off.'

'Not that door. The next,' shouted the Colonel, but Alleyn had already gone in.

She was dressed in a contemporary version of a garment that Alleyn had heard his mother refer to as a tea-gown: an elaborate confection worn, he rather thought, over pyjamas and held together by ribbons. Her hair had been arranged but insecurely so that it almost looked more dishevelled than it would have done if it had been left to itself. The same appraisement might have been made of her face. She was smoking.

When she saw Alleyn she gestured with both hands rather as if something fluttered near her nose. She took a step backwards and saw her husband in the doorway.

'Why've you come down, Chrissie?' he said. 'You're meant to stay in bed.'

'I – I'd run out of cigarettes.' She pointed a shaky finger at Alleyn. 'You again!' she said with a pretty awful attempt at playfulness.

'Me again, I'm afraid,' he said, 'I'm sorry to pounce like this but one or two things have cropped up.'

Her hands were at her hair, 'I'm in no state – Too shaming!' she cried. 'What *will* you think!'

'You'd better go back to bed,' her husband said brutally. 'Here! I'll take you.'

She's signalled, Alleyn thought. I can't prevent this.

'I'll just tidy up a bit,' she said. 'That's what I'll do.'

They went out, he holding her arm above the elbow.

And now, Alleyn thought, she'll tell him she's telephoned the Sanskrit. If it was the Sanskrit and I'll lay my shirt on it. They're cooking up what they're going to say to me.

He heard a door slam upstairs.

He looked round the drawing-room. Half conventional, half 'contemporary'. Different coloured walls, 'with-it' ornaments and one or two collages and a mobile mingled disconsolately with pouffes, simpering water-colours and martial photographs of the Colonel, one of which showed him in shorts and helmet with a Ng'ombwanan regiment forming a background. A ladylike desk upon which the telephone now gave out a click.

Alleyn was beside it. He lifted the receiver and heard someone dialling. The ringing sound set in. After a longish pause a muffled voice said 'Yes?'

'That you, Zenoclea?' The Colonel said, 'Chrissie rang you a moment ago, didn't she? All right. He's *here*.'

'Be careful.' (The Sanskrit, sure enough.)

'Of course. This is only to warn you.'

'Have you been drinking?'

'My dear Xenny! Look! He may call on you.'

'Why?'

'God knows. I'll come round later, or ring. 'Bye.'

A click and then the dialling tone.

Alleyn hung up and walked over to the window.

He was gazing at the distant prospect of the Basilica when the Colonel re-entered the room. Alleyn saw at once that he had decided on a change of manner. He came in jauntily.

'Ah!' he said. 'There we are! Chrissie's insisting on making herself presentable. She'll be down in a moment. Says she feels quite equal to it. Command take a pew. I think a drink while we wait is indicated, don't you? What shall it be?'

'Very civil of you,' Alleyn said, speaking the language, 'but it's not on for me, I'm afraid. Please don't let me stop you, though.'

'Not when you're on guard duty, what? Bad luck! Well, just to show there's no ill-feeling,' said the Colonel, 'I think I will.'

He opened a door at the far end of the room and went into what evidently was his study. Alleyn saw a martial collection of sword, service automatic and a massive hunting rifle hung on the wall. The Colonel returned with a bottle in one hand and a very large gin in the other.

'Your very good health,' he said and drank half of it.

Fortified and refreshed, it seemed, he talked away easily about the assassination. He took it for granted, or appeared to do so, that the spearsman had killed the Ambassador in mistake for the President. He said that you never could tell with blacks, that he knew them, that he'd had more experience of them, he ventured to claim, than most. 'Bloody good fighting men, mind you, but you can't trust them beyond a certain point.' He thought you could depend upon it that when the President and his entourage had got back to Ng'ombwana the whole thing would be dealt with in their way and very little would be heard of it. 'There'll be a new *mlinzi* on duty and no questions asked, I wouldn't wonder. On the other hand, he may decide to make a public example.'

'By that do you mean a public execution?'

'Don't take me up on that, old man,' said the Colonel, who was helping himself to another double gin. 'He hasn't gone in for that particular exercise, so far. Not like the late lamented, f'instance.'

'The Ambassador?'

'That's right. He had a pretty lurid past in that respect. Between you and me and the gatepost.'

'Really?'

'As a young man. Ran a sort of guerrilla group. When we were still here. Never brought to book but it's common knowledge. He's turned respectable of late years.'

His wife made her entrance: fully clothed, coiffured and regrettably made-up.

'Time for dinkies?' she asked. 'Super! Give me one, darling: kick-sticks.'

Alleyn thought: She's already given herself one or more. This is excessively distasteful.

'In a minute,' said her husband, 'sit down, Chris.'

She did, with an insecure suggestion of gaiety.

'What have you two been gossiping about?' she asked.

'I'm sorry,' Alleyn said, 'to bother you at an inopportune time and when you're not feeling well, but there is one question I'd like to ask you, Mrs Cockburn-Montfort.'

'Me? Is there? What?'

'Why did you fire off that Luger and then throw it in the pond?'

She gaped at him, emitted a strange whining sound that, incongruously enough, reminded him of Mrs Chubb. Before she could speak her husband said: 'Shut up, Chris. I'll handle it. I mean that. Shut up.'

He turned on Alleyn. The glass in his hand was unsteady but, Alleyn thought, he was in pretty good command of himself. One of those heavy drinkers who are seldom really drunk. He'd had a shock but he was equal to it.

He said: 'My wife will not answer any questions until we have consulted our solicitor. What you suggest is obviously unwarranted and quite ridiculous. And 'stremely 'fensive. You haven't heard the last of this, whatever-your-rank-is Alleyn.'

'I'm afraid you're right, there,' Alleyn said. 'And nor have you, perhaps. Good evening to you. I'll show myself out.'

IV

'And the odd thing about that little episode, Br'er Fox, is this: my bit of personal bugging on the Cockburn-Montfort telephone exchange copped Miss Xenoclea Sanskrit – Xenny for short – in an apparently motiveless lie. The gallant Colonel said: "He – " meaning me – "may call on you" and instead of saying: "He *has* called on me," she merely growled "Why?" Uncandid behaviour from a comrade, don't you think?'

'If,' said Fox carefully, 'this little lot, meaning the Colonel and his lady, the Sanskrit combination, the Sheridan gentleman and this chap Chubb, are all tied up in some hate-the-blacks club and *if*, as seems possible, seeing most of them were at the party, and seeing the way the lady carried on, they're mixed up in the fatality – ' He drew breath.

'I can't wait,' Alleyn said.

'I was only going to say it wouldn't, given all these circumstances, be anything out of the way if they got round to looking sideways at each other,' He sighed heavily. 'On the other hand,' he said, 'and I must say on the face of it this is the view I'm inclined to favour, we may have a perfectly straightforward job. The man with the spear used the spear and what else took place round about in the dark has little or no bearing on the matter.'

'How about Mrs C-M and her Luger in the ladies' loo?'

'Blast!' said Fox.

'The whole thing's so bloody untidy,' Alleyn grumbled

'I wouldn't mind going over the headings,' Fox confessed.

'Plough ahead and much good may it do you.'

'*A*.' said Fox, massively checking it off with finger and thumb. '*A*. The occurrence. Ambassador killed by spear. Spearsman stationed at rear in handy position. Says he was clobbered and his spear taken off him. Says he's innocent. *B*. Chubb. Ex-commando. Also at rear.

Member of this secret society or whatever it is. Suggestion that he's a black-hater. Says *he* was clobbered by black waiter. *C*. Mrs C-M. Fires shot, probably blank, from ladies' conveniences. Why? To draw attention? To get the President on his feet, so's he could be speared? By whom? This is the nitty-gritty one.' said Fox. 'If the club's an anti-black show would they collaborate with the spearsman or the waiter? The answer is: unlikely. Very unlikely. Where does this take us?'

'Hold on to your hats, boys.'

'To Chubb,' said Fox. 'It takes us to Chubb. Well, doesn't it? Chubb, set up by the club, clobbers the spearsman, and does the job on the Ambassador and afterwards says the waiter clobbered *him* and held him down.'

'But the waiter maintains that he stumbled in the dark and accidentally grabbed Chubb. If Chubb was the spearsman, what are we to make of this?'

'Mightn't it be the case, though? Mightn't he have stumbled and momentarily clung to Chubb?'

'Before or after Chubb clobbered the spearsman and grabbed the spear?'

Fox began to look disconcerted, 'I don't like it much,' he confessed. 'Still, after a fashion it fits. After a fashion it does.'

'It's a brave show, Br'er Fox, and does you credit. Carry on.'

'I don't know that I've all that much more to offer. This Sanskrit couple, now. At least there's a CRO on *him*. Fraud, fortune-telling and hard drugs, I think you mentioned. Big importer into Ng'ombwana until the present government turned him out. They're members of this club, if Mr Whipplestone's right when he says he saw them wearing the medallion.'

'Not only that,' Alleyn said. He opened a drawer in his desk and produced his black pottery cat. 'Take a look at this,' he said and exhibited the base. It bore, as a trademark, a wavy X. 'That's on the reverse of the medallions, too,' he said. 'X for Xenoclea, I suppose. Xenny not only wears a medallion, she makes 'em in her little kiln, fat witch that she is.'

'You're building up quite a case, Mr Alleyn, aren't you? But against whom? And for what?'

'You tell me. But whatever turns up in the ambassadorial department, I'll kick myself all round the Capricorns if I don't get something on the Sanskrits. What rot they talk when they teach us we should never get involved. Of course we get involved: we merely learn not to show it.'

'Oh, come now! *You* never do, Mr Alleyn.'

'Don't I? All right, Foxkin, I'm talking through my hat. But I've taken a scunner on la belle Xenny and Big Brother and I'll have to watch it. Look, let's get the CRO file and have a look for ourselves. Fred Gibson wasn't all that interested at that stage. One of his henchmen looked it up for him. There was nothing there that directly concerned security and he may not have given me all the details.'

So they called on the Criminal Records Office for the entry under Sanskrit.

Alleyn said, 'Just as Fred quoted it. Fraudulent practices. Fortune-telling. Suspected drug peddling. All in the past before he made his pile as an importer of fancy goods in Ng'ombwana. And he did, apparently, make a tidy pile before he was forced to sell out to a Ng'ombwanan interest.'

'That was recently?'

'Quite recently. I actually happened to catch sight of him standing outside the erstwhile premises when I was over there. He doesn't seem to have lost face – and God knows he's got plenty to lose – or he wouldn't have been asked to the party.'

'Wouldn't you say it was a bit funny their being invited, anyway?'

'Yes,' Alleyn agreed thoughtfully. 'Yes. I think I would.'

'Would you reckon this pottery business of the sister's was a money-spinner?'

'Not on a big scale.'

'Was she involved in any of the former charges?'

'She hasn't got a CRO. Wait a bit though. There's a cross reference. "See McGuigan, O." Fetch us down the Macs.' The sergeant on duty obliged.

'Here you are,' said Mr Fox presently. 'Take a look,' and without waiting for Alleyn to do so he continued in the slightly catarrhal voice he kept for reading aloud: '"McGuigan, Olive, supposed widow of Sean McGuigan of whom nothing known. Sister of Kenneth Sanskrit q.v. Later assumed as first name, Xenoclea. Sus. drug traffic with brother. Charged with fortune-telling for which, fined, June 1953. Reported to RSPCA cruelty to cat, 1967. Charged and convicted.

Fined with costs." Fred Gibson's henchmen left this out. He'll be getting some "advice" on this one,' said Fox.

'Ah. And Sam Whipplestone thinks she ill-treated his cat. Pretty little picture we're building up, aren't we? I must say I thought the "Xenoclea" bit was too good to be true,' Alleyn grunted.

'Is it a made-up job, then, that name?'

'Not by her, at least. Xenoclea was a mythical prophetess who wouldn't do her stuff for Hercules because he hadn't had a bath. After his Augean stables job, perhaps. I bet la belle Xenny re-christened herself and reverted to her maiden name when she took to her fortune-telling lay.'

'Where do they live?'

'Above the pottery pigs. There seems to be a flat up there: quite a sizeable one, by the look of it.'

'Does the brother live there with her – wait a bit,' said Fox interrupting himself. 'Where's the guest list we made last night?'

'In my office but you needn't worry. I looked it up. That's their joint address. While we're at it, Br'er Fox, let's see, for the hell of it, whether there's anything on Sheridan, A. R. G., 1a, Capricorn Walk.'

But Mr Sheridan had no criminal record.

'All the same,' Alleyn said, 'we'll have to get him sorted out. Even if it comes to asking the President if there's a Ng'ombwanan link. He wasn't asked to the reception, of course. Oh well, press on.'

They left the CRO and returned to Alleyn's rooms, where he managed to reach Superintendent Gibson on the telephone.

'What's horrible, Fred?'

'Nothing to report,' said that colourless man. 'All quiet inside the premises, seemingly. We've stopped the demolition. Routine precaution.'

'Demolition?'

'Clearing up after the party. The Vistas people and the electrics. It's silly really, seeing we can't go in. If nothing develops they may as well get on with it.'

'Any ingoings or outcomings of interest?'

'Post. Tradesmen. We looked over all deliveries which wasn't very popular. Callers offering condolences and leaving cards. The media of course. One incident.'

'What?'

'His Nibs, believe it or not.'

'The President?'

'That's right. Suddenly comes out by the front entrance with a dirty great dog on a leash and says he's taking it for a walk in the Park.'

Alleyn swore vigorously.

'What's that?' asked Gibson.

'Never mind. Go on.'

'My sergeant, on duty at the entrance, tries to reason with him. I'm doing a cruise round in a job car and they give me a shout and I come in and try to reason with him. He's very la-di-da, making out we're fussy. It's awkward,' said Mr Gibson drearily.

'How did you handle it, Fred?'

'I'm stuck with it, aren't I? So I say we'll keep with it and he says if it's a bodyguard I'm worried about he's got the dog and his own personal protection and with that the door opens and guess who appears?' invited Mr Gibson without animation.

'The spearsman of last night?'

'That's correct. The number one suspect in my book who we'd've borrowed last night, there and then, if we'd had a fair go. There he was, large as life.'

'You don't surprise me. What was the upshot?'

'Ask yourself. In flocks the media, telly, press, the lot. He says "no comment" and off he goes to his constitutional with the dog and the prime sus and five of my chaps in a panda doing their best in the way of protection. So they go and look at Peter Pan,' said Mr Gibson bitterly, 'and nobody shoots anybody or lobs in a bomb and they come home again. Tonight it's the Palace caper.'

'That's been scaled down considerably, hasn't it?'

'Yes. Nondescript transport. Changed route. Small party.'

'At least he's not taking the spearsman with him.'

'Not according to my info. It wouldn't surprise me.'

'Poor Fred!'

'Well, it's not what you'd pick in the way of a job,' said Gibson. 'Oh yes, and there's another thing. He wants to see you. Or talk to you.'

'Why? Did you gather?'

'No. He just chucks it over his shoulder when he walks away. He's awkward.'

'The visit may be cut short.'

'Can't be too short for me,' said Gibson and they took leave of each other.

'It's a case,' Alleyn said when he'd replaced the receiver, 'of "where do we go for honey?" I dunno, Br'er Fox. Press on, press on but in what direction?'

'This Mr Sheridan,' Fox ruminated. 'He seems to have been kind of side-tracked, doesn't he? I mean from the secret society or what-have-you angle.'

'I know he does. He wasn't at the party. That's why.'

'But he is a member of whatever they are.'

'Yes. Look here, Fox. The only reason – the only tenable reason – we've got for thinking there was some hanky-panky based on this idiot-group is the evidence, if you can call it that, of Mrs C-M having loosed off a Luger with a blank charge in the ladies' loo. I'm quite convinced, if only because of their reaction – hers and the gallant Colonel's – that she's the girl who did it, though proving it will be something else again. All right. The highly suspect, the generally inadmissible word "coincidental" keeps on rearing its vacant head in these proceedings but I'll be damned if I accept any argument based on the notion that two entirely unrelated attempts at homicide occurred within the same five minutes at an Ambassadorial party.'

'You mean,' said Fox, 'the idea that Mrs C-M and this little gang had something laid on and never got beyond the first move because the spearsman hopped in and beat them to it?'

'Is that what I mean? Yes, of course it is, but blow me down flat if it sounds as silly as I expected it to.'

'It sounds pretty silly to me.'

'You can't entertain the notion?'

'It'd take a big effort.'

'Well, God knows. You may have to make it. I tell you what, Foxkin. We'll try and get a bit more on Sheridan if only for tidiness's sake. And we'll take a long shot and give ourselves the dreary task of finding out how a girl of sixteen was killed in London on the first of May, 1969. Name Glenys Chubb.'

'Car accident?'

'We don't know. I get the impression that although the word accident was used, it was not used correctly. Lurking round the fringe of my rotten memory there's something or another, and it may be so much nonsense, about the name Chubb in connection with an unsolved homicide. We weren't involved. Not on our ground.'

'Chubb,' mused Fox. '*Chubb*, now. Yes. Yes, there *was* something. Now, what was it? Wait a bit, Mr Alleyn. Hold on.'

Mr Fox went into a glazed stare at nothing in particular from which he was roused by Alleyn bringing his palm down smartly on his desk.

'Notting Hill Gate,' Alleyn said. 'May 1969. Raped and strangled. Man seen leaving the area but never knocked off. That's it. We'll have to dig it out, of course, but I bet you that's it. Still open. He left a red scarf behind and it was identified.'

'You're dead right. The case blew out. They knew their man but they never got it tied up."

'No. Never.'

'He was coloured,' Fox said. 'A coloured chap, wasn't he?'

'Yes,' Alleyn said. 'He was. He was black. And what's more – Here! We'll get on to the Unsolved File for this one and we'll do it now, by gum.'

It didn't take long. The Unsolved Homicide file for May 1969 had a succinct account of the murder of Chubb, Glenys, aged sixteen, by a black person believed but never proved to be a native of Ng'ombwana.

CHAPTER 7

Mr Sheridan's Past

When they had closed the file for unsolved homicide, subsection rape and asphyxiation, 1969, Fox remarked that if Chubb hadn't seemed to have a motive before he certainly had one now. Of a far-fetched sort, Fox allowed, but a motive nevertheless. And in a sort of fashion he argued, this went some way to showing that the society – he was pleased to call it the 'fishy society' – had as its objective the confusion, subjection and downfall of The Black.

'I begin to fancy Chubb,' said Fox.

At this point Alleyn's telephone rang. To his great surprise it was Troy who was never known to call him at the Yard. He said: 'Troy! Anything wrong?'

'Not really and I'm sorry about this,' she said rapidly, 'but I thought you'd better know at once. It's your Boomer on the blower.'

'Wanting me?'

'Strangely enough, no. Wanting me.'

'Oh?' said Alleyn with an edge in his voice. 'Well, he'll have to wait. What for? No, don't tell me. It's about his portrait.'

'He's coming. Now. Here. In full fig to be painted. He says he can give me an hour and a half. I tried to demur but he just roared roughshod over my bleating. He said time was of the essence because his visit is to be cut short. He said the conversation can be continued in a few minutes when he arrives and with that he hung up and I think I hear him arriving.'

'By God, he's a daisy. I'll be with you in half an hour or earlier.'

146

'You needn't. It's not that I'm in the least flustered. It's only I thought you should know.'

'You couldn't be more right. Stick him up in the studio and get cracking. I'll be there in a jiffy.'

Alleyn clapped down his receiver and said to Fox: 'Did you get the gist of that? Whistle me up a car, Fox, and see if you can get the word through to Fred Gibson. I suppose he's on to this caper, but find out. And you stay here in case anything comes through and if it does, call me at home. I'm off.'

When he arrived at the pleasant cul-de-sac where he and Troy had their house, he found the Ng'ombwanan ceremonial car, its flag flying, drawn up at the kerb. A poker-faced black chauffeur sat at the wheel. Alleyn was not surprised to see, a little way along the street on the opposite side, a 'nondescript' which is the police term for a disguised vehicle, this time a delivery van. Two men with short haircuts sat in the driver's compartment. He recognized another of Mr Gibson's stalwarts sitting at a table outside the pub. A uniformed constable was on duty outside the house. When Alleyn got out of the police car this officer, looking self-conscious, saluted him.

'How long have *you* lot been keeping obbo on my pad?' Alleyn asked.

'Half an hour, sir. Mr Gibson's inside, sir. He's only just arrived and asked me to inform you.'

'I'll bet he did,' Alleyn said and let himself in.

Gibson was in the hall.

He showed something like animation on greeting Alleyn and appeared to be embarrassed. The first thing he had heard of the President's latest caper, he said, was a radio message that the Ambassadorial Rolls with the Ng'ombwanan flag mounted, had drawn up to the front entrance of the Embassy. His sergeant had spoken to the driver who said the President had ordered it and was going out. The sergeant reached Mr Gibson on radio but before he got to the spot the President, followed by his bodyguard, came out, swept aside the wretched sergeant's attempts to detain him and shouting out the address to his driver, had been driven away. Gibson and elements of the security forces outside the Embassy had then given chase and taken up the appropriate stations where Alleyn had seen them. When they arrived the President and his *mlinzi* were already in the house.

'Where is he now?'

'Mrs Alleyn,' said Gibson, coughing slightly, 'took him to the studio. She said I was to tell you. "The Studio", she said. He was very sarcastic about me being here. Seemed to think it funny,' said Gibson resentfully.

'What about the prime suspect?'

'Outside the studio door. I'm very, very sorry but without I took positive action I couldn't remove him. Mrs Alleyn didn't make a complaint. I'd've loved to've borrowed that chap then and there,' said Gibson.

'All right, Fred. I'll see what I can do. Give yourself a drink. In the dining-room, there. Take it into the study and settle down.'

'Ta,' said Gibson wearily, 'I could do with it.'

The studio was a separate building at the back of the house and had been built for a Victorian Academician of preposterous fame. It had an absurd entrance approached by a flight of steps with a canopy supported by a brace of self-conscious plaster caryatids that Troy had thought too funny to remove. Between these, in stunning incongruity, stood the enormous *mlinzi* only slightly less impressive in a dark suit than he had been in his lionskin and bracelets. He had his right forearm inside his jacket. He completely filled the entrance.

Alleyn said: 'Good evening.'

'Good day. Sir,' said the *mlinzi*.

'I – am – going – in,' said Alleyn very distinctly. When no move was made, he repeated this announcement, tapping his chest and pointing to the door.

The *mlinzi* rolled his eyes, turned smartly, knocked on the door and entered. His huge voice was answered by another, even more resonant and by a matter-of-fact comment from Troy: 'Oh, here's Rory,' Troy said.

The *mlinzi* stood aside and Alleyn, uncertain about the degree of his own exasperation, walked in.

The model's throne was at the far end of the studio. Hung over a screen Troy used for backgrounds was a lion's skin. In front of it, in full ceremonials, ablaze with decorations, gold lace and accoutrements, legs apart and arms akimbo, stood The Boomer.

Troy, behind a four-foot canvas, was setting her palette. On the floor lay two of her rapid exploratory charcoal drawings. A brush was clenched between her teeth. She turned her head and nodded vigorously at her husband, several times.

'Ho-ho!' shouted The Boomer. 'Excuse me, my dear Rory, that I don't descend. As you see, we are busy. Go away!' he shouted at the *mlinzi* and added something curt in their native tongue. The man went away.

'I apologize for him!' The Boomer said magnificently. 'Since last night he is nervous of my well-being. I allowed him to come.'

'He seems to be favouring his arm.'

'Yes. It turns out that his collar-bone was fractured.'

'Last night?'

'By an assailant, whoever he was.'

'Has he seen a doctor?'

'Oh, yes. The man who looks after the Embassy. A Doctor Gomba. He's quite a good man. Trained at St Luke's.'

'Did he elaborate at all on the injury?'

'A blow, probably with the edge of the hand since there is no indication of a weapon. It's not a break – only a crack.'

'What does the *mlinzi* himself say about it?'

'He has elaborated a little on his rather sparse account of last night. He says that someone struck him on the base of the neck and seized his spear. He has no idea of his assailant's identity. I must apologize,' said The Boomer affably, 'for my unheralded appearance, my dear old man. My stay in London has been curtailed. I am determined that no painter but your wife shall do the portrait and I am impatient to have it. Therefore I cut through the codswallop, as we used to say at Davidson's, and here, as you see, I am.'

Troy removed the brush from between her teeth. 'Stay if you like, darling,' she said and gave her husband one of the infrequent smiles that still afforded him such deep pleasure.

'If I'm not in the way,' he said and contrived not to sound sardonic. Troy shook her head.

'No, no, no,' said The Boomer graciously. 'We are pleased to have your company. It is permitted to converse. Provided,' he added with a bawling laugh, 'that one expects no reply. That is the situation. Am

I right *maestro?*' he asked Troy, who did not reply, 'I do not know the feminine of *maestro*,' he confessed. 'One must not say *maestress*. That would be in bad taste.'

Troy made a snuffling noise.

Alleyn sat down in a veteran armchair.

'Since I am here and as long as it doesn't disrupt the proceedings – ' he began.

'Nothing,' The Boomer interposed, 'disrupts *me*.'

'Good. I wonder then if your Excellency can tell me anything about two of your last night's guests.'

'My Excellency can try. He is so ridiculous,' The Boomer parenthesized to Troy, 'with his "Excellencies".' And to Alleyn: 'I have been telling your wife about our times at Davidson's.'

'The couple I mean are a brother and sister called Sanskrit.'

The Boomer had been smiling but his lips now closed over his dazzling teeth, 'I think perhaps I have moved a little,' he said.

'No,' Troy said. 'You are splendidly still,' She began to make dark, sweeping gestures on her canvas.

'Sanskrit,' Alleyn repeated. 'They are enormously fat.'

'Ah! Yes. I know the couple you mean.'

'Is there a link with Ng'ombwana?'

'A commercial one. Yes. They were importers of fancy goods.'

'Were?'

'Were,' said The Boomer without batting an eyelid. 'They sold out.'

'Do you know them personally?'

'They have been presented,' he said.

'Did they want to leave?'

'Presumably not, since they are coming back.'

'What?'

'I believe they are coming back. Some alteration in plans. I understand they intend to return immediately. They are persons of little importance.'

'Boomer,' said Alleyn, 'have they any cause to bear you a grudge?'

'None whatever. Why?'

'It's simply a check-up. After all, it seems somebody tried to murder you at your party.'

'Well, you won't have any luck with them. If anything, they ought to feel grateful.'

'Why?'

'It is under my regime that they return. They had been rather abruptly treated by the previous government.'

'When was the decision taken? To re-instate them?'

'Let me see – a month ago, I should say. More, perhaps.'

'But when I visited you three weeks ago I actually happened to see Sanskrit on the steps outside his erstwhile premises. The name had just been painted out.'

'You're wrong there, my dear Rory. It was, I expect, in process of being painted in again.'

'I see,' said Alleyn and was silent for some seconds. 'Do you like them?' he asked. 'The Sanskrits?'

'No,' said The Boomer. 'I find them disgusting.'

'Well, then – ?'

'The man had been mistakenly expelled. He made out his case,' The Boomer said with a curious air of restraint. 'He has every reason to feel an obligation and none to feel animosity. You may dismiss him from your mind.'

'Before I do, had he any reason to entertain personal animosity against the Ambassador?'

An even longer pause. 'Reason? He? None,' said The Boomer. 'None whatever.' And then: 'I don't know what is in your mind, Rory, but I'm sure that if you think this person could have committed the murder you are – you are – what is the phrase – you will get no joy from such a theory. But,' he added with a return of his jovial manner, 'we should not discuss these beastly affairs before Mrs Alleyn.'

'She hasn't heard us,' said Alleyn simply. From where he sat he could see Troy at work. It was as if her response to her subject was distilled into some sort of essence that flowed down arm, hand and brush to take possession of the canvas. He had never seen her work so urgently. She was making that slight breathy noise that he used to say was her inspiration asking to be let out. And what she did was splendid: a mystery in the making. 'She hadn't heard us,' he repeated.

'Has she not?' said The Boomer and added: 'That, I understand. I understand it perfectly.'

And Alleyn experienced a swift upsurge of an emotion that he would have been hard put to it to define. 'Do you Boomer?' he said, 'I believe you do.'

'A fraction more to your left,' said Troy. 'Rory – if you could move your chair. That's done it. Thank you.'

The Boomer patiently maintained his pose and as the minutes went by he and Alleyn had little more to say to each other. There was a kind of precarious restfulness between them.

Soon after half past six Troy said she needed her sitter no more for the present. The Boomer behaved nicely. He suggested that perhaps she would prefer that he didn't see what was happening. She came out of a long stare at her canvas, put her hand in his arm and led him round to look at it, which he did in absolute silence.

'I am greatly obliged to you,' said The Boomer at last.

'And I to you,' said Troy. 'Tomorrow morning, perhaps? While the paint is still wet?'

'Tomorrow morning,' promised The Boomer. 'Everything else is cancelled and nothing is regretted,' and he took his leave.

Alleyn escorted him to the studio door. The *mlinzi* stood at the foot of the steps. In descending Alleyn stumbled and lurched against him. The man gave an indrawn gasp, instantly repressed. Alleyn made remorseful noises and The Boomer, who had gone ahead, turned round.

Alleyn said: 'I've been clumsy. I've hurt him. Do tell him I'm sorry'

'He'll survive!' said The Boomer cheerfully. He said something to the man, who walked ahead into the house. The Boomer chuckled and laid his massive arm across Alleyn's shoulders.

He said: 'He really *has* a fractured collar-bone, you know. Ask Doctor Gomba or, if you like, have a look for yourself. But don't go on concerning yourself over my *mlinzi*. Truly, it's a waste of your valuable time.'

It struck Alleyn that if it came to being concerned, Mr Whipplestone and The Boomer in their several ways were equally worried about the well-being of their dependants. He said: 'All right, all right. But it's you who are my real headache. Look, for the last time, I most earnestly beg you to stop taking risks. I promise you, I honestly believe that there was a plot to kill you last night and that there's every possibility that another attempt will be made.'

'What form will it take do you suppose? A bomb?'

'And you might be right at that. Are you sure, are you absolutely sure, there's nobody at all dubious in the Embassy staff? The servants – '

'I am sure. Not only did your tedious but worthy Gibson's people search the Embassy but my own people did, too. Very, very thoroughly. There are no bombs. And there is not a servant there who is not above suspicion.'

'*How* can you be so sure! If, for instance, a big enough bribe was offered – '

'I shall never make you understand, my dear man. You don't know what I am to my people. It would frighten them less to kill themselves than to touch me. I swear to you that if there was a plot to kill me, it was not organized or inspired by any of these people. No!' he said and his extraordinary voice sounded like a gong. 'Never! It is impossible. No!'

'All right. I'll accept that so long as you don't admit unknown elements, you're safe inside the Embassy. But for God's sake don't go taking that bloody hound for walks in the Park.'

He burst out laughing, 'I am sorry,' he said, actually holding his sides like a clown, 'but I couldn't resist. It was so funny. There they were, so frightened and fussed. Dodging about, those big silly men. No! Admit! It was too funny for words.'

'I hope you find this evening's security measures equally droll.'

'Don't be stuffy,' said The Boomer. 'Would you like a drink before you go?'

'Very much, but I think I should return.'

'I'll just tell Gibson.'

'Where is he?'

'In the study. Damping down his frustration. Will you excuse me?'

Alleyn looked round the study door. Mr Gibson was at ease with a glass of beer at his elbow.

'Going,' Alleyn said.

He rose and followed Alleyn into the hall.

'Ah!' said The Boomer graciously. 'Mr Gibson. Here we go again, don't we, Mr Gibson?'

'That's right, your Excellency,' said Gibson tonelessly. 'Here we go again. Excuse me.'

He went out into the street, leaving the door open.

'I look forward to the next sitting,' said The Boomer, rubbing his hands. 'Immeasurably, I shall see you then, old boy. In the morning? Shan't I?'

'Not very likely, I'm afraid.'

'No?'

'I'm rather busy on a case,' Alleyn said politely. 'Troy will do the honours for both of us, if you'll forgive me.'

'Good, good, good!' he said genially. Alleyn escorted him to the car. The *mlinzi* opened the door with his left hand. The police car started up its engine and Gibson got into it. The Special Branch men moved. At the open end of the cul-de-sac a body of police kept back a sizeable crowd. Groups of residents had collected in the little street.

A dark, pale and completely bald man, well-dressed in formal clothes, who had been reading a paper at a table outside the little pub, put on his hat and strolled away. Several people crossed the street. The policeman on duty asked them to stand back.

'What *is* all this?' asked The Boomer.

'Perhaps it has escaped your notice that the media has not been idle. There's a front page spread with banner headlines in the evening papers.'

'I would have thought they had something better to do with the space.' He slapped Alleyn on the back. 'Bless you,' he roared. He got into the car, shouted, 'I'll be back at half past nine in the morning. Do try to be at home,' and was driven off. 'Bless *you*,' Alleyn muttered to the gracious salutes The Boomer had begun to turn on for the benefit of the bystanders. 'God knows you need it.'

The police car led the way, turning off into a side exit which would bring them eventually into the main street. The Ng'ombwanan car followed it. There were frustrated manifestations from the crowd at the far end which gradually dispersed. Alleyn, full of misgivings, went back to the house. He mixed two drinks and took them to the studio, where he found Troy still in her painting smock, stretched out in an armchair scowling at her canvas. On such occasions she always made him think of a small boy. A short lock of hair overhung her forehead, her hands were painty and her expression brooding. She got up, abruptly, returned to her easel and swept down a black line behind the head that started up from its tawny surroundings. She then backed away towards him. He moved aside and she saw him.

'How about it?' she asked.

'I've never known you so quick. It's staggering.'

'Too quick to be right?'

'How can you say such a thing? It's witchcraft.'

She leant against him. 'He's wonderful,' she said. 'Like a symbol of blackness. And there's something – almost desperate. Tragic? Lonely? I don't know. I hope it happens on that thing over there.'

'It's begun to happen. So we forget the comic element?'

'Oh that! Yes, of course, he is terribly funny. Victorian music-hall, almost. But I feel it's just a kind of trimming. Not important. Is that my drink?'

'Troy, my darling, I'm going to ask you something irritating.'

She had taken her drink to the easel and was glowering over the top of her glass at the canvas. 'Are you?' she said vaguely. 'What?'

'He's sitting for you again in the morning. Between now and then I want you not to let anybody or anything you don't know come into the house. No gas-meter inspectors or window-cleaners, no parcels addressed in strange hands. No local body representatives. Nothing and nobody that you can't account for.'

Troy, still absently, said, 'All right,' and then suddenly aware: 'Are you talking about *bombs?*'

'Yes, I am.'

'Good Lord!'

'It's not a silly notion, you know. Well, is it?'

'It's a jolly boring one, though.'

'Promise.'

'All right,' Troy said, and squeezed out a dollop of cadmium red on her palette. She put down her drink and took up a brush.

Alleyn wondered how the hell one kept one's priorities straight. He watched her nervous, paint-stained hand poise the brush and then use it with the authority of a fiddler. What she's up to, he thought, and what I am supposed to be up to are a stellar journey apart and yet ours, miraculously, is a happy marriage. Why?

Troy turned round and looked at him. 'I was listening,' she said, 'I do promise.'

'Well – thank you, my love,' he said.

II

That evening, at about the same time as The Boomer dined royally at Buckingham Palace, Alleyn, with Fox in attendance, set out to keep observation upon Mr Sheridan in his basement flat at No. la, Capricorn Walk. They drove there in a 'nondescript' equipped with a multi-channel radio set. Alleyn remembered that there had been some talk of Mr Whipplestone dining with his sister who had come up to London for the night, so there was no question of attracting his attention.

They had been advised by a panda on Unit Beat that the occupant of the basement flat was at home but his window curtains must be very heavy because they completely excluded the light. Alleyn and Fox approached from Capricorn Square and parked in the shadow of the plane trees. The evening was sultry and overcast and the precincts were given over to their customary quietude. From the Sun in Splendour, further back in the Square, came the sound of voices, not very loud.

'Hold on a bit. I'm in two minds about this one, Fox.' Alleyn said, 'It's a question of whether the coterie as a whole is concerned in last night's abortive attempt if that's what it was, or whether Mrs C-M and the Colonel acted quite independently under their own alcoholic steam. Which seems unlikely. If it was a concerted affair they may very well have called a meeting to review the situation. Quite possibly to cook up another attempt.'

'Or to fall out among themselves,' said Fox.

'Indeed. Or to fall out.'

'Suppose, for instance,' Fox said in his plain way, 'Chubb did the job, thinking it was the President: they won't be best pleased with *him*. And you tell me he seems to be nervous.'

'Very nervous.'

'What's in your mind, then? For now?'

'I thought we might lurk here for a bit to see if Mr Sheridan has any callers or if, alternatively, he himself steps out to take the air.'

'Do you know what he looks like?'

'Sam Whipplestone says he's dark, bald, middle height, well-dressed and speaks with a lisp. I've never seen him to my knowledge.' A pause. 'He's peeping,' said Alleyn.

A vertical sliver of light had appeared in the basement windows of No. la. After a second or two it was shut off.

'I wouldn't have thought,' Fox said, 'they'd fancy those premises for a meeting. Under the circs. With Mr Whipplestone living up above and all.'

'Nor would I.'

Fox grunted comfortably and settled down in his seat. Several cars passed down Capricorn Walk towards Baronsgate, the last being a taxi which stopped at No. 1. A further half-dozen cars followed by a delivery van passed between the watchers and the taxi and were held up, presumably by a block in Baronsgate itself. It was one of those sudden and rare incursions of traffic into the quiet of the Capricorns at night. When it had cleared a figure was revealed coming through the gate at the top of the basement steps at No. 1: a man in a dark suit and scarf wearing a 'City' hat. He set off down the Walk in the direction of Baronsgate. Alleyn waited for a little and then drove forward, he turned the corner, passed No. 1 and parked three houses further along.

'He's going into the Mews,' he said. And, sure enough, Mr Sheridan crossed the street, turned right and disappeared.

'What price he's making a call on the pottery pigs?' Alleyn asked. 'Or do you fancy the gallant Colonel and his lady? Hold on, Fox.'

He left Fox in the car, crossed the street and walked rapidly past the Mews for some twenty yards. He then stopped and returned to a small house-decorator's shop on the corner where he was able to look through the double windows down the Mews past the Napoli and the opening into Capricorn Place, where the Cockburn-Montforts lived, to the pottery at the far end. Mr Sheridan kept straight on, in and out of the rather sparse lighting until he reached the pottery. Here he stopped at a side-door, looked about him and raised his hand to the bell. The door was opened on a dim interior by an unmistakable vast shape. Mr Sheridan entered and the door was shut.

Alleyn returned to the car.

'That's it,' he said. 'The piggery it is. Away we go. We've got to play this carefully. He's on the alert, is Mr S.'

At the garage where Mr Whipplestone first met Lucy Lockett there was a very dark alley leading into a yard. Alleyn backed the car into it, stopped the engine and put out the lights. He and Fox opened the doors, broke into drunken laughter, shouted indistinguishably, banged the doors and settled down in their seats.

They had not long to wait before Colonel and Mrs Cockburn-Montfort turned out of Capricorn Place and passed them on the far side of the Mews, she teetering on preposterous heels, he marching with the preternatural accuracy of the seasoned toper.

They were admitted into the same door by the same vast shape.

'One to come,' Alleyn said, 'unless he's there already.'

But he was not there already. Nobody else passed up or down the Mews for perhaps a minute. The clock in the Basilica struck nine and the last note was followed by approaching footsteps on their side of the street. Alleyn and Fox slid down in their seats. The steps, making the customary rather theatrical, rather disturbing effect of footfalls in dark streets, approached at a brisk pace and Chubb passed by on his way to the pottery.

When he had been admitted Alleyn said: 'We don't, by the way, know if there are any more members, do we? Some unknown quantity?'

'What about it?'

'Wait and see, I suppose. It's very tempting, you know, Br'er Fox, to let them warm up a bit and then make an official call and politely scare the pants off them. It would stop any further attempts from that quarter on The Boomer unless, of course, there's a fanatic among them and I wouldn't put that past Chubb for one.'

'Do we try it, then?'

'Regretfully, we don't. We haven't got enough on any of them to make an arrest and we'd lose all chances of finally roping them in. Pity! Pity!'

'So what's the form?'

'Well, I think we wait until they break up and then, however late the hour, we might even call upon Mr Sheridan. Somebody coming,' Alleyn said.

'Your unknown quantity?'

'I wonder.'

It was a light footstep this time and approached rapidly on the far side of the Mews. There was a street lamp at the corner of Capricorn Place. The newcomer walked into its ambit and crossed the road coming straight towards them.

It was Samuel Whipplestone.

III

'Well, of course,' Alleyn thought. 'He's going for his evening constitutional, but why did he tell me he was dining with his sister?'

Fox sat quiet at his side. They waited in the dark for Mr
Whipplestone to turn and continue his walk.

But he stopped and peered directly into the alleyway. For a
moment Alleyn had the uncanny impression that they looked
straight into each other's eyes and then Mr Whipplestone, slipping
past the bonnet of the car, tapped discreetly on the driver's window.

Alleyn let it down.

'May I get in?' asked Mr Whipplestone. 'I think it may be important.'

'All right. But keep quiet if anybody comes. Don't bang the door,
will you? What's up?'

Mr Whipplestone began to talk very rapidly and precisely in a
breathy undertone, leaning forward so that his head was almost
between the heads of his listeners.

'I came home early,' he said. 'My sister Edith had a migraine. I
arrived by taxi and had just let myself in when I heard the basement
door close and someone came up the steps. I dare say I've become
hypersensitive to any occurrences down there. I went into the
drawing-room and without turning on the lights watched Sheridan
open the area gate and look about him. He was wearing a hat but for
a moment or two his face was lit by the headlamps of one of some
half-dozen cars that had been halted. I saw him very clearly. Very,
very clearly. He was scowling. I think I mentioned to you that I've
been nagged by the impression that I had seen him before, I'll return
to that in a moment.'

'So,' said Alleyn.

'I was still there, at my window, when this car pulled out of the
square from the shadow of the trees, turned right and parked a few
doors away from me. I noticed the number.'

'Ah!' said Alleyn.

'This was just as Sheridan disappeared up the Mews. The driver
got out of the car and – but I need not elaborate.'

'I was rumbled.'

'Well – yes. If you like to put it that way. I saw you station yourself at the corner and then return to this car. And I saw you drive

into the Mews. Of course, I was intrigued but believe me, Alleyn, I had no thought of interfering or indulging in any – ah – ah – '

'Counter-espionage?'

'Oh, my dear fellow! Well. I turned away from my window and was about to put on the lights when I heard Chubb coming down the stairs. I heard him walk along the hall and stop by the drawing-room door. Only for a moment. I was in two minds whether to put on the lights and say, "Oh, Chubb, I'm in," or something of that sort, or to let him go. So uncomfortable has the atmosphere been that I decided on the latter course. He went out, doublelocked the door and walked off in the same direction as Sheridan. And you. Into the Mews.'

Mr Whipplestone paused, whether for dramatic effect or in search of the precise mode of expression, he being invisible, it was impossible to determine.

'It was then,' he said, 'that I remembered. Why, at that particular moment the penny should drop, I have no notion. But drop it did.'

'You remembered?'

'About Sheridan.'

'Ah.'

'I remembered where I had seen him. Twenty-odd years ago. In Ng'ombwana.' Fox suddenly let out a vast sigh. 'Go on,' said Alleyn.

'It was a court of law. British law, of course, at that period. And Sheridan was in the dock.'

'Was he indeed!'

'He had another name in those days. He was reputed to come from Portuguese East and he was called Manuel Gomez. He owned extensive coffee plantations. He was found guilty of manslaughter. One of his workers – it was a revolting business – had been chained to a tree and beaten and had died of gangrene.'

Fox clicked his tongue several times.

'And that is not all. My dear Alleyn, for the prosecution there was a young Ng'ombwanan barrister who had qualified in London – the first, I believe, to do so.'

'The Boomer, by God.'

'Precisely. I seem to recollect that he pressed with great tenacity for a sentence of murder and the death penalty.'

'What *was* the sentence?'

'I don't remember – something like fifteen years, I fancy. The plantation is now in the hands of the present government, of course, but I remember Gomez was said to have salted away a fortune. In Portugal, I think. It may have been London. I am not certain of these details.'

'You *are* certain of the man?'

'Absolutely. And of the barrister. I attended the trial, I have a diary that I kept at that time and a pretty extensive scrapbook. We can verify. But I am certain. He was scowling in the light from the car. The whole thing flashed up most vividly, those one or two minutes later.'

'That's what actors call a double-take.'

'Do they?' Mr Whipplestone said absently, and then: 'He made a scene when he was sentenced. I'd never seen anything like it. It left an extraordinary impression.'

'Violent?'

'Oh yes, indeed. Screaming. Threatening. He had to be handcuffed and even then – It was like an animal,' said Mr Whipplestone.

'Fair enough,' Fox rumbled, pursuing some inward cogitation.

'You don't ask me,' Mr Whipplestone murmured, 'why I took the action I did. Following you here.'

'Why did you?'

'I felt sure *you* had followed *Sheridan* because you thought, as I did, that probably there was to be a meeting of these people. Whether at the Cockburn-Montforts' or at the Sanskrits' flat. And I felt most unhappily sure that Chubb was going to join them. I had and have no idea whether you actually intended to break in upon the assembly but I thought it might well be that this intelligence would be of importance. I saw Chubb being admitted to that place. I followed, expecting you would be somewhere in the Mews and I made out your car. So here I am, you see,' said Mr Whipplestone.

'Here you are and the man without motive is now supplied with what might even turn out to be the prime motive.'

'That,' said Mr Whipplestone, 'is what I rather thought.'

'You may say,' Fox ruminated, 'that, as far as motives go, it's now one apiece. Chubb: the daughter. The Sanskrits: losing their business. Sheridan – well, ask yourself. And the Colonel and Mrs C-M – what about them?'

'The Boomer tells me the Colonel was livid at getting the sack. He'd seen himself rigged out as a Field Marshal or as near as dammit. Instead of which he went into retirement and the bottle.'

'Would these motives apply,' Fox asked, 'equally to the Ambassador and the President? As victims, I mean.'

'Not in Sheridan's case, it would appear.'

'No,' Mr Whipplestone agreed. 'Not in this case.'

They were silent for a space. At last Alleyn said: 'I think this is what we do. We leave you here, Br'er Fox, keeping what I'm afraid may prove to be utterly fruitless observation. We don't know what decision they'll come to in the piggery-flat or indeed what exactly they're there to decide. Another go at The Boomer? The liquidation of the Ku-Klux-Fish or whatever it is? It's anybody's guess. But it's just possible you may pick up something. And, Sam, if you can stand up to another late night, I'd very much like to look at those records of yours.'

'Of course. Only too glad.'

'Shall we go, then?'

They had got out of the car when Alleyn put his head in at the window. 'The Sanskrits don't fit,' he said.

'No?' said Fox. 'No motive, d'you mean?'

'That's right. The Boomer told me that Sanskrit's been reinstated in his emporium in Ng'ombwana. Remember?'

'Now, that is peculiar,' said Fox. 'I'd overlooked that.'

'Something for you to brood on,' Alleyn said. 'We'll be in touch.'

He put his walkie-talkie in his pocket and he and Mr Whipplestone returned to No. 1, The Walk.

There was a card on the hall-table with the word OUT neatly printed on it. 'We leave it there to let each other know,' Mr Whipplestone explained. 'On account of the door chain.' He turned the card over to show 'IN', ushered Alleyn into the drawing-room, shut the door and turned on the lights.

'Do let's have a drink,' he said. 'Whisky and soda? I'll just get the soda. Sit down, do. I won't be a jiffy.'

He went out with something of his old sprightly air.

He had turned on the light above the picture over the fireplace. Troy had painted it quite a long time ago. It was a jubilant landscape half-way to being an abstract. Alleyn remembered it very well.

'Ah!' said Mr Whipplestone returning with a siphon in his hands and Lucy weaving in and out between his feet. 'You're looking at my treasure. I acquired it at one of the Group shows, not long after you married, I think. Look *out*, cat, for pity's sake! Now: shall we go into the dining-room where I can lay out the exhibits on the table? But first, our drinks. You begin yours while I search.'

'Steady with the scotch. I'm supposed to keep a clear head. Would you mind if I rang Troy up?'

'Do, do, do. Over there on the desk. The box I want is upstairs. It'll take a little digging out.'

Troy answered the telephone almost at once. 'Hello, where are you?' Alleyn asked.

'In the studio.'

'Broody?'

'That's right.'

'I'm at Sam Whipplestone's and will be, most probably, for the next hour or so. Have you got a pencil handy?'

'Wait a bit.'

He had a picture of her feeling about in the pocket of her painting smock.

'I've got a bit of charcoal,' she said. 'It's only to write down the number.'

'Hold on. Right.'

He gave it to her. 'In case anyone wants me,' he said. 'You, for instance.'

'Rory?'

'What?'

'Do you mind very much? About me painting The Boomer? Are you there?'

'I'm here, all right. I delight in what you're doing and I deplore the circumstances under which you're doing it.'

'Well,' said Troy, 'that's a straight answer to a straight question. Good night, darling.'

'Good night,' he said, 'darling.'

Mr Whipplestone was gone for some considerable time. At last he returned with a large, old-fashioned photograph album and an envelope full of press cuttings. He opened the connecting doors to the dining-room, laid his findings out on the table and displaced Lucy who affected a wayward interest in them.

'I was a great hoarder in those days,' he said. 'Everything's in order and dated. There should be no difficulty.'

There was none. Alleyn examined the album which had the faded melancholy aspect of all such collections while Mr Whipplestone looked through the cuttings. When the latter applied to items in the former, they had been carefully pasted beside the appropriate photographs. It was Alleyn who first struck oil.

'Here we are,' he said. And there, meticulously dated and annotated in Mr Whipplestone's neat hand, were three photographs and a yellowing page from the *Ng'ombwana Times* with the headline: 'Gomez trial. Verdict. Scene in Court.'

The photographs showed, respectively, a snapshot of a bewigged judge emerging from a dark interior, a crowd, mostly composed of black people, waiting outside a sunbaked court of justice, and an open car driven by a black chauffeur with two passengers in tropical kit, one of whom, a trim, decorous-looking person of about forty, was recognizable as Mr Whipplestone himself. 'Going to the Trial.' The press photographs were more explicit. There, unmistakably himself, in wig and gown, was the young Boomer. 'Mr Bartholomew Opala, Counsel for the Prosecution.' And there, already partially bald, dark, furious and snarling, a man handcuffed between two enormous black policemen and protected from a clearly menacing crowd of Ng'ombwanans. 'After the Verdict. The Prisoner,' said the caption, 'Leaving the Court.'

The letterpress carried an account of the trial with full journalistic appreciation of its dramatic highlights. There was also an editorial.

'And that,' Alleyn said, 'is the self-same Sheridan in your basement flat.'

'You would recognize him at once?'

'Yes. I thought I'd seen him for the first time – and that dimly – tonight, but it turns out that it was my second glimpse. He was sitting outside the pub this afternoon when The Boomer called on Troy.'

'No doubt,' said Mr Whipplestone drily, 'you will be seeing quite a lot more of him. I don't like this, Alleyn.'

'How do you think I enjoy it!' said Alleyn, who was reading the press cutting. 'The vows of vengeance,' he said, 'are quite Marlovian in their inventiveness, aren't they?'

'You should have heard them! And every one directed at your Boomer,' said Mr Whipplestone. He bent over the album, 'I don't suppose I've looked at this,' he said, 'for over a decade. It was stowed away in a trunk with a lot of others in my old flat. Even so, I might have remembered, one would have thought.'

'I expect he's changed. After all – twenty years!'

'He hasn't changed all that much in looks and I can't believe he's changed at all in temperament.'

'And you've no notion what became of him when he got out?'

'None. Portuguese East, perhaps. Or South America. Or a change of name. Ultimately, by fair means or foul, a British passport.'

'And finally whatever he does in the City?'

'Imports coffee perhaps,' sniffed Mr Whipplestone.

'His English is non-committal?'

'Oh, yes. No accent, unless you count a lisp which I suppose is a hangover. Let me give you a drink.'

'Not another, thank you, Sam. I must keep my wits about me, such as they are.' He hesitated for a moment and then said: 'There's one thing I think perhaps you should know. It's about the Chubbs. But before I go any further I'm going to ask you, very seriously indeed, to give an undertaking not to let what I tell you make any difference any difference at all – to your normal manner with the Chubbs. If you'd rather not make a blind commitment like this, then I'll keep my big mouth shut and no bones broken.'

Mr Whipplestone said quietly: 'Is it to their discredit?'

'No,' Alleyn said slowly, 'not directly. Not specifically. No.'

'I have been trained in discretion.'

'I know.'

'You may depend upon me.'

'I'm sure I can,' Alleyn said, and told Mr Whipplestone about the girl in the photograph. For quite a long time after Alleyn had finished he made no reply and then he took a turn about the room and said, more to himself than to Alleyn: 'That is a dreadful thing. I am very sorry. My poor Chubbs.' And after another pause. 'Of course, you see this as a motive.'

'A possible one. No more than that.'

'Yes. Thank you for telling me. It will make no difference.'

'Good. And now I mustn't keep you up any longer. It's almost midnight. I'll just give Fox a shout.'

Fox came through loud, clear and patient on the radio.

'Dead on cue, Mr Alleyn,' he said. 'Nothing till now but I think they're breaking up. A light in a staircase window. Keep with me.'

'Right you are,' said Alleyn and waited. He said to Mr Whipplestone. 'The party's over. We'll have Sheridan-Gomez and Chubb back in a minute.'

'Hullo,' said Fox.

'Yes?'

'Here they come. The Cockburn-Montforts. Far side of the street from me. Not talking. Chubb, this side, walking fast. Hold on. Wait for it, Mr Alleyn.'

'All right.'

Alleyn could hear the advancing and retreating steps.

'There he goes,' Fox said. 'He'll be with you in a minute and now, here comes Mr Sheridan, on his own. Far side of the street. The C-Ms have turned their corner. I caught a bit of one remark. From her. She said, "I was a fool. I knew at the time" and he seemed to shut her up. That's all. Over and – hold on. Hold on, Mr Alleyn.'

'What?'

'The door into the Sanskrit premises. Opening a crack. No light beyond but it's opening all right. They're being watched off.'

'Keep with it, Fox. Give me a shout if there's anything more. Otherwise, I'll join you in a few minutes. Over and out.'

Alleyn waited with Mr Whipplestone for about three minutes before they heard Chubb's rapid step, followed by the sound of his key in the lock.

'Do you want to see him?' Mr Whipplestone murmured. Alleyn shook his head. They heard the chain rattle. Chubb paused for a moment in the hall and then went upstairs.

Another minute and the area gate clicked. Mr Sheridan could be heard to descend and enter.

'There he goes,' said Mr Whipplestone, 'and there he'll be, rather like a bomb in my basement. I can't say I relish the thought.'

'Nor should I, particularly. If it's any consolation I don't imagine he'll be there for long.'

'No?'

'Well, I hope not. Before I leave you I'm going to try, if I may, to get on to Gibson. We'll have a round-the-clock watch on Gomez-cum-Sheridan until further notice.'

He roused Gibson, with apologies, from his beauty sleep and told him what he'd done, what he proposed to do and what he would like Gibson to do for him.

'And now,' he said, to Mr Whipplestone, 'I'll get back to my patient old Fox. Goodnight. And thank you. Keep the scrapbook handy, if you will.'

'Of course, I'll let you out.'

He did so, being, Alleyn noticed, careful to make no noise with the chain and to shut the door softly behind him.

As he walked down Capricorn Mews, which he did firmly and openly, Alleyn saw that there were a few more cars parked in it and that most of the little houses and the flats were dark now, including the flat over the pottery. When he reached the car and slipped into the passenger's seat, Fox said: 'The door was on the chink for about ten seconds and then he shut it. You could just make it out. Light catching the brass knocker. Nothing in it, I dare say. But it looked a bit funny. Do we call off the obbo, then?'

'You'd better hear this bit first.'

And he told Fox about the scrap-book and Mr Sheridan's past.

'Get away!' Fox said cosily. 'Fancy that now! So we've got a couple of right villains in the club. Him and Sanskrit. It's getting interesting, Mr Alleyn, isn't it?'

'Glad you're enjoying yourself, Br'er Fox. For my part I – ' He broke off. 'Look at this!' he whispered.

The street door of the Sanskrits' flat had opened and through it came, unmistakably, the elephantine bulk of Sanskrit himself, wearing a longish overcoat and a soft hat.

'*Now* what's he think he's doing!' breathed Mr Fox.

The door was locked, the figure turned outwards and for a moment the great bladder-like face caught the light. Then he came along the Mews, walking lightly as fat people so often do, and disappeared down Capricorn Place.

'That's where the C-Ms hang out,' said Fox.

'It's also the way to Palace Park Gardens where The Boomer hangs out. How long is it since you tailed your man, Fox?'

'Well – '

'We're off on a refresher course. Come on.'

CHAPTER 8

Keeping Obbo

Fox drove slowly across the opening into Capricorn Place.

'There he goes. Not into the C-Ms, though, I'm sure,' said Alleyn. 'Their lights are out and he's walking on the opposite side in deep shadow. Stop for a moment, Fox. Yes. He's not risking going past the house. Or is he? Look at that, Fox.'

A belated taxi drove slowly towards them up Capricorn Place. The driver seemed to be looking for a number. It stopped. The huge bulk of Sanskrit, scarcely perceptible in the shadows, light as a fairy, flitted on, the taxi screening it from the house.

'On you go, Fox. He's heading for the brick wall at the far end. We go left, left again into the Square, then right, and left again. Stop before you get to Capricorn Place.'

Fox executed this flanking manoeuvre. They passed by No. 1, The Walk, where Mr Whipplestone's bedroom light glowed behind his curtains, and by the Sun in Splendour, now in eclipse. They drove along the far end of the Square, turned left, continued a little way further and parked.

'That's Capricorn Place ahead,' said Alleyn. 'It ends in a brick wall with an opening into a narrow walk. That walk goes behind the Basilica and leads by an alleyway into Palace Park Gardens. It's my bet this is where he's heading but I freely admit it's a pretty chancy shot. Here he comes.'

He crossed the intersection rather like a walking tent with his buoyant fat-man's stride. They gave him a few seconds and then left the car and followed.

There was no sign of him when they turned the corner but his light footfall could be heard on the far side of the wall. Alleyn jerked his head at the gateway. They passed through it and were just in time to see him disappear round a distant corner.

'This is it,' Alleyn said. 'Quick, Fox, and on your toes.'

They sprinted down the walk, checked, turned quietly into the alleyway and had a pretty clear view of Sanskrit at the far end of it. Beyond him, vaguely declaiming itself, was a thoroughfare and the façade of an impressive house, from the second floor balcony of which protruded a flagpole. Two policemen stood by the entrance.

They moved into a dark doorway and watched.

'He's walking up as cool as you like!' Fox whispered.

'So he is.'

'Going to hand something in, is he?'

'He's showing something to the coppers. Gibson cooked up a pass system with the Embassy. Issued to their staff and immediate associates with the President's cachet. Quite an elaborate job. It may be, he's showing it.'

'Why would he qualify?'

'Well may you ask. Look at this, will you?'

Sanskrit had produced something that appeared to be an envelope. One of the policemen turned on his torch. It flashed from Sanskrit's face to his hands. The policeman bent his head and the light, dimmed, shone briefly up into his face. A pause. The officer nodded to his mate who rang the doorbell. It was opened by a Ng'ombwanan in livery: presumably a night-porter. Sanskrit appeared to speak briefly to the man, who listened, took the envelope, if that was what it was, stepped back and shut the door after him.

'That was quick!' Fox remarked.

'Now he's chatting to the coppers.'

They caught a faint high-pitched voice and the two policemen's 'Good night, sir.'

'Boldly does it, Br'er Fox,' said Alleyn. They set off down the alleyway.

There was a narrow footpath on their side. As the enormous tent figure, grotesque in the uncertain darkness, flounced towards them, it moved into the centre of the passage.

Alleyn said to Fox, as they passed it: 'As such affairs go I suppose it was all right. I hope you weren't too bored.'

'Oh no,' said Fox. 'I'm thinking of joining.'

'Are you? Good.'

They walked on until they came to the Embassy. Sanskrit's light footfalls died away in the distance. He had, presumably, gone back through the hole in the wall.

Alleyn and Fox went up to the two constables.

Alleyn said: 'Superintendent Alleyn, C Department.'

'Sir,' they said.

'I want as accurate and full an account of that incident as you can give me. Did you get the man's name? You?' he said to the constable who had seemed to be the more involved.

'No, sir. He carried the special pass, sir.'

'You took a good look at it?'

'Yes, sir.'

'But you didn't read the name?'

'I – I don't – I didn't quite get it, sir. It began with S and there was a K in it. "San" something, sir. It was all in order, sir, with his photograph on it, like a passport. You couldn't miss it being him. He didn't want to be admitted, sir. Only for the door to be answered. If he'd asked for admittance I'd have noted the name.'

'You should have noted it in any case.'

'Sir.'

'What precisely did he say?'

'He said he had a message to deliver, sir. It was for the First Secretary. He produced it and I examined it, sir. It was addressed to the First Secretary and had "For His Excellency The President's attention" written in the corner. It was a fairly stout manilla envelope, sir, but the contents appeared to me to be slight, sir.'

'Well?'

'I said it was an unusual sort of time to deliver it. I said he could hand it over to me and I'd attend to it, sir, but he said he'd promised to deliver it personally. It was a photograph, he said, that the President had wanted developed and printed very particular and urgent and a special effort had been made to get it done and it was only processed half an hour ago. He said he'd been instructed to hand it to the night-porter for the First Secretary.'

'Yes?'

'Yes. Well, I took it and put it over my torch, sir, and that showed up the shape of some rigid object like a cardboard folder inside it. There wasn't any chance of it being one of those funny ones, sir, and he *had* got a Special Pass and so we allowed it and – well, sir, that's all, really.'

'And you,' Alleyn said to the other man, 'rang the bell?'

'Sir.'

'Anything said when the night-porter answered it?'

'I don't think he speaks English, sir. Him and the bearer had a word or two in the native language I suppose it was. And then he just took delivery and shut the door and the bearer gave us good night and left.'

Mr Fox, throughout this interview, had gazed immovably, and to their obvious discomfort, at whichever of the constables was speaking. When they had finished he said in a sepulchral voice to nobody in particular that he wouldn't be surprised if this matter wasn't Taken Further upon which their demeanour became utterly wooden.

Alleyn said: 'You should have reported this at once. You're bloody lucky Mr Gibson doesn't know about it.'

They said in unison: 'Thank you very much, sir.'

'For what?' Alleyn said.

'Will you pass it on to Fred Gibson?' Fox asked as they walked back the way they had come.

'The incident? Yes. But I won't bear down on the handling of it. I ought to. Although it was tricky, that situation. He's got the Embassy go-ahead with his special pass. The copper had been told that anybody carrying one was *persona grata*. He'd have been taking quite a chance, if he'd refused.' Alleyn put his hand on Fox's arm. Look at that,' he said. 'Where did that come from?'

At the far end of the long alleyway, in deep shadow, someone moved away from them. Even as they glimpsed it, the figure slipped round the corner and out of sight. They could hear the soft thud of hurrying feet. They sprinted down the alley and turned the corner but there was no one to be seen.

'Could have come out of one of these houses and be chasing after a cab,' Fox said.

'They're all dark.'

'Yes.'

'And no sound of a cab. Did you get an impression?'

'No. Hat. Overcoat. Rubber soles. Trousers. I wouldn't even swear to the sex. It was too quick.'

'Damn,' Alleyn said and they walked on in silence.

'It would be nice to know what was in the envelope,' Fox said at last.

'That's the understatement of a lifetime.'

'Will you ask?'

'You bet I will.'

'The President?'

'Who else? And at the crack of dawn, I dare say, like it or lump it. Fox.' Alleyn said, 'I've been visited by a very disturbing notion.'

'Is that so, Mr Alleyn?' Fox placidly rejoined.

'And I'll be obliged if you'll just listen while I run through all the disjointed bits of information we have about this horrid fat man and see if some kind of pattern comes through in the end.'

'Be pleased to,' said Fox.

He listened with calm approval as they walked back into the now deserted Capricorns to pick up their car. When they were seated in it Alleyn said: 'There you are, Br'er Fox. Now then. By and large: what emerges?'

Fox laid his broad palm across his short moustache and then looked at it as if he expected it to have picked up an impression.

'I see what you're getting at,' he said, 'I think.'

'What I'm getting at,' Alleyn said, 'is – fairly simply – this – '

II

Alleyn's threat to talk to The Boomer at the crack of dawn was not intended to be, nor was it, taken literally. In the event, he himself was roused by Mr Gibson wanting to know if it really was true that the President was giving Troy another sitting at half past nine. When Alleyn confirmed this, Gibson's windy sighs whistled in the receiver. He said he supposed Alleyn had seen the morning's popular press and on Alleyn saying not yet, informed him that in each instance the front page carried a by-lined three-column spread with photographs of yesterday's visit by The Boomer. Gibson in a dreary voice began to quote some of the more offensive pieces of journalese. 'Rum Proceedings? Handsome Super's Famous Wife and African Dictator.' Alleyn, grinding his teeth, begged him to desist and he did so, merely observing that all things considered he wondered why Alleyn fancied the portrait proposition.

Alleyn felt it would be inappropriate to say that stopping the portrait would in itself be a form of homicide. He switched to the Sanskrit incident and learnt that it had been reported to Gibson. Alleyn outlined his and Fox's investigations and the conclusions he had drawn from them.

'It seems to look,' Mr Gibson mumbled, 'as if things might be coming to a head.'

'Keep your fingers crossed. I'm getting a search warrant. On the off-chance.'

'Always looks "active", applying for a warrant. By the way, the body's gone.'

'What?'

'The deceased. Just before first light. It was kept very quiet. Back entrance. Nondescript van. Special plane. All passed off nice and smooth. One drop of grief the less,' said Mr Gibson.

'You may have to keep obbo at the airport, Fred. Outgoing planes for Ng'ombwana,'

'Any time. You name it,' he said dismally.

'From now. We'll be in touch.' Alleyn said and they rang off.

Troy was in the studio making statements on the background. He told her that yesterday's protective measures would be repeated and that if possible he himself would be back before The Boomer arrived.

'That'll be fine,' she said. 'Sit where you did before, Rory, would you, darling? He's marvellous when he focuses on you.'

'You've got the cheek of the devil. Do you know that everybody but you thinks I'm out of my senses to let you go on with this?'

'Yes, but then you're you, aren't you, and you know how things are. And truly – it is – isn't it? – going – you know? Don't say it, but – isn't it?'

He said: 'It is. Strange as it may sound, I hardly dare look. It's leapt out of the end of your brush.'

She gave him a kiss. 'I *am* grateful,' she said. 'You know, don't you?'

He went to the Yard in a pleasant if apprehensive state of mind and found a message from Mr Whipplestone asking him to ring without delay. He put through the call and was answered at once.

'I thought you should know,' Mr Whipplestone began and the phrase had become familiar. He hurried on to say that, confronted by a leaking water-pipe, he had called at his land agents, Messrs Able & Virtue, at ten past nine o'clock that morning to ask if they could recommend a plumber. He found Sanskrit already there and talking to the young man with Pre-Raphaelite hair. When he saw Mr Whipplestone, Sanskrit had stopped short and then said in a counter-tenor voice that he would leave everything to them and they were to do the best they could for him.

The young man had said there would be no difficulty as there was always a demand in the Capricorns. Sanskrit said something indistinguishable and rather hurriedly left the offices.

'I asked casually,' said Mr Whipplestone, 'if the pottery premises were by any chance to let. I said I had friends who were flat-hunting. This produced a curious awkwardness on the part of the lady attendant and the young man. The lady said something about the place not being officially on the market as yet and in any case if it did come up it would be for sale rather than to let. The present occupant, she said, didn't want it made known for the time being. This, as you may imagine, intrigued me. When I left the agents I walked down Capricorn Mews to the Piggery. It had a notice on the door. "Closed for stocktaking". There are some very ramshackle curtains drawn across the shop window but they don't quite meet. I peered in. It was very ill-lit but I got the impression of some large person moving about among packing cases.'

'Did you, by George!'

'Yes. And on my way home I called in at the Napoli for some of their pâté. While I was there the Cockburn-Montforts came in. He was, I thought, rather more than three sheets in the wind but, as usual, holding it. She looked awful.'

Mr Whipplestone paused for so long that Alleyn said: 'Are you there, Sam?'

'Yes,' he said, 'yes, I am. To be frank, I'm wondering what you're going to think of my next move. Be quiet, Lucy. I don't habitually act on impulse. Far from it.'

'Very far, I'd have thought.'

'Although lately – However, I did act impulsively on this occasion. Very. I wanted to get a reaction. I gave them good morning, of course, and then, quite casually, you know, as I took my pâté from Mrs Pirelli, I said: 'I believe you're losing some neighbours, Mrs Pirelli?' She looked nonplussed. I said: "Yes. The people at the Pig-pottery. They're leaving, almost at once, I hear." This was not, of course, strictly true.'

'I wouldn't be so sure.'

'No? Well, I turned and was face to face with Cockburn-Montfort. I find it difficult to describe his look, or rather his succession of looks. Shock. Incredulity. Succeeded by fury. He turned even more purple in the process. Mrs Montfort quite gasped out: "I don't believe it!" and then gave a little scream. He had her by the arm and he hurt her. And without another word he turned her about and marched her out of the shop. I saw him wheel her round in the direction of the Piggery. She pulled back and seemed to plead with him. In the upshot they turned again and went off presumably to their own house. Mrs Pirelli said something in Italian and then: "If they go I am pleased." I left. As I passed the top of Capricorn Place, I saw the C-Ms going up their steps. He still held her arm and I think she was crying. That's all.'

'And this was – what? – half an hour ago?'

'About that.'

'We'll discuss it later. Thank you, Sam.'

'Have I blundered?'

'I hope not. I think you may have precipitated something.'

'I've got to have a word with Sheridan about the plumbing – a genuine word. He's at home. Should I – ?'

'I think you might but it's odds on the C-Ms will have got in first. Try.'

'Very well.'

'And the Chubbs?' Alleyn asked.

'Yes. Oh dear. If you wish.'

'Don't elaborate. Just the news, casually, as before.'

'Yes.'

'I'll be at home in about a quarter of an hour if you want me. If I don't hear from you I'll get in touch myself as soon as I can,' Alleyn said.

He checked with the man keeping observation and learned that Sanskrit had returned to the pottery after his visit to the land agents and had not emerged. The pottery was closed and the windows still curtained.

Five minutes later Alleyn and Fox found the entrance to the cul-de-sac, as on the former visit, cordoned off by police and thronged by an even larger crowd and quite a galaxy of photographers who were pestering Superintendent Gibson with loud cries against constabular arrogance. Alleyn had a word with Gibson, entered his own house, left Fox in the study and went straight to Troy in her studio. She had done quite a lot of work on the background.

'Troy,' he said, 'when he comes. I've got to have a word with him. Alone. I don't think it will take long and I don't know how much it will upset him.'

'Damn,' said Troy.

'Well. I know. But this is where it gets difficult. I've no choice.'

'I see. OK.'

'It's hell but there it is.'

'Never mind – I know. Here *he* is. You'd better meet him.'

'I'll be back. Much more to the point, I hope he will.'

'So do I. Good luck to whatever it is.'

'Amen to that, sweet powers,' Alleyn said and arrived at the front door at the same time as The Boomer, who had his *mlinzi* in attendance, the latter carrying a great bouquet of red roses and, most unexpectedly, holding the white Afghan hound on a scarlet leash. The Boomer explained that the dog seemed to be at a loose end. 'Missing his master,' said The Boomer.

He greeted Alleyn with all his usual buoyancy and then after a quick look at him said: 'Something is wrong, I think.'

'Yes,' Alleyn said. 'We must speak together, sir.'

'Very well, Rory. Where?'

'In here, if you will.'

They went into the study. When The Boomer saw Fox who had been joined by Gibson, he fetched up short.

'We speak together,' he said, 'but not, it seems, in private?'

'It's a police matter and my colleagues are involved.'

'Indeed? Good morning, gentlemen.'

He said something to the *mlinzi*, who handed him the roses, went out with the dog and shut the door.

'Will you sit down, sir?' Alleyn said.

This time The Boomer made no protest at the formalities. He said: 'By all means,' and sat in a white hide armchair. He wore the ceremonial dress of the portrait and looked superb. The red roses lent an extraordinary surrealist touch.

'Perhaps you will put them down somewhere?' he said and Alleyn laid them on his desk. 'Are they for Troy?' he asked. 'She'll be delighted.'

'What are we to speak about?'

'About Sanskrit. Will you tell me what was in the envelope he delivered at the Embassy soon after midnight this morning? It was addressed to the First Secretary. With a note to the effect that it was for your attention.'

'Your men are zealous in their performance of their tasks, Mr Gibson,' said The Boomer without looking at him.

Gibson cleared his throat.

'The Special Pass issued under my personal cachet evidently carried no weight with these policemen,' The Boomer added.

'Without it,' Alleyn said, 'the envelope would probably have been opened. I hope you will tell us what it contained. Believe me, I wouldn't ask if I didn't think it was of great importance.'

The Boomer who, from the time he had sat down, had not removed his gaze from Alleyn, said, 'It was opened by my secretary.'

'But he told you what it was?'

'It was a request. For a favour.'

'And the favour?'

'It was in connection with this person's return to Ng'ombwana. I think I told you that he has been reinstated.'

'Was it, perhaps, that he wants to return at once and asked for an immediate clearance – visas, permits, whatever is necessary? Procedures that normally, I think, take several days to complete?'

'Yes,' said The Boomer. 'That was it.'

'Why do you suppose he told the police officers that the envelope contained a photograph, one that you had ordered urgently, for yourself?'

For a second or two he looked very angry indeed. Then he said: 'I have no idea. It was a ridiculous statement. I have ordered no photographs.'

Alleyn said: 'Mr Gibson, I wonder if you and Mr Fox will excuse us?'

They went out with a solemn preoccupied air and shut the door after them.

'Well, Rory?' said The Boomer.

'He was an informer,' Alleyn said, 'wasn't he? He was what Mr Gibson would call so unprettily but so appropriately, a Snout.'

III

The Boomer had always, in spite of all his natural exuberance, commanded a talent for unexpected silences. He now displayed it. He neither moved nor spoke during a long enough pause for the clock in the study to clear its throat and strike ten. He then clasped his white gloved hands, rested his chin on them and spoke.

'In the old days,' he said, and his inordinately resonant voice, taking on the timbre of a recitative, lent the phrase huge overtones of nostalgia, 'at Davidson's, I remember one wet evening when we talked together, as youths of that age will, of everything under the sun. We talked, finally, of government and the exercise of power and suddenly, without warning, we found ourselves on opposite sides of a great gap – a ravine. There was no bridge. We were completely cut off from each other. Do you remember?'

'I remember, yes.'

'I think we were both surprised and disturbed to find ourselves in this situation. And I remember I said something like this: that we had stumbled against a natural barrier that was as old as our separate evolutionary processes – we used big words in those days. And you said there were plenty of territories we could explore without meeting such barriers and we'd better stick to them. And so, from that rainy evening onwards we did. Until now. Until this moment.'

Alleyn said: 'I mustn't follow you along these reminiscent byways. If you think for a moment, you'll understand why. I'm a policeman on duty. One of the first things we are taught is the necessity for non-involvement. I'd have asked to be relieved of this job if I had known what shape it would take.'

'What shape has it taken? What have you – uncovered?'

'I'll tell you. I think that the night before last a group of people, some fanatical, each in his or her own degree a bit demented and each with a festering motive of sorts, planned to have you assassinated in such a way that it would appear to have been done by your spearcarrier – your *mlinzi:* it's about these people that I'd like to talk to you. First of all, Sanskrit. Am I right or wrong in my conjecture about Sanskrit? Is he an informer?'

'There, my dear Rory, I must plead privilege.'

'I thought you might. All right. The Cockburn-Montforts. His hopes of military glory under the new regime came unstuck. He is said to have been infuriated. Has he to thank you, personally, for his compulsory retirement?'

'Oh, yes,' said The Boomer coolly, 'I got rid of him. He had become an alcoholic and quite unreliable. Besides, my policy was to appoint Ng'ombwanans to the senior ranks. We have been through all this.'

'Has he threatened you?'

'Not to my face. He was abusive at a personal interview I granted. I have been told that, in his cups, he uttered threats. It was all very silly and long forgotten.'

'Not on his part, perhaps. You knew he had been invited to the reception?'

'At my suggestion. He did good service in the past. We gave him a medal for it.'

'I see. Do you remember the Gomez case?'

For a moment, he looked surprised. 'Of course I remember it,' he said. 'He was a very bad man. A savage. A murderer. I had the pleasure of procuring him a fifteen-years stretch. It should have been a capital charge. He – ' The Boomer pulled up short. 'What of him?' he asked.

'A bit of information your sources didn't pass on to you, it seems. Perhaps they didn't know. Gomez has changed his name to Sheridan and lives five minutes away from your Embassy. He was not at your party but he is a member of this group and from what I have heard of him he's not going to let one setback defeat him. He'll try again.'

'That I can believe,' said The Boomer. For the first time he looked disconcerted.

Alleyn said: 'He watched this house from over the way while you sat to Troy yesterday morning. It's odds on he's out there again, now. He's being very closely observed. Would you say he's capable of going it alone and lobbing a bomb into your car or through my windows?'

'If he's maintained the head of steam he worked up against me at his trial – ' The Boomer began and checked himself. He appeared to take thought and then, most unconvincingly, let out one of his great laughs. 'Whatever he does,' he said, 'if he does anything, it will be a fiasco. *Bombs!* No, really, it's too absurd!'

For an alarming second or two Alleyn felt himself to be at explosion point. With difficulty, he controlled his voice and suggested, fairly mildly, that if any attempts made upon The Boomer turned out to be fiascos it would be entirely due to the vigilance and efficiency of the despised Gibson and his men.

'Why don't you arrest this person?' The Boomer asked casually.

'Because, as you very well know, we can't make arrests on what would appear to be groundless suspicion. He has done nothing to warrant an arrest.'

The Boomer scarcely seemed to listen to him, a non-reaction that didn't exactly improve his temper.

'There is one more member of this coterie,' Alleyn said. 'A servant called Chubb. Is he known to you?'

'Chubb? Chubb? Ah! Yes, by the way! I believe I *have* heard of Chubb. Isn't he Mr Samuel Whipplestone's man? He came up with drinks while I was having a word with his master who happened to mention it. You're not suggesting – !'

'That Sam Whipplestone's involved? Indeed I'm not. But we've discovered that the man is.'

The Boomer seemed scarcely to take this in. The enormous creature suddenly leapt to his feet. For all his great size he was on them, like an animal, in one coordinated movement.

'What am I thinking of!' he exclaimed. 'To bring myself here! To force my attention upon your wife with this silly dangerous person who, bombs or no bombs, is liable to make an exhibition of himself and kick up dirt in the street. I will take myself off at once. Perhaps I may see her for a moment to apologize and then I vanish.'

'She won't take much joy of that,' Alleyn said. 'She has gone a miraculously long way in an unbelievably short time with what promises to be the best portrait of her career. It's quite appalling to think of it remaining unfinished.'

The Boomer gazed anxiously at him and then, with great simplicity, said: 'I get everything wrong.'

He had made this observation as a solitary black schoolboy in his first desolate term and it had marked the beginning of their friendship. Alleyn stopped himself from saying, 'Don't look like that,' and, instead, picked up the great bouquet of roses, put them in his hands and said: 'Come and see her.'

'Shall I?' he said, doubtful but greatly cheered. 'Really? Good!'

He strode to the door and flung it open. 'Where is my *mlini?*' he loudly demanded.

Fox, who was in the hall, said blandly: 'He's outside Mrs Alleyn's studio, Your Excellency. He seemed to think that was where he was wanted.'

'We may congratulate ourselves,' Alleyn said, 'that he hasn't brought his spear with him.'

IV

Alleyn had escorted The Boomer to the studio and seen him established on his throne. Troy, tingling though she was with impatience, had praised the roses and put them in a suitable pot. She had also exultantly pounced upon the Afghan hound who, with an apparent instinct for aesthetic values, had mounted the throne and posed himself with killing effect against The Boomer's left leg and was in process of being committed to canvas.

Alleyn, possessed by a medley of disconnected anxieties and attachments, quitted the unlikely scene and joined Fox in the hall.

'Is it all right?' Fox asked, jerking his head in the direction of the studio. 'All that?'

'If you can call it all right for my wife to be settled cosily in there, painting a big black dictator with a suspected murderer outside the door and the victim's dog posing for its portrait: it's fine. Fine!'

'Well, it's unusual,' Fox conceded. 'What are you doing about it?'

'I'm putting one of those coppers on my doorstep outside the studio where he can keep the *mlinzi* company. Excuse me for a moment, Fox.'

He fetched the constable, a powerful man, from the pavement and gave him his directions.

'The man doesn't speak much English, if any,' he said, 'and I don't for a moment suppose he'll do anything but squat in the sun and stare. He's not armed and normally he's harmless. You're job's to keep close obbo on him till he's back in the car with Master.'

'Very good, sir,' said the officer and proceeded massively in the required direction.

Alleyn rejoined Fox.

'Wouldn't it be simpler,' Fox ventured, 'under the circumstances, I mean, to cancel the sittings?'

'Look here, Br'er Fox,' Alleyn said. 'I've done my bloody best to keep my job out of sight of my wife and by and large I've made a hash of it. But I'll tell you what: if ever my job looks like so much as coming between one dab of her brush and the surface of her canvas, I'll chuck it and set up a prep school for detectives.'

After a considerable pause Mr Fox said judicially: 'She's lucky to have you.'

'Not she,' said Alleyn. 'It's entirely the other way round. In the meantime, what's cooking? Where's Fred?'

'Outside. He's hoping for a word with you. Just routine, far as I know.'

Mr Gibson sat in a panda a little way down the cul-de-sac and not far from the pub. Uniformed men were distributed along the street and householders looked out of upstairs windows. The crowd at the entrance had thinned considerably.

Alleyn and Fox got into the panda.

'What's horrible?' they asked each other. Gibson reported that to the best of his belief the various members of the group were closeted in their respective houses. Mrs Chubb had been out of doors shopping but had returned home. He'd left a couple of men with radio equipment to patrol the area.

He was droning on along these lines when the door of Alleyn's house opened and the large officer spoke briefly to his colleague in the street. The latter was pointing towards the panda.

'This is for me,' Alleyn said. 'I'll be back.'

It was Mr Whipplestone on the telephone, composed but great with tidings. He had paid his plumbing call on Mr Sheridan and found him in a most extraordinary state.

'White to the lips, shaking, scarcely able to pull himself together and give me a civil hearing. I had the impression that he was about to leave the flat. At first I thought he wasn't going to let me in but he shot a quick look up and down the street and suddenly stepped back and motioned with his head for me to enter. We stood in the lobby. I really don't think he took in a word about the plumbers but he nodded and – not so much grinned as bared his teeth from time to time.'

'Pretty!'

'Not very delicious, I assure you. Do you know I was transported back all those years, into that court of justice in Ng'ombwana. He might have been standing in the dock again.'

'That's not an over-fanciful conceit, either. Did you say anything about the Sanskrits?'

'Yes. I did. I ventured. As I was leaving. I think I may say I was sufficiently casual. I asked him if he knew whether the pottery in the mews undertook china repairs. He looked at me as if I was mad and shook his head.'

'Has he gone out?'

'I'm afraid I don't know. You may be sure I was prepared to watch. I had settled to do so, but Mrs Chubb met me in the hall. She said Chubb was not well and would I mind if she attended to my luncheon – served it and so on. She said it was what she called a 'turn' that he's subject to and he had run out of whatever he takes for it and would like to go to the chemist's. I, of course, said I could look after myself and *she* could go to the chemist's. I said I would lunch out if it would help. In any case it was only ten o'clock. But she was distressed, poor creature, and I couldn't quite brush her aside and go into the drawing-room so I can't positively swear Sheridan – Gomez – didn't leave. It's quite possible that he did. As soon as I'd got rid of Mrs Chubb I went to the drawing-room window. The area gate was open and I'm certain I shut it.'

'I see. What about Chubb?'

'What, indeed! He *did* go out. Quite openly. I asked Mrs Chubb about it and she said he'd insisted. She said the prescription took some time to make up and he would have to wait.'

'Has he returned?'

'Not yet. Nor has Sheridan. If, in fact, he went out.'

'Will you keep watch, Sam?'

'Of course.'

'Good. I think I'll be coming your way.'

Alleyn returned to the car. He passed Mr Whipplestone's information on to Fox and Gibson and they held a brief review of the situation.

'What's important as I see it,' Alleyn said, 'is the way these conspirators are thinking and feeling. If I'm right in my guesses, they got a hell of a shock on the night of the party. Everything was set up. The shot fired. The lights went out. The expected commotion ensued. The anticipated sounds were heard. But when the lights went on again it was the wrong body killed by the right weapon wielded by they didn't know who. Very off-putting for all concerned. How did they react? The next thing they held a meeting at the Sanskrits. They'd had time to do a bit of simple addition and the answer had to be a rat in the wainscotting.'

'Pardon?' said Gibson.

'A traitor in their ranks, A snout.'

'Oh. Ah.'

'They must at the very least have suspected it. I'd give a hell of a lot to know what happened at that meeting while you and I, Fox, sat outside in the Mews.'

'Who did they suspect? Why? What did they plan? To have another go at the President? It seems unlikely that Sheridan-Gomez would have given up. Did any of them get wind of Sanskrit's visit to the Embassy last night? And who the devil was the shadow we saw sprinting round the alley-corner?'

'Come on, Mr Alleyn. What's the theory? Who, do you reckon?'

'Oh, I'll tell you *that*, Br'er Fox,' Alleyn said. And did.

'And if either of you lot,' he ended, 'so much as mumbles the word "conjecture" I'll put you both on dab for improper conduct.'

'It boils down to this, then,' said Fox. 'They may be contemplating a second attempt on the President or they may be setting their sights on the snout whoever they reckon him to be, or they may be split on their line of action. Or,' he added as an afterthought, 'they may have decided to call it a day, wind up the Ku-Klux-Fish and fade out in all directions.'

'How true. With which thought we, too, part company. We must be all-ways away, Br'er Fox. Some to kill cankers in the musk-rose buds – '

'What's all that about?' Gibson asked glumly.

'Quotations,' Fox said.

'Yes, Fred,' said Alleyn, 'and you can go and catch a red-hipped bumble-bee on the lip of a thistle while Fox and I war with rare mice for their leathern wings.'

'Who said all that bumph anyway?'

'Fairies. We'll keep in touch. Come on, Fox.'

They returned to their own anonymous car and were driven to the Capricorns. Here a discreet prowl brought them into touch with one of Gibson's men, a plainclothes sergeant, who had quite a lot to say for himself. The fishy brotherhood had not been idle. Over the last half-hour, the Cockburn-Montforts had been glimpsed through their drawing-room window, engaged in drinking and – or so it seemed – quarrelling in a desultory way between libations. Chubb had been followed by another plainclothes sergeant carrying artist's impedimenta, to a chemist's shop in Baronsgate where he handed in a prescription and sat down, presumably waiting for it to be made up. Seeing him settled there, the sergeant returned to Capricorn Mews where, having an aptitude in that direction, he followed a well-worn routine by sitting on a canvas stool and making a pencil sketch of the pig-pottery. He had quite a collection of sketches at home, some finished and prettily tinted with aquarelles, others of a rudimentary kind, having been cut short by an arrest or by an obligation to shift the area of investigation. For these occasions he wore jeans, a dirty jacket and an excellent wig of the Little Lord Fauntleroy type. His name was Sergeant Jacks.

Mr Sheridan, the Cockburn-Montforts and the Sanskrits had not appeared.

Fox parked the car in its overnight position under the plane trees in Capricorn Square from where he could keep observation on No. 1, the Walk, and Alleyn took a stroll down the Mews. He paused behind the gifted sergeant and, in the manner of the idle snooper, watched him tinker with a tricky bit of perspective. He wondered what opulent magic Troy, at that moment, might be weaving, over in Chelsea.

'Anything done?' he asked.

'Premises shut up, sir. But there's movement. In the back of the shop. There's a bit of a gap in the curtains and you can just get a squint. Not to see anything really. Nobody been in or out of the flat entrance.'

'I'll be within range. No. 1, Capricorn Walk. Give me a shout if there's anything. You could nip into that entry to call me up.'

'Yes, sir.'

Two youths from the garage strolled along and stared.

Alleyn said: 'I wouldn't have the patience, myself. Don't put me in it,' he added. These were the bystanders; remarks that Troy said were most frequently heard, 'Is it for sale?' he asked.

'Er,' said the disconcerted sergeant.

'I might come back and have another look,' Alleyn remarked and left the two youths to gape.

He pulled his hat over his left eye, walked very quickly indeed across the end of Capricorn Place and on into The Walk. He had a word with Fox in the car under the plane trees and then crossed the street to No. 1 where Mr Whipplestone, who had seen him coming, let him in.

'Sam,' Alleyn said. 'Chubb did go to the chemist.'

'I'm certainly glad to hear it.'

'But it doesn't necessarily mean he won't call at the piggery, you know.'

'You think not?'

'If he suffers from migraine the stresses of the past forty-eight hours might well have brought it on.'

'I suppose so.'

'Is his wife in?'

'Yes,' said Mr Whipplestone, looking extremely apprehensive.

'I want to speak to her.'

'Do you? That's – that's rather disturbing.'

'I'm sorry, Sam. It can't be helped, I'm afraid.'

'Are you going to press for information about her husband?'

'Probably.'

'How very – distasteful.'

'Police work is, at times, precisely that.'

'I know. I've often wondered how you can.'

'Have you?'

'You strike me, always, as an exceptionally fastidious man.'

'I'm sorry to disenchant you.'

'And I'm sorry to have been tactless.'

'Sam,' Alleyn said gently, 'one of the differences between police work and that of other and grander services is that we do our own dirty washing instead of farming it out at two or three removes.'

Mr Whipplestone turned pink. 'I deserved that,' he said.

'No, you didn't. It was pompous and out of place.'

Lucy Lockett, who had been washing herself with the zeal of an occupational therapist, made one of her ambiguous remarks, placed her forepaws on Alleyn's knee and leapt neatly into his lap.

'Now then, baggage,' Alleyn said, scratching her head, 'that sort of stuff never got a girl anywhere.'

'You don't know,' Mr Whipplestone said, 'how flattered you ought to feel. The demonstration is unique.'

Alleyn handed his cat to him and stood up. 'I'll get it over,' he said. 'Is she upstairs, do you know?'

'I think so.'

'It won't take long, I hope.'

'If I – if I can help in any way – ?'

'I'll let you know,' said Alleyn.

He climbed the stairs and tapped on the door. When Mrs Chubb opened it and saw him, she reacted precisely as she had on his former visit. There she stood, speechless with her fingers on her lips. When he asked to come in she moved aside with the predictable air of terrified reluctance. He went in and there was the enlarged photograph of the fresh-faced girl. The medallion, even, was, as before, missing from its place. He wondered if Chubb was wearing it.

'Mrs Chubb,' he said, 'I'm not going to keep you long and I hope I'm not going to frighten you. Yes, please, do sit down.'

Just as she did last time, she dropped into her chair and stared at him. He drew his up and leant forward.

'Since I saw you yesterday,' he said, 'we have learnt a great deal more about the catastrophe at the Embassy and about the people closely and remotely concerned in it. I'm going to tell you what I believe to be your husband's part.'

She moved her lips as if to say: 'He never – ' but was voiceless.

'All I want you to do is listen and then tell me if I'm right, partly right or wholly mistaken. I can't force you to answer as I expect you know, but I very much hope that you will.'

He waited a moment and then said: 'Well. Here it is. I believe that your husband, being a member of the group we talked about yesterday, agreed to act with them in an attack upon the President of Ng'ombwana. I think he agreed because of his hatred of blacks and of Ng'ombwanans in particular.' Alleyn looked for a moment at the smiling photograph, 'It's a hatred born of tragedy,' he said, 'and it has rankled and deepened, I dare say, during the last five years.

'When it was known that your husband was to be one of the waiters at the pavilion, the plan was laid. He had been given detailed instructions about his duties by his employers. The group was given even more detailed information from an agent inside the Embassy. And Chubb's orders were based on this information. He had been a commando and was very well suited indeed for the work in hand. Which was this. When the lights in the pavilion and the garden went out and after a shot was fired in the house, he was to disarm and disable the spearsman who was on guard behind the President, jump on a chair and kill the President with the spear.'

She was shaking her head to and fro and making inexplicit movements with her hands.

'No?' Alleyn said, 'Is that wrong? You didn't know about it? Not beforehand? Not afterwards? But you knew something was planned, didn't you? And you were frightened? And afterwards you knew it had gone wrong? Yes?'

She whispered. 'He never. He never done it.'

'No. He was lucky. He was hoist – He got the treatment he was supposed to hand out. The other waiter put him out of action. And what happened after that was no business of Chubb's.'

'You can't hurt him. You can't touch him.'

'That's why I've come to see you, Mrs Chubb. It may well be that we could, in fact, charge your husband with conspiracy. That means, with joining in a plan to do bodily harm. But our real concern is with the murder itself. If Chubb cuts loose from this group – and they're a bad lot, Mrs Chubb, a really bad lot – and gives me a straight answer to questions based on the account I've just given you, I think the police will be less inclined to press home attempted murder or charges of conspiracy. I don't know if you'll believe this but I do beg you, very seriously indeed, if you have any influence over him, to get him to make a complete break, not to go to any more meetings, above all, not to take part in any further action against anybody – Ng'ombwanan, white or what-have-you. Tell him to cut loose, Mrs Chubb. You tell him to cut loose. And at the same time not to do anything silly like making a bolt for it. That'd be about the worst thing he could do,'

He had begun to think he would get no response of any kind from her when her face wrinkled over and she broke into a passion of tears. At first it was almost impossible to catch sense of what she tried to say. She sobbed out words piecemeal, as if they escaped by haphazard compulsion. But presently phrases emerged and a sort of congruence of ideas. She said what had happened five years ago might have happened yesterday for Chubb. She repeated several times that he 'couldn't get over it', that he 'never hardly said anything, but she could tell'. They never talked about it, she said, not even on the anniversary, which was always a terrible day for both of them. She said that for herself something 'came over her at the sight of a black man', but for Chubb, Alleyn gathered, the revulsion was savage and implacable. There had been incidents. There were times when he took queer turns and acted very funny with headaches. The doctor had given him something.

'Is that the prescription he's getting made up now?'

She said it was. As for 'that lot', she added, she'd never fancied him getting in with them.

He had become secretive about the meetings, she said, and had shut her up when she tried to ask questions. She had known something was wrong. Something queer was going on.

'They was getting at him and the way he feels. On account of our Glen. I could tell that. But I never knew that.'

Alleyn gathered that after the event Chubb had been a little more communicative in that he let out he'd been 'made a monkey of'. He'd acted according to orders, he said, and what had he got for it? Him with his experience? He was very angry and his neck hurt.

'Did he tell you what really happened? Everything?'

No, she said. There was something about him 'getting in with the quick one according to plan' but being 'clobbered' from behind and making 'a boss shot of it'.

Alleyn caught back an exclamation.

It hadn't made sense to Mrs Chubb. Alleyn gathered that she'd felt, in a muddled way, that because a black man had been killed Chubb ought to have been pleased but that he was angry because something had, in some fashion, been put across him. When Alleyn suggested that nothing she had told him contradicted the version he had given to her, she stared hopelessly at him out of blurred eyes and vaguely shook her head.

'I suppose not,' she said.

'From what you've told me, my suggestion that you persuade him to break with them was useless. You've tried. All the same, when he comes back from the chemist's – '

She broke in: 'He ought to be back,' she cried. 'It wouldn't take that long! He ought to've come in by now. Oh Gawd: where is he?'

'Now don't you go getting yourself into a state before there's need,' Alleyn said. 'You stay put and count your blessings. Yes, that's what I said, Mrs Chubb. Blessings. If your man had brought off what he set out to do on the night of the party you *would* have had something to cry about. If he comes back, tell him what I've said. Tell him he's being watched. Keep him indoors and in the meantime brew yourself a strong cuppa and pull yourself together, there's a good soul. Good morning to you.'

He ran downstairs and was met at the drawing-room door by Mr Whipplestone.

'Well, Sam,' he said. 'Through no fault of his own your Chubb didn't commit murder. That's not to say – '

The telephone rang. Mr Whipplestone made a little exasperated noise and answered it.

'Oh!' he said. 'Oh, yes. He is. Yes, of course. Yes.'

'It's for you,' he said. 'It's Mrs Roderick.'

As soon as she heard Alleyn's voice, Troy said: 'Rory. Important. Someone with a muffled voice has just rung up to say there's a bomb in the President's car.'

CHAPTER 9

Climax

Alleyn said: 'Don't – ' but she cut in:

'No, listen! The thing is, he's gone. Five minutes ago. In his car.'

'Where?'

'The Embassy.'

'Right. Stay put.'

'Urgent,' Alleyn said to Mr Whipplestone. 'See you later.'

He left the house as Fox got out of the car under the trees and came towards him.

'Bomb scare,' said Fox. 'On the blower.'

'I know. Come on. The Embassy.'

They got into the car. On the way to the Embassy, which was more roundabout than the way through the hole in the Wall, Fox said a disguised voice had rung the Yard. The Yard was ringing Troy and had alerted Gibson and all on duty in the area.

'The President's on his way back,' Alleyn said. 'Troy's had the muffled voice, too.'

'The escort car will have got the message.'

'I hope so.'

'A hoax, do you reckon?'

'Considering the outlandish nature of the material we're supposed to be handling, it's impossible to guess. As usual, we take it for real. But I tell you what, Br'er Fox, I've got a nasty feeling that if it is a hoax it's a hoax with a purpose. Another name for it might be red-herring. We'll see Fred and then get back to our own patch. That Royal Academician in the Mews had better be keeping his eyes open. Here we are.'

They had turned out of a main thoroughfare, with their siren blaring, into Palace Park Gardens and there, outside the Embassy emerging from his police escort's car was The Boomer closely followed by his *mlinzi* and the Afghan hound. Alleyn and Fox left their car and approached him. He hailed them vigorously.

'Hullo, hullo!' shouted The Boomer, 'here are turnups for the books! You have heard the latest, I suppose?'

'We have,' said Alleyn. 'Where's the Embassy car?'

'Where? Where? Half-way between here and there, "there" being your own house, to be specific. The good Gibson and his henchmen are looking under the seats for bombs. Your wife required me no longer. I left a little early. Shall we go indoors?'

Alleyn excused himself and was glad to see them off. The driver of the official police car was talking into his radio. He said: 'Mr Alleyn's here now, sir. Yes, sir.'

'All right,' Alleyn said and got into the car.

It was Gibson. 'So you've heard?' he said. 'Nothing so far but we haven't finished.'

'Did *you* hear the call?'

'No. He or she rang the Yard. Info is that he probably spoke through a handkerchief.'

'He *or* she?'

'The voice was peculiar. A kind of squeaky whisper. They reckon it sounded frightened or excited or both. The exact words were: '*Is that Scotland Yard? There's a bomb in the Black Embassy car. Won't be long now*' Call not traced. They thought the car would be outside your place and a minute or so was lost ascertaining it was on the way here. All my chaps were alerted and came on the scene pronto. Oh, and they say he seemed to speak with a lisp.'

'Like hell they do! So would they with a mouthful of handkerchief. Who's on the Capricorn ground?'

'A copper in a wig with coloured chalks.'

'I know all about him. That all?'

'Yes,' said Gibson. 'The others were ordered round here,' and added with a show of resentment, 'My job's mounting security over this big, bloody black headache and a bloody gutty show it's turned out to be.'

'All right, Fred. I know. It's a stinker. I'll get back there myself. What about you?'

'Back to the suspect car scene. Look!' said Gibson with the nearest approach to shrillness that Alleyn would have thought possible, 'it's got to such a pitch that I'd welcome a straight case of bomb disposal and no nonsense. There you are! I'd welcome it.'

Alleyn was forming what conciliatory phrases he could offer when he was again called to the radio. It was the gifted Sergeant Jacks.

'Sir,' said the sergeant in some agitation, 'I better report.'

'What?'

'This bomb scare, sir. Just before it broke the military gentleman, Colonel Whatsit, beg pardon, came walking very rigid and careful up to the pig-pottery and leant on the bell of the door into their flat. And then the scare broke, sir, Mr Gibson's chap keeping obbo in a car near the entrance to Capricorn Passage, sir, came round and told me quick, through the driving window, that it was a general alert, sir. And while he was talking, a dirty great van pulled out of the garage and obscured my view of the pottery. Well, sir, I'd got my orders from you to stay where I am. And Mr Gibson's chap drove off. Meanwhile a traffic jam had built up in the Mews, behind the van. I couldn't get a sight of the pottery but I could hear the Colonel. He'd started up yelling. Something like: 'Open the bloody door, damn you, and let me in.' And then the drivers began sounding off their horns. It was like that for at least five minutes, sir.'

'Could anybody – could two enormous people – have got out and away while this lasted?'

'I reckon not, because it sorted itself out, sir, and when it had cleared, there was the Colonel still at the piggery door and still leaning on the bell. And he's leaning on it now. And yelling a bit but kind of fading out. I reckon he's so drunk he's had it. What'll I do, sir?'

'Where are you?'

'Ducked down behind my easel. It's a bit awkward but I thought I'd risk it. Could you hold on, sir?'

An interval of street noises. Alleyn held on and the voice returned, 'I'm up the alleyway, sir. I had to duck. The gentleman from the basement of No. 1, the Walk's passed the end of the alleyway going towards the pottery.'

'Get back to your easel and watch.'

'Sir.'

'I'm on my way. Over and out. Capricorn Square,' Alleyn said to the driver. 'Quick as you can make it but no siren.'

'What was all that, then?' asked Fox. When he was informed he remarked that the painter-chap seemed to be reasonably practical and active even if he did get himself up like a right Charlie. Mr Fox had a prejudice against what he called 'fancy-dress coppers'. His own sole gesture in that line was to put on an ancient Donegal tweed ulster and an out-of-date felt hat. It was surprising how effectively these lendings disguised his personality.

When they reached the Square Alleyn said: 'We'd better separate. This is tricky. Sheridan-Gomez is the only one of the gang that doesn't know me. The others might remember *you* from your checking out activities after the party. Have you got your nighty with you?'

'If you mean my Donegal ulster, yes I have. It's in the back.'

'And the head gear?'

'Rolled up in the pocket.'

'When you've dolled yourself up in them you might stroll to the piggery by the way of the Square and Capricorn Place. I'll take the Walk and the Mews. We'll no doubt encounter each other in the vicinity of the piggery.'

Fox went off looking like a North of Ireland corn chandler on holiday and Alleyn turned into Capricorn Walk looking like himself.

Lucy Lockett, taking the sun on the steps of No. 1, rolled over at him as he passed.

No doubt, Alleyn reflected, Gibson's men patrolling the Capricorns, who had been diverted to the Embassy on the bomb alarm, would soon return to their ground. At the moment there was no sign of them.

It was the busiest time of day in the Capricorns and a pretty constant two-way stream of traffic moved along the Walk. Alleyn used it to screen his approach to the house-decorator's shop on the corner of the Mews. From here, looking sideways through the windows, he had a view down the Mews to the pottery at the far end. Intermittently, he had glimpses of the gifted Sergeant Jacks at his easel but commercial vehicles backing and filing outside the garage, constantly shut him off. The pottery flashed in and out of view like the fractional revelations of commercial television. Now it was Colonel Cockburn-Montfort, still at the pottery flat door, with

Gomez beside him. And then, as if by sleight-of-hand, Chubb was there with them in consultation. Now a van drove into the Mews, fetched up outside the Napoli and began to deliver cartons and crates and there was no view at all.

Between the Napoli and the garage, and next door to the flower shop there was a tiny bistro, calling itself 'The Bijou'. On fine days it put four tables out on the pavement and served coffee and pâtisseries. One of the tables was unoccupied. Alleyn walked past the van and flower shop, sat at the table, ordered coffee and lit his pipe. He had his back to the pottery but got a fair reflection of it in the flower shop window.

Gomez and Chubb were near the flat door. The Colonel still leant against it, looking dreadfully groggy. Chubb stood back a little way with his fingers to his mouth. Gomez seemed to be peering in at the curtained shop window.

He was joined there by Inspector Fox, who had arrived via Capricorn Place. He appeared to search for an address and find it in the pottery. He approached the shop door, took out his spectacles, read the notice, 'Closed for Stocktaking' and evidently spoke to Gomez, who shrugged and turned his back.

Fox continued down the Mews. He paused by the talented Sergeant Jacks, again assumed his spectacles and bent massively towards the drawing. Alleyn watched with relish as his colleague straightened up, tilted his head appreciatively to one side, fell back a step or two, apologized to a passer-by and continued on his way. When he reached the table he said: 'Excuse me, is that chair taken?' and Alleyn said: 'No. Please.'

Fox took it, ordered coffee and when he had been served asked Alleyn the time.

'Come off it,' Alleyn said. 'Nobody's looking at you.'

But they both kept up the show of casual conversation between strangers.

Fox said: 'It's a funny set-up back there. They act as if they don't know each other. The Colonel seems to be on the blink. If you poked a finger at him, he'd fall flat.'

'What about the premises?'

'You can't see anything in the shop. There's curtains almost closed across the window and no light inside.'

He blew on his coffee and took a sip.

'They're in a funny sort of shape,' he said. 'The Gomez man's shaking. Very pale. Gives the impression he might cut up violent. Think they've skedaddled, Mr Alleyn? The Sanskrits?'

'It would have to be after 9.10 this morning when Sanskrit was seen to go home.'

'That copper with the crayons reckons they couldn't have made it since he's been on the job.'

'He dodged up the garage alley to talk to me, he might remember. Of course that damn bomb-scare drew Fred Gibson's men off. But no, I don't think they've flitted. I don't think so. I think they're lying doggo.'

'What's the drill, then?' Fox asked his coffee.

'I've got a search-warrant. Blow me down flat, Br'er Fox, if I don't take a chance and execute it. Look,' Alleyn said drawing on his pipe and gazing contentedly at the sky. 'We may be in a bloody awkward patch. You get back to the car and whistle up support. Fred's lot ought to be available again now. We'll move in as soon as they're on tap. Call us up on the artist's buzzer. Then we close in.'

'What about Gomez and the Colonel? And Chubb?'

'We keep it nice and easy but we hold them. See you on the doorstep.'

'Fox put down his empty cup, looked about him, rose, nodded to Alleyn and strolled away in the direction of Capricorn Walk. Alleyn waited until he had disappeared round the corner, finished his coffee and, at a leisurely pace rejoined Sergeant Jacks who was touching up his architectural details.

'Pack up,' Alleyn said, 'and leave your stuff up the alley there. You'll get a shout from Mr Fox in a matter of seconds.'

'Is it a knock-off, sir?'

'It may be. If that lot, there, start to move, we hold them. Nice and quiet, though. All right. Make it quick. And when you get the office from Mr Fox, come out here again where I can see you and we'll move in. Right?'

'Right, sir.'

The delivery van from the Napoli lurched noisily down the Mews, did a complicated turn-about in front of the pottery and went back the way it had come. Alleyn moved towards the pottery.

A police-car siren, braying in Baronsgate, was coming nearer. Another, closer at hand, approached from somewhere on the outer borders of the Capricorns.

Sergeant Jacks came out of the garage alleyway. Fox and Gibson had been quick.

Gomez walked rapidly up the Mews on the opposite side to Alleyn who crossed over and stopped in front of him. The sirens, close at hand now, stopped.

'Mr Sheridan?' Alleyn said.

For a moment the living image of an infuriated middle-aged man overlaid that of the same man fifteen years younger in Mr Whipplestone's album. He had turned so white that his close-shaved beard started up, blue-black, as if it had been painted across his face.

He said: 'Yes? My name is Sheridan.'

'Yes, of course. You've been trying to call upon the Sanskrits, haven't you?'

He made a very slight movement: an adjustment of his weight, rather like Mr Whipplestone's cat preparing to spring or bolt. Fox had come up behind Alleyn. Two of Gibson's uniformed men had turned into the Mews from Capricorn Place. There were more large men converging on the pottery. Sergeant Jacks was talking to Chubb and Fred Gibson loomed over Colonel Cockburn-Montfort by the door into the flat.

Gomez stared from Alleyn to Fox. 'What is this?' he lisped. 'What do you want? Who are you?'

'We're police officers. We're about to effect an entry into the pottery and I suggest that you come with us. Better not make a scene in the street, don't you think?'

For a moment Gomez had looked as if he meant to do so but he now said between his teeth: 'I want to see those people.'

'Now's your chance,' said Alleyn.

He glowered, hesitated and then said: 'Very well,' and walked between Alleyn and Fox, towards the pottery.

Gibson and the sergeant were having no trouble. Chubb was standing bolt upright and saying nothing. Colonel Cockburn-Montfort had been detached from the bell, deftly rolled round and propped against the door-jamb by Gibson. His eyes were glazed and his mouth slightly open but, like Chubb, he actually maintained a trace of his soldierly bearing.

Four uniformed men had arrived and bystanders had begun to collect.

Alleyn rang the bell and knocked on the top of the door. He waited for half a minute and then said to one of the policemen:

'It's a Yale. Let's hope it's not double-locked. Got anything?'

The policeman fished in his breast pocket, produced a small polythene ready-reckoner of a kind used for conversion to metric quantities. Alleyn slid it past the tongue of the lock and manipulated it.

'Bob's your uncle,' the constable murmured and the door was open.

Alleyn said to Fox and Gibson, 'Would you wait a moment with these gentlemen?' He then nodded to the constables who followed him in, one remaining inside the door.

'Hullo!' Alleyn called. 'Anyone at home?'

He had a resonant voice but it sounded stifled in the airless flat. They were in a narrow lobby hung with dim native cloth of some sort and smelling of dust and the stale fumes of sandarac. A staircase rose steeply on the left from just inside the door. At the far end, on the right was a door that presumably led into the shop. Two large suitcases strapped and labelled, leant against the wall.

Alleyn turned on a switch and a pseudo-oriental lamp with red panes came to life in the ceiling. He looked at the labels on the suitcases: 'Sanskrit, Ng'ombwana.'

'Come on,' he said.

He led the way upstairs. On the landing he called out again. Silence.

There were four doors, all shut.

Two bedrooms, small, exotically furnished, crowded and in disarray. Discarded garments flung on unmade beds. Cupboards and drawers, open and half-emptied. Two small, half-packed suitcases. An all-pervading and most unlovely smell.

A bathroom, stale and grubby, smelling of hot, wet fat. The wall-cupboard was locked.

Finally, a large, heavily furnished room with divans, deep rugs, horrid silk-shaded and beaded lamps, incense burners and a number of ostensibly African artifacts. But no Sanskrits.

They returned downstairs.

Alleyn opened the door at the end of the lobby and walked through.

He was in the piggery.

It was very dark. Only a thin sliver of light penetrated the slit between the heavy window curtains.

He stood inside the door with the two uniformed men behind him. As his eyes adjusted to the gloom, the interior began to emerge; a desk, a litter of paper and packing material, open cases and on the shelves, dimly flowering one or two pottery pigs. The end of the old stable, formed, as he remembered, a sort of alcove or cavern in which there were the kiln and a long work table. He saw a faint red glow there, now.

He was taken with a sensation of inertia that he had long ago learnt to recognize as the kind of nightmare which drains one of the power to move.

As now, when his hand was unable to grope about the dirty wall for a light switch.

The experience never lasted for more than a few seconds and now it had passed and left him with the knowledge that he was watched.

Someone at the far end of the shop, in the alcove room, sitting on the other side of the workbench, was watching him: a looming mass that he had mistaken for shadow.

It began to define itself. An enormous person, whose chin rested with a suggestion of doggy roguishness, on her arm and whose eyes were very wide open indeed.

Alleyn's hand found the switch and the room was flooded with light.

It was Miss Sanskrit who ogled him so coyly with her chin on her arm and her head all askew and her eyes wide open.

Behind the bench, with his back towards her, with his vast rump upheaved and with his head and arms and barrel submerged in a packing-case like a monstrous puppet doubled over its box, dangled her brother. They were both dead.

And between them, on the floor and the bench, were bloodied shards of pottery.

And in the packing-case lay the headless carcass of an enormous pig.

II

A whispered stream of obscenities had been surprised out of one of the constables but he had stopped when Alleyn walked into the alcove and had followed a short way behind.

'Stay where you are,' Alleyn said and then: 'No! One of you get that lot in off the street and lock the door. Take them to the room upstairs, keep them there and stay with them. Note anything that's said.

'The other call Homicide and give the necessary information. Ask Mr Fox and Mr Gibson to come here.'

They went out, shutting the door behind them. In a minute Alleyn heard sounds of a general entry and of people walking upstairs.

When Fox and Gibson arrived they found Alleyn standing between the Sanskrits. They moved towards him but checked when he raised his hand.

'This is nasty,' Fox said. 'What was it?'

'Come and see but walk warily.'

They moved round the bench and saw the back of Miss Sanskrit's head. It was smashed in like an egg. Beetroot-dyed hair, dark and wet, stuck in the wound. The back of her dress was saturated – there was a dark puddle on the table under her arm. She was dressed for the street. Her bloodied hat lay on the floor and her handbag was on the work table.

Alleyn turned to face the vast rump of her brother, clothed in a camel overcoat which was all that could be seen of him.

'Is it the same?' Gibson asked.

'Yes. A pottery pig. The head broke off on the first attack and the rest fell into the box after the second.'

'But – how exactly – ?' Fox said.

'Look what's on the table. Under her hand.'

It was a sheet of headed letter paper. 'The Piggie Pottery, 12 Capricorn Mews, SW3.' Written beneath this legend was: 'To Messrs Able and Virtue. Kindly . . .' And no more.

'A green ball-point,' Alleyn said, 'It's still in her right hand.'

'Fox touched the hand. 'Still warm,' he said.

'Yes.'

There was a checked cloth of sorts near the kiln. Alleyn masked the terrible head with it. 'One of the really bad ones,' he said.

'What was *he* doing?' Fox asked

'Stowing away the remaining pigs. Doubled up, and reaching down into the packing-case.'

'So you read the situation – how?'

'Like this, unless something else turns up to contradict it. She's writing. He's putting pigs from the bench into the packing-case. Someone comes between them. Someone who perhaps has offered to help. Someone, at any rate, whose presence doesn't disturb them. And this person picks up a pig, deals two mighty downward blows, left and right, quick as you please, and walks out.'

Gibson said angrily: 'Walks out! When? And when did he *walk in*? I've had these premises under close observation for twelve hours.'

'Until the bomb-scare, Fred.'

'Sergeant Jacks stayed put.'

'With a traffic jam building up between him and the pottery.'

'By God, this is a gutty job,' said Gibson.

'And the gallant Colonel was on the doorstep,' Alleyn added.

'I reckon *he* wouldn't have been any the wiser,' Fox offered, 'if the Brigade of Guards had walked in and out.'

'We'll see about that,' Alleyn said.

A silence fell between them. The room was oppressively warm and airless. Flies buzzed between the window curtains and the glass. One of them darted out and made like a bullet for the far end.

With startling unexpectedness the telephone on the desk rang. Alleyn wrapped his handkerchief round his hand and lifted the receiver.

He gave the number speaking well above his natural level. An unmistakably Ng'ombwanan voice said: 'It is the Embassy. You have not kept your appointment.'

Alleyn made an ambiguous falsetto noise.

'I said,' the voice insisted, 'you have not kept your appointment. To collect the passports. Your plane leaves at 5.30.'

Alleyn whispered: 'I was prevented. Please send them. Please.'

A long pause.

'Very well. It is not convenient but very well. They will be put into your letter-box. In a few minutes. Yes?'

He said nothing and heard a deep sound of impatience and the click of the receiver being replaced.

He hung up. 'For what it's worth,' he said, 'we now know that the envelope we saw Sanskrit deliver at the Embassy contained their passports. I'd got as much already from the President. In a few minutes they'll be dropping them in. He failed to keep his appointment to collect.'

Fox looked at the upturned remains of Sanskrit. 'He could hardly help himself,' he said. 'Could he?'

The front door bell rang. Alleyn looked through the slit in the curtains. A car had arrived with Bailey and Thompson, their driver and their gear. A smallish crowd had been moved down the Mews and into the passageway leading to Baronsgate.

The constable in the hallway admitted Bailey and Thompson. Alleyn said: 'The lot. Complete coverage. Particularly the broken pottery.'

Thompson walked carefully past the partition into the alcove and stopped short.

'Two, eh?' he said and unslipped his camera.

'Go ahead,' Alleyn said.

Bailey went to the table and looked incredulously from the enormous bodies to Alleyn, who nodded and turned his back. Bailey delicately lifted the checked cloth and said: 'Cor!'

'Not pretty,' Alleyn said.

Bailey, shocked into a unique flight of fancy, said: 'It's kind of not real. Like those blown-up affairs they run in fun shows. Giants. Gone into the horrors.'

'It's very much like that,' Alleyn said. 'Did you hear if they'd got through to Sir James?'

'Yes, Mr Alleyn. On his way.'

'Good. All right. Push on with it, you two.' He turned to Gibson and Fox. 'I suggest,' he said, 'that we let that lot upstairs have a look at this scene.'

'Shock tactics?' Gibson asked.

'Something like that. Agreed?'

'This is your ground, not mine,' said Gibson, still dully resentful, 'I'm only meant to be bloody security.'

Alleyn knew it was advisable to disregard these plaints.

He said: 'Fox, would you go upstairs? Take the copper in the hall with you. Leave him in the room and have a quiet word on the landing with the man who's been with them. If he's got anything I ought to hear, hand it on to me. Otherwise, just stick with them for a bit, would you? Don't give a clue as to what's happened. All right?'

'I think so,' said Fox placidly, and went upstairs.

Bailey's camera clicked and flashed. Miss Sanskrit's awful face started up and out in a travesty of life. Thompson collected pottery shards and laid them out on the far end of the work table. More exploratory flies darted down the room. Alleyn continued to watch through the curtains.

A Ng'ombwanan in civilian dress drove up to the door, had a word with the constable on guard and pushed something through the letter-box. Alleyn heard the flap of the clapper. The car drove away and he went into the hall and collected the package.

'What's that, then?' Gibson asked.

Alleyn opened it: two British passports elaborately stamped and endorsed and a letter on Embassy paper in Ng'ombwanan.

'Giving them the VIP treatment, I wouldn't be surprised,' Alleyn said and pocketed the lot.

Action known as 'routine' was now steadily under way. Sir James Curtis and his secretary arrived, Sir James remarking a little acidly that he would like to know this time whether he would be allowed to follow the usual procedure and hold his damned post mortems if, when and where he wanted them. On being shown the subjects he came as near to exhibiting physical repulsion as Alleyn had ever seen him and asked appallingly if they would provide him with bull-dozers.

He said that death had probably occurred within the hour, agreed with Alleyn's reading of the evidence, listened to what action he proposed to take and was about to leave when Alleyn said: 'There's a former record of drug-pushing against the man. No sign of them taking anything themselves, I suppose?'

'I'll look out for it but they don't often, do they?'

'Do we expect to find blood on the assailant?'

Sir James considered this. 'Not necessarily, I think,' he said. 'The size of the weapon might form a kind of shield in the case of the woman and the position of the head in the man.'

'Might the weapon have been dropped or hurled down on the man? They're extremely heavy, those things.'

'Very possible.'

'I see.'

'You'll send these monstrosities along then, Rory? Good day to you.'

When he'd gone Fox and the constable who had been on duty upstairs came down.

'Thought we'd better wait till Sir James had finished,' Fox said. 'I've been up there in the room with them. Chubb's very quiet but you can see he's put out.'

This, in Fox's language, could mean anything from being irritated to going berserk or suicidal. 'He breaks out every now and then,' he went on, 'asking where the Sanskrits are and why this lot's being kept. I asked him what he'd wanted to see them for and he comes with it that he *didn't* want to see them. He reckons he was on his way back from the chemist's by way of Capricorn Passage and just ran into the Colonel and Mr Sheridan. The Colonel was in such a bad way, Chubb makes out, he was trying to get him to let himself be taken home but all the Colonel would do was lean on the bell.'

'What about the Colonel?'

'It doesn't really make sense. He's beyond it. He said something or another about Sanskrit being a poisonous specimen who ought to be court-martialled.'

'And Gomez-Sheridan?'

'He's taking the line of righteous indignation. Demands an explanation. Will see there's information laid in the right quarters and we haven't heard the last of it. You'd think it was all quite ordinary except for a kind of twitch under his left eye. They all keep asking where the Sanskrits are.'

'It's time they found out,' Alleyn said, and to Bailey and Thompson: 'There's a smell of burnt leather. We'll have to rake out the furnace.'

'Looking for anything in particular, Mr Alleyn?'

'No. Well – No. Just looking. For traces of anything anyone wanted to destroy. Come on.'

He and Fox went upstairs.

As he opened the door and went in he got the impression that Gomez had leapt to his feet. He stood facing Alleyn with his bald head sunk between his shoulders and his eyes like black bootbuttons in his white kid face. He might have been an actor in a bad Latin-American film.

At the far end of the room Chubb stood facing the window with the dogged, conditioned look of a soldier in detention, as if whatever he thought or felt or had done must be thrust back behind a mask of conformity.

Colonel Cockburn-Montfort lay in an armchair with his mouth open, snoring profoundly and hideously. He would have presented a less distasteful picture, Alleyn thought, if he had discarded the outward showing of an officer and ambiguous addition – gentleman: the conservative suit, the signet ring on the correct finger, the handmade brogues, the regimental tie, the quietly elegant socks and, lying on the floor by his chair, the hat from Jermyn Street – all so very much in order. And Colonel Cockburn-Montfort so very far astray.

Gomez began at once: 'You are the officer in charge of these extraordinary proceedings, I believe. I must ask you to inform me, at once, why I am detained here without reason, without explanation or apology.'

'Certainly,' Alleyn said, 'It is because I hope you may be able to help us in our present job.'

'Police parrot talk!' he spat out, making a great thing of the plosives. The muscle under his eye flickered.

'I hope not,' Alleyn said.

'What is this "present job"?'

'We are making enquiries about the couple living in these premises. Brother and sister. Their name is Sanskrit.'

'Where are they!'

'They haven't gone far.'

'Are they in trouble?' he asked showing his teeth.

'Yes.'

'I am not surprised. They are criminals. Monsters.'

The Colonel snorted and opened his eyes. 'What?' he said. 'Who are you talking 'bout? Monsters?'

Gomez made a contemptuous noise. 'Go to sleep,' he said. 'You are disgusting.'

'I take 'ception that remark, sir,' said the Colonel and sounded exactly like Major Bloodknock, long ago. He shut his eyes.

'How do you know they are criminals?' Alleyn asked.

'I have reliable information,' said Gomez.

'From where?'

'From friends in Africa.'

'In Ng'ombwana?'

'One of the so-called emergent nations. I believe that is the name.'

'You ought to know,' Alleyn remarked, 'seeing that you spent so long there.' And he thought: He really is rather like an adder.

'You speak nonsense,' Gomez lisped.

'I don't think so, Mr Gomez.'

Chubb, by the window, turned and gaped at him.

'My name is Sheridan,' Gomez said loudly.

'If you prefer it.'

''Ere!' Chubb said with some violence. 'What is all this? *Names!*'

Alleyn said: 'Come over here, Chubb, and sit down. I've got something to say to all of you and for your own sakes you'd better listen to it. Sit down. That's right. Colonel Cockburn-Montfort – '

'Cert'n'ly,' said the Colonel, opening his eyes.

'Can you follow me or shall I send for a corpse-reviver?'

''Course I can follow you. F'what it's worth.'

'Very well. I'm going to put something to the three of you and it's this. You are members of a coterie which is motivated by racial hatred, more specifically, hatred of the Ng'ombwanan people in particular. On the night before last you conspired to murder the President.'

Gomez said, 'What is this idiot talk!'

'You had an informant in the Embassy: the Ambassador himself, who believed that on the death of the President and with your backing, he would achieve a *coup d'état* and assume power. In return, you, Mr Gomez, and you, Colonel Montfort, were to be reinstated in Ng'ombwana.'

The Colonel waved his hand as if these statements were too trivial to merit consideration. Gomez, his left ankle elegantly posed on his right thigh, watched Alleyn over his locked fingers. Chubb, wooden, sat bolt upright on the edge of his chair.

'The Sanskrits, brother and sister,' Alleyn went on, 'were also members of the clique. Miss Sanskrit produced your medallion in her pottery downstairs. They, however, were double agents. From the time the plan was first conceived to the moment for its execution and without the knowledge of the Ambassador, every move was being conveyed by the Sanskrits back to the Ng'ombwanan authorities. I think you must have suspected something of the sort when your plan miscarried. I think that last night after your meeting here broke up, one of the group followed Sanskrit to the Embassy and from a distance saw him deliver an envelope. He had passed by your house, Colonel Montfort.'

'I don't go out at night much nowadays,' the Colonel said, rather sadly.

'Your wife perhaps? It wouldn't be the first time you'd delegated one of the fancy touches to her. Well, it's of no great matter. I think the full realization of what the Sanskrits had done really dawned this morning when you learned that they were shutting up shop and leaving.'

'Have they made it?' Chubb suddenly demanded. 'Have they cleared out? Where are they?'

'To return to the actual event. Everything seemed to go according to plan up to the moment when, after the shot was fired and the guests' attention had been deflected, you, Chubb, made your assault on the spearcarrier. You delivered the chop from behind, probably standing on a subsequently overturned chair to do so. At the crucial moment you were yourself attacked from the rear by the Ng'ombwanan servant. He was a little slow off the mark. Your blow fell: not as intended on the spearsman's arm but on his collar-bone. He was still able to use his spear and he did use it, with both hands and full knowledge of what he was doing, on the Ambassador.'

Alleyn looked at the three men. There was no change in their posture or their expressions but a dull red had crept into Chubb's face and the Colonel's (which habitually looked as if it had reached saturation point in respect of purple) seemed to darken. They said nothing.

'I see I've come near enough the mark for none of you to contradict me,' Alleyn remarked.

'On the contrary,' Gomez countered. 'Your entire story is fantasy and a libel. It is too farcical to merit a reply.'

'Well, Chubb?'

'I'm not answering the charge, sir. Except what I said before. I was clobbered.'

'Colonel?'

'What? No comment. No bloody comment.'

'Why were you all trying to get in here, half an hour ago?'

'No comment,' they said together and Chubb added his former statement that he'd had no intention of calling on the Sanskrits but had merely stopped to offer his support to the Colonel and take him home.

The Colonel said something that sounded like: 'Most irregular and unnecessary.'

'Are you sticking to that?' Alleyn said. 'Are you sure you weren't, all three of you, going to throw a farewell party for the Sanskrits and give them, or at any rate, him, something handsome to remember you by?'

They were very still. They didn't look at Alleyn or at each other but for a moment the shadow of a fugitive smile moved across their faces.

The front doorbell was pealing again, continuously. Alleyn went out to the landing.

Mrs Chubb was at the street door, demanding to be let in. The constable on duty turned, looked up the stairs and saw Alleyn.

'All right,' Alleyn said. 'Ask her to come up.'

It was a very different Mrs Chubb who came quickly up the stairs, thrusting her shoulders forward and jerking up her head to confront Alleyn on the landing.

'Where is he?' she demanded, breathing hard. 'Where's Chubb? You said keep him home and now you've got him in here. And with them others. Haven't you? I know he's here. I was in the Mews and I seen. Why? What are you doing to him? Where,' Mrs Chubb reiterated, 'is my Chubb?'

'Come in,' Alleyn said. 'He's here.'

She looked past him into the room. Her husband stood up and she went to him. 'What are you doing?' she said. 'You come back with me. You've got no call to be here.'

Chubb said: 'You don't want to be like this. You keep out of it. You're out of place here, Min.'

'I'm out of place! Standing by my own husband!'

'Look – dear – '

'Don't talk to me!' She turned on the other two men. 'You two gentlemen,' she said, 'you got no call because he works for you to get him involved, stirring it all up again. Putting ideas in his head. It won't bring her back. Leave us alone. Syd – you come home with me. Come home.'

'I can't,' he said. 'Min. I can't.'

'Why can't you?' She clapped her hand to her mouth. 'They've arrested you! They've found out – '

'*Shut up!*' he shouted. 'You silly cow. You don't know what you're saying. *Shut up!*' They stared aghast at each other. 'I'm sorry, Min,' he said. 'I never meant to speak rough. I'm not arrested. It's not like that.'

'Where are they, then? Those two?'

Gomez said: 'You! Chubb! Have you no control over your woman? Get rid of her.'

'And that'll do from you,' Chubb said, turning savagely on him.

From the depths of his armchair, Colonel Cockburn-Montfort, in an astonishingly clear and incisive tone, said: 'Chubb!'

'Sir!'

'You're forgetting yourself.'

'Sir.'

Alleyn said: 'Mrs Chubb, everything I said to you this morning was said in good faith. Circumstances have changed profoundly since then in a way that you know nothing about. You *will* know before long. In the meantime, if you please will you either stay here, quietly, in this room – '

'You better, Min,' Chubb said.

' – or,' Alleyn said, 'just go home and wait there. It won't be for long.'

'Go on, then, Min. You better.'

'I'll stay,' she said. She walked to the far end of the room and sat down.

Gomez, trembling with what seemed to be rage, shouted: 'For the last time – where are they? Where have they gone? Have they escaped? I demand an answer. Where are the Sanskrits?'

'They are downstairs,' Alleyn said.

Gomez leapt to his feet, let out an exclamation – in Portuguese, Alleyn supposed – seemed to be in two minds what to say and at last with a sort of doubtful relish said: 'Have you arrested them?'

'No.'

'I want to see them,' he said. 'I am longing to see them.'

'And so you shall,' said Alleyn.

He glanced at Fox, who went downstairs. Gomez moved towards the door.

The constable who had been on duty in the room came back and stationed himself inside the door.

'Shall we go down?' Alleyn said and led the way.

III

It was from this point that the sequence of events in the pig-pottery shop took on such a grotesque, such a macabre aspect, that Alleyn was to look back on the episode as possibly the most out-landish in his professional career. From the moment when the corpse of Miss Sanskrit received the first of her gentlemen visitors, they all three in turn became puppet-like caricatures of them-selves, acting in a two-dimensional, crudely exaggerated style. In any other setting the element of black farce would have rioted. Even here, under the terrible auspices of the Sanskrits, it rose from time to time, like a bout of unseemly hysteria at the bad perfor-mance of a Jacobean tragedy.

The room downstairs had been made ready for the visit. Bailey and Thompson waited near the window, Gibson by the desk and Fox, with his notebook in hand, near the alcove. Two uniformed police stood inside the door and a third at the back of the alcove. The bodies of the Sanskrits, brother and sister, had not been moved or shrouded. The room was now dreadfully stuffy.

Alleyn joined Fox.

'Come in, Mr Gomez,' he said.

Gomez stood on the threshold, a wary animal, Alleyn thought, waiting with its ears laid back before advancing into strange territory. He looked, without moving his head, from one to another of the men in the room, seemed to hesitate, seemed to suspect and then, swaggering a little, came into the room.

He stopped dead in front of Alleyn and said: 'Well?'

Alleyn made a slight gesture. Gomez followed it, turned his head – and saw.

The noise he made was something between a retch and an exclamation. For a moment he was perfectly still and it was as if he and Miss Sanskrit actually and sensibly confronted each other. And because of the arch manner in which the lifeless head lolled on the lifeless arm and the dead eyes seemed to leer at him, it was as if Miss Sanskrit had done a Banquo and found Mr Gomez out.

He walked down the room and into the alcove. The policeman by the furnace gave a slight cough and eased his chin. Gomez inspected the bodies. He walked round the workbench and he looked into the packing-case. He might have been a visitor to a museum. There was no sound in the room other than the light fall of his feet on the wooden floor and the dry buzzing of flies.

Then he turned his back on the alcove, pointed to Alleyn and said: '*You!* What did you think to achieve by this? Make me lose my nerve? Terrify me into saying something you could twist into an admission? Oh no, my friend! I had no hand in the destruction of this vermin. Show me the man who did it and I'll kiss him on both cheeks and salute him as a brother, but I had no hand in it and you'll never prove anything else.'

He stopped. He was shaking as if with a rigor. He made to leave the room and saw that the door was guarded. And then he screamed out: 'Cover them up. They're obscene,' and went to the curtained window, turning his back on the room.

Fox, on a look from Alleyn, had gone upstairs. Thompson said under his breath, 'Could I have a second, Mr Alleyn?'

They went into the hallway. Thompson produced an envelope from his pocket and shook the contents out in his palm – two circular flattish objects about the size of an old sixpence, with concave upper surfaces. The under-surface of one had a pimple on it and on the other, a hole. They were blistered and there were tiny fragments of an indistinguishable charred substance clinging to them.

'Furnace?' Alleyn asked.

'That's right, sir.'

'Good. I'll take them.'

He restored them to their envelope, put them in his pocket and looked up the stairs to where Fox waited in the landing. 'Next,' he said, and thought: It's like a dentist's waiting-room.

The next was the Colonel. He came down in fairly good order with his shoulders squared and his chin up and feeling with the back of his heels for the stair-treads. As he turned into the shop he pressed up the corners of his moustache.

After the histrionics of Gomez, the Colonel's confrontation with the Sanskrits passed off quietly. He fetched up short, stood in absolute silence for a few seconds, and then said with an air that almost resembled dignity, 'This is disgraceful.'

'Disgraceful?' Alleyn repeated.

'They've been murdered.'

'Clearly.'

'The bodies ought to be covered. It's most irregular. And disgusting,' and he added, almost, it seemed, as an afterthought: 'It makes me feel sick.' And indeed he perceptibly changed colour.

He turned his back on the Sanskrits and joined Gomez by the window, 'I protest categorically,' he said, successfully negotiating the phrase, 'at the conduct of these proceedings. And I wish to leave the room.'

'Not just yet, I'm afraid,' Alleyn said as Gomez made a move towards the door, 'for either of you.'

'What right,' Gomez demanded, 'have you to keep me here? You have no right.'

'Well,' Alleyn said mildly, 'if you press the point we can note your objection, which I see Inspector Fox is doing in any case, and if you insist on leaving you may do so in a minute. In that case, of course, we shall ask you to come with us to the Yard. In the meantime: there's Chubb, Would you, Fox?'

In its own succint way Chubb's reaction was a classic. He marched in almost as if Fox was a sergeant-major's escort, executed a smart left turn, saw Miss Sanskrit, halted, became rigid, asked – unbelievably – 'Who done it?' and fainted backwards like the soldier he had been.

And the Colonel, rivalling him in established behaviour, made a sharp exasperated noise and said: 'Damn bad show.'

Chubb recovered almost immediately. One of the constables brought him a drink of water. He was supported to the only chair in the room and sat in it with his back to the alcove.

'Very sorry, sir,' he mumbled, not to Alleyn but to the Colonel. His gaze alighted on Gomez.

'You done it!' he said, sweating and trembling. 'Din' you? You said you'd fix it and you did. You fixed it.'

'Do you lay a charge against Mr Gomez?' Alleyn said.

'Gomez? I don't know any Gomez.'

'Against Mr Sheridan?'

'I don't know what it means, lay a charge, and I don't know how he worked it, do I? But he said last night if it turned out they'd ratted, he'd get them. And I reckon he's kept 'is word. He's got them.'

Gomez sprang at him like a released spring, so suddenly and with such venom that it took Gibson and both the constables all their time to hold him. He let out short, disjointed phrases, presumably in Portuguese, wetting his blue chin and mouthing at Alleyn. Perhaps because the supply of invective ran out he at last fell silent and watchful and seemed the more dangerous for it.

'That was a touch of your old Ng'ombwanan form,' Alleyn said. 'You'd much better pipe down, Mr Gomez. Otherwise, you know, we shall have to lock you up.'

'Filth!' said Mr Gomez, and spat inaccurately in Chubb's direction.

'Bad show. Damn bad show,' reiterated the Colonel, who seemed to have turned himself into a sort of Chorus to The Action.

Alleyn said: 'Has one of you lost a pair of gloves?'

The scene went silent. For a second or two nobody moved and then Chubb got to his feet. Gomez, whose arms were still in custody, looked at his hands with their garnish of black hair and the Colonel thrust his into his pockets. And then, on a common impulse, it seemed they all three began accusing each other incoherently and inanely of the murder of the Sanskrits, and would no doubt have gone on doing so if the front doorbell had not pealed once more. As if the sound-track for whatever drama was being ground out had been turned back for a re-play, a woman could be heard making a commotion in the hallway.

'I want to see my husband. Stop that. Don't touch me. I'm going to see my husband.'

The Colonel whispered, 'No! For Chrissake keep her out. *Keep her out.*'

But she was already in the room with the constable on duty in the hall making an ineffectual grab after her and the two men inside the door, taken completely by surprise, looking to Alleyn for orders.

He had her by the arms. She was dishevelled and her eyes were out of focus. It would be hard to say whether she smelt stronger of gin or scent.

Alleyn turned her with her back to the alcove and her face towards her husband. He felt her sagging in his grasp.

'Hughie!' she said. 'You haven't have you? Hughie, promise you haven't. *Hughie!*'

She fought with Alleyn, trying to reach her husband.

'I couldn't stand it, Hughie,' she cried. 'Alone, after what you said you'd do. I had to come. I had to know.'

And as Chubb had turned on his wife, so the Colonel, in a different key, turned on her.

'Hold your tongue!' he roared out. 'You're drunk.'

She struggled violently with Alleyn and in doing so swung round in his grasp and faced the alcove.

And screamed. And screamed. And poured out such a stream of fatal words that her husband made a savage attempt to get at her and was held off by Fox and Thompson and Bailey. And then she became terrified of him, begged Alleyn not to let him get to her and finally collapsed.

There being nowhere else to put her, they half carried her upstairs and left her with Mrs Chubb, gabbling wildly about how badly he treated her and how she knew when he left the house in a blind rage he would do what he said he would do. All of which was noted down by the officer on duty in the upstairs room.

In the downstairs room Alleyn, not having a warrant for his arrest, asked Colonel Cockburn-Montfort to come to the Yard where he would be formally charged with the murder of the Sanskrits.

'And I should warn you that – '

CHAPTER 10

Epilogue

'It was clear from the moment we saw the bodies,' Alleyn said, 'that Montfort was the man. The pig-pottery had been under strict surveillance from the time Sanskrit returned to it from the house-agents. The only gap came after Gibson's men had been drawn off by the bomb-scare. The traffic in the Mews piled up between Sergeant Jacks and the flat entrance where Montfort leant against the door-bell and for at least five minutes, probably longer, the façade was completely hidden by a van. During that time Montfort, who was beginning to make a scene in the street, had been admitted by one or other of the Sanskrits, with the object, one supposes, of shutting him up.

They were in a hurry. They had to get to the airport. They had planned to make their getaway within the next quarter of an hour and were packing up the last lot of pigs and writing a note for the agents. Leaving the drunken Colonel to grind to a halt, they returned to their jobs. Sanskrit put the penultimate pig in the case, his sister sat down to write the note. Montfort followed them up, found himself between the two of them, heaved up the last pig doorstop on the bench and in a drunken fury crashed it down left and right. The shock of what he'd done may have partly sobered him. His gloves were bloodied. He shoved them in the kiln, walked out and had the sense or the necessity to lean against the doorbell again. The van still blocked the view, and when it removed itself, there he still was.'

'Who raised the false alarm about the bomb?' asked Troy.

'Oh, one of the Sanskrits, don't you think? To draw Gibson's men off while the two of them did a bunk to Ng'ombwana. They were in a blue funk over the outcome of the assassination and an even bluer one at the thought of the Ku-Klux-Fish. They realized, as they were bound to do, that they'd been rumbled.'

'It would seem,' Mr Whipplestone said drily, 'that they did not over-estimate the potential.'

'It would indeed.'

'Rory – *how* drunk was the wretched man?' Troy asked.

'Can one talk about degrees of drunkenness in an alcoholic? I suppose one can. According to his wife, and there's no reason to doubt her, he was plug-ugly drunk and breathing murder when he left the house.'

'And the whole thing, you believe, was completely unpremeditated?' Mr Whipplestone asked.

'I think so. No coherent plan when he leant on the doorbell. Nothing beyond a blind alcoholic rage to get at them. There was the pig on the work table and there were their heads. Bang, bang and he walked out again. The traffic block was just drunkard's luck. I don't for a moment suppose he was aware of it and I think he'd have behaved in exactly the same way if it hadn't occurred.'

'He had the sense to put his gloves in the kiln,' Mr Whipplestone pointed out.

'It's the only bit of hard evidence we've got. I wouldn't venture a guess as to how far the shock of what he'd done sobered him. Or as to how he may have exaggerated his condition for our benefit. He's been given a blood test and the alcoholic level was astronomical.'

'No doubt he'll plead drunkenness,' said Mr Whipplestone.

'You may depend upon it. And to some purpose, I don't mind betting.'

'What about my poor, silly Chubb?'

'Sam, in the ordinary course of things he'd face a charge of conspiracy. If it does come to that, the past history – his daughter – and the dominance of the others will tell enormously in his favour. With a first-class counsel – '

'I'll look after that. And his bail. I've told him so.'

'I'm not sure we've got a case. Apart from the *mlinzi's* collar-bone there's no hard evidence. What we would greatly prefer would be for Chubb to make a clean breast about the conspiracy in return for his own immunity.'

Mr Whipplestone and Troy looked uncomfortable.

'Yes, I know,' Alleyn said. 'But just you think for a bit about Gomez. He's the only one, apart from Montfort himself who'd be involved and believe me, if ever there was a specimen who deserved what's coming to him, it's that one. We've got him on a forged passport charge which will do to go on with, and a search of his pseudo coffee-importing premises in the City has brought to light some very dubious transactions in uncut diamonds. And in the background is his Ng'ombwanan conviction for manslaughter of a particularly revolting nature.'

'What about the Embassy angle?' Troy asked.

'What indeed? What happened within those *opéra bouffe* walls is, as we keep telling ourselves, their affair although it will figure obliquely as motive in the case against Montfort. But for the other show – the slaughter of the Ambassador by the *mlinzi* – that's over to The Boomer and I wish the old so-and-so joy of it.'

'He leaves tomorrow, I'm told.'

'Yes. At 2.30. After giving Troy a final sitting.'

'*Really!*' Mr Whipplestone exclaimed, gazing in polite awe at Troy. She burst out laughing.

'Don't look so shocked,' she said and to her own, Alleyn's and Mr Whipplestone's astonishment dropped a kiss on the top of his head. She saw the pink scalp under the neat strands of hair turn crimson and said: 'Pay no attention. I'm excited about my work.'

'Don't ruin everything!' said Mr Whipplestone with tremendous dash. 'I'd hoped it was about me.'

II

'By all the rules, if there were any valid ones,' Troy said at half past eleven the following morning, 'it's an unfinished portrait. But even if you could give me another sitting I don't think I'd take it.'

The Boomer stood beside her looking at her work. At no stage of the sitting had he exhibited any of the usual shyness of the sitter who doesn't want to utter banalities and at no stage had he uttered any.

'There is something African in the way you have gone about this picture,' he said. 'We have no portraitists of distinction at present but if we had they would try to do very much as you have done, I think. I find it hard to remember that the painter is not one of my people.'

'You couldn't have said anything to please me more,' said Troy.

'No? I am glad. And so I must go: Rory and I have one or two things to settle and I have to change. So it is goodbye, my dear Mrs Rory, and thank you.'

'Goodbye,' Troy said, 'my dear President Boomer, and thank you.'

She gave him her painty hand and saw him into the house where Alleyn waited for him. This time he had come without his *mlinzi* who, he said, was involved with final arrangements at the Embassy.

He and Alleyn had a drink together.

'This has been in some ways an unusual visit,' The Boomer remarked.

'A little unusual,' Alleyn agreed.

'On your part, my dear Rory, it has been characterized by the tactful avoidance of difficult corners.'

'I've done my best. With the assistance, if that's the right word, of diplomatic immunity.'

The Boomer gave him a tentative smile. Alleyn reflected that this was a rare occurrence. The Boomer's habit was to bellow with laughter, beam like a lighthouse or remain entirely solemn.

'So those unpleasant persons,' he said, 'have been murdered by Colonel Cockburn-Montfort.'

'It looks like it.'

'They *were* unpleasant,' The Boomer said thoughtfully. 'We were sorry to employ them but needs must. You find the same sort of situation in your own service, of course.'

This being perfectly true, there was little to be said in reply.

'We regretted the necessity,' The Boomer said, 'to reinstate them in Ng'ombwana.'

'In the event,' Alleyn said drily, 'you don't have to.'

'No!' he cried gaily. 'So it's an ill wind, as the saying goes. We are spared the Sanskrits. *What* a good thing.'

Alleyn gazed at him, speechless.

'Is anything the matter, old boy?' The Boomer asked.

Alleyn shook his head.

'Ah!' said The Boomer, 'I think I know. We have come within sight of that ravine, again.'

'And again we can arrange to meet elsewhere.'

'That is why you have not asked me certain questions. Such as how far was I aware of the successful counterplot against my traitor-Ambassador. Or whether I myself dealt personally with the odious Sanskrits who served us so usefully. Or whether it was I, of my own design, who led our poor Gibson so far down the Embassy garden path.'

'Not only Gibson.'

An expression of extreme distress came over the large black face. His paws gripped Alleyn's shoulders and his enormous, slightly bloodshot eyes filled with tears.

'Try to understand,' he said. 'Justice has been done in accordance with our need, our grass-roots, our absolute selves. With time we shall evolve a change and adapt and gradually such elements may die out in us. At the present, my very dear friend, you must think of us – of me, if you like, as – '

He hesitated for a moment and then with a smile and a change in his huge voice: ' – as an unfinished portrait,' said The Boomer.

Coda

On a very warm morning in mid-summer, Lucy Lockett, wearing the ornamental collar in which she seemed to fancy herself, sat on the front steps of No. 1, Capricorn Walk, contemplating the scene and keeping an ear open on proceedings in the basement flat.

Mr Whipplestone had found a suitable tenant and the Chubbs were turning out the premises. A vacuum cleaner whined, there were sundry bumps. The windows were open and voices were heard.

Mr Whipplestone had gone to the Napoli to buy his Camembert and Lucy, who never accompanied him into the Mews, awaited his return.

The cleaner was switched off. The Chubbs interchanged peaceful remarks and Lucy, suddenly moved by the legendary curiosity of her species and sex, leapt neatly into the garden and thence through the basement window.

The chattels of the late tenant had been removed but a certain amount of litter still remained. Lucy pretended to kill a crumpled sheet of newspaper and then fossicked about in odd corners. The Chubbs paid little attention to her.

When Mr Whipplestone returned he found his cat on the top step, couchante, with something between her fore-paws. She gazed up at him and made one of her fetching little remarks.

'What have you got there?' he asked. He inserted his eyeglass and bent down to see.

It was a white pottery fish.

Last Ditch

For the family at Walnut Tree Farm

Contents

Cast of Characters

Young Roderick Alleyn (Ricky)
Chief Superintendent Roderick Alleyn   *His father*
Troy Alleyn   *His mother*
Inspector Fox   *His godfather*
Jasper Pharamond
Julia Pharamond   *His wife*
Selina & Julietta Pharamond   *Their daughters*
Louis Pharamond   *Their cousin*
Carlotta Pharamond   *His wife*
Bruno Pharamond   *Jasper's brother*
Susie de Waite
Dulcie Harkness   *An equestrienne*
Cuthbert Harkness   *Her uncle*
Gilbert Ferrant   *Of Deep Cove*
Marie Ferrant   *His wife*
Louis Ferrant   *Their son*
Sydney Jones   *A painter*
Bob Maistre   *Landlord of the*
                                                  Cod-and-Bottle

Sergeant Plank   *Of Deep Cove*
Mrs Plank   *His wife*
Their Daughter
Dr Carey   *Police surgeon, Montjoy*
Bob Blacker   *Veterinary surgeon*
Police Constables Moss & Cribbage
Jim Le Compte   *A sailor*
Sundry fishermen, waiters and innkeepers

CHAPTER 1

Deep Cove

With all their easy-going behaviour there was, nevertheless, something rarified about the Pharamonds. Or so, on his first encounter with them, did it seem to Ricky Alleyn.

Even before they came into their drawing-room, he had begun to collect this impression of its owners. It was a large, eccentric and attractive room with lemon-coloured walls, polished floor and exquisite, grubby Chinese rugs. The two dominant pictures, facing each other at opposite ends of the room, were of an irritable gentleman in uniform and a lavishly-bosomed impatient lady, brandishing an implacable fan. Elsewhere he saw, with surprise, several unframed sketches, drawing-pinned to the walls, one of them being of a free, if not lewd, character.

He had blinked his way round these incompatibles and had turned to the windows and the vastness of sky and sea beyond them when Jasper Pharamond came quickly in.

'Ricky Alleyn!' he stated. 'How pleasant. We're all delighted.'

He took Ricky's hand, gaily tossed it away and waved him into a chair. 'You're like both your parents,' he observed. 'Clever of you.'

Ricky, feeling inadequate, said his parents sent their best remembrances and had talked a great deal about the voyage they had taken with the Pharamonds as fellow passengers.

'They were *so* nice to us,' Jasper said. 'You can't think. VIPs as they were, and all.'

'They don't feel much like VIPs.'

'Which is one of the reasons one likes them, of course. But do tell me, exactly why have you come to the island, and is the lodging Julia found endurable?'

Feeling himself blush, Ricky said he hoped he had come to work through the Long Vacation and his accommodation with a family in the village was just what he had hoped for and that he was very much obliged to Mrs Pharamond for finding it.

'She adores doing that sort of thing,' said her husband. 'But aren't you over your academic hurdles with all sorts of firsts and glories? Aren't you a terribly young don?'

Ricky mumbled wildly and Jasper smiled. His small hooked nose dipped and his lip twitched upwards. It was a faunish smile and agreed with his cap of tight curls.

'I know,' he said, 'you're writing a novel.'

'I've scarcely begun.'

'And you don't want to talk about it. How wise you are. Here come the others, or some of them.'

Two persons came in: a young woman and a youth of about thirteen years, whose likeness to Jasper established him as a Pharamond.

'Julia,' Jasper said, 'and Bruno. My wife and my brother.'

Julia was beautiful. She greeted Ricky with great politeness and a ravishing smile, made enquiries about his accommodation and then turned to her husband.

'Darling,' she said. 'A surprise for you. A girl.'

'What do you mean, Julia? Where?'

'With the children in the garden. She's going to have a baby.'

'Immediately?'

'Of course not.' Julia began to laugh. Her whole face broke into laughter. She made a noise like a soda-water syphon and spluttered indistinguishable words. Her husband watched her apprehensively. The boy, Bruno, began to giggle.

'Who is this girl?' Jasper asked. And to Ricky: 'You must excuse Julia. Her life is full of drama.'

Julia addressed herself warmly to Ricky. 'It's just that we do seem to get ourselves let in for rather peculiar situations. If Jasper stops interrupting I'll explain.'

'I have stopped interrupting,' Jasper said.

'Bruno and the children and I,' Julia explained to Ricky, 'drove to a place called Leathers to see about hiring horses from the stable people. Harness, they're called.'

'Harkness,' said Jasper.

'Harkness. Mr and Miss. Uncle and niece. So they weren't in their office and they weren't in their stables. We were going to look in the horse-paddock when we heard someone howling. And I mean *really* howling. Bawling. And being roared back at. In the harness-room, it transpired, with the door shut. Something about Mr Harkness threatening to have somebody called Mungo shot because he'd kicked the sorrel mare. I think perhaps Mungo was a horse. But while we stood helpless it turned into Mr H. calling Miss H. a whore of Babylon. Too awkward. Well, what would you have done?'

Jasper said: 'Gone away.'

'Out of tact or fear?'

'Fear.'

Julia turned enormous eyes on Ricky.

'So would I,' he said hurriedly.

'Well, so might I, too, because of the children, but before I could make up my mind there came the sound of a really hard slap, and a yell, and the tack-room door burst open. Out flew Miss Harness.'

'Harkness.'

'Well, anyway, out she flew and bolted past us and round the house and away. And there in the doorway stood Mr Harkness with a strap in his hand, roaring out Old Testament anathemas.'

'What action did you take?' asked her husband.

'I turned into a sort of policewoman and said: "What seems to be the trouble, Mr Harkness?" and he strode away.'

'And then?'

'We left. We couldn't go running after Mr Harkness when he was in that sort of mood.'

'He might have hit *us*,' Bruno pointed out. His voice had the unpredictable intervals of adolescence.

'Could we get back to the girl in the garden with the children? A sense of impending disaster seems to tell me she is Miss Harkness.'

'But none other. We came upon her on our way home. She was standing near the edge of the cliffs with a very odd look on her face, so I stopped the car and talked to her and she's nine weeks gone.

My guess is that she won't tell Mr Harkness who the man is, which is why he set about her with the strap.'

'Did she tell you who the man is?'

'Not yet. One mustn't nag, don't you feel?' asked Julia, appealing to Ricky. 'All in good time. Come and meet her. She's not howling now.'

Before he could reply two more Pharamonds came in: an older man and a young woman, each looking very like Bruno and Jasper. They were introduced as 'our cousins, Louis and Carlotta'. Ricky supposed them to be brother and sister until Louis put his arms round Carlotta from behind and kissed her neck. He then noticed that she wore a wedding ring.

'Who,' she asked Julia, 'is the girl in the garden with the children? Isn't she the riding-school girl?'

'Yes, but I can't wade through it all again now, darling. We're going out to meet her, and you can come too.'

'We have met her already,' Carlotta said. 'On that narrow path one could hardly shove by without uttering. We passed the time of day.'

'Perhaps it would be kinder to bring her indoors.' Julia announced. 'Bruno darling, be an angel and ask Miss Harkness to come in.'

Bruno strolled away. Julia called after him: 'And bring the children, darling, for Ricky to meet.' She gave Ricky a brilliant smile: 'You *have* come in for a tricky luncheon, haven't you?' she said.

'I expect I can manage,' he replied, and the Pharamonds looked approvingly at him. Julia turned to Carlotta. 'Would you say you were about the same size?' she asked.

'As who?'

'Darling, as Miss Harkness. Her present size I mean, of course. Sufficient unto the day is the evil thereof.'

'What is all this?' Carlotta demanded in a rising voice. 'What's Julia up to?'

'No good, you may depend upon it,' Jasper muttered. And to his wife: 'Have you asked Miss Harkness to stay? Have you dared?'

'But where else is there for her to go? She can't return to Mr Harkness and be beaten up. In her condition. Face it.'

'They are coming,' said Louis, who was looking out of the windows. 'I don't understand any of this. Is she lunching?'

'And staying, apparently,' said Carlotta. 'And Julia wants me to give her my clothes.'

'Lend, not give, and only something for the night,' Julia urged. 'Tomorrow there will be other arrangements.'

Children's voices sounded in the hall. Bruno opened the door and two little girls rushed noisily in. They were aged about five and seven and wore nothing but denim trousers with crossover straps. They flung themselves upon their mother who greeted them in a voice fraught with emotion.

'*Dar* – lings!' cried Julia, tenderly embracing them.

Then came Miss Harkness.

She was a well-developed girl with a weather-beaten complexion and hands of such a horny nature that Ricky was reminded of hooves. A marked puffiness round the eyes bore evidence to her recent emotional contretemps. She wore jodhpurs and a checked shirt.

Julia introduced her all round. She changed her weight from foot to foot, nodded and sometimes said 'Uh.' The Pharamonds all set up a conversational breeze while Jasper produced a drinks-tray. Ricky and Bruno drank beer and the family either sherry or white wine. Miss Harkness in a hoarse voice asked for scotch and downed it in three noisy gulps. Louis Pharamond began to talk to her about horses and Ricky heard him say he had played polo badly in Peru.

How pale they all were, Ricky thought. Really, they looked as if they had been forced, like vegetables, under covers, and had come out severely bleached. Even Julia, a Pharamond only by marriage, was without colour. Hers was a lovely pallor, a dramatic setting for her impertinent eyes and mouth. She was rather like an Aubrey Beardsley lady.

At luncheon, Ricky sat on her right and had Carlotta for his other neighbour. Diagonally opposite, by Jasper and with Louis on her right, sat Miss Harkness with another whisky-and-soda, and opposite her on their father's left, the little girls, who were called Selina and Julietta. Louis was the darkest and much the most *mondain* of all the Pharamonds. He wore a thread-like black moustache and a silken jumper and was smoothly groomed. He continued to make one-sided conversation with Miss Harkness, bending his head towards her and laughing in a flirtatious manner into her baleful face. Ricky noticed that

Carlotta, who, he gathered, was Louis's cousin as well as his wife, glanced at him from time to time with amusement.

'Have you spotted our "Troy"?' Julia asked Ricky, and pointed to a picture above Jasper's head. He had, but had been too shy to say so. It was a conversation piece – a man and a woman, seated in the foreground, and behind them a row of wind-blown promenaders, dashingly indicated against a lively sky.

'Jasper and me,' Julia said, 'on board the *Oriana*. We adore it. Do you paint?'

'Luckily, I don't even try.'

'A policeman, perhaps?'

'Not even that, I'm afraid. An unnatural son.'

'Jasper,' said his wife, 'is a mathematician and is writing a book about the binomial theorem, but you musn't say I said so because he doesn't care to have it known. Selina, darling, one more face like that and out you go before the pudding, which is strawberries and cream.'

Selina, with the aid of her fingers, had dragged down the corners of her mouth, slitted her eyes and leered across the table at Miss Harkness. She let her face snap back into normality, and then lounged in her chair sinking her chin on her chest and rolling her eyes. Her sister, Julietta, was consumed with laughter.

'Aren't children awful,' Julia asked, 'when they set out to be witty? Yesterday at luncheon Julietta said: "My pud's made of mud," and they both laughed themselves sick. Jasper and I were made quite miserable by it.'

'It won't last,' Ricky assured her.

'It had better not.' She leant towards him. He caught a whiff of her scent, became startlingly aware of her thick immaculate skin and felt an extraordinary stillness come over him.

'So far, so good, wouldn't you say?' she breathed. 'I mean – at least she's not cutting up rough.'

'She's eating quite well,' Ricky muttered.

Julia gave him a look of radiant approval. He was uplifted. 'Gosh!' he thought. 'Oh, gosh, what is all this?'

It was with a sensation of having been launched upon unchartered seas that he took his leave of the Pharamonds and returned to his lodging in the village.

'That's an upsetting lady,' thought Ricky. 'A very lovely and upsetting lady.'

II

The fishing village of Deep Cove was on the north coast of the island: a knot of cottages clustered round an unremarkable bay. There was a general store and post office, a church and a pub: the Cod-and-Bottle. A van drove over to Montjoy on the south coast with the catch of fish when there was one. Montjoy, the only town on the island, was a tourist resort with three smart hotels. The Cove was eight miles away, but not many Montjoy tourists came to see it because there were no 'attractions', and it lay off the main road. Tourists did, however, patronize Leathers, the riding school and horse-hiring establishment run by the Harknesses. This was situated a mile out of Deep Cove and lay between it and the Pharamonds' house which was called L'Esperance, and had been in the possession of the family, Jasper had told Ricky, since the mid-eighteenth century. It stood high above the cliffs and could be seen for miles around on a clear day.

Ricky had hired a push-bicycle and had left it inside the drive gates. He jolted back down the lane, spun along the main road in grand style with salt air tingling up his nose and turned into the steep descent to the Cove.

Mr and Mrs Ferrant's stone cottage was on the waterfront; Ricky had an upstairs front bedroom and the use of a suffocating parlour. He preferred to work in his bedroom. He sat at a table in the window, which commanded a view of the harbour, a strip of sand, a jetty and the little fishing fleet when it was at anchor. Seagulls mewed with the devoted persistence of their species in marine radio-drama.

When he came into the passage he heard the thump of Mrs Ferrant's iron in the kitchen and caught the smell of hot cloth. She came out, a handsome dark woman of about thirty-five with black hair drawn into a knot, black eyes and a full figure. In common with most of the islanders, she showed her Gallic heritage.

'You're back, then,' she said. 'Do you fancy a cup of tea?'

'No, thank you very much, Mrs Ferrant. I had an awfully late luncheon.'

'Up above at L'Esperance?'

'That's right.'

'That would be a great spread, and grandly served?'

There was no defining her style of speech. The choice of words had the positive character almost of the West Country but her accent carried the swallowed r's of France. 'They live well up there,' she said.

'It was all very nice,' Ricky murmured. She passed her working-woman's hand across her mouth. 'And they would all be there. All the family?'

'Well, I think so, but I'm not really sure what the whole family consists of.'

'Mr and Mrs Jasper and the children. Young Bruno, when he's not at his schooling.'

'That's right,' he agreed. 'He was there.'

'Would that be all the company?'

'No,' Ricky said, feeling cornered, 'there were Mr and Mrs Louis Pharamond, too.'

'Ah,' she said, after a pause. 'Them.'

Ricky started to move away but she said: 'That would be all, then?'

He found her insistence unpleasing.

'Oh no,' he said, over his shoulder, 'there was another visitor,' and he began to walk down the passage.

'Who might that have been, then?' she persisted.

'A Miss Harkness,' he said shortly.

'What was *she* doing there?' demanded Mrs Ferrant.

'She was lunching,' Ricky said very coldly, and ran upstairs two steps at a time. He heard her slam the kitchen door.

He tried to settle down to work but was unable to do so. The afternoon was a bad time in any case and he'd had two glasses of beer. Julia Pharamond's magnolia face stooped out of his thoughts and came close to him, talking about a pregnant young woman who might as well have been a horse. Louis Pharamond was making a pass at her and the little half-naked Selina pulled faces at all of them. And there, suddenly, like some bucolic fury was Mrs Ferrant: 'You're back, then,' she mouthed. She's going to scream, he thought, and before she could do it, woke up.

He rose, shook himself and looked out of the window. The afternoon sun made sequined patterns on the harbour and enriched the colours of boats and the garments of such people as were abroad in the village. Among them, in a group near the jetty, he recognized his landlord, Mr Ferrant.

Mr Ferrant was the local plumber and general handyman. He possessed a good-looking car and a little sailing-boat with an auxiliary engine in which, Ricky gathered, he was wont to putter round the harbour and occasionally venture quite far out to sea, fishing. Altogether the Ferrants seemed to be very comfortably off. He was a big fellow with a lusty, rather sly look about him but handsome enough with his high colour and clustering curls. Ricky thought that he was probably younger than his wife and wondered if she had to keep an eye on him.

He was telling some story to the other men in the group. They listened with half-smiles, looking at each other out of the corners of their eyes. When he reached his point they broke into laughter and stamped about, doubled in two, with their hands in their trouser pockets. The group broke up. Mr Ferrant turned towards the house, saw Ricky in the window and gave him the slight, sideways jerk of the head which served as a greeting in the Cove. Ricky lifted his hand in return. He watched his landlord approach the house, heard the front door bang and boots going down the passage.

Ricky thought he would now give himself the pleasure of writing a bread-and-butter letter to Julia Pharamond. He made several shots at it but they all looked either affected or laboured. In the end he wrote:

Dear Mrs Pharamond,
It was so kind of you to have me and I did enjoy myself so *very* much.
With many thanks,
Ricky.
PS. I do hope your other visitor has settled in nicely.

He decided to go out and post it. He had arrived only last evening in the village and had yet to explore it properly.

There wasn't a great deal to explore. The main street ran along the front, and steep little cobbled lanes led off it through ranks of cottages, of which the one on the corner, next door to the Ferrants', turned out to be the local police station. The one shop there was, Mercer's Drapery and General Suppliers, combined the functions of post office, grocery, hardware, clothing, stationery and toy shops. Outside hung ranks of duffle coats, pea-jackets, oilskins and sweaters, all strung above secretive windows beyond which one could make out further offerings set out in a dark interior. Ricky was filled with an urge to buy. He turned in at the door and sustained a sharp jab below the ribs.

He swung round to find himself face to face with a wild luxuriance of hair, dark spectacles, a floral shirt, beads and fringes.

'Yow!' said Ricky, and clapped a hand to his waist. 'What's that for?'

A voice behind the hair said something indistinguishable. A gesture was made, indicating a box slung from the shoulder, a box of a kind very familiar to Ricky.

'I was turning round, wasn't I,' the voice mumbled.

'OK,' said Ricky. 'No bones broken. I hope.'

'Hurr,' said the voice, laughing dismally.

Its owner lurched past Ricky and slouched off down the street, the paintbox swinging from his shoulder.

'Very careless, that was,' said Mr Mercer, the solitary shopman, emerging from the shadows. 'I don't care for that type of behaviour. Can I interest you in anything?'

Ricky, though still in pain, could be interested in a dark-blue polo-necked sweater that carried a label 'Hand-knitted locally. Very special offer'.

'That looks a good kind of sweater,' he said.

'Beautiful piece of work, sir. Mrs Ferrant is in a class by herself.'

'Mrs Ferrant?'

'Quite so, sir. You are accommodated there, I believe. The pullover,' Mr Mercer continued, 'would be your size, I'm sure. Would you care to try?'

Ricky did try and not only bought the sweater but also a short blue coat of a nautical cut that went very well with it. He decided to wear his purchases.

He walked along the main street, which stopped abruptly at a flight of steps leading down to the strand. At the foot of these steps, with an easel set up before him, a palette on his arm and his paint-box open at his feet, stood the man he had encountered in the shop.

He had his back towards Ricky and was laying swathes of colour across a large canvas. These did not appear to bear any relation to the prospect before him. As Ricky watched, the painter began to superimpose in heavy black outline, a female nude with minuscule legs, a vast rump and no head. Having done this he fell back a step or two, paused, and then made a dart at his canvas and slashed down a giant fowl taking a peck at the nude. Leda, Ricky decided, and, therefore, the swan.

He was vividly reminded of the sketches pinned to the drawing-room wall at L'Esperance. He wondered what his mother, whose work was very far from being academic, would have had to say about this picture. He decided that it lacked integrity.

The painter seemed to think it was completed. He scraped his palette and returned it and his brushes to the box. He then fished out a packet of cigarettes and a matchbox, turned his back to the sea-breeze and saw Ricky.

For a second or two he seemed to lower menacingly, but the growth of facial hair was so luxuriant that it hid all expression. Dark glasses gave him a look of some dubious character on the Côte d'Azur.

Ricky said: 'Hullo, again. I hope you don't mind my looking on for a moment.'

There was movement in the beard and whiskers and a dull sound. The painter had opened his matchbox and found it empty.

'Got a light?' Ricky thought must have been said.

He descended the steps and offered his lighter. The painter used it and returned to packing up his gear.

'Do you find,' Ricky asked, fishing for something to say that wouldn't be utterly despised, 'do you find this place stimulating? For painting, I mean.'

'At least,' the voice said, 'it isn't bloody picturesque. I get power from it. It works for me.'

'Could I have seen some of your things up at L'Esperance – the Pharamonds' house?'

He seemed to take another long stare at Ricky and then said: 'I sold a few things to some woman the other day. Street show in

Montjoy. A white sort of woman with black hair. Talked a lot of balls, of course. They always do. But she wasn't bad, figuratively speaking. Worth the odd grope.'

Ricky suddenly felt inclined to kick him.

'Oh, well,' he said. 'I'll be moving on.'

'You staying here?'

'Yes.'

'For long?'

'I don't know,' he said, turning away.

The painter seemed to be one of those people whose friendliness increases in inverse ratio to the warmth of its reception.

'What's your hurry?' he asked.

'I've got some work to do,' Ricky said.

'Work?'

'That's right. Good evening to you.'

'You write, don't you?'

'Try to,' he said over his shoulder.

The young man raised his voice. 'That's what Gil Ferrant makes out, anyway. He reckons you write.'

Ricky walked on without further comment.

On the way back he reflected that it was highly possible every person in the village knew by this time that he lodged with the Ferrants – and tried to write.

So he returned to the cottage and tried.

He had his group of characters. He knew how to involve them, one with the other, but so far he didn't know where to put them: they hovered, they floated. He found himself moved to introduce among them a woman with a white magnolia face, black hair and eyes and a spluttering laugh.

Mrs Ferrant gave him his evening meal on a tray in the parlour. He asked her about the painter and she replied in an off-hand, slighting manner that he was called Sydney Jones and had a 'terrible old place up to back of Fisherman's Steps'.

'He lives here, then?' said Ricky.

'He's a foreigner,' she said, dismissing him, 'but he's been in the Cove a while.'

'Do you like his painting?'

'My Louis can do better.' Her Louis was a threatening child of about ten.

As she walked out with his tray she said: 'That's a queer old sweater you're wearing.'

'I think it's a jolly good one,' he called after her. He heard her give a little grunt and thought she added something in French.

Visited by a sense of well-being, he lit his pipe and strolled down to the Cod-and-Bottle.

Nobody had ever tried to tart up the Cod-and-Bottle. It was unadulterated pub. In the bar the only decor was a series of faded photographs of local worthies and a map of the island. A heavily-pocked dartboard hung on the wall and there was a shove-ha'penny at the far end of the bar. In an enormous fireplace, a pile of driftwood blazed a good-smelling welcome.

The bar was full of men, tobacco smoke and the fumes of beer. A conglomerate of male voices, with their overtones of local dialect, engulfed Ricky as he walked in. Ferrant was there, his back propped against the bar, one elbow resting on it, his body curved in a classic pose that was sexually explicit, and, Ricky felt, deliberately contrived. When he saw Ricky he raised his pint-pot and gave him that sidelong wag of his head. He had a coterie of friends about him.

The barman who, as Ricky was to learn, was called Bob Maistre, was the landlord of the Cod-and-Bottle. He served Ricky's pint of bitter with a flourish.

There was an empty chair in the corner and Ricky made his way to it. From here he was able to maintain the sensation of being an onlooker.

A group of dart players finished their game and moved over to the bar, revealing, to Ricky's unenthusiastic gaze, Sydney Jones, the painter, slumped at a table in a far corner of the room with his drink before him. Ricky looked away quickly, hoping that he had not been spotted.

A group of fresh arrivals came between them: fishermen, by their conversation. Ferrant detached himself from the bar and lounged over to them. There followed a jumble of conversation, most of it incomprehensible. Ricky was to learn that the remnants of a patois that had grown out of a Norman dialect, itself long vanished, could still be heard among the older islanders.

Ferrant left the group and strolled over to Ricky.

'Evening, Mr Alleyn,' he said. 'Getting to know us?'

'Hoping to, Mr Ferrant,' Ricky said.

'Quiet enough for you?'

'That's what I like.'

'Fancy that now, what you like, eh?'

His manner was half bantering, half indifferent. He stayed a minute or so longer, took one or two showy pulls at his beer, said: 'Enjoy yourself, then,' turned and came face to face with Mr Sydney Jones.

'Look what's come up in my catch,' he said. He fetched Mr Jones a shattering clap on the back and returned to his friends.

Mr Jones evidently eschewed all conventional civilities. He sat down at the table, extended his legs and seemed to gaze at nothing in particular. A shout of laughter greeted Ferrant's return to the bar and drowned any observation that, by a movement of his head, Mr Jones would seem to have offered.

'Sorry,' Ricky said. 'I can't hear you.'

He slouched across the table and the voice came through.

'Care to come up to my pad?' it invited.

There was nothing, at the moment, that Ricky fancied less.

'That's very kind of you,' he said. 'One of these days I'd like to see some of your work, if I may.'

The voice said, with what seemed to be an imitation of Ricky's accent, 'Not "one of these days". Now.'

'Oh,' Ricky said, temporizing, 'now? Well – '

'You won't catch anything,' Mr Jones sneered loudly. 'If that's what you're afraid of.'

'Oh God!' Ricky thought. 'Now he's insulted. What a bloody bore.'

He said: 'My dear man, I don't for a moment suppose anything of the sort.'

Jones emptied his pint-pot and got to his feet.

'Fair enough,' he said. 'We'll push off, then.'

And without another glance at Ricky he walked out of the bar.

It was dark outside and chilly, with a sea-nip in the air and misty haloes round the few street lamps along the front. The high tide slapped against the sea-wall.

They walked in silence as far as the place where Ricky had seen Mr Jones painting in the afternoon. Here they turned left into deep shadow and began to climb what seemed to be an interminable flight of wet, broken-down steps, between cottages that grew farther apart and finally petered out altogether.

Ricky's right foot slid under him, he lurched forward and snatched at wet grass on a muddy bank.

'Too rough for you?' sneered – or seemed to sneer – Mr Jones.

'Not a bit of it,' Ricky jauntily replied.

'Watch it. I'll go first.'

They were on some kind of very wet and very rough path. Ricky could only just see his host, outlined against the dim glow of what seemed to be dirty windows.

He was startled by a prodigious snort followed by squelching foot-steps close at hand.

'What the hell's that?' Ricky exclaimed.

'It's a horse,' Mr Jones tossed off.

The invisible horse blew down its nostrils.

They arrived at the windows and at a door. Mr Jones gave the door a kick and it ground noisily open. It had a dirty parody of a *portière* on the inside.

Without an invitation or, indeed, any kind of comment, he went in, leaving Ricky to follow.

He did so, and was astonished to find himself face to face with Miss Harkness.

CHAPTER 2

Syd Jones's Pad and Montjoy

Ricky heard a voice that might have been anybody's but his saying:

'Oh, hullo. Good evening. We meet again. Ha-ha.'

She looked at him with contempt. He said to Mr Jones:

'We met at luncheon up at L'Esperance.'

'Oh Christ!' Mr Jones said in a tone of utter disgust. And to Miss Harkness, 'What the hell were you doing up there?'

'Nothing,' she mumbled. 'I came away.'

'So I should bloody hope. Had they got some things of mine up there?'

'Yes.'

He grunted and disappeared through a door at the far end of the room. Ricky attempted a conversation with Miss Harkness but got nowhere with it. She said something inaudible and retired upon a record-player where she made a choice and released a cacophony.

Mr Jones returned. He dropped on to a sort of divan bed covered with what looked like a horse-rug. He seemed to be inexplicably excited.

'Take a chair,' he yelled at Ricky.

Ricky took an armchair, misjudging the distance between his person and the seat, which, having lost its springs, thudded heavily on the floor. He landed in a ludicrous position, his knees level with his ears. Mr Jones and Miss Harkness burst into raucous laughter. Ricky painfully joined in – and they immediately stopped.

He stretched out his legs and began to look about him.

As far as he could make out in the restricted lighting provided by two naked and dirty bulbs, he was in the front of a dilapidated cottage whose rooms had been knocked together. The end where he found himself was occupied by a bench bearing a conglomeration of painter's materials. Canvases were ranged along the walls including a work which seemed to have been inspired by Miss Harkness herself or at least by her breeches, which were represented with unexpected realism.

The rest of the room was occupied by the divan bed, chairs, a filthy sink, a colour television and a stereophonic record-player. A certain creeping smell as of defective drainage was overlaid by the familiar pungency of turpentine, oil and lead.

Ricky began to ask himself a series of unanswerable questions. Why had Miss Harkness decided against L'Esperance? Was Mr Jones the father of her child? How did Mr Jones contrive to support an existence combining extremes of squalor with colour television and a highly sophisticated record-player? How good or how bad was Mr Jones's painting?

As if in answer to this last conundrum, Mr Jones got up and began to put a succession of canvases on the easel, presumably for Ricky to look at.

This was a familiar procedure for Ricky. For as long as he could remember, young painters fortified by an introduction or propelled by their own hardihood, would bring their works to his mother and prop them up for her astringent consideration. Ricky hoped he had learnt to look at pictures in the right way, but he had never learned to talk easily about them and in his experience the painters themselves, good or bad, were as a rule extremely inarticulate. Perhaps, in this respect, Mr Jones's formidable silences were merely occupational characteristics.

But what would Troy, Ricky's mother, have said about the paintings? Mr Jones had skipped through a tidy sequence of styles. As representation retired before abstraction and abstraction yielded to collage and collage to surrealism, Ricky fancied he could hear her crisp dismissal: 'Not much cop, I'm afraid, poor chap.'

The exhibition and the pop music came to an end and Mr Jones's high spirits seemed to die with them. In the deafening silence that followed Ricky felt he had to speak. He said: 'Thank you very much for letting me see them.'

'Don't give me that,' said Mr Jones, yawning hideously. 'Obviously you haven't understood what I'm doing.'

'I'm sorry.'

'Stuff it. You smoke?'

'If you mean what I think you mean, no, I don't.'

'I didn't mean anything.'

'My mistake,' Ricky said.

'You ever take a trip?'

'No,'

'Bloody smug, aren't we?'

'Think so?' Ricky said, and not without difficulty struggled to his feet. Miss Harkness was fully extended on the divan bed and was possibly asleep.

Mr Jones said: 'I suppose you think you know what you like.'

'Why not? Anyway, that's a pretty crummy old crack, isn't it?'

'Do you ever look at anything that's not in the pretty peep department?'

'Such as?'

'Oh, you wouldn't know,' Mr Jones said. 'Such as Troy. *Does* the name Troy mean anything to you, by the way?'

'Look,' Ricky said, 'it really is bad luck for you and I can't answer without making it sound like a pay-off line. But, yes, the name Troy does mean quite a lot to me. She's – I feel I ought to say "wait for it, wait for it" – she's my mother.'

Mr Jones's jaw dropped. This much could be distinguished by a change of direction in his beard. There were, too, involuntary movements of the legs and arms. He picked up a large tube of paint which he appeared to scrutinize closely. Presently he said in a voice which was pitched unnaturally high:

'I couldn't be expected to know that, could I?'

'Indeed, you couldn't.'

'As a matter of fact, I've really gone through my Troy phase. You won't agree, of course, but I'm afraid I feel she's painted herself out.'

'Are you?'

Mr Jones dropped the tube of paint on the floor.

Ricky picked it up.

'Jerome et Cie,' he said. 'They're a new firm, aren't they? I think they sent my Mum some specimens to try. Do you get it direct from France?'

Jones took it from him.

'I generally use acrylic,' he said.

'Well,' Ricky said, 'I think I'll seek my virtuous couch. It was nice of you to ask me in.'

They faced each other as two divergent species in a menagerie might do.

'Anyway,' Ricky said, 'we do both speak English, don't we?'

'You reckon?' said Mr Jones. And after a further silence: 'Oh Christ, forget the lot and have a beer.'

'I'll do that thing,' said Ricky.

II

To say that after this exchange all went swimmingly at Mr Jones's pad would not be an accurate account of that evening's strange entertainment but at least the tone became less acrimonious. Indeed, Mr Jones developed high spirits of a sort and instructed Ricky to call him Syd. He was devoured by curiosity about Ricky's mother, her approach to her work and – this was a tricky one – whether she took pupils. Ricky found this behavioural change both touching and painful.

Miss Harkness took no part in the conversation but moodily produced bottled beer of which she consumed rather a lot. It emerged that the horse Ricky had shrunk from in the dark was her mount. So, he supposed, she would not spend the night at Syd's pad, but would ride, darkling, to the stables or – was it possible? – all the way to L'Esperance and the protection, scarcely, it seemed, called for, of the Pharamonds.

By midnight Ricky knew that Syd was a New Zealander by birth, which accounted for certain habits of speech. He had left his native soil at the age of seventeen and had lived in his pad for a year. He did some sort of casual labour at Leathers, the family riding-stables to which Miss Harkness was attached but from which she seemed to have been evicted.

'He mucks out,' said Miss Harkness in a solitary burst of conversation and, for no reason that Ricky could divine, gave a hoarse laugh.

It transpired that Syd occasionally visited St Pierre-des-Roches, the nearest port on the Normandy coast to which there was a weekly ferry service.

At a quarter to one Ricky left the pad, took six paces into the night and fell flat on his face in the mud. He could hear Miss Harkness's horse giving signs of equine consternation.

The village was fast asleep under a starry sky, the sound of the night tide rose and fell uninterrupted by Ricky's rubber-shod steps on the cobbled front. Somewhere out on the harbour a solitary light bobbed, and he wondered if Mr Ferrant was engaged in his hobby of night fishing. He paused to watch it and realized that it was nearer inshore than he had imagined and coming closer. He could hear the rhythmic dip of oars.

There was an old bench facing the front. Ricky thought he would wait there and join Mr Ferrant, if indeed it was he, when he landed.

The light vanished round the far side of the jetty. Ricky heard the gentle thump of the boat against a pier followed by irregular sounds of oars being stowed and objects shifted. A man with a lantern rose into view and made fast the mooring lines. He carried a pack on his back and began to walk down the jetty. He was too far away to be identified.

Ricky was about to get up and go to meet him when, as if by some illusionist's trick, there was suddenly a second figure beside the first. Ricky remained where he was, in shadow.

The man with the lantern raised it to the level of his face, and Ricky saw that he was indeed Ferrant, caught in a Rembrandt-like golden effulgence. Ricky kept very still, feeling that to approach them would be an intrusion. They came towards him. Ferrant said something indistinguishable and the other replied in a voice that was not that of the locals: 'OK, but watch it. Good night.' They separated. The newcomer walked rapidly away towards the turning that led up to the main road and Ferrant crossed the street to his own house.

Ricky ran lightly and soundlessly after him. He was fitting his key in the lock and had his back turned.

'Good morning, Mr Ferrant,' Ricky said.

He spun round with an oath.

'I'm sorry,' Ricky stammered, himself jolted by this violent reaction. 'I didn't mean to startle you.'

Ferrant said something in French, Ricky thought, and laughed, a little breathlessly.

'Have you been making a night of it, then?' he said, 'Not much chance of that in the Cove.'

'I've been up at Syd Jones's.'

'Have you now,' said Ferrant. 'Fancy that.' He pushed the door open and stood back for Ricky to enter.

'Good night then, Mr Alleyn,' said Ferrant.

As Ricky entered he heard in the distance the sound of a car starting. It seemed to climb the steep lane out of Deep Cove, and at that moment he realized that the second man on the wharf had been Louis Pharamond.

The house was in darkness. Ricky crept upstairs making very little noise. Just before he shut his bedroom door he heard another door close quite near at hand.

For a time he lay awake listening to the sound of the tide and thinking what a long time it seemed since he arrived in Deep Cove. He drifted into a doze, and found the scarcely-formed persons of the book he hoped to write, taking upon themselves characteristics of the Pharamonds, of Sydney Jones, of Miss Harkness and the Ferrants, so that he scarcely knew which was which.

The next morning was cold and brilliant with a March wind blowing through a clear sky. Mrs Ferrant gave Ricky a grey mullet for his breakfast, the reward, it emerged, of her husband's night excursion.

By ten o'clock he had settled down to a determined attack on his work.

He wrote in longhand, word after painful word. He wondered why on earth he couldn't set about this job with something resembling a design. Once or twice he thought possibilities – the ghosts of promise – began to show themselves. There was one character, a woman, who had stepped forward and presented herself to be written about. An appreciable time went by before he realized he was dealing with Julia Pharamond.

It came as quite a surprise to find that he had been writing for two hours. He eased his fingers and filled his pipe. I'm feeling better, he thought.

Something spattered against the window-pane. He looked out and down, and there, with his face turned up, was Jasper Pharamond.

'Good morning to you,' Jasper called in his alto voice, 'are you *incommunicado*? Is this a liberty?'

'Of course not. Come up.'

'Only for a moment.'

He heard Mrs Ferrant go down the passage, the door open and Jasper's voice on the stairs: 'It's all right, thank you, Marie. I'll find my way.'

Ricky went out to the landing and watched Jasper come upstairs. He pretended to make heavy weather of the ascent, rocking his shoulders from side to side and thumping his feet.

'Really!' he panted when he arrived. 'This is the authentic setting. Attic stairs and the author embattled at the top. You must be sure to eat enough. May I come in?'

He came in, sat on Ricky's bed with a pleasant air of familiarity, and waved his hand at the table and papers. 'The signs are propitious,' he said.

'The place is propitious,' Ricky said warmly. 'And I'm very much obliged to you for finding it. Did you go tramping about the village and climbing interminable stairs?'

'No, no. Julia plumped for Marie Ferrant.'

'You knew her already?'

'She was in service up at L'Esperance before she married. We're old friends,' said Jasper lightly.

Ricky thought that might explain Mrs Ferrant's curiosity.

'I've come with an invitation,' Jasper said. 'It's just that we thought we'd go over to Montjoy to dine and trip a measure on Saturday and we wondered if it would amuse you to come.'

Ricky said: 'I ought to say no, but I won't. I'd love to.'

'We must find somebody nice for you.'

'It won't by any chance be Miss Harkness?'

'My dear!' exclaimed Jasper excitedly. 'Apropos the Harkness! Great drama! Well, great drama in a negative sense. She's gone!'

'When?'

'Last night. Before dinner. She prowled down the drive, disappeared and never came back. Bruno wonders if she jumped over the cliff – too awful to contemplate.'

'You may set your minds at rest,' said Ricky. 'She didn't do that.' And he told Jasper all about his evening with Syd Jones and Miss Harkness.

'Well!' said Jasper. 'There you are. What a very *farouche* sort of girl. No doubt the painter is the partner of her shame and the father of her unborn babe. What's he like? His work, for instance?'

'You ought to be the best judge of that. You've got some of it pinned on your drawing-room walls.'

'I might have known it!' Jasper cried dramatically. 'Another of Julia's finds! She bought them in the street in Montjoy on Market Day. I can't wait to tell her,' Jasper said, rising energetically. 'What fun! No. We must both tell her.'

'Where is she?'

'Down below, in the car. Come and see her, do.'

Ricky couldn't resist the thought of Julia so near at hand. He followed Jasper down the stairs, his heart thumping as violently as if he had run up them.

It was a dashing sports car and Julia looked dashing and expensive to match it. She was in the driver's seat, her gloved hands drooping on the wheel with their gauntlets turned back so that her wrists shone delicately. Jasper at once began to tell about Miss Harkness, inviting Ricky to join in. Ricky thought how brilliantly she seemed to listen and how this air of being tuned-in invested all the Pharamonds. He wondered if they lost interest as suddenly as they acquired it.

When he had answered her questions she said briskly: 'A case, no doubt, of like calling to like. Both of them naturally speechless. No doubt she's gone into residence at the pad.'

'I'm not so sure,' Ricky said. 'Her horse was there, don't forget. It seemed to be floundering about in the dark.'

Jasper said, 'She would hardly leave it like that all night. Perhaps it was only a social call after all.'

'How very odd,' Julia said, 'to think of Miss Harkness in the small hours of the morning, riding through the Cove. I wonder she didn't wake you up.'

'She may not have passed by my window.'

'Well,' Julia said, 'I'm beginning all of a sudden to weary of Miss Harkness. It was very boring of her to be so rude, walking out on us like that.'

'It'd have been a sight more boring if she'd stayed, however,' Jasper pointed out.

There was a clatter of shoes on the cobblestones and the Ferrant son, Louis, came running by on his way home from school. He slowed up when he saw the car and dragged his feet, staring at it and walking backwards.

'Hullo, young Louis,' Ricky said.

He didn't answer. His sloe eyes looked out of a pale face under a dark thatch of hair. He backed slowly away, turned and suddenly ran off down the street.

'That's Master Ferrant, that was,' said Ricky.

Neither of the Pharamonds seemed to have heard him. For a second or two they looked after the little boy and then Jasper said lightly: 'Dear me! It seems only the other day that his Mum was a bouncing tweeny or parlourmaid, or whatever it was she bounced at.'

'Before my time,' said Julia. 'She's a marvellous laundress and still operates for us. Darling, we're keeping Ricky out here. Who can tell what golden phrase we may have aborted. Super that you can come on Saturday, Ricky.'

'Pick you up at eightish,' cried Jasper, bustling into the car. They were off, and Ricky went back to his room.

But not, at first, to work. He seemed to have taken the Pharamonds upstairs, and with them little Louis Ferrant, so that the room was quite crowded with white faces, black hair and brilliant pitch-ball eyes.

III

Montjoy might have been on another island from the Cove and in a different sea. Once a predominantly French fishing village, it was now a fashionable place with marinas, a yacht club, surfing, striped umbrellas and, above all, the celebrated Hotel Montjoy itself with its Stardust Ballroom, whose plateglass dome and multiple windows could be seen, airily glowing, from far out to sea. Here, one dined and danced expensively to a famous band, and here, on Saturday night at a window-table sat the Pharamonds, Ricky and a girl called Susie de Waite.

They ate lobster salad and drank champagne. Ricky talked to and danced with Susie de Waite as was expected of him and tried not to look too long and too often at Julia Pharamond.

Julia was in great form, every now and then letting off the spluttering firework of her laughter. He had noticed at luncheon that she had uninhibited table-manners and ate very quickly. Occasionally she sucked her fingers. Once when he had watched her doing this he found Jasper looking at him with amusement.

'Julia's eating habits,' he remarked, 'are those of a partially-trained marmoset.'

'Darling,' said Julia, waggling the sucked fingers at him, 'I love you better than life itself.'

'If only,' Ricky thought, 'she would look at me like that' – and immediately she did, causing his unsophisticated heart to bang at his ribs and the blood mount to the roots of his hair.

Ricky considered himself pretty well adjusted to the contemporary scene. But, he thought, every adventure that he had experienced so far had been like a bit of fill-in dialogue leading to the entry of the star. And here, beyond all question, she was.

She waltzed now with her cousin Louis. He was an accomplished dancer and Julia followed him effortlessly. They didn't talk to each other, Ricky noticed. They just floated together – beautifully.

Ricky decided that he didn't perhaps quite like Louis pharamond. He was too smooth. And anyway, what had he been up to in the Cove at one o'clock in the morning?

The lights were dimmed to a black-out. From somewhere in the dome, balloons, treated to respond to ultraviolet ray, were released in hundreds and jostled uncannily together, filling the ballroom with luminous bubbles. The band reduced itself to the whispering shish-shish of waves on the beach below. The dancers, scarcely moving, resembled those shadows that seem to bob and pulse behind the screen of an inactive television set.

'May we?' Ricky asked Susie de Waite.

He had once heard his mother say that a great deal of his father's success as an investigating officer stemmed from his gift for getting people to talk about themselves. 'It's surprising,' she had said, 'how few of them can resist him.'

'Did you?' her son asked.

'Yes,' Troy said, and after a pause, 'but not for long.'

So Ricky asked Susie de Waite about herself and it was indeed surprising how readily she responded. It was also surprising how unstimulating he found her self-revelations.

And then, abruptly, the evening was set on fire. They came alongside Julia and Louis and Julia called to Ricky.

'Ricky, if you don't dance with me again at once I shall take umbrage.' And then to Louis. 'Goodbye, darling. I'm off.'

And she was in Ricky's arms. The stars in the sky had come reeling down into the ballroom and the sea had got into his eardrums and bliss had taken up its abode in him for the duration of a waltz.

They left at two o'clock in the large car that belonged, it seemed, to the Louis Pharamonds. Louis drove with Susie de Waite next to him and Bruno on her far side. Ricky found himself at the back between Julia and Carlotta, and Jasper was on the tip-up seat facing them.

When they were clear of Montjoy on the straight road to the Cove, Louis asked Susie if she'd like to steer, and on her rapturously accepting, put his arm round her. She took the wheel.

'Is this all right?' Carlotta asked at large. 'Is she safe?'

'It's fantastic,' gabbled Susie. 'Safe as houses. Promise! Ow! Sorry!'

She really is rather an ass of a girl, Ricky thought.

Julia picked up Ricky's hand and then Carlotta's. 'Was it a pleasant party?' she asked, gently tapping their knuckles together. 'Have you liked it?'

Ricky said he'd adored it. Julia's hand was still in his. He wondered whether it would be all right to kiss it under, as it were, her husband's nose, but felt he lacked the style. She gave his hand a little squeeze, dropped it, leant forward and kissed her husband.

'Sweetie,' Julia cried extravagantly, 'you *are* such heaven! Do look, Ricky, that's Leathers up there where Miss Harkness does her stuff. We really must all go riding with her before it's too late.'

'What do you mean,' her husband asked, 'by your "too late"?'

'Too late for Miss Harkness, of course. Unless, of course, she does it on purpose, but that would be very silly of her. Too silly for words,' said Julia severely.

Susie de Waite let out a scream that modulated into a giggle. The car shot across the road and back again.

Carlotta said sharply: 'Louis, do keep your techniques for another setting.'

Louis gave what Ricky thought of as a bedroom laugh, cuddled Susie up and closed his hand over hers on the wheel.

'Behave,' he said. 'Bad girl.'

They arrived at the lane that descended precipitously into the Cove. Louis took charge, drove pretty rapidly down it and pulled up in front of the Ferrant cottage.

'Here we are,' he said. 'Abode of the dark yet passing-fair Marie. Is she still dark and passing-fair, by the way?'

Nobody answered.

Louis said very loudly: 'Any progeny? Oh, but of course. I forgot.'

'Shut up,' Jasper said, in a tone of voice that Ricky hadn't heard from him before.

He and Julia and Carlotta together said good night to Ricky, who by this time was outside the car. He shut the door as quietly as he could and stood back. Louis reversed noisily and much too fast. He called out something that sounded like: 'Give her my love.' The car shot away in low gear and roared up the lane.

Upstairs on the dark landing Ricky could hear Ferrant snoring prodigiously and pictured him with his red hair and high colour and his mouth wide open. Evidently he had not gone fishing that night.

IV

In her studio in Chelsea, Troy shoved her son's letter into the pocket of her painting smock and said:

'He's fallen for Julia Pharamond.'

'Has he, now?' said Alleyn. 'Does he announce it in so many words?'

'No, but he manages to drag her into every other sentence of his letter. Take a look.'

Alleyn read his son's letter with a lifted eyebrow. 'I see what you mean,' he said presently.

'Oh well,' Troy muttered. 'It'll be one girl and then another, I suppose, and then, with any luck, just one and that a nice one. In the meantime, she's very attractive. Isn't she?'

'A change from dirty feet, jeans, and beads in the soup, at least.'

'She's beautiful,' said Troy.

'He may tire of her heavenly inconsequence.'

'You think so?'

'Well, I would. They seem to be taking quite a lot of trouble over him. Kind of them.'

'He's a jolly nice young man,' Troy said firmly.

Alleyn chuckled and read on in silence.

'Why,' Troy asked presently, 'do you suppose they live on that island?'

'Dodging taxation. They're clearly a very clannish lot. The other two are there.'

'The cousins that came on board at Acapulco?'

'Yes,' Alleyn said. 'It was a sort of enclave of cousins.'

'The Louis's seem to live with the Jaspers, don't they?'

'Looks like it.' Alleyn turned a page of the letter. 'Well,' he said, 'besotted or not, he seems to be writing quite steadily.'

'I wonder if his stuff's any good, Rory? Do you wonder?'

'Of course I do,' he said, and went to her.

'It can be tough going, though, can't it?'

'Didn't you swan through a similar stage?'

'Now I come to think of it,' Troy said, squeezing a dollop of flake white on her palette, 'I did. I wouldn't tell my parents anything about my young men and I wouldn't show them anything I painted. I can't imagine why.'

'You gave me the full treatment when I first saw you, didn't you? About your painting?'

'Did I? No, I didn't. Shut up,' said Troy, laughing. She began to paint.

'That's the new brand of colour, isn't it? Jerome et Cie?' said Alleyn, and picked up a tube.

'They sent it for free. Hoping I'd talk about it, I suppose. The white and the earth colours are all right but the primaries aren't too hot. Rather odd, isn't it, that Rick should mention them?'

'Rick? Where?'

'You haven't got to the bit about his new painting chum and the pregnant equestrienne.'

'For the love of Mike!' Alleyn grunted and read on. 'I must say,' he said, when he'd finished, 'he *can* write, you know, darling. He can indeed.'

Troy put down her palette, flung her arm round him and pushed her head into his shoulder. 'He'll do us nicely,' she said, 'won't he? But it was quite a coincidence, wasn't it? About Jerome et Cie and their paint?'

'In a way,' said Alleyn, 'I suppose it was.'

V

On the morning after the party, Ricky apologized to Mrs Ferrant for the noisy return in the small hours, and although Mr Ferrant's snores were loud in his memory, said he was afraid he had been disturbed.

'It'd take more than that to rouse *him*,' she said. She never referred to her husband by name. '*I* heard you. Not *you* but him. Pharamond. The older one.'

She gave Ricky a sideways look that he couldn't fathom. Derisive? Defiant? Sly? Whatever lay behind her manner, it was certainly not that of an ex-domestic cook, however emancipated. She left him with the feeling that the corner of a curtain had been lifted and dropped before he could see what lay beyond it.

During the week he saw nothing of the Pharamonds except in one rather curious incident on the Thursday evening. Feeling the need of a change of scene, he had wheeled his bicycle up the steep lane, pedalled along the road to Montjoy and at a point not far from L'Esperance had left his machine by the wayside and walked towards the cliff-edge.

The evening was brilliant and the Channel, for once, blue with patches of bedazzlement. He sat down with his back to a warm rock at a place where the cliff opened into a ravine through which a rough path led between clumps of wild broom, down to the sea. The air was heady and a salt breeze felt for his lips. A lark sang and Ricky would have liked a girl – any girl – to come up through the broom from the sea with a reckless face and the sun in her eyes.

Instead, Louis Pharamond came up the path. He was below Ricky, who looked at the top of his head. He leant forward, climbing, swinging his arms, his chin down.

Ricky didn't want to encounter Louis. He shuffled quickly round the rock and lay on his face. He heard Louis pass by on the other side. Ricky waited until the footsteps died away, wondering at his own behaviour.

He was about to get up when he heard a displaced stone roll down the path. The crown of a head and the top of a pair of shoulders appeared below him. Grossly foreshortened though they were, there was no mistaking who they belonged to. Ricky sank down behind his rock and let Miss Harkness, in her turn, pass him by.

He rode back to the cottage.

He was gradually becoming *persona grata* at the pub. He was given a 'good evening' when he came in and warmed up to when, his work having prospered that day, he celebrated by standing drinks all round. Bill Prentice, the fish-truck driver, offered to give him a lift into Montjoy if ever he fancied it. They settled for the coming morning. It was then that Miss Harkness came into the bar alone.

Her entrance was followed by a shuffling of feet and by the exchange of furtive smiles. She ordered a glass of port. Ferrant, leaning back against the bar in his favourite pose, looked her over. He said something that Ricky couldn't hear and raised a guffaw. She smiled slightly. Ricky realized that with her entrance the atmosphere in the Cod-and-Bottle had become that of the stud. And that not a man there was unaware of it. So this, he thought, is what Miss Harkness is about.

The next morning, very early, Ricky tied his bicycle to the roof of the fish-truck and himself climbed into the front seat.

He was taken aback to find that Syd Jones was to be a fellow-passenger. Here he came, hunched up in a dismal mackintosh, with his paintbox slung over his shoulder, a plastic carrier-bag and a large and superior suitcase which seemed to be unconscionably heavy.

'Hullo,' Ricky said. 'Are you moving into the Hotel Montjoy, with your grand suitcase?'

'Why the hell would I do that?'

'All right, all right, let it pass. Sorry.'

'I'm afraid I don't fall about at upper-middle-class humour.'

'My mistake,' said Ricky. 'I do better in the evenings.'

'I haven't noticed it.'

'You may be right. Here comes Bill. Where are you going to put your case? On the roof with my upper-middle-class bike?'

'In front. Shift your feet. Watch it.'

He heaved the case up, obviously with an effort, pushed it along the floor under Ricky's legs and climbed up. Bill Prentice, redolent of fish, mounted the driver's seat, Syd nursed his paintbox and Ricky was crammed in between them.

It was a sparkling morning. The truck rattled up the steep lane, they came out into sunshine at the top and banged along the main road to Montjoy. Ricky was in good spirits.

They passed the entry into Leathers with its signboard: 'Riding Stables. Hacks and Ponies for hire. Qualified Instructors.' He wondered if Miss Harkness was up and about. He shouted above the engine to Syd: 'You don't go there every day, do you?'

'Definitely bloody not,' Syd shouted back. It was the first time Ricky had heard him raise his voice.

The road made a blind turn round a dense copse. Bill took it on the wrong side at forty miles an hour.

The windscreen was filled with Miss Harkness on a plunging bay horse, all teeth and eyes and flying hooves. An underbelly and straining girth reared into sight. The brakes shrieked, the truck skidded, the world turned sideways, and the passenger's door flew open. Syd Jones, his paintbox and his suitcase shot out. The van rocked and sickeningly righted itself on the verge in a cloud of dust. The horse could be seen struggling on the ground and its rider on her feet with the reins still in her hands. The engine had stopped and the air was shattered by imprecations – a three-part disharmony from Bill, Syd and, predominantly, Miss Harkness.

Bill turned off the ignition, dragged his hand-brake on, got out and approached Miss Harkness, who told him with oaths to keep off. Without a pause in her stream of abuse she encouraged her mount to clamber to its feet, checked its impulse to bolt and began gently to examine it; her great horny hand passed with infinite delicacy down its trembling legs and heaving barrel. It was, Ricky saw, a wall-eyed horse.

'Keep the hell out of it,' she said softly. 'You'll hear about this.'

She led the horse along the far side of the road and past the truck. It snorted and plunged but she calmed it. When they had gone some distance, she mounted. The sound of its hooves, walking, diminished. Bill began to swear again.

Ricky slid out of the truck on the passenger's side. The paintbox had burst open and its contents were scattered about the grass. The catches on the suitcase had been sprung and the lid had flown back. Ricky saw that it was full of unopened cartons of Jerome et Cie's paints. Syd Jones squatted on the verge, collecting tubes and fitting them back into their compartments.

Ricky stooped to help him.

'Cut that out!' he snarled.

'Very well, you dear little man,' Ricky said, with a strong inclination to throw one at his head. He took a step backwards, felt something give under his heel and looked down. He had trodden on a large tube of vermilion and burst the end open. Paint had spurted over his shoe.

'Oh damn, I'm sorry,' he said. 'I'm most awfully sorry.'

He reached for the depleted tube. It was snatched from under his hand. Syd, on his knees, the tube in his grasp and his fingers reddened, mouthed at him. What he said was short and unprintable.

'Look,' Ricky said. 'I've said I'm sorry. I'll pay for the paint and if you feel like a fight you've only to say so and we'll shape up and make fools of ourselves here and now. How about it?'

Syd was crouched over his task. He mumbled something that might have been 'Forget it.' Ricky, feeling silly, walked round to the other side of the truck. It was being inspected by Bill Prentice with much the same intensity as Miss Harkness had displayed when she examined her horse. The smell of petrol now mingled with the smell of fish.

'She's OK,' Bill said at last and climbed into the driver's seat. 'Silly bitch,' he added, referring to Miss Harkness, and started up the engine.

Syd loomed up on the far side with his suitcase, round which he had buckled his belt. His jeans drooped from his hip-bones as if from a coat-hanger.

'Hang on a sec,' Bill shouted.

He engaged his gear and the truck lurched back on the road. Syd waited. Ricky walked round to the passenger's side. To his astonishment, Syd observed on what sounded like a placatory note: 'Bike's OK, then?'

They climbed on board and the journey continued. Bill's strictures upon Miss Harkness were severe and modified only, Ricky felt, out of consideration for Syd's supposed feelings. The burden of his plaint was that horse-traffic should be forbidden on the roads.

'What was she on about?' he complained. 'The horse was OK.'

'It was Mungo,' Syd offered. 'She's crazy about it. Savage brute of a thing.'

'That so?'

'Bit me. Kicked the old man. He wants to have it destroyed.'

'Is it all right with her?' asked Ricky.

'So she reckons. It's an outlaw with everyone else.'

They arrived at the only petrol station between the Cove and Montjoy. Bill pulled into it for fuel and oil and held the attendant rapt with an exhaustive coverage of the incident.

Syd complained in his dull voice: 'I've got a bloody boat to catch, haven't I?'

Ricky, who was determined not to make advances, looked at his watch and said that there was time in hand.

After an uncomfortable silence Syd said, 'I'm funny about my painting gear. You know? I can't do with anyone else handling it. You know? If anyone else scrounges my paint, you know, borrows some, I can't use that tube again. It's kind of contaminated. Get what I mean?'

Ricky thought that what he seemed to mean was a load of high-falutin' balls, but he gave a tolerant grunt and after a moment or two Syd began to talk. Ricky could only suppose that he was try-ing to make amends. His discourse was obscure but it transpired that he had been given some kind of agency by Jerome et Cie. He was to leave free samples of their paints at certain shops and with a number of well-known painters, in return for which he was given his fare, as much of their products for his own use as he cared to ask for and a small commission on sales. He produced their business card with a note, 'Introducing Mr Sydney Jones', written on it. He showed Ricky the list of painters they had given him. Ricky was not altogether surprised to find his mother's name at the top.

With as ill a grace as could be imagined, he said he supposed Ricky 'wouldn't come at putting the arm on her', which Ricky interpreted as a suggestion that he should give Syd an introduction to his mother.

'When are you going to pay your calls?' Ricky asked.

The next day, it seemed. And it turned out that Syd was spending the night with friends who shared a pad in Battersea. Jerome et Cie had expressed the wish that he should modify his personal appearance.

'Bloody commercial shit,' he said violently. 'Make you vomit, wouldn't it?'

They arrived at the wharves in Montjoy at half past eight. Ricky watched the crates of fish being loaded into the ferry and saw Syd Jones go up the gangplank. He waited until the ferry sailed. Syd had vanished, but at the last moment he re-appeared on deck wearing his awful raincoat and with his paintbox still slung over his shoulder.

Ricky spent a pleasant day in Montjoy and bicycled back to the Cove in the late afternoon.

Rather surprisingly, the Ferrants had a telephone. That evening Ricky put a call through to his parents advising them of the approach of Sydney Jones.

CHAPTER 3

The Gap

'As far as I can see,' Alleyn said, 'he's landing us with a sort of monster.'

'He thinks it might amuse us to meet him after all we've heard.'

'It had better,' Alleyn said mildly.

'It's only for a minute or two.'

'When do you expect him?'

'Some time in the morning, I imagine.'

'What's the betting he stays for luncheon?'

Troy stood before her husband in the attitude that he particularly enjoyed, with her back straight, her hands in the pockets of her painting smock and her chin down rather like a chidden little boy.

'And what's the betting,' he went on, 'my own true love, that before you can say Flake White, he's showing you a little something he's done himself.'

'That,' said Troy grandly, 'would be altogether another pair of boots and I should know how to deal with them. And anyway he told Rick he thinks I've painted myself out.'

'He grows more attractive every second.'

'It was funny about the way he behaved when Rick trod on his vermilion.'

Alleyn didn't answer at once. 'It was, rather,' he said at last. 'Considering he gets the stuff free.'

'Trembling with rage, Rick said, and his beard twitching.'

'Delicious.'

'Oh well,' said Troy, suddenly brisk. 'We can but see.'

'That's the stuff. I must be off.' He kissed her. 'Don't let this Jones fellow make a nuisance of himself,' he said. 'As usual, my patient Penny-lope, there's no telling when I'll be home. Perhaps for lunch or perhaps I'll be in Paris. It's that narcotics case. I'll get them to telephone. Bless you.'

'And you,' said Troy cheerfully.

She was painting a tree in their garden from within the studio. At the heart of her picture was an exquisite little silver birch just starting to burgeon and treated with delicate and detailed realism. But this tree was at the core of its own diffusion a larger and much more stylized version of itself and that, in turn, melted into an abstract of the two trees it enclosed. Alleyn said it was like the unwinding of a difficult case with the abstractions on the outside and the implacable 'thing itself' at the hard centre. He had begged her to stop before she went too far.

She hadn't gone any distance at all when Mr Sydney Jones presented himself.

There was nothing very remarkable, Troy thought, about his appearance. He had a beard, close-cropped, revealing a full, vaguely sensual but indeterminate mouth. His hair was of a medium length and looked clean. He wore a sweater over jeans. Indeed, all that remained of the Syd Jones Ricky had described was his huge silly-sinister pair of black spectacles. He carried a suitcase and a newspaper parcel.

'Hullo,' Troy said, offering her hand. 'You're Sydney Jones, aren't you? Ricky rang up and told us you were coming. Do sit down, won't you?'

'It doesn't matter,' he mumbled, and sniffed loudly. He was sweating.

Troy sat on the arm of a chair. 'Do you smoke?' she said. 'I'm sorry I haven't got any cigarettes but do if you'd like to.'

He put his suitcase and the newspaper parcel down and lit a cigarette. He then picked up his parcel.

'I gather it's about Jerome et Cie's paints, isn't it?' Troy suggested. 'I'd better say that I wouldn't want to change to them and I can't honestly give you a blurb. Anyway I don't do that sort of thing. Sorry.' She waited for a response but he said nothing. 'Rick tells us,' she said, 'that you paint.'

With a gesture so abrupt that it made her jump, he thrust his parcel at her. The newspaper fell away and three canvases tied together with string were exposed.

'Is that,' Troy said, 'some of your work?'

He nodded.

'Do you want me to look at it?'

He muttered.

Made cross by having been startled, Troy said: 'My dear boy, do for pity's sake speak out. You make me feel as if I were giving an imitation of a woman talking to herself. Stick them up there where I can see them.'

With unsteady hands he put them up, one by one, changing them when she nodded. The first was the large painting Ricky had decided was an abstraction of Leda and the Swan. The second was a kaleidoscopic arrangement of shapes in hot browns and raucous blues. The third was a landscape, more nearly representational than the others. Rows of perceptible houses with black, staring windows stood above dark water. There was some suggestion of tactile awareness but no real respect, Troy thought, for the medium.

She said: 'I think I know where we are with this one. Is it St Pierre-des-Roches on the coast of Normandy?'

'Yar,' he said.

'It's the nearest French port to your island, isn't it? Do you often go across?'

'Aw – yar,' he said, fidgeting. 'It turns me on. Or did. I've worked that vein out, as a matter of fact.'

'Really,' said Troy. There was a longish pause. 'Do you mind putting up the first one again. The Leda.'

He did so. Another silence. 'Well,' she said, 'do you want me to say what I think? Or not?'

'I don't mind,' he mumbled, and yawned extensively.

'Here goes, then. I find it impossible to say whether I think you'll develop into a good painter or not. These three things are all derivative. That doesn't matter while you're young: if you've got something of your own, with great pain and infinite determination you will finally prove it. I don't think you've done that so far. I do get something from the Leda thing – a suggestion that you've got a strong sense of rhythm, but it is no more than a suggestion. I don't think you're very self-critical.' She looked hard at him. 'You don't fool about with drugs, do you?' asked Troy.

There was a very long pause before he answered quite loudly, 'No.'

'Good. I only asked because your hands are unsteady and your behaviour erratic, and – ' She broke off. 'Look here,' she said, 'you're *not* well, are you? Sit down. No, don't be silly, sit down.'

He did sit down. He was shaking, sweat had started out under the line of his hair and he was the colour of a peeled banana. He gaped and ran a dreadful tongue round his mouth. She fetched him a glass of water. The dark glasses were askew. He put up his trembling hand to them and they fell off, disclosing a pair of pale ineffectual eyes. Gone was the mysterious Mr Jones.

'I'm all right,' he said.

'I don't think you are.'

'Party. Last night.'

'What sort of party?'

'Aw. A fun thing.'

'I see.'

'I'll be OK.'

Troy made some black coffee and left him to drink it while she returned to her work. The spirit trees began to enclose their absolute inner tree more firmly.

When, at a quarter past one, Alleyn walked into the studio, it was to find his wife at work and an enfeebled young man avidly watching her from an armchair.

'Oh,' said Troy, grandly waving her brush and staring fixedly at Alleyn. 'Hullo, darling. Syd, this is my husband. This is Rick's friend, Syd Jones, Rory. He's shown me some of his work and he's going to stay for luncheon.'

'Well!' Alleyn said, shaking hands. 'This *is* an unexpected pleasure. How are you?'

II

Three days after Ricky's jaunt to Montjoy Julia Pharamond rang him up at lunch-time. He had some difficulty in pulling himself together and attending to what she said.

'You do ride, don't you?' she asked.

'Not at all well.'

'At least you don't fall off?'

'Not very often.'

'There you are, then. Super. All settled.'

'What,' he asked, 'is settled?'

'My plan for tomorrow. We get some Harkness hacks and ride to Bon Accord.'

'I haven't any riding things.'

'No problem. Jasper will lend you any amount. I'm ringing you up while he's out because he'd say I was seducing you away from your book. But I'm not, am I?'

'Yes,' said Ricky, 'you are, and it's lovely,' and heard her splutter.

'Well, anyway,' she said, 'it's all settled. You must leap on your *bicyclette* and pedal up to L'Esperance for breakfast and then we'll all sweep up to the stables. Such fun.'

'Is Miss Harkness coming?'

'No. How can you ask! Before we knew where we were she'd miscarry.'

'If horse-exercise was going to make her do that it would have done so already, I fancy,' said Ricky, and told her about the mishap on the road to Montjoy. Julia was full of exclamations and excitement. 'How,' she said, 'you dared not to ring up and tell us immediately!'

'I thought you'd said she was beginning to be a bore.'

'She's suddenly got interesting again. So she's back at Leathers and reconciled to Mr Harkness?'

'I've no idea.'

'But couldn't you *tell*? Couldn't you *sense* it?'

'How?'

'Well, from her conversation.'

'It consisted exclusively of oaths.'

'I can't wait to survey the scene at Leathers. Will Mr Jones be there mucking-out?'

'He was in London quite recently.'

'In London! Doing what?'

'Lunching with my parents, among other things.'

'You really are *too* provoking. I can see that all sorts of curious things are happening and you're being furtive and sly about them.'

'I promise to disclose all. I'm not even fully persuaded, by the way, that she and Syd Jones *are* lovers.'

'I shall be the judge of that. Here comes Jasper and I'll have to tell him I've seduced you. Goodbye.'

'Which is no more than God's truth,' Ricky shouted fervently. He heard her laugh and hang up the receiver.

The next morning dawned brilliantly, and at half past nine Ricky, dressed in Jasper's spare jodhpurs and boots and his own Ferrant sweater, proposed to take a photograph of the Pharamonds, including the two little girls produced for the purpose. They assembled in a group on the patio. The Pharamonds evidently adored being photographed, especially Louis, who looked almost embarrassingly smooth in breeches, boots, sharp hacking jacket and gloves.

'Louis, darling,' Julia said, surveying him, *'très snob presque cad!* You lack only the polo stick!'

'I don't understand how it is,' Carlotta said, 'but nothing Louis wears ever looks even a day old.'

Ricky thought that this assessment didn't work if applied to Louis's face. His very slight tan looked almost as if it had been laid on, imposing a spurious air of health over a rather dissipated foundation.

'I bought this lot in Acapulco eight years ago,' said Louis.

'I remember. From a dethroned Prince who'd lost his all at the green baize tables,' said Julia.

'My recollection,' Carlotta said, 'is of a *déclassé* gangster but I may be wrong.'

Selina, who had been going through a short repertoire of exhibitionist antics, ignored by her seniors, suddenly flung herself at Louis and hung from his wrist, doubling up her legs and shrieking affectedly.

'You little monster,' he said, 'you've nearly torn off a button,' and examined his sleeve.

Selina walked away with a blank face.

Bruno said, 'Do let's get posed-up for Ricky and then take off for the stables.'

'Let's be ultra-mondains,' Julia decided. She sank into a swinging chaise-longue, dangled an elegantly breeched leg and raised a drooping hand above her head.

Jasper raised it to his lips. 'Madame is enchanting – nay, irresistible – *ce matin*,' he said.

Selina stuck out her tongue.

Bruno, looking impatient, merely stood.

'Thank you,' said Ricky.

They piled into Louis's car and drove to Leathers.

The avenue, a longish one, led to an ugly Victorian house, and continued round the back into the stable yard, and beyond this to a barn at some distance from the other buildings.

'Hush!' Julia said dramatically. 'Listen! Louis, stop.'

'Why?' asked Louis, but stopped nevertheless.

Somewhere round the corner of the house a man was shouting.

'My dears!' said Julia. 'Mr Harkness in a rage again. How too awkward.'

'What should we do about it?' Carlotta asked. 'Slink away or what?'

'Oh, nonsense,' Jasper said. 'He may be ticking off a horse or even Mr Jones for all we know.'

'Ricky says Mr Jones is in London.'

'*Was*,' Ricky amended.

'Anyway, I refuse to be done out of our riding treat,' said Bruno. 'Press on, Louis.'

'Be quiet, Bruno. Listen.'

Louis wound down the window. A female voice could be clearly heard.

'*And if I want to bloody jump the bloody hedge, by God I'll bloody jump it, I'll jump it on Mungo, by God.*'

'*Anathema! Blasphemy!*'

'*Don't you lay a hand on me: I'm pregnant,*' bellowed Miss Harkness.

'*Harlot!*'

'*Shut up.*'

'*Strumpet!*'

'*Stuff it.*'

'Oh, do drive on, Louis,' said Carlotta crossly. 'They'll stop when they see us. It's so boring, all this.'

Louis said, 'It would be nice if people made up their minds.'

'We have. Press on.'

He drove into the stable yard.

The picture that presented itself was of a row of six loose-boxes, each with a horse's bridled head looking out of the upper half, flanked at one end by a tack-room and at the other by an open coach-house containing a small car, coils of old wire discarded gear, tools, and empty sacks: all forming a background for a large red man with profuse whiskers towering over Miss Harkness, who faced him with a scowl of defiance.

'Lay a hand on me and I'll call the police,' she threatened.

Mr Harkness, for undoubtedly it was he, had his back to the car. Arrested, no doubt, by a sudden glaze that overspread his niece's face, he turned and was transfixed.

His recovery was almost instantaneous. He strode towards them, all smiles.

'Morning, morning. All ready for you. Six of the best,' shouted Mr Harkness. He opened car doors, offered a large freckled hand with ginger bristles, helped out the ladies and, laughing merrily, piloted them across the yard.

'Dulcie's got 'em lined up,' he said.

Julia beamed upon Mr Harkness and, to his obvious bewilderment, gaily chided Miss Harkness for deserting them. He shouted: 'Jones!'

Syd Jones slid out of the tack-room door, and with a sidelong scowl at Ricky, approached the loose-boxes.

Julia advanced upon him with extended hand. She explained to Mr Harkness that she and Syd were old friends. It would be difficult to say which of the two men was the more embarrassed.

Syd led out the first horse, a sixteen-hand bay, and Mr Harkness said he would give Jasper a handsome ride. Jasper mounted, collecting the bay and walking it round the yard. The others followed, Julia on a nice-looking grey mare. It was clear to Ricky that the Pharamonds were accomplished horse people. He himself was given an aged chestnut gelding who, Mr Harkness said, still had plenty of go in him if handled sympathetically. Ricky walked and then jogged him round the yard in what he trusted was a sympathetic manner.

Bruno was mounted on a lively, fidgeting sorrel mare and was told she would carry twelve stone very prettily over the sticks. 'You asked for a lively ride,' Mr Harkness said to Bruno, 'and you'll get it. Think you'll be up to her?'

Bruno said with dignity that he did think so. Clearly not averse to showing-off a little, he rode out into the horse-paddock where three hurdles had been set up. He put the sorrel at them and flew over very elegantly. Ricky, with misgivings, felt his mount tittuping under him. 'You shut up,' he muttered to it. Julia, who had come alongside, leant towards him, her face alive with entertainment.

'Ricky!' she said. 'Are you feeling precarious?'

'Precarious!' he shouted. 'I'm terror-stricken. And now you're going to laugh at me,' he added, hearing the preliminary splutter.

'If you fall off, I'll try not to. But you're sitting him like a rock.'

'Not true, alas.'

'Nearly true. Good God! He's at it again!'

Mr Harkness had broken out into the familiar roar but this time his target was Bruno. The horse-paddock sloped down-hill towards a field from which it was separated by a dense and pretty high blackthorn hedge. Bruno had turned the sorrel to face a gap in the hedge and the creature, Ricky saw, was going through the mettlesome antics that manifest an equine desire to jump over something.

'No, stop! You can't! Here! Come back!' Mr Harkness roared. And to Jasper: 'Call that kid back. He'll break his neck. He'll ruin the mare. Stop him!'

The Pharamonds shouted but Bruno dug in his heels and put the sorrel at the gap. It rose, its quarters flashed up, it was gone and there was no time, or a lifetime, before they heard an earthy thump and a diminishing thud of hooves.

Mr Harkness was running down the horse-paddock. Jasper had ridden past him when, on the slope beyond the hedge, Bruno appeared, checking his dancing mount. Farther away, on the hillside, a solitary horse reared, plunged and galloped idiotically up and down a distant hedge. Ricky thought he recognized the wall-eyed Mungo.

Bruno waved vaingloriously.

Julia had ridden alongside Ricky. 'Horrid, showing-off little brute,' said Julia. 'Wait till I get at him.' And she began shakily to laugh.

Mr Harkness bawled infuriated directions to Bruno about how to rejoin them by way of gates and a lane. The Pharamonds collected round Julia and Ricky.

'I am ashamed of Bruno,' said Jasper.

'What's it like,' Carlotta asked, 'on the other side?'

'A sheer drop to an extremely deep and impossibly wide ditch. The mare's all Harkness said she was to clear it.'

'Bruno's good, though,' said Julia.

'He's given you a fright and he's shown like a mountebank.'

Julia said: 'Never mind!' and leant along her horse's neck to touch her husband's hand. Ricky suddenly felt quite desolate.

The Pharamonds waited ominously for the return of the errant Bruno while Mr Harkness enlarged upon the prowess of Sorrel Lass which was the stable name of the talented mare. He also issued a number of dark hints as to what steps he would have taken if she had broken a leg and had to be destroyed.

In the middle of all this and just as Bruno, smiling uneasily, rode his mount into the stable-yard, Miss Harkness, forgotten by all, burst into eloquence.

She was 'discovered' leering over the lower half-door of an empty loose-box. With the riding crop, from which she appeared never to be parted, she beat on the half-door and screamed in triumph.

'Yar! Yar! Yar!' Miss Harkness screamed, 'Old bloody Unk! She's bloody done it, so sucks boo to rotten old you.'

Her uncle glared upon her but made no reply. Jasper, Carlotta and Louis were administering a severe if inaudible wigging to Bruno, who had unwillingly dismounted. Syd Jones had disappeared.

Julia said to Ricky: 'We ought to bring Bruno and Dulcie together; they seem to have something in common, don't you feel? What have you lot been saying to him?' she asked her husband who had come across to her.

'I've asked for another mount for him.'

'Darling!'

'He's got to learn, sweetie. And in any case Harkness doesn't like the idea of him riding her. After that performance.'

'But he rode her beautifully, we must admit.'

'He was told not to put her at the hedge.'

Syd Jones came out and led away the sorrel. Presently he reappeared with something that looked like an elderly polo pony, upon which Bruno gazed with evident disgust.

The scene petered out. Miss Harkness emerged from the loose-box, strode past her uncle, shook hands violently with sulking Bruno and continued into the house, banging the door behind her.

Mr Harkness said: 'Dulcie gets a bit excitable.'

Julia said: 'She's a high-spirited girl, isn't she? Carlotta, darling, don't you think we ought to hit the trail? Come along, boys. We're off.'

There was, however, one more surprise to come. Mr Harkness approached Julia with a curious, almost a sheepish smile, and handed up an envelope.

'Just a little thing of my own,' he said. 'See you this evening. Have a good day.'

When they reached the end of the drive Julia said, 'What can it be?'

'Not the bill,' Carlotta said. 'Not when he introduced it like that.'

'Oh, I don't know. The bill, after all, would be a little thing of his own.'

Julia had drawn what appeared to be a pamphlet from the envelope. She began to read. 'Not true!' she said, and looked up, wide-eyed, at her audience. 'Not true,' she repeated.

'What isn't?' Carlotta asked crossly. 'Don't go on like that, Julia.'

Julia handed the pamphlet to Ricky. 'You read it,' she said. 'Aloud.'

'DO YOU KNOW,' Ricky read, 'that you are in danger of HELL-FIRE?'

'DO YOU KNOW, that the DAY of JUDGEMENT *is AT HAND?*

'WOE! WOE! WOE!!! cries the Prophet – '

'Obviously,' Julia interrupted, 'Mr Harkness is the author.'

'Why?'

'Such very horsy language. "Whoa! Whoa! Whoa!" '

'He seems to run on in the same vein for a long time,' Ricky said, turning the page. 'It's all about the last trump and one's sins lying bitter in one's belly. Wait a bit. Listen.'

'What?'

'Regular gatherings of the Inner Brethren at Leathers on Sunday evenings at seven-thirty to which you are Cordially Invited. Bro. Cuthbert ("Cuth") Harkness will lead. Discourse and Discussion. Light Supper. Gents fifty p. Ladies a basket. All welcome.'

'Well,' said Jasper after a pause, 'that explains everything. Or does it?'

'I *suppose* it does,' said Julia doubtfully. 'Mr Harkness, whom we must learn to call Cuth, even if it sounds as if one had lost a tooth – '

'How do you mean, Julia?'

'Don't interrupt. "Cuspid",' Julia said hurriedly. 'Clearly, he's a religious fanatic and that's why he's taken Miss Harkness's pregnancy so hard.'

'Of course. Evidently they're extremely strict,' Jasper agreed.

'I wonder what they do at their parties. Would it be fun – '

'No, Julia,' said Louis, 'it would not be fun; ladies a basket, or no.'

Carlotta said, 'Do let's go. We can discuss Mr Harkness later. There's a perfect green lane round the corner.'

So all the Pharamonds and Ricky rode up the hill. They showed for some moments on the skyline, elegant against important clouds. Then the lane dipped into a valley and they followed it and disappeared.

III

They lunched at a little pub in Bon Accord on the extreme northern tip of the island. It was called the Fisherman's Rest and was indeed full of guernseys, gumboots and the smell of fish. The landlord turned out to be a cousin of Bob Maistre at the Cod-and-Bottle.

Jasper stood drinks all round and Julia captivated the men by asking about the finer points of deep-sea fishing. From here she led the conversation to Mr Harkness, evoking a good deal of what Louis afterwards referred to as bucolic merriment.

'Cuth Harkness,' the landlord said, 'was a sensible enough chap when he first came. A riding instructor or some such in the army, he were. Then he took queer with religion.'

'He were all right till he got cranky-holy,' someone said. 'Druv himself silly brooding on hell-fire, I reckon.'

'Is Miss Harkness a member of the group?' Louis asked, and Ricky saw that mention of Miss Harkness evoked loose-mouthed grins and sidelong looks.

'Dulce?' somebody blurted out as if the name itself was explicit. 'Her?' and there was a general outbreak of smothered laughter.

'Reckon her's got better things to do,' the landlord said. This evoked a further round of stifled merriment.

'Quite a girl, our Dulcie, isn't she?' Louis said easily. He passed a white hand over the back of his patent-leather head. 'Mind you,' he added, 'I wouldn't know.'

Carlotta and Julia walked out into the fresh air where Ricky joined them.

'I wish he wouldn't,' Carlotta said.

'Louis?' Julia asked.

'Yes,' said Carlotta. 'That's right. Louis. My husband, you know. Shouldn't we be moving on?' She smiled at Ricky. 'But we're an ever-so-jolly family, of course,' she said. 'Aren't we, Julia?'

'Come on,' Julia said. 'Let's get the fiery steeds. Where's Bruno?'

'With them, I expect. Still a bit huffy.'

But Bruno left off being huffy when they all rode a fine race across a stretch of open turf. Ricky's blood tingled in his ears and his bottom began to be sore.

When they had pulled up Louis gave a cry. He dismounted and hopped about on his elegant left foot.

'Cramp?' asked Jasper.

'What do you suppose it is, love, hopscotch? Blast and hell, I'll have to get this boot off,' groaned Louis. 'Here. Bruno!'

Bruno very efficiently pulled off the boot. Louis wrenched at his foot, hissing with pain. He stood up, stamped and limped.

'It's no good,' he said. 'I'll have to go back.'

'I'll come with you, darling,' his wife offered.

'No, you won't, damn it,' he said. He mounted, holding the boot in his right hand. He flexed his right foot, keeping it out of the iron and checking his horse's obvious desire to break away.

'Will you be OK?' asked Jasper.

'I will if you'll all be good enough to move off,' he said. He turned his horse and began to walk it back along the turf.

'Leave it,' Carlotta said. 'He'll be cross if we don't. He knows what he's doing.'

In spite of a marked increase in his saddle-soreness, Ricky enjoyed the rest of the day's outing. They took roundabout lanes back to the Cove and the sun was far in the west when, over a rise in the road, L'Esperance came unexpectedly into view, a romantic silhouette, distant and very lonely against a glowing sky.

'Look at our lovely house!' cried Julia. She began to sing a Spanish song and the other Pharamonds joined in. They sang, off and on, all the way to Leathers and up the drive.

'Will Louis have taken the car or is he waiting for us?' Bruno wondered.

'It'd be a hell of a long wait,' said Jasper.

'I fancy he'll be walking home,' Carlotta said. 'It's good for his cramp to walk.'

As they turned the corner of the house into the stable yard, they saw the car where Louis had left it. It was unoccupied.

'Yes, he's walking,' said Jasper. 'We'll catch up with him.'

There was nobody about in the yard. Everything seemed very quiet.

'I'll dig someone up,' Jasper said. He turned his hack into a loose-box and walked off.

Bruno, who had recovered from the effects of his wigging and showed signs of wanting to brag about his exploit, said: 'Julia, come down and look at my jump. Ricky, will you come? Carlotta, come and look. Come on.'

'If we do, it doesn't mean to say we approve,' Julia said sternly. 'Shall we?' she asked Ricky and Carlotta. 'I'd rather like to.'

They rode their bored horses into the paddock and down the hill. A long shadow from the blackthorn hedge reached towards them and the air struck cold as they entered it.

Ricky felt his horse's barrel expand between his knees. It lifted its head, neighed and reared on its hind legs.

'Here!' he exclaimed. 'What's all this!' It dropped back on its forefeet and danced. From far beyond the hedge, on the distant hill-side, there came an answering scream.

Julia crammed her own now agitated mount up to the gap in the hedge where Bruno had jumped. Ricky watched her bring the horse round and heard it snort. It stood and trembled. Julia leant forward in the saddle and patted its neck. She looked over the gap and down. Ricky saw her gloved hand clench. For a moment she was perfectly still. Then she turned towards him and he thought he had never seen absolute pallor in a face until now.

Behind him Carlotta said: 'What's possessing the animals?' and then: 'Julia, what is it?'

'Ricky,' Julia said in somebody else's voice, 'let Bruno take your horse and come here. Bruno, take Carlotta and the horses back to the yard and stay there. Do what I tell you, Carlotta. Do it at once. And find Jasper. Send him down here.'

They did what she told them. Ricky walked down the slope to Julia, who dismounted.

'You'd better look,' she said. 'Down there. Down.'

Ricky looked through the gap. Water glinted below in the shadows. Trampled mud stank and glistened. Deep scars and slides ploughed the bank. Everything was dead still down there. Particularly the interloper, who lay smashed and discarded, face upwards, in the puddled ditch, her limbs all higgledy-piggledy at impossible angles, her mouth awash with muddy water, and her foolish eyes wide open and staring at nothing at all. On the hillside the sorrel mare, saddled, bridled and dead lame, limped here and there, snatching inconsequently at the short grass. Sometimes she threw up her head and whinnied. She was answered from the hilltop by Mungo, the wall-eyed bay.

IV

'I told her,' Mr Harkness sobbed. 'I told her over and over again not to. I reasoned with her. I even chastised her for her soul's sake, but she would! She was consumed with pride and she would do it and the Lord has smitten her down in the midst of her sin.' He knuckled his eyes like a child, gazed balefully about him and suddenly roared out: 'Where's Jones?'

'Not here, it seems,' Julia ventured.

'I'll have the hide off him. He's responsible. He's as good as murdered her.'

'Jones!' Carlotta exclaimed. 'Murdered!'

'Orders! He was ordered to take her to the smith. To be re-shod on the off-fore. If he'd done that she wouldn't have been here. I ordered him on purpose to get her out of the way.'

Julia and Carlotta made helpless noises. Bruno kicked at a loose-box door. Ricky felt sick. Inside the house Jasper could be heard talking on the telephone.

'What's he doing?' Mr Harkness demanded hopelessly. 'Who's he talking to? What's he saying!'?

'He's getting a doctor,' Julia said, 'and an ambulance.'

'And the vet?' Mr Harkness demanded. 'Is he getting the vet? Is he getting Bob Blacker, the vet? She may have broken her leg, you know. She may have to be destroyed. Have you thought of that? And there she lies looking so awful. Somebody ought to close the eyes. I can't, but somebody ought to.'

Ricky, to his great horror, felt hysteria rise in his throat. Mr Harkness rambled on, his voice clotted with tears. It was almost impossible to determine when he spoke of his niece and when of his sorrel mare. 'And what about the hacks?' he asked. 'They ought to be unsaddled and rubbed down and fed. She ought to be seeing to them. She sinned. She sinned in the sight of the Lord! It may have led to hell-fire. More than probable. What about the hacks?'

'Bruno,' Julia said. 'Could you?'

Bruno, with evident relief, went into the nearest loose-box. Characteristic sounds – snorts, occasional stamping, the clump of a saddle dumped across the half-door and the bang of an iron against wood – lent an air of normality to the stable yard.

Mr Harkness dived into the next-door box so suddenly that he raised a clatter of hooves.

He could be heard soothing the grey hack: 'Steady girl. Stand over,' and interrupting himself with an occasional sob.

'This is too awful,' Julia breathed. 'What can one do?'

Carlotta said: 'Nothing.'

Ricky said: 'Shall I see if I can get him a drink?'

'Brandy? Or something?'

'He may have given it up because of hell-fire,' Julia suggested. 'It might send him completely bonkers.'

'I can but try.'

He went into the house by the back-door, and following the sound of Jasper's voice, found him at the telephone in an office where Mr Harkness evidently did his bookkeeping.

Jasper said: 'Yes. Thank you. As quick as you can, won't you?' and hung up the receiver. 'What now?' he asked. 'How is he?'

'As near as damn it off his head. But he's doing stables at the moment. The girls thought, perhaps a drink.'

'I doubt if we'll find any.'

'Should we look?'

'I don't know. Should we? Might it send him utterly cuckoo?'

'That's what we wondered,' said Ricky.

Jasper looked round the room and spotted a little corner cupboard. After a moment's hesitation he opened the door and was confronted with a skull-and-crossbones badly drawn in red ink and supported by a legend:

BEWARE!
This Way Lies Damnation!!!

The card on which this information was inscribed had been hung round the neck of a whisky bottle.

'In the face of that,' Ricky said, 'what should we do?'

'I've no idea. But I know what I'm going to do,' said Jasper warmly. He unscrewed the cap and took a fairly generous pull at the bottle. 'I needed that,' he gasped and offered it to Ricky.

'No, thanks,' Ricky said. 'I feel sick already.'

'It takes all sorts,' Jasper observed, wiping his mouth and returning the bottle to the cupboard. 'The doctor's coming,' he said. 'And so's the vet.' He indicated a list of numbers above the telephone. 'And the ambulance.'

'Good,' said Ricky.

'They all said: "Don't move her." '

'Good.'

'The vet meant the mare.'

'Naturally.'

'God,' said Jasper. 'This is awful.'

'Yes. Awful.'

'Shall we go out?'

'Yes.'

They returned to the stable yard. Bruno and Mr Harkness were still in the loose-boxes. There was a sound of munching and an occasional snort.

Jasper put his arm round his wife. 'OK?' he asked.

'Yes. You've been drinking.'

'Do you want some?'

'No.'

'Where's Bruno?'

Julia jerked her head at the loose-boxes. 'Come over here,' she said, and drew the two men towards the car. Carlotta was in the driver's seat, smoking.

'Listen,' Julia said. 'About Bruno. You know what he's thinking, of course?'

'What?'

'He's thinking it's his fault. Because he jumped the gap first. So she thought she could.'

'Not his fault if she did.'

'That's what I say,' said Carlotta.

'Try and persuade Bruno of it! He was told not to and now see what's come of it. That's the way he's thinking.'

'Silly little bastard,' said his brother uneasily.

Ricky said: 'She'd made up her mind to do it before we got here. She'd have done it if Bruno had never appeared on the scene.'

'Yes, Ricky,' Julia said eagerly. 'That's just it. That's the line we must take with Bruno. Do say all that to him, won't you? How right you are.'

'There'll be an inquest, of course, and it'll come out,' Jasper said. 'Bruno's bit'll come out.'

'Hell,' said Carlotta.

A car appeared, rounded the corner of the house and pulled up. The driver, a man in a tweed suit carrying a professional bag, got out.

'Dr Carey?' Jasper asked.

'Blacker's the name. I'm the vet. Where's Cuth? What's up, anyway?'

'I should explain,' Jasper said, and was doing so when a second car arrived with a second man in a tweed suit carrying a professional bag. This was Dr Carey. Jasper began again. When he had finished Dr Carey said: 'Where is she, then?' and, being told, walked off down the horse-paddock. 'When the ambulance comes – ' he threw over his shoulder – 'will you show them where? I'll see her uncle when I get back.'

'I'd better talk to Cuth,' said the vet. 'This is a terrible thing. Where is he?'

As if in answer to a summons, Mr Harkness appeared, like a woebegone Mr Punch, over the half-door of a loose-box.

'Bob,' he said. 'Bob, she's dead lame. The sorrel mare, Bob. Bob, she's dead lame and she's killed Dulcie.'

And then the ambulance arrived.

Ricky stood in a corner of the yard feeling extraneous to the scenes that followed. He saw the vet move off and Mr Harkness, talking pretty wildly, make a distracted attempt to follow him and then stand wiping his mouth and looking from one to the other of the two retreating figures, each with its professional bag, rather like items in a surrealistic landscape.

Then Mr Harkness ran across the yard and bailed up the two ambulance men who were taking out a stretcher and canvas cover. Lamentations rolled out of him like sludge. The men seemed to calm him after a fashion and they listened to Jasper when he pointed the way. But Mr Harkness kept interrupting and issuing his own instructions: 'You can't miss it,' he kept saying. 'Straight across there. Where there's the gap in the hedge. I'll show you. You can't miss it.'

'We've got it, thank you, sir,' they said. 'Don't trouble yourself. Take it easy.'

They walked away, carrying the stretcher between them. He watched them and pulled at his underlip and gabbled under his breath. Julia went to him. She was still very white and Ricky saw that her hand trembled. She spoke with her usual quick incisiveness.

'Mr Harkness,' Julia said, 'I'm going to take you indoors and give you some very strong black coffee and you're going to sit down and drink it. Please don't interrupt because it won't make the smallest difference. Come along.'

She put her hand under his elbow and, still talking, he suffered himself to be led indoors.

Carlotta remained in the car. Jasper went over to talk to her. Bruno was nowhere to be seen.

It occurred to Ricky that this was a situation with which his father was entirely familiar. It would be at about this stage, he supposed, that the police car would arrive and his father would stoop over death in the form it had taken with Miss Harkness and would dwell upon that which Ricky turned sick to remember. Alleyn did not discuss his cases with his family but Ricky, who loved him, often wondered how so fastidious a man could have chosen such work.

And here he pulled up. I must be barmy, he told himself. I'm think-ing about it as if it were not a bloody accident but a crime.

Presently Julia came out of the house.

'He's sitting in his parlour,' she said, 'drinking instant coffee with a good dollop of scotch in it. I don't know whether he's spotted the scotch and is pretending he hasn't or whether he's too bonkers to know.'

There was the sound of light wheels on gravel and round the corner of the house came a policeman on a bicycle.

'Good evening, all,' said the policeman, dismounting. 'What seems to be the trouble?'

Julia walked up to him with outstretched hand.

'You say it!' she cried. 'You really do say it! How perfectly super.'

'Beg pardon, madam?' said the policeman, sizing her up.

'I thought it was only a joke thing about policemen asking what seemed to be the trouble and saying "Evening all".'

'It's as good a thing to say as anything else,' reasoned the policeman.

'Of *course* it is,' she agreed warmly. 'It's a splendid thing to say.'

Jasper intervened. 'My wife's had a very bad shock. She made the discovery.'

'That's right,' Julia said, in a trembling voice. 'My name's Julia Pharamond and I made the discovery and I'm not quite myself.'

The policeman – he was a sergeant – had removed his bicycle clips and produced his notebook. He made a brief entry.

'Is that the case?' he said. 'Mrs J. Pharamond of L'Esperance, that would be, wouldn't it? I'm sure I'm very sorry. It was you that rang the station, sir, was it?'

'No. I expect it was Dr Carey. I rang him. Or perhaps it was the ambulance.'

'I see, sir. And I understand it's a fatality. A horse-riding accident?' They made noises of assent. 'Very sad, I'm sure,' said the sergeant. 'Yes. So if I might just take a wee look-see.'

Once more Jasper pointed the way. The sergeant in his turn tramped down the horse-paddock to the blackthorn hedge.

'You could do with some of that coffee and grog yourself, darling,' Jasper said.

'I did take a sly gulp. I can't think why I rushed at Sergeant Dixon like that.'

'He's not Sergeant Dixon.'

'There! You see! I'll be calling him that to his face if I'm not careful. Too rude. I suppose you're right. I suppose I'm like this on account of my taking a wee look-see.' She burst into sobbing laughter and Jasper took her in his arms.

He looked from Ricky to Carlotta. 'We ought to get her out of this,' he said.

'Why don't we all just go? We can't do any good hanging about here,' said Carlotta.

'We can't leave Mr Harness,' Julia sobbed into her husband's coat. 'We don't know what he mightn't get up to. Besides Sergeant Thing will want me to make a statement and Ricky, too, I expect. That's very important, isn't it, Ricky? Taking statements on the scene of the crime.'

'What crime?' Carlotta exclaimed. 'Have you gone dotty, Julia?'

'Where's Bruno got to now?' Jasper asked.

'He went away to be sick,' said Carlotta. 'I expect he'll be back in a minute.'

Jasper put Julia into the back of the car and stayed beside her for some time. Bruno returned looking ghastly and saying nothing. At last the empty landscape became reinhabited. First, along a lane beyond a distant hedge, appeared the vet leading the sorrel mare. They could see her head, pecking up and down, and the top of the vet's tweed hat. Then, beyond the gap in the blackthorn hedge, partly obscured by leafy twigs, some sort of activity was seen to be taking place. Something was being half-lifted, half-hauled up the bank on the far side. It was Miss Harkness on the stretcher, decently covered.

CHAPTER 4

Intermission

Miss Harkness, parcelled in canvas, lay in the ambulance, her uncle was in his office with the doctor, and Julia and Bruno had been driven home to L'Esperance by Carlotta. Ricky and Jasper still waited in the stable yard because they didn't quite like to go away. Ricky wandered about in a desultory fashion, half-looking at what there was to be seen but unable to dismiss his memory of Dulcie Harkness. He drifted into the old coach-house. Beside the car, a broken-down gig, pieces of perished harness and a heap of sacks; a coil of old and discarded wire hung from a peg. Ricky idly examined it and found that the end had recently been cut.

He could hear the sorrel mare blowing through her nostrils – she was in a loose-box with her leg bandaged, having a feed. The vet came out.

'It's a hell of a sprain, in her near fore,' said the vet. 'And a bad cut in front, half-way down the splint bone. I can't quite understand the cut. There must have been *something* in the gap to cause it. I think I'll go down and have a look at the terrain. Now they've taken away . . . now – er – it's all clear.'

'The police sergeant's there,' Ricky said. 'He went back after he'd seen Mr Harkness.'

'Old Joey Plank?' said the vet. 'He's all right. I'd be obliged if you'd come down with me, though. I'd like to see just where this young hopeful of yours took off when he cleared the jump. I don't like being puzzled. Of course, anything can happen. For one thing, he'll be very much lighter than Dulcie. She's a big girl, but all the same it's a pretty good bet Dulcie Harkness wouldn't go wrong over the same sticks on the same mount as a kid of thirteen. She's – she would have been in the top class if she'd liked to go in for it. Be glad if you'd stroll down. OK?'

In one way, there was nothing in the wide world Ricky wanted to do less, and he fancied Jasper felt much the same, but they could hardly refuse and at least they would get away from the yard and the ambulance with its two men sitting in front and its closed doors with Miss Harkness behind them. Jasper did point out that they were the width of the paddock away when Bruno jumped, but Mr Blacker paid no attention and led the way downhill.

The turf was fairly soft and copiously indented with hoof prints. When they got to within a few feet of the gap the vet held up his hand and they all stopped.

'Here you are, then,' he said. 'Here's where they took off and here are the marks of the hind hooves, the first lot with the boy up being underneath, with the second overlapping at the edges and well dug in. Tremendous thrust, you know, when the horse takes off. See the difference between these and the prints left by the forefeet.'

Sergeant Plank, in his shirtsleeves and red with exertion, loomed up in the gap.

'This is a nasty business, Joey,' said the vet.

'Ah. Very. And a bit of a puzzle, at that. Very glad these two gentlemen have come down. If it's all the same, I'll just get a wee statement about how the body was found, like. We have to do these things in the prescribed order, don't we? Halfa mo'.'

He didn't climb through the gap but edged his way down the hedge to where he'd hung his tunic. From this he extracted his note-book and pencil. He joined them and fixed his gaze – his eyes were china-blue and very bright – upon Ricky.

'I understand you was the first to see the deceased, sir,' he said.

Ricky experienced an assortment of *frissons*.

'Mrs Pharamond was the first,' he said. 'Then me.'

'Pardon me. So I understood. Could I have the name, if you please, sir?'

'Roderick Alleyn.'

A longish silence followed.

'Oh yes?' said the sergeant. 'How is that spelt, if you please?'

Ricky spelt it.

'You wouldn't,' Sergeant Plank austerely suggested, 'be trying to take the micky, would you, sir?'

'Me? Why? Oh!' said Ricky, blushing. 'No, Sergeant, I wouldn't dream of it. I'm his son.'

A further silence.

'I had the pleasure,' said Sergeant Plank, clearing his throat, 'of working under the Chief Superintendent on a case in the West Country. In a very minor capacity. Guard duty. He wouldn't remember, of course.'

'I'll tell him,' said Ricky.

'He still wouldn't remember,' said Sergeant Plank, 'but it *was* a pleasure, all the same.'

Yet another silence was broken by Mr Blacker. 'Quite a coincidence,' he said.

'It is that,' Sergeant Plank said warmly. And to Ricky: 'Well then, sir, even if it seems a bit funny, perhaps you'll give me a few items of information.'

'If I can, Mr Plank, of course.'

So he gave, at dictation speed, his account of what he saw when Julia called him down to the gap. He watched the sergeant laboriously begin every line of his notes close to the edge of the page and fill in to the opposite edge in the regulation manner. When that was over he took a statement from Jasper. He then said that he was sure they realized that he would, as a matter of routine, have to get statements from Julia and Bruno.

'There'll be an inquest, sir, as I'm sure you'll realize, and no doubt your wife will be called to give formal evidence, being the first to sight the body. And your young brother may be asked to say something about the nature of his own performance. Purely a matter of routine.'

'I suppose so,' said Jasper. 'I wish it wasn't, however. The boy's very upset. He's got the idea, we think, that she wouldn't have tried to jump the gap if he hadn't done it first. She seemed to be very excited about him doing it.'

'Is that so? Excited?'

Mr Blacker said: 'She would be. From what I can make out from Cuth Harkness, it'd been a bit of a bone of contention between them.

He told her she shouldn't try it on and she kind of defied him. Or that's what I made out. Cuth's in a queer sort of state.'

'Shock,' said the sergeant, still writing. 'I wouldn't be surprised. Who broke the news?'

'My wife and I did,' said Jasper. 'He insisted on coming down here to look for himself.'

'He's fussed. One minute it's the mare and the next it's the niece. He didn't seem,' Sergeant Plank said, 'to be able to tell the difference, if you can understand.'

'Only too well.'

The vet had moved away. He was peering through the gap at the ditch and the far bank. The remains of a post-and-rail fence ran through the blackthorn hedge and was partly exposed. He put his foot on the lower rail as if to test whether it would take his weight.

'I'd be obliged, Mr Blacker,' said the sergeant, raising his china-blue gaze from his notes, 'if you didn't. Just a formality but it's what we're instructed. No offence.'

'What? Oh. Oh, all right,' said Blacker. 'Sorry, I'm sure.'

'That's quite all right, sir. I wonder,' said the sergeant to Ricky, 'If you'd just indicate where you and Mrs Pharamond were when you noticed the body.'

For the life of him, Ricky could not imagine why this should be of interest, but he described how Julia had called him to her and how he had dismounted, giving his horse to Bruno, and had gone to her, and how she, too, had dismounted and he had peered through the gap. He parted some branches near the end of the gap.

'Like that,' he said.

He noticed that the post at his left hand was loose in the ground. Near the top on the outer side and almost obscured by brambles was a fine scar that cut through the mossy surface and bit into the wood. The opposite post at the other end of the gap was overgrown with blackthorn. He crossed and saw broken twigs and what seemed to be a scrape up the surface of the post.

'Would you have noticed,' Sergeant Plank said behind him, making him jump, 'anything about the gap, sir?'

Ricky turned to meet the sergeant's blue regard.

'I was too rattled,' he said, 'to notice anything.'

'Very natural,' Plank said, still writing. Without looking up he pointed his pencil at the vet. 'And would you have formed an opinion, Mr Blacker, as to how, exactly, the accident took place? Like – would you think that what went wrong, went wrong on this side after the horse took off? Or would you say it cleared the gap and crashed on the far bank?'

'If you'd let me go and take a look,' Blacker said, a trifle sourly, 'I'd be better able to form an opinion, wouldn't I?'

'Absolutely correct,' said the disconcerting sergeant. 'I agree with every word of it. And if you can notice the far bank – it's nice and clear from here – I've marked out the position of the body (which was, generally speaking, eccentric, owing to the breakage of limbs, etcetera, etcetera) with pegs. Not but what the impression in the mud doesn't speak for itself quite strong. I dare say you can see the various other indications; they stand out, don't they? Can be read like a book, I dare say, by somebody as up in the subject as yourself, Mr Blacker.'

'I wouldn't go as far as all that,' Blacker said, mollified. 'What I *would* say is that the mare came down on the far bank – you can see a clear impression of a stirrup iron in the mud – and seems to have rolled on Dulcie. Whether Dulcie pitched forward over the mare's head or fell with her isn't so clear.'

'Very well put. And borne out by the nature of the injuries. I don't think you've seen the body, have you, Mr Blacker?'

'No.'

'No. Quite so. The head's in a nasty mess. Kicked. Shocking state, really. You'll have remarked the state of the face, I dare say, Mr Alleyn.'

Ricky nodded. His mouth went dry. He had indeed remarked it.

'Yes. Well, now, I'd better go up and have a wee chat with the uncle,' said Mr Plank.

'You won't find that any too easy,' Jasper said.

Sergeant Plank made clucking noises. He struggled into his tunic, buttoned up his notebook and led the way back to the house. 'Very understandable, I'm sure,' he threw out rather vaguely. 'There'll be the little matter of identification. By the next-of-kin, you know.'

'Oh God!' Ricky said. 'You can't do that to him.'

'We'll make it as comfortable as we can.'

'Comfortable!'

'I'll just have a wee chat with him first.'

'You don't want us any more, do you?' Jasper asked him.

'No, no, no,' he said. 'We know where to find you, don't we? I'll drop in at L'Esperance if you don't object, sir, and just pick up a little signed statement from your good lady and maybe have a word with this young show-jumper of yours. Later on this evening, if it suits.'

'It'll have to, won't it, Sergeant? But I can't pretend,' Jasper said with great charm, 'that I hadn't hoped that they'd be let off any more upsets for today at least.'

'That's right,' said Sergeant Plank cordially. 'You would, too. We can't help it, though, can we, sir! So if you'll excuse me, I ought to give Superintendent Curie at Montjoy a tinkle about this. It's been a pleasure, Mr Alleyn. Quite a coincidence. *À ce soir,*' added the sergeant.

He smiled upon them, crossed over to the ambulance and spoke to the men, one of whom got out and went round to the rear doors. He opened them and disappeared inside. The doors clicked to. Sergeant Plank nodded in a reassuring manner to Jasper and Ricky and walked into the house.

'Would you say,' Jasper asked Ricky, 'that Sergeant Plankses abound in our police force?'

'Not as prolifically as they used to, I fancy.'

'Well, my dear Ricky, I suppose we now take our bracing walk to L'Esperance.'

'You don't think – '

'What?'

'We ought to stay until he's – done it? Looked.'

'The doctor's with him.'

'Yes. So he is.'

'Well, then – '

But as if the ambulance and its passengers had laid some kind of compulsion on them, they still hesitated. Jasper lit a cigarette. Ricky produced his pipe but did nothing with it.

'The day,' said Jasper, 'has not been without incident.'

'No.'

They began to move away.

'I'm afraid you have been distressed by it,' said Jasper. 'Like my poorest Julia and, for a different reason, my tiresome baby brother.'

'Haven't *you*?' Ricky asked.

Jasper came to a halt. 'Been distressed? Not profoundly, I'm afraid. I didn't see her, you know. I have a theory that the full shock and horror of a death is only experienced when it has been seen. I must, however, confess to a reaction in myself at one point of which I dare say I should be ashamed. I don't know that I am, however.'

'Am I to hear what it was?'

'Why not? It happened when the ambulance men came into the yard, here, carrying Miss Harkness on their covered stretcher. I had been thinking: thank God I wasn't the one to find them. The remains, as of course they will be labelled. And then, without warning, there came upon me a – really a quite horribly strong impulse to go up to the stretcher and uncover them. I almost believe that if it could have been accomplished in a flash with a single flourish I would have done it – like Antony revealing Caesar's body to the Romans. But of course the cover was fastened down and it would have been a fiddling, silly business and they would have stopped me. But why on earth should such a notion come upon me? Really we do *not* know ourselves, do we?'

'It looks like it.'

'Confession may be good for the soul,' Jasper said lightly, 'but I must say I find it a profoundly embarrassing exercise.'

'He's coming.'

Mr Harkness came out of the house under escort like the victim of an accident. Dr Carey and Sergeant Plank had him between them, their hands under his arms. The driver got down and opened the rear doors. His colleague looked out.

'It'll only take a moment,' they heard Dr Carey say.

On one impulse they turned and walked away, round the house and down the drive, not speaking to each other. A motor-cycle roared down the cliff road, turned in at the gates and, with little or no diminution of speed, bore down upon them.

'Look who's here,' said Jasper.

It was Syd Jones. At first it seemed that he was going to ignore them but at the last moment he cut down his engine and skidded to a halt.

'G' day,' he said morosely, and exclusively to Jasper. 'How's tricks?'

They looked wildly at each other.

'Seen Dulce?' asked Syd.

II

Any number of distracted reactions tumbled about in Ricky's head. For an infinitesimal moment he actually thought Syd wanted to know if he'd seen dead Dulce with the broken body. Then he thought 'we've got to tell him,' and then that dead Dulce might be carrying Syd's baby and this was the first time he'd remembered about what would doubtless be referred to as her 'condition'. He had no idea how long this state of muddled thinking persisted, but their silence or their manner must have been strange because Syd said:

'What's wrong?' He spoke directly to Jasper and had not looked at Ricky.

Jasper said: 'There's been an accident. I'm afraid this is going to be a shock.'

'It's bad news, Syd,' Ricky said. Because he thought he ought to and because he was unexpectedly filled with a warmth of compassion for Syd, he laid a hand on his arm and was much discomforted when Syd shook him off without a glance.

'It's about Dulcie Harkness,' Jasper said.

'What about her? Did you say an accident? Here!' Syd demanded. 'What are you on about? Is she dead? Or what?'

'I'm afraid she is, Syd.' Ricky ventured.

After a considerable pause he said: 'Poor old Dulce.' And then to Jasper: 'What happened?'

Jasper told him. He was, Ricky knew, a quite remarkably inexpressive person and allowances had to be made for that. He seemed to be sobered, taken aback, even perturbed, but, quite clearly, not shattered. And still he would not look at Ricky.

'You can hardly credit it,' he mumbled.

He seemed to turn the information over in his mind and after doing so for some time said: 'She was pregnant. Did you know that?'

'Well, yes,' Jasper said. 'Yes, we did.'

'They'll find that out, won't they?'

'Yes, I expect they will.'

'Too bad,' he said.

Jasper caught Ricky's eye and made a slight face at him.

'Who,' he asked, 'is the father?'

'I dunno,' said Syd, almost cheerfully. 'And I reckon she didn't. She was quite a girl.'

Somebody else had used the phrase about her. Recently. It was Louis, Ricky remembered; Louis Pharamond in the Fisherman's Rest at Bon Accord.

'Where's the old man?' Syd asked Jasper.

'In the house. The doctor's there. And a police sergeant.'

'What's *he* want?' Syd demanded.

'They have to make a formal appearance at fatal accidents,' Ricky said, and was ignored.

'He's very much upset,' said Jasper.

'Who is?'

'Mr Harkness.'

'He warned her. Didn't he? You heard him.'

'Of course he did.'

'Fair enough, then. What's he got to worry about?'

'Good God!' Jasper burst out and then checked himself. 'My dear Jones,' he urged. 'The man's had a monstrous shock. His niece has been killed. He's had to identify her body. He's – '

'Aw,' said Syd. 'That, yeah.'

And to Ricky's bewilderment he actually turned pale.

'That's different, again,' he said. 'That could be grotty, all right.'

He stood for a moment or two with his head down, looking at his boots. Then he hitched his shoulder, settled himself on his seat and revved up his engine.

'Where are you going?' Jasper shouted.

'Back,' he said. 'No sense going on, is there? It was her I wanted to see.'

They stood and watched him. He kicked the ground, turned his machine and roared off the way he had come.

'That creature's a monster,' said Jasper.

'He may be a monster,' Ricky said, 'but there's one thing we can be sure he's not.'

'Really? Oh, I see what you mean. Yes, I suppose we can.'

The sound of the motor-cycle faded.

'That's a bloody expensive machine,' Ricky said.

'Oh?'

'New.'

'Really?' said Jasper without interest. 'Shall we go?'

It was an opulent evening, as if gold dust had been shaken out of some heavenly sifter, laying a spell over an unspectacular landscape. Even the effects of chiaroscuro were changed, so that details normally close-at-hand were set at a golden remove. L'Esperance itself was enskied by inconsequent drifts of cloud at its base. The transformation would have been a bit too much of a good thing, Ricky thought, if its impermanence had not lent it a sort of austerity. Even as they saw the glow on each other's faces, it faded and the evening was cold.

'Ricky,' Jasper said, 'come up and have a drink and supper with us. We would like you to come.'

But Ricky thought it best to say no and they parted at the entrance to the drive. He mounted his bicycle and was sharply reminded of his saddle-soreness.

When he got back to the Cove it was to find that news of the accident was already broadcast. Mrs Ferrant met him in the passage.

'This is a terrible business, then,' she said, without any preliminaries and stared at Ricky out of her stewed-prune eyes. He had no mind to discuss it with her, anticipating a series of greedy questions. He remembered Mrs Ferrant's former reactions to mention of Dulcie Harkness.

'They're saying it was a horse-riding accident,' she probed. 'That's correct, is it? They're. saying there was arguments with the uncle, upalong, over her being too bold with her jumping. Is it true, then, what they're saying, that you was a witness to the accident? Was it you that found her, then? There's a terrible retribution for you, isn't it, whatever she may have been in the past?'

Ricky staved her off as best he could but she served his supper – one of her excellent omelettes – with a new batch of questions at each re-appearance, and he fought a losing battle. In the end he was obliged to give an account of the accident.

While this was going on he became aware of sundry bumps and shufflings in the passage outside.

'That's him,' Mrs Ferrant threw out. 'He's going on one of his holidays over to St Pierre-des-Roches by the morning boat.'

'I didn't know there was one.'

'The *Island Belle*. She calls once a week on her way from Montjoy.'

'Really?' said Ricky, glad to steer Mrs Ferrant herself into different waters. 'I might take the trip one of these days.'

'It's an early start. Five a.m.'

She had left the door ajar. From close on the other side, but without showing himself, Ferrant called peremptorily: 'Marie! *Hé!*'

'Yes,' she said quickly and went out, shutting the door.

Ricky heard them walk down the passage.

He finished his supper and climbed up to his room, suddenly very tired; too tired and too sore and becoming too stiff to go along to the Cod-and-Bottle, where in any case he would be avidly questioned about the accident. And much too tired to write. He had a hot bath, restraining a yelp when he got into it, applied with difficulty first-aid plasters to the raw discs on his bottom and went to bed, where he fell at once into a heavy sleep.

He woke to find his window pallid in the dawnlight. He was aware of muted sounds in the downstairs passage. The heavy front door was shut. Footsteps sounded on the outside path.

Wide awake, he got out of bed, went to his open window and looked down.

Mr Ferrant, with two suitcases, walked towards the jetty where the *Island Belle* was coming in. There was something unexpected, unreal even, about her, sliding alongside in the dawnlight. Quiet voices sounded and the slap of rope on the wet jetty. Mr Ferrant was a solitary figure with his baggage and his purposeful tread. But what very grand suitcases they were: soft hide, surely, not plastic, and coming, Ricky was sure, from some very smart shop. As for Mr Ferrant, one could hardly believe it was he, in a camel-hair overcoat, pork-pie hat, suede shoes and beautiful gloves. He turned his head and Ricky saw that he wore dark glasses.

He watched Mr Ferrant, the only embarking passenger, go up the gangplank and disappear. Some packages and a mailbag were taken aboard, and then the *Island Belle*, with a slight commotion from her propeller, pulled out, her lights wan in the growing morning.

Ricky returned to bed and to sleep. When he finally awoke at nine o'clock, Mr Ferrant's departure seemed unreal as a dream and enclosed, like a dream, between sleep and sleep.

Three days later the inquest was held in the Cove village hall. The coroner came out from Montjoy. The jury was made up of local characters, some of whom were known to Ricky as patrons of the Cod-and-Bottle.

Julia and Ricky were called to give formal evidence as to sighting the body, and Mr Harkness as to its identity. He was subdued and shaky and extremely lugubrious, answering in a low, uneven voice. He tried to say something about the dangerous nature of the jump and about the warning? he had given his niece and the rows this had led to.

'I allowed anger to take hold of me,' he said, and looked round the assembly with washed-out eyes. 'I went too far and I said too much. I may have driven her to it.' He broke down and was allowed to leave the room.

Dr Carey gave evidence as to the nature of the injuries, which were multiple and extensive. Some of the external ones could be seen to have been caused by a horse's hoof, others were breakages. The internal ones might have been brought about by the mare rolling on her rider. It was impossible, on the evidence, to arrive at a more precise conclusion. She was some eight or nine weeks pregnant, Dr Carey added, and a little eddy of attention seemed to wash through the court. Superintendent Curie, from Montjoy, nominally in charge of the police investigation, was ill in hospital, but to the obvious surprise of the jury, applied, through Sergeant Plank, for an adjournment, which was agreed to.

Outside in the sunshine Ricky talked to Julia and Jasper. It was his first meeting with them since the accident although they had spoken on the telephone. Nobody could have been more simply dressed than Julia and nobody could have looked more exquisite, he thought, or more exotic in that homespun setting.

'I don't in the least understand all this,' Julia said. 'Why an adjournment? Ricky, you're the one to explain to us.'

'Why me?'

'Because your gorgeous papa is a copper. Is he perpetually asking for adjournments when everyone longs for the whole thing to be – ' she stopped, looked for a moment into his eyes and then said rapidly – 'to be dead, buried and forgotten?'

'Honestly, I don't know anything at all about police goings-on. He never speaks of his cases. We've so much else to talk about,' Ricky said simply. 'I imagine they have to be almost insanely thorough and exhaustive.'

'I can't think that it makes any difference to anyone, not even Mr Harkness in all his righteous anguish, whether poor Dulcie fell forwards, sideways or over the horse's tail. Oh God, Jasper darling, why does everything I say always have to sound so perfectly heartless and beastly.'

'Because you're a realist, my love, and anyway it doesn't,' said Jasper. 'You'd be the most ghastly fake if you pretended to be heartbroken over the wretched girl. You had a beastly shock because you saw her. If you'd only *heard* she'd been killed you'd have said: "How awful for poor Cuth," and sent flowers to the funeral. Which, by the way, we ought perhaps to do. What do you think?'

But Julia paid no attention.

'Ricky,' she said. 'It couldn't be – or could it? – that the police – what is it that's always said in the papers – don't rule out the possibility of "foul play"? Could it be that, Ricky?'

'I don't know. Truly I don't know,' Ricky said. And then, acutely conscious of their fixed regard, he blurted out what he had in fact been thinking.

'I had wondered,' said Ricky.

III

' "So I thought," ' Alleyn read aloud, ' "I'd ask you if the idea's just plain silly. And if you don't think it's silly, whether you think I ought to say anything to Sergeant Plank or whether that would be behaving like the typical idiot layman. Or, finally, whether it's a guinea to a gooseberry, Sergeant Plank will have thought of it for himself – " which,' Alleyn said, looking up from the letter, 'will certainly be the case if Sergeant Plank's worth his stripes.'

'Wouldn't we much rather Rick kept out of it, whatever it may be, and got on with his book?' asked Ricky's mother.

'Very much rather. Drat the boy, why does he want to go and get himself involved?' Alleyn rubbed his nose and looked sideways at his wife. 'Quite neat of him to spot that bit, though, wasn't it? "Obviously recent," he says.'

'Should we suggest he comes home?' Troy wondered, and then: 'No. Silly of me. Why on earth, after all?'

'He may be called when the inquest is re-opened, in which case he'd have to go trundling back. No, I shouldn't worry. It's odds on there's nothing in it, and he's perfectly well able to cope, after all, with anything that may turn up.' Alleyn returned to the letter. 'I see,' he said, 'that Julia was dreadfully upset but rallied gallantly and gave her evidence quite beautifully. So that's still on the *tapis*, one gathers.'

'I hope she's not finding him a bore.'

'Does a woman ever dislike the admiration of a reasonably presentable young chap?'

'True.'

'He really does seem to have struck a rum set-up one way or another,' said Alleyn, still reading. 'What with his odd-jobbing plumber of a landlord dressed up like a con man at the crack of dawn and going on holiday to St Pierre-des-Roches.'

'It's a pretty little peep of a place. I painted it when I was a student. The egregious Syd has made a regrettable slosh at it. But it's hardly the spot for camel-hair coats and zoot-suits.'

'Perhaps Ferrant uses it as a jumping-off place for the sophisticated south.'

'And then there's Louis Pharamond,' said Troy, pursuing her own thoughts, 'having had some sort of affair with poor Miss Harkness, doesn't it seem? Or does it?'

'In company with your visitor with the free paints and the dizzy spell. And listen to this,' said Alleyn. ' "My Mrs Ferrant reacts very acidly to mention of Dulcie Harkness, even though she does make obligatory *non nisi* noises. I can't help wondering if Mr Ferrant's roving eye has lit some time or another on Miss Harkness." Really!' said Alleyn, 'The Island jollities seem to be of a markedly uninhibited kind. And Miss Harkness of an unusually obliging disposition.'

'Bother!' said Troy.

'I know. And then, why should the egregious Jones scream with rage when Ricky trod on his vermilion? There's plenty more where that came from, it seems. For free. And if it comes to that, why should Jones take it into his head to cut Rick? Apparently he would neither look at, nor speak to him. Not a word about having taken a luncheon off us, it appears.'

'He's a compulsive boor, of course. Mightn't we be making far too much of a series of unrelated and insignificant little happenings?'

'Of course we might,' Alleyn agreed warmly. He finished reading his son's letter, folded it and put it down. 'He's taken pains over that,' he said. 'Very long and very detailed. He even goes to the trouble of describing the contents of the old coach-house.'

'The whole thing's on his mind and he thinks writing it all out may help him to get shot of it.'

'He's looking for a line. It's rather like those hidden picture-games they used to put in kid's books. A collection of numbered dots and you joined them up in the given order and found you'd got a pussy-cat or something. Only Rick's dots aren't numbered and he can't find the line.'

'If there is one.'

'Yes. There may be no pussy-cat.'

'It's the sort of thing you're doing all the time, isn't it?'

'More or less, my treasure. More or less.'

'Oh!' Troy exclaimed. 'I do *hope* there isn't a line and I do hope Miss Harkness wasn't – '

'What?'

'Murdered,' said Troy. 'That, really, is what the letter's all about, isn't it?'

'Oh yes,' Alleyn agreed. 'That's what it's all about.'

The telephone rang and he answered it. It was his Assistant Commissioner. Being a polite man he made his usual token apology.

'Oh, Rory,' he said. 'Sorry to disturb you at home. Did I hear you mention your boy was staying on that island where Sunniday Enterprises, if that's what they call themselves, have set up a holiday resort of sorts?'

It pleased the AC – nobody knew why – when engaged in preliminaries, to affect a totally false vagueness about names, places and activities.

Alleyn said: 'Yes, sir, he's there,' and wondered why he was not surprised. It was as if he had been waiting for this development, an absurd notion to entertain.

'Staying at this place of theirs? What's it called? Mount something?'

'Hotel Montjoy. Lord, no. He's putting up at a plumber's cottage on the non-u side of the island.'

'The Bay. Or Deep Bay, would that be?'

'Deep Cove,' Alleyn said, beginning to feel exasperated as well as apprehensive.

'To be sure. Yes. I remember now, you did say something about a plumber and Deep Cove,' said the bland AC.

Alleyn thought: You devious old devil, what *are* you up to? and waited.

'Well,' said the AC, 'the thing is, I wondered if he might be helpful. You remember the dope case you tidied up in Rome? Some of the Ziegfeldt group?'

'Oh *that*,' Alleyn said, greatly relieved. 'Yes.'

'Well, as we all know to our discomfort, Ziegfeldt himself still operates in a very big way.'

'Quite. I understand,' said Alleyn, 'there have been extensive improvements to his phoney castle in the Lebanon. Loos on every landing.'

'Sickening, isn't it?' said the AC. 'Well, my dear Rory, the latest intelligence through Interpol and from chaps in our appropriate branch is that the route has been altered. From Izmir to Marseilles it still rings the changes between the Italian ports and the morphine-heroin transformation is still effected in laboratories outside Marseilles. But from there on there's a difference. Some of the heroin now gets away through a number of French seaports, some of them quite small. You can guess what I'm coming to, I dare say.'

'Not to St Pierre-des-Roches, by any chance?'

'And from there to this island of yours – '

'It's not mine. With respect,' said Alleyn.

' – from where it finds its way to the English market. We don't *know* any of this,' said the AC, 'but it's been suggested. There are pointers! There's a character with a bit of a record who shows signs of unexpected affluence. That kind of thing.'

'May I ask, sir,' Alleyn said, 'the name of the character who shows signs of unexpected affluence?'

'Of course you may. He's a plumber and odd-job man living in Deep Cove and he is called Ferrant.'

'Fancy that,' Alleyn said tonelessly.

'Quite a coincidence, isn't it?'

'Life is full of them.'

'So I just wondered if your young man had noticed anything.'

'He's noticed his landlord, who is called Ferrant and is a plumber, leaving at dawn by a channel packet, if that's what it is, dressed up to kill with leather suitcases and bound for St Pierre-des-Roches.'

'There now!' cried the AC. 'Splendid fellow, your son. Jolly good! Super!' He occasionally adopted the mannerisms of an effusive scout-master.

'Has anything been said by the appropriate branch about a painter called Jones?' Alleyn asked.

'A house-painter?'

'No, though you might make the mistake. A picture painter.'

'Jones. Jones. Jones. No. No Joneses. Why?'

'He travels in artists' materials for a firm called Jerome et Cie with a factory in St Pierre-des-Roches. Makes frequent visits to London.'

'Artists' materials?'

'In half-pound tubes. Oil colours.'

There was a longish silence.

'Oh yes?' said the AC in a new voice. The strange preliminaries evidently were over and they were down to the hard stuff.

'First name?' snapped the AC.

'Sydney.'

'Living?'

'In Deep Cove. The firm's handing out free colour to one or two leading painters, including Troy. He called on us here, with an introduction from Rick. I'd say he was getting over a hang-up.'

'They don't like that. The bosses. It doesn't work out – pusher into customer.'

'Of course not. But I wouldn't think he was a habitual. There'd been a party the night before. My guess would be that he was suffering from withdrawal symptoms, but on what Ricky says of him, he doesn't seem to be hooked. Yet. It may amount to nothing.'

'Anything else about him?'

Alleyn told him about the roadside incident when Ricky trod on the vermilion.

'Got into a stink, did he?'

'Apparently.'

'It's worth watching.'

'I wondered.'

'We haven't got anyone on the island so far. The lead on St Pierre's only just come through. What's the young chap doing there, Rory?'

Alleyn said very firmly: 'He's writing a book, sir. He went over there to put himself out of the way of distraction and has set himself a time limit.'

'Writing!' repeated the AC discontentedly. 'A book!' And he added: 'Extraordinary what they get up to nowadays, isn't it? One of mine runs a discotheque.'

Alleyn was silent.

'Nothing official, of course, but you might suggest he keeps his eyes open,' said the AC.

'They'll be down on his book, I hope.'

'All right. All right. Oh, by the way, there's something else come through. About an hour ago. Another coincidence in a way, I suppose one might call it. From this island of yours.'

'Oh?'

'Yes. The sergeant at Montjoy rang up. Sergeant Plank he is. There's been a riding fatality. A fortnight ago. Looked like a straightforward accident but they're not satisfied. Inquest adjourned. Thing is: his Super's been inconsiderate enough to perforate his appendix and they want us to move in. Did you say anything?'

'No.'

'There's a funny noise.'

'It may be my teeth. Grinding.'

The AC gave a high whinnying laugh.

'You can take Fox with you, of course,' he said. 'And while you're at it you may find – '

His voice, edgy and decisive, continued to issue unpalatable instructions.

IV

After posting his long letter to his parents, Ricky thought that now, perhaps, he could push the whole business of Dulcie Harkness into the background and get on with his work. The answer couldn't reach him for at least three days, and when it came it might well give half a dozen good suggestions why there should be fresh scars, as of wire, on the posts of the broken-down fence and why the wire that might have made them had been removed and why there was a gash that the vet couldn't explain on a sorrel mare's near foreleg and why there was a new-looking cut end to a coil of old wire in the coach-house. And perhaps his father would advise him to refrain from teaching his grandmother, in the unlikely person of Sergeant Plank, to suck eggs.

Tomorrow was the day when the *Island Belle* made her dawn call at the Cove. There was a three-day-a-week air service but Ricky liked the idea of the little ship. He came to a sudden decision. If the day was fine he would go to St Pierre-des-Roches, return in the evening to Montjoy, and either walk the eight miles or so to the Cove or stand himself a taxi. The break might help him to get things into perspective. He wondered if he was merely concocting an elaborate excuse for not getting on with his work.

'I may run into Mr Ferrant,' he thought, 'taking his ease at his inn. I might even have a look at Jerome et Cie's factory. Anyway, I'll go.'

He told Mrs Ferrant of his intention and that disconcerting woman bestowed one of her protracted stares upon him and then said she'd give him something to eat at half past four in the morning. He implored her to do no such thing but merely fill his Thermos flask overnight with her excellent coffee and allow him to cut himself a 'piece'.

She said, 'I don't know why you want to go over there; it's no great masterpiece, that place.'

'Mr Ferrant likes it, doesn't he?'

'Him.'

'If there's anything you want to send him, Mrs Ferrant, I'll take it with pleasure.'

She gave a short laugh that might as well have been a snort.

'He's got everything *he* wants,' she said, and turned away. Ricky thought that on her way downstairs she said something about the unlikelihood of his encountering Mr Ferrant but he couldn't be sure of this.

He woke himself up at four to a clear sky and a waning moon. The harbour was stretched like silk between its confines, with the inverted village for a pattern. A party of gulls sat motionless on their upside-down images and the jetty was deserted.

When he was dressed and shaved he stole down to the kitchen. It was much the biggest room in the house and the Ferrants used it as a living-room. It had television and radio, armchairs and a hideous dresser with a great array of china. Holy oleographs abounded. The stove and refrigerator looked brand new and so did an array of pots and pans. Ricky felt as if he had disturbed the kitchen in a night-life of its own.

It was warm and smelt of recent cooking. His Thermos stood in the middle of the table and, beside it, a message on the back of an envelope: 'Mr Allen. Food in warm drawer.'

When he opened the drawer he found a dish of toasted bacon sandwiches. She must have come down and prepared them while he was getting up. They were delicious. When he had finished them and drunk his coffee he washed up in a gingerly fashion. It was now twenty to five. Ricky felt adventurous. He wondered if perhaps he would want to stay in St Pierre-des-Roches, and on an impulse returned to his room and pushed overnight gear and an extra shirt and jeans into his rucksack.

And now, there was the *Island Belle* coming quietly into harbour with not a living soul to see her, it seemed, but Ricky.

He went downstairs and wrote on the envelope: 'Thank you. Delicious. May stay a day or two, but more likely back tonight.'

Then he let himself out and walked down the empty street to the jetty. The sleeping houses in the Cove looked pallid and withdrawn. He felt as if he saw them for the first time.

The *Island Belle* was already alongside. Two local men, known to Ricky at the pub, were putting a few crates on board. He exchanged a word with them and then followed them up the gangway. A sailor took charge of the crates and wished him good morning.

The *Belle* was a small craft, not more than five hundred tons. She did not make regular trips to the Devon and Cornwall coast, but generally confined herself to trading between the islands and nearby French ports. The captain was on the bridge, an elderly bearded man, who gave Ricky an informal salute. A bell rang. The gangway was hauled up, and one of the Cove men freed the mooring-ropes. The *Belle* slid out into the harbour.

Ricky watched the village shift back, rearrange itself and become a picture rather than a reality. He went indoors and found a little box of a purser's office where a man in a peaked cap sold him a return ticket. He looked into the empty saloon with its three tables, wall benches and shuttered miniature bar.

When he returned on deck they were already outside the heads and responding, he found with misgiving, to a considerable swell. The chilly dawn breeze caught him, and he began to walk briskly along the starboard side, past the wheel-house and towards the forward hatch.

Cargo, including crates of fish covered with tarpaulins, was lashed together on the deck. Ricky stopped short of it. Someone was standing motionless on the far side of the crates with his back turned. This person wore a magenta woollen cap, pulled down over his ears, with the collar of his coat turned up to meet it. A sailor, Ricky supposed.

Conscious of a feeling of inward uneasiness, he moved forward, seeking a passageway round the cargo, and had found one when the man in the magenta cap turned. It was Sydney Jones.

Ricky hadn't seen him since they met in the drive to Leathers on the day of the accident. On that occasion, Syd's inexplicable refusal to speak to or look at him seemed to put a stop to any further exchanges. Ricky's mother had written a brief account of his visit. 'When he dropped to it that your poor papa was a policeman,' she wrote, 'which was just before he went back to the Yard, Jones lost not a second in shaking our dust off his sandals. Truly, we *were* nice to him. Daddy thinks he was suffering from a hangover. I'm afraid his work isn't much cop, poor chap. Sorry, darling.'

And here they were, confronted. Not for long, however. Syd, grey in the face, jerked away, and Ricky was left staring at his back across a crate of fish.

'Ah, to hell with it,' he thought, and walked round the cargo.

'Look here,' he said. 'What *is* all this? What've I done?'

Syd made a plunge, an attempt, it seemed, to dodge round him, but they were both caught by an ample roll of the *Island Belle* and executed an involuntary *pas de deux* that landed them nose to nose across the fish crate as if in earnest and loving colloquy. Syd's dark glasses slid away from his washed-out eyes.

In spite of growing queasiness, Ricky burst out laughing. Syd mouthed at him. He was re-growing his beard.

'Come on,' Ricky said. 'Let's know the worst. You can't insult me! Tell me all.' He was beginning to be cold. Quite definitely all was not well within. Syd contemplated him with unconcealed disgust.

'Come on,' Ricky repeated with an awful attempt at jauntiness. 'What's it all about, for God's sake?'

Clinging to the fish crate and exhibiting intense venom, Syd almost shrieked at him: 'It's about me wanting to be on my bloody pat, that's what it's about. Get it? It's about I can't take you crawling round after me. It's about I'm not one of those. It's not my scene, see? No way. See? *No way*. So do me a favour and – '

Another lurch from the *Island Belle* coincided with a final piece of obscene advice.

'You unspeakable – ' Ricky shouted and pulled himself up. 'I was wrong,' he said. 'You can insult me, can't you, or have a bloody good try, and if I thought you meant what you said I'd knock your bloody little block off. "Crawl round after *you*",' quoted Ricky, failing to control a belch. 'I'd rather crawl after a caterpillar. You make me sick,' he said. He attempted a dismissive gesture and, impelled by the ship's motion, broke into an involuntary canter down the sloping deck. He fetched up clinging to the taffrail where, to his fury, he was indeed very sick. When it was over, he looked back at Syd. He, too, had retired to the taffrail where he was similarly engaged.

Ricky moved as far aft as he was able, and for the remainder of the short voyage divided his time between a bench and the side.

St Pierre-des-Roches lay in a shallow bay between two nondescript headlands. Rows of white houses stared out to sea through blank windows. A church spire stood over them and behind it on a hillside appeared buildings of a commercial character.

As the ship drew nearer some half-dozen small hotels sorted themselves out along the front. Little streets appeared and shop fronts with titles that became readable: 'Dupont Frères', 'Occasions', 'Chatte Noire', and then, giving Ricky – wan and shaky but improving – quite a little thrill: 'Jerome et Cie', above a long roof on the hillside.

Determined to avoid another encounter, Ricky watched Syd Jones go ashore, gave him a five-minute start and then himself went down the gangway. He passed through the *douanes* and a *bureau de change* and presently was walking up a cobbled street in St Pierre-des-Roches.

Into one of the best smells in all the world: the smell of fresh-brewed coffee and fresh-baked brioches and croissants. His sea-sickness was as if it had never been. There was *'La Chatte Noire'* with an open door through which a gust of warm air conveyed these delectable aromas, and inside were work-people having their break-fasts; perhaps coming off night-shift. Suddenly Ricky was ravenous.

The little bistro was rather dark. Its lamps were out and the early morning light was still tentative. A blue drift of tobacco smoke hung on the air. Although the room was almost full of customers there was not much conversation.

Ricky went to the counter and gave his order in careful French to the *patronne, a* large lady with an implacable bosom. He was vaguely conscious as he did so that another customer had come in behind him.

He took the only remaining single seat, facing the street door, and was given his *petit déjeuner.* No coffee is ever quite as good as it smells but this came close to it. The butter and *confitures* in little pots were exquisite and he slapped sumptious dollops of them on his warm brioches. This was adventure.

He had almost finished when there was a grand exodus from the bistro with much scraping of chair-legs, clearing of throats and exchange of pleasantries with the *patronne.* Ricky was left with only three other customers in view.

Or was it only three? Was there perhaps not someone still there in the corner of the room behind his back? He had the feeling that there was and that it would be better not to turn round and look.

Instead he raised his eyes to the wall facing him and looked straight into the disembodied face of Sydney Jones.

The shock was so disconcerting that seconds passed before he realized that what he saw was Syd's reflection, dark glasses and all, in a shabby looking-glass, and that it was Syd who sat in the corner behind his back and had been watching him.

There is always something a little odd, a little uncomfortable about meeting another person's eyes in a glass: it is as if the watchers had simultaneously caught each other out in a furtive exercise. In this case the sensation was much exaggerated. For a moment Ricky and

Syd stared at each other's images with something like horror and then Ricky scrambled to his feet, paid his bill and left in a hurry.

As he walked up the street with his rucksack on his back he wondered if Syd was going to ruin his visit to St Pierre-des-Roches by cropping up like a malignant being in a Hans Andersen tale. Since Dulcie Harkness's death he hadn't thought much about Syd's peculiar behaviour, being preoccupied with misgivings of another kind concerning freshly cut wire scars on wooden posts and a gash on a sorrel mare's leg. He thought: how boring it was of Syd to be like that. If they were on friendly terms he could have asked him about the wire. And then he thought, with a nasty jolt, that perhaps it mightn't be a good idea to ask Syd about the wire.

He passed several shops and an *estaminet* and arrived at a square with an hôtel de ville, central gardens, a frock-coated statue of a portentous gentleman with whiskers, a public lavatory, a cylindrical billboard and a newsagent. There were also several blocks of offices, a consequential house or two and L'Hôtel des Roches which Ricky liked the look of.

The morning was now well established, the sun shone prettily on the Place Centrale, as the little square was called, and Ricky thought it would be fun to stay overnight in St Pierre and perhaps not too extravagant to put up at L'Hôtel des Roches. He went in and found it to be a decorous hostelry, very provincial in tone and smelling of beeswax. In a parlour opening off the entrance hall, a bourgeois family sat like caricatures of themselves and read their morning papers. A dim clerk said they could accommodate Monsieur and an elderly porter escorted him by way of a cautious old lift to a room with a double bed, a wash-hand stand, an armchair, a huge wardrobe and not much else. Left alone, he took the opportunity to wash the legacy of the fish crate from his hands, and then looked down from his lattice window at a scene that might have been painted by a French Grandmère Moses. Figures, dressed mostly in black, walked briskly about the Place Centrale, gentlemen removed hats, ladies inclined their heads, children in smocks, bow-ties and berets skittered in the central gardens, housewives in shawls marched steadfastly to market. And behind all this activity was the harbour with the *Island Belle* at her moorings.

This didn't look like Syd Jones's scene, Ricky thought, still less like Mr Ferrant with his camel-hair coat and pork-pie hat. Days rather than hours might have passed since he sailed away from the Cove: it was a new world.

He changed into jeans and a T-shirt, left his rucksack in his room and went out to explore. First, he would go uphill. The little town soon petered out. Some precipitous gardens, a flight of steps and a road to a cemetery led to the church, not surprisingly dedicated to St Pierre-des-Roches. It turned out to be rather commonplace except perhaps for a statue of the Saint himself in pastel colours wearing his custodial keys and stationed precariously on an unconvincing rock. *'Tu es Pierre,'* said a legend, *'et sur cette pierre Je bâtirai Mon èglise.'*

One could, for a small sum, climb the tower. Ricky did so and was rewarded by a panorama of the town, its environs, the sparkling sea and a fragile shadow that was his own island out there in the Channel.

And there quite near at hand, were the premises of Jerome et Cie with their own legend in electric lights garnished with the image of a tube from which erupted a sausage of paint. At night, this, by a quaint device, would seem to gush busily. It reminded Ricky of the morning when he trod on Syd's vermilion. Perhaps Syd had come over to St Pierre to renew his stocks of samples and to this end would be calling on Messrs Jerome et Cie. Ricky rested his arms on the balustrade and watched the humanoids moving about in the street below: all heads and shoulders. A funeral crawled up the road. He looked down into a wreath of lilies on top of the hearse. The cortège turned into the cemetery and presently there was a procession with a priest, a boy swinging a censer and a following of black midgets. He imagined he could catch a whiff of incense. The cortège disappeared behind a large monument.

Ricky, caught in a kind of indolence, couldn't make up his mind to leave the balcony. He still lounged on the balustrade and stared down at the scene below. Into a straggle of pedestrians there emerged from beneath him someone who seemed to have come out of the church itself; a figure with a purplish-red cap. It wore a belted coat and something square hung from its shoulder.

Ricky was not really at all surprised.

A frightful rumpus outraged his ear-drums and upheaved his diaphragm. The church clock, under his feet, was striking ten.

CHAPTER 5

Intermezzo With Storm

The last stroke of ten still rumbled on the air as Ricky watched the midget that was Syd walk up the street and, sure enough, turn in at the gateway to Jerome et Cie's factory. Had he come out of the church? Had he already been lurking in some dark corner when Ricky came in? Or had he followed Ricky? Why had he gone there? To say his prayers? To look for something to paint? To rest his legs? The box, loaded as it always seemed to be with large tubes of paint, must be extremely heavy. And yet he had shifted it casually from one shoulder to the other and there was nothing in the movement to suggest weight. Perhaps it was empty and he was going to get a load of free paints from Jerome et Cie.

Ricky was visited by a sequence of disturbing notions. Did Sydney Jones really think that he, Ricky, was following him round, spying on him or – unspeakable thought – lustfully pursuing him? Or was the boot on the other foot? Was Syd, in fact, keeping observation on Ricky? Had Syd, for some unguessable reason, followed him on board the *Island Belle?* Into the bistro? Up the hill to the church? When cornered, were the abuse and insults a shambling attempt to throw him off the scent? Which was the hunter and which the hunted?

It had been after Syd's return from London and after Dulcie's death that he had, definitely, turned hostile. Why? Had anything happened when he lunched with Ricky's parents to make him so peculiar? Was it because Troy had not thought well of his paintings? Or had asked if he was messing about with drugs?

And here Ricky suddenly remembered Syd's face, six inches from his own, when they were *vis-à-vis* across the fish crate and Syd's dark glasses had slid down his nose. Were his eyes not pin-pupilled? And did he not habitually snuffle and sweat? And what about the night at Syd's pad when he asked if Ricky had ever taken a trip? And behaved very much as if he'd taken something-or-another himself? Could drugs in fact be the explanation? Of everything? The scene he made when vermilion paint burst out of the wrong end of the tube? The sulks? The silly violence? Everything?

A squalid, boring explanation, he thought, and one that didn't really satisfy him. There was something else. It came to him that he would very much like to rake the whole thing over with his father.

He descended the church tower and went out to the street. Which way? On up the hill to Jerome et Cie or back to the town? Without consciously coming to a decision he found he had turned to the right and was approaching the entrance to the factory.

Opposite to it was a café with chairs and tables set out under an awning. The day was beginning to be hot. He had walked quite a long way and climbed a tower. He chose a table beside a potted rubber plant whose leaves shielded him from the factory entrance but were not dense enough to prevent him watching it. He ordered beer and a roll and began to feel like a character in a *roman policier*. He supposed his father had often done this sort of thing and tried to imagine him, with his air of casual elegance, 'keeping observation' hour after hour with a pile of saucers mounting on the table. 'At a certain little café in the suburbs of St Pierre-des-Roches,' thought Ricky. That was how they began *romans policiers* in the salad days of the genre.

The beer was cold and delicious. It was fun to be keeping his own spot of observation, however pointless it might turn out to be.

Someone had left a copy of *Le Monde* on the table. He picked it up and began laboriously to read it, maintaining through the rubber plant leaves a pretty constant watch on the factory gates.

Feeling as if the waiters and every customer in the café observed him with astonishment, he contrived to make a hole in the paper which might be useful if, by some freakish chance, Syd should take it into his head to refresh himself when he emerged from the factory. Time went by slowly. It really was getting awfully hot. The newspaper tipped forward. He gave a galvanic jerk, opened his eyes and found himself looking through the rubber plant leaves at Syd Jones, crossing the street towards him.

Ricky whipped the paper up in front of his face and found that the peephole he had made was virtually useless. He stole a quick look over the top and there was Syd, sure enough, seating himself at a distant table with his back to Ricky. He dumped his paintbox on the unoccupied seat. There was no doubt that now it was extremely heavy.

Ricky asked himself what the devil he thought he was up to and why it had become so important to find a reason for Syd Jones taking a scunner to him. And why was he so concerned to find out if Syd doped himself? Was it because these were details in a pattern that refused to emerge and somehow or another – yes, that, absurdly, was it – could be associated with the death of Dulcie Harkness?

Having arrived at this preposterous conclusion, what was he going to do about it? Waste his little holiday by playing an inane game of hide-and-seek with Syd Jones and return to the Island no wiser than when he left it?

There were no looking-glasses in this café and Syd had his back to Ricky, who had widened the hole in *Le Monde*. He was assured that his legs were unrecognizable since he had changed into jeans and espadrilles.

The waiter took an order from Syd and came back with *café-nature* and a glass of water.

And now Ricky became riveted to the hole in his paper. Syd looked round furtively. There were only four other people including Ricky in the café and he had chosen a table far removed from any of them. Suddenly, as far as Ricky could make out, he put the glass on the seat of his chair, between his thighs. He then appeared to take something out of the breast pocket of his shirt. His head was sunk on his chest and he leant forward as if to rest his left forearm on his knee and seemed intent on some hidden object. He became very still. After a few seconds his right arm jerked slightly, there was a further manipulation of some sort, he raised his head and his body seemed to relax as if in the gift of the sun.

'That settles the drug question, poor sod,' thought Ricky.

But he didn't think it settled anything else.

Syd began to tap the ground with his foot as though keeping time with an invisible band. With the fingers of his right hand he beat a tattoo on the lid of his paintbox. Ricky heard him laugh contentedly. The waiter walked over to his table and looked at him. Syd groped in his pocket and dropped quite a little handful of coins on the table. The waiter picked up what was owing and waited for his tip. Syd made a wide extravagant gesture. 'Help yourself,' Ricky heard him say. *'Servez-vous, mon vieux,'* in execrable French. *'Prenez le tout.'* The man bowed and swept up the coins. He turned away, and for the benefit of his fellow-waiter, lifted his shoulders and rolled his head. Syd had not touched his coffee.

'Good morning, Mr Alleyn.'

Every nerve in Ricky's body seemed to leap. He let out an exclamation, dropped the newspaper and turned to find Mr Ferrant smiling down at him.

II

After the initial shock, Ricky's reaction was one of hideous embarrassment joined to fury. He sat there with a flaming face knowing himself to look the last word in abysmal foolishness. How long, Oh God, how long had Mr Ferrant stood behind him and watched him squint with screwed-up countenance through a hole in a newspaper at Syd Jones? Mr Ferrant, togged out in skin-tight modishly flared white trousers, a pink striped T-shirt, white buckskin sandals and a medallion on a silver chain. Mr Ferrant of the clustering curls and impertinent smile. Mr Ferrant, incongruously enough, the plumber and odd-job man.

'You made me jump,' Ricky said. 'Hullo. Mrs Ferrant said you might be here.'

Mr Ferrant snapped his fingers at the waiter.

'Mind if I join you?' he asked Ricky.

'No. Please do. What,' Ricky invited in a strange voice, 'will you have?'

He would have beer. Ricky ordered two beers and felt that he himself would be awash with it.

Ferrant, whose every move seemed to Ricky to express a veiled insolence, slid into a chair and stretched himself. 'When did you come over, then?' he asked.

'This morning.'

'Is that right?' he said easily. 'So did *he*,' and nodded across at Syd, who now fidgeted and looked at his watch. At any moment, Ricky thought, he might turn round and see them and what could that not lead to?

The waiter brought their beer. Ferrant lit a cigarette. He blew out smoke and wafted it away with a workman's hand. 'And what brought you over, anyway?' he asked.

'Curiosity,' said Ricky, and then hurriedly: 'To make a change from work.'

'Work? That'd be writing, wouldn't it?' he said, as if there was something suspect in the notion. 'Where you staying?' Ricky told him.

'That's a crummy little old place, that is,' he said. 'I go to Le Beau Rivage myself.'

He took the copy of *Le Monde* out of Ricky's nerveless grasp and stuck his blunt forefinger through the hole. 'Quite fascinating what you was reading, seemingly. Couldn't take your eyes off of it, could you, Mr Alleyn?'

'Look here,' Ricky said. He put his hand up to his face and felt its heat. 'I expect you think there was something a bit off about – about – my looking – about – But there wasn't. I can't explain but – '

'Me!' said Ferrant. 'Think! I don't think nothing.'

He drained his glass and clapped it down on the table. 'We all get our little fancies, like,' he said. 'Right? And why not? Nice drop of ale, that.' He was on his feet. 'Reckon I'll have a word with Syd,' he said. 'Quite a coincidence. He came in the morning boat, too. Lovely weather, isn't it? Might turn to thunder later on.'

He strolled across between the empty tables with slight but ineffable shifts of his vulgar little stern. Ricky could have kicked him but he could have kicked himself still harder.

It seemed an eternity before Ferrant reached Syd, who appeared to have dozed off. Ricky, held in a nightmarish inertia, could not take his eyes off them. Ferrant laid his hand on Syd's head and rocked it, not very gently, to and fro.

Syd opened his eyes. Ferrant twisted the head towards Ricky. He said something that didn't seem to register. Syd blinked and frowned as if unable to focus his eyes, but he made a feeble attempt to shake

Ferrant off. Ferrant released him with a bully's playful buffet. Ricky saw awareness dawn on Syd's face and a mounting anger.

Ferrant shifted the paintbox to the ground and sat down. He put his hand on Syd's knee and leant towards him. He might have been giving him some important advice. The waiter strolled towards Ricky, who paid and tipped him. He said something about, '*Un drôle de type, celui-là*', meaning Ferrant.

Ricky left the café. On his way out Ferrant waved to him.

He walked back into the town, chastened.

Perhaps the circumstance that most mortified him was the certainty that Ferrant by this time had told Syd about the hole in the newspaper.

The day had turned into a scorcher and the soles of his feet were cobbled with red-hot marbles. He reached the front and sought the shade of a wooden pavilion facing the sea. He shuffled out of his espadrilles, lit his pipe and began to feel a little better.

The *Island Belle* was still at her berth. After the upset with Syd Jones on the way over, Ricky hadn't thought of finding out when she sailed for Montjoy. He wondered whether he should call it a day, sail with her and retire upon his proper occupation of writing a book and perhaps licking the wounds in his self-esteem.

He was unable to make up his mind. French holiday-makers came and went, with the approach of noon the day grew hotter and the little pavilion less endurable. Ricky left it and walked painfully along the front to a group of three hotels, each of which had private access to a beach. He went into the first, Le Beau Rivage, hired bathing drawers and a towel and swam about among the decorous *bourgeoisie* hoping to become refreshed and in better heart.

What he did become was hungry. Unable to face the walk along scorching pavements, he took a taxi to his hotel, lunched there in a dark little *salon à manger* and retired to his room, where he fell into a very heavy sleep.

He woke, feeling awful, at three o'clock. The room had darkened. When he looked out of his window it was to the ominous rumble of thunder and at steely clouds rolling in from the north. The harbour had turned grey and choppy and the *Island Belle* jounced at her moorings. There were very few people about in the town and those that were to be seen walked quickly, seeking shelter.

Ricky was one of those beings who respond uncomfortably to electric storms. They produced a nervous tingling in his arms and legs and a sense of impending disaster. As a small boy they had aroused a febrile excitement, so that at one moment he wanted to hide and at the next to stand at the window or even go out of doors for the sheer terror of doing so. Although he had learned to control these reactions and to give little outward sign of them, the restlessness they induced even now was almost unbearable.

The room flashed up and out. Ricky counted the seconds automatically, scarcely knowing that he did so. 'One – a – b, Two – a – b – ' up to seven when the thunder broke. That meant, or so he had always believed, that the core of the storm was seven miles away and might or might not come nearer.

The sky behaved in the manner of a Gustave Doré engraving. A crack opened and a shaft of vivid sunlight darted down like God's vengeance upon the offending sea.

Ricky tingled from head to foot. The room had stealthily become much too small. He was invaded by an urge to prove himself to himself. 'I may have made a muck of my espionage,' he thought, 'but, by gum, I'm not going to stay in my bedroom with pins and needles because a couple of clouds are having it off up there. To hell with them.'

He fished a light raincoat out of his rucksack and ran downstairs, pulling it on as he went. The elderly clerk was asleep behind his desk.

Outside there was a stifled feeling in the air as if the town held its breath. Sounds – isolated footsteps, desultory voices and the hiss of tyres on the road – were all exaggerated. The sky was now so black that twilight seemed to have fallen on St Pierre-des-Roches.

Forked lightning wrote itself with a flourish across the Heavens and almost simultaneously a gigantic tin tray banged overhead. A woman in the street crossed herself and broke into a shuffle. Ricky thought: 'If I combed my hair it would crackle.'

A few big drops fell like bullets in the dust and then, tremendously, the rain came down.

It was a really ferocious storm. The streets were running streams, lightning whiplashed almost continuously, thunder mingled with the din made by rain on roofs, sea and stone. Ricky's espadrilles felt as if they dissolved on his feet.

But he went on downhill to the sea, taking a kind of satisfaction in pandemonium. Here was the bistro where he had breakfasted, here the first group of shops. And here the deserted front, not a soul on it, pounded by the deluge and beyond it the high tide pocked all over with rain. Le Beau Rivage overlooked this scene. Ricky could see a number of people staring out from its glassed-in portico and wondered if Ferrant was among them.

The *Island Belle* rocked at her moorings. Her gangway grated on the wharf.

Ricky saw that the administrative offices were shut, but a goods shed, in which three cars were parked, was open. He sheltered there. It was very dark. The rain drummed remorselessly on the roof. He got an impression of somebody else being in the shed: an impression so strong that he called out, 'Hullo! Anyone at home?' but there was no answer. He shook the rain from his mackintosh and hood and fished out his handkerchief to wipe his face. 'This has been a rum sort of a day,' he thought, and wondered how best to wind it up.

Evidently the *Island Belle* would not sail for some time. The cars and a number of crates were yet, he supposed, to be put aboard her. He thought he remembered that a notice of some sort was exhibited at the foot of the gangway: probably the time of sailing. The Cove and his own familiar island began to seem very attractive. He would find out when the *Island Belle* sailed, return to the hotel for his ruck-sack, pay his bill and rejoin her.

He pulled his hood well over his face and squelched out of the shed into the storm.

It was only a short distance to the ship's moorings. Her bows rose and fell and above the storm he could hear her rubbing-strake grind against the jetty. He walked forward into the rain and was half-blinded. When he came alongside the ship he stopped at the edge of the jetty and peered up, wondering if there was a watchman aboard.

The blow came as if it was part of the storm, a violence that struck him below the shoulders. The jetty had gone from under his feet. The side of the ship flew upwards. He thought: 'This is abominable,' and was hit in the face. Green cold enclosed him and his mouth was full of water. Then he knew what had happened.

He had fallen between the turn of the bilge and the jetty, had struck against something on his way down and had sunk and risen. Salt water stung the back of his nose and lodged in his throat. He floundered in a narrow channel between the legs of the jetty and the sloping side of the bilge.

'Did he fall or was he pushed?' thought Ricky, struggling in his prison, and knew quite definitely that he had been pushed.

III

He had no idea how much leeway the ship's moorings allowed her or whether she might roll to such a degree that he could be crushed against the legs of the jetty, the only motionless things in a heaving universe.

His head cleared. Instinctive physical reactions had kept him afloat for the first moments. He now got himself under control. 'I ought to yell,' he thought, and a distant thunderclap answered him. He turned on his back; the ship rolled and disclosed a faint daylight moon careering across a gap in the clouds. With great difficulty he began to swim, sometimes touching the piles and grazing his hands and feet on barnacles. The turn of the bilge passed slowly above him and at last was gone. He had cleared the bows of the *Island Belle*. There was St Pierre-des-Roches with the Hotel Beau Rivage and the hill and the church spire above it.

Now, should he yell for help? But there was still Somebody up there perhaps who wanted him drowned, crushed, whatever way – dead. He trod water, bobbing and ducking, and looked about him.

Not three feet away was a steel ladder.

When he reached and clung to it he still thought of the assailant who might be up there, waiting. He was now so cold that it would be better to risk anything rather than stay where he was. So he climbed, slowly. He had lost his espadrilles and the rungs bit into his feet. There was a sound like a voice very far away: In his head, he thought: Not real. Half-way up he paused. Everything had become quiet. It no longer rained.

'Hey! Hey there! Are you all right?'

For a moment he didn't know where to look. The voice seemed to have come out of the sky. Then he saw, in the bows of the ship, leaning over the taffrail, a man in oilskins and sou'wester. He waved at Ricky.

'Are you OK, mate?' shouted the man.

Ricky tried to answer but could only produce a croak.

'Hang on, I'll be with you. Hang on.'

Ricky hauled himself up another three rungs. His reeling head was just below the level of the jetty. He pushed his left arm through the rungs of the ladder and hung there, clinging with his right hand. He heard boots clump down the gangway and along the jetty towards him.

'You'll be all right,' said the voice, close above him. He let his head flop back. The face under the sou'wester was red and concerned and looked very big against the sky. An arm and a purplish hand reached down. 'Come on, then,' said the voice, 'only a couple more.'

'I'm sort of – gone – ' Ricky whispered.

'Not you. You're fine. Make the effort, Jack.'

He made the effort and was caught by the arms and saved.

He lay on the jetty saying: 'I'm sorry. I'm so sorry,' and being sick.

The man was very kind. He took off his oilskin and spread it over Ricky, whose teeth now chattered like castanets. He lay on his back and saw the clouds part and disperse. He felt the sun on his face.

'You're doing good, mate,' said the man. 'How's about we go on board and take a drop of something for the cold? You was aboard us this morning? That right?'

'Yes. This morning.'

'Up she rises. Take it easy. Lovely.'

He was on his feet. They began to move along the jetty.

'Is there anybody else?' Ricky said.

'How'd you mean, anybody else?'

'Watching.'

'You're not yourself. You'll be all right. Here we go, then.'

Ricky made heavy work of the gangway. Once on board he did what he was told. The man took him into the little saloon. He helped him strip and brought him a vest and heavy underpants. He lay on a bench and was covered with a blanket and overcoats and given half a tumbler of raw whisky. It made him gasp and shudder, but it ran through him like fire. 'Super,' he said. 'That's super.'

'What happened, then? Did you slip on the jetty or what?'

'I was pushed. No, I'm not wandering and I'm not tight – yet. I was given a bloody great shove in the back. I swear I was. Listen.'

The man listened. He scraped his jaw and eyed Ricky and every now and then wagged his head.

'I was looking up at the deck, trying to see if anyone was about. I wanted to know when she sails. I was on the edge almost. I can feel it now – two hands hard in the small of my back. I took a bloody great stride into damn-all and dropped. I hit something. Under my eye, it was.'

The man leant forward and peered at his face. 'It's coming up lovely,' he admitted. 'I'll say that for you.'

'Didn't you see anybody?'

'Me! I was taking a bit of kip, mate, wasn't I? Below. Something woke me, see. Thunder or what-have-you and I come up on deck and there you was, swimming and ducking and grabbing the ladder. I hailed you but you didn't seem to take no notice. Not at first you didn't.'

'He must have been hiding in the goods shed. He must have followed me down and sneaked into the shed.'

'Reckon you think you know who done it, do you? Somebody got it in for you, like?' He stared at Ricky. 'You don't look the type,' he said. 'Nor yet you don't sound like it, neither.'

'It's hard to explain,' Ricky sighed. He was beginning to feel sleepy.

'Look,' said the man, 'we sail at six. Was you thinking of sailing with us, then? Just to know, like. No hurry.'

'Oh, yes,' Ricky said. 'Yes, please.'

'Where's your dunnage?'

Ricky pulled himself together and told him. The man said his mate, the second deckhand, was relieving him as watchman at four-thirty. He offered to collect Ricky's belongings from the hotel and pay his bill. Ricky fished his waterproof wallet out of an inside pocket of his raincoat and found that the notes were not too wet to be presentable.

'I can't thank you enough,' he said. 'Look. Take a taxi. Buy yourself a bottle of scotch from me. You will, won't you?'

He said he would. He also said his name was Jim le Compte and they'd have to get Ricky dressed proper and sitting up before the Old Man came aboard them.

And by six o'clock Ricky was sitting in the saloon fully dressed with a rug over his knees. It was a smoother crossing than he had feared and rather to his surprise he was not sea-sick, but slept through most of it. At Montjoy he said goodbye to his friend. 'Look,' he said, 'Jim, I owe you a lot already. Will you do something more for me?'

'What would that be?'

'Forget about there being anyone else in it. I just skidded and fell. Please don't think,' Ricky added, 'that I'm in any sort of trouble. Believe me, I'm not. Word of honour. But – will you be a good chap and leave it that way?'

Le Compte looked at him for some moments with his head on one side. 'Fair enough, squire,' he said at last. 'If that's the way you want it. You skidded and fell.'

'You *are* a good chap,' said Ricky. He went ashore carrying a rucksack full of wet clothes and took a taxi to the Cove.

He let himself in and went straight upstairs, passing Mrs Ferrant who was speaking on the telephone.

When he entered his room a very tall man got up out of the armchair.

It was his father.

IV

'So you see I'm on duty,' said Alleyn. 'Fox and I have got a couple of tarted-up apartments at the Neo-Ritz, or whatever it calls itself, in Montjoy, the use of a police car and a tidy programme of routine work ahead. I wouldn't have any business talking to you, Rick, except that by an exasperating twist, you may turn out to be a source of information.'

'Hi!' said Ricky excitedly. 'Is it about Miss Harkness?'

'Why?' Alleyn asked sharply.

'I only wondered.'

'I wouldn't dream of telling you what it's about normally, but if we're to get any further I think I'll have to. And Rick – I want an absolute assurance that you'll discuss this business with nobody. But nobody. In the smallest degree. It must be as if it'd never been. Right?'

'Right,' said Ricky, and his father thought he heard a tinge of regret.

'Nobody,' Alleyn repeated. 'And certainly not Julia Pharamond.'

Ricky blushed.

'As far as you're concerned, Fox and I have come over to discuss a proposed adjustment to reciprocal procedure between the island constabulary and the mainland police. We shall be sweating it out at interminable and deadly-boring meetings. That's the story. Got it?'

'Yes, Cid.'

'Cid', deriving from CID, was the name Ricky and his friends gave his father.

'Yes. And nobody's going to believe it when we start nosing round at the riding stables. But never mind. Let's say that as we were here, the local chaps thought they'd like a second opinion. By the way, talking about local chaps, the Super at Montjoy hasn't helped matters by bursting his appendix and having an urgent operation. The local sergeant at the Cove – Plank – but, of course, you know Plank – is detailed to the job.'

'He's nobody's fool.'

'Good. Now, coming back to you. The really important bit to remember is that we must be held to take no interest whatever in Mr Ferrant's holidays and we've never even heard of Sydney Jones.'

'But,' Ricky ventured, 'I've told the Pharamonds about his visit to you and Mum.'

'Damn. All right, then. It passed off quietly and nothing has ever come of it.'

'If you say so.'

'I do say so. Loud and clear.'

'Yes, Cid.'

'Good. All right. Are you hungry, by the way?'

'Now you mention it.'

'Could that formidable lady downstairs be persuaded to give us both something to eat?'

'I'm sure. I'll ask her.'

'You'd better tell her you slid on the wet wharf and banged your cheek on a stanchion.'

'She'll think I was drunk.'

'Good. You smell like a scotch hangover anyway. Are you sure you're all right, old boy? Sure?'

'Fine. Now. I'll have a word with Mrs F.'

When he'd gone, Alleyn looked out of the window at the darkening Cove and turned over Ricky's account of his visit to St Pierre-des-Roches and the events that preceded it. People, he reflected, liked to talk about police cases in terms of a jigsaw puzzle and that was fair enough as far as it went. But in this instance he couldn't be sure that the bits all belonged to the same puzzle. 'Only connect,' Forster owlishly laid down as the novelist's law. He could equally have been setting out a guide for investigating officers.

There had never been any question of Ricky following in his father's footsteps. From the time when his son went to his first school, Alleyn had been at pains to keep his job at a remove as far as the boy was concerned. Ricky's academic career had been more than satisfactory and about as far removed from the squalor, boredom, horror and cynicism of a policeman's lot as it would be possible to imagine.

And now? Here they were, both of them, converging on a case that might well turn out to be all compact of such elements. And over and above everything else, here was Ricky, escaped from what, almost certainly, had been a murderous attack, the thought of which sent an icy spasm through his father's stomach. Get him out of it, smartly, now, before there was any further involvement, he thought – and then had to recognize that already Ricky's involvement was too far advanced for this to be possible. He must be treated as someone who might, himself in the clear, provide the police with 'helpful information'.

And at the back of his extreme distaste for this development, why was there an indefinable warmth, a latent pleasure? He wondered if perhaps an old loneliness had been, or looked to become, a little assuaged.

Ricky came back with the assurance that Mrs Ferrant was concocting a dish, the mere smell of which would cause the salivary glands of a hermit to spout like fountains.

'She's devoured by curiosity,' he said. 'About you. Why you're here. What you do. Whether you're cross with me. The lot. She'd winkle information out of a Trappist monk, that one would. I can't wait.'

'For what?'

'For her to start on you.'

'Rick,' Alleyn said. 'She's Mrs Ferrant, and Ferrant, you tell me, is mysteriously affluent, goes in for solitary night-fishing, pays dressy visits to St Pierre-des-Roches and seems to be thick with Jones. With Jones who also visits there and goes to London carrying paint and who, since he's found out your father is a cop, has taken a scunner to you. You think Jones dopes. So do I. Ferrant seems to have a bully's ascendancy over Jones. One of them, you think, tried to murder you. It follows that you watch your step with Mrs Ferrant, don't you agree?'

'Yes. Of course. And I always have. Not because of any of that but because she's so bloody insatiable. About the Pharamonds in particular. Especially about Louis.'

'Yes?'

'Yes. And I'll tell you what. I think when she was cooking or whatever she did up at L'Esperance, she had a romp on the side with Louis.'

'Why?'

'Because of the way he talks about her. The bedside manner. And – well, because of that kid.'

'The Ferrant kid?'

'That's right. There's a look. Unmistakable, I'd have thought. Dark and cheeky and a bit of a slyboots.'

'Called?'

'Wait for it.'

'Louis?'

Ricky nodded.

'It's as common a French name as can be,' said Alleyn.

'Yes, of course,' Ricky agreed, 'and it'd be going altogether too far, one would think, wouldn't one? To christen him that if Louis was – ' He made a dismissive gesture. 'It's probably just my dirty mind after all. And – well – '

'You don't like Louis Pharamond?'

'Not much. Does it show?'

'A bit.'

'He was on that voyage when you met them, wasn't he?' Ricky asked. Alleyn nodded. 'Did you like him?'

'Not much.'

'Good.'

'Which signifies," Alleyn said, 'damn all.'

'He had something going with Miss Harkness.'

'For pity's sake!' Alleyn exclaimed. 'How many more and why do you think so?'

Ricky described the incident on the cliffs. 'It had been a rendez-vous,' he said rather importantly. 'You could tell.'

'I don't quite see how when you say you were lying flat on your face behind a rock, but let that pass.'

Ricky tried not to grin. 'Anyway,' he said, 'I bet I'm right. He's a prowler.'

'Rick,' Alleyn said after a pause, 'I'm here on a sort of double job which is my Assistant Commissioner's Machiavellian idea of econ-omy. I'm here because the local police are worried about the death of Dulcie Harkness and have asked us to nod in, and I'm also supposed in an off-hand, carefree manner to look into the possibility of this island being a penultimate station in one of the heroin routes into Great Britain.'

'Lawks!'

'Yes. Of course you've read about the ways the trade is run. Every kind of outlandish means of transit is employed – electric light-fittings, component parts for hearing aids, artificial limbs, fat men's navels, anything hollow – you name it. If the thing's going on here there's got to be some way of getting the stuff out of Marseilles, where the con-version into heroin is effected, across to St Pierre, from there to the island and thence to the mainland. Anything suggest itself?'

'Such as why did Jones cut up so rough when I trod on his paint?'

'Go on.'

'He does seem to make frequent trips – Hi!' Ricky said, interrupt-ing himself. 'Would this mean Jerome et Cie were in it or that Jones was on his own?'

'Probably the former, but it's anyone's guess.'

'And Ferrant? The way he behaved with Syd at St Pierre. Could they be in cahoots? Is there anything on Ferrant?'

'The narcotics boys say he's being watched. Apparently he makes these pleasure trips rather often and has been known to fly down to Marseilles and the Côte d'Azur where he's been seen hob-nobbing with recognized traders.'

'But what's he supposed to *do*?'

'They've nothing definite. He may have the odd rendezvous on calm nights when he goes fishing. Suppose – and this is the wildest guesswork – but suppose a gentleman with similar propensities puts out from St Pierre with a consignment of artists' paints. They've been opened at the bottom and capsules of heroin pushed up and filled in nice and tidy with paint. Then a certain amount is squeezed out at the top and the tubes messed about to look used. And in due course they go into Syd Jones's paintbox among his rightful materials and he takes one of his trips over to London. The stuff he totes round to shops and artists' studios is of course pure as pure. The Customs people have got used to him and his paintbox. They probably did their stuff at some early stages before he began to operate. Even now, if they got curious, the odds are they'd hit on the wrong tube. One would suppose he doesn't distribute more than a minimum of the doctored jobs among his legitimate material. Of which the vermilion you put your great hoof on was one.'

Alleyn stopped. He looked at his son and saw a familiar glaze of incredulity and interest on his open countenance.

'Don't get it wrong,' he said. 'That may be all my eye. Mr Jones may be as pure as the driven snow. But if you can find another reason for him taking such a scunner to you, let's have it. Rick, consider. You visit his pad and show an interest in his Jerome et Cie paint. A few days later you tread on his vermilion and try to pick up the tube. You send him to us and when he gets there he's asked if he's messing about with drugs. On top of that he learns that your pop's a cop. He sets out on a business trip to headquarters and who does he find dodging about among the cargo? You, chummy. He's rattled and lets fly, accusing you of the first offence he can think of that doesn't bear any relation to his actual on-goings. And to put the lid on it you dog his footsteps almost to the very threshold of Messrs Jerome et Cie. And don't forget, all this may be a farrago of utter nonsense.'

'It adds up, I suppose. Or does it?'

'If you know a better "ole" – '

'What about Ferrant, then? Are they in cahoots over the drug racket?'

'It could be. It looks a bit like it. And Ferrant it is who finds you – What exactly *were* you doing? Show me.'

'Have a heart.'

'Come on.' Alleyn picked up a copy of yesterday's *Times*. 'Show me.' Ricky opened it and tore a hole in the centre fold. He then advanced his eye to the hole, screwed up his face and peered through.

Alleyn looked over the top of *The Times*. 'Boh!' he said.

Mrs Ferrant came in.

'Your bit of supper's ready,' she said, regarding them with surprise. 'In the parlour.'

Self-conscious, they followed her downstairs.

The aroma – delicate, pervasive and yet discreet – welcomed them into the parlour. The dish, elegantly presented, was on the table. The final assembly had been completed, the garniture was in place. Mrs Ferrant, saucepan in hand, spooned the shell-fish sauce over hot fillets of sole.

'My God!' Alleyn exclaimed. '*Sole à la Dieppoise!*'

His success with the cook could only be compared with that of her masterpiece with him. Ricky observed, with mounting wonderment and small understanding, since the conversation was in French, the rapport his father instantly established with Mrs Ferrant. He questioned her about the sole, the shrimps, the mussels. In a matter of minutes he had elicited the information that Madame (as he was careful to call her) had a maman who actually came from Dieppe and from whom she inherited her art. He was about to send Ricky out at the gallop to purchase a bottle of white Burgundy, when Mrs Ferrant, a gratified smirk twitching at her lips, produced one. He kissed her hand and begged her to join them. She consented. Ricky's eyes opened wider and wider.

As the strange little feast progressed he became at least partially tuned in. He gathered that his father had steered the conversation round to the Pharamonds and the days of her service up at L'Esperance. 'Monsieur Louis' came up once or twice. He was sophisticated. A very mondain type, was he not? One might say so, said Mrs Ferrant with a shrug. It was her turn to ask questions. Monsieur Alleyn was well acquainted with the family, for example? Not to say 'well'. They had been fellow-passengers on an ocean voyage. Monsieur's visit was unanticipated by his son, was it not? But entirely so. It had been pleasant to surprise him. So droll the expression, when he walked in. Jaw dropped, eyes bulging, Alleyn gave a lively imitation and slapped his son jovially on the shoulder.

Ah yes, for example, his black eye, Mrs Ferrant enquired, and switching to English asked Ricky what he'd been doing with himself, then, in St Pierre. Had he got into bad company? Ricky offered the fable of the iron stanchion. Her stewed prune eyes glittered and she said something in French that sounded like *à d'autres*: Ricky wondered whether it was the equivalent of 'tell us another'.

'You got yourself in a proper mess,' she pointed out. 'Dripping wet those things are in your rucksack.'

'I got caught in the thunderstorm.'

'Did it rain seaweed, then?' asked Mrs Ferrant, and for the first time in their acquaintance gave out a cackle of amusement in which, to Ricky's fury, his father joined.

'*Ah, madame!*' said Alleyn with a comradely look at Mrs Ferrant. '*Les jeunes hommes!*'

She nodded her head up and down. Ricky wondered what the hell she supposed he'd been up to.

The *sole à la Dieppoise* was followed by the lightest of sorbets, a cheese board, coffee and cognac.

'I have not eaten so well,' Alleyn said, 'since I was last in Paris. You are superb, madame.'

The conversation proceeded bilingually and drifted round to Miss Harkness and what Alleyn, with, as his son felt, indecent understatement, referred to as *son contretemps équestre*.

Mrs Ferrant put on an air of grandeur, of sombre loftiness. It had been unfortunate, she conceded. Miss Harkness's awful face and sightless glare flashed up in Ricky's remembrance.

She had perhaps been of a reckless disposition, Alleyn hinted. In more ways than one, Mrs Ferrant agreed, and sniffed very slightly.

'By the way, Rick,' Alleyn said. 'Did I forget to say? Your Mr Jones called on us in London.'

'Really?' said Ricky, managing to sound surprised. 'What on earth for? Selling Mummy his paints?'

'Well – advertising them, shall we say. He showed your mother some of his work.'

'What did she think?'

'I'm afraid, not a great deal.'

It was Mrs Ferrant's turn again. Was Mrs Alleyn, then, an artist? An artist of great distinction, perhaps? And Alleyn himself? He was on holiday, no doubt? No, no, Alleyn said. It was a business trip. He would be staying in Montjoy for a few days but had taken the opportunity to visit his son. Quite a coincidence, was it not, that Ricky should be staying at the Cove. Lucky fellow! Alleyn cried, catching him another buffet and bowing at the empty dishes.

Mrs Ferrant didn't in so many words ask Alleyn what his job was, but she came indecently close to it. Ricky wondered if his father would side-step the barrage, but no, he said cheerfully that he was a policeman. She offered a number of exclamations. She would never have dreamt of it! A policeman! In English she accused him of 'having her on', and in French of not being the type. It was all very vivacious and Ricky didn't believe a word of it. His ideas on Mrs Ferrant were undergoing a rapid transformation, due in part, he thought, to her command of French. He couldn't follow much of what she said, but the sound of it lent a gloss of sophistication to her general demeanour. It put her into a new category. She had become more formidable. As for his father: it was as if some frisky stranger laughed and flattered and almost flirted. Was this The Cid? What were they talking about now? About Mr Ferrant and his trips to St Pierre and how he would never eat as well abroad as he did at home. He had business connections in France perhaps? No. Merely family ones. He liked to keep up with his aunts . . .

Ricky had had a long, painful and distracting day of it. Impossible to believe that only this morning he and Sydney Jones had leant nose-to-nose across a crate of fish on a pitching deck. And how odd those people looked, scuttling about so far below. Like woodlice. Awful to fall from the balcony among them. But he *was* falling: down, down into the disgusting sea.

'Arrrach!' he tried to shout, and looked into his father's face and felt his hands on his shoulders. Mrs Ferrant had gone.

'Come along, old son,' Alleyn said, and his deep voice was very satisfactory. 'Bed. Call it a day.'

V

Inspector Fox was discussing a pint of mild-and-bitter when Alleyn walked into the bar at the Cod-and-Bottle. He was engaged in dignified conversation with the landlord, three of the habituals and

Sergeant Plank. Alleyn saw that he was enjoying his usual success. They hung upon his words. His massive back was turned to the door and Alleyn approached him unobserved.

'That's where you hit the nail smack on the head, Sergeant,' he was saying. 'Calm, cool and collected. You've had the experience of working with him?'

'Well,' said Sergeant Plank, clearing his throat, 'in a very subsidiary position, Mr Fox. But I remarked upon it.'

'You remarked upon it. Exactly. So've I. For longer than you might think, Mr Maistre,' said Fox, drawing the landlord into closer communion. 'And a gratifying experience it's been. However,' said Mr Fox, who had suddenly become aware of Alleyn's approach, '*Quoi qu'il en soit.*'

The islanders were bilingual, and Mr Fox never let slip an opportunity to practise his French or to brag, in a calm and stately manner, of the excellencies of his superior officer. It was seldom that Alleyn caught him at this exercise and when he did, he gave him fits. But that made little difference to Fox, who merely pointed out that the technique had proved a useful approach to establishing comfortable relations with persons from whom Alleyn hoped to obtain information.

'By and large,' Mr Fox had said, 'people like to know about personalities in the Force so long as they're in the clear themselves. They get quite curious to meet you, Mr Alleyn, when they hear about your little idiosyncrasies: it takes the stiffness out of the first enquiries, if you see what I mean. In theatrical parlance,' Fox had added, 'they call it building up an entrance.'

'In common-or-garden parlance,' Alleyn said warmly, 'it makes a bloody great fool out of me.' Fox had smiled slightly.

On this occasion it was clear that the Foxian method had been engaged and, it was pretty obvious, abetted, by Sergeant Plank. Alleyn found himself the object of fixed and silent attention in the bar of the Cod-and-Bottle and the evident subject of intense speculation.

Mr Fox, who was infallible in remembering names at first hearing, performed introductions and Alleyn shook hands all round. Throats were cleared and boots were shuffled. Bob Maistre deployed his own technique as host and asked Alleyn how he'd found the young chap, then, and what was all this they'd heard about him getting himself into trouble over to St Pierre? Alleyn gave a lively account of his son losing his footing on the wet jetty, hitting his jaw on an iron stanchion and falling between the jetty and the *Island Belle*.

'Could have been a serious business,' he said, 'as far as I can make out. No knowing what might have happened if it hadn't been for this chap aboard the ship – Jim le Compte, isn't it?'

It emerged that Jim le Compte was a Cove man and this led easily to the introduction of local gossip, easing round under Plank's pilotage, to Mr Ferrant and to wags of the head and knowing grins suggesting that Gil Ferrant was a character, a one, a bit of a lad.

'He's lucky,' Alleyn said lightly, 'to be able to afford jaunts in France, I wish I could.'

This drew forth confused speculations as to Gil Ferrant's resources: his rich aunties in Brittany, his phenomenal luck on the French lotteries, his being, in general, a pretty warm customer.

This turn of conversation was, to Alleyn's hidden fury, interrupted by Sergeant Plank, who offered the suggestion that no doubt the Chief Super's professional duties sometimes took him across the Channel. Seeing it was expected of him, Alleyn responded with an anecdote or two about a sensational case involving the pursuit and arrest in Marseilles, with the assistance of the French force, of a notable child-killer. This, as Fox said afterwards, went down like a nice long drink, but, as he pointed out to Sergeant Plank, had the undesirable effect of cutting off any further local gossip. 'It was well-meant on your part, Sarge,' Mr Fox conceded, 'but it broke the thread. It stopped the flow of info.'

'I'm a source of local info myself, Mr Fox,' Sergeant Plank ventured. 'In my own person, I am.'

'True enough as far as it goes, Sarge, but you're overlooking a salient factor. As the Chief Super has frequently remarked, ours is a solitary class of employment. We can, and in your own type of patch, the village community, we often do, establish friendly relations. Trespassing, local vandalism, creating nuisances, trouble with neighbours and they're all over you, but let something big turn up and you'll find yourself out on your own. They'll herd together like sheep and you won't be included in the flock. It can be uncomfortable till you get used to it.'

Fox left a moment or two for this to sink in. He then cleared his throat and continued. 'The effect of the diversion,' he said, 'was this.

The thread of local gossip being broken, what did they do? They got all curious about the Chief. What's he here for? Is it the Harkness fatality, and if not, what is it? And if it is, why is it? Enough to create the wrong atmosphere at the site of investigation.'

Whether or not these pronouncements were correct, the atmosphere at Leathers the next morning, as disseminated by Mr Harkness, the sole occupant, was far from comfortable. Alleyn, Fox and Plank arrived at eight-thirty to find shuttered windows and a notice pinned to the front door: 'Stables Closed till Further Notice.' They knocked and rang to no effect.

'He'll be round at the back,' Plank said, and led the way to the stables.

At first they seemed to be deserted. A smell of straw and horse-droppings hung on the air, flies buzzed, and in the old open coach-house a couple of pigeons waddled about the floor, pecked here and there and flew up to the rafters where they defecated off-handedly on the roof of the battered car. In the end loose-box the sorrel mare reversed herself, looked out, rolled her eyes, pricked her ears at them and trembled her nostrils in an all but inaudible whinny.

'Will I see if I can knock Cuth Harkness up, sir?' offered Plank.

'Wait a bit, Plank. Don't rush it.'

Alleyn strolled over to the loose-box. 'Hullo, old girl,' he said, 'how goes it?' He leant on the half-door and looked her over. The near foreleg was still bandaged. She nibbled his ear with velvet lips. 'Feeling bored, are you?' he said, and moved down the row of empty loose-boxes to the coach-house.

There was the coil of old wire where Ricky had seen it, hanging from a peg above a pile of empty sacks. It was rather heavier than picture-hanging wire and looked as if it had been there for a long time. But as Ricky had noticed, there was a freshly-cut end. Alleyn called Fox and the sergeant over. Plank's boots, being of the regulation sort, loudly announced his passage across the yard. He changed to tip-toe and an unnerving squeak.

'Take a look,' Alleyn murmured.

'I reckon,' Plank said after a heavy-breathed examination, 'that could be it, Mr Alleyn. I reckon that would fit.'

'Do you, by George,' Alleyn said.

There was an open box in the corner filled with a jumble of odds-and-ends and a number of tools, among them a pair of wire-cutters. With uncanny speed Alleyn used them to nip off three inches of wire from the reverse end.

'That, Sergeant Plank,' he said, as he replaced the cutters, 'is something we must never, never do.'

'I'll try to remember, sir,' said Sergeant Plank demurely.

'Mr Harkness,' Fox said, 'seems to be coming, Mr Alleyn.'

And indeed he could be heard coughing hideously inside the house. Alleyn reached the door in a breath and the other two stood behind him. He knocked briskly.

Footsteps sounded in the passage and an indistinguishable grumbling. A lock was turned and the door dragged open a few inches. Mr Harkness, blinking and unshaven, peered out at them through a little gale of Scotch whisky.

'The stables are closed,' he said thickly, and made as if to shut the door. Alleyn's foot was across the threshold.

'Mr Harkness?' he said. 'I'm sorry to bother you. We're police officers. Could you give us a moment?'

For a second or two he neither spoke nor moved. Then he pulled the door wide open.

'Police, are you?' Mr Harkness said. 'What for? Is it about my poor sinful niece again, God forgive her, but that's asking too much of Him? Come in.'

He showed them into his office and gave them chairs and seemed to become aware, for the first time, of Sergeant Plank.

'Joey Plank,' he said. 'You again. Can't you let it alone? What's the good? It won't bring her back. Vengeance is mine, saith the Lord, and she's finding that out for herself where she's gone. Who are these gentlemen?'

Plank introduced them: 'The Chief Superintendent is on an administrative visit to the island, Mr Harkness,' he said, 'and has kindly offered to take a wee look-see at our little trouble.'

'Why do you talk in that silly way about it?' Mr Harkness asked fretfully. 'It's not a little trouble, it's hell and damnation and she's brought it on herself and I'm the cause of it. I'm sorry,' he said, and turned to Alleyn with a startling change to normality. 'You'll think me awfully rude but I dare say you'll understand what a shock this has been.'

'Of course we do,' Alleyn said. 'We're sorry to break in on you like this, but Superintendent Curie in Montjoy suggested it.'

'I suppose he thinks he knows what he's talking about,' Mr Harkness grumbled. His manner now suggested a mixture of hopelessness and irritation. His eyes were bloodshot, his hands unsteady and his breath was dreadful. 'What's this about the possibility of foul play? What do they think I am, then? If there was any chance of foul play, wouldn't I be zealous in the pursuit of unrighteousness? Wouldn't I be sleepless night and day as the hound of Heaven until the awful truth was hunted down?' He glared moistly at Alleyn. 'Well,' he shouted. 'Come on! *Wouldn't I?*'

'I'm sure you would,' Alleyn hurriedly agreed.

'Very natural and proper,' said Fox.

'You shut up,' said Mr Harkness, but absently and without rancour.

'Mr Harkness,' Alleyn began, and checked himself. 'I'm sorry – should I be giving you your rank? I don't know – '

The shaky hand drifted to the toothbrush moustache. 'I don't insist on it,' the thick voice mumbled. 'Might of course. But let it pass. Mr's good enough.' The wraith of the riding-master faded and the distracted zealot returned. 'Pride,' said Mr Harkness, 'is the deadliest of all the sins. You were saying?'

He leant towards Alleyn with a parody of anxious attentiveness.

Alleyn was very careful. He explained that in cases of fatality the police had a duty to eliminate the possibility of any verdict but that of accident. Sometimes, he said, there were features that at first sight seemed to preclude this. 'More often than not,' he said, 'these features turn out to be of no importance, but we do have to make sure of it.'

With an owlish and insecure parody of the conscientious officer, Mr Harkness said: 'Cer'nly. Good show.'

Alleyn, with difficulty, took him through the period between the departure and return of the riding-party. It emerged that Mr Harkness had spent most of the day in the office concocting material for religious handouts. He gave a disjointed account of locking his niece in her room and of her presumed escape, and said distractedly that some time during the afternoon, he could not recall when, he had gone into the barn to pray but had noticed nothing untoward and had met nobody. He began to wilt.

'Where did you have your lunch?' Alleyn asked.

'Excuse me,' said Mr Harkness, and left the room.

'Now what!' Mr Fox exclaimed.

'Call of nature?' Sergeant Plank suggested.

'Or the bottle,' Alleyn said. 'Damn.'

He looked about the office: at faded photographs of equestrian occasions; of a barely recognizable and slim Mr Harkness in the uniform of a mounted-infantry regiment. A more recent photograph displayed a truculent young woman in jodhpurs displaying a sorrel mare.

'That's Dulce,' said Sergeant Plank. 'That was,' he added.

The desk was strewn with bills, receipts and a litter of brochures and pamphlets, some of a horsy description, others proclaiming in dated, execrable type the near approach of judgement and eternal damnation. In the centre was a letter pad covered in handwriting that began tidily and deteriorated into an illegible scrawl. This seemed to be a draft for a piece on the lusts of the flesh. Above and to the left of the desk was the corner-cupboard spotted by Ricky and Jasper Pharamond. The door was not quite closed and Alleyn flipped it open. Inside was the whisky bottle and behind this, as if thrust out of sight but still distinguishable, the card with a red ink skull-and-crossbones and the legend – 'BEWARE! This Way Lies Damnation! ! !' The bottle was empty.

Alleyn reached out a long finger and lifted a corner of the card, exposing a small carton half-filled with capsules.

'Look at this, Br'er Fox,' he said.

Fox put on his spectacles and peered.

'Well, well,' he said, and after a closer look: 'Simon Frères. Isn't there something, now, about Simon Frères?'

'Amphetamines. Dexies. Prohibited in Britain,' Alleyn said. He opened the carton and shook one capsule into his palm. He had replaced the carton and pocketed the capsule when Fox said, 'Coming.'

Alleyn shut the cupboard door and was back in his chair as an uneven footstep announced the return of Mr Harkness. He came in on a renewed fog of scotch.

'Apologize,' he said, 'Bowels all to blazes. Result of shock. You were saying?'

'I'd said all of it, I think,' Alleyn replied. 'I was going to ask, though, if you'd mind our looking over the ground outside. Where it happened and so on.'

'Go where you like,' he said, 'but don't, please, please don't, ask me to come.'

'Of course, if you'd rather not.'

'I dream about that gap,' he whispered. There was a long and difficult silence. 'They made me see her,' he said at last. 'Identification. She looked awful.'

'I know.'

'Well,' he said with one of his most disconcerting changes of manner, 'I'll leave you to it. Good hunting.' Incredibly he let out a bark of what seemed to be laughter, and rose, with difficulty, to his feet. He had begun to weep.

They had reached the outside door when he erupted into the passage, and ricocheting from one wall to the other, advanced towards Alleyn, upon whom he thrust a pink brochure.

Alleyn took it and glanced at flaring headlines.

'WINE IS A MOCKER,' he saw. 'STRONG DRINK IS RAGING.'

'Read,' Mr Harkness said with difficulty, 'mark, learn and inwardly indigest. See you on Sunday.'

He executed an abrupt turn and once more retired, waving airily as he did so. His uneven footsteps faded down the passage.

Fox said thoughtfully: 'He won't last long at that rate.'

'He's not himself, Mr Fox,' Plank said, rather as if he felt bound to raise excuses for a local product. 'He's very far from being himself. It's the liquor.'

'You don't tell me.'

'He's not used to it, like.'

'He's learning, though,' Fox said.

Alleyn said: 'Didn't he drink? Normally?'

'TT. Rabid. Hell-fire, according to him. Since he was Saved,' Plank added.

'Saved from what?' Fox asked. 'Oh, I see what you mean. Eternal damnation and all that carry-on. What was that about "See you Sunday?" Has anything been said about seeing him on Sunday?'

'Not by me,' Alleyn said. 'Wait a bit.'

He consulted the pink brochure. Following some terrifying information about the evils of intemperance, it went on to urge a full attendance at the Usual Sunday Gathering in the Old Barn at Leathers with Service and Supper, Gents 50p, Ladies a Basket.

Across these printed instructions a wildly irregular hand had scrawled: 'Special! Day of Wrath! ! May 13th! ! ! Remember! ! ! !'

'What's funny about May 13th?' asked Plank and then: 'Oh. Of course. Dulcie.'

'Will it be a kind of memorial service?' Fox speculated.

'Whatever it is, we shall attend it,' said Alleyn. 'Come on.' And he led the way outside.

The morning was sunny and windless. In the horse-paddock two of the Leathers string obligingly nibbled each others' flanks. On the hillside beyond the blackthorn hedge three more grazed together, swishing their tails and occasionally tossing up their heads.

'Peaceful scene, sir?' Sergeant Plank suggested.

'Isn't it?' Alleyn agreed. 'Would that be the Old Barn?' He pointed to a building at some distance from the stables.

'That's it, sir. That's where they hold their meetings. It's taken on surprising in the district. By all accounts he's got quite a following.'

'Ever been to one, Plank?'

'Me, Mr Alleyn? Not in my line. We're C of E., me and my missus. They tell me this show's very much in the blood-and-thunder line.'

'We'll take a look at the barn later.'

They walked down to the gap in the hedge.

An improvised but sturdy fence had been built enclosing the area where the sorrel mare had taken off for her two jumps. Pieces of raised weather-board covered the hoof prints.

'Who ordered all this?' Alleyn asked. 'The Super?'

After a moment Plank said: 'Well, no, sir.'

'You did it on your own?'

'Sir.'

'Good for you, Plank. Very well done.'

'Sir,' said Plank, crimson with gratification.

He lifted and replaced the boards for Alleyn. 'There wasn't anything much in the way of human prints,' he said. 'There's been heavy rain. And, of course, horses' hoof prints all over the shop.'

'You've saved these.'

'I took casts,' Plank murmured.

'You'll be getting yourself in line for a halo,' said Alleyn, and they moved to the gap itself. The blackthorn in the gap had been considerably knocked about. Alleyn looked over it and down and across to the far bank where a sort of plastic tent had been erected. Above and around this a shallow drain had been dug.

'That's one hell of a dirty great jump,' Alleyn said.

There was a massive slide down the near bank and a scramble of hoof prints on the far one.

'As I read them,' Plank ventured, 'it looks as if the mare made a mess of the jump, fell all ways down this bank and landed on top of her rider on the far side.'

'And it looks to me,' Alleyn rejoined, 'that you're not far wrong.'

He examined the two posts on either side of the gap. They were half hidden by blackthorn, but when this was held aside, scars, noticed by Ricky, were clearly visible: on one post thin rounded grooves, obviously of recent date, on the other, similar grooves dragged upwards from the margin. Both posts were loose in the ground.

At considerable discomfort to himself, Alleyn managed to clear a way to the base of the left-hand post and crawl into it.

'The earth's been disturbed,' he grunted. 'Round the base.'

He backed out, groped in his pocket and produced his three inches of fencing wire from the coach-house.

'Here comes the nitty-gritty bit,' said Fox.

He and Plank wrapped handkerchiefs round their hands and held back obstructing brambles. Alleyn cupped his scratched left hand under one of the grooves, and with his right finger and thumb insinuated his piece of wire into it. It fitted snugly.

'Bob's your uncle,' said Fox.

'A near relation at least. Let's try elsewhere.'

They did so, with the same result on both posts.

'Well, Plank,' Alleyn said, sucking the back of his hand, 'how do you read the evidence?'

'Sir, like I did before, if you'll excuse my saying so, though I hadn't linked it up with that coil in the coachhouse. Should have done, of course, but I missed it.'

'Well?'

'It looks like there was this wire, strained between the posts. It'd been there a long time, because coming, as we now know, from the lot in the coach-house it must have been rusty.' Plank caught himself up. 'Here. Wait a mo,' he said. 'Forget that. That was silly.'

'Take your time.'

'Ta. No. Wipe that. Excuse me, sir. But it had been there a long time because the wire marks are overgrown by thorn.'

Fox cleared his throat.

'What about that one, Fox?' Alleyn said.

'It doesn't follow. Not for sure. It wants closer examination,' Fox said. 'It could have been rigged from the far side.'

'I think so. Don't you, Plank?'

'Sir,' said Plank, chastened.

'Go on, though. When was it removed from the barn?'

'Recently. Recently it was, sir. Because the cut end was fresh.'

'Where is it?'

'We don't know that, do we, sir?'

'Not on the peg in the coach-house, at least. That lot's in one piece. What does all this seem to indicate?'

'I'd kind of thought,' said Plank carefully, 'it pointed to her having cut it away before she attempted the jump. It's very dangerous, sir, isn't it, in horse-jumping – wire is. Hidden wire.'

'Very.'

'Would the young chap,' Fox asked, 'have noticed it if it was in place when he jumped?'

Alleyn walked back to the prints of the sorrel mare's take-off and looked at the gap.

'Old wire. It wouldn't catch the light, would it? We'll have to ask the young chap.'

Plank cleared his throat. 'Excuse me, sir,' he said. 'I did carry out a wee routine check along the hedgerow, and there's no wire there. I'd say, never has been.'

'Right.' Alleyn hesitated for a moment. 'Plank,' he said, 'I can't talk to your Super till he's off the danger list, so I'll be asking you about matters I'd normally discuss with him.

'Sir,' said Plank, fighting down any overt signs of gratification.

'Why was it decided to keep the case open?'

'Well, sir, on account really of the wire. I reported what I could make out of the marks on the posts and the Super had a wee look-see. That was the day he took bad with the pain, like. It were that evening his appendix bust and they operated on him, and his last instructions to me was: "Apply for an adjournment and keep your trap shut. It'll have to be the Yard." '

'I see. Has anything been said to Mr Harkness about the wire?'

'There has, but bloody-all come of it. Far's I could make out it's been there so long he'd forgotten about it. *Was* there, in fact, before he bought the place. He reckons Dulcie went down and cut it away before she jumped, which is what I thought seemed to make sense if anything he says can be so classed. But Gawd knows,' said Plank, removing his helmet and looking inside it as if for an answer, 'he was that put about there was no coming to grips with the man. Would you care to take a look at the far bank, sir? Where she lay?'

They took a look at it and the horses in the field came and took a look at them, blowing contemptuously through their nostrils. Plank removed his tent and disclosed the pegs he had driven into the ground round dead Dulcie Harkness.

'And you took photographs, did you?' Alleyn asked.

'It's a bit of a hobby with me,' Plank said, and drew them from a pocket in his tunic. 'I carry a camera round with me,' he said. 'On the off-chance of a nice picture.'

Fox placed his glasses, looked and clicked his tongue. 'Very nasty,' he said. 'Very unpleasant. Poor girl.'

Plank, who contemplated his handiwork with a proprietary air, his head slightly tilted, said absently: 'You wouldn't hardly recognize her if it wasn't for the shirt. I used a sharper aperture for this one,' and he gave technical details.

Alleyn thought of the picture in the office of a big blowzy girl in a check shirt, exhibiting the sorrel mare. He returned the photographs to their envelope and put them in his pocket. Plank replaced the tent.

Alleyn said: 'From the time the riding-party left until she was found, who was here? On the premises?'

'There again!' Plank cried out in vexation. 'What've we got? Sir, we've got Cuth Harkness and that's it. Now then!' He produced his notebook, wetted his thumb and turned pages. 'Harkness. Cuthbert,' he said, and changed to his police-court voice.

'I asked Mr Harkness where he and Miss Harkness and Mr Sydney Jones were situated and how employed subsequent to the departure of the riding-party. Mr Harkness replied that he instructed Jones to drive into Montjoy and collect horse fodder, which he later did. At this point Mr Harkness broke down and spoke very confusedly about Mr Jones – something about him not having got the mare re-shod as ordered. He shed tears considerably. Mr Jones, on being interviewed, testified that Mr Harkness had words with deceased who was in her room but who looked out of her window and spoke to him, he being at that time in the stable yard. I asked Mr Harkness: "Was she locked in her room?" He said she had carried on to that extent that he went quietly upstairs and turned the key in her door, which at this point was in the outside lock. When I examined the door, the key was in the inside lock and was in the unlocked position. I noted a gap of three-quarters of an inch between door and floor. I noted a thin rug laying in the gap. I pointed this out to Mr Harkness, who told me that he had left the key in the outside lock. I examined the rug and the area where it lay and formed the opinion it had been dragged into the room. The displacement of dust on the floor caused me to form this opinion, which was supported by Mr Harkness to the extent that the deceased had effected an escape in this manner when a schoolgirl.'

Plank looked up. 'I have the key, sir,' he said.

'Right. So your reading is that she waited until her uncle was gone and then poked the key on to the mat. With what?'

'She carried one of those old-time pocket knives with a spike for getting stones out of hooves. It was in her breeches pocket.'

'*First Steps in Easy Detection*,' Alleyn murmured.

'Sir?'

'Yes, all right. Could be. So you read it that at some stage after this performance she let herself out, went downstairs, cut away the wire and dumped it we don't know where. But replaced the cutters – '

Fox said: 'Ah. Yes. There's that.'

' – and then saddled up the mare and rode to her death. I can't,' said Alleyn, rubbing his nose, 'get it to run smoothly. It's got a spurious feel about it. But then, of course, one hasn't known that poor creature. What was she like, Plank?'

After a considerable pause Plank said: 'Big.'

'One could see that. As a character? Come on, Plank.'

'Well,' said Plank, a countryman, 'if she'd been a mare you'd of said she was always in season.'

'That's a peculiar way of expressing yourself, Sergeant Plank,' Fox observed austerely.

'My son said something to much the same effect,' said Alleyn.

They returned to the yard. When they were half-way up the horse-paddock, Alleyn stooped and poked at the ground. He came up with a small and muddy object in the palm of his hand.

'Somebody's lost a button?' he said. 'Rather a nice one. Off a sleeve, I should think.'

'I never noticed it,' said Plank.

'It'd been trodden by a horse into the mud.'

He put it in his pocket.

'What's the vet called, Plank?' he asked.

'Blacker, sir, Bob.'

'Did you see the cut on the mare's leg?'

'No, sir. He'd bandaged her up when I looked at her.'

'Like it or lump it, he'll have to take it off. Ring him up, Plank.'

When Mr Blacker arrived, he seemed to be, if anything, rather stimulated to find police on the spot. He didn't even attempt to hide his curiosity and darted avid little glances from one to the other.

'Something funny in the wind, is there?' he said, 'or what?'

Alleyn asked if he could see the injury to the mare's leg. Blacker demurred but more as a matter of form, Alleyn thought, than with any real concern. He went to the mare's loose-box and was received with that air of complete acceptance and non-interest which animals seem to reserve for veterinary surgeons.

'How's the girl, then?' asked Mr Blacker.

She was wearing a halter. He moved her about the loose-box and then walked her round the yard and back.

'Nothing much the matter *there*, is there?' Plank ventured.

The mare stretched out her neck towards Alleyn and quivered her nostrils at him.

'Like to take hold of her?' the vet said.

Alleyn did. She butted him uncomfortably, drooled slightly and paid no attention to the removal of the bandage.

'There we are,' said Mr Blacker. 'Coming along nicely.'

Hair was growing in where it had been shaved off round the cut, which ran horizontally across the front of the foreleg about three inches above the hoof. It had healed, as Mr Blacker said, good and pretty and they'd have to get those two stitches out, wouldn't they? This was effected with a certain display of agitation on the part of the patient.

Alleyn said: 'What caused it?'

'Bit of a puzzle, really. There were scratches from the blackthorn, which you'll have seen was knocked about, and bruises and one or two superficial grazes, but she came down in soft ground. I couldn't find anything to account for this cut. It went deep, you know. Almost to the bone. There wasn't anything of the sort in the hedge but, my God, you'd have said it was wire.'

'Would you indeed?' Alleyn put his hand in his pocket and produced the few inches of wire he had cut from the coil in the coach-house. He held it alongside the scar.

'Would that fit?' he asked.

'By God,' said Mr Blacker, 'it certainly would.'

Alleyn said, 'I'm very much obliged to you, Blacker.'

'Glad to be of any help. Er – yes – er,' said Mr Blacker, 'I suppose, er, I mean, er . . .'

'You're wondering why we're here? On departmental police business, but your Super, finding himself out of action, suggested we might take a look at the scene of the accident.'

They were in the stable yard. The Leathers string of horses had moved to the brow of the hill. 'Which,' Alleyn asked, 'is Mungo, the wall-eyed bay?'

'That thing!' said Blacker. 'We put it down a week ago. Cuth always meant to, you know, it was a wrong 'un. He'd taken a scunner to it after it kicked him. Way he talked about it, you'd have thought it was possessed of a devil. It was a real villain, I must say. Dulce fancied it, though. Thought she'd make a show-jumper of it. Fantastic! Well, I'll be on my way. Morning to you.'

When he had gone Alleyn said: 'Shall we take a look at the barn? If open.'

It was a stone building standing some way beyond the stables and seemed to bear witness to the vanished farmstead, said by Plank to have pre-dated Leathers. There were signs of a thatched roof having been replaced by galvanized iron. They found a key above the door which carried the legend 'Welcome to all' in amateurish capitals.

'That lets us in,' said Fox drily.

The interior was well-lit from uncurtained windows. There was no ceiling to hide the iron roof and birds could be heard scuffling about outside. The hall wore that air of inert expectancy characteristic of places of assembly, caught, as it were, by surprise. A group of about a hundred seats, benches of various kinds and a harmonium faced a platform approached by steps, on which stood a table, a large chair and six smaller ones. The table carried a book-prop and an iron object that appeared to symbolize fire, flanked by a cross and a sword.

'That'll be Chris Beale, the smith's, work,' said Plank, spotting it. 'He's one of them.'

The platform, flanked by curtains, was backed by a whitewashed wall with a central door. This was unlocked and opened into a room fitted with a gas boiler, a sink and cupboards with crockery. ' "Ladies a basket", we must remember,' Alleyn muttered, and returned to the platform. Above the door and occupying half the width of the wall hung an enormous placard, scarlet and lettered in white. 'THE WAGES OF SIN,' it alarmingly proclaimed, 'ARE DEATH.'

The side walls, also, were garnished with dogmatic injunctions including quotations from the twenty-seventh chapter of Deuteronomy. One of these notices attracted Mr Fox's attention: 'Watch,' it said, 'for ye know not at what hour the Master cometh.'

'Do they reckon they do?' Fox asked Plank.

'Do what, Mr Fox?'

'Know,' Fox said. 'When.'

As if in answer to his enquiry, the front door opened to reveal Mr Harkness. He stood there, against the light, swaying a little and making preliminary noises. Alleyn moved towards him.

'I hope,' he began, 'you don't mind our coming in. It does say on the door – '

A voice from within Mr Harkness said, 'Come one, come all. All are called. Few are chosen. See you Sunday.'

He suddenly charged down the hall and up the steps, most precariously, to the door on the platform. Here he turned and roared in his more familiar manner. 'It will be an unexamplimented experience. Thank you.'

He gave a military salute and plunged out of sight.

'I'll think we'll have it at that,' said Alleyn.

CHAPTER 6

Morning at the Cove

At half past nine on that same morning, Ricky chucked his pen on his manuscript, ran his fingers through his hair and plummeted into the nadir of doubt and depression that from time to time so punctually attends upon dealers in words.

'I'm no good,' he thought, 'it's all a splurge of pretension and incompetence. I write about one thing and something entirely different is trying to emerge. Or is there quite simply nothing there *to* emerge? Over and out.'

He stared through the window at a choppy and comfortless harbour and his thoughts floated as inconsequently as driftwood among the events of the past weeks. He wallowed again between ship and jetty at St Pierre-des-Roches. He thought of Julia Pharamond and that teasing face was suddenly replaced by the frightful caved-in mask of dead Dulcie. Ferrant returned to make a fool of him and he asked himself for the hundredth time if it had been Ferrant or Syd Jones who had tried to drown him. And for the hundredth time he found it a preposterous notion that anybody should try to drown him. And yet he knew very well that it had been so and that his father believed him when he said as much.

So now he thought of his father and of Br'er Fox, who was his godfather. He wondered how exactly they behaved when they worked together on a case and if at that moment they were up at Leathers, detecting. And then, with a certainty that quite astonished him, Ricky tumbled to it that the reason why he couldn't write that morning was not because the events of the day before had distracted him or because he was bruised and sore and looked a sight or because the horror of Dulcie Harkness had been revived, but simply because he wanted very badly indeed to be up there with his father, finding out about things.

'Oh *no*!' he thought. 'I won't take that. That's not my scene. I've other things to do. Or have I?' He was very disturbed.

He hadn't seen any of the Pharamonds since the day of the postponed inquest. Jasper had rung up and asked him to dinner, but Ricky had said he was in a bad patch with his work and had promised himself there would be no more junketings until he had got over it. He could hear Julia in the background shouting instructions.

'Tell him to bring his book and we'll all write it for him.'

Jasper had explained that Julia was in the bath and she, in the background, screamed that umbrage would be taken if Ricky didn't come. It had emerged that the next day the Pharamonds were flying over to London to see the ballet and meant to stay on for a week or so if anything amusing offered. Ricky had stuck to his guns and not dined at L'Esperance, and had wasted a good deal of the evening regretting it.

He wondered if they were still in London. Did they always hunt in a pack? Were they as rich as they seemed to be? Julia had said that Jasper had inherited a fortune from his Brazilian grandfather. And had Louis also inherited a fortune? Louis didn't seem to do work of any description. Jasper was at least writing a book about the binomial theorem, but Louis – Ricky wouldn't be surprised if Louis was a bit hot: speculated rashly perhaps, or launched slightly dubious companies. But then he didn't care for Louis and his bedroom eyes. Louis was the sort of man that women, God knew why, seemed to fall for. Even his cousin Julia when they danced together.

Julia. It would perhaps be just as well, bearing in mind his father's strictures upon talkativeness, if Julia was still in London. If she was at L'Esperance she would wish to know why his father was here, she would ask them both to dinner and say – he could see her magnolia face and her impertinent eyes – that they were slyboots both of them. Perhaps his father would not go, but sooner or later he, Ricky, would, and once under the spell, could he trust himself not to blurt something out? No, it would be much better if the Pharamonds had decided to prolong their London visit. Much better.

And having settled that question he felt braced and took up his pen.

He heard the telephone ring and Mrs Ferrant come out of the kitchen, releasing televisual voices from within.

He knew it was going to be for him and he knew it would be Julia.

Mrs Ferrant shouted from the foot of the stairs and returned to the box.

As usual Ricky felt as if he had sunk much too rapidly in a fast lift. The telephone was in the passage, and before he picked up the receiver he could hear it gabbling. Julia was admonishing her daughter. 'All I can say, Selina, is this. Putting mud in Nanny's reticule is the unfunniest thing you could possibly do and just *so* boring that I can't be bothered talking about it. Please go away.'

'I've only just come,' Ricky said.

'Ricky?'

'None other.'

'You sound peculiar.'

'I'm merely breathless.'

'Have you been running?'

'No,' said Ricky crossly. He took a plunge. 'You have that effect on me,' he said.

'Smashing! I must tell Jasper.'

'When did you come back?'

'Just this moment. The ballet was out of this world. And there were some fantastic parties. Lots of jolly chums.'

Ricky was stabbed by jealousy. 'How lovely,' he said.

'I've rung up to know if it can possibly be true that your superb papa is among us.'

'Here we go,' Ricky thought. He said, 'How did you know?'

'Louis caught sight of him in the hotel last night.'

'But – I thought you said you'd only just got back.'

'Louis didn't come to London. He doesn't like the ballet. He stayed at the Hotel Montjoy to escape from Selina and Julietta. Has Troy come too?'

'No, she's busily painting a tree in London.'

'Louis says your papa seemed to be hob-nobbing with an elderly policeman.'

'There's meant to be some sort of re-organization going on in the force.'

'Are they going to raise Sergeant Plank to dizzy heights? I'd like that, wouldn't you?'

'Very much.'

'You're huffy, aren't you?'

'No!' Ricky cried. 'I'm not. Never less.'

'Nevertheless what?'

'I didn't say "nevertheless", I said I was never less huffy.'

'Well then, you're being a slyboots as usual and not divulging some dynamic bit of gossip.' A pause, and then the voice said, 'Ricky, dear, I don't know why I tease you.'

'I don't mind.'

'Promise? Very well, then, is it in order for us to ring up your father and ask him to dine? Or lunch?'

'Yes – well – yes, of course. He'd adore it. Only thing: he *is* very much occupied, it seems.'

'Does it? Well – one can but try,' she said coolly. Ricky felt inclined to say, 'Who's being huffy now?' but he only made vague noises and felt wretched.

'Of course you'd be invited too,' she threw out.

'Thank you, Julia.'

'You still sound odd.'

'I fell in the sea at St Pierre.'

'How too extraordinary! What were you doing in St Pierre? Or in the sea if it comes to that. Never mind. You should have said so at once and we wouldn't have been at cross-purposes like funny men on the box. Ricky?'

'Yes, Julia.'

'Has the inquest been re-opened?'

'No.'

'I see. I feel we shall never get rid of Miss Harness.'

'Harkness.'

'I don't do it on purpose. To me she is Harness.'

'I know.'

'I hoped in my shallow way that the ballet and fun things would put her out of my head. But they haven't.' She added hurriedly, furtively almost, 'I dream about it. Seeing her. Isn't that awful?'

'I'm so terribly sorry. So do I, if it's any comfort.'

'You do? Not fair to say I'm glad. Ricky – don't answer if you mustn't – but Ricky – was she murdered?'

'I don't know. Honestly. How could I?'

'Your father.'

'Julia – please don't.'

'I'm sorry. How's your book going?'

'Not very fast.'

'How's Mr Jones? At least I can ask you how Mr Jones is.'

'Oh, God!' Ricky said under his breath and aloud: 'He's away. Over at St Pierre-des-Roches.'

'I see. I think I must find out what Selina is doing. It's Nanny's evening off and there's an ominous silence. Goodbye.'

'I've been thinking a lot about all of you.'

'Have you?'

'Goodbye.'

'Goodbye.'

Ricky was cast down by this exchange. It had been miserably unsatisfactory. He felt that the relationship so elegantly achieved with Julia had been lost in a matter of minutes and there he was floundering about among evasions and excuses while she got more and more remote. She hadn't spluttered. Not once.

Mrs Ferrant opened the kitchen door, releasing the honeyed cajolements of a commercial jingle and the subtle aroma of a *sauce béarnaise*.

'I didn't think to ask,' she said, 'did you happen to see him over in St Pierre?'

'Yes,' said Ricky. 'We ran into each other.'

'Any message?'

'No. Nothing particular.'

She said: 'That black eye of yours is a proper masterpiece, isn't it?'

Ricky returned to his room.

II

Alleyn had finished out-of-doors at Leathers. He went inside to ask Mr Harkness if he might look at his niece's bedroom and found him snoring hideously in his office chair. He could not be roused to a sensible condition. Alleyn, in Fox's presence, formally put his request and took the snort that followed it as a sign of consent.

They all went upstairs to Dulcie's room.

It was exactly what might have been expected. The walls were covered in horsy photographs, the drawers and wardrobe were stuffed with equestrian gear. Riding boots stood along the floor. The bed was dragged together rather than made. On a table beside it were three battered pornographic paperbacks. A tube of contraceptive pills was in the drawer: half empty.

'Must have been careless,' Fox said. They began a systematic search.

After an unproductive minute or two Plank said: 'You don't suppose she thought taking that dirty great jump might do the trick, do you, sir?'

'Who can tell? On what we've got it sounds more as if the jump was the climax of a blazing row with her uncle. Did they blast off at each other as a regular practice, do you know, Plank?'

'Only after he took up with this funny religion, or so they reckon in the Cove. Before that they was thought to be on very pleasant terms. He taught her to ride and was uncommon proud of the way she shaped up.'

Fox threw his head back in order to contemplate from under his spectacles an item of Miss Harkness's underwear. 'Free in her ways,' he mused, 'by all accounts. *By your* account if it comes to that, Sarge.'

Sergeant Plank reddened. 'According to the talk,' he said, 'that was the trouble between them. After he took queer with his Inner Brethren he cut up rough over Dulcie's life-style. The general opinion is he tried to hammer it out of her, but what a hope. I dare say her being in the family way put the lid on it.' He entered the wardrobe and was enveloped in overcoats.

'When the Pharamonds and my son went to pick up their horses they interrupted a ding-dong go during which she roared out that she was pregnant and he called her a whore of Babylon.'

'I never knew that,' said Plank's voice, stuffy with clothes. 'Is that a fact?'

'You wouldn't get round to wondering,' Fox suggested, 'if his attitude could have led to anything serious?'

Plank, still red-faced, emerged from the wardrobe, 'No, Mr Fox,' he said loudly. 'Not to him rigging wire in the gap. Not Cuth

Harkness. Not a chap like him, given over to horses and their management. And that mare the apple of his eye! It's not in the man to
do it, drunk or sober, dotty or sane.' He appealed to Alleyn. 'I've
known the man for four years and it's not on, sir, it's not bloody
on. Excuse me. Like you was saying yourself, sir, about this being
an affair of character. Well, there's no part of this crime, if it is a
crime, in Cuth Harkness's character, and I'd stake my promotion
on it.'

Alleyn said:'It's a point well taken. You might just remember
something else they tell us.'

'What's that, sir?'

'Don't get emotionally involved.'

'Ah,' said Fox. 'There's always that, Sarge. There's always that.'

'Well, I know there is, Mr Fox. But it does seem to me – well . . .
Considering – '

'Considering,' Alleyn said, 'that Harkness locked her up in her
room and on pain of hell-fire and damnation forbade her to jump –
Considering that, would you say, Plank?'

'Yes, sir. I would.'

Mr Fox, who was replacing Miss Harkness's undergarments with
the careful devotion of a lady's maid, said generously, 'Which is what
you might call a glimpse of the obvious, I'll say that for it.'

'Well, ta, Mr Fox,' said Plank, mollified.

Alleyn was going through the pockets of a hacking-jacket that
hung from the back of a chair. They yielded a grubby handkerchief,
small change and a rumpled envelope of good paper addressed in a
civilized hand. It had been opened. Alleyn drew out a single sheet
with an engraved heading: L'Esperance and the address. On it was
written in the same hand. 'Cliffs. Thursday. Usual time. L.P.'

He showed it to the others.

' "L.P." eh,' Fox remarked.

'It doesn't stand for "long playing",' said Alleyn, 'although I suppose, in a cockeyed sense, it just might.'

'Plank,' he said, as they drove away from Leathers, 'I want you to
go over everything that Sydney Jones told you about the dialogue
with Harkness after the riding party left. Not only the row with
Dulcie but what he said to Jones himself. We won't need your notebook again: just tell me.'

Plank, who was driving, did so. Jones had described Harkness in the yard and Dulcie at her bedroom window, hurling insults at each other. Dulcie had said she could take not only the sorrel mare, but also the wall-eyed Mungo over the gap in the blackthorn hedge. Her uncle violently forbade her, under threat of a hiding, to make the attempt on any of the horses, least of all the mare. He had added the gratuitous opinion that she sat a jumping horse like a sack of potatoes. She had sworn at him and banged down the window.

'And then?'

'According to Jones, Harkness had told him to drive the car to a corn merchant on the way to Montjoy and pick up some sacks of fodder.'

'Rick remembers,' Alleyn said, 'that after the body was found, Mr Harkness said Jones had been told to take the mare to the smith to be re-shod and that he'd given this order to get the mare out of Dulcie's way. Harkness had added that because Jones didn't carry out this order he was as good as a murderer. Didn't Jones tell you about this?'

'Not a word, sir. No, he never.'

'Sure?'

'Swear to it, sir.'

Fox said: 'Mr Harkness isn't what you'd call a reliable witness. He could have invented the bit about the blacksmith.'

'He wasn't drinking then, Mr Fox. That set in later,' said Plank, who seemed set upon casting little rays of favourable light upon the character of Mr Harkness. 'But he was very much upset,' he added. 'I will say that for him. Distracted is what he was.'

'However distracted,' Alleyn said, 'one would hardly expect him to cook up a pointless fairy-tale, would one? I'd better talk to Rick about this,' he said vexedly, and asked Plank to drive into the Cove. 'Come and take a look at your godson, Br'er Fox,' he suggested, and to Plank: 'Drop us round the corner at the station. You'll be able to put in half an hour catching up on routine.'

'Don't make me laugh, sir,' said Plank.

They passed the Ferrants' house, turned into the side lane and pulled up at the corner cottage, which was also the local police station. A compact little woman with tight hair and rosy cheeks was hoeing vigorously in the garden. Nearby a little girl with Plank's face at the wrong end of a telescope was knocking up a mud pie in a flowerpot.

Plank, all smartness, was out of the driver's seat and opening the doors in a flash.

'Is this Mrs Plank?' Alleyn said, and advanced upon her, bare-headed. She was flustered and apologized for her mucky hand. Fox was presented. He and Alleyn admired the garden.

'It's beginning to look better,' Mrs Plank said. 'It was a terrible old mess when we first came four years ago.'

'Have you had many moves?' Alleyn asked them, and they said this was the third.

'And that makes things difficult,' Alleyn said, knowing constant transfers to be a source of discontent.

He had them talking freely in no time: about the disastrous effect on the children's education and the problems of settling into a new patch where you never knew what the locals would be like: friendly or suspicious, helpful or resentful; of how, on the whole, the Cove people were not bad, but you had to get used to being kept at a distance.

Alleyn edged the conversation round to the neighbours. Did Mrs Plank know the Ferrants round the corner with whom his son lodged? Not well, she said shortly. Mrs Ferrant kept herself to herself. Mrs Plank felt sorry for her. 'Really,' Alleyn asked. 'Why?'

Finding herself in the delicious situation where gossip could be regarded as a duty, Mrs Plank said that what with Ferrant away in France half the time, and where they got the money for it nobody knew, and never taking her with him and when he was home the way he carried on so free for all that he gave her washing machines and fridges and the name he had in the Cove for his bold behaviour and yet being secretive with it: well, the general feeling was that Mrs Ferrant was to be pitied. Although, come to that, Mrs Ferrant herself wasn't all that –

'Now then, Mother,' said Plank uneasily.

'Well, I know,' she said, 'and so do you, Joe.' Alleyn had a picture of the village policeman's wife, cut off from the cosy interchange of speculative gossip, always having to watch her tongue and always conscious of being on the outside.

'I'm sure Mrs Plank's the soul of discretion,' he said. 'And we're grateful for any tips about the local situation, aren't we, Plank? About Mrs Ferrant – you were saying?'

It emerged that Mrs Plank had acquired one friend only with whom she was on cosy terms: her next-door neighbour in the lane, a widow who, in the past, had been a sewing-maid up at L'Esperance at the time when Mrs Ferrant was in service there. Ten years ago that would be, said Mrs Plank, and added with a quick glance at her husband that Mrs Ferrant had left to get married. The boy was not yet eleven. Louis, they called him. 'Mind you,' Mrs Plank ended, 'they're French.'

'So are most of the islanders, mother,' said Plank. She tossed her head at him. 'You know yourself, Joe,' she said, 'there's been trouble. With him.'

'What sort of trouble?' Alleyn asked.

'Maintenance,' said Plank. 'Child. Up to Bon Accord.'

'Ah. Don't tell me. He's no good, that one,' cried Mrs Plank in triumph.

Mr Fox said, predictably, that they'd have to get her in the Force, and upon that playful note they parted.

Alleyn and Fox turned right from the lane on to the front. They crossed over to the far side and looked up at Ricky's window, which was wide open. There he was with his tousled head of hair, so like his mother's, bent over his work. Alleyn watched him for a moment or two, willing him to look up. Presently he did and a smile broke over his bruised face.

'Good morning, Cid me dear,' said Ricky. 'Good morning, Br'er Fox. Coming up? Or shall I come down?'

'We'll come up.'

Ricky opened the front door to them. He wore a slightly shame-faced air and had a postcard in his hand.

'Mrs F. is out marketing,' he said. 'Look. On the mat, mixed up with my mail. Just arrived.' He shut the door.

The postcard displayed a hectically-coloured view of a market-square and bore a legend: *La place du marché, La Tournière.'* Ricky turned it over. It had a French stamp and was addressed in an awk-ward hand to 'M. Ferrant', but carried no message.

'It's his writing,' Ricky said. 'He's given me receipts. That's how he writes his name. Look at the postmark, Cid.'

'One a.m. La Tournière. Posted yesterday. Air mail.'

'But he was in St Pierre yesterday. Even if it wasn't Ferrant who shoved me off the jetty, it certainly was Ferrant who made me look silly in the café. Where is La Tournière?'

'North of Marseilles,' said his father.

'Marseilles! But that's – what?'

'At a guess, between six and seven hundred kilometres by air from St Pierre. Come upstairs,' said Alleyn.

He dropped the card on the mat and was on the top landing before the other two reached half-way. They all moved into Ricky's room as Mrs Ferrant fitted her key in the front door.

'How did you know she was coming?' Ricky asked.

'What? Oh, she dumped her shopping bag against the door while she fished for her key. Didn't you hear?'

'No,' said Ricky.

'We haven't all got radioactive ears,' said Mr Fox, looking benignly upon his godson.

Alleyn said abruptly: 'Rick, why do you think it was Ferrant who shoved you overboard?'

'Why? I don't know why. I just felt sure it was he. I can't say more than that – I just – I dunno. I was certain. Come to think of it, it might have been Syd.'

'For the sake of argument we'll suppose it was Ferrant. He may have felt he'd better remove to a distant spot, contrived to get himself flown to La Tournière and posted this card at the airport. What time was it when you took the plunge?'

'According to my ruined wrist watch, eight minutes past three.'

Fox said: 'When we came into St Pierre at four yesterday a plane for Marseilles was taking off. If it calls at – ' Mr Fox arranged his mouth in an elaborate pout – 'La Tournière, it could be there by six-thirty, couldn't it? Just?'

'Is there anything,' Ricky ventured, 'against him having been staying at La Tournière, and deciding to fly up to St Pierre by an early plane yesterday morning?'

'What was it you used to say, Mr Alleyn?' Mr Fox asked demurely. ' "Stop laughing. The child's quite right"!'

'My very words,' said Alleyn. 'All right, Rick, that may be the answer. Either way, Fox, the *peloton des narcotiques,* as you would no doubt call the French drug squad, had better be consulted. Ferrant's on their list as well as ours. He's thought to consort with someone in the upper strata of the trade.'

'Where?' Ricky asked.

'In Marseilles.'

'I say! Could he have been under orders to get rid of me? Because Syd had reported I'd rumbled his game with the paints?'

Fox shot a quick look at Alleyn and made a rumbling noise in his throat.

Alleyn said, 'Remember we haven't anything to show for the theory about Jones and his paints. It may be as baseless as one of those cherubim that so continually do cry. But we've got to follow it up. Next time, if there is a next time, that Master Syd sets out for London with his paintbox they'll take him and his flake white to pieces at Weymouth and they won't find so much as a lone pep pill in the lot. Either he's in the clear or he'll have seen the light and shut up shop.'

'Couldn't you – couldn't it be proved one way or the other?' Ricky asked.

'Such as?' said Fox, who was inclined to treat his godson as a sort of grown-up infant prodigy.

'Well,' said Ricky with diminishing assurance, 'such as searching his pad.'

'Presumably, he's still in France,' said Alleyn.

'All the better.'

'Troy and I agreed,' Alleyn said to Fox, 'that taking one consideration with another it was better to keep our child uninformed about the policeman's lot. Clearly, we have succeeded brilliantly.'

'Come off it, Cid,' said Ricky, grinning.

'However, we haven't come here to discuss police law but to ask you to recall something Harkness said about his orders to Syd Jones. Do you remember?'

'Do you mean when he said he'd ordered Syd to take the sorrel mare to the blacksmith and he was in an awful stink because Syd hadn't done it? He said Syd was as good as a murderer.'

'What *did* Jones do with himself?'

'I suppose he cleared off quite early. After he'd collected some horse-feed, I think.'

'We don't know,' Fox said heavily, 'who was on the premises from the time the riding-party left until they returned. Apart from the two Harknesses. Or has Plank gone into that, would you say?'

'We'll ask him. All right, Rick. I don't think we'll be hounding you any more.'

'I'd rather be hounded than kept out.'

Fox said: 'I dare say you don't care to talk about work in progress.' He looked with respect at the weighted heap of manuscript on Ricky's table.

'It's a struggle, Br'er Fox.'

'Would I be on the wrong wavelength if I said it might turn out to be all the better for that?'

'You couldn't say anything nicer,' said Ricky. 'And I only hope you're right.'

'He often is,' said Alleyn.

'About people at Leathers during that afternoon,' Ricky said. 'There is, of course, Louis Pharamond.' And he described Louis's cramp and early return.

'Nobody tells us anything,' Alleyn cheerfully complained. 'What time would he have got back?'

'If he pushed along, I suppose about three-ish. When he left he was carrying his right boot and had his right foot out of its stirrup. He's very good on a horse.'

'Has he said anything about the scene at Leathers when he got there?'

Ricky stared at his father. 'Funny,' he said. 'I don't know.'

'Didn't he give evidence at the inquest, for pity's sake?'

'No. No, he didn't. I don't think they realized he returned early.'

'But surely one of you must have said something about it?'

'I dare say the others did. I haven't seen them since the inquest. I should think he probably unsaddled his horse, left it in the loose-box and came away without seeing anybody. It was there when we got back. Of course if there'd been anything untoward, he'd have said so, wouldn't he?'

After a considerable pause, during which Fox cleared his throat, Alleyn said he hoped so, and added that as investigating officers they could hardly be blamed if they didn't know at any given time whether they were looking into a possible homicide or a big deal in heroin. It would be tidier, he said, if some kind of link could be found.

Ricky said: 'Hi.'

'Hi, what?' asked his father.

'Well – I'd forgotten. You might say there *is* a link.'

' "Define, define, well-educated infant," ' Alleyn quoted patiently.

'I'm sure it's of no moment, mind you, but the night I came home late from Syd's pad . . . ' and he described the meeting on the jetty between Ferrant and Louis Pharamond.

'What time,' Alleyn said, after a long pause, 'was this?'

'About one-ish.'

'Funny time to meet, didn't you rather think?'

'I thought Louis Pharamond might go fishing with Ferrant. I didn't know whether they'd been together in the boat or what. It was jolly dark,' Ricky said resentfully.

'It was your impression, though, that they had just met?'

'Yes. Well – yes, it was.'

'And all you heard was Louis Pharamond saying, "All right?" or "OK, careful", or "Watch it". Yes?'

'Yes. I'm sorry, Cid,' said Ricky. 'Subsequent events have kind of wiped it.'

Fox said : 'Understandable.'

Alleyn said perhaps it was and added that he would have to wait upon the Pharamonds anyway. Upon this Ricky looking very uncomfortable, told him about Julia's telephone call and intention of asking them to dinner. 'I said I knew you'd adore to but were horribly busy. Was that OK?'

'Half of it was, at least. Yes, old boy, you were the soul of tact. Sure you don't fancy the Diplomatic after all? How did she know I was here?'

'Louis caught sight of you in the hotel. Last night.'

'I see. I don't, on the whole, think this is an occasion for dinner-parties. Will they all be at home this morning, do you suppose?'

'Probably.'

'One other thing, Rick. I'm afraid we may have to cut short your sojourn at the Cove.'

Ricky stared at him: 'Oh *no!*' he exclaimed. 'Why?'

Alleyn walked over to the door, opened it and had an aerial view of Mrs Ferrant on her knees, polishing the stairs. She raised her head and they looked into each other's faces.

'*Bonjour, madame!*' Alleyn called out jovially. '*Comment ça va?*'

'*Pas si mat, monsieur,*' she said.

'*Toujours affairée, n'est pas?*'

She agreed. That was how it went. He said he was about to look for her. He had lost his ball-point pen and wondered if she had come across it in the *petit salon* last evening after he left. Alas, no. Definitely, it was not in the *petit salon*. He thanked her and with further compliments re-entered the room and shut the door.

Ricky began in a highish voice. 'Now, look here, Cid – '

Alleyn and Fox simultaneously raised their forefingers. Ricky, against his better judgement, giggled. 'You look like mature Gentlemen of the Chorus,' he said, but he said it quietly. 'Shall I shut the window? In case of prowlers on the pavement?'

'Yes,' said his father.

Ricky did so and changed his mind about introducing a further note of comedy. 'Sorry,' he said. 'But why?'

'Principally because it would be inappropriate, supposing Ferrant returns, for you to board in the house of your would-be murderer – if indeed he is that.'

'I want to stay. My work's going better, I think. And – I'm sorry, but I *am* mixed up in the on-goings. And anyway he hasn't come back. Much more than all that, I want to see it out.'

They looked so gravely at him that he felt extremely uneasy.

From the street below there came seven syncopated toots from a car horn.

Ricky said in an artificial voice: 'That's Julia.'

Alleyn opened the window and leaned out. Ricky heard the familiar and disturbing voice.

'*You?*' Julia shouted. 'What fun! We've been hunting you.'

'I'll come down. Hold on.'

He nodded to Fox. 'Meet you at Plank's,' he said, and to Ricky: 'See you later, old boy.'

As he went downstairs he thought: 'Damn. He went white. He *has* got it badly.'

III

Julia was in her dashing sports car and Bruno was doubled up in the token seat behind her. She was dressed in white, as Alleyn remembered seeing her on the ship, with a crimson scarf on her head and those elegant gloves. Enormous dark glasses emphasized her pallor and her remarkable mouth. She had a trick when she laughed of lifting her lip up and curving it in. This changed her into a gamine and was extremely appealing. 'Poor old Rick,' Alleyn thought, 'He hadn't a chance. On the whole I dare say it's been good for him.'

Ricky, standing back from his closed window, was able to see his father shake hands with Julia and at her suggestion get into the passenger's seat. She looked at him as she sometimes looked at Ricky and had taken off her black glasses to smile at him. She talked – vividly, Ricky was sure – and he wondered at his father's air of polite attention. When she talked like that to Ricky he felt himself develop a fatuous expression and indeed was sometimes obliged to pull his face together and shut his mouth.

His father did not look in the least fatuous.

Now Julia stopped talking and laughing. She leant towards Alleyn and seemed to listen closely as he, still with that air of formal courtesy, spoke to her. So might her doctor or solicitor have behaved.

What could they be saying? he wondered. Something about Louis? Or could it be about him, by any chance? The thought perturbed him.

'Ricky,' Alleyn was saying, 'was in a bit of a spot. I'd told him not to gossip.'

'And there have I been badgering him. Wretched Ricky!' cried Julia, and broke into her splutter.

'He'll recover. It must be pretty obvious to everybody in the Cove, in spite of all Sergeant Plank's diplomacy, that there's something in the wind.'

'About the accident, you mean?'

'Yes.'

'That it wasn't an accident?'

'That it hasn't been conclusively shown that it was. Is your cousin with you this morning?'

'Louis? Or Carlotta?'

'Louis.'

'You're sitting on his coat. He's gone to buy cigarettes.'

'I'm sorry.' He hitched the coat from under him and straightened it, pulling down the sleeves. 'What a very smart hacking-jacket,' he said.

'It goes too far in my opinion. He hooks it over his shoulders and looks like a mass-produced David Niven.'

'He's lost a sleeve button. Have I sat it off? How awful, I'd better look.'

'You needn't bother. I think my daughter wrenched it off. Why do you want to see Louis?'

'In case he noticed anything out of the way when he returned to Leathers.'

Julia twisted round to look at her young brother-in-law. 'I don't think he did, do you, Bruno?'

Bruno said in an uncomfortable voice, 'I think he just said he didn't see anybody or something like that.'

'And, by the way,' Alleyn said, 'when you jumped that gap – a remarkable feat, if I may say so – did you go down and inspect it beforehand?'

A pause. 'No,' Bruno muttered at last.

'Really? So you wouldn't have noticed anything particular about it – about the actual gap?'

Bruno shook his head.

'No rail, for instance, running through the thorn?'

'There wasn't a rail.'

'Just the thorn? No wire?'

For a moment Alleyn thought Bruno was going to respond to this but he didn't. He shook his head, looked at the floor of the car and said nothing.

Julia winked at Alleyn and bumped her knee against his.

Bruno said: 'OK if I go to the shop?'

'Of course, darling. If you see Louis tell him who's here, will you? He's buying cigarettes, probably in the Cod-and-Bottle.'

Bruno slid out of the car and walked along the front with his shoulders hunched.

'You musn't mind,' Julia said. 'He's got a thing about jumping the gap.'

'What sort of thing?'

'He thinks he may have been an incentive to the Harness.'

'Harness?'

'I've got a fixation about her name. The others think I do it to be funny but I don't, poor thing.'

'I gather she was hell-bent on the jump anyway.'

'So she was, but Bruno fancies he may have brought her up to boiling-point and it makes him miserable. Only if it's mentioned. He forgets in between and goes cliff-climbing and bird-watching. How's Cuth?' asked Julia, and when he didn't reply at once, said: 'Come on, you must know Cuth. The uncle.'

'In retirement.'

'Well, we all know that. The maids told Nanny he's drinking himself to death out of remorse. I can't imagine how they know. Well, one can guess: postman; customers wanting hacks; Ricky's chum Syd before he bolted.'

'Has he bolted?'

'Cagey old Ricky just said he'd gone over to St Pierre-des-Roches, but the village thinks he bolted. According to Nanny. She has a wide circle of friends and all of them say Syd's done a bunk.'

'Why do they think he's done that?'

'Well, it's really – you mustn't mind this, either,' said Julia, opening her eyes very wide and beginning to gabble, 'but you see, to begin with, Nanny says they all thought there must be funny business afloat when the inquest was adjourned and on top of that everyone knew she was going to have a baby. Well, I mean, Cuth seems to have bellowed away about it, far and wide. And as she was a constant caller at Syd's pad they put two and two together.' Julia stopped short. 'Have you ever thought,' she said in a different voice, 'how *very* appropriate that expression would be if it was "one and one together".'

'It hadn't occurred to me.'

'I make you a present of it. Where was I?'

'I think you were going to tell me something that you hoped I wouldn't mind.'

'Ah! Thank you. It was just that your arrival on the scene led everyone to believe that you were hard on Syd's trail because Syd was the – what does "putative" mean? Not that Nanny used the expression.'

' "Supposed" or "presumed".'

'That's what I thought. The putative papa. Somehow I don't favour the theory. The next part gets vague: Nanny hurries over it rather, but the general idea seems to be that Syd was afraid Cuth would horsewhip him into marrying Dulcie.'

'And what steps is Syd supposed to have taken?'

'They don't say it in so many words.'

'What do they say? It doesn't matter how many words.'

'They hint.'

'What do they hint?'

'That Syd egged her on. To jump. Hoping.'

'I see,' said Alleyn.

'And then, of course, your arriving on the scene – '

'I only arrived last night.'

'Nanny was at a whist-drive last night, The WI. Some of the husbands picked their ladies up on the way home from the Cod-and-Bottle where they had been introduced to you by Sergeant Plank.'

'I see,' said Alleyn again.

'That's what I hoped you wouldn't mind: the whist-drive ladies all saying it looked pretty funny. It seems nobody really believes you merely came to give Sergeant Plank and the boys in blue a new look. They're all very thrilled to have you, I may say.'

'Too kind.'

'So are we, of course. Here they come. I expect you'd like to have your word with Louis, wouldn't you? I'll pay Ricky a little visit.'

'He's got a black eye and will be self-conscious but enchanted.'

Alleyn, a quick mover, was out of the car and had the door open for her. She gave him a steady look. 'How very kind,' she said, and left him.

The presence of Louis Pharamond on the front had the effect of turning it into some kind of resort – some little harbour only just 'discovered', perhaps, but shortly to be developed and ruined. His blue silk polo-necked jersey, his sharkskin trousers, his golden wrist watch, even the medallion he wore on a thin chain, were none of them excessive, but one felt it was only by a stroke of good luck that he hadn't gone too far with, say, some definitely regrettable ring or even an ear-ring.

Bruno, who trailed after Louis with his hands in his denim pockets, turned into the shop. Louis advanced alone and bridged the awkward gap between himself and Alleyn with smiles and expressions of pleasurable recognition.

'This *is* a nice surprise!' he cried, with outstretched hand. 'Who'd have thought we'd meet again so soon!'

There was the weather-worn bench close by where Ricky had sat in the early hours of the morning. Village worthies sometimes gathered there as if inviting the intervention of some TV commentator. Alleyn, having negotiated Louis's effusive greetings, suggested that they might move to this bench, and they did so.

'I gather,' he said, 'you've guessed that I'm here on a job.' Louis was all attention; appropriately grave, entirely correct.

'Well, yes, we have wondered, actually. The riding-school girl, isn't it? Rotten bad show.' He added with an air of diffidence that one didn't of course want to speak out-of-turn, but did this mean there was any suspicion that it wasn't an accident?

Alleyn wondered how many more times he was to say that they were obliged to make sure.

'Anything else,' said Louis, 'is unbelievable. It's – well, I mean, what could it be but an accident?' And he rehearsed the situation as it had presented itself to the Pharamonds. 'I mean,' he said, 'she was hell-bent on doing it. And with her weight up – she was a great hefty wench, you know, not to put too fine a point on it. I'd say she must have ridden every ounce of eleven stone. Well, it was a foregone conclusion.'

Alleyn said it looked like that, certainly.

'We're trying to find out,' he said, 'as closely as may be, when it happened. The medical report very tentatively puts it at between four and five hours of when she was found. But even that is uncertain. She may have survived the injuries for some considerable time or she may have died immediately.'

'Yes, I see.'

'When did you arrive back at Leathers? I know about the cramp.'

Louis sat with his lightly-clasped hands between his knees. Perhaps they tightened their grasp of each other: if so, that was his only movement.

'I?' he said. 'I don't know exactly. I suppose it would have been about three o'clock. I rode back by the shortest route. The cramp cleared up quite soon and I put on my boot and took most of it at an easy canter.'

'When you arrived was anybody about?'

'Not a soul. I unsaddled the hack and walked home.'

'Meeting anybody?'

'Meeting nobody.'

'Did you happen to look across the horse-paddock to the hedge?'

Louis ran his hand down the back of his head.

'I simply don't remember,' he said. 'I suppose I might have. If I did there was nothing out of the way to be seen.'

'No obvious break in the gap, for instance?'

He shook his head.

'No sign of the sorrel mare on the hillside?'

'Certainly not. But I really don't think I looked in that direction.'

'I thought you might have been interested in young Bruno's jump.'

'Young Bruno behaved like a clodhopper. No, I'm sorry. I'm no good to you, I'm afraid.'

'You knew Miss Harkness, didn't you?'

'She came to lunch one day at L'Esperance – on Ricky's first visit, by the way. I suppose he told you.'

'Yes, he did. Apart from that?'

'Not to say "knew",' Louis said. He seemed to examine this remark and hesitated as if about to qualify it. For a second one might have almost thought it had suggested some equivocation. 'She came into the pub sometimes when I was there,' he said. 'Once or twice, I wouldn't remember. She wasn't,' Louis said, 'exactly calculated to snatch one's breath away. Poor lady.'

'Did you meet her on a Thursday afternoon near the foot of a track going down the cliffs?'

The movement Louis made was like a reflex action, slight but involving his whole body and instantly repressed. It almost came as a shock to find him still sitting quietly on the bench.

'Good Lord!' he said. 'I believe I did. How on earth did you know? Yes. Yes, it was an afternoon when I'd been for a walk along the bay. So I did.'

'Did you meet by appointment?'

That brought him to his feet. Against a background of sparkling harbour and cheerful sky he stood like an advertisement for men's wear, leaning back easily against the sea-wall. An obliging handful of wind lifted his hair.

'Look here,' Louis said, 'I don't much like all this. Do you mind explaining?'

'Not a bit. Your note was in the pocket of her hacking-jacket.'

'Damn,' said Louis quietly. He waited for a moment, and then with a graceful, impetuous movement re-seated himself by Alleyn.

'I wouldn't have had this happen for the world,' he said.

'No?'

'On several counts. There's Carlotta, first of all, and most of all. I mean, I know I'm a naughty boy sometimes and so does she, but this is different. In the light of what's happened. It'd be horrid for Carlotta.'

He waited for Alleyn to say something but Alleyn was silent.

'You do understand, I'm sure. I mean it was nothing. No question of any – attachment. You might say, she simply happened to be damn good at one thing and made no bones about it. As was obvious to all. But – well, you'll understand – I'd hate Carlotta to know. For it to come out. Under the circs.'

'It won't unless it's relevant.'

'Thank God for that. I don't see how it possibly could be.'

'Was this meeting at the cliffs the first time?'

'I'm not sure – yes, I think it might have been.'

'Not according to the note. The note said "Usual time".'

'All right, then. It wasn't. I said I wasn't sure.'

'One would have thought,' Alleyn said mildly, 'you'd remember.'

'Basically the whole thing meant so little. I've tried to explain. It was nothing. Absolutely casual. It would have petered out, as you might say, without leaving a trace.'

'You're sure of that?'

'What the hell do you mean?'

'She was pregnant.'

'If you're trying to suggest – ' Louis broke off. He had spoken loudly, but now, after a quick look up at Ricky's window, stopped short. In the silence that followed Julia's voice could be heard. Alleyn looked round and was in time to see her appear briefly at the closed window. She waved to them and then turned away. Ricky could be dimly seen in the background.

'There is absolutely no question of that,' Louis said. 'You can dismiss any such notion.'

'Have you any theory on the parentage?'

For a moment or two he hesitated and then said that 'not to put too fine a point on it', it might be anybody. By one of those quirks of foresight Alleyn knew what his next remark would be and out it came. 'She was quite a girl,' Louis said.

'So I've been told,' said Alleyn.

Louis waited. 'Is that all you wanted to see me about?' he said at last.

'Pretty well, I think. We'd just like to be sure about any possible callers at Leathers during the day. A tidying-up process. Routine.'

'Yes, I see. I'm sorry if I didn't take kindly to being grilled.'

'It was hardly that, I hope.'

'Well – you did trick me over that unlucky note, didn't you?'

'You should see us when we get really nasty,' Alleyn said.

'It's just because of Carlotta. You do understand?'

'I think so.'

'I suppose I'm pretty hopeless,' said Louis. 'But still.' He stretched elaborately as if freeing himself from the situation. 'Ricky seems to be enjoying the giddy pleasures of life in Deep Cove and La Maison Ferrant,' he said. 'I can't imagine what he finds to do with himself when he's not writing.'

'There's been some talk of night-fishing and assignations with his landlord in the early hours of the morning, but I don't think anything's come of it. Do you ever go in for that?'

Louis didn't answer. It was as if for a split second he had become the victim of suspended animation, a 'still' introduced into a motion picture with the smile unerased on his face. This hitch in time was momentary: so brief that it might have been an illusion. The smile broadened and he said: 'Me? Not my scene, I'm afraid. Too keen on my creature comforts.'

He took out his cigarette case and filled it with a steady hand from a new packet. 'Is there anything else?' he asked.

'Not that I can think of,' Alleyn said cheerfully. 'I'm sorry I had to raise uncomfortable ghosts.'

'Oh,' Louis said, 'I'll survive. I wish I could have been more help.' He looked up at Ricky's window. 'What's all this we hear about him taking a plunge?'

Alleyn said it appeared that Ricky had slipped on the wet wharf, knocked his face against a gangway stanchion and fallen in.

'He's a pretty picture,' he said, 'and loath to display himself'

Louis said they'd soon see about that, and with a sudden and uncomfortable display of high spirits, threw a handful of fine gravel at the window. Some of it miscarried and spattered on the front door. Ricky loomed up, empurpled and unwilling, behind the glass. Louis gestured for him to open the window and when he had done so shouted: ' "But soft, what light from yonder window breaks" ' in a stagy voice. Julia appeared beside Ricky and took his arm.

'Do pipe down, Louis,' she said. 'You're inflaming the populace.'

And indeed the populace, in the shape of one doubled-up ancient-of-days on his way to the Cod-and-Bottle and three pre-school-aged children, had paused to gape at Louis. Two windows were opened. Mr Mercer came out of his shop and went in again.

More dramatically, the front door of the Ferrants' house was thrown wide and out stormed Mrs Ferrant, screaming as she came: *'Louis: assez de bruit!* What are you doing! *Petit méchant.'*

She came face to face with Louis Pharamond, stopped dead and shut her mouth like a trap.

'Good morning, Marie,' he said. 'Were you looking for me?'

Her eyes narrowed and her hands clenched. For a moment Alleyn thought she was going to have a go at Louis, but she turned instead to him. 'Pardon, M. Alleyn,' she said. 'A stupid mistake. My son occasionally has the bad manners to throw stones.' And with a certain magnificence she returned indoors.

'Let's face it,' said Louis, 'I am *not*, in that department, a popular boy.' He looked up at Julia in the window. 'We'll be late for luncheon,' he called. 'Coming?'

'Go and find Bruno, then,' she said. 'I'll be down in a moment.'

Alleyn looked at his watch. 'I'm running shamefully late,' he said. 'Will you forgive me?'

'For almost anything,' Julia called, 'except not coming to see us. *Au revoir.'*

IV

Ricky would not have chosen for Julia to see him with his black eye which was half-closed and made him look as if he lewdly winked at people. He had felt sheepish and uncomfortable when

she walked into his room, but, although she did laugh, it was sympathetically, and at first she didn't ask him to elaborate on his accident.
This surprised him because after all it would have been a natural
thing to do. Perversely, although relieved, he felt slightly hurt at
the avoidance.

Nor did she tease him with questions about his father's activities,
but related the Pharamonds' London adventures, asked him about
his writing and repeated her nonsense offer to help him with it. She
dodged about from one topic to another. The children, she said, had
become too awful. 'They writhe and ogle and have suddenly turned
just *so* common that I begin to think they must be changelings and
not Jasper's and mine at all.'

'Oh, come,' said Ricky.

'I promise! Of course, I love them to distraction and put it all
down to everybody but me spoiling them. We've decided that they
shall have a tutor.'

'Aren't they rather small for that?' Ricky ventured.

'Not at all. He needn't teach them anything: just rule them with
a rod of iron and think of strenuous and exhausting games. I had
rather wondered if Mr Jones might do.'

'You can't by any chance mean that?'

'Not really. It did just cross my mind that perhaps he could teach
them painting. Selina's style is rather like his own. With guidance
she might develop into a sort of Granddaughter Moses. Still, as you
tell me he's junketing in St Pierre-des-Roches, these ideas are only
wishful thinking on my part. I merely throw them out.'

'I don't know where he is.'

'Didn't you go jaunting together in St Pierre?'

'No, no,' he said in a hurry. 'Not together. Only, as it happened,
at the same time. I was just a day-tripper.'

'Well,' said Julia, gazing at his face, 'you certainly do seem to have
tripped in a big way.'

Ricky joined painfully in her amusement. It was at this point that
Julia had walked over to the window and waved to Alleyn and
Louis.

'They look portentous,' she said, and then, with an air of understatement that was not quite successful, she said: 'It's not fair.'

'I don't understand? What isn't?'

'The two of them, down there. The "confrontation". Isn't that one of the *in* words? Oh, come off it, Ricky. You know what I mean. Diamond-cut-paste. One guess which is which.'

This was so utterly unlike anything Julia had ever said to him in their brief acquaintanceship and, in its content, so acutely embarrassing, that he could find no reply. She had come close to him and looked into his face searchingly as if hesitating on the edge of some further extravagance or indiscretion.

Ricky's hands began to tingle and his heart to thump.

'Poorest Ricky,' she said, and gently laid her palm against his unbruised cheek, 'I've muddled you. Never mind.'

Ricky's thoughts were six-deep and simultaneous. He thought: 'That's torn it,' and at the same time, 'This is it: this is Julia in my arms and these are her ribs,' and 'If I kiss her I'll probably hurt my face,' and even, *bouleversé* though he was, 'What *does* she mean about Louis?' And then he was kissing her.

'No, no,' Julia was saying. 'My dear boy, no. What *are* you up to! Ricky, please.'

Now they stood apart. She said: 'Bless my soul, you *did* take me by surprise,' and made a shocked face at him. ' "Out upon you, fie upon you, bold-faced jig," ' she quoted.

'She's not even disconcerted,' he thought. 'I might be Selina for all she feels about it.'

He said: 'I'm sorry, but you do sort of trigger one off, you know.'

'Do I? How lovely! It's very gratifying to know one hasn't lost the knack. I must tell Jasper, it'll be good for him.'

'How can you?' Ricky said quietly.

'My dear, I'm sorry. That was beastly of me. I won't tell Jasper. I wouldn't dream of it.'

She waited for a moment and then began to make conversation as if he were an awkward visitor who had, somehow or another, to be put at his ease. He did his best to respond and in some degree succeeded, but he was humiliated and confusedly resentful.

'Have you,' she said at last, 'had your invitation to Cuth's party?'

'His party? No.'

'Not exactly a party perhaps, although it's "ladies a basket", we must remember. *You* must remember. It's one of his services. In the Barn at Leathers on Sunday. You're sure to be asked. Do come and

bring your papa. Actually, it seems anyone is welcome. Gents fifty p.
We've all been invited and I think we're all going, although Louis
may be away. It has "The Truth!" written by hand all over it with
rows of exclamation marks and "Revelation!" in enormous capitals
on the last page. You must come back to L'Esperance afterwards for
supper in case the baskets are not very filling.'

It had been at this point that Louis threw gravel at the window.
When Ricky looked down and saw him there with Alleyn standing
behind him, it was as if they were suddenly exhibited as an illustra-
tion to Julia's extraordinary observations. He was given, as he afterwards thought, a new look at his father – at his quietude and his air
of authority. And there was handsome Louis in the foreground, all
eyes and teeth, acting his boots off. Ricky understood what Julia had
meant when she said it wasn't fair.

In response to Louis's gesture, he opened the window and was
witness to the idiotic quotation from Romeo, Julia's quelling of Louis
and Mrs Ferrant's eruption into the scene and departure from it.

When Julia had dealt crisply with the remaining situation, she
shut the window and returned to Ricky.

'High time the Pharamonds removed themselves,' she said. She
looked directly into his eyes, broke into her laugh, kissed him rapidly
on his unbruised side and was gone.

She gave a cheerful greeting to Mrs Ferrant as she saw herself off.

Ricky stood stock-still in his room. He heard the car start up and
climb the hill to the main road. When he looked out his father had
gone and the little street was deserted.

'And after all that,' he thought, 'I suppose I'm meant to get on
with my book.'

V

Round the corner in Sergeant Plank's office, Alleyn talked to his contact in Marseilles: M. l'Inspecteur Dupont. They spoke in French and
were listened to with painful concentration by Mr Fox. Dupont had
one of those Provençal voices that can be raised to a sort of metallic
clatter guaranteed to extinguish any opposition. It penetrated every
corner of the little room and caused Mr Fox extreme consternation.

At last, when Alleyn, after an exchange of compliments, hung up the receiver, Fox leant back in his chair, un-knitted his brow and sighed deeply.

'It's the pace,' he said heavily. 'That's what gets you: that and the noise. I suppose,' he added wistfully, turning to Sergeant Plank, 'you had no difficulty?'

'Me, Mr Fox? I don't speak French. We only came here four years ago. We've tried to learn it, the missus and me, but we don't seem to make much headway and in any case the lingo they use over here's a patois. The chaps always seem to drop into it when I look in at the Cod-and-Bottle,' said Plank in his simple way. Another symptom, Alleyn thought, of the country policeman's loneliness.

'Well,' he said, 'for what it's worth, Ferrant has been spotted in La Tournière and in Marseilles.'

'I got that all right,' said Fox, cheering up a little.

'And he's made a trip to a place outside Marseilles where one of the big boys hangs out in splendour and is strongly suspected. They haven't been able to pin anything on him. The old, old story.'

'What are they doing about it?'

'A lot. Well – quite a lot. No flies, by and large, on the narcotics squad in Marseilles: they get the practice if they look for it and could be very active. But, again, it's the old story. The French are never madly enthusiastic about something they haven't set up themselves. Nor, between you and me and the junkie, are they as vigilant at the ports as they might be. Still, Dupont's one of their good numbers. He's all right as long as you don't step on his *amour propre*. He says they've got a dossier as fat as a bible on this character – a Corsican, he is, like most of them: a qualified chemist and a near millionaire with a château half-way between Marseilles and La Tournière and within easy distance of a highly sophisticated laboratory disguised as an innocent research set-up where this expert turns morphine into heroin.'

'Well!' said Fox. 'If they've got all this why don't they pull chummie in?'

'French law is very fussy about the necessity for detailed, conclusive and precise evidence before going in for a knock-off. And they haven't got enough of that. What they *have* got is a definite line on Ferrant. He's been staying off and on in an expensive hotel in La Tournière known to be a rendezvous for heroin merchants. He left there unexpectedly yesterday morning. Yes, I know. Rick's idea. They've been keeping obbo on him for weeks. Apparently the tip-off came from an ex-mistress in the hell-knows-no-fury department.'

'Did I catch the name Jones?' asked Fox.

'You did. Following up their line on Ferrant, they began to look out for anybody else from the island who made regular trips to St Pierre and they came up with Syd. So far they haven't got much joy out of that, but, as you may have noticed, when I told Inspecteur Dupont that Jones is matey with Ferrant, the decibel count in his conversation rose dramatically. There's one other factor, a characteristic of so many cases in the heroin scene: they keep getting shadowy hints of another untraced person somewhere on a higher rung in the hierarchy, who controls the island side of operations. One has to remember the rackets are highly sophisticated and organized down to the last detail. In a way they work rather like labour gangs in totalitarian countries: somebody watching and reporting and himself being watched and reported upon all the way up to the top. One would expect an intermediary between, say, an operative like Ferrant and a top figure like the millionaire in a château outside Marseilles. Dupont feels sure there is such a character.'

'What do we get out of all this?' Fox asked.

Alleyn got up and moved restlessly about the little office. A bluebottle banged at the window-pane. In the kitchen, Mrs Plank could be heard talking to her daughter.

'What I get,' Alleyn said at last, 'is no doubt a great slab of fantasy. It's based on conjecture and, as such, should be dismissed.'

'We might as well hear it,' said Fox.

'All right. If only to get it out of my system. It goes like this. Ferrant is in La Tournière and Syd Jones is in St Pierre, having arrived at the crack of dawn yesterday morning. Syd is now persuaded that Rick is spying on him and has followed him to St Pierre for that purpose. He has grown more and more worried and, on landing, rings up Ferrant. The conversation is guarded but they have an alarm code that means "I've got to talk to you." Ferrant comes to St Pierre by the early morning plane – Dupont says there's one leaves at seven. They are to meet in the café opposite the premises of Jerome et Cie. Rick sits in the café being a sleuth and squinting through a hole in *Le Monde* at Syd. At which ludicrous employment he is caught by Ferrant. Rick leaves the café. Syd, who seems to have gone to pieces and given himself a jolt of something, heroin one supposes, now tells Ferrant his story and Ferrant, having seen for himself my poor child's antics with the paper and bearing in mind that I'm a copper, decides that Rick is highly expendable. One of the two keeps tabs on Rick, is rewarded by a thunderstorm and takes the opportunity to shove him overboard between the jetty and the ship.' Alleyn's eyes closed for half a second. 'The ship,' he repeated, 'was rolling. Within a couple of feet of the legs of the jetty.'

He walked over to the window and stood there with his back to the other men. 'I suppose,' he said, 'he was saved by the turn of the bilge. If the ship had been lower in the water – ' He broke off. 'Yes. Quite so,' Fox said. Plank cleared his throat.

For a moment or two none of them spoke. Mrs Plank in her kitchen sang mutedly and the little girl kept up what seemed to be a barrage of questions.

Alleyn turned back into the room.

'He thought it was Ferrant,' he said. 'I don't know quite why; apart from the conjectural motive.'

'How doped up was this other type – Jones?'

'Exactly, Br'er Fox. We don't know.'

'If he's on the mainline racket – and it seems he is – '

'Yes.'

'And under this Ferrant's influence – '

'It's a thought, isn't it? Well, there you are,' Alleyn said. 'A slice of confectionery from a plain cook and you don't have to swallow it.'

There was a long pause which Fox broke by saying, 'It fits.'

Plank made a confirmatory noise in his throat.

'So what happens next?' asked Fox. 'Supposing this is the case?'

Alleyn said: 'All right. For the hell of it – supposing. What *does* Ferrant do? Hang about St Pierre waiting,' Alleyn said rapidly, 'for news of a body found floating under the jetty? Does he go back to La Tournière and report? If so, to whom? And what is Syd Jones up to? Supposing that he's got his next quota of injected paint tubes, if in fact they are injected, does he hang about St Pierre? Or does he lose his nerve and make a break for Lord knows where?'

'If he's hooked on dope,' Fox said, 'he's had it.'

Plank said: 'Excuse me, Mr Fox. Meaning?'

'Meaning as far as his employers are concerned.'

Alleyn said: 'Drug merchants don't use heavy consumers inside the organization, Plank. Beyond a certain point they become unpredictable and much too dangerous. If Jones is in process of becoming a junkie, he's out automatically, and if his bosses think he's a risk he might very easily be out altogether.'

'Would he go to earth somewhere over there in France?' Fox wondered. And then: 'Never mind that for the moment, Mr Alleyn. True or not, and I'd take long odds on your theory being the case, I don't at all fancy the position our young man has got himself into. And I don't suppose you do either.'

'Of course I don't,' Alleyn said, with a violence that made Sergeant Plank blink. 'I'm in two minds whether to pack him off home or what the devil to do about him. He's hell-bent on sticking round here and I'm not sure I don't sympathize with him.'

Fox said: 'And yet, wouldn't you say that when they do find out he escaped and came back here, they'll realize that anything he knows he'll have already handed on to you so there won't be the same reason for getting rid of him? The beans, as you might say, are spilt.'

'I'd thought of that too, Br'er Fox. These people are far too sophisticated to go about indulging in unnecessary liquidations. All the same – '

He broke off, and glanced at Sergeant Plank, whose air of deference was heavily laced with devouring curiosity. 'The fact of the matter is,' Alleyn said quickly, 'I find it difficult to look objectively at the position, which is a terrible confession from a senior cop. I don't know what the drill ought to be. Should I ask to be relieved from the case because of personal involvement?'

'Joey,' Mrs Plank called from the kitchen, and her husband excused himself.

'Fox,' Alleyn said, 'what the hell should a self-respecting copper do when his boy gets himself bogged down, and dangerously so, in a case like this? Send him abroad somewhere? If they are laying for him that'd be no solution. This lot is one of the big ones with fingers everywhere. And I can't treat Rick like a kid. He's a man, and what's more, I don't think he'd take it if I did and, by God, I wouldn't want him to take it.'

Fox, after some consideration, said it was an unusual situation. 'I can't say,' he admitted, 'that I can recollect anything of the sort occurring in my experience, or yours either, Mr Alleyn, I dare say. Very unusual. You could think, if you weren't personally concerned, that there's a piquant element.'

'For the love of Mike, Fox!'

'It was only a passing fancy. You were wondering what would be the correct line to take?'

'I was.'

'With respect, then, I reckon he should do as I think he wants to do. Stay put and act under your orders.'

'Here?'

'Here.'

'If Ferrant comes back? Or Jones?'

'It would be interesting to see the reaction when they met.'

'Always supposing Ferrant's the man. Or Jones.'

'That's right. It's possible that Ferrant may still be waiting for the body – you'll excuse me, won't you, Mr Alleyn – to rise. He may think it's caught up under the pier. Unless, of course, the chap in the ship has talked.'

'The ship doesn't return to St Pierre for some days. And Ricky got the man to promise he *wouldn't* talk. He thinks he'll stick to his word.'

'Yerse,' said Fox. 'But we all know what a few drinks will do.'

'Anyway, Ferrant has probably telephoned his wife and heard that Rick's home and dry. I wonder,' Alleyn said, 'if he's in the habit of sending her postcards with no message.'

'Just to let her know where he is?'

'And I wonder – I do very much wonder how far, if any distance at all, that excellent cook is wise to her husband's proceedings.'

Sergeant Plank returned with a plateload of enormous cheese and pickle sandwiches and a jug of beer.

'It's getting on for three o'clock,' he said, 'and the missus reckons you must be fair clemmed for a snack, Mr Alleyn.'

'Your missus, Sergeant Plank,' said Alleyn, 'is a pearl among ladies and you may tell her so with our grateful compliments.'

CHAPTER 7

Syd's Pad Again

When Ricky had eaten his solitary lunch he was unable to settle to anything. He had had a most disturbing morning and himself could hardly believe in it. The memory of Julia's blouse creasing under the pressure of his fingers and of herself warm beneath it, her scent and the smooth resilience of her cheek were at once extraordinarily vivid yet scarcely to be believed. Much more credible was the ease with which she had dealt with him.

'She stopped *my* nonsense,' he thought, 'with one arm tied behind her back. I suppose she's a dab hand at disposing of excitable young males.' For the first time he was acutely aware of the difference in their ages and began to wonder uncomfortably how old Julia, in fact, might be.

Mixed up with all this and in a different though equally disturbing key was his father's suggestion that he, Ricky, should take himself off. This he found completely unacceptable and wondered unhappily if they were about to have a family row about it. He was much attached to his father.

And then there was the case itself, muddling to a degree, with its shifting focus, its inconsistencies and lack of perceptible design. He thought he would write a kind of résumé, and did so and was, he felt, none the wiser for it. Turn to his work, he could not.

The harbour glittered under an early afternoon sun and beyond the heads there was a lovely blue and white channel. He decided to take a walk, first looking in his glass to discover, he thought, a slightly less grotesque face. His eye, at least, no longer leered, although the area beneath it still resembled an over-ripe plum.

Since his return he had felt that Mrs Ferrant, not perhaps spied upon him, but kept an eye on him. He had an impression of doors being shut a fraction of a second after he left or returned to his room. As he stepped down into the street he was almost sure one of the parlour curtains moved slightly. This was disagreeable.

He went into Mr Mercer's shop to replace his lost espadrilles with a pair from a hanging cluster inside the door. Mr Mercer, in his dual role of postmaster, was in the tiny office reserved for Her Majesty's Mail. On seeing Ricky he hurried out, carrying an air-letter and a postcard.

'*Good* afternoon, sir,' said Mr Mercer winningly, after a startled look at the eye. '*Can* I have the pleasure of helping you? And *may* I impose upon your kindness? Today's post was a little delayed and the boy had started on his rounds. *If* you would – You *would!* Much obliged, I'm sure.'

The letter was from Ricky's mother and the postcard he saw at a glance was from St Pierre-des-Roches with a view of that fateful jetty. For Mrs Ferrant.

When he was out in the street he examined the card. Ferrant's writing again and again no message. He turned back to the house and pushed the card and the espadrilles through the letter flap. He put his mother's letter in his pocket, and walked briskly down the front towards the Cod-and-Bottle and past it.

Here was the lane, surely, that he had taken that dark night when he visited Syd's pad – a long time ago, as it now seemed. The name, roughly painted on a decrepit board, hung lop-sided from its signpost: 'Fisherman's Steps'.

'Blow me down flat,' thought Ricky, 'if I don't case the joint.'

In the dark he had scarcely been aware of the steps, so worn, flattened and uneven had they become, but had stumbled after Syd like a blind man, only dimly conscious of the two or three cottages on either side. He saw now that they were unoccupied and falling into ruin. Clear of them the steps turned into a steep and sleazy path that separated areas of rank weeks littered with rusting tins. The path was heavily indented with hoof prints. 'How strange,' he thought, 'those were left, I suppose, by Dulcie's horse, Mungo: "put down" now, dead and buried, like its rider.'

And here was Syd's pad.

It must originally have been a conventional T-plan cottage with rooms on either side of a central passage. At some stage of its decline the two front rooms had been knocked into one, making the long disjointed apartment he had visited that night. The house was in a state of dismal neglect. At the back an isolated privy faced a desolation of weeds.

The hoof prints turned off to the right and ended in a morass overhung by a high bramble to which, Ricky thought, the horse must have been tethered.

It was through the marginal twigs of this bush that he surveyed the pad and from here, with the strangest feeling of involvement in some repetitive expression of antagonism, thought he caught the slightest possible movement in one of the grimy curtains that covered the windows.

Ricky may be said to have kept his head. He realized that if there was anybody looking out they could certainly see him. The curtains, he remembered, were of a flimsy character, an effective blind from outside but probably semi-transparent from within. Suppose Syd Jones had returned and was there at the window, Ricky himself would seem to be the spy, lurking but perfectly visible behind the brambles.

He took out his pipe, which was already filled, and lit it, making a show of sheltering from the wind. When it was going he emerged and looked about him as if making up his mind where he would go and then, with what he hoped was an air of purposeful refreshment and enjoyment of the exercise, struck up the path, passing close by the pad. The going became steeper and very rough and before he had covered fifty feet the footpath had petered out.

He continued, climbing the hill until he reached the edge of a grove of stunted pines that smelled warm in the afternoon sun. Three cows stared him out of countenance and then tossed their heads contemptuously and returned to their grazing. The prospect was mildly attractive: he looked down on cottage roofs and waterfront and away over the harbour and out to sea where the coast of Normandy showed up clearly. He sat down and took thought, keep-

ing an eye on Syd's pad and asking himself if he had only imagined
he was watched from behind the curtain; if what he thought he had
seen was merely some trick of light on the dirty glass.

Suppose Syd had returned, when and how had he come?

How far down the darkening path to subservience had Syd gone?
Ricky called up the view of him through that shaming hole in *Le
Monde:* the grope in the pockets, the bent head, hunched shoulders,
furtively busy movements, slight jerk.

Had Syd picked up a load of doctored paint tubes from Jerome et
Cie? Did Syd himself, perhaps, do the doctoring in his pad? Was he
at it now, behind his dirty curtains? If he was there, how had he
come back? By air, last evening? Or early this morning? Or could
there have been goings-on in the small hours – a boat from St
Pierre? Looking like Ferrant at his night fishing?

What had happened between Ferrant and Syd after Ricky left the
café? Further bullying? Had they left together and gone somewhere
for Syd to sleep it off? Or have a trip? Or what?

Ricky fetched up short. Was it remotely possible that Ferrant
could by some means have injected Syd with the idea of getting rid
of him, Ricky? He knew nothing of the effects of heroin, if in fact
Syd had taken heroin, or whether it would be possible to lay a subject on to commit an act of violence.

And finally: had it after all been Syd who, under the influence of
Ferrant or heroin or both, hid on the jetty and knocked him overboard?

The more he thought of this explanation, the more likely he felt
it to be.

Almost, had he known it, he was following his father's line of rea-
soning as he expounded it, not half a mile away, over in Sergeant
Plank's office. Almost, but not quite, because, at that point or thereabouts, Alleyn finished the last of Mrs Plank's sandwiches and said:
There is another possibility, you know. Sydney Jones may have cut
loose from Ferrant and, inspired by dope, acted on his own. Ricky
says he got the impression that there was someone else in the goods
shed when he sheltered there.'

'Might have sneaked in for another jolt of the stuff,' Fox speculated, 'and acted on the "rush". It takes different people different
ways.'

'Incidentally, Br'er Fox, his addiction might have been the reason why he didn't take the sorrel mare to the smith.'

'Nipped off somewhere for a quickie?'

'And now we *are* riding high on the wings of fancy.'

'I do wonder, though, if Jones supplied Mr Harkness with those pills. "Dexies", you say they are. And sold in France.'

'Sold in St Pierre quite openly, Dupont tells me.'

'Excuse me,' Plank asked, 'but what's a dexie?'

'Street name for amphetamines,' Alleyn replied. 'Pep pills to you. Comparatively harmless taken moderately, but far from so when used to excess. Some pop artists take them to induce, I suppose, their particular brand of professional hysteria. Celebrated orators have been said to take them – ' He stopped short. 'We shall see how Mr Harkness performs in that field on Sunday,' he said.

'If he can keep on his feet,' Fox grunted.

'He'll contrive to do that, I fancy. He's a zealot, he's hag-ridden, he's got something he wants to loose off if it's only a dose of hell-fire, and he's determined we shall get an earful. I back him to perform, pep-pills and scotch or no pep-pills and scotch.'

'Might that,' Plank ventured, 'be why Syd Jones got these pills for him in the first place? To kind of work him up to it.'

' "Might, might, might",' Alleyn grunted. 'Yes, of course, Plank. It might indeed, if Jones *is* the supplier.'

'It'd be nice to know,' Fox sighed, 'where Jones and Ferrant are. Now.'

And Ricky, up on his hillside, thought so too. He was becoming very bored with the prospect of the rusted roof and outside privy at Syd's pad.

He could not, however, rid himself of the notion that Syd might be on the watch down there, just as he'd got it into his head that Mrs Ferrant was keeping observation on him in her cottage. Had Syd crept out of his pad and did he lie in wait behind the bramble bush, for instance, with a blunt instrument?

To shake off this unattractive fancy, he took out his mother's letter and began to read it.

Troy wrote as she talked and Ricky enjoyed her letters very much. She made exactly the right remarks, and not too many of them, about his work and told him sparsely about her own. He became absorbed and no longer aware of the countrified sounds around him: seagulls down in the Cove, intermittent chirping from the pine grove and an occasional stirring of its branches; even the distant and inconsequent pop of a shotgun where somebody might be shooting rabbits. And if subconsciously he heard, quite close at hand, footfalls on the turf, he attributed them to the three cows.

Until a shadow fell across Troy's letter and he looked up to find Ferrant standing over him with a grin on his face and a gun in his hand.

II

At about this same time – half past three in the afternoon – Sergeant Plank was despatched to Montjoy under orders to obtain a search-warrant, and if he was forced to do so, execute it at Leathers, collecting to that end two local constables from the central police station.

'We'll get very little joy up there,' Alleyn said, 'unless we find that missing length of wire. Remember the circumstances. Some time between about ten-thirty in the morning and sixish in the evening and before Dulcie Harkness jumped the gap, somebody rigged the wire. And the same person, after Dulcie had crashed, removed and disposed of it. Harkness, when he wasn't haranguing his niece and ineffectually locking her up, was in his office cooking up hell-fire pamphlets. Jones took a short trip to the corn-chandler's and back and didn't obey orders to take the mare to the smith's. We don't know where he went or what he may have done. Louis Pharamond came and went, he says, round about three. He says he saw nobody and nothing untoward. As a matter of interest, somebody has dropped an expensive type of leather button in the horse-paddock, which he says he didn't visit. He's lost its double from his coat sleeve.

'I think you'll do well, Plank, to work out from the fence, taking in the stables and the barn. Unless you're lucky you won't finish today. And on a final note of jolly optimism there's always the possibility that somebody from outside came in, rigged the trap, hung about until Dulcie was killed in it and then dismantled the wire and did a bunk, taking it with him.'

'Oh, dear,' said Plank primly.

'On which consideration you'd better get cracking. All right?'

'Sir.'

'Good. I don't need to talk about being active, thorough and diligent, do I?'

'I hope not,' said Plank. And then: 'I *would* like to ask, Mr Alleyn: *is* there any connection between the two investigations – Dulcie's death and the dope scene?'

Alleyn said slowly: 'That's the hundred-guinea one. There do seem to be very tenuous links, so tenuous that they may break down altogether, but for what they're worth I'll give them to you.'

Plank listened with carefully restrained avidity.

When Alleyn had finished they made their final arrangements. They telephoned the island airport for details of disembarking passengers. There had been none bearing a remote resemblance to Ferrant or Jones. Plank was to telephone his own station at five-thirty to report progress. If neither Alleyn nor Fox was there, Mrs Plank would take the message. 'If by any delicious chance,' Alleyn said, 'you find anything before then, you'd better pack up and bring your booty here and be wary about dabs.'

'And I take the car, sir?'

'You do. You'd better lay on some form of tranport to be sent here for us in case of an emergency. Can you do this?'

'The Super said you were to have the use of his own car, sir, if required.'

'Very civil of him.'

'I'll arrange for it to be brought here.'

'Good for you. Off you go.'

'Sir.'

'With our blessing, Sergeant Plank.'

'Much obliged, I'm sure, sir,' said Plank, and left after an inaudible exchange with his wife in the kitchen.

'And what for us?' Fox asked when he had gone.

' "And what for me, my love, and what for me?" ' Alleyn muttered. 'I think it's about time we had a look at Mr Ferrant's sea-going craft.'

'Do we know where he keeps it exactly?'

'No, and I don't want to ask Madame. We'll take a little prowl. Come and say goodbye to Mrs P.'

He took the tray into the kitchen. Mrs Plank was ironing. 'That *was* kind,' he said, and unloaded crockery into the sink. 'Is this the drill?' he asked, and turned on the tap.

'Don't you touch them things!' she shouted. Beg pardon, sir, I'm sure. It's very kind but Joe'd never forgive me.'

'Why on earth not?'

'It wouldn't be fitting,' she said in a flurry. 'Not the thing at all.'

'I don't see why. Here!' he said to the little girl who was ogling him round the leg of the table. 'Can you dry?'

She swung her barrel of a body from side to side and shook her head.

'No, she can't,' said her mother.

'Well, Fox can,' Alleyn announced as his colleague loomed up in the doorway. 'Can't you?'

'Pleasure,' he said, and they washed up together.

'By the way, Mrs Plank,' Alleyn asked, 'do you happen to know where Gil Ferrant berths his boat?'

She said she fancied it was anchored out in the harbour. He makes great use of it, said Mrs Plank.

'When he goes night fishing?'

'If that's what it is.'

This was a surprising reaction, but it turned out that Mrs Plank referred to the possibility of philandering escapades after dark in *Fifi*, which was the name of Ferrant's craft. 'How *she* puts up with it, I'm sure I don't know,' said Mrs Plank. 'No choice in the matter, I dare say.'

Fox clicked his tongue against his palate and severely contemplated the glass he polished. 'Fancy that,' he said.

Unhampered by the austere presence of her husband, Mrs Plank elaborated. She said that mind you, Mr Fox, she wouldn't go so far as to say for certain but her friend next door knew for a fact that the poor girl had been seen embarking *Fifi* after dark with Ferrant in attendance, and as for her and that Jones . . . She laughed shortly and told her daughter to go into the garden and make another mud pie. The little girl did so by inches, retiring backwards with her eyes on Alleyn as if he were royalty. Predictably she tripped on the doorstep and fell backwards on to the wire mat. She was still roaring when they left.

'Didn't amount to much joy,' Fox said disparagingly as they walked down to the front. 'All this about the girl. We knew she was – what's that the prince called the tom in the play?'

' "Some road"?'

'That's right. The young chap took me to see it,' said Fox, who usually referred in this fashion to his god-son. 'Very enjoyable piece. Well, as I was saying, we knew already what this unfortunate girl was.'

'We didn't know she'd had to do with Ferrant, though. If it's true. Or that she went boating with him after dark.'

'If it's true,' they said together.

'Might be the longed-for link, if it *is* true,' Fox said. 'In any case I suppose we add him to the list.'

'Oh yes. Yes. We prick him down. And if Rick's got the right idea about the attack on him, I suppose we add a gloss to the name. "Prone to violence".'

'There is that, too,' said Fox.

They were opposite the Ferrants' cottage. Alleyn looked up at Ricky's window. It was shut and there was no sign of him at his work table.

'I think I'll just have a word with him,' he said. 'If he's at home. I won't be a moment.'

But Ricky was not at home. Mrs Ferrant said he'd gone out about half an hour ago: she couldn't say in what direction. He had not left a message. His bicycle was in the shed. She supposed the parcel in the hall must be his.

'Freshening himself up with a bit of exercise, no doubt,' said Fox gravely. 'Heavy work, it must be, you know, this writing. When you come to think of it.'

'Yes, Foxkin, I expect it must,' Ricky's father said, with a friendly glance at his old colleague. 'Meanwhile one must pursue the elusive *Fifi*. From Rick's story of the dead-of-night encounter between Ferrant and Louis Pharamond, it looks as if she sometimes ties up at the end of the pier. But if she anchors out in the harbour, he'll need a dinghy. There are only four boats out there. Can you pick up the names?'

Fox, who was long-sighted, said: '*Tinker, Marleen, Bonny Belle*. Wait a bit. She's coming round. Hold on. Yes. That's her. Second from the right, covered with a tarpaulin. *Fifi:*

'Damn.'

'Could we get a dinghy and row out?'

'With Madame Ferrant's beady eye at the front parlour window.'

'Do you reckon?'

'I'd take a bet on it. Let's trip blithely down the pier.'

They walked down the pier and stood with their hands in their pockets, ostensibly gazing out to sea. Alleyn pointed to the distant coast of France.

'To coin a phrase, don't look now, but *Fifi's* dinghy's below, moored to the jetty with enough line to accommodate to the tide.'

'Is she, though? Oh, yes,' said Fox, slewing his eyes down and round. 'I see. *Fifi* on the stern. Would she normally be left like that though? Wouldn't she knock herself out against the pier?'

'There are old tyres down there for fenders. But you'd think she'd be hauled up the beach with the others. Or, of course, if the owner was aboard, tied up to *Fifi:*

'Do we get anything out of this, then?'

'Let's go back, shall we?'

They returned to the front and sat on the weatherworn bench. Alleyn got out his pipe.

'I've got news for you, Br'er Fox,' he said. 'Last evening that dinghy *was* hauled up on the beach. I'm sure of it. I waited up in Rick's room for an hour until he arrived and spent most of the time looking out of the window. There she was, half-blue and half-white, and her name across her stern. She was just on the seaward side of high-water mark with her anchor in the sand. She'd be afloat at high tide.'

'Is that so? Well, well. Now, how do you read that?' asked Fox.

'Like everything else that's turned up – with modified rapture. Ferrant may let one of his mates in the Cove have the use of his boat while he's away.'

'In which case, wouldn't the mate return it to the beach?'

'Again, you'd think so, wouldn't you?' Alleyn said. And after a pause: 'When I left last night, at ten o'clock, the tide was coming in. The sky was overcast and it was very dark. The dinghy wasn't on the beach this morning.'

He lit his pipe. They were silent for some time.

Behind them the Ferrants' front door banged. Alleyn turned quickly, half-expecting to see Ricky, but it was only the boy, Louis,

with his black hair sleeked like wet fur to his head. He was unnaturally tidy and French-looking in his matelot jersey and very
short shorts.

He stared at them, stuck his hands in his pockets and crossed the
road, whistling and strutting a little.

'Hullo,' Alleyn said. 'You're Louis Ferrant, aren't you?'

He nodded. He walked over to the low wall and lounged against
it as Louis Pharamond had lounged that morning: self-consciously,
deliberately. Alleyn experienced the curious reaction that is induced
by unexpected crosscutting in a film as if the figure by the wall
blinked by split seconds from child to man to child again.

'Where are you off to?' he asked. 'Do you ever go fishing?'

The boy shook his head and then said: 'Sometimes,' in an indifferent voice.

'With your father, perhaps?'

'He's not here,' Louis said very quickly.

'You don't go out by yourself? In the dinghy?'

He shrugged his shoulders.

'Or perhaps you can't row,' Alleyn casually suggested.

'Yes. I can. I can so, row. My papa won't let anybody but me row
the dinghy. Not anybody. I can row by myself even when it's *gros
temps*. Round the *musoir*, I can, and out to the *cap*. Easy.'

'I bet you wouldn't go out on your own at night.'

'Huh! Easy! Often! I – '

He stopped short, looked uncomfortably at the house and turned
sulky. 'I can so, row,' he muttered, and began to walk away.

'I'll get you to take me out one of these nights,' Alleyn said.

But Louis let out a small boy's whoop and ran suddenly, down the
road and round the corner.

'Let me tell you a fairy-tale, Br'er Fox,' said Alleyn.

'Any time,' said Fox.

'It's about a little boy who stayed up late because his mother told
him to. When it was very dark and very late indeed and the tide was
high, she sent him down to the strand where his papa's dinghy was
anchored and just afloat and he hauled up the anchor and rowed the
dinghy out to his papa's motor-boat, which was called *Fifi*, and he
tied her up to *Fifi* and waited for his papa who was not really his

papa at all. Or *perhaps* as it was a calm night, he rowed right out to the heads – the *cap* – and waited there. And presently his papa arrived in a boat from France which went back to France. So the little boy and his papa rowed all the way back to the pier and came home. And they left the dinghy tied up to the pier.'

'And what did the papa do then?' Fox asked in falsetto.

'That,' Alleyn said, 'is the catch. He can hardly have bedded down with his lawful wedded wife, and be lying doggo in the bedroom. Or can he?'

'Possible.'

'Yes. Or,' Alleyn said, 'he may be bedded down somewhere else.'

'Like where?'

'Like Syd's pad, for example.'

'And why's he come back? Because things are getting too hot over there?' Fox hazarded.

'Or, while we're in the inventive vein, because they might be potentially even hotter over here and he wants to clean up damning evidence.'

'Where? Don't tell me. At Syd's pad. Or,' Fox said, 'could it be, don't laugh, to clean up Syd.'

'Because, wait for it, Syd it was who made the attempt on Rick and bungled it and has become unreliable and expendable. Your turn.'

'A digression. Reverting to the deceased. While on friendly terms with Syd at his pad, suppose she stumbled on something,' said Fox.

'What did she stumble on? Oh, I'm with you. On a doctored tube of emerald oxide of chromium or on the basic supply of dope.'

'And fell out with Jones on account of it being his baby and he not being prepared to take responsibility and so she threatened to grass on him,' said Fox, warming to his work. 'Or alternatively, yes, by gum, for Syd read Ferrant. It was *his* baby and *he* did her in. Shall I go on?'

'Be my guest.'

'Anyway, one, or both of them, fixes up the death trap and polishes her off,' said Fox. 'There you are! Bob's your uncle.' He chuckled.

Alleyn did not reply. He got up and looked at Ricky's window. It was still shut. The village was very quiet at this time in the afternoon.

'I wonder where he went for his walk,' he said. 'I suppose he could have come back while we were on the pier.'

'He couldn't have failed to see us.'

'Yes, but he wouldn't butt in. He's not at his table. When he's there you can see him very clearly from the street. Good God, I'm behaving like a clucky old hen.'

Fox looked concerned but said nothing.

Alleyn said: 'We're not exactly active at the moment, are we? What the hell have we got in terms of visible, tangible, put-on-table evidence? Damn all.'

'A button.'

'True.'

'It wasn't anywhere near the fence,' said Fox. 'Might he just have forgotten?'

'He might, but I don't think so. Fox, I'm going to get a search-warrant for Syd's pad.'

'You are?'

'Yes. We can't leave it any longer. Even if we've done no better than concoct a fairy-tale, Jones does stand not only as an extremely dubious character but as a kind of link between the two crackpot cases we're supposed to be handling. I've been hoping Dupont at his end might turn up something definite and in consequence haven't taken any action with the sprats that might scare off the mackerel. But there's a limit to masterly inactivity and we've reached it.'

'So we search,' Fox said. He fixed his gaze upon the distant coast of France. 'What d'you reckon, Mr Alleyn?' he asked. 'Has he got back? Have they both got back? Jones and Ferrant?'

'Not according to the airport people.'

'By boat, then, like we fancied. In the night?'

'We'll find out soon enough, won't we? Here comes a copper in the Super's car. It's ho for the nearest beak and a search-warrant.'

'It'll be a pity,' Fox remarked, 'if nobody's there after all. Bang goes the fairy-tale. Back to square one.' He considered this possibility for a moment. 'All the same,' he said, 'although I don't usually place any reliance on hunches, I've got a funny kind of feeling there's somebody in Syd's pad.'

III

The really extraordinary feature of Ricky's situation was his inability to believe in it. He had to keep reminding himself that Ferrant had a real gun of sorts and was pointing it into the small of his back. Ferrant had shown it to him and said it was real and that he would use it if Ricky did not do as he was told. Even then Ricky's incredulity nearly got the better of him and he actually had to pull himself together and stop himself calling his bluff and suddenly bolting down the hill.

The situation was embarrassing rather than alarming. When Syd Jones slouched out of the pad and met them and fastened his arms behind his back with a strap, Ricky thought that all three of them looked silly and not able to carry the scene off with style. This reaction was the more singular in that, at the same time, he knew they meant business and that he ought to be deeply alarmed.

And now, here he was, back in Syd's pad and in the broken-down chair he had occupied on his former visit, very uncomfortable because of his pinioned arms. The room smelt and looked as it had before and was in the same state of squalor. He saw that blankets had been rigged up over the windows, A solitary shaded lamp on the work table gave all the light there was. His arms hurt him and broken springs dug into his bottom.

There was one new feature apart from the blankets. Where there had been sketches drawing-pinned to the wall there now hung a roughly framed canvas. He recognized the work that had Leda and the Swan as its subject.

Ferrant lounged against the table with unconvincing insolence. Syd lay on his bed and looked seldom and furtively at Ricky. Nothing was said and, grotesquely, this silence had the character of a social hiatus. Ricky had some difficulty in breaking it.

'What is all this?' he asked, and his voice sounded like somebody else's. 'Am I kidnapped or what?'

'That's right, Mr Alleyn,' Ferrant said. 'That's correct. You are our hostage, Mr Alleyn.'

He was smoking. He inhaled and blew smoke down his nostrils. 'What an act!' Ricky thought.

'Do you mind telling me why?' he asked.

'A pleasure, Mr Alleyn, A great pleasure.'

Ricky thought: 'If this was fiction it would be terrible stuff. One would write things like "sneered Ferrant" and "said young Alleyn, very quietly".'

He said: 'Well, come on, then. Let's have it.'

'You're going to write a little note to your papa, Mr Alleyn.'

For the first time an authentic cold trickle ran down Ricky's spine. 'To say what?' he asked.

Ferrant elaborated with all the panache of a B Grade film gangster. The message Ricky was to write would be delivered to the Cove police station: never mind by whom. Ricky said tartly that he couldn't care less by whom: what was he expected to say?

'Take it easy, take it easy,' Ferrant snarled out of the corner of his mouth. He moved round the table and sat down at it. He cocked up his feet in their co-respondent shoes on the table and levelled his gun between his knees at Ricky. It was not a pose that Ricky, himself in acute discomfort, thought that Ferrant would find easy or pleasant to sustain.

He noticed that among the litter on the table were the remains of a meal: an open jack-knife, cups and a half-empty bottle of cognac. A piece of drawing paper lay near the lamp with an artist's conté pencil beside it. There was a chair on that side of the table, opposite Ferrant.

'That's the idea,' said Ferrant: (' "Purred", no doubt, would be the chosen verb,' thought Ricky.) 'We'll have a little action, shall we?'

He nodded magnificently at Syd, who got off the bed and moved to Ricky. He bent over him, not looking in his face.

'Your breath stinks, Syd,' said Ricky,

Syd made a very raw reply. It was the first time he had spoken. He hauled ineffectually at Ricky and they floundered about aimlessly before Ricky got his balance. It was true that Syd smelt awful.

Obviously they wanted him on the chair, facing Ferrant. He managed to shoulder Syd off and sit on it.

'Now then,' he said. 'What's the drill?'

'We'll take it ve-ry nice and slow,' said Ferrant, and Ricky thought he'd been wanting to get the phrase off his chest, appropriate or not, as the situation developed. He repeated it: 'Nice and slow.'

'If you want me to write you'll have to untruss me, won't you?'
Ricky pointed out.

'I'm giving the orders in this scene, mate, do you mind?' said
Ferrant. He nodded again to Syd, who moved behind Ricky but did
not release him.

Ricky had pins and needles in his forearms. It was difficult to
move them. His upper arms, still pinioned, had gone numb. Ferrant
raised the gun slightly.

'And we won't try any funny business, will we?' he said. 'We'll
listen carefully and do what we're told like a good boy. Right?'

He waited for an answer and, getting none, began to lay down the
law.

He said Ricky was to write a message in his own words and if he
tried anything on he'd have to start again. He was to say that he was
held as a hostage and the price of his release was absolute inactivity
on the part of the police until Ferrant and Syd had gone.

'Say,' Ferrant ordered, 'that if they start anything you'll be fixed.
For keeps.'

That was to be the message.

How many strata of thought are there at any given moment in a
human brain? In Ricky's there was a kind of lethargy, a profound
unbelief in the situation, a sense of non-reality as if, in an approaching moment, he would find himself elsewhere and unmolested.
With this, a rising dry terror and an awareness of the neccessity to
think clearly about the immediate threat. And, overall, a desolate
longing for his father.

'Suppose I won't write it,' he said. 'What about that?'

'Something not very nice about that. Something we don't want to
do.'

'If you mean you'll shoot me you must be out of your mind.
Where would that get you?' Ricky asked, forcing himself, and it cost
him an enormous effort, to take hold of what he supposed must be
reality. 'Don't be silly,' he said. 'What do you want? To do a bolt
because you're up to your eyebrows in trouble? The hostage ploy's
exploded, you ought to know that. They'll call your bluff. *You're* not
going to shoot me.'

Syd Jones mumbled, 'You ought to know we mean business.
What about yesterday? What about – '

'Shut up,' said Ferrant.

'All right,' said Ricky. 'Yesterday. What about it? A footling attempt to do me in and a dead failure at that.'

To his own surprise he suddenly lost his temper with Syd. 'You've been a bloody fool all along,' he shouted. 'You thought I was on to whatever your game is with drugs, didn't you? It wouldn't have entered my head if you hadn't made such an ass of yourself. You thought I sent you to see my parents because my father's a cop. I sent you out of bloody kindness. You thought I was spying on you and tailed you over to St Pierre. You were dead wrong all along the line and did yourself a lot of harm. Now, God save the mark, you're trying to play at kidnappers. You fool, Syd. If you shot me here, it'd be the end of you. What do you think my father'd do about that one? He'd hunt you both down with the police of two nations to help him. *You* don't mean business. Ferrant's making a monkey of you and you're too bloody dumb or too bloody doped to see it. Call yourself a painter. You're a dirty little drug-runner's side-kick and a failure at that.'

Syd hit him across the mouth. His upper lip banged against his teeth. Tears ran down his face. He lashed out with his foot. Syd fell backwards and sat on the floor. Ricky saw through his tears that Syd had the jack-knife in his hand.

Ferrant, in command of a stream of whispered indecencies, rose and was frightening. He came round the table and winded Ricky with a savage jab under the ribs. Ricky doubled up in his chair and through the pain felt them lash his ankles together. Ferrant took his shoulders and jerked him upright. He began to hit him methodically with hard open-handed slaps on his bruised face. 'This is the worst thing that has ever happened to me,' Ricky thought.

Now Ferrant had the knife. He forced Ricky's head back by the hair and held the point to his throat.

'Now,' whispered Ferrant, 'who's talking about who means business? Another squeal out of you, squire, and you'll be gagged. And listen. Any more naughty stuff and you'll end up with a slit windpipe at the bottom of the earth bog behind this shack. Your father won't find you down there in a hurry and when he does he won't fancy what he sees. *Filth*,' said Ferrant, using the French equivalent. He shook Ricky by the hair of his head and slapped his face again.

Ricky wondered afterwards if this treatment had for a moment or two actually served to clear rather than fuddle his wits and even to extend his field of observation. Whether this was so or not, it was a fact that he now became aware, beyond the circle of light cast by the single lamp, of suitcases that were vaguely familiar. Now he recognized them – The ultra smart pieces of luggage ('*Très snob presque cad*' – who had said that?) suspended from Ferrant's gloved hands as he walked down the street to the jetty in the early hours of the morning.

He saw, blearily, the familiar paintbox lying open on the table with a litter of tubes and an open carton beside it. He even saw that one tube had been opened at the bottom and was gaping.

'They're cleaning up,' he thought. And then: 'They're cooking up a getaway with the stuff. Tonight. They saw me watching the pad, and they saw me up by the pine-grove, and they hauled me in. Now they don't know what to do with me. They're improvising.'

Ferrant thrust his face at him: 'That's for a start,' he said. 'How about it. You'll write this message? Yes?'

Ricky tried to speak but found that his tongue was out of order and his upper lip bled on the inside and wouldn't move. He made ungainly noises. Syd said: 'Christ, you've croaked him.'

Ricky made an enormous effort. 'Won't work,' he hoped he'd said. Ferrant listened with exaggerated attention.

'What's that? Won't work? Oh, it'll work, don't worry,' he said. 'Know how? You're going down to the pier with us, see? And if your papa and his bloody fuzz start anything, you'll croak.' He touched Ricky's throat with the point of the knife. 'See? Feel that? Now get to it. Tell him.'

They released his right arm and strapped the left to the chair. Ferrant pushed the drawing paper towards him and tried to shove the pencil into his tingling hand. 'Go on,' he said. 'Go on. Take it. Take it.'

Ricky flexed his fingers and clenched and unclenched his hand. He felt horribly sick. Ferrant's voice receded into the distance and was replaced by a thrumming sound. Something hard pressed against his forehead. It was the table. 'But I haven't passed out,' he thought. 'Not quite.'

Syd Jones was saying: 'No, Gil, don't. Hell, Gil, not now. Not yet. Look, Gil, why don't we gag him and tie him up and leave him?

Why don't we finish packing the stuff and stay quiet till it's time and just leave him?'

'Do I have to go over it again! Look. So he doesn't turn up. So his old man's asking for him. Marie reckons he's suspicious. They'll be watching, don't you worry. All right. So we leave him here and we walk straight into it. But if we've got him between us and look like we mean business, they won't do a bloody thing. They can't. We'll take him in the dinghy as far as the boat and tip him overboard. By the time they've fished him out, we're beyond the heads and on our way.'

'I don't like it. Look at him. He's passed out.'

Ricky stayed as he was. When Ferrant jerked his head back he groaned, opened his eyes, shut them again, and, when released, flopped forward on the table. 'I must listen, listen, listen,' he thought. It was a horrid task – so much easier to give up, to yield, voluptuously almost, to whatever punch, slap or agonizing tweak they chose to deal out. And what to do about writing? What would be the result if he did write – write what? What Ferrant had said – write to his father.

'Go on,' Ferrant was saying. 'Get to it. You know what to put. Go on.'

His head was jerked up again by the hair. Perhaps his scalp rather than his mouth hurt most.

His fingers closed round the conté pencil. He dragged his hand over the paper.

'Kidnapped,' he wrote, 'OK. They say if you're inactive till they've gone I won't be hurt. If not I will. Sorry.' He made a big attempt at organized thinking. 'P.A.D.' he wrote as a signature, and let the pencil slide out of his grip.

Ferrant read the message. 'What's this P.A.D.?' he demanded.

'Initials. Patrick Andrew David,' Ricky lied, and thought it sounded like royalty.

'What's this "Ricky" stuff then?'

'Nickname. Always sign P.A.D.'

The paper was withdrawn. His face dropped painfully on his forearm and he closed his eyes. Their voices faded and he could no longer strain to listen. It would be delicious if in spite of the several pains that competed for his attention, he could sleep.

There was no such thing as time, only the rise and ebbing of pain to which a new element had been added, cutting into his ankles as if into the sorrel mare's near fore.

IV

It took much longer than they had anticipated to get their search-warrant. The magistrates court had risen and Alleyn was obliged to hunt down a Justice of the Peace in his home. He lived some distance on the far side of Montjoy in an important house at the foot of a precipitous lane. They had trouble in finding him and when found he turned out to be a fusspot and a ditherer. On the return journey the car jibbed at the steep ascent and wouldn't proceed until Fox had removed his considerable weight and applied it to the rear. Whereupon Alleyn, using a zigzagging technique, finally achieved the summit and was obliged to wait there for his labouring colleague. They then found that there was next to no petrol left in the tank and stopped at the first station to fill up. The man asked them if they knew they had a slow puncture.

By the time they got back to the Cove dusk was falling and Sergeant Plank had twice rung up from Leathers.

Mrs Plank, the victim of redundancy, reported that there was nothing to report but that he would report again at seven-thirty. She offered them high tea which they declined. Alleyn left Fox to take the call, saying he would look in for a fleeting moment on Ricky, who would surely have returned from his walk.

So he went round the corner to the Ferrants' house. Ricky's window was still shut. The boy, Louis, admitted Alleyn.

Mrs Ferrant came out of her kitchen to the usual accompaniment of her television.

'Good evening, monsieur,' she said. 'Your son has not yet returned.'

The idiot insistence of a commercial jingle blared to its conclusion before Alleyn spoke.

'He's rather late, isn't he?' Alleyn said.

She lifted her shoulders. 'He has perhaps walked to Bon Accord and is eating there.'

'He didn't say anything about doing that?'

'No. There was no need.'

'You would wish to know because of the meal, madame. It was inconsiderate of him.'

'*C'est pen de chose.*'

'Has he done this before?'

'Once perhaps. Or more than once. I forget. You will excuse me, monsieur. I have the boy's meal to attend to.'

'Of course. Forgive me. Your husband has not returned?'

'No, monsieur. I do not expect him. Excuse me.'

When she had shut the kitchen door after her, Alleyn lifted his clenched fist to his mouth, took in a deep breath, waited a second and then went upstairs to Ricky's room. Perhaps there would be a written message there that he had not, for some reason, wished to leave with Mrs Ferrant.

There was no message. Ricky's manuscript, weighted by a stone, was on his table. A photograph of his parents stared past his father at the empty room. The smell of Ricky – a tweed and shaving-soap smell, mixed with his pipe – hung on the air.

'She was lying,' he thought. 'He hasn't gone to Bon Accord. What the hell did he say was the name of that pub, where they lunched?' 'Fisherman's Rest' clicked up in his police-drilled memory. He returned to the work table. On a notepad Ricky had written a telephone number and after it L'E.

'He'd not go there,' Alleyn thought. 'Or would he? If Julia rang him up? Not without letting me know. But he couldn't let me know.'

There was more writing – a lot of it – on an underleaf of the notepad. Alleyn saw that it was a quite exhaustive breakdown of the circumstances surrounding Ricky's experiences before and during his visit to St Pierre-des-Roches.

Alleyn momentarily closed his eyes. 'Madame F.,' he thought, 'has no doubt enjoyed a good read.'

He took down the L'Esperance number and left a message under the stone: 'Sorry I missed you. Cid.'

'She'll read it, of course,' he thought, and went downstairs. The kitchen door was ajar and the television silent.

'*Bon soir, madame,*' he called out cheerfully, and let himself out.

Back at the police station he rang the Fisherman's Rest at Bon Accord, and to a background of bar-conviviality was told that Ricky was not, and had not been, there. Fox, who had yielded to Mrs Plank's renewed hospitality, listened with well-controlled consternation.

Alleyn then rang L'Esperance. He was answered by a voice that he recognized as Bruno's.

'Hullo,' he said. 'Alleyn here. I'm sorry to bother you but is Rick by any chance with you?'

'No, sir, we haven't seen him since – '

He faded out. Alleyn heard his own name and then, close and unmistakable, Julia's voice.

'It's you! What fun. Have you mislaid your son?'

'I seem to have, for the moment.'

'We've not seen him since this morning. Could he be hunting you down in your smart hotel? Perhaps he's met Louis and they're up to no good in Montjoy.'

'Is Louis in Montjoy?'

'I think so. *Carlotta*,' cried Julia musically, 'is Louis in Montjoy?' And after a pause, into the receiver: 'She doesn't seem to know.'

'I'm so sorry to have bothered you.'

'You needn't be. Quite to the contrary. Hope you find him.'

'I expect I shall,' he said, quite gaily. 'Goodbye and thank you.'

When he had hung up, he and Fox looked steadily at each other.

Fox said: 'There'll be a simple explanation, of course.'

'If there is,' Alleyn said, 'I'll knock his block off,' and contrived to laugh. 'You think of one, Fox,' he said. 'I can't.'

'Such as gone for a walk and sprained an ankle?'

'All right. Yes. That.'

'He wouldn't be up at Leathers? No. Plank would have said.'

The telephone rang.

'That'll *be* Plank,' said Fox, and answered it. 'Fox here. Yes. Nothing, eh? I'll ask the Chief.' He looked at Alleyn who, with a most uncharacteristic gesture, passed his hand across his eyes.

'Tell him to – no, wait a moment. Tell them to knock off and report back here. And – you might just ask – '

Fox asked and got the expected reply.

'By God,' said Alleyn. 'I wish this hadn't happened. Damn the boy, I ought to have got him out of it to begin with.'

After a longish pause, Fox said: 'I'm not of that opinion, if you don't mind my saying so, Mr Alleyn.'

'I don't mind, Br'er Fox. I hope you're right.'

'It'll just turn out he's taken an extra long walk.'

'You didn't hear Mrs Ferrant. I think she knows something.'

'About the young chap?'

'Yes.'

Fox was silent.

'We must, of course, do what we'd do if someone came into the station and reported it,' Alleyn said.

'Tell them to wait,' Fox said promptly. 'Give him until it gets dark and then if he hadn't turned up we'd – well – '

'Set up a search.'

'That's right,' said Fox uncomfortably.

'In the meantime we've got the official search on hand. Did Plank say what he'd beaten up in the way of help?'

'The chaps he's got with him. A couple of coppers from the Montjoy factory,' said Fox, meaning the police station.

'We'll take them with us. After all, we don't know what we'll find there, do we?' said Alleyn.

CHAPTER 8

Night Watches

The thing they got wrong in the gangster films, Ricky thought, was what it did to you being tied up. The film victims, once they were released, did one or two obligatory staggers and then became as nimble as fleas and started fighting again. He knew that when, if ever, he was released, his legs would not support him, his arms would be senseless and his head so compounded of pain that it would hang down and wobble like a wilted dahlia.

He could not guess how long it was since they gagged him. Jones had made a pad out of rag and Ferrant had forced it between his teeth and bound it with another rag, It tasted of turpentine and stung his cut lip. They had done this when Syd said he'd heard something outside. Ferrant had switched off the light and they were very still until there was a scratching at the door.

'It's the kid,' Ferrant said.

He opened the door a little way and after a moment shut it again very quietly. Syd switched on the light. Young Louis was there. He wore a black smock like a French schoolboy and a beret, He had a satchel on his back. His stewed-prune eyes stared greedily at Ricky out of a blackened face.

Ferrant held out his hand and Louis put a note in it. Ferrant read it – it was evidently very short – and gave it to Syd.

Louis said: 'Papa, he asked me if I could row the boat.'

'Who did?'

'The fuzz. He asked if I was afraid to go out in her at night.'

'What'd you say?'

'I said I wasn't. I didn't say anything else, Papa. Honest.'

'By God, you better not.'

'Maman says he's getting worried about *him*.' Louis pointed to Ricky. 'You got him so he can't talk, haven't you, Papa? Have you worked him over? His face looks like you have. What are you going to do with him, Papa?'

'*Tais-toi donc*. Keep your tongue behind your teeth. *Passe-moi la boustifaille.*'

Louis gave him the satchel.

'Good. Now, there is more for you to do. Take this envelope. Do not open it. You see it has his name on it. The detective's name. Listen carefully. You are to push it under the door at the police station and nobody must see you. Do not put it through the slot. Under the door. Then push the bell and away home quick and silent before the door is opened. Very quick. Very silent. And nobody to see you. Repeat it.'

He did, accurately.

'That is right. Now go.'

'I've blacked my face. Like a gunman. So's nobody can see me.'

'Good. The light, Syd.'

Syd switched it off and on again when the door was shut.

'Is he safe?' Syd asked.

'Yes. Get on with it.'

'We can't take – ' Syd stopped short and looked at Ricky – 'everything,' he said.

They had paid no attention to him for a long time. It was as if by trussing him up they had turned him into an unthinking as well as an inaminate object.

They had been busy. His chair had been turned away from the table and manhandled excruciatingly to bring him face to the wall. There had been some talk of a blindfold, he thought, but he kept his eyes shut and let his head flop, and they left him there, still gagged, and could be heard moving purposefully about the room.

He opened his eyes. Leda and the Swan had gone from their place on the wall and now lay face down on the floor close to his feet. He recognized the frame and wondered bemusedly by what means it had hung up there because there was no cord or wire to be seen, although there were the usual ring-screws.

Ferrant and Syd went quietly about their business. They spoke seldom and in low voices but they generated a floating sense of urgency and at times seemed to argue. He began to long for the moment to come when they would have to release whatever it was that bound and cut into his ankles. If he was to walk between them down to the boat, that was what they would have to do. And where would The Cid be, then? Watching with Br'er Fox from the window in Ricky's room? Unable to do anything because if he did . . . Would The Cid ever get that message? Where was he now? Now, when Ricky wanted him so badly. 'It's too much,' he thought. 'Yesterday and the thunder and lightning and the sea and blacking my eye and now all this: face, jaw, mouth, ankle: no, it's too much. The wall poured upwards, his eyes closed and he fainted.

The boy Louis did not follow the path down to the front but turned off it to his right and slithered, darkling, along tortuous passages that ran uphill and down, behind the backs of cottages, some occupied and some deserted.

The moon had not yet risen and the going was tricky, but he was sure-footed and knew his ground. He was excited and thought of himself in terms of his favourite comic strip as a Miracle Kid.

He came out of his labyrinth at the top of the lane that ran down to the police station.

Here he crouched for a moment in the blackest of the shadows. There was no need to crouch, the lane was deserted, but he enjoyed doing it and then flattening himself against a wall and edging downhill.

The blue lamp was on, but the station windows were dark while those in the living-quarters glowed. He could hear music: radio or telly, with the fuzz family watching it and the Miracle Kid, all on his own, out in the dark.

'*Whee-ee! !*'

Across the lane like the Black Shadow. Envelope. Under the door. Stuck. Push. Bell. Push. 'Zing! ! !'

In by the back door with Maman waiting. Hands in pockets. Cool. Slouch in wagging the hips.

'*Eh bien?*' said Mrs Ferrant, nodding her head up and down. '*Tu es fort satisfait de ta petite personne, hein?*'

Round the corner in the police station, Mrs Plank, peering up and down the lane, told herself it was too late for a runaway knock. Unless, she thought, it was that young Louis from round the corner who was allowed to wait up till all hours and was not a nice type of child. Then she noticed the envelope at her feet. She picked it up. Addressed to the Super and sealed. She shut the front door, went into the kitchen and turned the envelope over and over in her hands.

There was no telling how late it might be when they returned, all of them. Joe had been very quiet when he came in, but she knew he was gratified by the way the corners of his mouth twitched. He had told her they were going to search Syd Jones's premises but it was not to be mentioned. He knew, thought Mrs Plank, that he could trust her.

It had been a most irregular way of delivering the note, if it was a note. Suppose it was important? Suppose Mr Alleyn should know of it at once and suppose that by leaving it until he came in, if he did come in and not drive straight back to Montjoy, some irreparable damage was done? On the other hand Joe and Mr Alleyn and Mr Fox might be greatly displeased if she butted in at that place with a note that turned out to be some silly prank.

She worried it over, this way and that. She examined the envelope again and again, particularly the direction, written in capital letters with some sort of crayon, it looked like: 'MR ALLEN'. Someone who didn't know how to spell his name.

The flap was not all that securely gummed down.

'Well, I don't care, I will,' she thought.

She manœuvred it open and read the message.

II

Before they set out for Syd's pad, Alleyn had held a short briefing at the station with Fox, Plank and the two constables from Montjoy: Cribbage and Moss.

'We're going into the place,' he had told them, 'because I think we've sufficient grounds to justify a search for illicit drugs. It will have to be an exhaustive search and as always in these cases it may bring us no joy. The two men we're interested in are known to have been in St Pierre yesterday, and, as far as we've been able to find out, haven't returned to the island. Certainly not by air. There has been no official passage to the Cove by sea and your chaps – ' he looked at the two constables – 'checked the ferry at Montjoy. This doesn't take in the possibility that they came back during the night in a French chum's craft and were transhipped somewhere near the heads into Ferrant's dinghy and brought ashore. We've no evidence – ' he hesitated for a moment and caught Fox's eye – 'no evidence,' he repeated, 'to support any such theory: it is pure speculation. If, however, it had so happened, it might mean that Ferrant as well as Jones was up at the pad and they might turn naughty. Mr Fox and Sergeant Plank are carrying handcuffs.' He looked round at the four impassive faces. 'Well,' he said, 'that's it. Shall we push off? Got your lamps?'

Plank had produced two acetylene lamps in addition to five powerful hand torches because, as he said, they didn't know but what the power might be off. He had also provided himself with a small torch with a blue light.

They had driven along the front, past the Cod-and-Bottle, and parked their car near Fisherman's Steps.

Ricky had described his visit to Syd's pad so vividly that Alleyn felt as if he himself had been there before. They didn't say much to each other as they climbed the steps. Plank, who in the course of duty beats had become familiar with the ground, led the way and used his torch to show awkward patches.

'We don't want to advertise ourselves,' Alleyn had said. 'On the other hand, we're making a routine search, not scaling the cliffs of Abraham in black-face. If there's somebody at home and won't answer the door we effect an entrance. If nobody's there we still effect an entrance. And that's it.'

They were about half-way up the steps and had passed the last of the cottages, when Plank said: 'The place is up on the right, sir. If there was lights in the front windows we'd see them from here.'

'I can just make out the roof

'Somebody might be in a back room,' said Fox.

'Of course. We'll take it quietly from here – Plank, you're familiar with the lie of the land. When we get there you take a man with
you and move round to the back door as quietly as you can. We
three will go to the front door. *If* there's anybody at home he might
try a break. From now on, softly's the word. Don't rush it and don't
use your torch unless you've got to and then keep it close to the
ground.'

They moved on slowly. The going became increasingly difficult,
their feet slipped, they breathed hard and once the larger of the
Montjoy men fell heavily, swore and said, 'Pardon.' Plank admin-
istered a stern rebuke. They continued uphill, still led by Plank,
who turned every now and then to make sure they were all
together.

On the last of these occasions he put out his hand and touched
Alleyn.

'Sir,' Plank breathed, 'has someone fallen back?'

No, they were all there.

'What is it?'

'We're being followed.'

Alleyn turned. Some way below them a torchlight darted
momentarily about the steps, blacked out and reappeared, nearer.

'One of the locals? Coming home?' Fox speculated.

'Wait.'

No. It showed again for a fraction of a second and was much
nearer. They could hear uneven footfalls and laboured breathing.
Whoever it was must be scrambling, almost running up the steps.

'Christ!' Plank broke out. 'It's the missus.'

It was Mrs Plank, so out of breath that she clung to Alleyn with
one hand and, with the other, shoved the paper at him.

'Sh-sh!' she panted. 'Don't speak. Don't say anything. Read it.'

Alleyn opened his jacket as a shield to her torch, and read.

Fox, who was at his elbow, saw the paper quiver in his hand. The
little group was very still. Voices of patrons leaving the Cod-and-
Bottle broke the silence and even the slap of the incoming tide along
the front. Alleyn motioned with his head. The others closed about
him, bent over and formed a sort of massive scrum round the torch-
lit paper. Fox was the first to break the silence.

'Signed P.A.D.?' Fox said. 'Why?'

'It's his writing. Weak. But his. It's a tip-off. *"Pad"*. They didn't drop to it or they'd have cut it out.'

'Practical,' said Fox unevenly. And then: 'What do we do?'

Alleyn read the message again, folded it, and put it in his pocket. Mrs Plank switched off her torch. The others waited.

'Mrs Plank,' Alleyn said, 'you don't know how grateful I am to you. How did this reach you?'

She told him. 'I got the notion,' she ended, 'that it might be that young Louis Ferrant. I suppose because he's a one for runaway knocks.'

'Is he, indeed? Now, please, you must go back. Go carefully and thank you.'

'Will it – they won't? – will it be all right?'

'You cut along, Mother,' said her husband. ''Course it will.'

'Goodnight, then,' she said, and was gone.

Fox said: 'She's not using her torch.'

'She's good on her feet,' said Plank.

Throughout, they had spoken just above a whisper. When Alleyn talked now it was more slowly and unevenly than was his custom, but in a level voice.

'It's a question, I think, of whether we declare ourselves and talk to them from outside the house or risk an unheard approach and a break-in. I don't think – ' he stopped for a moment – 'I don't think I dare do that.'

'No,' said Fox. 'No. Not that way. Too risky.'

'Yes. It seems clear that already they've. . . given him a bad time – the writing's very shaky.'

'It does say "OK", though. Meaning he is.'

'It says that. There's a third possibility. He says "till they've gone", and I can't think of them making a getaway by any means other than the way we discussed, Fox. If so, they'll come out at some time during the night, carrying their stuff. With Ricky between them. They've worked it out that we won't try anything because of the threat to Rick. We carry on now, with the old plan. We don't know which door they'll use so we'll have two at the back and three at the front. And wait for them to emerge.'

'And jump them?'

'Yes,' Alleyn said. 'And jump them.'

'Hard and quick?'

'Yes. They'll be armed.'

'It's good enough,' Fox said, and there were satisfied noises from the other three men.

'I think it's the best we can do. It may be – ' for the first time Alleyn's voice faltered – 'a long wait. That won't – be easy.'

It was not easy. As they drew near the house they could make it out in a faint diffusion of light from the village below. They moved very slowly now, over soft, uneven ground, Plank leading them. He would stop and put back a warning hand when they drew near an obstacle, such as the bramble bush where Miss Harkness had tethered her horse and Ricky had so ostentatiously lit his pipe. No chink of light showed from window or door.

They inched forward with frequent stops to listen and grope about them. A breeze had sprung up. There were rustlings, small indeterminate sounds, and from the pine-grove further up the hill, a vague soughing. This favoured their approach.

It was always possible, Alleyn thought, that they were being watched, that the lights had been put out and a chink opened at one of the windows. What would the men inside do then? And there was, he supposed, another possibility – that Ricky was being held somewhere else – in one of the deserted cottages, for instance, or even gagged and out in the open. But no. Why 'Pad' in the message? Unless they'd moved after sending the message. Should Fox return and try to screw a statement out of Mrs Ferrant? But then the emergence from the pad might happen and they would be a man short.

They had come to the place where a rough path branched off, leading round to the back of the house. Plank breathed this information in Alleyn's ear: 'We'll get back to you double-quick, sir, if it's the front. Can you make out the door?' Alleyn squeezed his elbow and sensed rather than saw Plank's withdrawal with PC Moss.

There was the door. They crept up to it, Alleyn and Fox on either side, with PC Cribbage behind Fox. There was a sharp crackle as Cribbage fell foul of some bush or dry stick. They froze and waited. The breeze carried a moisture with it that tasted salt on Alleyn's lips. Nothing untoward happened.

Alleyn began to explore with his fingers the wall, the door and a step leading up to it. He sensed that Fox, on his side, was doing much the same thing.

The door was weather-worn and opened inwards. The handle was on Alleyn's side. He found the keyhole, knelt and put his eye to it but could see nothing. The key was in the lock, evidently. Or hadn't Ricky, describing the pad, talked about a heavy curtain masking the door? Alleyn thought he had.

He explored the bottom of the door. There was very little gap between it and the floor, but as he stared fixedly at the place where his finger rested he became aware of a lesser darkness, of the faintest possible thinning out of non-visibility that increased, infinitesimally, when he withdrew his hand.

Light, as faint as light could be, filtered through the gap between the door and the floor.

He slid his finger away from him along the gap and ran into something alive. Fox's finger. Alleyn closed his hand round Fox's and then traced on its hairy back the word LIGHT. Fox reversed the process. YES.

Alleyn knelt. He laid his right ear to the door and stopped up the left one.

There was sound. Something being moved. The thud of stockinged or soft-shod feet and then, only just perceptibly, voices.

He listened and listened, unconscious of aching knees, as if all his other faculties had been absorbed by the sense of hearing. The sounds continued. Once, one of the voices was raised. Of one thing he was certain – neither of them belonged to Ricky.

To Ricky, on the other side of the door. Quite close? Or locked up in some back room? Gagged? What had they done to him to turn his incisive Italianate script into the writing of an old man?

Monstrous it was, to wait and to do nothing. Should he, after all, have decided to break in? Suppose they shot him and Fox before the others could jump on them, what would they do to Ricky?

The sounds were so faint that the men must be at the end of the room farthest from the door. He wondered if Fox had heard them, or Cribbage.

He got to his feet, surprised to find how stiff he was. He waited for a minute or two and then eased across until he found Fox, who was leaning with his back to the wall, and whispered: 'Hear them?'

'Yes.'

'At least we've come to the right place.'

'Yes.'

Alleyn returned to his side of the door.

The minutes dragged into an hour. The noises continued intermittently, and, after a time, became more distant as if the men had
moved to another room. They changed in character. There was a
scraping metallic sound, only just detectable, and then silence.

It was no longer pitch dark. Shapes had begun to appear, shadows
of definite form and patches of light. The moon, in its last quarter,
had risen behind the pine-grove and soon would shine full upon
them. Already he could see Fox and beyond him PC Cribbage,
propped against the wall, his head drooping, his helmet inclined
forward above his nose. He was asleep.

Even as Alleyn reached out to draw Fox's attention to his neighbour, Cribbage's knees bent. He slid down the wall and fell heavily
to the ground, kicking the acetylene lamp. Wakened, he began to
scramble to his feet and was kicked by Fox. He rose with abject
caution.

Absolute silence had fallen inside the house.

Alleyn motioned to Fox, and Fox, with awful grandeur, motioned
to the stricken Cribbage. They cat-walked across to Alleyn's side of
the door and stood behind him, all three of them pressed back
against the wall.

'If – ' Alleyn breathed, 'we act.'

'Right.'

They moved a little apart and waited, Alleyn with his ear to the
door. The light that had shown so faintly across the threshold went
out. He drew back and signalled to Fox. After a further eternal interval they all heard a rustle and clink as of a curtain being drawn.

The key was turned in the lock.

The deep framework surrounding the door prevented Alleyn
from seeing it open, but he knew it *had* opened, very slightly. He
knew that the man inside now looked out and saw nothing untoward where Fox and Cribbage had been. To see them, he would
have to open up wide enough to push his head through and look to
his right.

The door creaked.

In slow motion a black beret began to appear. An ear, a temple,
the flat of a cheek and then, suddenly, the point of a jaw and an eye.

The eye looked into his. It opened wide and he drove his fist hard at the jaw.

Ferrant pitched forward. Fox caught him under the arms and Cribbage took him by the knees. Alleyn closed the door.

Ferrant's right hand opened and Alleyn caught the gun that fell from it. 'Lose him. Quick,' he said. Fox and Cribbage carried Ferrant, head lolling and arms dangling, round the corner of the house. The operation had been virtually soundless and occupied a matter of seconds.

Alleyn moved back to his place by the door. There was still no sound from inside the house. Fox and Cribbage returned.

'Still out,' Fox muttered, and intimated that Ferrant was hand-cuffed to a small tree with his mouth stopped.

They took up their former positions, Alleyn with Ferrant's gun – a French army automatic – in his hand. This one, he thought, was going to be simpler.

Two loud thumps came from within the house, followed by an exclamation that sounded like an oath. Then, soft but unmistakable, approaching footsteps and again the creak of the opening door.

'Gil!' Syd Jones whispered into the night. 'What's up? Where are you? Are you there, Gil?'

Like Ferrant, he widened the door-opening and like Ferrant, thrust his head out.

They used their high-powered torches. Syd's face, a bearded mask, started up, blinking and expressionless. He found himself looking into the barrel of the automatic. 'Hands up and into the room,' Alleyn said. Fox kicked the door wide open, entered the house and switched on the light. Alleyn followed Syd, with Cribbage behind him.

At the far end of the room, face to wall, gagged and bound in his chair, was Ricky.

'Fox,' Alleyn said. Fox took the automatic and began the obliga-tory chant – 'Sydney Jones, I arrest . . .' Plank arrived and put on the handcuffs.

Alleyn, stooping over his son, was saying: 'It's me, old boy. You'll be all right. It's me.' He removed the bloodied gag. Ricky's mouth hung open. His tongue moved and he made a sound. Alleyn took his head carefully between his hands.

Ricky contrived to speak. 'Oh, golly, Cid,' he said. 'Oh, *golly*!'

'I know. Never mind. Won't be long now. Hold on.'

He unstrapped the arms and they fell forward. He knelt to release the ankles.

Ricky's white socks were bloodied and overhung his shoes. Alleyn turned the socks back and exposed wet ridges that had closed over the bonds.

From between the ridges protruded a twist of wire and two venomous little prongs.

III

Ricky lay on the bed. In the filthy little kitchen, PC Moss boiled up a saucepan of water and tore a sheet into strips. Sergeant Plank was at the station, telephoning for a doctor and ambulance.

Ferrant and Syd Jones, handcuffed together, sat side by side facing the table. Opposite them Alleyn stood with Fox beside him and Cribbage modestly in the background. The angled lamp had been directed to shine full in the prisoners' faces.

On the table, stretched out to its full length on a sheet of paper, lay the wire that had bound Ricky's ankles and cut into them. It left a trace of red on the paper.

To Ricky himself, lying in the shadow, his injuries thrumming through his nerves like music, the scene was familiar. It was an interrogation scene with obviously dramatic lighting, barked questions, mulish answers, suggested threats. It looked like a standard offering from a police story on television.

But it didn't sound like one. His father and Fox did not bark their questions. Nor did they threaten, but were quiet and deadly cold and must, Ricky thought, be frightening indeed.

'This wire,' Alleyn was saying to Syd, 'it's yours, is it?'

Syd's reply, if he made one, was inaudible.

'Is it off the back of the picture frame there? It is? Where did you get it? Where?' A pause. 'Lying about? Where?'

'I don't remember.'

'At Leathers?'

'S'right.'

'When?'

'I wouldn't know.'

'You know very well. When?'

'I don't remember. It was some old junk. We didn't want it.'

'Was it before the accident?'

'Yes. No. After.'

'Where?'

'In the stables.'

'Where, exactly?'

'I don't know.'

'You know. Where?'

'Hanging up. With a lot more.'

'Did you cut it off?'

'No. It was on its own. A separate bit. What's the idea?' Syd broke out with a miserable show of indignation. 'So it's a bit of old wire. So I took it to hang a picture. So what?'

Ferrant, on a jet of obscenities, French and English, told him to hold his tongue.

'I didn't tie him up,' Syd said. 'You did.'

'*Merde.*'

Alleyn said: 'You will both be taken to the police station in Montjoy and charged with assault. Anything you say now – and then – will be taken down and may be used in evidence. For the moment, that's all.'

'Get up,' said Fox.

Cribbage got them to their feet. He and Fox marshalled them towards the far end of the room. As they were about to pass the bed, looking straight before them, Fox laid massive hands upon their shoulders and turned them to confront it.

Ricky, from out of the mess they had made of his face, looked at them. Ferrant produced the blank indifference of the dock. Syd, whose face, as always, resembled the interior of an old-fashioned mattress, showed the whites of his eyes.

Fox shoved them round again and they were taken, under Cribbage's surveillance, to the far end of the room.

PC Moss emerged from the kitchen with a saucepan containing boiled strips of sheet and presented it before Alleyn.

Alleyn said: 'Thank you, Moss. I don't know that we should do anything before the doctor's seen him. Perhaps clean him up a bit.'

'They're sterile, sir,' said Moss. 'Boiled for ten minutes.'

'Splendid.'

Alleyn went into the kitchen. Boiled water had been poured into a basin. He scrubbed his hands with soap that Syd evidently used on his brushes if not on himself. Alleyn returned to his son. Moss held the saucepan for him and he very cautiously swabbed Ricky's mouth and eyes.

'Better,' said Ricky.

Alleyn looked again at the ankles. The wire had driven fibres from Ricky's socks into the cuts.

'I'd better not meddle,' Alleyn said. 'We'll get on with the search, Fox.' He bent over Ricky. 'We're getting the quack to have a look at you, old boy.'

'I'll be OK.'

'Of course you will. But you're bloody uncomfortable, I'm afraid.'

Ricky tried to speak, failed, and then with an enormous effort said: 'Try some of the dope,' and managed to wink.

Alleyn winked back, using the serio-comic family version with one corner of the mouth drawn down and the opposite eyebrow raised, a grimace beyond his son's achievement at the moment. He hesitated and then said: 'Rick, it's important or I wouldn't nag. How did you get here?'

With an enormous effort Ricky said: 'Went for a walk.'

'I see: you went for a walk? Past this pad? Is that it?'

'Thought I'd case the joint.'

'Dear God,' Alleyn said quietly.

'They copped me.'

'That,' said Alleyn, 'is all I wanted to know. Sorry you've been troubled.'

'Don't mention it,' said Ricky faintly.

'Fox,' Alleyn said. 'We search. All of us.'

'What about them?' Fox asked with a jerk of his head and an edge in his voice that Alleyn had never heard before. 'Should we wire them up?'

'No,' Alleyn said. 'We shouldn't.' And he instructed Cribbage to double-handcuff Ferrant and Syd, using the second pair of bracelets to link their free hands together behind their backs. They were sat on the floor with their shoulders to the wall. The search began.

At the end of half an hour they had opened the bottom ends of thirty tubes of paint and found capsules in eighteen of them. Dollops of squeezed-out paint neatly ornamented the table. Alleyn withdrew Fox into the kitchen.

'Fair enough,' he said. 'We've got the *corpus delicti*. What we don't know yet is the exact procedure. Jones collected the paints in St Pierre, but were they already doctored or was he supplied with the capsules and drugs and left to do the job himself? It looks like the latter.'

'Stuff left over?'

'Yes. They were about to do a bolt, probably under orders to hide any stuff they couldn't carry. And along came my enterprising son, "casing", as he puts it, "the joint".'

'That,' Fox murmured, 'would put them about a bit.'

'Yes. What to do with him? Pull him in, which they did. But if they held him, sooner or later we'd set up a search. I imagine that they were in touch with Madame F. through that nefarious kid. Well, in their fluster, they hit on the not uningenious idea of using Rick as a screen for their getaway. And if Mrs Plank had not been the golden lady she undoubtedly is, they might well have brought it off. I wish to hell that bloody quack would show up.'

'I'm sure he'll be all right,' said Fox, meaning Ricky.

The meticulous search went on, inch by inch through the littered room, under the bed, stereo table, in the shelves and cupboards and through heaps of occulted junk. They were about to move into an unspeakable little bedroom at the back when Alleyn said: 'While we were outside, before Ferrant came to the door, I heard a metallic sound. Very faint.'

'In the house?'

'Yes. Did you?'

'I didn't catch it. No,' said Fox.

'Let's try the kitchen. You two,' he said to Cribbage and Moss, 'carry on here.' He took off his jacket and rolled up his sleeves.

The kitchen was in the same state of squalor as the rest of the pad. Its most conspicuous feature was a large and decrepit coal range of an ancient make with a boiler and tap on one side of the grate and an oven on the other. It looked as if it was never used, On top of it was a small modern electric stove. Alleyn removed this to the table and started on the range. He lifted the iron rings and probed inside with a bent poker, listening to the sound. He opened the oven, played his torch round the interior and tapped the lining. He had let down the front of the grate and lifted the top when Fox gave a grunt.

'What?' Alleyn asked.

'His personal supply. Syringe. Dope. It's "horse" all right,' said Fox, meaning heroin. 'There's one tablet left.'

'Where?'

'Top shelf of the dresser. Behind an old cook-book. Rather appropriate.'

A motor-siren sounded down on the front. 'This'll be the ambulance,' said Fox. 'And the doctor. We hope.'

When Alleyn didn't answer, Fox turned and found him face down in the open top of the range. 'There should be a cavity over the oven,' he said, 'and there isn't and – Yes. Surprise, surprise.'

He began pulling. A flat object was edged into view. The siren sounded again and nearer.

'It *is* the ambulance,' Alleyn said. 'You get this lot out, Br'er Fox, and no reward for guessing what's the prize.'

He was back with Ricky before Fox had collected himself or anything else.

Ricky took a bleary look at his father and begged him, in a stifled voice, not to make him laugh.

'Why should you laugh?'

'When did you join the Black and White Minstrels? Your face. Oh God, I mustn't laugh.'

Alleyn returned to the kitchen and looked at it in a cracked glass on the wall. The nose was black. He swabbed it with an unused bandage and again washed his hands. Fox had extracted a black attaché case from the stove and had forced the lock and opened it. 'What's that lot worth on the street market?' he asked.

'Two thousand quid if a penny,' said Alleyn, and returned to his son. 'We've got Jones's very own dope,' he said, 'and we've got the consignment in transit.' He walked down the room to Ferrant and Jones, seated in discomfort on the floor. 'You heard that, I suppose,' he said.

Ferrant, in his sharp suit and pink floral shirt, spat inaccurately at Alleyn. He had not spoken since his passage with Syd.

But Syd gazed up at Alleyn. He shivered and yawned and his nose ran. 'Look,' he said, 'give me a fix. Just one. Look, I need it. I got to have it. Look – for God's sake.' He suddenly screamed. 'Give it to me! I'll tell you the lot! Get me a fix!'

IV

Ricky was in the Montjoy Hospital, having managed a fuller account of his misadventures before being given something to settle him down for the night.

At half past two in the morning, the relentlessly-lit charge-room at Montjoy police station smelt of stale bodies, breath and tobacco with an elusive background of Jeyes fluid.

Ferrant, who had refused to talk without the advice of a solicitor, had been taken to the cells while the station sergeant tried to raise one. Syd Jones whimpered, suffered onsets of cramp, had to be taken to the lavatory, yawned, ran at the nose and repeatedly pleaded for a fix. Dr Carey, called in to watch, said that no harm would be done if the drug was withheld for the time being.

Everything that Jones said confirmed their guesswork. He even showed signs of a miserable sort of complacence over his ingenuity in the matter of the paint tubes. He admitted, as if it was of little account, that it was he who tried to drown Ricky at St Pierre.

On one point only he was obdurate: he could not or would not say anything about Louis Pharamond, contriving, when questioned, to recover something of his old intransigence.

'Him,' he said. 'Don't give me him!' and then looked frightened and would say no more about Louis Pharamond.

Alleyn said: 'Why didn't you take the sorrel mare to the smith, as you were told to, after you got back with the horse-feed?'

Syd drove his fingers through his thicket of hair. 'What are you on about now?' he moaned. 'What's that got to do with anything? OK, OK, so I biked back to my pad, didn't I? So what?'

'To get yourself a fix?'

'Yeah. OK. Yeah.'

For the twentieth time he got up and shambled about the room, stamping and grabbing at the calf of his leg. 'I got cramp,' he said. He fetched up in front of Fox. 'I'll make a complaint,' he said. 'I'll have it in for you lot the way you're treating me. Sadists. Fascist pigs.'

'Don't be silly,' said Fox.

Syd appealed to Dr Carey. 'Doc,' he said, 'you'll look after me. Won't you, Doc? You got to, haven't you? For Christ's sake, Doc'

'You'll have to hang on a bit longer,' said Doctor Carey, and glanced at Alleyn. Syd broke down completely and wept.

Alleyn said: 'Give him what he needs.'

'Really?'

'Yes. Really.'

Dr Carey went out of the room.

Syd, fingering his beard and biting his dirty fingers, let out a kind of laugh. 'I couldn't help it, could I?' he gabbled, and looked sideways at Alleyn, who had turned away from him and didn't reply.

'It was Gil used the wire on him, not me,' Syd said to Alleyn's back.

Fox walked over to Plank, who throughout the long hours had taken notes. Fox leant over him and turned the pages back.

'Is this correct?' he asked Syd. 'What you've deposed about the wire? Where you got it and what you wanted it for?'

'I've said so, haven't I? Yes. Yes. Yes. For the picture.'

'Why won't you talk about Mr Louis Pharamond?'

'There's nothing to say.'

'Who's the next above Ferrant? Who gives the orders?'

'I don't know. I've told you. Where's the doc? Where's he gone?'

'He'll be here,' said Fox. 'You'll get your fix if you'll talk about your boss. And I don't mean Harkness. I mean who gives the orders? Is it Louis Pharamond?'

'I can't. I can't. They'd knock me off. I would if I could. They'd get me. Honest. I can't.' Syd returned to his chair and wept.

Without turning round Alleyn said: 'Let it be, Fox.'

Dr Carey came back with a prepared syringe and a swab. Syd, with a trembling hand, pushed up his sleeve.

'Good God,' said the doctor, 'you've been making a mess of yourself, haven't you?' He gave the injection.

The reaction was instantaneous. It was a metamorphosis – as if Syd's entire person thawed and re-formed into a blissful transfiguration of itself. He lolled back in his chair and giggled. 'Fantastic,' he said.

Dr Carey watched him for a moment and then joined Alleyn at the far end of the room.

'He's well away,' he said. He's had ten milligrammes and he's full of well-being: the classic euphoria. You've seen for yourselves what the withdrawal symptoms can be like.'

Alleyn said: 'May I put a hypothetical case to you? There may be no answer to it. It may be just plain silly.'

'We can give it a go,' said Dr Carey.

'Suppose, on the afternoon of Dulcie Harkness's death, having taken himself off to his pad, he treated himself, to an injection of heroin. Is it within the bounds of possibility that he could return on his motor-bike to Leathers, help himself to a length of wire from the stables, rig it across the gap in the fence, wait until Dulcie Harkness was dying or dead, remove the wire and return to his pad, to reappear on his bike, apparently in full control of himself, later on in the evening?'

Dr Carey was silent for some time. Syd Jones had begun to hum tunelessly under his breath.

Carey said at last, 'Frankly, I don't know how to answer you. Since my time in the casualty ward at St Luke's I've had no experience of drug addiction. I know symptoms vary widely from case to case. You'd do better to consult a specialist.'

'You wouldn't rule it out altogether?'

'For what it's worth – I don't think I'd do that, quite.'

'I'll get that bugger,' Syd Jones announced happily. 'I'll bloody well get him.'

'What bugger?' Fox asked.

'That'd be telling. Think I'd let you in? You got to be joking, Big Fuzz.'

'About my son?' Alleyn asked Dr Carey.

'Ah yes, of course. He's settled down nicely.'

'Yes?'

'He'll be all right. There's been quite a bit of pain and considerable shock. He's had something that'll help him sleep. And routine injections against tetanus and so on. The cuts round the ankles were nasty. We'd like to keep him under observation.'

'Thank you,' Alleyn said. 'I'll tell his mother.'

'Of course I'm completely in the dark,' said Dr Carey. 'Or nearly so. But, damn it all, I *am* supposed to be the police surgeon round here. And there *is* an adjourned inquest coming up.'

'My dear chap,' said Alleyn, pulling himself together, 'I know, and I'm sorry. You shall hear all. In the meantime what shall we do with this specimen?'

Syd Jones, gloomily surveyed by Fox, laughed, talked incomprehensibly and drifted into song.

'You won't get any sense out of him. I'd put him in the cells and have him supervised. He'll go to sleep sooner or later,' said Dr Carey.

Syd was removed, laughing heartily as he went. Fox went out to arrange for a constable to sit in his cell until he fell asleep, and Alleyn, who now felt as if he'd been hauled through a mangle, pulled himself together and gave Dr Carey a succinct account of the case as it had developed. They sat on the hideously uncomfortable wall bench. It was now ten minutes past three in the morning. The station sergeant came in with cups of strong tea: the third brew since they'd arrived five hours ago.

Dr Carey said: 'No, thanks, I'm for my bed.' He stood up, stretched, held out his hand and was professionally alerted. 'You look done up,' he said. 'Not surprising. Will you get off now?'

'Oh yes. Yes, I expect so.'

'Where are you staying?'

'At the Montjoy.'

'Like anything to help you sleep?'

'Lord, no,' said Alleyn, 'I'd drop off in a gravel pit. Nice of you to offer, though. Good night.'

He went to bed at his hotel, fell instantly and profoundly asleep and, having ordered breakfast in his room at 7.30 and arranged with himself to wake at 7, did so and put in a call to his wife. It went through at once.

'That's your waking-up voice,' he said.

'Never mind. Is anything the matter?'

'There was but it's all right now.'

'Ricky?'

'Need you ask? But darling, repeat, it's all right now. I promise.'

'Tell me.'

He told her.

'When's the first plane?' Troy asked.

'Nine-twenty from Heathrow. You transfer at St Pierre-des-Roches.'

'Right.'

'Hotel Montjoy and George VI Hospital.'

'Rory, say if you'd rather I didn't. You will, won't you?'

'I'd rather you did, but God knows where I'll be when you get here. We may well blow up for a crisis.'

'Could you book a room?'

'I could. This one.'

'Right. I'll be in it.'

Troy hung up. Alleyn rang up the hospital and was told Ricky had enjoyed a fairly comfortable night and was improving. He bathed, dressed, ate his breakfast and was about to call the hotel office when the telephone rang again. He expected it would be Fox and was surprised and not overjoyed to hear Julia Pharamond's voice.

'Good morning,' said Julia. She spoke very quietly and sounded hurried and unlike herself. 'I'm very sorry indeed to bother you and at such a ghastly hour. I wouldn't have, only we're in trouble and I – well, Jasper and I – thought we'd better.'

'What's the matter?'

'And Carlotta agrees.'

'Carlotta does?'

'Yes. I don't want,' Julia whispered piercingly into the mouthpiece, 'to talk down the telephone. À cause des domestiques. Damn, I'd forgotten they speak French.'

'Can you give me an inkling?'

After a slight pause Julia said in a painstakingly casual voice. 'Louis.'

'I'll come at once,' said Alleyn.

He called Fox up. On his way out, while Fox rang Plank, Alleyn left the L'Esperance number at the hotel office, ordered a taxi to meet Troy's plane and booked her in. 'And you might get flowers for the room. Lilies-of-the-valley if you can.'

'How many?' asked the grand lady at Reception.

'Lots,' said Alleyn. 'Any amount.'

The lady smiled indulgently and handed him a letter. It had just been sent in from the police station, she said. It was addressed to him. The writing was erratic. There was much crossing out and some omissions, but on the whole he thought it rather more coherent than might have been expected. It was written on headed paper with a horse's head printed in one corner.

Sir: I am in possession of certain facts – in re slaying of my niece – and have been guided to make All Known Before The People since they sit heavy on my conscience. Therefore on Sunday next (please see enclosure) I will proclaim All to the multitude the Lord of Hosts sitteth on my tongue and He Will Repay. The Sinner will be called an Abomination before the Lord and before His People. Amen. Amen. *I* will be greatly obliged if you will be kind enough to attend.

With compliments

Yrs etc. etc.

C. Harkness.

(Brother Cuth)

He showed the letter, together with the enclosure – a new pamphlet – to Fox, who read it when they had set off in Superintendent Curie's car.

'He doesn't half go on, doesn't he?' said Fox. 'Do you make out he thinks he knows who chummy is?'

'That's how I read it.'

'What'll we do about this service affair?'

'Attend in strength.'

They drove on in silence. The morning was clear and warm, the channel sparkled and the Normandy coast looked as if it was half its actual distance away.

'What do you reckon Mr L. Pharamond's been up to?' asked Fox.

'I'll give you one guess.'

'Skedaddled?'

'Skedaddled. And if we'd known, how could we have stopped him?'

'We could have kept him under obbo,' Fox mused.

'But couldn't have prevented him lighting out. Well, could we? Under what pretext? Seen conversing with G. Ferrant at one o'clock in the morning? Query: Involved in drug running? Dropped a sleeve button in the horse-paddock at Leathers. Had previously denied going into horse-paddock. Now says he forgot. End of information. Query: Murdered Dulcie Harkness? He wouldn't be able to keep a straight face over that lot, Br'er Fox.'

Up at L'Esperance they found Jasper waiting on the terrace. Alleyn introduced Fox. Jasper, though clearly surprised that he had come, was charming. He led them to a table and a group of chairs, canopied and overlooking the sea.

'Julia's coming down in a minute,' he said. 'We thought we'd like to see you first. Will you have coffee? And things? We're going to. It's our breakfast.'

It was already set out, with croissants and brioches on the table. It smelt superb. When Alleyn accepted, Fox did too.

'It really is extremely odd,' Jasper continued, heaping butter and honey on a croissant. 'And very worrying. Louis has completely vanished. Here comes Julia.'

Out of the house she hurried in a white trouser suit and ran down the steps to them with her hands extended. Fox was drinking coffee. He rose to his feet and was slightly confused.

'How terribly kind of you both to come,' said Julia. 'No, *too* kind, when one knows you're being so active and fussed. How's Ricky?'

'In hospital,' said Alleyn, shaking hands.

'*No*! Because of his black eye?'

'Partly. Could we hear about Louis?'

'Hasn't Jasper said? He's vanished. Into thin air.'

'Since when?'

Jasper, whose mouth was full, waved his wife on.

'Since yesterday,' said Julia. 'You remember yesterday morning when he was as large as life in his zoot-suit and talked to you on the front? In the Cove?'

'I remember,' Alleyn said.

'Yes. Well, we drove back here for luncheon. And when we got here, he sort of clapped his hand to his brow and said he'd forgotten to send a business cable to Lima and it was important and he'd have to attend to it. Louis has – what does one call them? – in Peru.'

Jasper said: 'Business interests. We came originally from Peru. But he's the only one of us to have any business links. He's jolly rich, old Louis is.'

'Well, then,' said Julia. 'He often has to ring up Lima or cable to it. They're not very clever at the Cove about cables in Spanish or long-distance calls to Peru. So he goes into Montjoy. At first we thought he'd probably lunched there.'

'Did you see him again before he left?'

'No. We were at luncheon,' said Julia.

'We heard him come downstairs and start his car. Now I come to think of it,' said Jasper, 'it was some little time after we'd sat down.'

'Have you looked to see if he's taken anything with him – an overnight bag, for instance?'

'Yes,' said Julia, 'but not a penny the wiser are we. Louis has so many zoot-suits and silken undies and pyjamas and terribly doggy pieces of luggage that one couldn't tell. Even Carlotta couldn't. She's still looking.'

'What else have you done about it?' asked Alleyn. He thought of his own gnawing anxieties during Ricky's disappearance and wondered if Carlotta, for example, suffered anything comparable: Jasper and Julia, though worried, clearly did not.

'Well,' Julia was saying, 'for a long time we didn't do anything. We'd expected him simply to whizz into Montjoy, send his cable and whizz back. Then when he didn't we supposed he'd decided to lunch at the Montjoy and perhaps stay the night. He often does that when the little girls get too much for him. But he *always* rings up to tell us. When he didn't ring and didn't come back for dinner, Carlotta telephoned the hotel and he hadn't been there at all. And still we haven't had sniff nor sight of him.'

'I even rang the pub at Belle Vue,' said Jasper.

'What about his car?'

'We rang the park where he always leaves it and it's there. He clocked in about twenty minutes after he left here.'

'The thing that really is pretty bothering,' Julia said, 'is that he was in a peculiar sort of state yesterday morning. After we left you. We wondered if you noticed anything.'

Alleyn gave himself a moment's respite. He thought of Louis: over-elegant, over-facetious, giving his performance on the front. 'How do you mean "peculiar"?' he asked.

'For him, very quiet, and at the same time, *I* felt he was in a rage. You mustn't mind my asking but did you have words, the two of you?'

'No.'

'I only wondered. He wouldn't say anything about being grilled by you and didn't seem to enjoy me calling it that – I was just being funny-man. You know? But he didn't relish it. So I wondered.'

'Was that why you asked me to come?'

Jasper said: 'What we really hoped you'd do is give us some advice about what action we could take. One doesn't want to make a sort of public display but at the same time one can't just loll about in the sun supposing that he'll come bounding back.'

'Has he ever done anything of this sort before?'

Julia and Jasper spoke simultaneously.

'Not like this,' said Jasper.

'Not exactly,' said Julia.

They looked at Fox and away.

Fox said: 'I wonder if I could be excused, Mrs Pharamond? We started a slow puncture on the way up. If I'm not required at the moment, sir, perhaps I should change the wheel?'

'Would you, Fox? We'll call out if we need you.'

Fox rose. 'A very enjoyable cup of coffee,' he said, with a slight bow in Julia's direction and descended the steps to the lower terrace where the car was parked. It was just as well, thought Alleyn, that it was out of sight.

'Not true!' said Julia with, wide-open eyes. 'My dear! The tact! Have you many like that?'

'We have a finishing-school,' said Alleyn, 'at the CID.'

Jasper said: 'Answering your question. No, Louis, as Julia said, always lets us know if he's going to be away unexpectedly.'

'Is he often away unexpectedly?'

'Well – '

Julia burst out. 'Oh, let's not be cagey and difficult, darling. After all, we asked the poor man to come, so why shuffle and snuffle when he wants to know about things? Yes, Louis does quite often leave us for reasons undisclosed and probably not very respectable. He can't keep his hands off the ladies.'

'Julia! *Darling!*'

'And *what* ladies some of them are. But then, it appears that Louis bowls them over like ninepins and has only to show himself at a casino in Lima for them to swarm. This we find puzzling. Perhaps he's been hijacked and taken away for a sort of gentlemanly white-slave trade, to be offered to sex-starved señoritas, which would really suit him very well as he could combine their pleasure with his business.'

'No, honestly,' Jasper protested and giggled.

'Darling, admit. You're not all that keen on him yourself. But we do love Carlotta *very* dearly,' said Julia, 'and we've got sort of inoculated to Louis like one does with sandflies, blood being thicker than water as far as Jasper is concerned.'

Jasper said: 'What steps *do* you think we should take?'

Alleyn found it odd to repeat the advice that he and Fox had offered each other yesterday. He said they could report Louis's disappearance to the police now or wait a little longer. He thought he would advise the latter course.

'Have you,' he said, 'looked to see if his papers – passport and medical certificates and so on – are in his room? You say he often makes business trips to Peru. Isn't it just possible that something cropped up – say a cable – calling him there on urgent business and that you'll get a telegram to this effect?'

Jasper and Julia looked at each other and shook their heads. Alleyn was trying to remember in which South American countries extradition orders could be operated.

'Speaking as a policeman,' said Julia, 'which it's so difficult to remember you are, would the force be very bored if asked to take a hand? I mean, busy as you all seem to be over the Harkness affair? Wouldn't they think Louis's on-goings of no account?'

'No,' Alleyn said. 'They wouldn't think that.'

A stillness came over the group of three. Jasper, who had reached out to the coffee-pot, withdrew his hand. He looked very hard at Alleyn and then at his wife.

Julia said: 'Is there something – you know and we don't? About Louis?'

Carlotta came out of the house and down the steps. She was very pale, even for a Pharamond. She came to the table and sat down as if she needed to.

'I've made a discovery,' she said. 'Louis's passport and his attaché case and the file he always takes when he goes to Lima are missing. I forced open the drawer in his desk. So I imagine, don't you,' said Carlotta, 'that he's walked out on me?'

'You sound as if you're not surprised,' said Julia.

'Nor am I. He's been precarious for quite a time. You've seen it, haven't you? You must have.' They were silent. 'I always knew, of course,' Carlotta said, 'that by and large you thought him pretty ghastly. But there you are. I have a theory that quite a lot of women require a touch of the bounder in their man. I'm one of them. So, true to type, he's bounded away.'

Jasper said: 'Carla, darling, aren't you rushing your fences a bit? After all, we don't know why he's gone. If he's gone.'

Julia said: 'I've got a feeling that Roderick, if we're still allowed to call him that, knows. And I don't believe he thinks it's anything to do with you, Carla.' She turned to Alleyn. 'Am I right?' she asked.

Alleyn said slowly: 'If you mean do I know definitely he's gone, I don't. I've no information at all as to his recent movements.'

'He's in trouble, though. Isn't he? It's best we should all realize. Really.'

'What's he done?' Carlotta demanded. 'He has done something, hasn't he? I've known he was up to something. I can always tell.'

Jasper said with an unfamiliar note in his voice: 'I think we'd better remember, girls, that we are talking, however much we may like him, to a policeman.'

'Oh, dear. I suppose we should,' Julia agreed, and sounded vexed rather than alarmed. 'I suppose we must turn cagey and evasive and he'll set traps for us and when we fall into them he'll say things like "I didn't know but you've just told me." They always do that. Don't you?' she asked Alleyn.

'I don't fancy it's going to be my morning for aphorisms,' he said.

'Somehow,' Julia mused, 'I've always thought – you won't mind my saying, Carla darling? I prefer to be open – I've always thought Louis was a tiny bit the absconding type.'

Carlotta looked thoughtfully at her. 'Have you?' she said, as if her attention had been momentarily caught. 'Well, it looks as though you're right. Or doesn't it?' she added, turning to Alleyn.

He stood up. The three of them contemplated him with an air of – what? Polite interest? Concern? One would have said no more than that, if it had not been for Carlotta's pallor, the slightest tremor in Jasper's hand as he put down his coffee-cup, and – in Julia? – the disappearance, as if by magic, of her immense vitality.

'I think,' Alleyn said, 'that in a situation which for me, if not for you, poses a problem, I'll have to spill the beans. The not very delicious beans. As you say, I'm a policeman. I'm what is known as an "investigating officer", and if something dubious crops up I've got to investigate it. That is why I'm here, on the island. Now, such is the nature of the investigation, anybody doing a bolt for no discernible reason becomes somebody the police want to see. Your cousin is now somebody I want to see.'

After a long silence Jasper said: 'I don't like your chances.'

'Nor do I, much.'

'I suppose we aren't to know what you want to see him about?'

'I've gone further than I should already.'

Carlotta said: 'It's not about that girl, is it? Oh God, it's not about her?'

'It's no good, Carla,' Julia said, and put her arm round Carlotta. 'Obviously, he's not going to tell you.' She looked at Alleyn and the ghost of her dottiness revisited her. 'And we actually asked you to come and help us,' she said. 'It's like the flies asking the spider to walk into their parlour, isn't it?'

'Alas!' said Alleyn. 'It is, a bit. I'm sorry.'

The child Selina appeared on the steps from the house. She descended them in jumps with her feet together.

'Run away, darling,' her parents said in unison.

Selina continued to jump.

'Selina,' said her father. 'What did we tell you?'

She accomplished the final jump. 'I can't,' she said.

'Nonsense,' said her mother. 'Why can't you?'

'I got a message.'

'A message? What message? Tell us later and run away now.'

'It's on the telephone. I answered it.'

'Why on earth couldn't you say so?'

'For him,' said Selina. She pointed at Alleyn and made a face.

Julia said automatically: 'Don't do that and don't point at people. It's for you,' she said to Alleyn.

'Thank you. Selina,' he said. 'Will you show me the way.'

'Okey-dokey-pokey,' said Selina, and seized him by the wrist.

'You see?' Julia appealed to Alleyn. 'Quite awful!'

'One is helpless,' said Jasper.

As they ascended the steps Selina repeated her jumping technique, retaining her hold on Alleyn's wrist. When they were half-way up she said: 'Cousin Louis is a dirty old man.'

Alleyn, nonplussed, gazed down at her. In her baleful way Selina was a pretty child.

'Why do you talk like that?' he temporized.

'What *is* a dirty old man?' asked Selina.

'Father Christmas in a chimney.'

'You're cuckoo.' She slid her hand into his and adopted a normal manner of ascent. 'Anyway,' she said, 'Louis says he is.'

'What do you mean?'

'Louis Ferrant says his mother says Cousin Louis is a DOM.'

'Do you know Louis Ferrant?'

'Nanny knows his mother. We meet them in the village. He's bigger than me. He says things.'

'What sort of things?'

'I forget,' said Selina, and looked uncomfortable.

'I don't think Louis Ferrant's an awfully good idea,' Alleyn said. He hoisted Selina up to his shoulder. She gave a shriek of pleasure and they entered the house.

It was Plank on the telephone.

'I thought you'd like to know, sir,' he said. 'They've rung through from Montjoy. Jones wants to bargain.'

'He does? What's he offering?'

'As far as we can make out – info on Dulcie. He won't talk to anyone but you. He's drying out and in a funny mood.'

'I'll come.'

'One other thing, Mr Alleyn. Mr Harkness rang up. He's on about this service affair tomorrow. He's very keen on everybody attending it. There was a lot of stuff about Vengeance Is Mine says the Lord and the Book of Leviticus. He said he's been guided to make known before the multitude the sinner in Israel.'

'Oh, yes?'

'Yes. Something about it being revealed to him in a dream. He sounded very wild.'

'Drunk?'

'Damn near DT's, I reckon.'

'Do you suppose there'll be a large attendance?'

'Yes,' said Plank, 'I do. There's a lot of talk about it. He's sent some dirty big announcements to the pub and the shop.'

'Sent them? By whom?'

'The delivery boy from the Cod-and-Bottle. Mr Harkness was very upset when I told him Jones and Ferrant wouldn't be able to be present. He said the Lord would smite the police hip and thigh and cast them into eternal fires if Jones and Ferrant didn't attend the meeting. Particularly Jones. He's far gone, sir.'

'So it would seem. We'll have to go to his party, of course. But first things first, Plank, and that means Jones. Is there anything to keep you in the Cove?'

'No, sir. I've informed Mrs Ferrant her husband's in custody and will come before the court on Monday.'

'How did she take that?'

'She never said a word but, my oath, she looked at me old-fashioned.'

'I dare say. I'll get down as soon as I can,' said Alleyn, and hung up.

When he came out of the house he found the Pharamonds still sitting round the table. They were not speaking and looked as if they had been that way ever since he left.

He went over to them. Jasper stood up.

'That was Sergeant Plank,' Alleyn said. 'I'm wanted. I wish I could tell you how sorry I am that things have fallen out as they have.'

'Not your fault,' said Julia. 'Or ours if it comes to that. We're what's called victims of circumstance. Why's Ricky in hospital?'

'He was beaten up.'

'Not – ?' Carlotta broke out.

'No, no. By Gil Ferrant and Syd Jones. They come up before the beak tomorrow. Rick's all right.'

Julia said: 'Poorest Ricky, what a time he's having! Give him our love.'

'I will, indeed,' said Alleyn.

'Of course, if Louis should turn up, the Pharamonds, however boring the exercise, will close their ranks.'

'Of course.'

'And I with them. Because it behoves me so to do.' She reached out her hand to Carlotta, who took it. 'But then again,' she said, 'I'm not a Pharamond. I'm a Lamprey. I think, ages ago, you met some of my relations.'

'I believe I did,' said Alleyn.

CHAPTER 9

Storm Over

'Back to square one,' Alleyn thought when they brought Sydney Jones before him with once again all the unlovely symptoms of the deprived addict. Dr Carey had evidently not been over-generous with the fix.

He began at once to say he would only talk to Alleyn and wouldn't have any witnesses in the room.

'It won't make any difference, you silly chap,' Fox said with a low degree of accuracy. But Syd knew a thing worth two of that, and stuck to it.

In the end Fox and Alleyn exchanged glances and Fox went away.

Syd said: 'You going to fix me up?'

'Not without the doctor's approval.'

'I've got something I can tell you. About Dulcie. It'd make a difference.'

'What is it?'

'Oh no!' said Syd. 'Oh, dear me, no! Fair's fair.'

'If you can give me information that will lead substantially to a charge, the fact that you did so and did it of your own accord would be taken into consideration. If it turns out to be something that we could get from another source – Ferrant, for instance – '

Syd, with a kind of febrile intensity, let fling a stream of obscenities. It emerged that Syd now laid all his woes at Ferrant's door. It was Ferrant who had introduced him to hard-line drugs, Ferrant who established Syd's link with Jerome et Cie, Ferrant who egged him on to follow Ricky about the streets in St Pierre-des-Roches, Ferrant who kidnapped Ricky and brought him into the pad.

'And this information you say you have, is about Ferrant, is it?' Alleyn asked.

'If they got on to it I'd shopped him, they'd get me.'

'Who would?'

'Them. Him. Up there.'

'Are you talking about Mr Louis Pharamond?'

'*Mister. Mister* Philistine. *Mister* Bloody Fascist Sod Pharamond. You don't know,' Syd said, 'why I wanted that wire. Well? Do you?'

'To hang a picture.'

'That's right. Because she said it gave her a feeling that I've got a strong sense of rhythm. That's what she said.'

'This,' Alleyn thought, 'is the unfairest thing that has ever happened to me.'

He said: 'Get back to what you can tell me. Is it about Ferrant?'

'More or less that's what she said,' Syd mumbled.

'*Ferrant!*' Alleyn insisted, and could have shouted it. 'What about Ferrant?'

'What'll I get for it? For assault?'

'It depends on the magistrates. You can have a solicitor and a barrister to defend you.'

'Will *he* get longer? Seeing he laid it all on? Gil?'

'Possibly. If you can satisfy the court that he did.'

Syd wiped the back of his hand across his face. 'Not like that,' he said, 'not in front of him. In court. Not on your Nelly.'

'Why not?'

'They'd get me,' he said.

'Who would?'

'Them. The organization. That lot.'

Alleyn moved away from him. 'Make up your mind,' he said, and looked at his watch. 'I can't give you much longer.'

'I never wanted to do him over. I never meant to make it tough. You know? Tying him up with the wire and that. It was Gil.'

'For the last time: if you have something to say about Ferrant, say it.'

'I want a fix.'

'Say it.'

Syd bit his fingers, wiped his nose, blinked, and with a travesty of pulling himself together, cleared his throat and whispered: 'Gil did it.'

'Did what?'

'Did her. Dulcie.'

And then, as if he'd turned himself on like a tap, he poured out his story.

Dulcie Harkness, he said, had found out about the capsules in the paint tubes. It had happened one night when she was 'going with' Syd. It might have been the night he took Ricky to the pad. Yes – it was that night. Before they arrived she had taken it into her head to tidy up the paint-table and had come across a tube that was open at the wrong end. When Ricky had gone she had pointed it out to Syd. Alleyn gathered that this rattled Syd. He told her it was because the cap had jammed. Dulcie had unscrewed the cap with ease and 'got nosy'. Syd had lost his temper – he was, he said, by that time 'high' on grass. There was a fine old scene between them and she'd left the pad saying she expected to be made an honest woman by him. Or else.

After that she kept on at him both before and after his trip to London. Her uncle was giving her hell and she wanted to cut loose and the shortest route to that desired end, she argued, was a visit to the registry office with Syd. By this time, it emerged, she was 'going with somebody else' and threatened to talk.

'Do you mean to Louis Pharamond?'

Never mind who. She got Syd so worried he'd confided in Gil Ferrant and Gil had gone crook, Syd said, revealing his antipodean origin. Gil had taken it very seriously indeed. He'd tackled Dulcie, tried to scare her with threats about what would happen to her if she talked, but she laughed at him and said two could play at that game.

That was the situation on the morning before the accident. When he returned from his trip to the corn-chandler Syd found Ferrant lurking round the stables. He had driven up in his car. Alleyn heard with surprise that Mrs Ferrant was with him. It appeared that she did the fine laundering for L'Esperance and they had called there to deliver it. Ferrant said that within the next few days he was going over to St Pierre under orders from above and Syd was to hold himself in readiness to follow, to collect a consignment. Ferrant wanted to know how Dulcie was behaving herself. Syd gave him an account of the fence-jumping incident, her threat to try it herself and the subsequent row with her uncle.

Ferrant had asked where she was and Syd had said up in her room but that wouldn't be for long. She'd broken out before and she would again and if he knew anything about her she'd take the mare over the jump.

'Where,' Alleyn asked, 'was her uncle at this time?'

In his office, writing hell-fire pamphlets, Syd supposed. And where was the sorrel mare? In her loose-box. And Mrs Ferrant? She remained in the car.

'Go on.'

Well, Ferrant supplied Syd's stuff and he'd brought a packet and he said why didn't Syd doss down somewhere and do himself a favour. He was friendlier than Syd had known him since the row over Dulcie. They were in the old coach-house at the time and Syd noticed how Ferrant looked round at everything.

Well. So Syd had said he didn't mind if he did. He went into one of the unoccupied loose-boxes where he settled himself down on the clean straw and gave himself a fix.

The next thing he could be sure about was that it was quite a lot later in the afternoon. He pulled himself together and went into the coach-house where he had parked his bike. It was then that he noticed the length of wire that had been newly cut off from the main coil. He thought it would do to hang his picture and he took it. He then remembered he was supposed to take the sorrel mare to the smith. He looked in her loose-box but she wasn't there. It was too late to do anything about it now so he biked down to the cliffs and had another fix. After a time he got round to wondering what had gone on at Leathers. He returned there and met Ricky and Jasper Pharamond who told him about Dulcie.

Here Syd came to a stop. He gazed at Alleyn and pulled at his beard.

'Well,' Alleyn said, 'is that all?'

'All! God, it's everything. He did it. I know. I could tell, the way he carried on afterwards when I talked about it. He was pleased with himself. You could tell.'

At this point Syd became hysterical. He swore that if they put him in the witness-box he wouldn't say a word about heroin or against

Ferrant because if he did he'd 'be in for it'. It was for Alleyn to follow up the information he'd given him, but he, Syd, wasn't going to be made a monkey of. It was remarkable that however frantic he became he never mentioned Ferrant's name or alluded to him in any way without lowering his voice, as if Ferrant might overhear him. But when he pleaded for his fix he became vociferous and at last began to scream.

Alleyn said he'd ask Dr Carey to look at Syd and saw him taken back to his cell. He and Fox then called on Gil Ferrant and were received with a great show of insolence. Ferrant lounged on his bed. He still wore his sharp French suit and pink shirt but they were greatly dishevelled and he had an overnight beard. He chewed gum with his mouth open and looked them up and down through half-shut eyes. Almost, Alleyn thought, he preferred Syd.

'Good morning,' he said.

Ferrant raised his eyebrows, stretched elaborately and yawned.

'No doubt,' Alleyn said, 'it's been explained to you that you haven't much hope of avoiding a conviction and the maximum sentence. If you plead guilty you may get off with less. Do you want to make a statement?'

Ferrant shook his head slowly from side to side and made a great thing of shifting the wad of gum.

'Advised not to,' he drawled.

Alleyn said: 'We've found enough heroin at Jones's place to send you up for years.'

Ferrant said, 'That's his affair.'

'And yours. Believe me, yours.'

'No comment,' he said, and shut his eyes.

'You're out on a limb,' said Alleyn. 'Your master's cleared off. Did you know that?'

Ferrant didn't open his eyes but the lids quivered.

'You'd do better to co-operate,' Fox advised.

Ferrant, still lolling on the bed, opened his eyes and looked at Alleyn. 'And how's Daddy's Baby-boy this morning?' he asked, and smiled as he chewed.

In the silence that followed this quip, Alleyn, as if desire could actually change places with action, saw – almost felt – his fist drive into the bristled chin. His fingernails bit into his palm. He looked at Fox, whose neck seemed to have swollen and whose face was red.

A long-forgotten phrase from *Little Dorrit* came into Alleyn's mind: 'Count five-and-twenty, Tattycoram.' He had actually begun to count the seconds in his head when Plank came in to say he was wanted on the telephone by Mrs Pharamond. In the passage he said to Plank, 'Ferrant won't talk. Mr Fox is having a go. Take your notebook.'

Plank, after a startled glance at him, went off.

When Alleyn spoke to Julia she sounded much more like her usual self.

'What luck!' said Julia. 'I rang the Cove station and a nice lady said you might be where you are. It's to tell you Carlotta's had a message from Louis. Are you pleased? We are.'

'Am I to hear what it is?'

'It's a picture postcard of the Montjoy Hotel. Someone has written in a teeny-weeny hand: 'Picked up in street' and it's very grubby. It says, "Everything OK. Writing. L." and it's addressed, of course, to Carla. Would you like to know how we interpret it?'

'Very much.'

'We think Louis has flown to Brazil. I, for one, hope he stays there and so I bet, between you and me and the gatepost, does Carlotta. He was becoming altogether too *difficile*. But *wasn't* it kind of whoever it was to fish the card out of some gutter and pop it in the post?'

'Very kind. Can you read the postmark? The time?'

'Wait a sec. No, I can't. There's a muddy smudge all over it.'

'Will you let me see it?'

'Not,' said Julia promptly, 'if it'll help you haul him back. But we thought it only fair to let you know about it.'

'Thank you,' Alleyn said.

'So we're all feeling relieved and in good heart for Mr Harkness's party tomorrow. I suppose poorest Ricky won't attend, will he? How boring for him to be in hospital. We're going to see him. After the party, so as to tell him all about it. He's allowed visitors I hope?'

'Oh, yes. His mother's arriving today.'

'Troy! But how too exciting! *Jasper*,' screamed Julia. 'Troy's coming to see Ricky.'

Alleyn heard Jasper exclaiming buoyantly in the background.

'I must go, I'm afraid,' he said into the receiver. 'Thank you for telling me about the postcard.'

'You aren't at all huffy, I suppose? You sound like Ricky when he's huffy.'

'A fat lot of good it would do me if I was. Oh, by the way, does Mrs Ferrant do your laundry?'

'The fine things. Tarty blouses. Frills and pleats. Special undies. She's a wizard with the iron. Like Mrs Tiggywinkle. Why?'

'Does she collect and deliver?'

'We usually drop and collect. Why?'

'I must fly. Thank you so much.'

'Wait a bit. Do you suppose Louis dropped the postcard on purpose so that we wouldn't get it until he'd skedaddled?'

'The idea does occur, doesn't it? Goodbye.'

On the way to the Cove he reflected that a great many people in the Pharamonds' boots would be secretly enchanted to get rid of Louis but only the Pharamonds would loudly say so.

II

'First stop, Madame Ferrant,' said Alleyn as they drove into Deep Cove. 'I want you both to come in with me. I don't fancy the lady is easily unseated but we'll give it a go.'

She opened the door to them. Her head was neatly tied up in a black handkerchief. She was implacably aproned and her sleeves were rolled up. Her face, normally sallow, was perhaps more so than usual and this circumstance lent emphasis to her eyes.

'Good morning,' she said.

Alleyn introduced Fox and produced the ostensible reason for the call. He would pack up his son's effects and, of course, settle his bill. Perhaps she would be kind enough to make it out.

'It is already prepared,' said Mrs Ferrant, and showed them into the parlour. She opened a drawer in a small bureau and produced her account. Alleyn paid and she receipted it.

'Madame will understand,' Alleyn said in French, 'that under the circumstances it would regrettably be unsuitable for my son to remain.'

'*Parfaitement*,' said Mrs Ferrant.

'Especially since the injuries from which he suffers were inflicted by Madame's husband.'

Not a muscle of her face moved.

'You have, of course,' Alleyn went on, changing to English, 'been informed of his arrest. You will probably be required to come before the court on Monday.'

'I have nothing to say.'

'Nevertheless, Madame, you will be required to attend.' She slightly inclined her head.

'In the meantime, if you wish to see your husband you will be permitted to do so.'

'I have no desire to see him.'

'No?'

'No.'

'I should perhaps explain that although he has been arrested on a charge of assault there may well follow a much graver accusation: trading in illicit drugs.'

'As to that, it appears to me to be absurd,' said Mrs Ferrant.

'Oh, Madame, I think not. May I remind you of your son's errands last night to and from the premises occupied by Sydney Jones? Where your husband and Jones handled a consignment of heroin and where, with your connivance, they planned their escape?'

'I know nothing of all this. Nothing. My boy is a mere child.'

'In years, no doubt,' said Alleyn politely.

She remained stoney.

'Tell me,' Alleyn said. 'How long have you known the real object of your husband's trips to Marseilles and the Côte d'Azur?'

'I don't know what you mean.'

'Are they for pleasure? Do you accompany him?'

She gave a slight snort.

'A little romance, perhaps?'

She looked disgusted.

'To take a job?'

She was silent.

'Plumbing?' Alleyn hinted, and after another fruitless pause: 'Ah, well, at least he sends postcards. To let you know where he is to be found if anything urgent crops up, no doubt.'

She began to count the money he had put on the table.

'There is another small matter,' he said, 'on which I think you can help us. Will you be so kind as to carry your memory back to the day on which Dulcie Harkness was murdered.'

She put her hands behind her back – suddenly, as if to hide them – and made to adjust her apron strings. 'Murdered?' she said. 'There has been no talk of murder.'

'There has, however, been talk. On that day, late in the morning, did you and your husband visit Leathers?'

Her mouth was a tight line, locked across her face.

'Madame,' said Alleyn, 'why are you so unwilling to speak? It may be I should not have used the word you object to. It may be that the "accident" *was* an accident. In order to settle it either way, we welcome any information, however trivial, about the situation at Leathers on that morning. We understand you and your husband called there. Why should you make such a great matter of this visit? Was it connected with your husband's business activities abroad?'

A metaphysician might, however fancifully, have said of Mrs Ferrant that her body, at this moment, "thought", so still did she hold it and so deeply did it breathe. Alleyn saw the pulse beating at the base of her neck. He wondered if there was to be a sudden rage.

But no: she unlocked her mouth and achieved composure.

'I am sorry,' she said. 'You will understand that I have had a shock and am, perhaps, not quite myself. It is a matter of distress to me that my husband is in trouble.'

'But of course.'

'As for this other affair: yes, we called at Leathers on the morning you speak of. My husband had been asked to do a job there – a leaking pipe, I think he said it was – and had called to say that he could not undertake it at that time.'

'You saw Mr Harkness?'

'I remained in the car. My husband may have seen him. But I think not.'

'Did you see Sydney Jones?'

'Him! *He* was there. There was some talk about a quarrel between Harkness and the girl.' Her eyes slid round at him. 'Perhaps it is Harkness to whom you should speak.'

'Do you remember if there were any horses in the stables?'

'I did not see. I did not notice the stables.'

'Or in the horse-paddock? Or the distant hillside?'

'I didn't notice.'

'What time was it?'

'Possibly about ten-thirty. Perhaps later.'

'Had you been anywhere else that morning?'

'To L'Esperance.'

'Indeed?'

'I do *le blanchissage de fin* for the ladies, I delivered it there.'

'Is that the usual procedure?'

'No,' she said composedly. 'Usually one of their staff picks it up. As we were driving in that direction and the washing was ready, I delivered it.'

'Speaking of deliveries, you do know, don't you, that young Louis – to distinguish him,' said Alleyn, 'from the elder Louis – delivered a note from your husband addressed to me. At the police station? Here, very late last night? He pushed it under the door, rang the bell and ran away.'

'That's a bloody lie,' said Mrs Ferrant. In English.

The conversation so far had been conducted in a lofty mixture of French and English and, in both languages, at a high level of decorum. It was startling to hear Mrs Ferrant come out strongly in basic British fishwife.

'But it isn't, you know,' Alleyn said mildly. 'It's what happened.'

'No! I swear it. The boy has done nothing. Nothing. He was in bed and asleep by nine o'clock.' The front door banged.

'Maman! *Maman!*' cried a treble voice. 'Where are you?'

Mrs Ferrant's hand went to her mouth.

They heard young Louis run down the passage and in and out of the kitchen.

'Maman! Are you upstairs. Where are you?'

'*Ferme ton bec,*' she let out in the standard maternal screech. 'I am busy. Stop that noise.'

But he returned, running up the passage, and burst into the parlour.

'Maman,' he said, 'they have nicked Papa. The boys are saying it. They nicked him last night at the house where he gave me the letter.' He stared at Alleyn. 'Him,' he said, and pointed. 'The fuzz. He's nicked Papa.'

Mrs Ferrant raised her formidable right arm in what no doubt was a familiar gesture.

Louis said: 'No, Maman!' and cringed.

Alleyn said: 'Do you often give Louis a *coup* for speaking the truth, Mrs Ferrant?'

She thrust the receipted bill at him. 'Take it and remove yourself,' she said. 'I have nothing more to say to you.'

'I shall do so. With the fondest remembrances of your *Sole à la Dieppoise.*'

Upstairs in Ricky's room Fox said: 'What do we get out of that lot?'

'Apart from confirmation of various bits of surmise and conjecture, I should say damn all, or very nearly so. If it's of interest, I think she's jealous of her husband and completely under his thumb. I think she hates his guts and would go to almost any length to obey his orders. Otherwise, damn all.'

They packed up Ricky's belongings. The morning had turned sunny and the view from the window, described with affection in his letters, was at its best. The harbour was spangled, seagulls stooped and coasted, and down on the front a covey of small boys frisked and skittered. Louis was not among them.

Alleyn laid his hand on the stack of paper that was Ricky's manuscript and wondered how long the view from the window would remain vivid in his son's memory, All his life, perhaps, if anything came of the book. He covered the pile with a sheet of plain paper and put it into an attaché case, together with a quantity of loose notes. Fox packed the clothes. In a drawer of the wardrobe he found letters Ricky had received from his parents.

'Mrs F. will have enjoyed a good read,' said Alleyn grimly.

When everything was ready and the room had taken on the blank look of unoccupation, they put Ricky's baggage in the car. Alleyn, for motives he would have found hard to define but suspected to be less than noble, left five pounds on the dressing-table.

Before they shut the front door they heard her cross the passage and mount the stairs.

'She'll chuck it after you,' predicted Fox.

'What's the betting? Give her a chance.'

They waited. Mrs Ferrant did not throw the five pounds after them. She snapped the window curtains across the upstairs room. A faint tremor seemed to suggest that she watched them through the crack.

They returned to Montjoy, after a brief visit to Syd's pad where they found Moss and Cribbage, who had completed an exhaustive search and had assembled the fruits of it on the work table: a tidy haul, Alleyn said. He pressed his thumb down on tubes of paint and felt the presence of buried capsules. He looked at the collection, still nestling under protective rows of flake white: capsules waiting to be inserted, and at a chair, the legs of which were scored with wire and smudged with blood.

'You've done very well,' he said, and turned to Plank. 'Normally,' he said, 'I'd have sent for Detective-Sergeant Thompson, who's my particular chap at the Yard, but seeing you're an expert, Plank, I think we'll ask you to take the photographs of this area for us. How do you feel about tackling the job?'

Scarlet with gratification, Plank intimated that he felt fine and was dropped at his station to collect photographic gear. Moss and Cribbage were to take alternate watches at the pad until the exhibits were removed. Fox and Alleyn returned to Montjoy.

As their car climbed up the steep lane to the main road, Alleyn looked down on the Cove and wondered whether or not he would have occasion to return to it.

When he walked into his room at the Hotel Montjoy, he found Troy there waiting for him.

III

Sunday came in to the promise of halcyon weather. A clear sky and a light breeze brought an air of expectation to the island.

Ricky's progress was satisfactory and though his face resembled, in Troy's words, one of Turner's more intemperate sunsets, no bones were broken and no permanent disfigurement need be expected. His ankles were still very swollen and painful but there was no sign of infection and with the aid of sticks he hoped to be able to hobble out of hospital tomorrow.

In the morning Alleyn and Fox had a session on the balcony outside the Alleyns' room. They trudged through the body of evidence point by point, in familiar pursuit of an overall pattern.

'You know,' Fox said, pushing his spectacles up his forehead, when they paused for Alleyn to light his pipe, 'the unusual feature of this case, as I see it, is its lack of definition. Take the homicide aspect, now. As a general rule we know who we're after. There's no mystery. It's a matter of finding enough material to justify an arrest. It's not *like* that this time,' Fox said vexedly. 'You may have your ideas and so may I, Mr Alleyn. We may even think there's only the one possibility that doesn't present an unanswerable objection, but there's not what I'd call a hard *case* to be made out. We've got the drug scene on the one hand and this poor girl on the other. Are they connected? Well, *are* they? *Was* she knocked off because she threatened to shop them on account of requiring a husband? And if so, which would she shop? Or all? We've got three names which could, as you might say, qualify – but only one available for the purpose of marriage.'

'The miserable Syd.'

'Quite so. Then there's this uncle. There were all these scenes with him. Threats and all the rest of it. Motive, you might think. But he wasn't drinking at that time and you can't imagine him risking his own horseflesh. The mare he's so keen on was just as likely to be killed as the girl. And in any case he'd threatened to give her what for if she had a go. *And* he ordered Jones to remove the mare so's she couldn't try. No, I reckon we've got to boil it down to those three unless – by crikey, I wonder.'

'What?'

'What was it you quoted yesterday about a female informant in France? I've got it,' said Fox, and repeated it. He thought it over, became restless, shook his head and broke out again. 'We've no nice, firm *times* for anything,' he lamented. 'Mr and Mrs Ferrant, S. Jones, *Mr* Louis Pharamond all flitting about the premises, in and out and round about, and Mr Harkness locking the girl up. The girl getting out and getting herself killed. Mr Harkness writing these silly pamphlets, *I* don't know,' Fox said, and readjusted his glasses. 'It's mad.'

'It's half past eleven,' said Alleyn. 'Have a drink.'

Fox looked surprised. 'Really?' he said. 'This is unusual, Mr Alleyn. Well, since you've suggested it I'll take a light ale.'

Alleyn joined him. They sat on the hotel balcony and looked not towards France but westwards across the *Golfe* to the Atlantic. They saw that battlements of cloud had built up on the horizon.

'What does that mean?' wondered Troy, who had come out to join them. 'Is that the weather quarter?'

'There's no wind to speak of,' Alleyn said.

'Very sultry,' said Fox. 'Humid.'

'The cloud's massing while you look at it,' Troy said. 'Swelling up over the edge of the ocean as fast as fast can be.'

'Perhaps it's getting ready for Mr Harkness's service. Flashes of lightning,' said Alleyn. 'An enormous beard lolloping over the top of the biggest cloud and a gigantic hand chucking thunderbolts. Very alarming.'

'They say it's the season on the island, for that class of weather,' Fox observed.

'And in St Pierre-des-Roches, judging by Rick's experience.'

'Oppressive,' sighed Fox.

The western sky slowly darkened. By the time they had finished work on the file, cloud overhung the Channel and threatened the island. After luncheon it almost filled the heavens and was so low that the church spire on the hill above Montjoy looked as if it would prick it and bring down a deluge. But still it didn't rain. Alleyn and Troy walked to the hospital and Fox paid a routine visit to the police station.

By tea-time the afternoon had so darkened that it might have been evening.

At five o'clock Julia rang up, asking Troy if they would like to be collected for what she persisted in calling 'Cuth's Party'. Troy explained that she would not be attending it and that Alleyn and Fox had a car. Jasper shouted greetings down the telephone. They both seemed to be in the best of spirits. Even Carlotta joined in the fun.

Troy said to Alleyn: 'You'd say they rejoiced over the bolting of the egregious Louis.'

'They've good cause to.'

'Is he in deep trouble, Rory?'

'Might well be. We don't really know and it's even money that we'll never find out.'

The telephone rang again and Alleyn answered it. He held the receiver away from his ear and Troy could hear the most remarkable noises coming through as of a voice being violently tuned in and out on a loud-speaker. Every now and then words would belch out in a roar: 'Retribution' was one and 'Judgement' another. Alleyn listened with his face screwed up.

'I'm coming,' he said, when he got the chance. 'We are all coming. It has been arranged.'

'Jones!' the voice boomed. *'Jones!'*

'That may be a bit difficult, but I think so.'

Expostulations rent the air.

'This is too much,' Alleyn said to Troy. He laid the receiver down and let it perform. When an opportunity presented itself he snatched it up and said: 'Mr Harkness, I am coming to your service. In the meantime, goodbye,' and hung up.

'Was that really Mr Harkness?' asked Troy, 'or was it an elemental on the rampage?'

'The former. Wait a jiffy.'

He called the office and said there seemed to be a lunatic on the line and would they be kind enough to cut him off if he rang again.

'How can he possibly hold a service?' Troy asked.

'He's hell-bent on it. Whether he's in a purely alcoholic frenzy or whether he really has taken leave of his senses or whether in fact he has something of moment to reveal, it's impossible to say.'

'But what's he *want?*'

'He wants a full house. He wants Ferrant and Jones, particularly.'

'Why?'

'Because he's going to tell us who killed his niece.'

'For crying out loud!' said Troy.

'That,' said Alleyn, 'is exactly what he intends to do.'

The service was to be at six o'clock. Alleyn and Fox left Montjoy at a quarter to the hour under a pall of cloud and absolute stillness. Local sounds had become isolated and clearly defined: voices, a car engine starting up, desultory footfalls. And still it did not rain.

After a minute or two on the road a police van overtook them and sailed ahead.

'Plank,' said Alleyn, 'with his boys in blue and their charges. Only they're not in blue.'

'I suppose it's OK,' Fox said, rather apprehensively.

'It'd better be,' said Alleyn.

As they passed L'Esperance, the Pharamonds' largest car could be seen coming down the drive. And on the avenue to Leathers they passed little groups of pedestrians and fell in behind a procession of three cars.

'Looks like capacity all right,' said Fox.

Two more cars were parked in front of the house and the police van was in the stable yard. Out in the horse-paddock the sorrel mare flung up her head and stared at them. The loose-boxes were empty.

'Is he looking after all this himself?' Fox wondered. 'You'd hardly fancy he was up to it, would you?'

Mr Blacker, the vet, got out of one of the cars and came to meet them.

'This is a rum go and no mistake,' he said. 'I got the most peculiar letter from Cuth. Insisting I come. Not my sort of Sunday afternoon at all. Apparently he's been canvassing the district. Are you chaps mixed up in it, or what?'

Alleyn was spared the necessity of answering by the arrival of the Pharamonds.

They collected round Alleyn and Fox, gaily chattering as if they had met in the foyer of the Paris Opera. Julia and Carlotta wore black linen suits with white lawn blouses: exquisite tributes to Mrs Ferrant's art as a *blanchisseuse de fin*.

'Shall we go in?' Julia asked as if the bells had rung for curtain-up. 'We mustn't miss anything, must we?' She laid her gloved hand on Alleyn's arm. 'The baskets!' she said. 'Should we take them in or leave them in the car?'

'*Baskets?*'

'You must remember? "Ladies a Basket". Carlotta and I have brought *langouste* and mayonnaise sandwiches. Do you think – suitable?'

'I'm not sure if the basket arises this time.'

'We must wait and see. If unsuitable we shall wolf them up when we get home. As a kind of *hors d'oevre*. You're dining, aren't you? You and Troy? And Mr Fox, *of course?*'

'Julia,' Alleyn said, 'Fox and I are policemen and we're on duty and however delicious your *langouste* sandwiches, I doubt if we can accept your kind invitation. And now, like a dear creature, go and assemble your party in the front stalls and don't blame me for what you are about to receive. It's through there on your right.'

'Oh, dear!' said Julia. 'Yes. I see. Sorry.'

He watched them go off and then looked into the police van. Plank and Moss were in the front, Cribbage and a very young constable in the back, with Ferrant and Syd Jones attached to them. The police were in civilian dress

Alleyn said: 'Wait until everyone else has gone in and then sit at the back. OK? If there aren't any seats left, stand.'

'Yes, sir,' said Plank.

'Where are your other chaps?'

'They went in, Mr Alleyn. As far front as possible. And there's an extra copper from the mainland, like you said. Outside the back door.'

'How are your two treasures in there?'

'Ferrant's a right monkey, Mr Alleyn. Very uncooperative. He doesn't talk except to Jones and then it's only the odd curse. The doctor came in to see Jones before we left and gave him a reduced fix. The doctor's here.'

'Good.'

'He says Mr Harkness called him in to give him something to steady him up, but he reckons he'd already taken something on his own account.'

'Where is Dr Carey?'

'In the audience. He's just gone in. He said to tell you Mr Harkness is in a very unstable condition but not incapable.'

'Thank you. We'll get moving. Come on, Fox.'

They joined the little stream of people who walked round the stables and along the path to the Old Barn.

A man with a collection plate stood inside the door. Alleyn, fishing out his contribution, asked if he could by any chance have a word with Mr Harkness and was told that Brother Cuth was at prayer in the back room and could see nobody. 'Alleluia,' he added, apparently in acknowledgement of Alleyn's donation.

Alleyn and Fox found seats half-way down the barn. Extra chairs and boxes were being brought in, presumably from the house. The congregation appeared to be a cross-section of Cove and countryside in its Sunday clothes with a smattering of rather more stylish persons who might hail from Montjoy or even be tourists come out of curiosity. Alleyn recognized one or two faces he had seen at the Cod-and-Bottle. And there, stony in the fourth row with Louis beside her, sat Mrs Ferrant.

A little further forward from Alleyn and Fox were the Pharamonds, looking like a stand of orchids in a cabbage patch and behaving beautifully.

In the front three rows sat, or so Alleyn concluded, the hard-core brethren. They had an air of proprietorship and kept a smug eye on their books.

The curtains were closed to exclude the stage.

An audience, big or small, as actors know, generates its own flavour and exudes it like a pervasive scent. This one gave out the heady smell of suspense.

The tension increased when a thin lady with a white face seated herself at the harmonium and released strangely disturbing strains of unparalleled vulgarity.

'Shall we gather at the River?' invited the harmonium. 'The Beautiful, The Beautiful, The Ree-iv-a?'

Under cover of this prelude Plank and his support brought in their charges. Alleyn and Fox could see them reflected in a glazed and framed scroll that hung from a beam: 'The Chosen Brethren', it was headed, and it set out the professions of the sect.

Plank's party settled themselves on a bench against the back wall.

The harmonium achieved its ultimate *fortissimo* and the curtains opened jerkily to reveal six men seated behind a table on either side of a more important but empty chair. The congregation, prompted by the elect, rose.

In the commonplace light of early evening that filled the hall and in a total silence that followed a last deafening *roulade* on the organ, Mr Harkness entered from the inner room at the back of the platform.

One would have said that conditions were not propitious for dramatic climax: it had, however, been achieved.

He was dressed in a black suit and wore a black shirt and tie. He had shaved, and his hair, cut to regimental length, was brushed. His eyes were bloodshot, his complexion was blotched and his hands unsteady, but he seemed to be more in command of himself than he had been on the occasions when Alleyn had encountered him. It was a star entrance and if Mr Harkness had been an actor he would have been accorded a round of applause.

As it was he sat in the central chair. There he remained motionless throughout the ensuing hymn and prayers. These latter were extempore and of a highly emotional character, and were given out in turn by each of the six supporting brethren, later referred to by Plank as 'Cuth's side-kicks'.

With these preliminaries accomplished and all being seated, Cuthbert Harkness rose to deliver his address. For at least a minute and in complete silence he stood with head bent and eyes closed while his lips moved, presumably in silent prayer. The wait was hard to bear.

From the moment he began to speak he generated an almost intolerable tension. At first he was quiet but it would have come as a relief if he had spoken at the top of his voice.

He said: 'Brethren: This is the Day of Reckoning. We are sinners in the sight of the Great Master. Black as hell are our sins and only the Blood of Sacrifice can wash us clean. We have committed abominations. Our unrighteousness stinks in the nostrils of the All-Seeing Host. Uncleanliness, lechery and defilement stalk through our ranks. And Murder.'

It was as if a communal nerve had been touched, causing each member of his audience to stiffen. He himself actually 'came to attention' like a soldier. He squared his shoulders, lifted his chin, inflated his chest and directed his bloodshot gaze over the heads of his listeners. He might have been addressing a parade.

'Murder,' roared Mr Harkness. 'You have Murder here in your midst, brethren, here in the very temple of righteousness. And I shall reveal its Name unto you. I have nursed the awful knowledge like a viper in my bosom, I have wrestled with the Angel of Darkness. I have suffered the torments of the Damned but now the Voice of Eternal Judgement has spoken unto me and all shall be made known.'

He stopped dead and looked wildly round his audience. His gaze alighted on the row against the back wall and became fixed. He raised his right arm and pointed.

'Guilt!' he shouted. 'Guilt encompasseth us on every hand. The serpent is coiled in divers bosoms. I accuse! Sydney Jones – '

'You lay off me,' Syd screamed out, 'you shut up.'

Heads were turned. Sergeant Plank could be heard expostulating. Harkness, raising his voice, roared out a sequence of anathemas, but no specific accusation. The accusing finger shifted.

'Gilbert Ferrant! Woe unto you Gilbert Ferrant – '

By now half the audience had turned in their seats. Gilbert Ferrant, tallow-faced, stared at Harkness.

'Woe unto you, Gilbert Ferrant. Adulterer! Trader in forbidden fruits!'

It went on. Now only the inner brethren maintained an eyes-front demeanour. Consternation mounted in the rest of the congregation. Mr Harkness now pointed at Mrs Ferrant. He accused her of stony-heartedness and avarice. He moved on to Bob Maistre (wine-bibbing) and several fishermen unknown to Alleyn (blasphemy).

He paused. His roving and ensanguined gaze alighted on the Pharamonds. He pointed: 'And ye,' he apostrophized them, 'wallowers in the flesh-pots . . .'

He rambled on at the top of his voice. They were motionless throughout. At last he stopped, glared, and seemed to prepare himself for some final and stupendous effort. Into the silence desultory sounds intruded. It was as if somebody outside the barn had begun to pepper the iron roof with pellets, only a few at first but increasing. At last the clouds had broken and it had begun to rain.

One might be forgiven, Alleyn thought afterwards, for supposing that some celestial stage-management had taken charge, decided to give Mr Harkness the full treatment, and grossly overdone it. Mr Harkness himself seemed to be unaware of the mounting fusilade on the roof. As the din increased he broke out anew. He stepped up his parade-ground delivery. He shouted anathemas: on his niece and her sins, citing predictable Biblical comparisons, notably Jezebel and the whore of Babylon. He referred to Leviticus 20.6 and to the Cities of the Plains. He began to describe the circumstances of her death. He was now very difficult to hear, for the downpour on the iron roof was all-obliterating.

'And the Sinner . . .' could be made out '. . . Mark of Cain . . . before you all . . . now proclaim . . . Behold the man . . .'

He raised his right arm to the all-too-appropriate accompaniment of a stupendous thunder-clap and turned himself into a latter-day Lear. He beat his bosom and seemed at last to become aware of the storm.

An expression of bewilderment and frustration appeared. He stared wildly about him, gestured, clasped his hands and looked beseechingly round his audience.

Then he covered his face with his hands and bolted into the inner room. The door shut behind him with such violence that the framed legend above it crashed to the floor. Still the rain hammered on the iron roof.

Alleyn and Fox were on the stage with Plank hard at their heels. Nothing they said could be heard. Alleyn was at the door. It was locked. He and Fox stood back from it, collected themselves and shoulder-charged it. It resisted but Plank was there and joined in the next assault. It burst open and they plunged into the room.

Brother Cuth hung from a beam above the chair he had kicked away. His confession was pinned to his coat. He had used a length of wire from the coil in the old coach-house.

IV

Alleyn pushed the confession across the table to Fox. 'It's all there,' he said. 'He may have written it days ago or whenever he first made up his mind.

'He was determined to destroy the author, as he saw her, of his damnation, and then himself. The method only presented itself after their row about Dulcie jumping the gap. He seems to have found some sort of satisfaction, some sense of justice in the act of her dis-obedience being the cause of her death. He must have . . . made his final preparations during the time he was locked up in the back room before the service began. If we'd broken in the door on the first charge we might just have saved him. He wouldn't have thanked us for it.'

'I don't get it, sir,' Plank said. 'Him risking the sorrel mare. It seems all out of character.'

'He didn't think he was risking the mare. He'd ordered Jones to take her to the smith and he counted on Dulcie trying the jump with Mungo, the outlaw, the horse he wanted to destroy. In the verbal battle they exchanged, he told her the mare had gone to the smith and she said she'd do it on Mungo. It's there, in the confession. He's been very thorough.'

'When did he rig the wire in the gap?' Fox asked. He was read-ing the confession. 'Oh, yes. I see. As soon as Jones went to the corn-chandler's, believing that on his return he would remove the sorrel mare to the blacksmith's.'

'And unrigged it after the Ferrants left when Jones was sleeping it off in the loose-box.'

Fox said: 'And that girl lying in full view there in the ditch, looking the way she did! You can't wonder he went off the rails.' He read on.

Plank said: 'And yet, Mr Alleyn, by all accounts he used to be fond of her, too. She was his niece. He'd adopted her.'

'What's all this he's on about? Leviticus 20.6,' Fox asked.

'Look it up in the Bible they so thoughtfully provide in your room, Br'er Fox. I did. It says: "None of you shall approach to any that is near of kin to him to uncover their nakedness." '

Fox thought it over and was scandalized. 'I see,' he said. 'Yes, I see.'

'To him,' Alleyn said, 'she was the eternal temptress. The Scarlet Woman. The cause of his undoing. In a way, I suppose, he thought he was handing over the outcome to the Almighty. If she obeyed him and stayed in her room, nothing would happen. If she defied him, everything would. Either way the decision came from on high.'

'Not my idea of Christianity,' Plank muttered. 'The missus and I are C of E,' he added.

'You know,' Alleyn said to Fox, 'one might almost say Harkness was a sort of cross between Adam and the Ancient Mariner. "The woman tempted me", you know. And the subsequent revulsion followed by the awful necessity to talk about it, to make a proclamation before all the world and then to die.'

They said nothing for some time. At last Fox cleared his throat.

'What about the button?' he asked.

'In the absence of its owner, my guess would be that he went into the horse-paddock out of curiosity to inspect Bruno's jump and saw dead Dulcie – Dulcie who'd been threatening to shop her drug-running boyfriends; that, true to his practice of a strictly background figure of considerable importance, Louis decided to have seen nothing and removed himself from the terrain. Too bad he dropped a button.'

'Well,' Fox said, after a further pause, 'we haven't had what you'd call a resounding success. Missed out with our homicide by seconds, lost a big fish on the drug scene and ended up with a couple of tiddlers. *And* we've seen the young chap turn into a casualty on the way. How is he, Mr Alleyn?'

'We've finished for the time being. Come and see,' said Alleyn.

Ricky had been discharged from hospital and was receiving in his bedroom at the hotel. Julia, Jasper and Troy were all in attendance. The Pharamonds had brought grapes, books, champagne and some more *langouste* sandwiches because the others had been a success. They had been describing, from their point of view, Cuth's Party, as Julia only just continued not to call it.

'Darling,' she said to Ricky, 'your papa was quite wonderful.' And to Troy, 'No, but I promise. Superb.' She appealed to Fox. 'You'll bear me out, Mr Fox.' Rather to his relief she did not wait for Fox to do so. 'There we all were,' Julia continued at large. 'I can't tell you – the noise! And poor, poorest Cuth, trying with all his might to compete, rather, one couldn't help thinking, like Mr Noah in the deluge. I don't mean to be funny but it did come into one's head at the time. And really, you know, it was rather impressive. Especially when he pointed us out and said we were wallowers in the flesh-pots of Egypt, though why Egypt, one asks oneself. And then all those . . . "effects" don't they call them – and – and – '

Julia stopped short. 'Would you agree,' she said, appealing to Alleyn, 'that when something really awful happens it's terribly important not to work up a sort of phoney reaction? You know? Making out you're more upset than you really are. Would you say that?'

Alleyn said: 'In terms of self-respect I think I would.'

'Exactly,' said Julia. 'It's like using a special sort of pious voice about somebody that's dead when you don't really mind all that much.' She turned to Ricky and presented him with one of her most dazzling smiles. 'But then you see,' she said, 'thanks to your papa we only saw the storm scene, as I expect it would be called in Shakespeare. Because after they broke in the door a large man pulled the stage curtains across and then your papa came through, like men in dinner-jackets do in the theatre, and asked for a doctor and told us there's been an accident and would we leave quietly. So we did. Of course if we'd – ' Julia stopped. Her face had gone blank. 'If we'd seen,' she said rapidly, 'it would have been different.'

Ricky remembered what she had been like after she had seen Dulcie Harkness. And then he remembered Jasper saying: 'The full shock and horror of a death is only experienced when it has been seen.'

Julia and Jasper said they must go and Alleyn went down with them to their car. Jasper touched Alleyn's arm and they let Julia go ahead and get into the driver's seat.

'About Louis,' Jasper said. 'Is it to do with drugs?'

'We think it may be.'

'I've thought from time to time that something like that might be going on. But it all seemed unreal. We've never known anybody who was hooked.'

Alleyn echoed Julia. 'If you had,' he said, 'it would have been different.'

When he returned, it was to find Fox and Troy and Ricky quietly contented with each other's company.

Alleyn put his arm round Troy.

'Well, Br'er Fox,' he said, 'tomorrow is another day.'

Grave Mistake

For Gerald Lascelles

Contents

Cast of Characters

Verity Preston	*Of Keys House, Upper Quintern*
The Hon. Mrs Foster (Sybil)	*Of Quintern Place, Upper Quintern*
Claude Carter	*Her stepson*
Prunella Foster	*Her daughter*
Bruce Gardener	*Her gardener*
Mrs Black	*His sister*
The Rev. Mr Walter Cloudesley	*Vicar of St Crispin-in-Quintern*
Nikolas Markos	*Of Mardling Manor, Upper Quintern*
Gideon Markos	*His son*
Jim Jobbin	*Of Upper Quintern Village*
Mrs Jim	*His wife. Domestic helper*
Dr Field-Innis, MB	*Of Upper Quintern*
Mrs Field-Innis	*His wife*
Basil Schramm (neé Smythe)	*Medical incumbent, Greengages Hotel*
Sister Jackson	*His assistant*
G. M. Johnson	*Housemaids, Greengages Hotel*
Marleena Biggs	
The Manager	*Greengages Hotel*
Daft Artie	*Upper Quintern Village*
Young Mr Rattisbon	*Solicitor*
Chief Superintendent Roderick Alleyn	*CID*
Detective-Inspector Fox	*CID*
Detective-Sergeant Thompson	*CID Photographic Expert*
Sergeant Bailey	*CID Fingerprint Expert*
Sergeant McGuiness	*Upper Quintern Police Force*
PC Dance	*Upper Quintern Police Force*
A Coroner	
A Waiter	

CHAPTER 1

Upper Quintern

' "Bring me," ' sang the ladies of Upper Quintern, ' "my Bow of Burning Gold." '

' "Bring me," ' itemized the Hon. Mrs Foster, sailing up into a thready descant, ' "my Arrows of Desire." '

' "Bring me," ' stipulated the vicar's wife, adjusting her pince-nez and improvising into seconds, ' "my Chariot of Fire." '

Mrs Jim Jobbin sang with the rest. She had a high soprano and a sense of humour and it crossed her mind to wonder what Mrs Foster would do with Arrows of Desire or how nice Miss Preston of Keys House would manage a Spear, or how the vicar's wife would make out in a Chariot of Fire. Or for a matter of that how she herself, hard-working creature that she was, could ever be said to rest or stay her hand, much less build Jerusalem here in Upper Quintern or anywhere else in England's green and pleasant land.

Still, it was a good tune and the words were spirited if a little far-fetched.

Now they were reading the minutes of the last meeting and presently there would be a competition and a short talk from the vicar, who had visited Rome with an open mind.

Mrs Jim, as she was always called in the district, looked round the drawing-room with a practised eye. She herself had 'turned it out' that morning and Mrs Foster had done the flowers, picking white japonica with a more lavish hand than she would have dared to use had she known that McBride, her bad-tempered jobbing gardener, was on the watch.

Mrs Jim, pulling herself together as the chairwoman, using a special voice, said she knew they would all want to express their sympathy with Mrs Black in her recent sad loss. The ladies murmured and a little uncertain woman in a corner offered soundless acknowledgement.

Then followed the competition. You had to fill in the names of ladies present in answer to what were called cryptic clues. Mrs Jim was mildly amused but didn't score very highly. She guessed her own name, for which the clue was 'She doesn't work out'. 'Jobb-in'. Quite neat but inaccurate, she thought because her professional jobs were, after all, never 'in'. Twice a week she obliged Mrs Foster here at Quintern Place, where her niece, Beryl, was a regular. Twice a week she went to Mardling Manor to augment the indoor staff. And twice a week, including Saturdays, she helped Miss Preston at Keys House. From these activities she arrived home in time to get the children's tea and her voracious husband's supper. And when Miss Preston gave one of her rare parties, Mrs Jobbin helped out in the kitchen, partly because she could do with the extra money but mostly because she liked Miss Preston.

Mrs Foster she regarded as being a bit daft; always thinking she was ill and turning on the gushing act to show how nice she could be to the village.

Now the vicar, having taken a nervy look at the Vatican City, was well on his way to the Forum. Mrs Jobbin made a good-natured effort to keep him company.

Verity Preston stretched out her long corduroy legs, looked at her boots and wondered why she was there. She was fifty years old but carried about her an air of youth. This was not achieved by manipulation; rather it was as if, inside her middle-aged body, her spirit had neglected to grow old. Until five years ago she had worked in the theatre, on the production side. Then her father, an eminent heart-specialist, had died and left Keys House to her with just enough money to enable her to live in it and write plays, which she did from time to time with tolerable success.

She had been born at Keys, she supposed she would die there, and she had gradually fallen into a semi-detached acceptance of the rhythms of life at Upper Quintern which, in spite of war, bombs, crises and inflations, had not changed all that much since her childhood.

The great difference was that, with the exception of Mr Nikolas Markos, a newcomer to the district, the gentry had very much less money nowadays and, again with the exception of Mr Markos, no resident domestic help. Just Mrs Jim, her niece Beryl, and some dozen lesser ladies who were precariously available and all in hot demand. Mrs Foster was cunning in securing their services and was thought to cheat by using bribery. She was known, privately, as the Pirate.

It was recognized on all hands that Mrs Jim was utterly impervious to bribery. Mrs Foster had tried it once and had invoked a reaction that made her go red in the face whenever she thought of it. It was only by pleading the onset of a genuine attack of lumbago that she had induced Mrs Jim to return.

Mrs Foster was a dedicated hypochondriac and nobody would have believed in the lumbago if McBride, the Upper Quintern jobbing gardener, had not confided that he had come across her on the gravelled drive, wearing her best tweeds, hat and gloves and crawling on all fours towards the house. She had been incontinently smitten on her way to the garage.

The vicar saw himself off at the Leonardo da Vinci airport, said his visit had given him much food for thought and ended on a note of ecumenical wistfulness.

Tea was announced and a mass move to the dining-room accomplished.

'Hullo, Syb,' said Verity Preston. 'Can I help?'

'Darling!' cried Mrs Foster. *'Would* you? Would you pour? I simply can't cope. *Such* arthritis! In the wrists.'

'Sickening for you.'

'Honestly. *Too* much. Not a wink all night and this party hanging over one, and Prue's off somewhere watching hang-gliding' (Prunella was Mrs Foster's daughter), 'so she's no use. And to put the final pot on it, ghastly McBride's given notice. Imagine!'

'*McBride* has? Why?'

'He *says* he feels ill. If you ask me it's bloody-mindedness.'

'Did you have words?' Verity suggested, rapidly filling up cups for ladies to carry off on trays.

'Sort of. Over my picking the japonica. This morning.'

'Is he still here? Now?'

'Don't ask me. Probably flounced off. Except that he hasn't been paid. I wouldn't put it past him to be sulking in the tool shed.'

'I must say I hope he won't extend his embargo to take me in.'

'Oh, dear me no!' said Mrs Foster, with a hint of acidity. 'You're his adored Miss Preston. You, my dear, can't do wrong in McBride's bleary eyes.'

'I wish I could believe you. Where will you go for honey, Syb? Advertise or what? Or eat humble pie?'

'Never that! Not on your life! Mrs *Black!*' cried Mrs Foster in a voice of mellifluous cordiality. '*How* good of you to come. *Where* are you sitting? Over there, are you? *Good.* Who's died?' she muttered as Mrs Black moved away. 'Why were we told to sympathize?'

'Her husband.'

'That's all right then. I wasn't overdoing it.'

'Her brother's arrived to live with her.'

'He wouldn't happen to be a gardener, I suppose.'

Verity put down the teapot and stared at her. 'You won't believe this,' she said, 'but I rather think I heard someone say he is. Mrs Jim, it was. Yes, I'm sure. A gardener.'

'My dear! I wonder if he's any good. My dear, *what* a smack in the eye that would be for McBride. Would it be all right to tackle Mrs Black now, do you think? Just to find out?'

'Well – '

'Darling, you know me. I'll be the soul of tact.'

'I bet you will,' said Verity.

She watched Mrs Foster insinuate herself plumply through the crowd. The din was too great for anything she said to be audible, but Verity could guess at the compliments sprinkled upon the vicar, who was a good-looking man, the playful badinage with the village. And all the time, while her pampered little hands dangled from her wrists, Mrs Foster's pink coiffure tacked this way and that, making towards Mrs Black, who sat in her bereavement upon a chair at the far end of the room.

Verity, greatly entertained, watched the encounter, the gradual response, the ineffable concern, the wide-open china-blue stare, the compassionate shakes of the head and, finally, the withdrawal of both ladies from the dining-room, no doubt into Syb's boudoir. Now, thought Verity, she'll put in the hard tackle.

Abruptly, she was aware of herself being under observation.

Mrs Jim Jobbin was looking at her and with such a lively expression on her face that Verity felt inclined to wink. It struck her that of all the company present – county, gentry, trade and village, operating within their age-old class structure – it was for Mrs Jim that she felt the most genuine respect.

Verity poured herself a cup of tea and began, because it was expected of her, to circulate. She was a shy woman but her work in the theatre had helped her to deal with this disadvantage. Moreover, she took a vivid interest in her fellow creatures.

'Miss Preston,' Mr Nikolas Markos had said, the only time they had met, 'I believe you look upon us all as raw material,' and his black eyes had snapped at her. Although this remark was a variant of the idiotic 'don't put me in it', it had not induced the usual irritation. Verity, in fact, had been wondering at that very moment if she could build a black comedy round Upper Quintern ingredients.

She reached the french windows that opened on lawns, walks, rose-gardens and an enchanting view across the Weald of Kent.

A little removed from the nearest group, she sipped her tea and gazed with satisfaction at this prospect. She thought that the English landscape, more perhaps than any other, is dyed in the heraldic colours of its own history. It is *there*, she thought, and until it disintegrates, earth, rock, trees, grass, turf by turf, leaf by leaf and blade by blade, it will remain imperturbably itself. To it, she thought, the reed really *is* as the oak and she found the notion reassuring.

She redirected her gaze from the distant prospect to the foreground and became aware of a human rump, elevated above a box hedge in the rose-garden.

The trousers were unmistakable: pepper-and-salt, shape less, earthy and bestowed upon Angus McBride or purchased by him at some long-forgotten jumble sale. He must be doubled up over a treasured seedling, thought Verity. Perhaps he had forgiven Sybil Foster or perhaps, with his lowland Scots rectitude, he was working out his time.

'Lovely view, isn't it?' said the vicar. He had come alongside Verity, unobserved.

'Isn't it? Although at the moment I was looking at the person behind the box hedge.'

'McBride,' said the vicar.

'I thought so, by the trousers.'

'I know so. They were once my own.'

'Does it,' Verity asked, after a longish pause, 'strike you that he is sustaining an exacting pose for a very long time?'

'Now you mention it.'

'He hasn't stirred.'

'Rapt, perhaps over the wonders of nature,' joked the vicar.

'Perhaps. But he must be doubled over at the waist like a two-foot rule.'

'One would say so, certainly.'

'He gave Sybil notice this morning on account of health.'

'Could he be feeling faint, poor fellow,' hazarded the vicar, 'and putting his head between his knees?' And after a moment, 'I think I'll go and see.'

'I'll come with you,' said Verity. 'I wanted to look at the rose-garden in any case.'

They went out by the french window and crossed the lawn. The sun had come out and a charming little breeze touched their faces.

As they neared the box hedge the vicar, who was over six feet tall, said in a strange voice, 'It's very odd.'

'What is?' Verity asked. Her heart, unaccountably, had begun to knock at her ribs.

'His head's in the wheelbarrow. I fear,' said the vicar, 'he's fainted.'

But McBride had gone further than that. He was dead.

II

He had died, the doctor said, of a heart attack and his condition was such that it might have happened any time over the last year or so. He was thought to have raised the handles of the barrow, been smitten and tipped forward, head first, into the load of compost with which it was filled.

Verity Preston was really sorry. McBride was often maddening and sometimes rude but they shared a love of old-fashioned roses and respected each other. When she had influenza he brought her primroses in a jampot and climbed a ladder to put them on her window-sill. She was touched.

An immediate result of his death was a rush for the services of Mrs Black's newly arrived brother. Sybil Foster got in first, having already paved the way with his sister. On the very morning after McBride's death, with what Verity Preston considered indecent haste, she paid a follow-up visit to Mrs Black's cottage under cover of a visit of condolence. Ridiculously inept, Verity considered, as Mr Black had been dead for at least three weeks and there had been all those fulsomely redundant expressions of sympathy only the previous afternoon. She'd even had the nerve to take white japonica.

When she got home she telephoned Verity.

'My dear,' she raved, 'he's *perfect.* So sweet with that dreary little sister and *such* good manners with me. Called one Madam which is more than – well, never mind. He knew at once what would suit and said he could sense I had an understanding of the "bonny wee flooers". He's Scotch.'

'Clearly,' said Verity.

'But quite a different *kind* of Scotch from McBride. Highland I should think. Anyway – very superior.'

'What's he charge?'

'A little bit more,' said Sybil rapidly, 'but, my dear, the *difference?'*

'References?'

'Any number. They're in his luggage and haven't arrived yet. *Very* grand, I gather.'

'So you've taken him on?'

'Darling! What do you think? Mondays and Thursdays. All day. He'll tell me if it needs more. It well may. After all, it's been shamefully neglected – I know you won't agree, of course.'

'I suppose I'd better do something about him.'

'You'd better hurry. Everybody will be grabbing. I hear Mr Markos is a man short up at Mardling. Not that I think my Gardener would take an under-gardener's job.'

'What's he called?'

'Who?'

'Your gardener.'

'You've just said it. Gardener.'

'You're joking.'

Sybil made an exasperated noise into the receiver.

'So he's gardener-Gardener,' said Verity. 'Does he hyphenate it?'

'Very funny.'

'Oh, come *on*, Syb!'

'All right, my dear, you may scoff. Wait till you see him.'

Verity saw him three evenings later. Mrs Black's cottage was a short distance along the lane from Keys House and she walked to it at 6.30, by which time Mrs Black had given her brother his tea. She was a mimbling little woman, meekly supporting the prestige of recent widowhood. Perhaps with the object of entrenching herself in this state, she spoke in a whimper.

Verity could hear television blaring in the back parlour and said she was sorry to interrupt. Mrs Black, alluding to her brother as Mr Gardener, said without conviction that she supposed it didn't matter and she'd tell him he was wanted.

She left the room. Verity stood at the window and saw that the flower-beds had been recently dug over and wondered if it was Mr Gardener's doing.

He came in. A huge sandy man with a trim golden beard, wide mouth and blue eyes, set far apart and slightly, not unattractively, strabismic. Altogether a personable figure. He contemplated Verity quizzically from aloft, his head thrown back and slightly to one side and his eyes half-closed.

'I didna just catch the name,' he said, 'ma-am.'

Verity told him her name and he said, ou aye, and would she no' tak' a seat.

She said she wouldn't keep him a moment and asked if he could give her one day's gardening a week.

'That'll be the residence a wee piece up the lane, I'm thinking. It's a bonny garden you have there, ma-am. What I call perrrsonality. Would it be all of an acre that you have there, now, and an orchard, forby?'

'Yes. But most of it's grass and that's looked after by a contractor,' explained Verity, and felt angrily that she was adopting an apologetic, almost a cringing attitude.

'Ou aye,' said Mr Gardener again. He beamed down upon her. 'And I can see fine that it's highly prized by its leddy-mistress.'

Verity mumbled self-consciously.

They got down to brass tacks. Gardener's baggage had arrived. He produced glowing references from, as Sybil had said, grand employers, and photographs of their quellingly superior grounds. He was accustomed, he said, to having at the verra least a young laddie working under him but realized that in coming to keep his sister company in her ber-r-rievement, pure lassie, he would be obliged to dra' in his horns a wee. Ou, aye.

They arrived at wages. No wonder, thought Verity, that Sybil had hurried over the topic: Mr Gardener required almost twice the pay of Angus McBride. Verity told herself she ought to say she would let him know in the morning and was just about to do so when he mentioned that Friday was the only day he had left and in a panic she suddenly closed with him.

He said he would be glad to work for her. He said he sensed they would get along fine. The general impression was that he preferred to work at a derisive wage for somebody he fancied rather than for a pride of uncongenial millionaires and/or noblemen, however open-handed.

On that note they parted.

Verity walked up the lane through the scents and sounds of a spring evening. She told herself that she could afford Gardener, that clearly he was a highly experienced man and that she would have kicked herself all round her lovely garden if she'd funked employing him and fallen back on the grossly incompetent services of the only other jobbing gardener now available in the district.

But when she had gone in at the gate and walked between burgeoning lime trees up to her house, Verity, being an honest-minded creature, admitted to herself that she had taken a scunner on Mr Gardener.

As soon as she opened her front door she heard the telephone ringing. It was Sybil, avid to know if Verity had secured his services. When she learnt that the deed had been done she adopted an irritatingly complacent air as if she herself had scored some kind of triumph.

Verity often wondered how it had come about that she and Sybil seemed to be such close friends. They had known each other all their lives, of course, and when they were small had shared the same governess. But later on, when Verity was in London and Sybil,

already a young widow, had married her well-heeled, short-lived
stockbroker, they seldom met. It was after Sybil was again widowed,
being left with Prunella and a highly unsatisfactory stepson from her
first marriage, that they picked up the threads of their friendship.
Really they had little in common.

Their friendship in fact was a sort of hardy perennial, reappearing
when it was least expected to do so.

The horticultural analogy occurred to Verity while Sybil gushed
away about Gardener. He had started with her that very day, it transpired, and, my dear, the *difference!* And the *imagination!* And the
work, the sheer *hard* work. She raved on. She really is a bit of an ass,
is poor old Syb, Verity thought.

'And don't you find his Scots *rather* beguiling?' Sybil was asking.

'Why doesn't his sister do it?'

'Do what, dear?'

'Talk Scots?'

'Good Heavens, Verity, how should I know? Because she came
south and married a man of Kent, I dare say. Black spoke broad
Kentish.'

'So he did,' agreed Verity pacifically.

'I've got news for you.'

'Have you?'

'You'll never guess. An invitation. From *Mardling Manor,* no less,'
said Sybil in a put-on drawing-room-comedy voice.

'Really?'

'For dinner. Next Wednesday. He rang up this morning. Rather
unconventional if one's to stickle, I suppose, but that sort of tommy-
rot's as dead as the dodo in my book. And we *have* met. When he
lent Mardling for that hospital fund-raising garden-party. Nobody
went inside, of course. I'm told lashings of lolly have been poured
out – redecorated, darling, from attic to cellar. You were there,
weren't you? At the garden-party?'

'Yes.'

'Yes. I was sure you were. Rather intriguing, I thought, didn't
you?'

'I hardly spoke to him,' said Verity inaccurately.

'I hoped you'd been asked,' said Sybil much more inaccurately.

'Not I. I expect you'll have gorgeous grub.'

'I don't know that it's a *party*.'

'Just you?'

'My dear. Surely not! But no. Prue's come home. She's met the son somewhere and so she's been asked – to balance him, I suppose. Well,' said Sybil on a dashing note, 'we shall see what we shall see.'

'Have a lovely time. How's the arthritis?'

'Oh, *you* know. Pretty ghastly, but I'm learning to live with it. Nothing else to be done, is there? If it's not that it's my migraine.'

'I thought Dr Field-Innis had given you something for the migraine.'

'Hopeless, my dear. If you ask me Field-Innis is getting beyond it. *And* he's become very offhand, I don't mind telling you.'

Verity half-listened to the so-familiar plaints. Over the years Sybil had consulted a procession of general practitioners and in each instance enthusiasm had dwindled into discontent. It was only because there were none handy, Verity sometimes thought, that Syb had escaped falling into the hands of some plausible quack.

' – and I had considered,' she was saying, 'taking myself off to Greengages for a fortnight. It does quite buck me up, that place.'

'Yes, why don't you?'

'I think I'd like to just be *here*, though, while Mr Gardener gets the place into shape.'

'One calls him "Mr Gardener", then?'

'Verity, he *is* very superior. Anyway I hate those old snobby distinctions. You don't, evidently.'

'I'll call him the Duke of Plaza-Toro if he'll get rid of my weeds.'

'I really must go,' Sybil suddenly decided, as if Verity had been preventing her from doing so. 'I can't make up my mind about Greengages.'

Greengages was an astronomically expensive establishment; a hotel with a resident doctor and a sort of valetudinarian sideline where weight was reduced by the exaction of a deadly diet while appetites were stimulated by compulsory walks over a rather dreary countryside. If Sybil decided to go there, Verity would be expected to drive through twenty miles of dense traffic to take a luncheon of inflationary soup and a concoction of liver and tomatoes garnished with mushrooms to which she was uproariously allergic.

She had no sooner hung up her receiver when the telephone rang again.

'Damn,' said Verity, who hankered after her cold duck and salad and the telly.

A vibrant male voice asked if she were herself and on learning that she was, said it was Nikolas Markos speaking.

'Is this a bad time to ring you up?' Mr Markos asked. 'Are you telly-watching or thinking about your dinner, for instance?'

'Not quite yet.'

'But almost, I suspect. I'll be quick. Would you like to dine here next Wednesday? I've been trying to get you all day. Say you will, like a kind creature. Will you?'

He spoke as if they were old friends and Verity, accustomed to this sort of approach in the theatre, responded.

'Yes,' she said. 'I will. I'd like to. Thank you. What time?'

III

Nobody in Upper Quintern knew much about Nikolas Markos. He was reputed to be fabulously rich, widowed and a financier. Oil was mentioned as the almost inescapable background. When Mardling Manor came on the market Mr Markos had bought it, and when Verity went to dine with him, had been in residence, off and on, for about four months.

Mardling was an ugly house. It had been built in mid-Victorian times on the site of a Jacobean mansion. It was large, pepper-potted and highly inconvenient; not a patch on Sybil Foster's Quintern Place, which was exquisite. The best that could be said of Mardling was that, however hideous, it looked clumsily important both inside and out.

As Verity drove up she saw Sybil's Mercedes parked alongside a number of other cars. The front door opened before she got to it and revealed that obsolete phenomenon, a manservant.

While she was being relieved of her coat she saw that even the ugliest of halls can be made beautiful by beautiful possessions. Mr Markos had covered the greater part of the stupidly carved walls with smoky tapestries. These melted upwards into an almost invisible gallery and relinquished the dominant position above an enormous fireplace to a picture. Such a picture! An imperious quattrocento man, life-size, ablaze in a scarlet cloak on a round-rumped charger. The rider pointed his sword at an immaculate little Tuscan town.

Verity was so struck with the picture that she was scarcely conscious that behind her a door had opened and closed.

'Ah!' said Nikolas Markos, 'you like my arrogant equestrian? Or are you merely surprised by him?'

'Both,' said Verity.

His handshake was quick and perfunctory. He wore a green velvet coat. His hair was dark, short and curly at the back. His complexion was sallow and his eyes black. His mouth, under a slight moustache, seemed to contradict the almost too plushy ensemble. It was slim-lipped, and, Verity thought, extremely firm.

'Is it a Uccello?' she asked, turning back to the picture.

'I like to think so, but it's a borderline case. "School of" is all the pundits will allow me.'

'It's extraordinarily exciting.'

'Isn't it, just? I'm glad you like it. And delighted, by the way, that you've come.'

Verity was overtaken by one of her moments of middle-aged shyness. 'Oh. Good,' she mumbled.

'We're nine for dinner: my son, Gideon, a Dr Basil Schramm who's yet to arrive, and you know all the rest, Mrs Foster and her daughter, the vicar (*she's* indisposed) and Dr and Mrs Field-Innis. Come and join them.'

Verity's recollection of the drawing-room at Mardling was of a great ungainly apartment, over-furnished and nearly always chilly. She found herself in a bird's-egg blue and white room, sparkling with firelight and a welcoming elegance.

There, expansively on a sofa, was Sybil at her most feminine, and that was saying a great deal. Hair, face, pampered little hands, jewels, dress and, if you got close enough, scent – they all came together like the ingredients of some exotic pudding. She fluttered a minute handkerchief at Verity and pulled an arch grimace.

'This is Gideon,' said Mr Markos.

He was even darker than his father and startlingly handsome. 'My dear, an Adonis,' Sybil was to say of him, and later was to add that there was 'something' wrong and that she was never deceived, she sensed it at once, let Verity mark her words. When asked to explain herself she said it didn't matter but she always *knew*. Verity thought that she knew, too. Sybil was hell-bent on her daughter Prunella encouraging the advances of a hereditary peer with the unlikely name of Swingletree and took an instant dislike to any attractive young man who hove into view.

Gideon looked about twenty, was poised and had nice manners. His black hair was not very long and was well kept. Like his father, he wore a velvet coat. The only note of extravagance was in the frilled shirt and flowing tie. These lent a final touch to what might have been an unendurably romantic appearance, but Gideon had enough natural manner to get away with them.

He had been talking to Prunella Foster, who was like her mother at the same age; ravishingly pretty and a great talker. Verity never knew what Prunella talked about as she always spoke in a whisper. She nodded a lot and gave mysterious little smiles and, because it was the fashion of the moment, seemed to be dressed in expensive rags partly composed of a patchwork quilt. Under this supposedly evening attire she wore a little pair of bucket boots.

Dr Field-Innis was an old Upper Quintern hand. The younger son of a brigadier, he had taken to medicine instead of arms and had married a lady who sometimes won point-to-points and more often fell off.

The vicar we have already met. He was called Walter Cloudesley, and ministered, a little sadly, to twenty parishioners in a very beautiful old church that had once housed three hundred.

Altogether, Verity thought, this was a predictable Upper Quintern dinner-party with an unpredictable host in a highly exceptional setting.

They drank champagne cocktails.

Sybil, sparkling, told Mr Markos how clever he was and went into an ecstasy over the house. She had a talent that never failed to tickle Verity's fancy, for making the most unexceptionable remark to a gentleman sound as if it carried some frisky innuendo. She sketched an invitation for him to join her on the sofa but he seemed not to notice. He stood over her and replied in kind. Later on, Verity thought, she will tell me he's a man of the world.

He moved to his hearthrug and surveyed his guests with an air of satisfaction. 'This is great fun,' he said. 'My first Quintern venture. Really, it's a kind of christening party for the house, isn't it? What a good thing you could come, Vicar.'

'I certainly give it my blessing,' the vicar hardly countered. He was enjoying a second champagne cocktail.

'And, by the way, the party won't be undiluted Quintern. There's somebody still to come. I do hope he's not going to be late. He's a man I ran across in New York, a Basil Schramm. I found him – ' Mr Markos paused and an odd little smile touched his mouth – 'quite interesting. He rang up out of a clear sky this morning, saying he was going to take up a practice somewhere in our part of the world and was driving there this evening. We discovered that his route would bring him through Upper Quintern and on the spur of the moment I asked him to dine. He'll unbalance the table a bit but I hope nobody's going to blench at that.'

'An American?' asked Mrs Field-Innis. She had a hoarse voice.

'He's Swiss by birth, I fancy.'

'Is he taking a locum,' asked Dr Field-Innis, 'or a permanent practice?'

'The latter, I supposed. At some hotel or nursing home or convalescent place or something of the sort. Green – something.'

'*Not* "gages",' cried Sybil, softly clapping her hands.

'I knew it made me think of indigestion. Greengages it is,' said Mr Markos.

'Oh,' said Dr Field-Innis. 'That place.'

Much was made of this coincidence, if it could be so called. The conversation drifted to gardeners. Sybil excitedly introduced her find. Mr Markos became *grand signorial* and when Gideon asked if they hadn't taken on a new man, said they had but he didn't know what he was called. Verity, who, a-political at heart, drifted guiltily from left to right and back again, felt her redder hackles rising. She found that Mr Markos was looking at her in a manner that gave her the sense of having been rumbled.

Presently he drew a chair up to hers.

'I very much enjoyed your play,' he said. 'Your best, up to date, I thought.'

'Did you? Good.'

'It's very clever of you to be civilized as well as penetrating. I want to ask you, though – '

He talked intelligently about her play. It suddenly dawned on Verity that there was nobody in Upper Quintern with whom she ever discussed her work and she felt as if she spoke the right lines in the wrong theatre. She heard herself eagerly discussing her play and fetched up abruptly.

'I'm talking shop,' she said. 'Sorry.'

'Why? What's wrong with shop? Particularly when your shop's one of the arts.'

'Is yours?'

'Oh,' he said, 'mine's as dull as ditchwater.' He looked at his watch. 'Schramm *is* late,' he said. 'Lost in the Weald of Kent, I dare say. We shall not wait for him. Tell me – '

He started off again. The butler came in. Verity expected him to announce dinner but he said, 'Dr Schramm, sir.'

When Dr Schramm walked into the room it seemed to shift a little. Her mouth dried. She waited through an unreckoned interval for Nikolas Markos to arrive at her as he performed the introductions.

'But we have already met,' said Dr Schramm. 'Some time ago.'

IV

Twenty-five years to be exact, Verity thought. It was ludicrous – grotesque almost – after twenty-five years, to be put out by his reappearance.

'Somebody should say "What a small world",' said Dr Schramm.

He had always made remarks like that. And laughed like that and touched his moustache.

He didn't know me at first, she thought. That'll learn me.

He had moved on towards the fire with Mr Markos and been given, in quick succession, two cocktails. Verity heard him explain how he'd missed the turn-off to Upper Quintern.

But why 'Schramm'? she wondered. He could have hyphenated himself if 'Smythe' wasn't good enough. And 'Doctor'? So he qualified after all.

'Very difficult country,' Mrs Field-Innis said. She had been speaking for some time.

'Very,' Verity agreed fervently and was stared at.

Dinner was announced.

She was afraid they might find themselves together at the table but after, or so she fancied, a moment's hesitation, Mr Markos put Schramm between Sybil and Dr Field-Innis who was on Verity's right, with the vicar on her left. Mr Markos himself was on Sybil's right. It was a round table.

She managed quite well at dinner. The vicar was at all times prolific in discourse and, being of necessity as well as by choice, of an abstemious habit, he was a little flown with unaccustomed wine. Dr Field-Innis was also in talkative form. He coruscated with anecdotes concerning high jinks in his student days.

On his far side, Dr Schramm, whose glass had been twice replenished, was much engaged with Sybil Foster, which meant that he was turned away from Dr Field-Innis and Verity. He bent towards Sybil, laughed a great deal at everything she said and established an atmosphere of flirtatious understanding. This stabbed Verity with the remembrance of long-healed injuries. It had been his technique when he wished to show her how much another woman pleased him. He had used it at the theatre in the second row of the stalls, prolonging his laughter beyond the rest of the audience so that she, as well as the actress concerned, might become aware of him. She realized that even now, idiotically after twenty-five years, he aimed his performance at her.

Sybil, she knew, although she had not looked at them, was bringing out her armoury of delighted giggles and upward glances.

'And then,' said the vicar, who had returned to Rome, 'there was the Villa Giulia. I can't describe to you – '

In turning to him, Verity found herself under observation from her host. Perhaps because the vicar had now arrived at the Etruscans, it occurred to Verity that there was something knowing about Mr Markos's smile. You wouldn't diddle that one in a hurry, she thought.

Evidently he had asked Mrs Field-Innis to act as hostess.

When the port had gone round once she surveyed the ladies and barked out orders to retire.

Back in the drawing-room it became evident that Dr Schramm had made an impression. Sybil lost no time in tackling Verity. Why, she asked, had she never been told about him? Had Verity known him well? Was he married?

'I've no idea. It was a thousand years ago,' Verity said. 'He was one of my father's students, I think. I ran up against him at some training-hospital party as far as I can remember.'

Remember? He had watched her for half the evening and then, when an 'Excuse me' dance came along, had relieved her of an unwieldy first-year student and monopolized her for the rest of the evening.

She turned to the young Prunella, whose godmother she was, and asked what she was up to these days, and made what she could of a reply that for all she heard of it might have been in mime.

'Did you catch any of that?' asked Prunella's mother wearily.

Prunella giggled.

'I think I may be getting deaf,' Verity said.

Prunella shook her head vigorously and became audible. 'Not you, Godmama V,' she said. 'Tell us about your super friend. What a dish!'

'*Prue*,' expostulated Sybil, punctual as clockwork.

'Well, Mum, he is,' said her daughter, relapsing into her whisper. 'And you can't talk, darling,' she added. 'You gobbled him up like a turkey.'

Mrs Field-Innis said, 'Really!' and spoilt the effect by bursting into a gruff laugh.

To Verity's relief this passage had the effect of putting a stop to further enquiries about Dr Schramm. The ladies discussed local topics until they were joined by the gentlemen.

Verity had wondered whether anybody – their host or the vicar or Dr Field-Innis – had questioned Schramm as she had been questioned about their former acquaintanceship, and if so, how he had answered and whether he would think it advisable to come and speak to her. After all, it would look strange if he did not.

He did come. Nikolas Markos, keeping up the deployment of his guests, so arranged it. Schramm sat beside her and the first thought that crossed her mind was that there was something unbecoming about not seeming, at first glance, to have grown old. If he had appeared to her, as she undoubtedly did to him, as a greatly changed person, she would have been able to get their confrontation into perspective. As it was he sat there like a hangover. His face at first glance was scarcely changed, although when he turned it into a stronger light, a system of lines seemed to flicker under the skin. His eyes were more protuberant, now, and slightly bloodshot. A man, she thought, of whom people would say he could hold his liquor. He used the stuff she remembered, on hair that was only vestigially thinner at the temples.

As always he was, as people used to say twenty-five years ago, extremely well turned out. He carried himself like a soldier.

'How are you, Verity?' he said. 'You look blooming.'

'I'm very well, thank you.'

'Writing plays, I hear.'

'That's it.'

'Absolutely splendid. I must go and see one. There is one, isn't there? In London?'

'At the Dolphin.'

'Good houses?'

'Full,' said Verity.

'Really! So they wouldn't let me in. Unless you told them to. Would you tell them to? Please?'

He bent his head towards her in the old way. Why on earth, she thought, does he bother?

'I'm afraid they wouldn't pay much attention,' she said.

'Were you surprised to see me?'

'I was, rather.'

'Why?'

'Well – '

'Well?'

'The name for one thing.'

'Oh, that!' he said, waving his hand. 'That's an old story. It's my mother's maiden name. Swiss. She always wanted me to use it. Put it in her Will, if you'll believe it. She suggested that I made myself "Smythe-Schramm" but that turned out to be such a wet mouthful I decided to get rid of Smythe.'

'I see.'

'So I qualified after all, Verity.'

'Yes.'

'From Lausanne, actually. My mother had settled there and I joined her. I got quite involved with that side of the family and decided to finish my course in Switzerland.'

'I see.'

'I practised there for some time – until she died to be exact. Since then I've wandered about the world. One can always find something to do as a medico.' He talked away, fluently. It seemed to Verity that he spoke in phrases that followed each other with the ease of frequent usage. He went on for some time, making, she thought, little sorties against her self-possession. She was surprised to find how ineffectual they proved to be. Come, she thought, I'm over the initial hurdle at least, and began to wonder what all the fuss was about.

'And now you're settling in Kent,' she said politely.

'Looks like it. A sort of hotel-cum-convalescent home. I've made rather a thing of dietetics – specialized actually – and this place offers the right sort of scene. Greengages, it's called. Do you know it at all?'

'Sybil – Mrs Foster – goes there quite often.'

'Yes,' he said. 'So she tells me.'

He looked at Sybil who sat, discontentedly, beside the vicar. Verity had realized that Sybil was observant of them. She now flashed a meaning smile at Schramm as if she and he shared some exquisite joke.

Gideon Markos said, 'Pop, may I show Prue your latest extravagance?'

'Do,' said his father. 'By all means.'

When they had gone he said, 'Schramm, I can't have you monopolizing Miss Preston like this. You've had a lovely session and must restrain your remembrance of things past. I'm going to move you on.'

He moved him on to Mrs Field-Innis and took his place by Verity.

'Gideon tells me,' he said, 'that when I have company to dine I'm bossy, old hat and a stuffed shirt or whatever the "in" phrase is. But what should I do? Invite my guests to wriggle and jerk to one of his deafening records?'

'It might be fun to see the vicar and Florence Field-Innis having a go.'

'Yes,' he said, with a sidelong glance at her, 'it might indeed. Would you like to hear about my "latest extravagance"? You would? It's a picture. A Troy.'

'From her show at the Arlington?'

'That's right.'

'How lovely for you. Which one? Not by any chance "Several Pleasures"?'

'But you're brilliant!'

'It *is*?'

'Come and look.'

He took her into the library where there was no sign of the young people: a large library it was, and still under renovation. Open cases of books stood about the floors. The walls, including the backs of shelves, had been redone in a lacquer-red Chinese paper. The Troy painting stood on the chimney-piece – a glowing flourish of exuberance, all swings and roundabouts.

'You *do* collect lovely pictures,' she said.

'Oh, I'm a dedicated magpie. I even collect stamps.'

'Seriously?'

'Passionately,' he said. He half-closed his eyes and contemplated his picture.

Verity said, 'You're going to hang it where it is, are you?'

'I think so. But whatever I do with it in this silly house is bound to be a compromise,' he said.

'Does that matter very much?'

'Yes, it does. I lust,' said Mr Markos, 'after Quintern Place.'

He said this with such passion that Verity stared at him.

'Do you?' she said. 'It's a lovely house, of course. But just seeing it from the outside – '

'Ah, but I've seen it from inside too.'

Verity thought what a slyboots old Syb was not to have divulged this visit but he went on to say that on a househunting drive through Kent he saw Quintern Place from afar and had been so struck that he had himself driven up to it there and then.

'Mrs Foster,' he said, 'was away but a domestic was persuaded to let me catch a glimpse of the ground floor. It was enough. I visited the nearest land agency only to be told that Quintern was not on their or anybody else's books and that former enquiries had led to the flattest of refusals. Mine suffered a like fate; there was no intention to sell. So, you may say that in a fit of pique, I bought this monster where I can sit down before my citadel in a state of fruitless siege.'

'Does Sybil know about all this?'

'Not she. The approach has been discreet. Be a dear,' said Mr Markos, 'and don't tell her.'

'All right.'

'How nice you are.'

'But I'm afraid you haven't a hope.'

'One can but try,' he said and Verity thought if ever she saw fixity of purpose in a human face, she saw it now, in Mr Markos's.

V

As she drove home, Verity tried to sort out the events of the evening but had not got far with them when, at the bottom of the drive, her headlamps picked up a familiar trudging figure. She pulled up alongside.

'Hullo, Mrs Jim,' she said. 'Nip in and I'll take you home.'

'It's out of your way, Miss Preston.'

'Doesn't matter. Come on.'

'Very kind, I'm sure. I won't say no,' said Mrs Jim.

She got in neatly and quickly but settled in her seat with a kind of relinquishment of her body that suggested fatigue.

Verity asked her if she'd had a long day and she said she had, a bit.

'But the money's good,' said Mrs Jim, 'and with Jim on half-time you can't say no. There's always something,' she added and Verity understood that she referred to the cost of living.

'Do they keep a big staff up there?' she asked.

'Five if you count the housekeeper. Like the old days,' Mrs Jim said, 'when I was in regular service. You don't see much of them ways now, do you? Like I said to Jim, they're selling the big houses when they can, for institutions and that. Not trying all out to buy them, like Mr Markos.'

'Is Mr Markos doing that?'

'He'd like to have Quintern,' said Mrs Jim. 'He come to ask if it was for sale when Mrs Foster was at Greengages a year ago last April. He was that taken with it, you could see. I was helping spring-clean at the time.'

'Did Mrs Foster know?'

'He never left 'is name. I told her a gentleman had called to enquire, of course. It give me quite a turn when I first see him after he come to the Manor.'

'Did you tell Mrs Foster it was he who'd called?'

'I wasn't going out to Quintern Place at the time,' said Mrs Jim shortly, and Verity remembered that there had been a rift.

'It come up this evening in conversation. Mr Alfredo, that's the butler,' Mrs Jim continued, 'reckons Mr Markos is still dead set on Quintern. He says he's never known him not to get his way once he's made up his mind to it. You're suited with a gardener, then?'

Mrs Jim had a habit of skipping, without notice, from one topic to another. Verity thought she detected a derogatory note but could not be sure. 'He's beginning on Friday,' she said. 'Have you met him, Mrs Jim?'

'Couldn't miss 'im, could I?' she said, rubbing her arthritic knee. 'Annie Black's been taking him up and down the village like he was Exhibit A in the horse show.'

'He'll be company for her.'

'He's all of that,' she said cryptically.

Verity turned into the narrow lane where the Jobbins had their cottage. When they arrived no light shone in any of the windows. Jim and the kids all fast alseep, no doubt. Mrs Jim was slower leaving the car than she had been in entering it and Verity sensed her weariness. 'Have you got an early start?' she asked.

'Quintern at eight. It was very kind of you to bring me home, Miss Preston. Ta, anyway. I'll say good night.'

That's two of us going home to a dark house, Verity thought as she turned the car.

But being used to living alone, she didn't mind letting herself into Keys House and feeling for the light switch.

When she was in bed she turned over the events of the evening and a wave of exhaustion came upon her together with a nervous condition she thought of as 'restless legs'. She realized that the encounter with Basil Schramm (as she supposed she should call him) had been more of an ordeal than she had acknowledged at the time. The past rushed upon her, almost with the impact of her initial humiliation. She made herself relax, physically, muscle by muscle, and then tried to think of nothing.

She did not think of nothing but she thought of thinking of nothing and almost, but not quite, lost the feeling of some kind of threat waiting offstage like the return of a baddie in one of the old moralities. And at last after sundry heart-stopping jerks she fell asleep.

CHAPTER 2

Greengages (I)

There were no two ways about it, Gardener was a good gardener. He paid much more attention to his employer's quirks and fancies than McBride had ever done and he was a conscientious worker.

When he found his surname caused Verity some embarrassment, he laughed and said it wad be a' the same to him if she calt him by his first name which was Brrruce. Verity herself was no Scot but she couldn't help thinking his dialect was laid on with a trowel. However, she availed herself of the offer and Bruce he became to all his employers. Praise of him rose high in Upper Quintern. The wee laddie he had found in the village was nearly six feet tall and not quite all there. One by one as weeks and then months went by, Bruce's employers yielded to the addition of the laddie, with the exception of Mr Markos's head gardener who was adamant against him.

Sybil Foster continued to rave about Bruce. Together they pored over nurserymen's catalogues. At the end of his day's work at Quintern he was given a pint of beer and Sybil often joined him in the staff sitting-room to talk over plans. When odd jobs were needed indoors he proved to be handy and willing.

'He's such a comfort,' she said to Verity. 'And, my dear, the energy of the man! He's made up his mind I'm to have home-grown asparagus and has dug two enormous deep, deep graves, beyond the tennis court of all places, and is going to fill them up with all sorts of stuff – seaweed, if you can believe me. The maids have fallen for him in a big way, thank God.'

She alluded to her 'outside help', a girl from the village, and Beryl, Mrs Jim's niece. Both, according to Sybil, doted on Bruce and she hinted that Beryl actually had designs. Mrs Jim remained cryptic on the subject. Verity gathered that she thought Bruce 'hated himself', which meant that he was conceited.

Dr Basil Schramm had vanished from Upper Quintern as if he had never appeared there and Verity, after a time, was almost, but not quite, able to get rid of him.

The decorators had at last finished their work at Mardling and Mr Markos was believed to have gone abroad. Gideon however, came down from London most weekends, often bringing a house-party with him. Mrs Jim reported that Prunella Foster was a regular attendant at these parties. Under this heading Sybil displayed a curiously ambivalent attitude. She seemed on the one hand to preen herself on what appeared, in her daughter's highly individual argot, to be a 'grab'. On the other hand she continued to drop dark, incomprehensible hints about Gideon, all based, as far as Verity could make out, on an infallible instinct. Verity wondered if, after all, Sybil merely entertained some form of maternal jealousy. It was OK for Prue to be all set about with ardent young men, but it was less gratifying if she took a fancy to one of them. Or was it simply that Sybil had set her sights on the undynamic Lord Swingletree for Prue?

'Of course, darling,' she had confided on the telephone one day in July, 'there's lots of lovely lolly but you know me, that's not everything, and one doesn't know, does one, anything *at all* about the background. Crimpy hair and black eyes and large noses. Terribly good-looking, I grant you, like profiles on old pots, but what is one to think?' And sensing Verity's reaction to this observation she added hurriedly, 'I don't mean what you mean, as you very well know.'

Verity said, 'Is Prue serious, do you suppose?'

'Don't ask me,' said Sybil irritably. 'She whispers away about him. Just when I was so pleased about John Swingletree. *Devoted,* my dear. All I can say is, it's playing havoc with my health. Not a wink last night and I dread my back. She sees a lot of him in London. I prefer not to know what goes on there. I really can't take much more, Verry. I'm going to Greengages.'

'When?' asked Verity, conscious of a jolt under her ribs.

'My dear, on Monday. I'm hoping your chum can do something for me.'

'I hope so, too.'

'What did you say? Your voice sounded funny.'

'I hope it'll do the trick.'

'I wrote to him personally, and he answered at once. A charming letter, so understanding and informal.'

'Good.'

When Sybil prevaricated she always spoke rapidly and pitched her voice above its natural register. She did so now and Verity would have taken long odds that she fingered her hair at the back of her head.

'Darling,' she gabbled, 'you couldn't give me a boiled egg, could you? For lunch? Tomorrow?'

'Of course I could,' said Verity.

She was surprised, when Sybil arrived, to find that she really did look unwell. She was a bad colour and clearly had lost weight. But apart from that there was a look of – how to define it? – a kind of blankness, of a mask almost. It was a momentary impression and Verity wondered if she had only imagined she saw it. She asked Sybil if she'd seen a doctor and was given a fretful account of a visit to the clinic in Great Quintern, the nearest town. An unknown practitioner, she said, had 'rushed over her' with his stethoscope, 'pumped up her arm' and turned her on to a dim nurse for other indignities. Her impression had been one of complete professional detachment. 'One might have been drafted, darling, into some yard, for all he cared. The deadliest of little men with a signet ring on the wrong finger. All right, I'm a snob,' said Sybil crossly and jabbed at her cutlet.

Presently she reverted to her gardener. Bruce as usual had been 'perfect', it emerged. He had noticed that Sybil looked done up and had brought her some early turnips as a present. 'Mark my words,' she said. 'There's something *in* that man. You may look sceptical, but there is.'

'If I look sceptical it's only because I don't understand. What sort of thing is there in Bruce?'

'You know *very* well what I mean. To be perfectly frank and straightforward – breeding. Remember,' said Sybil surprisingly, 'Ramsay MacDonald.'

'Do you think Bruce is a blue-blooded bastard? Is that it?'

'Stranger things have happened,' said Sybil darkly. She eyed Verity for a moment or two and then said airily, 'He's not very comfortable with the dreary little Black sister – tiny dark room and nowhere to put his things.'

'Oh?'

'Yes. I've been considering,' said Sybil rapidly, 'the possibility of housing him in the stable block – you know, the old coachman's quarters. They'd have to be done up, of course. It'd be a good idea to have somebody on the premises when we're away.'

'You'd better watch it, old girl,' Verity said, 'or you'll find yourself doing a Queen Victoria to Bruce's Brown.'

'Don't be ridiculous,' said Sybil.

She tried without success to get Verity to fix a day when she would come to a weight-reducing luncheon at Greengages.

'I do think it's the least you can do,' she said piteously. 'I'll be segregated among a tribe of bores and dying for gossip. And besides you can bring me news of Prue.'

'But I don't see Prue in the normal course of events.'

'Ask her to lunch, darling. Do – '

'Syb, she'd be bored to sobs.'

'She'd adore it. You *know* she thinks you're marvellous. It's odds on she'll confide in you. After all, you're her godmother.'

'It doesn't follow as the night the day. And if she should confide I wouldn't hear what she said.'

'There *is* that difficulty, I know,' Sybil conceded. 'You must tell her to scream. After all, her friends seem to hear her. Gideon Markos does, presumably. And that's not all.'

'Not all what?'

'All my woe. Guess who's turned up?'

'I can't imagine. *Not,*' Verity exclaimed on a note of real dismay, '*not* Charmless Claude? Don't tell me!'

'I do tell you. He left Australia weeks ago and is working his way home on a ship called *Poseidon*. As a steward. I've had a letter.'

The young man Sybil referred to was Claude Carter, her stepson – a left-over from her first marriage in whose favour not even Verity could find much to say.

'Oh Syb,' she said, 'I *am* sorry.'

'He wants me to forward a hundred pounds to Tenerife.'

'Is he coming to Quintern?'

'My dear, he doesn't say so but of course he will. Probably with the police in hot pursuit.'

'Does Prue know?'

'I've told her. Horrified, of course. She's going to make a bolt to London when the time comes. This is why, on top of everything else, I'm hell-bent for Greengages.'

'Will he want to stay?'

'I expect so. He usually does. I can't stop that.'

'Of course not. After all – '

'Verry, he gets the very generous allowance his father left him and blues the lot. I'm always having to yank him out of trouble. And what's more – absolutely for your ears alone – when I pop off he gets everything his father left me for my lifetime. God knows what he'll do with it. He's been in jail and I dare say he dopes. I'll go on paying up, I suppose.'

'So he'll arrive and find – who?'

'Either Beryl, who's caretaking, or Mrs Jim who's relieving her and springcleaning, or Bruce, if it's one of his days. They're all under strict instructions to say I'm away ill and not seeing anybody. If he insists on being put up nobody can stop him. Of course he might – '

There followed a long pause. Verity's mind misgave her.

'Might what?' she said.

'Darling, I wouldn't know but he *might* call on you. Just to enquire.'

'What,' said Verity, 'do you want me to do?'

'Just not tell him where I am. And then let me know and come to Greengages. Don't just ring or write, Verry. Come. Verry, as my oldest friend I ask you.'

'I don't promise.'

'No, but you will. You'll come to awful lunch with me at Greengages and tell me what Prue says and whether Charmless Claude has called. Think! You'll meet your gorgeous boyfriend again.'

'I don't want to.'

As soon as she had made this disclaimer, Verity realized it was a mistake. She visualized the glint of insatiable curiosity in Sybil's large blue eyes and knew she had aroused the passion that, second only to her absorption in gentlemen, consumed her friend – a devouring interest in other people's affairs.

'*Why* not?' Sybil said quickly. 'I knew there was something. That night at Nikolas Markos's dinner-party. I sensed it. What was it?'

Verity pulled herself together. 'Now, then,' she said. 'None of that. Don't you go making up nonsenses about me.'

'There *was* something,' Sybil repeated. 'I'm never wrong. I sensed there was something. I know!' she sang out. 'I'll ask Basil Schramm – Dr Schramm I mean – himself. He'll tell me.'

'You'll do nothing of the sort,' Verity said, and tried not to sound panicstricken. She added too late, 'He wouldn't know what on earth you were driving at. Syb – please don't go making a fool of me. And of yourself.'

'*Tum-te-tiddily. Tum-te-tee,*' sang Sybil idiotically. 'See what a tizzy we've got into.'

Verity kept her temper.

Wild horses, she decided, would not drag her to luncheon at Greengages. She saw Sybil off with the deepest misgivings.

II

Gideon Markos and Prunella Foster lay on a magnificent hammock under a striped canopy beside the brand-new swimming pool at Mardling Manor. They were brown, wet and almost nude. Her white-gold hair fanned across his chest. He held her lightly as if some photographer had posed them for a glossy advertisement.

'Because,' Prunella whispered, 'I don't want to.'

'I don't believe you. You do. Clearly, you want me. Why pretend?'

'All right, then. I do. But I'm not going to. I don't choose to.'

'But why, for God's sake? Oh,' said Gideon with a change of voice, 'I suppose I know. I suppose, in a way, I understand. It's the "Too rash, too ill-advised, too sudden" bit. Is that it? What?' he asked, bending his head to hers. 'What did you say? Speak up.'

'I like you too much.'

'Darling Prue, it's extremely nice of you to like me too much but it doesn't get us anywhere, now does it?'

'It's not meant to.'

Gideon put his foot to the ground and swung the hammock violently. Prunella's hair blew across his mouth.

'Don't,' she said and giggled. 'We'll capsize. Stop.'

'No.'

'I'll fall off. I'll be sick.'

'Say you'll reconsider the matter.'

'Gideon, *please.*'

'Say it.'

'I'll reconsider the matter, damn you.'

He checked the hammock but did not release her.

'But I'll come to the same conclusion,' said Prunella. 'No, darling. Not again! *Don't.* Honestly, I'll be sick. I promise you I'll be sick.'

'You do the most dreadful things to me,' Gideon muttered after an interval. 'You beastly girl.'

'I'm going in again before the sun's off the pool.'

'Prunella, are you really fond of me? Do you think about me when we're not together?'

'Quite often.'

'Very well, then, would you like – would you care to entertain the idea – I mean, couldn't we try it out? To see if we suit?'

'How do you mean?'

'Well – in my flat? Together. You like my flat, don't you? Give it, say, a month and then consider?'

She shook her head.

'I could beat you like a gong,' said Gideon. 'Oh, come *on*, Prunella, for Christ's sake. Give me a straight answer to a straight question. Are you fond of me?'

'I think you're fantastic. You know I do. Like I said, I'm too fond of you for a jolly affair. Too fond to face it all turning out to be a dead failure and us going back to square one and wishing we hadn't tried. We've seen it happen among our friends, haven't we? Everything super to begin with. And then the not-so-hot situation develops.'

'Fair enough. One finds out and no bones broken, which is a damn sight better than having to plough through the divorce court. Well, isn't it?'

'It's logical and civilized and liberated but it's just not on for me. No way. I must be a throwback or simply plain chicken. I'm sorry.

Darling Gideon,' said Prunella, suddenly kissing him. 'Like the song said, "I do, I do, I do, I do".'

'What?'

'Love you,' she mumbled in a hurry. 'There. I've said it.'

'God!' said Gideon with some violence. 'It's not fair. Look here, Prue. Let's be engaged. Just nicely and chastely and frustratingly engaged to be married and you can break it off whenever you want to. And I'll swear, if you like, not to pester you with my ungentlemanly attentions. No. Don't answer. Think it over and in the meantime, like Donne says, "for God's sake hold your tongue and let me love".'

'He didn't say it to the lady. He said it to some irritating acquaintance.'

'Come here.'

The sun-baked landscape moved into late afternoon. Over at Quintern Place, Bruce having dug a further and deeper asparagus bed, caused the wee lad, whose name was Daft Artie, to fill it up with compost, fertilizer and soil while he himself set to work again with his long-handled shovel. Comprehensive drainage and nutrition was needed if his and his employer's plans were to be realized.

Twenty miles away at Greengages in the Weald of Kent, Dr Basil Schramm completed yet another examination of Sybil Foster. She had introduced into her room a sort of overflow of her own surplus femininity – beribboned pillows, cushions, a negligée and a bedcover both rose-coloured. Photographs. Slippers trimmed with marabou, a large box of *petit-fours au massepain* from the 'Marquise de Sévigné' in Paris, which she had made but a feeble attempt to hide from the dietetic notice of her doctor. Above all, there was the pervasive scent of oil enclosed in a thin glass container that fitted over the light bulb of her table-lamp. Altogether the room, like Sybil herself, went much too far but, again like Sybil, contrived to get away with it.

'Splendid,' said Dr Schramm, withdrawing his stethoscope. He turned away and gazed out of the window with professional tact while she rearranged herself.

'There!' she said presently.

He returned and gazed down at her with the bossy, possessive air that she found so satisfactory.

'I begin to be pleased with you,' he said.

'Truly?'

'Truly. You've quite a long way to go, of course, but your general condition is improved. You're responding.'

'I feel better.'

'Because you're not allowed to take it out of yourself. You're a highly strung instrument, you know, and mustn't be at the beck and call of people who impose upon you.'

Sybil gave a deep sigh of concealed satisfaction.

'You do so understand,' she said.

'Of course I do. It's what I'm here for. Isn't it?'

'Yes,' said Sybil, luxuriating in it. 'Yes, indeed.'

He slid her bracelet up her arm and then laid his fingers on her pulse. She felt sure it was going like a train. When, after a final pressure, he released her she said as airily as she could manage, 'I've just written a card to an old friend of yours.'

'Really?'

'To ask her to lunch on Saturday. Verity Preston.'

'Oh yes?'

'It must have been fun for you, meeting again after so long.'

'Well, yes. It was,' said Dr Schramm, 'very long ago. We used to run up against each other sometimes in my student days.' He looked at his watch. 'Time for your rest,' he said.

'You must come and talk to her on Saturday.'

'That would have been very pleasant.'

But it turned out that he was obliged to go up to London on Saturday to see a fellow medico who had arrived unexpectedly from New York.

Verity, too, was genuinely unable to come to Greengages, having been engaged for luncheon elsewhere. She rang Sybil up and said she hadn't seen Prue but Mrs Jim reported she was staying with friends in London.

'Does that mean Gideon Markos?'

'I've no idea.'

'I'll bet it does. What about ghastly C.C.?'

'Not a sign of him as far as I know. I see by the shipping news that *Poseidon* came into Southampton the day before yesterday.'

'Keep your fingers crossed. Perhaps we'll escape after all.'

'I think not,' said Verity.

She was looking through her open window. An unmistakable figure shambled towards her up the avenue of limes.

'Your stepson,' she said, 'has arrived.'

III

Claude Carter was one of those beings whose appearance accurately reflects their character. He looked, and in fact was, damp. He seemed unable to face anything or anybody. He was well into his thirties but maintained a rich crop of post-adolescent pimples. He had very little chin, furtive eyes behind heavy spectacles, a vestigial beard and mouse-coloured hair which hung damply, of course, half way down his neck.

Because he was physically so hopeless, Verity entertained a kind of horrified pity for him. This arose from a feeling that he couldn't be as awful as he looked and that anyway he had been treated unfairly – by his Maker in the first instance and probably in the second by his masters (he had been sacked from three schools), his peers (he had been bullied at all of them) and life in general. His mother had died in childbirth and he was still a baby when Sybil married his father, who was killed in the blitz six months later and of whom Verity knew little beyond the fact that he collected stamps. Claude was brought up by his grandparents who didn't care for him. These circumstances, when she thought of them, induced in Verity a muddled sense of guilt for which she could advance no justification and which was certainly not shared by Claude's stepmother.

When he became aware of Verity at her window he pretended, ineffectually, that he hadn't seen her and approached the front door with his head down. She went out to him. He did not speak but seemed to offer himself feebly for her inspection.

'Claude,' said Verity.

'That's right.'

She asked him in and he sat in her sunny drawing-room as if, she thought, he had been left till called for. He wore a T-shirt that had been made out of a self-raising-flour bag and bore the picture of a lady who thrust out a vast bosom garnished with the legend 'Sure to

Rise'. His jeans so far exceeded in fashionable shrinkage as to cause him obvious discomfort.

He said he'd been up to Quintern Place where he'd found Mrs Jim Jobbin who told him Mrs Foster was away and she couldn't say when she would return.

'Not much of a welcome,' he said. 'She made out she didn't know Prue's address, either. I asked who forwarded their letters.' He blew three times down his nose, which was his manner of laughing, and gave Verity a knowing glance. 'That made Mrs Jim look pretty silly,' he said.

'Sybil's taking a cure,' Verity explained. 'She's not seeing anybody.'

'What, again! What is it this time?'

'She was run down and needs a complete rest.'

'I thought you'd tell me where she was. That's why I came.'

'I'm afraid not, Claude.'

'That's awkward,' he said fretfully. 'I was counting on it.'

'Where are you staying?'

'Oh, up there for the time being. At Quintern.'

'Did you come by train?'

'I hitched.'

Verity felt obliged to ask him if he'd had any lunch and he said, not really. He followed her into the kitchen where she gave him cold meat, chutney, bread, butter, cheese and beer. He ate a great deal and had a cigarette with his coffee. She asked him about Australia and he said it was no good, really, not unless you had capital. It was all right if you had capital.

He trailed back after her to the drawing-room and she began to feel desperate.

'As a matter of fact,' he said, 'I was depending on Syb. I happen to be in a bit of a patch. Nothing to worry about really, but, you know.'

'What sort of patch?' she asked against her will.

'I'm short.'

'Of money?'

'What else is there to be short of?' he asked and gave his three inverted sniffs.

'How about the hundred pounds she sent to Tenerife?'

He didn't hesitate or look any more hang-dog than he was already.

'Did she *send* it!' he said. 'Typical of the bloody Classic Line, that is. Typical inefficiency.'

'Didn't it reach you?'

'Would I be cleaned out if it had?'

'Are you sure you haven't spent it?'

'I resent that, Miss Preston,' he said, feebly bridling.

'I'm sorry if it was unfair. I can let you have twenty pounds. That should tide you over. And I'll let Sybil know about you.'

'It's a bit off not telling where she is. But thanks, anyway, for helping out. I'll pay it back of course, don't worry.'

She went to her study to fetch it and again he trailed after her. Horrid to feel that it was not a good idea for him to see where she kept her housekeeping money.

In the hall she said, 'I've a telephone call to make. I'll join you in the garden. And then I'm afraid we'll have to part. I've got work on hand.'

'I quite understand,' he said with an attempt at dignity.

When she rejoined him he was hanging about outside the front door. She gave him the money. 'It's twenty-three pounds,' she said. 'Apart from loose change, it's all I've got in the house at the moment.'

'I quite understand,' he repeated grandly, and after giving her one of his furtive glances said, 'Of course, if I had my own I wouldn't have to do this. Do you know that?'

'I don't think I understand.'

'If I had the Stamp.'

'The Stamp?'

'The one my father left me. The famous one.'

'I'd forgotten about it.'

'You wouldn't have if you were in my boots. The Black Alexander.'

Then Verity remembered. The story had always sounded like something out of a boy's annual. Claude's father had inherited the stamp which was one of a set that had been withdrawn on the day of issue because of an ominous fault: a black spot in the centre of the Czar Alexander's brow. It was reputed to be the only specimen known to be extant and worth a fabulous amount. Maurice Carter had been killed in the blitz while on leave. When his stamp collection was uplifted from his bank the Black Alexander was missing. It was never recovered.

'It was a strange business, that,' Verity said.

'From what they've told me it was a very strange business indeed,' he said, with his laugh.

She didn't answer. He shuffled his feet in the gravel and said he supposed he'd better take himself off.

'Goodbye then,' said Verity.

He gave her a damp and boneless handshake and had turned away when a thought seemed to strike him.

'By the way,' he said. 'If anyone asks for me I'd be grateful if you didn't know anything. Where I am and that. I don't suppose they will but, you know, if they do.'

'Who would they be?'

'Oh – boring people. You wouldn't know them.' He smiled and for a moment looked fully at her. 'You're so good at not knowing where Syb is,' he said, 'the exercise ought to come easy to you, Miss Preston.'

She knew her face was red. He had made her feel shabby.

'Look here. Are you in trouble?' she asked.

'Me? Trouble?'

'With the police?'

'Well, I must say! Thank you very much! What on earth could have given you that idea!' She didn't answer. He said, 'Oh well, thanks for the loan anyway,' and walked off. When he had got half way to the gate he began, feebly, to whistle.

Verity went indoors meaning to settle down to work. She tried to concentrate for an hour, failed, started to write to Sybil, thought better of it, thought of taking a walk in the garden and was called back by the telephone.

It was Mrs Jim, speaking from Quintern Place. She sounded unlike herself and said she was sure she begged pardon for giving the trouble but she was that worried. After a certain amount of preliminary explanation it emerged that it was about 'that Mr Claude Carter'.

Sybil had told the staff it was remotely possible that he might appear and that if he did and wanted to stay they were to allow it. And then earlier this afternoon someone had rung up asking if he was there and Mrs Jim had replied truthfully that he wasn't and wasn't expected and that she didn't know where he could be found. About half an hour later he arrived and said he wanted to stay.

'So I put him in the green bedroom, according,' said Mrs Jim, 'and I told him about the person who'd rang and he says he don't want to take calls and I'm to say he's not there and I don't know nothing about him. Well, Miss Preston, I don't like it. I won't take the responsibility. There's something funny going on and I won't be mixed up. And I was wondering if you'd be kind enough to give me a word of advice.'

'Poor Mrs Jim,' Verity said. 'What a bore for you. But Mrs Foster said you were to put him up and, difficult as that may be, that's what you've done.'

'I didn't know then what I know now, Miss Preston.'

'What do you know now?'

'I didn't like to mention it before. It's not a nice thing to have to bring up. It's about the person who rang earlier. It was – somehow I knew it was, before he said – it was the police.'

'Oh lor', Mrs Jim.'

'Yes, miss. And there's more. Bruce Gardener come in for his beer when he finished at five and he says he'd run into a gentleman in the garden, only he never realized it was Mr Claude. On his way back from you, it must of been, and Mr Claude told him he was a relation of Mrs Foster's and they got talking and – '

'Bruce doesn't know – ? Does he know? – Mrs Jim, Bruce didn't tell him where Mrs Foster can be found?'

'That's what I was coming to. She won't half be annoyed, won't she? Yes, Miss Preston, that's just what he did.'

'Oh *damn*,' said Verity after a pause. 'Well, it's not your fault, Mrs Jim. Nor Bruce's if it comes to that. Don't worry about it.'

'But what'll I say if the police rings again?'

Verity thought hard but any solution that occurred to her seemed to be unendurably shabby. At last she said, 'Honestly, Mrs Jim, I don't know. Speak the truth, I suppose I ought to say, and tell Mr Claude about the call. Beastly though it sounds, at least it would probably get rid of him.'

There was no answer. 'Are you there, Mrs Jim?' Verity asked. 'Are you still there?'

Mrs Jim had begun to whisper, 'Excuse me, I'd better hang up.' And in loud, artificial tones added, 'That will be all, then, for today, thank you.' And did hang up. Charmless Claude, thought Verity, was in the offing.

Verity was now deeply perturbed and at the same time couldn't help feeling rather cross. She was engaged in making extremely tricky alterations to the last act of a play which, after a promising try-out in the provinces, had attracted nibbles from a London management. To be interrupted at this stage was to become distraught.

She tried hard to readjust and settle to her job but it was no good. Sybil Foster and her ailments and problems, real or synthetic, weighed in against it. Should she, for instance, let Sybil know about the latest and really most disturbing news of her awful stepson. Had she any right to keep Sybil in the dark? She knew that Sybil would be only too pleased to be kept there but that equally some disaster might well develop for which she, Verity, would be held responsible. She would be told she had been secretive and had bottled up key information. It wouldn't be the first time that Sybil had shovelled responsibility all over her and then raised a martyred howl when the outcome was not to her liking.

It came to Verity that Prunella might reasonably be expected to take some kind of share in the proceedings but where, at the moment, was Prunella and would she become audible if rung up and asked to call?

Verity read the same bit of dialogue three times without reading it at all, cast away her pen, swore and went for a walk in her garden. She loved her garden. There was no doubt that Bruce had done all the right things. There was no greenfly on the roses. Hollyhocks and delphiniums flourished against the lovely brick wall round her elderly orchard. He had not attempted to foist calceolarias upon her or indeed any objectionable annuals, only night-scented stocks. She had nothing but praise for him and wished he didn't irritate her so often.

She began to feel less badgered, picked a leaf of verbena, crushed and smelt it and turned back towards the house.

I'll put the whole thing aside, she thought, until tomorrow. I'll sleep on it.

But when she came through the lime trees she met Prunella Foster streaking hot-foot up the drive.

IV

Prunella was breathless, a condition that did nothing to improve her audibility. She gazed at her godmother and flapped her hands in a manner that reminded Verity of her mother.

'Godma,' she whispered, 'are you alone?'

'Utterly,' said Verity.

'Could I talk to you?'

'If you can contrive to make yourself heard, darling, of course you may?'

'I'm sorry,' said Prunella, who was accustomed to this admonishment. 'I will try.'

'Have you walked here?'

'Gideon dropped me. He's in the lane. Waiting.'

'Come indoors. I wanted to see you.'

Prunella opened her eyes very wide and they went indoors where without more ado she flung her arms round her godmother's neck, almost shouted the information that she was engaged to be married, and burst into excitable tears.

'My dear child!' said Verity. 'What an odd way to announce it. Aren't you pleased to be engaged?'

A confused statement followed during which it emerged Prunella was very much in love with Gideon but was afraid he might not continue to be as much in love with her as now appeared because one saw that sort of thing happening all over the place, didn't one, and she knew if it happened to her she wouldn't be able to keep her cool and put it into perspective and she had only consented to an engagement because Gideon promised that for him it was for keeps but how could one be sure he knew what he was talking about?

She then blew her nose and said that she was fantastically happy.

Verity was fond of her god-daughter and pleased that she wanted to confide in her. She sensed that there was more to come.

And so there was.

'It's about Mummy,' Prunella said. 'She's going to be livid.'

'But why?'

'Well, first of all she's a roaring snob and wants me to marry John Swingletree because he's a peer. Imagine!'

'I don't know John Swingletree.'

'The more lucky, you. The bottom. And then, you see, she's got one of her things about Gideon and his papa. She thinks they've sprung from a mid-European ghetto.'

'None the worse for that,' said Verity.

'Exactly. But you know what she is. It's partly because Mr Markos didn't exactly make a big play for her at that dinner-party when they first came to Mardling. You know,' Prunella repeated, 'what she is. Well, don't you, Godma?'

There being no way out of it, Verity said she supposed she did.

'Not,' Prunella said, 'that she's all that hooked on him. Not now. She's all for the doctor at Greengages – you remember? Wasn't he an ex-buddy of yours, or something?'

'Not really.'

'Well, anyway, she's in at the deep end, boots and all. Potty about him. I do so wish,' Prunella said as her large eyes refilled with tears, 'I didn't have to have a mum like that. Not that I don't love her.'

'Never mind.'

'And now I've got to tell her. About Gideon and me.'

'How do you think of managing that? Going to Greengages? Or writing?'

'Whatever I do she'll go ill at me and say I'll be sorry when she's gone. Gideon's offered to come too. He's all for taking bulls by the horns. But I don't want him to see what she can be like if she cuts up rough. You know, don't you? If anything upsets her applecart when she's nervy it can be a case of screaming hysterics. Can't it?'

'Well – '

'You know it can. I'd hate him to see her like that. Darling, darling Godma V, I was wondering – '

Verity thought, She can't help being a bit like her mother, and was not surprised when Prunella said she had *just* wondered if Verity was going to visit her mother and if she did whether she'd kind of prepare the way.

'I hadn't thought of going. I really am busy, Prue.'

'Oh,' said Prunella, falling back on her whisper and looking desolate. 'Yes. I see.'

'In any case, shouldn't you and Gideon go together and Gideon – well – '

'Ask for my hand in marriage like Jack Worthing and Lady
Bracknell?'

'Yes.'

'That's what *he* says. Darling Godma V,' said Prunella, once more
hanging herself round Verity's neck, 'if we took you with us and you
just sort of – you know – first. Couldn't you? We've come all the way
from London just this minute almost, to ask. She pays more attention to you than anybody. Please.'

'Oh, Prue.'

'You *will?* I can see you're going to. And you can't possibly refuse
when I tell you my other hideous news. Not that Gideon-and-me is
hideous but just you wait.'

'Charmless Claude?'

'You *knew!* I rang up Quintern from Mardling and Mrs Jim told me.
Isn't it *abysmal?* When we all thought he was safely stowed in Aussie.'

'Are you staying tonight?'

'There! With Claudie-boy? Not on your Nelly. I'm going to
Mardling. Mr Markos is back and we'll tell him about us. He'll be
super about it. I ought to go.'

'May I come to the car and meet your young man?'

'Oh, you mustn't trouble to do that. He'll come,' Prunella said.
She put a thumb and finger between her teeth, leant out of the window and emitted a piercing whistle. A powerful engine started up in
the lane, a rakish sports model shot through the drive in reverse and
pulled up at the front door. Gideon Markos leapt out.

He really was an extremely good-looking boy, thought Verity, but
she could see, without for a moment accepting the disparagement,
what Sybil had meant by her central European remark. He was an
exotic. He looked like a Latin member of the jet set dressed by an
English tailor. But his manner was unaffected as well as assured and
his face alive with a readiness to be amused.

'Miss Preston,' he said, 'I gather you're not only a godmother but
expected to be a fairy one. Are you going to wave your wand and
give us your blessing?'

He put his arm around Prunella and talked away cheerfully about
how he'd bullied her into accepting him. Verity thought he was
exalted by his conquest and that he would be quite able to manage
not only his wife but if need be his mother-in-law as well.

'I expect Prue's confided her misgivings,' he said, 'about her mama being liable to cut up rough over us. I don't quite see why she shoud take against me in such a big way, but perhaps that's insufferable. Anyway, I hope *you* don't feel I'm not a good idea?' He looked quickly at her and added, 'But then, of course, you don't know me so that was a pretty gormless remark, wasn't it?'

'The early impression,' said Verity, 'is not unfavourable.'

'Well, thank the Lord for that,' said Gideon.

'Darling,' breathed Prunella, 'she's coming to Greengages with us. You are, Godma, you know you are. To temper the wind. Sort of.'

'That's very kind of her,' he said and bowed to Verity.

Verity knew she had been out-manoeuvred, but on the whole did not resent it. She saw them shoot off down the drive. It had been settled that they would visit Greengages on the coming Saturday but not, as Prunella put it, for a cabbage-water soup and minced grass luncheon. Gideon knew of a super restaurant en route.

Verity was left with a feeling of having spent a day during which unsought events converged upon her and brought with them a sense of mounting unease, of threats, even. She suspected that the major ingredient of this discomfort was an extreme reluctance to suffer another confrontation with Basil Schramm.

The following two days were uneventful but Thursday brought Mrs Jim to Keys for her weekly attack upon floors and furniture. She reported that Claude Carter kept very much to his room up at Quintern, helped himself to the food left out for him and, she thought, didn't answer the telephone. Beryl, who was engaged to sleep in while Sybil Foster was away, had said she didn't fancy doing so with that Mr Claude in residence. In the upshot the difficulty had been solved by Bruce who offered to sleep in, using a coachman's room over the garage formerly occupied by a chauffeur-handyman.

'I knew Mrs Foster wouldn't have any objections to *that*,' said Mrs Jim, with a stony glance out of the window.

'Perhaps, though, she ought just to be asked, don't you think?'

'He's done it,' said Mrs Jim sparsely. 'Bruce. He rung her up.'

'At Greengages?'

'That's right, miss. He's been over there to see her,' she added. 'Once a week. To take flowers and get orders. By bus. Of a Saturday. She pays.'

Verity knew that she would be expected by her friends to snub
Mrs Jim for speaking in this cavalier manner of an employer but she
preferred not to notice.

'Oh, well,' she generalized, 'you've done everything you can, Mrs
Jim.' She hesitated for a moment and then said, 'I'm going over
there on Saturday.'

After a fractional pause Mrs Jim said, 'Are you, miss? That's very
kind of you, I'm sure,' and switched on the vacuum-cleaner. 'You'll
be able to see for yourself,' she shouted above the din.

Verity nodded and returned to the study. But what? she
wondered. *What* shall I be able to see?

V

Gideon's super restaurant turned out to be within six miles of
Greengages. It seemed to be some sort of club of which he was a
member and was of an exalted character with every kind of discreet
attention and very good food. Verity seldom lunched at this level
and she enjoyed herself. For the first time she wondered what
Gideon's occupation in life might be. She also remembered that
Prunella was something of a *partie.*

At half past two they arrived at Greengages. It was a converted
Edwardian mansion approached by an avenue, sheltered by a stand
of conifers and surrounded by ample lawns in which flower-beds
had been cut like graves.

There were a number of residents strolling about with visitors or
sitting under brilliant umbrellas on exterior furnishers' contraptions.

'She does know we're coming, doesn't she?' Verity asked. She
had begun to feel apprehensive.

'You and me, she knows,' said Prunella. 'I didn't mention Gideon.
Actually.'

'Oh, Prue!'

'I thought you might sort of ease him in,' Prue whispered.

'I really don't think – '

'Nor do I,' said Gideon. 'Darling, why can't we just – '

'There she is!' cried Verity. 'Over there beyond the calceolarias
and lobelia under an orange brolly. She's waving. She's seen us.'

'Godma V, *please*. Gideon and I'll sit in the car and when you wave we'll come. Please.'

Verity thought, I've eaten their astronomical luncheon and drunk their champagne so now I turn plug-ugly and refuse? 'All right,' she said, 'but don't blame me if it goes haywire.'

She set off across the lawn.

Nobody has invented a really satisfactory technique for the gradual approach of people who have already exchanged greetings from afar. Continue to grin while a grin dwindles into a grimace? Assume a sudden absorption in the surroundings? Make as if sunk in meditation? Break into a joyous canter? Shout? Whistle? Burst, even, into song?

Verity tried none of these methods. She walked fast and when she got within hailing distance cried, 'There you are!'

Sybil had the advantage in so far as she wore enormous dark sunglasses. She waved and smiled and pointed, as if in mock astonishment or admiration at Verity and when she arrived extended her arms for an embrace.

'Darling Verry!' she cried. 'You've come after all.' She waved Verity into a canvas chair, seemed to gaze at her fixedly for an uneasy moment or two and then said with a change of voice, 'Whose car's that? Don't tell me. It's Gideon Markos's. He's driven you both over. You needn't say anything. They're engaged!'

This, in a way, was a relief. Verity, for once, was pleased by Sybil's prescience. 'Well, yes,' she said, 'they are. And honestly, Syb, there doesn't seem to me to be anything against it.'

'In that case,' said Sybil, all cordiality spent, 'why are they going on like this? Skulking in the car and sending you to soften me up. If you call that the behaviour of a civilized young man! Prue would never be like that on her own initiative. He's persuaded her.'

'The boot's on the other foot. He was all for tackling you himself.'

'Cheek! Thick-skinned push. One knows where he got that from.'

'Where?'

'God knows.'

'You've just said you do.'

'Don't quibble, darling,' said Sybil.

'I can't make out what, apart from instinctive promptings, sets you against Gideon. He's intelligent, eminently presentable, obviously rich – '

'Yes, and where does it come from?'

' – and, which is the only basically important bit, he seems to be a young man of good character and in love with Prue.'

'John Swingletree's devoted to her. Utterly devoted. And she was – ' Sybil boggled for a moment and then said loudly – 'she was getting to be very fond of him.'

'The Lord Swingletree, would that be?'

'Yes, it would, and you needn't say it like that.'

'I'm not saying it like anything. Syb, they're over there waiting to come to you. Do be kind. You won't get anywhere by being anything else.'

Sybil was silent for a moment and then said, 'Do you know what I think? I think it's a put-up job between him and his father. They want to get their hands on Quintern.'

'Oh, my *dear* old Syb!'

'All right. You wait. Just you wait.'

This was said with all her old vigour and obstinacy and yet with a very slight drag, a kind of flatness in her utterance. Was it because of this that Verity had the impression that Sybil did not really mind all that much about her daughter's engagement? There was an extraordinary suggestion of hesitancy and yet of suppressed excitement – almost of jubilation.

The pampered little hand she raised to her sunglasses quivered. It removed the glasses and for Verity the afternoon turned cold.

Sybil's face was blankly smooth as if it had been ironed. It had no expression. Her great china-blue eyes really might have been those of a doll.

'All right,' she said. 'On your own head be it. Let them come. I won't make scenes. But I warn you I'll never come round. Never.'

A sudden wave of compassion visited Verity.

'Would you rather wait a bit?' she asked. 'How are you, Syb? You haven't told me. Are you better?'

'Much, much better. Basil Schramm is fantastic. I've never had a doctor like him. Truly. He so *understands*. I expect,' Sybil's voice luxuriated, 'he'll be livid when he hears about this visit. He won't let me be upset. I told him about Charmless Claude and he said I must on no account see him. He's given orders. Verry, he's quite fantastic,' said

Sybil. The warmth of these eulogies found no complementary expression in her face or voice. She wandered on, gossiping about Schramm and her treatment and his nurse, Sister Jackson, who, she said complacently, resented his taking so much trouble over her. 'My dear,' said Sybil, 'jealous! Don't worry, I've got that one buttoned up.'

'Well,' Verity said, swallowing her disquietude, 'perhaps you'd better let me tell these two that you'll see Prue by herself for a moment. How would that be?'

'I'll see them both,' said Sybil. 'Now.'

'Shall I fetch them, then?'

'Can't you just wave?' she asked fretfully.

As there seemed to be nothing else for it, Verity walked into the sunlight and waved. Prunella's hand answered from the car. She got out, followed by Gideon, and they came quickly across the lawn. Verity knew Sybil would be on the watch for any signs of a conference however brief and waited instead of going to meet them. When they came up with her she said under her breath, 'It's tricky. Don't upset her.'

Prunella broke into a run. She knelt by her mother and looked into her face. There was a moment's hesitation and then she kissed her.

'Darling Mummy,' she said.

Verity returned to the car.

There she sat and watched the group of three under the orange canopy. They might have been placed there for a painter like Troy Alleyn. The afternoon light, broken and diffused, made nebulous figures of them so that they seemed to shimmer and swim a little. Sybil had put her sunglasses on again so perhaps, thought Verity, Prue won't notice anything.

Now Gideon had moved. He stood by Sybil's chair and raised her hand to his lips. She ought to like that, Verity thought. That ought to mean she's yielding but I don't think it does.

She found it intolerable to sit in the car and decided to stroll back towards the gates. She would be in full view. If she was wanted Gideon could come and get her.

A bus had drawn up outside the main gates. A number of people got out and began to walk up the drive. Among them were two men, one of whom carried a great basket of lilies. He wore a countrified tweed suit and hat and looked rather distinguished. It came as quite a shock to recognize him as Bruce Gardener in his best clothes. Sybil would have said he was 'perfectly presentable'.

And a greater and much more disquieting shock to realize that his shambling, ramshackle companion was Claude Carter.

VI

When Verity was a girl there had been a brief craze for what were known as rhymes of impending disaster – facetious couplets usually on the lines of 'Auntie Maude's mislaid her glasses and thinks the burglar's making passes', accompanied by a childish drawing of a simpering lady being man-handled by a masked thug.

Why was she now reminded of this puerile squib? Why did she see her old friend in immediate jeopardy, threatened by something undefined but infinitely more disquieting than any nuisance Claude Carter could inflict upon her? Why should Verity feel as if the afternoon, now turned sultry, was closing about Sybil? Had she only imagined that there was an odd immobility in Sybil's face?

And what ought she to do about Bruce and Claude?

Bruce was delighted to see her. He raised his tweed hat high in the air, beamed across the lilies and greeted her in his richest and most suspect Scots. He was, he said, paying his usual wee Saturday visit to his pure leddy and how had Miss Preston found her the noo? Would there be an improvement in her condeetion, then?

Verity said she didn't think Mrs Foster seemed very well and that at the moment she had visitors to which Bruce predictably replied that he would bide a wee. And if she didna fancy any further visitors he'd leave the lilies at the desk to be put in her room. 'She likes to know her garden prospers,' he said. Claude had listened to this exchange with a half-smile and a shifting eye.

'You found your way here, after all?' Verity said to him, since she could scarcely say nothing.

'Oh yes,' he said. 'Thanks to Bruce. He's sure she'll be glad to see me.'

Bruce looked, Verity thought, as if he would like to disown this remark and indeed began to say he'd no' put it that way when Claude said, 'That's her, over there, isn't it? Is that Prue with her?'

'Yes,' said Verity shortly.

'Who's the jet-set type?'

'A friend.'

'I think I'll just investigate,' he said with a pallid show of effrontery and made as if to set out.

'Claude, please wait,' Verity said, and in her dismay turned to Bruce. He said at once, 'Ou, now, Mr Carter, would you no' consider it more advisable to bide a while?'

'No,' said Claude, over his shoulder, 'thank you, I wouldn't,' and continued on his way.

Verity thought, I can't run after him and hang on his arm and make a scene. Prue and Gideon will have to cope.

Prue certainly did. The distance was too great for words to be distinguished and the scene came over like a mime. Sybil reached out a hand and clutched her daughter's arm. Prue turned, saw Claude and rose. Gideon made a gesture of enquiry. Then Prue marched down upon Claude.

They faced each other, standing close together, Prue very upright, rather a dignified little figure, Claude with his back to Verity, his head lowered. And in the distance Sybil being helped to her feet by Gideon and walked towards the house.

'She'll be better indoors,' said Bruce in a worried voice, 'she will that.'

Verity had almost forgotten him but there he stood gazing anxiously over the riot of lilies he carried. At that moment Verity actually liked him.

Prue evidently said something final to Claude. She walked quickly towards the house, joined her mother and Gideon on the steps, took Sybil's arm and led her indoors. Claude stared after them, turned towards Verity, changed his mind and sloped off in the direction of the trees.

'It wasna on any invitation of mine he came,' said Bruce hotly. 'He worrumed the information oot of me.'

'I can well believe it,' said Verity.

Gideon came to them.

'It's all right,' he said to Verity. 'Prue's taking Mrs Foster up to her room.' And to Bruce, 'Perhaps you could wait in the entrance hall until Miss Prunella comes down.'

'I'll do that, sir, thank you,' Bruce said and went indoors.

Gideon smiled down at Verity. He had, she thought, an engaging smile. 'What a very bumpy sort of a visit,' he said.

'How was it shaping up? Before Charmless Claude intervened?'

'Might have been worse, I suppose. Not much worse, though. The reverse of open arms and cries of rapturous welcome. You must have done some wonderful softening-up, Miss Preston, for her to receive me at all. We couldn't be more grateful.' He hesitated for a moment. 'I hope you don't mind my asking but is there – is she – Prue's mother – I don't know how to say it. Is there something – ?' He touched his face.

'I know what you mean. Yes. There is.'

'I only wondered.'

'It's new.'

'I think Prue's seen it. Prue's upset. She managed awfully well but she *is* upset.'

'Prue's explained Charmless Claude, has she?'

'Yes. Pretty ghastly specimen. She coped marvellously,' said Gideon proudly.

'Here she comes.'

When Prunella joined them she was white-faced but perfectly composed. 'We can go now,' she said and got into the car.

'Where's your bag?' asked Gideon.

'What? Oh, *damn;* said Prunella, 'I've left it up there. Oh, *what* a fool! Now I'll have to go back.'

'Shall I?'

'It's in her room. And she's been pretty beastly to you.'

'Perhaps I could better myself by a blithe change of manner.'

'*What* a good idea,' cried Prunella. 'Yes, do let's try it. Say she looks like Mrs Onassis.'

'She doesn't. Not remotely. Nobody less.'

'She thinks she does.'

'One can but try,' Gideon said. 'There's nothing to lose.'

'No more there is.'

He was gone for longer than they expected. When he returned with Prunella's bag he looked dubious. He started up the car and drove off.

'Any good?' Prunella ventured.

'She didn't actually throw anything at me.'

'Oh,' said Prunella. 'Like that, was it?'

She was very quiet on the homeward drive. Verity, in the back seat, saw her put her hand on Gideon's knee. He laid his own hand briefly over it and looked down at her. He knows exactly how to handle her, Verity thought. There's going to be no doubt about who's the boss.

When they arrived at Keys she asked them to come in for a drink but Gideon said his father would be expecting them.

'I'll see Godma V in,' said Prue as Gideon prepared to do so.

She followed Verity indoors and kissed and thanked her very prettily. Then she said, 'About Mummy. Has she had a stroke?'

'My dear child, why?'

'You noticed. I could see you did.'

'I don't think it looked like that. In any case they – the doctor – would have let you know if anything serious was wrong.'

'P'raps he didn't know. He may not be a good doctor. Sorry, I forgot he was a friend.'

'He's not. Not to matter.'

'I think I'll ring him up. I think there's something wrong. Honestly, don't you?'

'I did wonder.'

'And yet – '

'What?'

'In a funny sort of way she seemed – well – excited, pleased.'

'I thought so, too.'

'It's very odd,' said Prunella. 'Everything was odd. Out of focus, kind of. Anyway, I will ring up that doctor. I'll ring him tomorrow. Do you think that's a good idea?'

Verity said, 'Yes, darling. I do. It should put your mind at rest.'

But it was going to be a long time before Prunella's mind would be in that enviable condition.

VII

At five minutes past nine that evening, Sister Jackson, the resident nurse at Greengages, paused at Sybil Foster's door. She could hear the television. She tapped, opened and after a long pause approached the bed. Five minutes later she left the room and walked rather quickly down the passage.

At eleven o'clock Dr Schramm telephoned Prunella to tell her that her mother was dead.

CHAPTER 3

Alleyn

Basil looked distinguished, Verity had to admit, exactly as he ought to look under the circumstances, and he behaved as one would wish him to behave, with dignity and propriety, with deference and with precisely the right shade of controlled emotion.

'I had no reason whatever to suspect that, beyond symptoms of nervous exhaustion which had markedly improved, there was anything the matter,' he said. 'I feel I must add that I am astonished that she should have taken this step. She was in the best of spirits when I last saw her.'

'When was that, Dr Schramm?' asked the Coroner.

'On that same morning. About eight o'clock. I was going up to London and looked in on some of my patients before I left. I did not get back to Greengages until a few minutes after ten in the evening.'

'To find?'

'To find that she had died.'

'Can you describe the circumstances?'

'Yes. She had asked me to get a book for her in London – the autobiography of a Princess somebody – I forget the name. I went to her room to deliver it. Our bedrooms are large and comfortable and are often used as sitting-rooms. I have been told that she went up to hers late that afternoon. Long before her actual bedtime. She had dinner there, watching television. I knocked and there was no reply but I could hear the television and presumed that because of it she had not heard me. I went in. She was in bed and lying on her back. Her bedside table-lamp was on and I saw at once that a bottle of tablets was overturned and several – five, in fact – were scattered over the surface of the table. Her drinking glass was empty but had been used and was lying on the floor. Subsequently, a faint trace of alcohol – whisky – was found in the glass. A small whisky bottle, empty, was on the table. She sometimes used to take a modest night-cap. Her jug of water was almost empty. I examined her and found that she was dead. It was then twenty minutes past ten.'

'Can you give a time for when death occurred?'

'Not exactly, no. Not less than an hour before I found her.'

'What steps did you take?'

'I made absolutely certain there was no possibility of recovery. I then called up our resident nurse. We employed a stomach pump. The results were subsequently analysed and a quantity of barbiturates was found.' He hesitated and then said, 'I would like, sir, if this is an appropriate moment, to add a word about Greengages and its general character and management.'

'By all means, Dr Schramm.'

'Thank you. Greengages is not a hospital. It is a hotel with a resident medical practitioner. Many, indeed most, of our guests are not ill. Some are tired and in need of a change and rest. Some come to us simply for a quiet holiday. Some for a weight-reducing course. Some are convalescents preparing to return to normal life. A number of them are elderly people who are reassured by the presence of a qualified practitioner and a registered nurse. Mrs Foster had been in the habit of coming from time to time. She was a nervy subject and a chronic worrier. I must say at once that I had not prescribed the barbiturate tablets she had taken and have no idea how she had obtained them. When she first came I did, on request, prescribe phenobarbiturates at night to help her sleep but after her first week they were discontinued as she had no further need of them. I apologize for the digression but I felt it was perhaps indicated.'

'Quite. Quite. Quite,' chattered the complacent Coroner.

'Well then, to continue. When we had done what had to be done, I got in touch with another doctor. The local practitioners were all engaged or out but finally I reached Dr Field-Innis of Upper Quintern. He very kindly drove over and together we made a further examination.'

'Finding?'

'Finding that she had died of an overdose. There was no doubt of it at all. We found three half-dissolved tablets at the back of the mouth and one on the tongue. She must have taken the tablets, four or five at a time and lost consciousness before she could swallow the last ones.'

'Dr Field-Innis is present, is he not?'

'He is,' Basil said, with a little bow in the right direction. Dr Field-Innis bobbed up and down in his seat.

'Thank you very much, Dr Schramm,' said the Coroner with evident respect.

Dr Field-Innis was called.

Verity watched him push his glasses up his nose and tip back his head to adjust his vision just as he always did after he had listened to one's chest. He was nice. Not in the least dynamic or lordly, but nice. And conscientious. And, Verity thought, at the moment very clearly ill-at-ease.

He confirmed everything that Basil Schramm had deposed as to the state of the room and the body and the conclusion they had drawn and added that he himself had been surprised and shocked by the tragedy.

'Was the deceased a patient of yours, Dr Field-Innis?'

'She consulted me about four months ago.'

'On what score?'

'She felt unwell and was nervy. She complained of sleeplessness and general anxiety. I prescibed a mild barbiturate. *Not* the propri-etary tranquillizer she was found to have taken that evening, by the way.' He hesitated for a moment. 'I suggested that she should have a general overhaul,' he said.

'Had you any reason to suspect there was something serious the matter?'

There was a longer pause. Dr Field-Innis looked for a moment at Prunella. She sat between Gideon and Verity who thought, irrele-vantly, that like all blondes, especially when they were as pretty as Prunella, mourning greatly became her.

'That,' said Dr Field-Innis, 'is not an easy question to answer. There were, I thought, certain possible indications, very slight indeed, that should be followed up.'

'What were they?'

'A gross tremor in the hands. That does not necessarily imply a conspicuous tremor. And – this is difficult to define – a certain appearance in the face. I must emphasize that this was slight and possibly of no moment but I had seen 'something of the sort before and felt it should not be disregarded.'

'What might these symptoms indicate, Dr Field-Innis? A stroke?' hazarded the Coroner. 'Not necessarily.'

'Anything else?'

'I say this with every possible reservation. But yes. Just possibly – Parkinson's disease.'

Prunella gave a strange little sound, half cry, half sigh. Gideon took her hand.

The Coroner asked, 'And did the deceased, in fact, follow your advice?'

'No. She said she would think it over. She did not consult me again.'

'Had she any idea you suspected – ?'

'Certainly not,' Dr Field-Innis said loudly. 'I gave no indication whatever. It would have been most improper to do so.'

'Have you discussed the matter with Dr Schramm?'

'It has been mentioned, yes.'

'Had Dr Schramm remarked these symptoms?' The Coroner turned politely to Basil Schramm. 'Perhaps,' he said, 'we may ask?'

He stood up. 'I had noticed the tremor,' he said. 'On her case-history and on what she had told me I attributed this to the general nervous condition.'

'Quite,' said the Coroner. 'So, gentlemen, we may take it, may we not, that fear of this tragic disease cannot have been a motive for suicide? We may rule that out?'

'Certainly,' they said together and together they sat down. Tweedledum and Tweedledee, Verity thought.

The resident nurse was now called, Sister Jackson, an opulent lady of good looks, a highish colour and an air of latent sexiness, damped down, Verity thought, to suit the occasion. She confirmed the doctors' evidence and said rather snootily that of course if Greengages had been a hospital there would have been no question of Mrs Foster having a private supply of any medicaments.

And now Prunella was called. It was a clear day outside and a ray of sunlight slanted through a window in the parish hall. As if on cue from some zealous stage-director it found Prunella's white-gold head and made a saint of her.

'How lovely she is,' Gideon said quite audibly. Verity thought he might have been sizing up one of his father's distinguished possessions. 'And how obliging of the sun,' he added and gave her a friendly smile. This young man, she thought, takes a bit of learning.

The Coroner was considerate with Prunella. She was asked about the afternoon visit to Greengages. Had there been anything unusual in her mother's behaviour? The Coroner was sorry to trouble her but would she mind raising her voice, the acoustics of the hall no doubt were at fault. Verity heard Gideon chuckle.

Prunella gulped and made a determined attempt to become fully vocal. 'Not really,' she said. 'Not unusual. My mother was rather easily fussed and – well – you know. As Dr Schramm said, she worried.'

'About anything in particular, Miss Foster?'

'Well – about me, actually.'

'I beg your pardon?'

'About *me*,' Prunella shrilled and flinched at the sound of her own voice. 'Sorry,' she said.

'About you?'

'Yes. I'd just got engaged and she fussed about that, sort of. But it was all right. Routine, really.'

'And you saw nothing particularly unusual?'

'Yes. I mean,' said Prunella, frowning distressfully and looking across at Dr Field-Innis, 'I did think I saw something – different – about her.'

'In what way?'

'Well, she was – her hands – like Dr Field-Innis said were trembly. And her speech I thought – you know – kind of dragged. And there was – or I thought there was – something about her face. As if it had kind of, you know, blanked out or sort of smoothed over, sort of – well – slowed up. I can't describe it. I wasn't even sure it was there.'

'But it troubled you?'

'Yes. Sort of,' whispered Prunella.

She described how she and Gideon took her mother back to the house and how she went up with her to her room.

'She said she thought she'd have a rest and go to bed early and have dinner brought up to her. There was something she wanted to

see on television. I helped her undress. She asked me not to wait. So
I turned the box on and left her. She truly seemed all right, apart
from being tired and upset about – about me and my engagement.'
Prunella's voice wavered into inaudibility, and her eyes filled with
tears.

'Miss Foster,' said the Coroner, 'just one more question. Was
there a bottle of tablets on her bedside table?'

'Yes, there was,' Prunella said quickly. 'She asked me to take it
out of her beauty box, you know, a kind of face box. It was on the
table. She said they were sleeping-pills she'd got from a chemist ages
ago and she thought if she couldn't go to sleep after her dinner she'd
take one. I found them for her and put them out. And there was a
lamp on the table, a book and an enormous box of *petits-fours au
massepain*. She gets – she used to get them from that shop the
"Marquise de Sévigné" – in Paris. I ate some before I left.'

Prunella knuckled her eyes like a small girl and then hunted for
her handkerchief. The Coroner said they would not trouble her any
more and she returned to Gideon and Verity.

Verity heard herself called and found she was nervous. She was
taken over the earlier ground and confirmed all that Prunella had
said. Nothing she was asked led to any mention of Bruce Gardener's
and Claude Carter's arrival at Greengages and as both of them had
been fended off from meeting Sybil she did not think it incumbent
on her to say anything about them. She saw that Bruce was in the
hall, looking stiff and solemn as if the inquest was a funeral. He
wore his Harris tweed suit and a black tie. Poor Syb would have
liked that. She would have probably said there was 'good blood
there' and you could tell by the way he wore his clothes. Meaning
blue blood. And suddenly and irrelevantly there came over Verity
the realization that she could never believe ridiculous old Syb had
killed herself.

She had found Dr Field-Innis's remarks about Sybil's appearance
deeply disturbing, not because she thought they bore the remotest
relation to her death but because she herself had for so long paid so
little attention to Sybil's ailments. Suppose, all the time, there had
been ominous signs? Suppose she had felt as ill as she said she did?
Was it a case of 'wolf, wolf'? Verity was miserable.

She did not pay much attention when Gideon was called and said that he had returned briefly to Mrs Foster's room to collect Prunella's bag and that she had seemed to be quite herself.

The proceedings now came to a close. The Coroner made a short speech saying in effect that the jury might perhaps consider it was most unfortunate that nothing had emerged to show why the deceased had been moved to take this tragic and apparently motiveless step, so out of character according to all that her nearest and dearest felt about her. Nevertheless, in face of what they had heard they might well feel that the circumstances all pointed in one direction. However – at this point Verity's attention was distracted by the sight of Claude Carter, whom she had not noticed before. He was sitting at the end of a bench against the wall, wearing a superfluous raincoat with the collar turned up and feasting quietly upon his fingernails.

' – and so,' the Coroner was saying, 'you may think that in view of the apparent absence of motive and notwithstanding the entirely appropriate steps taken by Dr Schramm, an autopsy should be carried out. If you so decide I shall, of course, adjourn the inquest *sine die.'*

The jury, after a short withdrawal, brought in a verdict along these lines and the inquest was accordingly adjourned until after the autopsy.

The small assembly emptied out into the summery quiet of the little village.

As she left the hall Verity found herself face to face with Young Mr Rattisbon. Young Mr Rattisbon was about sixty-five years of age and was the son of Old Mr Rattisbon who was ninety-two. They were London solicitors of eminent respectability and they had acted for Verity's family and for Sybil's unto the third and fourth generation. His father and Verity's were old friends. As the years passed, the son grew more and more like the father, even to adopting his eccentricities. They both behaved as if they were character-actors playing themselves in some dated comedy. Both had an extraordinary mannerism – when about to pronounce upon some choice point of law they exposed the tips of their tongues and vibrated them as if they had taken sips of scalding tea. They prefaced many of their remarks with a slight whinny.

When Mr Rattisbon saw Verity he raised his out-of-date city hat very high and said, 'Good morning' three times and added, 'Very sad, yes,' as if she had enquired whether it was or was not so. She asked him if he was returning to London but he said no, he would find himself something to eat in the village and then go up to Quintern Place if Prunella Foster found it convenient to see him.

Verity rapidly surveyed her larder and then said, 'You can't lunch in the village. There's only the Passcoigne Arms and it's awful. Come and have an omelette and cheese and a glass of reasonable hock with me.'

He gave quite a performance of deprecating whinnies but was clearly delighted. He wanted, he said, to have a word with the Coroner and would drive up to Keys when it was over.

Verity, given this start, was able to make her unpretentious preparations. She laid her table, took some cold sorrel soup with cream from the refrigerator, fetched herbs from the orchard, broke eggs into a basin and put butter in her omelette pan. Then she paid a visit to her cellar and chose one of the few remaining bottles of her father's sherry and one of the more than respectable hock.

When Mr Rattisbon arrived she settled him in the drawing-room, joined him in a glass of sherry and left him with the bottle at his elbow while she went off to make the omelette.

They lunched successfully, finishing off with ripe Stilton and biscuits. Mr Rattisbon had two and a half glasses of hock to Verity's one. His face, normally the colour of one of his own parchments, became quite pink.

They withdrew into the garden and sat in weather-worn deckchairs under the lime trees.

'How very pleasant, my dear Verity,' said Mr Rattisbon. 'Upon my word, how quite delightful! I suppose, alas, I must keep my eye upon the time. And, if I may, I shall telephone Miss Prunella. I mustn't overstay my welcome.'

'Oh, fiddle, Ratsy!' said Verity, who had called him by this Kenneth Grahameish nickname for some forty years. 'What did you think about the inquest?'

The professional change came over him. He joined his fingertips, rattled his tongue and made his noise.

'M'nah,' he said. 'My dear Verity. While you were preparing our delicious luncheon I thought a great deal about the inquest and I may say that the more I thought the less I liked it. I will not disguise from you, I am uneasy.'

'So am I. What exactly is *your* worry? Don't go all professionally rectitudinal like a diagram. Confide. Do, Ratsy, I'm the soul of discretion. My lips shall be sealed with red-tape, I promise.'

'My dear girl, I don't doubt it. I had, in any case, decided to ask you. You were, were you not, a close friend of Mrs Foster?'

'A very *old* friend. I think perhaps the closeness was more on her side than mine, if that makes sense.'

'She confided in you?'

'She'd confide in the Town Crier if she felt the need, but yes, she did quite a lot.'

'Do you know if she has recently made a Will?'

'Oh,' said Verity, 'is that your trouble?'

'Part of it, at least. I must tell you that she did in fact execute a Will four years ago. I have reason to believe that she may have made a later one but have no positive knowledge of such being the case. She – yah – she wrote to me three weeks ago advising me of the terms of a new Will she wished me to prepare. I was – frankly appalled. I replied, as I hoped, temperately, asking her to take thought. *She* replied at once that I need concern myself no further in the matter with additions of a – of an intemperate – I would go so far as to say a hostile, character. So much so that I concluded that I had been given the – not to put too fine a point upon it – sack.'

'Preposterous!' cried Verity. 'She couldn't!'

'As it turned out she didn't. On my writing a formal letter asking if she wished the return of the Passcoigne documents which we hold, and, I may add, have held since the barony was created, she merely replied by telegram.'

'What did it say?'

'It said "Don't be silly".'

'How like Syb!'

'Upon which,' said Mr Rattisbon, throwing himself back in his chair, 'I concluded that there was to be no severance of the connection. That is the last communication I had from her. I know not if she

made a new Will. But the fact that I – yah – jibbed, might have led
her to act on her own initiative. Provide herself,' said Mr Rattisbon,
lowering his voice as one who speaks of blasphemy, 'with a Form.
From some stationer. Alas.'

'Since she was in cool storage at Greengages, she'd have had to
ask somebody to get the form for her. She didn't ask me.'

'I think I hear your telephone, my dear,' Mr Rattisbon said.

It was Prunella. 'Godma V,' she said with unusual clarity, 'I saw
you talking to that fantastic old Mr Rattisbon. Do you happen to
know where he was going?'

'He's here. He's thinking of visiting you.'

'Oh, good. Because I suppose he ought to know. Because, actually, I've found something he ought to see.'

'What have you found, darling?'

'I'm afraid,' Prunella's voice escalated to a plaintive squeak, 'it's a
Will.'

When Mr Rattisbon had taken his perturbed leave and departed,
bolt upright, at the wheel of his car, Prunella rang again to say she
felt that before he arrived she must tell her godmother more about
her find.

'I can't get hold of Gideon,' she said, 'so I thought I'd tell you.
Sorry, darling, but you know what I mean.'

'Of course I do.'

'Sweet of you. Well. It was in Mummy's desk in the boudoir,
top-drawer. In a stuck-up envelope with "Will" on it. It was signed
and witnessed ten days ago. At Greengages, of course, and it's on a
printed form thing.'

'How did it get to Quintern?'

'Mrs Jim says Mummy asked Bruce Gardener to take it and put it
in the desk. He gave it to Mrs Jim and she put it in the desk. Godma
V, it's a stinker.'

'Oh dear.'

'It's – you'll never believe this – I can't myself. It starts off by
saying she leaves half her estate to me. You do know, don't you, that
darling Mummy was a Rich Bitch. Sorry, that's a fun-phrase. But
true.'

'I did suppose she was.'

'I mean *really* rich. Rolling.'

'Yes.'

'Partly on account of Grandpapa Passcoigne and partly because Daddy was a wizard with the lolly. Where was I?'

'Half the estate to you,' Verity prompted.

'Yes. That's over and above what Daddy entailed on me if that's what it's called. And Quintern's entailed on me, too, of course.'

'Nothing the matter with *that*, is there?'

'Wait for it. You'll never, never believe this – half to me *only* if I marry awful Swingles – John Swingletree. I wouldn't have thought it possible. Not even with Mummy, I wouldn't. It doesn't *matter*, of course, I mean, I've got more than is good for me with the entailment. Of course it's a lot less on account of inflation and all that but I've been thinking, actually, that I ought to give it away when I marry. Gideon doesn't agree.'

'You astonish me.'

'But he wouldn't stop me. Anyway, he's rather more than OK for lolly.' Prunella's voice trembled. 'But Godma V,' she said, 'how she *could*! How she could think it'd make me do it! Marry Swingles and cut Gideon just for the cash. It's repulsive.'

'I wouldn't have believed it of her. Does Swingletree *want* you to marry him, by the way?'

'Oh yes,' said Prunella impatiently. 'Never stops asking, the poor sap.'

'It must have been when she was in a temper,' said Verity. 'She'd have torn it up when she came round.'

'But she didn't, did she? And she'd had plenty of time to come round. And you haven't heard anything yet. Who do you suppose she's left the rest to? – well, all but £25,000? She's left £25,000 to Bruce Gardener, as well as a super little house in the village that is part of the estate and provision for him to be kept on as long as he likes at Quintern. But the rest – including the half if I don't marry Swingles – to whom do you suppose?'

A wave of nausea came over Verity. She sat down by her telephone and saw with detachment that the receiver shook in her hand.

'Are you there?' Prunella was saying. 'Hullo! Godma V?'

'I'm here.'

'I give you three guesses. You'll never get it. Do you give up?'

'Yes.'

'Your heart-throb, darling. Dr Basil Schramm.'

A long pause followed. Verity tried to speak but her mouth was dry.

'Godma, are you there? Is something the matter with your telephone? Did you hear me?'

'Yes, I heard. I – I simply don't know what to say.'

'Isn't it awful?'

'It's appalling.'

'I told you she was crackers about him, didn't I?'

'Yes, yes, you did and I saw it for myself. But to do this – !'

'I know. When I don't marry that ass Swingles, Schramm'll get the lot.'

'Good God!' said Verity.

'Well, won't he? *I* don't know. Don't ask me. Perhaps it'll turn out to be not proper. The Will, I mean.'

'Ratsy will pounce on that – Mr Rattisbon – if it is so. Is it witnessed?'

'It seems to be. By G. M. Johnson and Marleena Biggs. Housemaids at Greengages I should think, wouldn't you?'

'I dare say.'

'Well, I thought I'd just tell you.'

'Yes. Thank you.'

'I'll let you know what Mr Rats thinks.'

'Thanks.'

'Goodbye then, Godma darling.'

'Goodbye, darling. I'm sorry. Especially,' Verity managed, 'about the Swingletree bit.'

'I know. Bruce is chicken feed, compared,' said Prunella.

'And what a name!' she added. 'Lady Swingletree! I ask you!' and hung up.

It was exactly a week after this conversation and on just such another halcyon afternoon that Verity answered her front doorbell to find a very tall man standing in the porch.

He took off his hat. 'Miss Preston?' he said. 'I'm sorry to bother you. I'm a police officer. My name is Alleyn.'

II

Afterwards, when he had gone away, Verity thought it strange that her first reaction had not been one of alarm. At the moment of encounter she had simply been struck by Alleyn himself, by his voice, his thin face and – there was only one word she could find – his distinction. There was a brief feeling of incredulity and then the thought that he might be on the track of Charmless Claude. He sat there in her drawing-room with his knees crossed, his thin hands clasped together and his eyes, which were bright, directed upon her. It came as a shock when he said, 'It's about the late Mrs Foster that I hoped to have a word with you.'

Verity heard herself say, 'Is there something wrong?'

'It's more a matter of making sure there isn't,' he said. 'This is a routine visit and I know that's what we're always supposed to say.'

'Is it because something's turned up at the – examination – the – I can't remember the proper word.'

'Autopsy?'

'Yes. Stupid of me.'

'You might say it's arisen out of that, yes. Things have turned out a bit more complicated than was expected.'

After a pause, Verity said, 'I'm sure one's not meant to ask questions, is one?'

'Well,' he said, and smiled at her, 'I can always evade answering but the form is supposed to be for me to ask.'

'I'm sorry.'

'Not a bit. You shall ask me anything you like as the need arises. In the meantime, shall I go ahead?'

'Please.'

'My first one is about Mrs Foster's room.'

'At Greengages?'

'Yes.'

'I was never in it.'

'Do you know if she habitually used a sort of glass sleeve contraption filled with scented oil that fitted over a lamp bulb?'

' "Oasis"? Yes, she used it in the drawing-room at Quintern and sometimes, I think, in her bedroom. She adored what she called a really groovy smell.'

' "Oasis", if that's what it was, is all of that. They tell me the memory lingers on in the window curtains. Did she usually have a nightcap, do you know? Whisky?'

'I think she did, occasionally, but she wasn't much of a drinker. Far from it.'

'Miss Preston, I've seen the notes of your evidence at the inquest but if you don't mind I'd like to go back to the talk you had with Mrs Foster on the lawn that afternoon. It's simply to find out if by any chance, and on consideration, hindsight if you like, something was said that now seems to suggest she contemplated suicide.'

'Nothing. I've thought and thought. Nothing.' And as she said this Verity realized that with all her heart she wished there had been something and at the same time told herself how appalling it was that she could desire it. I shall never get myself sorted out over this, she thought and realized that Alleyn was speaking to her.

'If you could just run over the things you talked about. Never mind if they seem irrelevant or trivial.'

'Well, she gossiped about the hotel. She talked a lot about – the doctor – and the wonders of his cure and about the nurse – Sister something – who she said resented her being a favourite. But most of all we talked about Prunella – her daughter's – engagement.'

'Didn't she fancy the young man?'

'Well – she *was* upset,' Verity said. 'But – well, she was often upset. I suppose it would be fair to say she was inclined to get into tizzies at the drop of a hat.'

'A fuss-pot?'

'Yes.'

'Spoilt, would you say?' he asked, surprisingly.

'Rather indulged, perhaps.'

'Keen on the chaps?'

He put this to her so quaintly that Verity was startled into saying, 'You *are* sharp!'

'A happy guess, I promise you,' said Alleyn.

'You must have heard about the Will,' she exclaimed.

'Who's being sharp now?'

'I don't know,' Verity said crossly, 'why I'm laughing.'

'When, really, you're very worried, aren't you? Why?'

'I don't *know*. Not really. It's all so muddling,' she broke out. 'And I *hate* being muddled.'

She stared helplessly at Alleyn. He nodded and gave a small affirmative sound.

'You see,' Verity began again, 'when you asked if she said anything that suggested suicide I said "nothing" didn't I? And if you'd known Syb as well as I did, there *was* nothing. But when you ask if she's ever suggested anything of the sort – well, yes. If you count her being in a bit of a stink over some dust-up and throwing a temperament and saying life wasn't worth living and she might as well end it all. But that was just histrionics. I often thought Syb's true métier was the theatre.'

'Well,' said Alleyn, 'you ought to know.'

'Have you seen Prunella? Her daughter?' Verity asked.

'Not yet. I've read her evidence. I'm on my way there. Is she at home, do you know?'

'She has been, lately. She goes up to London quite a lot.'

'Who'll be there if she's out?'

'Mrs Jim Jobbin. General factotum. It's her morning at Quintern.'

'Anyone else?'

Damn! thought Verity, here we go. She said, 'I haven't been in touch. Oh, it's the gardener's day up there.'

'Ah yes. The gardener.'

'Then you *do* know about the Will?'

'Mr Rattisbon told me about it. He's an old acquaintance of mine. May we go back to the afternoon in question? Did you discuss Miss Foster's engagement with her mother?'

'Yes. I tried to reconcile her to the idea.'

'Any success?'

'Not much. But she did agree to see them. Is it all right to ask – did they find – did the pathologist find – any signs of disease?'

'He thinks on Dr Field-Innis's report that she might have had Parkinson's disease.'

'If she had known that,' Verity said, 'it might have made a difference. If she was told – but Dr Field-Innis didn't tell her.'

'And Dr Schramm, apparently, didn't spot it.'

Sooner or later it had to come. They'd arrived at his name.

'Have you met Dr Schramm?' Alleyn asked casually.

'Yes.'

'Know him well?'

'No. I used to know him many years ago but we had entirely lost touch.'

'Have you seen him lately?'

'I've only met him once at a dinner-party some months ago. At Mardling – Mardling Manor, belonging to Mr Nikolas Markos. It's his son who's engaged to Prunella.'

'The millionaire Markos would that be?'

'Not that I know. He certainly seems to be extremely affluent.'

'The millionaire who buys pictures,' said Alleyn, 'if that's any guide.'

'This one does that. He'd bought a Troy.'

'That's the man,' said Alleyn. 'She called it "Several Pleasures".'

'But – how did you – ? Oh, I see,' said Verity, 'you've been to Mardling.'

'No. The painter is my wife.'

'Curiouser,' said Verity, after a long pause, 'and curiouser.'

'Do you find it so? I don't quite see why.'

'I should have said how lovely. To be married to Troy.'

'Well, we like it,' said Troy's husband. 'Could I get back to the matter in hand, do you think?'

'Of course. Please,' said Verity, with a jolt of vertigo under her diaphragm.

'Where were we?'

'You asked me if I'd met Basil Smythe.'

'*Smythe?*'

'I should have said Schramm,' Verity amended quickly. 'I believe Schramm was his mother's maiden name. I think she wanted him to take it. He said something to that effect.'

'When would that have happened, would you suppose?'

'Some time after I knew him, which was in 1951, I think,' Verity added and hoped it sounded casual.

'How long had Mrs Foster known him, do you imagine?'

'Not – very long. She met him first at that same dinner-party. But,' said Verity quickly, 'she'd been in the habit of going to Greengages for several years.'

'Whereas he only took over the practice last April,' he said casually. 'Do you like him? Nice sort of chap?'

'As I said, I've only met him that once.'

'But you knew him before?'

'It was – so very long ago.'

'I don't think you liked him very much,' he murmured as if to himself. 'Or perhaps – but it doesn't matter.'

'Mr Alleyn,' Verity said loudly and, to her chagrin, in an unsteady voice. 'I know what was in the Will.'

'Yes, I thought you must.'

'And perhaps I'd better just say it: the Will might have happened at any time in the past if Sybil had been thoroughly upset. On the rebound from a row, she could have left anything to anyone who was in favour at the time.'

'But did she to your knowledge ever do this in the past?'

'Perhaps she never had the same provocation in the past.'

'Or was not sufficiently attracted?'

'Oh,' said Verity, 'she took fancies. Look at this whacking great legacy to Bruce.'

'Bruce? Oh yes. The gardener. She thought a lot of him, I suppose? A faithful and tried old retainer? Was that it?'

'He'd been with her about six months and he's middle-aged and rather like a resurrection from the more dubious pages of J. M. Barrie, but Syb thought him the answer to her prayers.'

'As far as the garden was concerned?'

'Yes. He does my garden too.'

'It's enchanting. Do you dote on him as well?'

'No. But I must say I like him better than I did. He took trouble over Syb. He visited her once a week with flowers and I don't think he was sucking up. I just think he puts on a bit of an act like a guide doing his sob-stuff over Mary Queen of Scots in Edinburgh Castle.'

'I've never heard of a guide doing sob-stuff in Edinburgh Castle.'

'They drool. When they're not having a go at William and Mary, they get closer and closer to you and the tears seem to come into their eyes and they drool about Mary Queen of Scots. I may have been unlucky of course. Bruce is positively taciturn in comparison. He overdoes the nature-lover bit but only perhaps because his employers encourage it. He *is*, in fact, a dedicated gardener.'

'And he visited Mrs Foster at Greengages?'

'He was there that afternoon.'

'While you were there?'

Verity explained how Bruce and she had encountered in the grounds and how she'd told him Sybil wouldn't be able to see him then and how Prunella had suggested later on that he left his lilies at the desk.

'So he did just that?'

'I think so. I suppose they both went back by the next bus.'

'*Both?*'

'I'd forgotten Charmless Claude.'

'What?'

'He's Syb's ghastly stepson.'

Verity explained Claude but avoided any reference to his more dubious activities, merely presenting him as a spineless drifter. She kept telling herself she ought to be on her guard with this atypical policeman in whose company she felt so inappropriately conversational. At the drop of a hat, she thought, she'd find herself actually talking about that episode of the past that she had never confided to anyone and which still persisted so rawly in her memory.

She pulled herself together. He had asked her if Claude was the son of Sybil's second husband.

'No, of her first husband, Maurice Carter. She married him when she was seventeen. He was a very young widower. His first wife died in childbirth – leaving Claude who was brought up by his grandparents. They didn't like him very much, I'm afraid. Perhaps he might have turned out better if they had, but there it is. And then Maurice married Syb who was in the WRNS. She was on duty somewhere in Scotland when he got an unexpected leave. He came down here to Quintern – Quintern Place is *her* house, you know – and tried to ring her up but couldn't get through so he wrote a note. While he was doing this he was recalled urgently to London. The troop-train he caught was bombed and he was killed. She found the note afterwards. That's a sad story, isn't it?'

'Yes. Was this stepson, Claude, provided for?'

'Very well provided for, really. His father wasn't an enormously rich man but he left a trust fund that paid for Claude's upbringing. It still would be a reasonable standby if he didn't contrive to lose it as fast as it comes in. Of course,' Verity said, more to herself than to Alleyn, 'it'd have been different if the stamp had turned up.'

'Did you say "stamp"?'

'The Black Alexander. Maurice Carter inherited it. It was a pre-revolution Russian stamp that was withdrawn on the day it was issued because of a rather horrid little black flaw that looked like a bullet-hole in the Czar's forehead. Apparently no other specimen was known to be in existence and so this one was worth some absolutely fabulous amount of money. Maurice's own collection was medium-valuable and it went to Claude, who sold it, but the Black Alexander couldn't be found. He was known to have taken it out of his bank the day before he died. They searched and searched but with no luck and it's generally thought he must have had it on him when he was killed. It was a direct hit. It was bad luck for Claude about the stamp.'

'Where is Claude now?'

Verity said uncomfortably that he had been staying at Quintern but she didn't know if he was still there.

'I see. Tell me, when did Mrs Foster re-marry?'

'In – when was it? In 1958. A large expensive stockbroker who adored her. He had a heart condition and died of it in 1964. You know,' Verity said suddenly, 'when one tells the whole story, bit by bit, it turns almost into a classic tragedy, and yet, somehow one can't see poor old Syb as a tragic figure. Except when one remembers the *look*.'

'The look that was spoken of at the inquest?'

'Yes. It would have been quite frightful if she, of all people, had suffered that disease.'

After a longish pause, Verity said, 'When will the inquest be reopened?'

'Quite soon. Probably early next week. I don't think you will be called again. You've been very helpful.'

'In what way? No, don't tell me,' said Verity. 'I – I don't think I want to know. I don't think I want to be helpful.'

'Nobody loves a policeman,' he said cheerfully and stood up. So did Verity. She was a tall woman but he towered over her.

He said, 'I think this business has upset you more than you realize. Will you mind if I give you what must sound like a professionally motivated word of advice? If it turns out that you're acquainted with some episode or some piece of behaviour, perhaps quite a long way back in time, that might throw a little light on – say, on the character of one or other of the people we have discussed – don't withhold it. You never know. By doing so you might be doing a disservice to a friend.'

'We're back to the Will again. Aren't we?'

'Oh, that? Yes. In a sense we are.'

'You think she may have been influenced? Or that in some way it might be a cheat? Is that it?'

'The possibility must be looked at when the terms of a Will are extravagant and totally unexpected and the Will itself is made so short a time before the death of the testator.'

'But that's not all? Is it? You're not here just because Syb made a silly Will. You're here because she died. You think it wasn't suicide. Don't you?'

He waited so long and looked so kindly at her that she was answered before he spoke.

'I'm afraid that's it,' he said at last. 'I'm sorry.'

Again he waited, expecting, perhaps, that she might ask more questions or break down but she contrived, as she put it to herself, to keep up appearances. She supposed she must have gone white because she found he had put her back in her chair. He went away and returned with a glass of water.

'I found your kitchen,' he said. 'Would you like brandy with this?'

'No – why? There's nothing the matter with me,' said Verity and tried to steady her hand. She took a hurried gulp of water.

'Dizzy spell,' she improvised. '"Age with his stealing steps" and all that.'

'I don't think he can be said to have "clawed you in his clutch".'

'Thank you.'

'Anyway, I shan't bother you any longer. Unless there's something I can do?'

'I'm perfectly all right. Thank you very much, though.'

'Sure? I'll be off then. Goodbye.'

Through the drawing-room window she watched him go striding down the drive and heard a car start up in the lane.

Time, of course, does heal as people say in letters of condolence, she thought. But they don't mention the scars and twinges that crop up when the old wound gets an unexpected jolt. And this is a bad jolt, thought Verity. This is a snorter.

And Alleyn, being driven by Inspector Fox to Quintern Place, said, 'That's a nice intelligent creature, Br'er Fox. She's got character and guts but she couldn't help herself going white when I talked about Schramm. She was much concerned to establish that they hadn't met for many years and then only once. Why? An old affair? On the whole, I can't wait to meet Dr Schramm.'

III

But first they must visit Quintern Place. It came into view, unmistakably as soon as they had passed through the village – a Georgian house half way up a hill, set in front of a stand of oaks and overlooking a rose-garden, lawns, a ha-ha and a sloping field and woodlands. Facing this restrained and lovely house, and separated from it by a shallow declivity, was a monstrous Victorian pile, a plethora of towers and pepper-pots approached by a long avenue which opened, by way of grandiloquent gates, off the lane leading to Quintern. 'That's Mardling Manor, that is,' said Alleyn, 'the residence of Mr Nikolas Markos who had the good sense and taste to buy Troy's "Several Pleasures".'

'I wouldn't have thought the house was quite his style,' said Mr Fox.

'And you'd have been dead right. I can't imagine what possessed him to buy such a monumental piece of complacency unless it was to tease himself with an uninterrupted view of a perfect house,' said Alleyn and little knew how close to the mark he had gone.

'Did you pay a call on the local Super?' he asked.

'Yes. He's looking forward to meeting you. I got a bit of info out of him,' said Mr Fox, 'which came in handy, seeing I've only just been brought in on the case. It seems they're interested in the deceased lady's stepson, a Mr Carter. He's a bit of a ne'er-do-well. Worked his way home from Australia in the *Poseidon* as a ship's steward. He's done porridge for attempted blackmail and he's sussy for bringing the hard stuff ashore but they haven't got enough for a catch. He's staying up at Quintern Place.'

'So Miss Preston thought. And here we go.'

The approach was through a grove of rhododendrons from which they came out rather unexpectedly on a platform in front of the house.

Looking up at the façade, Alleyn caught a fractional impression of someone withdrawing from a window at the far end of the first floor. Otherwise there was no sign of life.

The door was opened by a compact little person in an apron. She looked quickly at the car and its driver and then, doubtfully, at Alleyn who took off his hat.

'You must be Mrs Jim Jobbin,' he said.

Mrs Jim looked hard at him. 'That's correct,' she said.

'Do you think Miss Foster could give me a moment if she's in?'

'She's not.'

'Oh.'

Mrs Jim gave a quick look across the little valley to where Mardling Manor shamelessly exhibited itself. 'She's out,' she said.

'I'm sorry about that. Would you mind if I came in and had a word with you ? I'm a police officer but there's no need to let that bother you. It's only to tidy up some details about the inquest on Mrs Foster.'

He had the impression that Mrs Jim listened for something to happen inside the house and, not hearing it, waited for him to speak and not hearing that either, was relieved. She gave him another pretty hard look and then stood away from the door.

'I'll just ask my colleague to wait if I may?' Alleyn said and returned to the car.

'A certain amount of caginess appears,' he murmured. 'If anything emerges and looks like melting away ask it if it's Mr Carter and keep it here. Same goes for the gardener.' Aloud he said, 'I won't be long,' and returned to the house.

Mrs Jim stood aside for him and he went into a large and beautifully proportioned hall. It was panelled in parchment-coloured linenfold oak with a painted ceiling and elegant stairway. 'What a lovely house,' Alleyn said. 'Do you look after it?'

'I help out,' said Mrs Jim guardedly.

'Miss Preston told me about you. Mrs Foster's death must have been a shock after knowing her for so long.'

'It seemed a pity,' Mrs Jim conceded economically.

'Did you expect anything of the kind?'

'I didn't expect anything. I never thought she'd make away with herself if that's what's meant. She wasn't the sort.'

'Everybody seems to think that,' Alleyn agreed.

The hall went right through the house and at the far end looked across rose-gardens to the misty Weald of Kent. He moved to the windows and was in time to see a head and shoulders bob up and down behind a box hedge. The owner seemed to be crouched and running.

'You've got somebody behaving rather oddly in your garden,' said Alleyn. 'Come and look.'

She moved behind him.

'He's doubled up,' Alleyn said, 'behind that tallish hedge. Could he be chasing some animal?'

'I don't know, I'm sure.'

'Who could it be?'

'The gardener's working here today.'

'Has he got long fair hair?'

'No,' she said quickly, and passed her hand across her mouth. 'Would the gentleman in the garden, by any chance, be Mr Claude Carter?'

'It might.'

'Perhaps he's chasing butterflies.'

'He might be doing anything,' said Mrs Jim woodenly.

Alleyn, standing back from the window and still watching the hedge, said: 'There's only one point I need bother you with, Mrs Jobbin. It's about the envelope that I believe you put in Mrs Foster's desk after her death.'

'She give it to the gardener about a week before she died and said he was to put it there. He give it to me and asked me to. Which I did.'

'And you told Miss Foster it was there?'

'Correct. I remembered it after the inquest.'

'Do you know what was in it?'

'It was none of my business, was it, sir?' said Mrs Jim, settling for the courtesy title. 'It had "Will" written on the outside and Miss Prue said it was a stinker. She give it to the lawyer.'

'Was it sealed, do you remember?'

'It was gummed up. Sort of.'

'Sort of, Mrs Jim?'

'Not what you'd call a proper job. More of a careless lick. She was like that with her letters. She'd think of something she'd meant to say and open them up and then stick them down with what was left of the gum. She was great on afterthoughts.'

'Would you mind letting me see the desk?'

Mrs Jim's face reddened and she stuck out her lower lip.

'Mrs Jobbin,' Alleyn said, 'don't think we're here for any other purpose than to try and sort matters out in order that there shall be no injustice done to anybody, including Miss Prunella Foster, or if it comes to that, to the memory of her mother. I'm not setting traps at the moment, which is not to say a copper never does. As I expect you very well know. But not here and not now. I would simply like to see the desk, if you'll show me where it is.'

She looked fixedly at him for an appreciable interval, then broke out, 'It's no business of mine, this isn't. I don't know anything that goes on up here, sir, and if you'll excuse my speaking out, I don't want to. Miss Prue's all right. She's a nice young lady, for all you can't hear half she says and anyone can see she's been upset. But she's got her young man and he's sharp enough for six and he'll look after her. So'll his old – his father,' amended Mrs Jim. 'He's that pleased, anyway, with the match seeing he's getting what he'd set his heart on.'

'Really? What was that?' Alleyn asked, still keeping an eye on the box hedge.

'This property. He wanted to buy it and they say he would have paid anything to get it. Well, in a sort of way he'll get his wish now, won't he? It's settled he's to have his own rooms – self-contained, like. I'll show you the desk, then, if you'll come this way.'

It was in a smallish room known in her lifetime as Sybil's boudoir, which lay between the great drawing-room and the dining-room where, on the day of the old gardener's death, the Upper Quintern ladies had held their meeting. The desk, a nice piece of Chippendale, stood in the window. Mrs Jim indicated the centre drawer and Alleyn opened it. Letter paper, stamps and a diary were revealed.

'The drawer wasn't locked?' he asked.

'Not before, it wasn't. I left the envelope on the top of some papers and then I thought it best to turn the key in the lock and keep it. I handed the key to Miss Prue. She doesn't seem to have locked it.'

'And was the envelope sealed?'

'Like I said.' She waited for a moment and then, for the second time, broke out: 'If you want to know any more about it you can ask Bruce. He fetched it. Mrs Foster give it to him.'

'Do you think he knows what was in it? The details, I mean?'

'Ask him. I don't know. *I* don't discuss the business of the house and I don't ask questions, no more than I expect them to ask me.'

'Mrs Jobbin, I'm sure you don't and I won't bother you much further.'

He was about to shut the drawer when he noticed a worn leather case. He opened it and it disclosed a photograph, in faded sepia, of a group from a Scottish regiment. Among the officers was a second lieutenant, so emphatically handsome as to stand out from among his fellows.

'That's her first,' said Mrs Jim, at Alleyn's back. 'Third from the left. Front row. Name of Carter.'

'He must have been a striking chap to look at.'

'Like a Greek god,' Mrs Jim startled him by announcing, still in her wooden voice. 'That's what they used to say, them in the village that remembered him.'

Wondering which of the Upper Quintern worthies had employed this classy simile, Alleyn pushed the drawer shut and looked at the objects on the top of the desk. Prominent among them was a photograph of pretty Prunella Foster, one of the ultra-conservative kind, destined for glossy magazines and thought of, by Alleyn, as 'Cabinet Pudding'. Further off, and equally conventional, was a middle-aged man of full habit and slightly prominent eyes who had signed himself 'John'. That would be Foster, the second husband and Prunella's father. Alleyn looked down into the pink-shaded lamp on Sybil Foster's desk. The bulb was covered by a double-glass slipper. A faint odour of sweet almonds still hung about it.

'Was there anything else you was wanting?' asked Mrs Jim.

'Not from you, thank you, Mrs Jobbin. I'd like a word with the gardener. I'll find him somewhere out there, I expect.' He waited for a moment and then said cheerfully, 'I gather you're not madly keen on him.'

'Him,' said Mrs Jim. 'I wouldn't rave and that's a fact. Too much of the Great I Am.'

'The – ?'

'Letting on what a treat he is to all and sundry.'

'Including Mrs Foster?'

'Including everybody. It's childish. One of these days he'll burst into poetry and stifle himself,' said Mrs Jim and then seemed to think better of it. 'No harm in 'im, mind,' she amended. 'Just asking for attention. Like a child, pathetic, reely. And good at his work, he is. You've got to hand it to him. He's all right at bottom even if it is a long way down.'

'Mrs Jobbin,' said Alleyn, 'you are a very unexpected and observant lady. I will leave my card for Miss Foster and I wish you a grateful good morning.'

He held out his hand. Mrs Jobbin, surprised into a blush, put her corroded little paw into it and then into her apron pocket.

'Bid you good day, then,' she said. 'Sir. You'll likely find him near the old stables. First right from the front door and right again. Growing mushrooms, for Gawd's sake.'

Bruce was not near the old stables but in them. As Alleyn approached he heard the drag and slam of a door and when he 'turned right again' found his man.

Bruce had evidently taken possession of what had originally been some kind of open-fronted lean-to abutting on the stables. He had removed part of the flooring and dug up the ground beneath. Bags of humus and a heap of compost awaited his attention.

In response to Alleyn's greeting he straightened up, squared his shoulders and came forward. 'Guid day, sir,' he said. 'Were you looking for somebody?'

'For you,' Alleyn said, 'if your name's Gardener?'

'It is that. Gardener's the name and gardener's the occupation,' he said, evidently cracking a vintage quip. 'What can I do for you, then?'

Alleyn made the usual announcement.

'Police?' said Bruce loudly and stared at him. 'Is that a fact? Ou, aye, who'd have thowt it?'

'Would you like me to flash a card at you?' Alleyn asked lightly. Bruce put his head on one side, gazed at him, waited for a moment and then became expansive.

'Och, na, na, na, na,' he said. 'Not at a', not at a'. There's no call for anything o' the sort. You didna strike me at first sight as a constabulary figure, just. What can I do for you?'

Members of the police force develop a sixth sense about the undeclared presence of offstage characters. Alleyn had taken the impression that Bruce was aware, but not anxiously, of a third person somewhere in the offing.

'I wanted to have a word with you, if I might,' he said, 'about the late Mrs Foster. I expect you know about the adjourned inquest?'

Bruce looked fixedly at him. He's re-focusing, thought Alleyn. He was expecting something else.

'I do that,' Bruce said. 'Aye. I do that.'

'You'll realize, of course, that the reason for the adjournment was to settle, beyond doubt, the question of suicide.'

Bruce said slowly, 'I wad never have believed it of her. Never. She was aye fu' of enthusiasm. She liked fine to look ahead to the pleasures of her garden. Making plans! What for would we be planning for mushrooms last time I spoke with her if she was of a mind to make awa' wi' herself?'

'When was that?'

He pushed his gardener's fingers through his sandy hair and said it would have been when he visited her a week before it happened and that she had been in great good humour and they had drawn plans on the back of an envelope for a lily-pond and had discussed making a mushroom bed here in the old stables. He had promised to go into matters of plumbing and mulching and here he was, carrying on as if she'd be coming home to see it. Something, he said, must have happened during that last week to put sic' awfu' thoughts into her head.

'Was it on that visit,' Alleyn asked, 'that she gave you her Will to put in her desk here at Quintern?'

Bruce said aye, it was that, and intimated that he hadn't fancied the commission but that her manner had been so light-hearted he had not entertained any real misgivings.

Alleyn said, 'Did Mrs Foster give you any idea of the terms of this Will?'

For the first time he seemed to be discomfited. He bent his blue unaligned gaze on Alleyn and muttered she had mentioned that he wasn't forgotten.

'I let on,' he said, 'that I had no mind to pursue the matter.'

He waited for a moment and then said Alleyn would consider maybe that this was an ungracious response but he'd not like it to be thought he looked for anything of the sort from her. He became incoherent, shuffled his boots and finally burst out, 'To my way of thinking it wasna just the decent thing.'

'Did you say as much to Mrs Foster?'

'I did that.'

'How did she take it?'

'She fetched a laugh and said I'd no call to be sae squeamish.'

'And that was all?'

'Ou aye. I delivered the thing into the hand of Mrs Jim, having no mind to tak' it further and she told me she'd put it in the desk.'

'Was the envelope sealed?'

'No' sealed in the literal sense but licked up. The mistress wasna going to close it but I said I'd greatly prefer that she should.' He waited for a moment. 'It's no' that I wouldna have relished the acquisition of a wee legacy,' he said. 'Not a great outlandish wallop, mind, but a wee, decent amount. I'd like that. I would so. I'd like it fine and put it by, remembering the bonny giver. But I wouldna have it thowt or said I took any part in the proceedings.'

'I understand that,' said Alleyn. 'By the way, did Mrs Foster ask you to get the form for her?'

'The forrum? What forrum would that be, sir?'

'The Will. From a stationer's shop?'

'Na, na,' he said, 'I ken naething o' that.'

'And while we're on the subject, did she ask you to bring things in for her? When you visited her?'

It appeared that he had from time to time fetched things from Quintern to Greengages. She would make a list and he would give it to Mrs Jim. 'Clamjampherie', mostly, he thought, things from her dressing-table. Sometimes, he believed, garments. Mrs Jim would put them in a small case so that he wasn't embarrassed by impedimenta unbecoming to a man. Mrs Foster would repack the case with things to be laundered. Alleyn gathered that the strictest decorum was observed. If he was present at these exercises he would withdraw to the window. He was at some pains to make this clear, arranging his mouth in a prim expression as he did so.

A picture emerged from these recollections of an odd, rather cosy relationship, enjoyable, one would think, for both parties. Plans had been laid, pontifications exchanged. There had been, probably, exclamatory speculation as to what the world was coming to, consultations over nurserymen's catalogues, strolls round the rose-garden and conservatory. Bruce sustained an air of rather stuffy condescension in letting fall an occasional reference to these observances and still he gave, as Mrs Jim in her own fashion had given, an impression of listening for somebody or something.

Behind him in the side wall was a ramshackle closed door leading, evidently, into the main stables. Alleyn saw that it had gaps between the planks and had dragged its course through loose soil and what was left of the floor.

He made as if to go and then looking at Bruce's preparations asked if this was in fact to be the proposed mushroom bed. He said it was.

'It was the last request she made,' he said. 'And I prefer to carry it out.' He expanded a little on the techniques of mushroom culture and then said, not too pointedly, if that was all he could do for Alleyn he'd better get on with it and reached for his long-handled shovel.

'There was one other thing,' Alleyn said. 'I almost forgot. You did actually go over to Greengages on the day of her death, didn't you?'

'I did so. But I never saw her,' he said and described how he had waited in the hall with his lilies and how Prunella – 'the wee lassie' he predictably called her – had come down and told him her mother was very tired and not seeing anybody that evening. He had left the lilies at the desk and the receptionist lady had said they would be attended to. So he had returned home by bus.

'With Mr Claude Carter?' asked Alleyn.

Bruce became very still. His hands tightened on the shovel. He stared hard at Alleyn, made as if to speak and changed his mind. Alleyn waited.

'I wasna aware, just,' Bruce said at last, 'that you had spoken to that gentleman.'

'Nor have I. Miss Preston mentioned that he arrived with you at Greengages.'

He thought that over. 'He arrived. That is so,' said Bruce, 'but he did not depart with me.' He raised his voice. 'I wish it to be clearly understood,' he said. 'I have no personal relationship with that gentleman.' And then very quietly and with an air of deep resentment, 'He attached himself to me. He worrumed the information out of me as to her whereabouts. It was an indecent performance and one that I cannot condone.'

He turned his head fractionally towards the closed door. 'And that is the total sum of what I have to say in the matter,' he almost shouted.

'You've been very helpful. I don't think I need pester you any more. Thank you for co-operating.'

'There's no call for thanks. I'm a law-abiding man,' Bruce said, 'and I canna thole mysteries. Guid day to you, sir.'

'This is a lovely old building,' Alleyn said. 'I'm interested in Georgian domestic architecture. Do you mind if I have a look around?'

Without waiting for an answer he passed between Bruce and the closed door, dragged it open and came face to face with Claude Carter.

'Oh, hullo,' said Claude. 'I thought I heard voices.'

CHAPTER 4

Routine

The room was empty and smelt of rats with perhaps an undertone of long-vanished fodder. There was a tumbledown fireplace in one corner and in another a litter of objects that looked as if they had lain there for a century: empty tins, a sack that had rotted, letting out a trickle of cement, a bricklayer's trowel, rusted and handleless, a heap of empty manure bags. The only window was shuttered. Claude was a dim figure.

He said, 'I was looking for Bruce. The gardener. I'm afraid I don't know – ?'

The manner was almost convincing, almost easy, almost that of a son of the house. Alleyn thought the voice was probably pitched a little above its normal level but it sounded quite natural. For somebody who had been caught red-eared in the act of eavesdropping, Claude displayed considerable aplomb.

Alleyn shut the door behind him. Bruce Gardener, already plying his long-handled shovel, didn't look up.

'And I was hoping to see you,' said Alleyn. 'Mr Carter, isn't it?'

'That's right. You have the advantage of me.'

'Chief Superintendent Alleyn.'

After a considerable pause, Claude said, 'Oh. What can I do for you, Chief Superintendent?'

As soon as Alleyn told him he seemed to relax. He answered all the questions readily. Yes, he had spoken to Miss Preston and Prue Foster but had not been allowed to visit his stepmother. He had gone for a stroll in the grounds, had missed the return bus and had walked into the village and picked up a later one there.

'A completely wasted afternoon,' he complained. 'And I must say I wasn't wildly enthusiastic about the reception I got. Particularly in the light of what happened. After all, she was my stepmother.'

'When was the last time you saw her?'

'When? I don't know when. Three – four years ago.'

'Before you went to Australia?'

He shot a sidelong look at Alleyn. 'That's right,' he said, and after a pause, 'You seem to be very well informed of my movements, Chief Superintendent.'

'I know you returned as a member of the ship's complement in the *Poseidon.*'

After a much longer pause, Claude said, 'Oh yes?'

'Shall we move outside and get a little more light and air on the subject?' Alleyn suggested.

Claude opened a door that gave directly on the yard. As they walked into the sunshine a clock in the stable turret tolled eleven very sweetly. The open front of the lean-to faced the yard. Bruce, shovelling vigorously, was in full view, an exemplar of ostentatious non-intervention. Claude stared resentfully at his stern and walked to the far end of the yard. Alleyn followed him.

'How long,' he asked cheerfully, 'had you been in that dark and rather smelly apartment?'

'How *long?* I don't know. No time at all really. Why?'

'I don't want to waste my breath and your time repeating myself, if you've already heard about the Will. And I think you must have heard it because, as I came up, the adjoining door in there was dragged shut.'

Claude gave a rather shrill titter. 'You *are* quick, aren't you?' he said. He lowered his voice. 'As I said,' he confided, 'I was looking for that gardener-man in there. As a matter of fact I thought he might be in the other room and then when you came in and began talking it was jolly awkward. I didn't want to intrude so I – I mean I – you know – it's difficult to explain – '

'You're making a brave shot at it, though, aren't you ? Your sense of delicacy prompted you to remove into the next room, shut that same openwork door and remain close by it throughout our conversation. Is that it?'

'Not at all. You haven't understood.'

'You'd seen us arrive in a police car, perhaps, and you left the house in a hurry for the rose-garden and thence proceeded round the left wing to the stables?'

'I don't know,' said Claude, with a strange air of frightened effrontery, 'why you're taking this line with me, Superintendent, but I must say I resent it.'

'Yes, I thought you might be a bit put out by our appearance. Because of an irregularity in your departure from the *Poseidon.*'

Claude began feverishly to maintain that there had been some mistake and the police had had to climb down and he was thinking of lodging a complaint only it didn't seem worthwhile.

Alleyn let him talk himself to a standstill and then said his visit had nothing to do with any of this and that he only wanted to be told if Claude did in fact know of a recent Will made by Mrs Foster shortly before her death.

An elaborate shuffling process set in, hampered, it seemed, by the proximity of the ever-industrious Bruce. By means of furtive little nods and becks Claude indicated the desirability of a remove. Alleyn disregarded these hints and continued on a loudish, cheerful note.

'It's a perfectly simple question,' he said. 'Nothing private about it. Have you, in fact, known of such a Will?'

Claude made slight jabs with his forefinger, in the direction of Bruce's rear elevation.

'As it happens, yes,' he mouthed.

'You have? Do you mind telling me how it came to your knowledge?'

'It's – I – it just so happened – '

'What did?'

'I mean to say – '

'*Havers!*' Bruce suddenly roared out. He became upright and faced them. 'What ails you, man?' he demanded. 'Can you no' give a straight answer when you're speired a straight question? Oot wi' it, for pity's sake. Tell him and ha' done. There's nothing wrong wi' the facts o' the matter.'

'Yes, well, all right, all right,' said the wretched Claude and added with a faint show of grandeur, 'And you may as well keep a civil tongue in your head.'

Bruce spat on his hands and returned to his shovelling.

'Well, Mr Carter?' Alleyn asked.

By painful degrees it emerged that Claude had happened to be present when Bruce came into the house with the Will and had happened to see him hand it over to Mrs Jim and had happened to notice what it was on account of the word Will being written in large letters on the envelope.

'And had happened,' Bruce said, without turning round but with a thwack of his shovel on the heap of earth he had raised, 'to enquire with unco' perrrsistence as to the cirrrcumstances.'

'Look here, Gardener, I've had about as much of you as I can take,' said Claude, with a woeful show of spirit.

'You can tak' me or leave me, Mr Carter, and my preference would be for the latter procedure.'

'Do you know the terms of the Will?' Alleyn cut in.

'No, I don't. I'm not interested. Whatever they are, they don't affect me.'

'How do you mean?'

'My father provided for me. With a trust fund or whatever it's called. Syb couldn't touch that and she's not bloody likely to have added to it,' said Claude with a little spurt of venom.

Upon this note Alleyn left them and returned deviously, by way of a brick-walled vegetable garden, to Fox. He noticed two newly made asparagus beds, and a multitude of enormous cabbages and wondered where on earth they all went and who consumed them. Fox, patient as ever, awaited him in the car.

'Nothing to report,' Fox said. 'I took a walk round but no signs of anyone.'

'The gardener's growing mushrooms in the stables and the stepson's growing butterflies in the stomach,' said Alleyn and described the scene.

'Miss Preston,' he said, 'finds Bruce's Scots a bit hard to take.'

'Phoney?'

'She didn't say that. More, "laid on with a trowel". She might have said with a long-handled shovel if she'd seen him this morning. But –

I don't know. I'm no expert on dialects, Scots or otherwise, but it seemed to me he uses it more in the manner of someone who has lived with the genuine article long enough to acquire and display it inconsistently and inaccurately. His last job was in Scotland. He may think it adds to his charm or pawkiness or whatever.'

'What about the stepson?'

'Oh, quite awful, poor devil. Capable of anything if he had the guts to carry it through.'

'We move on?'

'We do. Hark forrard, hark forrard away to Greengages and the point marked x if there is one. Shall I drive and you follow the map?'

'Fair enough, if you say so, Mr Alleyn. What do I look for?'

'Turn right after Maidstone and follow the road to the village of Greenvale. Hence "Greengages", no doubt.'

'Colicky sort of name for a hospital.'

'It's not a hospital.'

'Colicky sort of a name for whatever it is.'

'There's no suggestion that the lady in question died of that, at least.'

'Seeing I've only just come in, could we re-cap on the way? What've we got for info?'

'We've got the lady who is dead. She was in affluent circumstances, stinking rich in fact, and probably in the early stages of Parkinson's disease but unaware of it, and we've got the medical incumbent of an expensive establishment that is neither hospital nor nursing home but a hotel that caters for well-to-do invalids, whose patient the lady was, and who did not spot the disease. We've got a local doctor called Field-Innis and a police pathologist who did. We've got the lady's daughter who on the afternoon of her mother's death announced her engagement to a rich young man who did not meet with the lady's approval. We've got the rich young man's millionaire papa who coveted the lady's house, failed to buy it but will now live in it when his son marries the daughter.'

'Hold on,' said Fox, after a pause. 'OK, I'm with you.'

'We've got an elderly Scottish gardener, possible pseudoish, to whom the lady has left twenty-five thousand deflated quid in a recent Will. The rest of her fortune is divided between her daughter if she marries a peer called Swingletree and the medical incumbent who didn't diagnose Parkinson's disease. If the daughter doesn't marry Swingletree the incumbent gets the lot.'

'That would be Dr Schramm?'

'Certainly. The rest of the cast is made up of the lady's stepson by her first marriage who is the archetype of all remittance-men and has a police record. Finally, we have a nice woman of considerable ability called Verity Preston.'

'That's the lot?'

'Give and take a trained nurse and a splendid lady called Mrs Jim who obliges in Upper Quintern, that's the lot.'

'What's the score where we come in? Exactly, I mean?'

'The circumstances are the score really, Br'er Fox. The Will and the *mise-en-scène*. The inquest was really adjourned because everybody says the lady was such an unlikely subject for suicide and had no motive. An extended autopsy seemed to be advisable. Sir James Curtis performed it. The undelicious results of Dr Schramm's stomach pump had been preserved and Sir James confirms that they disclosed a quantity of the barbiturate found in the remaining tablets on the bedside table and in the throat and at the back of the tongue. The assumption had been that she stuffed down enough of the things to become so far doped as to prevent her swallowing the last lot she put in her mouth.'

'Plausible?'

'Dr Schramm thought so. Sir James won't swallow it but says she would have – if you'll excuse a joke in bad taste, Br'er Fox. He points out that there's a delay of anything up to twenty minutes before the barbiturate in question, which is soluble in alcohol, starts to work and it's hard to imagine her waiting until she was too far under to swallow before putting the final lot in her mouth.'

'So what do we wonder about?'

'Whether somebody else put them there. By the way, Sir James looked for traces of cyanide.'

'Why?' Mr Fox asked economically.

'There'd been a smell of almonds in the room and in the contents of the stomach but it turned out that she used sweet almond oil in one of those glass-slipper things they put over lamp bulbs and that she'd wolfed quantities of marzipan petits-fours from the "Marquise de Sévigné" in Paris. The half-empty box was on her bedside table along with the vanity box and other litter.'

'Like – the empty bottle of scotch?'

'And the overturned glass. Exactly.'

'Anybody know how much there'd been in the bottle? That day, for instance?'

'Apparently not. She kept it in a cupboard above the handbasin. One gathers it lasted her a good long time.'

'What about dabs?'

'The local chaps had a go before calling us in. Bailey and Thompson are coming down to give the full treatment.'

'Funny sort of set-up though, isn't it?' Fox mused.

'The funniest bit is yet to come. Cast your mind back, however reluctantly, to the contents of the stomach as examined by Doctor Field-Innis and Schramm.'

'Oodles of barbiturate?'

'According to Schramm. But according to Sir James an appreciable amount but not enough, necessarily, to have caused death. You know how guarded he can be. Even allowing for what he calls "a certain degree of excretion" he would not take it as a matter of course that death would follow. He could find nothing to suggest any kind of susceptibility or allergy that might explain why it did.'

'So now we begin to wonder about the beneficiaries in the recent and eccentric Will?'

'That's it. And who provided her with the printed form. Young Mr Rattisbon allowed me to see it. It looks shop-new-fresh creases, sharp corners and edges.'

'And all in order?'

'He's afraid so. Outrageous though the terms may be. I gather, by the way, that Miss Prunella Foster would sooner trip down the aisle with a gorilla than with the Lord Swingletree.'

'So her share goes to this Dr Schramm?'

'In addition to the princely dollop he would get in any case.'

'It scarcely seems decent,' said Fox primly. 'You should hear the Rattisbons, *pète et fils,* on the subject.'

'It's twenty to one,' Fox said wistfully as they entered a village, 'there's a nice-looking little pub ahead.'

'So there is. Tell me your thoughts.'

'They seem to dwell upon Scotch eggs, cheese and pickle sandwiches and a pint of mild-and-bitter.'

'So be it,' said Alleyn and pulled in.

II

Prunella Foster arrived from London at Quintern Place on her way to lunch with her fiancé and his father at Mardling. At Quintern Mrs Jim informed her of Alleyn's visit earlier in the morning. As a *raconteuse*, Mrs Jim was strong on facts and short on atmosphere. She gave a list of events in order of occurrence, answered Prunella's questions with the greatest possible economy and expressed no opinion of any sort whatsoever. Prunella was flustered.

'And he was a *policeman*, Mrs Jim?'

'That's what he said.'

'Do you mean there was any doubt about it?'

'Not to say doubt. It's on his card.'

'Well-what?'

Cornered, Mrs Jim said Alleyn had seemed a bit on the posh side for it. 'More after the style of one of your friends, like,' she offered and added that he had a nice way with him.

Prunella got her once more to rehearse the items of the visit, which she did with accuracy.

'So he asked about – ?' Prunella cast her eyes and jerked her head in the direction, vaguely, of that part of the house generally frequented by Claude Carter.

'That's right,' Mrs Jim conceded. She and Prunella understood each other pretty well on the subject of Claude. 'But it was only to remark he'd noticed him dodging up and down in the rose-garden. He went out, after, to the stables. The gentleman did.'

'To find Bruce?'

'That's right. Mr Claude, too, I reckon.'

'Oh?'

'Mr Claude come in after the gentleman had gone and went into the dining-room.'

This, Prunella recognized, was a euphemism for 'helped himself to a drink'.

'Where is he now?' she asked.

Mrs Jim said she'd no idea. They'd come to an arrangement about his meals, it emerged. She prepared a hot luncheon for one o'clock and laid the table in the small morning-room. She then beat an enormous gong and left for home. When she returned to Quintern in two days' time she would find the *disjecta membra* of this meal together with those of any subsequent snacks, unpleasantly congealed upon the table.

'How difficult everything is,' Prunella muttered. 'Thank you, Mrs Jim. I'm going to Mardling for lunch. We're making plans about Quintern – you know, arranging for Mr Gideon's father to have his own quarters with us. He's selling Mardling, I think. After all that he'd done to it! Imagine! And keeping the house in London for his headquarters.'

'Is that right, miss?' said Mrs Jim, and Prunella knew by the wooden tone she employed that she was deeply stimulated. 'We'll be hearing wedding-bells one of these days, then?' she speculated.

'Well – not yet, of course.'

'No,' Mrs Jim agreed. 'That wouldn't be the thing. Not just yet.'

'I'd really rather not have a "wedding", Mrs Jim. I'd rather be just married early in the morning in Upper Quintern with hardly anyone there. But he – Gideon – wants it the other way, so I suppose my aunt – Auntie Boo – ' she whispered her way into inaudibility and her eyes filled with tears. She looked helplessly at Mrs Jim and thought how much she liked her. For the first time since her mother died it occurred to Prunella that, apart of course from Gideon, she was very much alone in the world. She had never been deeply involved with her mother and had indeed found her deviousness and vanities irritating when not positively comical and even that degree of tolerance had been shaken by the preposterous terms of this wretched Will. And yet now, abruptly, when she realized that Sybil was not and never would be there to be laughed at or argued with, that where she had been there was – nothing, a flood of desolation poured over Prunella and she broke down and cried with her face in Mrs Jim's cardigan which smelt of floor polish.

Mrs Jim said, 'Never mind, then. It's been a right shock and all. We know that.'

'I'm sorry,' Prunella sobbed, 'I'm awfully sorry.'

'You have your cry out, then.'

This invitation had the opposite result to what had been intended. Prunella blew her nose and pulled herself together. She returned shakily to her wedding arrangements. 'Somebody will have to give me away,' she said.

'As long as it's not that Mr Claude,' said Mrs Jim loudly.

'God forbid. I wondered – I don't know – can one be given away by a woman? I could ask the vicar.'

'Was you thinking of Miss Verity?'

'She *is* my godmother. Yes, I was.'

'Couldn't do better,' said Mrs Jim.

'I must be off,' said Prunella, who did not want to run into Claude. 'You don't happened to know where those old plans of Quintern are? Mr Markos wants to have a look at them. They're in a sort of portfolio thing.'

'Library. Cupboard near the door. Bottom shelf.'

'How clever of you, Mrs Jim.'

'Your mother had them out to show Bruce. Before she went to that place. She left them out and *he* – ' the movement of the head they both used to indicate Claude – 'was handling them and leaving them all over the place so I put them away.'

'Good for you. Mrs Jim – tell me. Does he – well – does he sort of peer and prowl ? Do you know what I mean? Sort of?'

'Not my place to comment,' said Mrs Jim, 'but as you've brought it up, yes, he do. I can tell by the way things have been interfered with – shifted, like.'

'Oh dear.'

'Yes. Specially them plans. He seemed to fancy them particular. I seen him looking at that one of the grounds through the magnifying glass in the study. He's a proper nosey-parker if you ask me and don't mind my mentioning it,' said Mrs Jim rapidly. She brought herself up with a jerk. 'Will I fetch them, then? Put out your washing,' said Mrs Jim as an afterthought.

'Bless you. I'll just collect some things from my room.'

Prunella ran up a lovely flight of stairs and across a first-floor landing to her bedroom – a muslin and primrose affair with long windows opening over terraces, rose-gardens and uncluttered lawns that declined to the ha-ha, meadows, hayfields, spinneys and the tower of St Crispin-in-Quintern. A blue haze veiled the more distant valleys and hills and turned the chimneys of a paper-making town into minarets. Prunella was glad that after she had married she would still live in this house.

She bathed her eyes, repacked her suitcase and prepared to leave. On the landing she ran into Claude.

There was no reason why he should not be on the landing or that she should have been aware that he had arrived there but there was something intrinsically furtive about Claude that gave her a sensation of stealth.

He said, 'Oh, hullo, Prue, I saw your car.'

'Hullo, Claude. Yes. I just looked in to pick up some things.'

'Not staying, then?'

'No.'

'I hope I'm not keeping you away,' he said, and looked at his feet and smiled.

'Of course not. I'm mostly in London these days.'

He stole a glance at her left hand.

'Congratulations are in order, I see.'

'Yes. Thank you.'

'When's it to be?'

She said it hadn't been decided and began to move towards the stairs.

'Er – ' said Claude, 'I was wondering – '

'Yes?'

'Whether I'm to be handed the push.'

Prunella made a panic decision to treat this as a joke.

'Oh,' she said jauntily, 'you'll be given plenty of notice.'

'Too kind. Are you going to live here?'

'As a matter of fact, yes. After we've made some changes. You'll get fair warning, I promise.'

'Syb said I could be here, you know.'

'I know what she said, Claude. You're welcome to stay until the workmen come in.'

'Too kind,' he repeated, this time with an open sneer. 'By the way, you don't mind my asking, do you? I would like to know when the funeral is to be.'

Prunella felt as if winter had come into the house and closed about her heart. She managed to say, 'I don't – we won't know until after the inquest. Mr Rattisbon is going to arrange everything. You'll be let know, Claude, I promise.'

'Are you going to this new inquest?'

'I expect so. I mean, yes. Yes, I am.'

'So am I. Not that it affects me, of course.'

'I really must go. I'm running late.'

'I never wrote to you. About Syb.'

'There was no need. Goodbye.'

'Shall I carry your case down?'

'No, thanks. Really. It's quite light. Thank you very much, though.'

'I see you've got the old plans out. Of Quintern.'

'Goodbye,' Prunella said desperately and made a business of getting herself downstairs.

She had reached the ground floor when his voice floated down to her. 'Hi!'

She wanted to bolt but made herself stop and look up to the first landing. His face and hands hung over the balustrade.

'I suppose you realize we've had a visit from the police,' said Claude. He kept his voice down and articulated pedantically.

'Yes, of course.'

One of the dangling hands moved to cup the mouth. 'They seem to be mightily interested in your mother's horticultural favourite,' Claude mouthed. 'I wonder why.'

The teeth glinted in the moon-face.

Prunella bolted. She got herself and her baggage through the front door and into her car and drove, much too fast, to Mardling.

'Honestly,' she said ten minutes later to Gideon and his father, 'I almost feel we should get in an exorcizer when Claude goes. I wonder if the vicar's any good on the bell, book and candle lay.'

'You enchanting child,' said Mr Markos in his florid way and raised his glass to her. 'Is this unseemly person really upsetting you?

Should Gideon and I advance upon him with threatening gestures? Can't he be dispensed with?'

'I must say,' Gideon chimed in, 'I really do think it's a bit much he should set himself up at Quintern. After all, darling, he's got no business there, has he? I mean, no real family ties or anything. Face it.'

'I suppose not,' she agreed. 'But my mama did feel she ought not to wash her hands of him completely, awful though he undoubtedly is. You see, she was very much in love with his father.'

'Which doesn't, if one looks at it quite cold-bloodedly, give his son the right to impose upon her daughter,' said Mr Markos.

Prunella had noticed that this was a favourite phrase – 'quite cold-bloodedly' – and was rather glad that Gideon had not inherited it. But she liked her father-in-law-to-be and became relaxed and expansive in the atmosphere (anything, she reflected, but 'cold-blooded') that he created around himself and Gideon. She felt that she could say what she chose to him without being conscious of the difference in their ages, and that she amused and pleased him.

They sat out of doors on swinging seats under canopies. Mr Markos had decided that it was a day for pre-prandial champagne – 'a sparkling, venturesome morning', he called it. Prunella, who had skipped breakfast and was unused to such extravagance, rapidly expanded. She downed her drink and accepted another. The horrors, and lately there really had been moments of horror, slipped into the background. She became perfectly audible and began to feel that this was the life for her and was meant for her and she for it, that she blossomed in the company of the exotic Markoses, the one so delightfully mundane, the other so enchantingly in love with her. Eddies of relief, floating on champagne, lapped over her and if they were vaguely disturbed by little undertows of guilt (for after all she had a social conscience) that, however reprehensibly, seemed merely to add to her exhilaration. She took a vigorous pull at her champagne and Mr Markos refilled her glass.

'Darling,' said Gideon, 'what *have* you got in that monstrous compendium or whatever it is in your car?'

'A surprise,' cried Prunella, waving her hand. 'Not for you, love. For Pil.' She raised her glass to Mr Markos and drank to him.

'For *whom?*' asked the Markoses in unison.

'For my papa-in-law-to-be. I've been too shy to know what to call you,' said Prunella. 'Not for a moment, that you *are* a Pill. Far from it. *Pillycock sat on Pillycock hill,*' she sang before she could stop herself. She realized she had shaken her curls at Nikolas, like one of Dickens's more awful little heroines and was momentarily ashamed of herself.

'You shall call me whatever you like,' said Mr Markos and kissed her hand. Another Dickens reference swam incontinently into Prunella's dizzy ken, *'Todgers were going it.'* For a second or two she slid aside from herself and saw herself 'going it' like mad in a swinging chair under a canopy and having her hand kissed. She was extravagantly pleased with life.

'Shall I fetch it?' Gideon asked.

'Fetch what?' Prunella shouted recklessly.

'Whatever you've brought for your papa-in-law-to-be.'

'Oh, *that.* Yes, darling, do, and I think perhaps no more champagne.'

Gideon burst out laughing. 'And I think perhaps you may be right,' he said and kissed the top of her head. He went to her car and took out the portfolio.

Prunella said to Mr Markos, 'I'm tightish. How awful.'

'Are you? Eat some olives. Stuff down lots of those cheese things. You're not really very tight.'

'Promise? All right, I will,' said Prunella and was as good as her word. A car came up the avenue.

'Here is Miss Verity Preston,' said Mr Markos. 'Did we tell you she was lunching?'

'No!' she exclaimed and blew out a little shower of cheese straws. 'How too frightful, she's my godmother.'

'Don't you like her?'

'I adore her. But *she* won't like to see *me* flown with fizz so early in the day. Or ever. And as a matter of fact it's not my form at all, by and large,' said Prunella, swallowing most of an enormous mouthful of cheese straws and helping herself to more. 'I'm a sober girl.'

'You're a divine girl. I doubt if Gideon deserves you.'

'You're absolutely right. The cheese straws and olives are doing the trick. I shan't go on about being drunk. People who do that are such a bore always, don't you feel? And anyway I'm rapidly becoming sober.' As if to prove it, she had begun to whisper again.

The Markoses went to meet Verity. Prunella thought of following them but compromised by getting up from her swinging seat, which she did in a quickly controlled flounder.

'Godma V,' she said. And when they were close enough to each other she hung herself about Verity's neck and was glad to do so.

'Hullo, young party,' said Verity, surprised by this effusion and not knowing what to do about it. Prunella sat down abruptly and inaccurately on the swinging chair.

The Markoses, father and son, stood one on each side of her, smiling at Verity, who thought that her godchild looked like a briar rose between a couple of succulent exotics. They will absorb her, Verity thought, into their own world and one doesn't know what that may be. Was Syb by any chance right? And ought I to take a hand? What about her Aunt Boo? Boo was Syb's flighty sister. I'd better talk to Prue and I suppose write to Boo, who ought to have come back and taken some responsibility, instead of sending vague cables from Acapulco. She realized that Nikolas Markos was talking to her.

' – hope you approve of champagne at this hour.'

'Lovely,' Verity said hastily, 'but demoralizing.'

'That's what I found, Godma V,' whispered Prunella, lurching about in her swinging chair.

For Heaven's sake, thought Verity, the child's tipsy.

But when Mr Markos had opened the portfolio, tenderly drawn out its contents and laid them on the garden table, which he dusted with his handkerchief, Prunella had so far recovered as to give a fairly informed comment on them.

'They're the original plans, I think. He was meant to be rather a grand architect. The house was built for my I-don't-know-how-many-times-great grandfather. You can see the date is 1780. He was called Lord Rupert Passcoigne. My mama was the last Passcoigne of that family and inherited Quintern from her father. I hope I've got it right. The plans are rather pretty, aren't they, with the coat-of-arms and all the trimmings and nonsense?'

'My dear child,' said Mr Markos, poring over them, 'they're exquisite. It's – I really can't tell you how excited I am to see them.'

'There are some more underneath.'

'We mustn't keep them too long in this strong light. Gideon, put this one back in the portfolio. Carefully. Gently. No, let me do it.'

He looked up at Verity. 'Have you seen them?' he asked. 'Come and look. Share my gloat, do.'

Verity had seen them, as it happened, many years ago, when Sybil had first married her second husband, but she joined the party round the table. Mr Markos had arrived at a plan for the gardens at Quintern and dwelt on it with greedy curiosity.

'But this has never been carried out,' he said. 'Has it? I mean, nicest possible daughter-in-law-to-be, the gardens today bear little resemblance in concept to this exquisite *schema*. Why?'

'Don't ask me,' said Prunella. 'Perhaps they ran out of cash or something. I rather think Mummy and Bruce were cooking up a grand idea about carrying out some of the scheme but decided we couldn't afford it. If only they hadn't lost the Black Alexander Claude could have done it.'

'Yes, indeed,' said Verity.

Mr Markos looked up quickly. 'The Black Alexander!' he said. 'What can you mean? You can't mean – '

'Oh, yes, of course. You're a collector.'

'I am indeed. Tell me.'

She told him and when she had done so he was unusually quiet for several seconds.

'But how immensely rewarding it would be – ' he began at last and then pulled himself up. 'Let us put the plans away,' he said. 'They arouse insatiable desires. I'm sure you understand, don't you, Miss Preston? I've allowed myself to build – not castles in Spain but gardens in Kent, which is much more reprehensible. Haven't I?'

How very intelligent, Verity thought, finding his black eyes focused on hers, this Mr Markos is. He seems to be making all sorts of assumptions and I seem to be liking it.

'I don't remember that I saw the garden plan before,' she said. 'It would have been a perfect marriage, wouldn't it?'

'Ah. And you have used the perfect phrase for it.'

'Would you like to keep the plans here,' asked Prunella, 'to have another gloat?'

He thanked her exuberantly and, luncheon having been announced, they went indoors.

Since that first dinner-party, which now seemed quite a long time ago, and the visit to Greengages on the day of Sybil's death, Verity had not seen much of the Markoses. She had been twice asked to Mardling for cocktail-parties and on each occasion had been unable to go and one evening Markos Senior had paid an unheralded visit to Keys House, having spotted her, as he explained, in her garden and acted on the spur of the moment. They had got on well, having tastes in common and he showing a pretty acute appreciation of the contemporary theatre. Verity had been quite surprised to see the time when he finally took his stylish leave of her. The next thing that she had heard of him was that he had 'gone abroad', a piece of information conveyed by village telegraph through Mrs Jim. And 'abroad', as far as Verity knew, he had remained until this present reappearance.

They had their coffee in the library, now completely finished. Verity wondered what would happen to all the books if, as Mrs Jim had reported, Mr Markos really intended to sell Mardling. This was by no means the sterile, unhandled assembly made by a moneyed person more interested in interior decoration than the written word.

As soon as she came in she saw above the fireplace the painting called 'Several Pleasures' by Troy.

'So you did hang it there,' she said. 'How well it looks.'

'Doesn't it?' Mr Markos agreed. 'I dote on it. Who would think it was painted by a policeman's missus.'

Verity said, 'Well, I can't see why not. Although, I suppose you'd say a rather exceptional policeman.'

'So you know him?'

'I've met him, yes.'

'I see. So have I. I met him when I bought the picture. I should have thought him an exotic in the Force, but perhaps the higher you go at the Yard the rarer the atmosphere.'

'He visited me this morning.'

Prunella said, 'You don't tell me!'

'But I do,' said Verity.

'And me. According to Mrs Jim.'

Gideon said, 'Would it be about the egregious Claude?'

'No,' said Verity. 'It wouldn't. Not so far as I was concerned. Not specifically, anyway. It seemed to be – ' she hesitated – 'as much about this new Will as anything.'

And in the silence that followed the little party in the library quietly collapsed. Prunella began to look scared and Gideon put his arm round her.

Mr Markos had moved in front of his fireplace. Verity thought she saw a change in him – the subtle change that comes over men when something has led a conversation into their professional field – a guarded attentiveness.

Prunella said, 'I've been pushing things off. I've been pretending to myself nothing is really very much the matter. It's not true. Is it?' she insisted, appealing to Verity.

'Perhaps not quite, darling,' Verity said, and for a moment it seemed to her that she and Prunella were, in some inexplicable way, united against the two men.

III

It was half past two when Alleyn and Fox arrived at Greengages. The afternoon being clement, some of the guests were taking their post-prandial ease in the garden. Others, presumably, had retired to their rooms. Alleyn gave his professional card in at the desk and asked if they might have a word with Dr Schramm.

The receptionist stared briefly at Alleyn and hard at Mr Fox. She tightened her mouth, said she would see, appeared to relax slightly and left them.

'Know us when she sees us again,' said Fox placidly. He put on his spectacles and, tilting back his head, contemplated an emaciated water-colour of Canterbury Cathedral. 'Airy-fairy,' he said. 'Not my notion of the place at all,' and moved to a view of the Grand Canal.

The receptionist returned with an impeccably dressed man who had Alleyn's card in his hand and said he was the manager of the hotel. 'I hope,' he added, 'that we're not in for any further disruption.' Alleyn cheerfully assured him that he hoped so too and repeated that he would like to have a word or two with Dr Schramm. The manager retired to an inner office.

Alleyn said to the receptionist, 'May I bother you for a moment? Of course you're fussed we're here to ask tedious questions and generally make nuisances of ourselves about the death of Mrs Foster.'

'You said it,' she returned, 'not me.' But she touched her hair and she didn't sound altogether antagonistic.

'It's only a sort of tidying-up job. But I wonder if you remember anything about flowers that her gardener left at the desk for her.'

'I wasn't at the desk at the time.'

'Alas!'

'Pardon? Oh yes. Well, as a matter of fact I *do* happen to remember. The girl on duty mentioned that the electrical repairs man had taken them up when I was off for a minute or two.'

'When would that be?'

'I really couldn't say.'

'Is the repairs man a regular visitor?'

'Not that I know. He wasn't called in from the desk, that I can tell you.'

'Could you by any merciful chance find out when, where and why he was here?'

'Well, I must say!'

'It would be *very* kind indeed. Really.'

She said she would see what she could do and retired into her office. Alleyn heard the whirr of a telephone dial. After a considerable interlude a highly starched nurse of opulent proportions appeared.

'Dr Schramm will see you now,' she said in a clinical voice. Only the copies of *Punch,* Alleyn felt, were missing.

The nurse rustled them down a passage to a door bearing the legend: 'Dr Basil Schramm, MB. Hours 3-5 p.m. and by appointment.'

She ushered them into a little waiting-room and there, sure enough, were the copies of *Punch* and *The Tatler.* She knocked at an inner door, opened it and motioned them to go in.

Dr Schramm swivelled round in his desk chair and rose to greet them.

A police officer of experience and sensibility may come to recognize mannerisms common to certain persons with whom he has to deal. If he is wise he will never place too much reliance on this simplification. When, for instance, he is asked by the curious layman if the police can identify certain criminal types by looking at them, he will probably say no. Perhaps he will qualify this denial by adding that he does find that certain characteristics tend to crop up – shabby stigmata – in sexual offenders. He is not referring to raincoats or to sidelong lurking but to a look in the eyes and about the mouth, a look he is unable to define.

To Alleyn it seemed that there were traits held in common by men who, in Victorian times, were called ladykillers – a display, covert or open, of sexual vainglory that sometimes, not always, made less heavily endowed acquaintances want, they scarcely knew why, to kick the possessors.

If ever he had recognized this element he did so now in Dr Basil Schramm. It declared itself in the brief, perfectly correct but experienced glance which he gave his nurse. It was latent in the co-ordinated ease with which he rose to his feet and extended his hand, in the boldish glance of his widely separated eyes and in the fold that joined his nostrils to the corners of his mouth. Dr Schramm was not unlike a better-looking version of King Charles II.

As a postscript to these observations he thought that Dr Schramm looked like a heavy, if controlled, drinker.

The nurse left them.

'I'm so sorry to keep you waiting,' said Dr Schramm. 'Do sit down.' He glanced at Alleyn's card and then at him. 'Should I say Superintendent or Mr or just plain Alleyn?'

'It couldn't matter less,' said Alleyn. 'This is Inspector Fox.'

'Sit, sit, sit, do.'

They sat.

'Well, now, what's the trouble?' asked Dr Schramm. 'Don't tell me it's more about this unhappy business of Mrs Foster?'

'I'm afraid I do tell you. It's just that, as I'm sure you realize, we have to tidy up rather exhaustively.'

'Oh yes. That – of course.'

'The local Force has asked us to come in on the case. I'm sorry, but this does entail a tramp over ground that I dare say you feel has already been explored *ad nauseam*.'

'Well – ' He raised his immaculately kept hands and let them fall. 'Needs must,' he said and laughed.

'That's about it,' Alleyn agreed. 'I believe her room has been kept as it was at the time of her death? Locked up and sealed.'

'Certainly. Your local people asked for it. To be frank it's inconvenient, but never mind.'

'Won't be long now,' said Alleyn cheerfully.

'I'm glad to hear it. I'll take you up to her room.'

'If I could have a word before we go.'

'Oh? Yes, of course.'

'I really wanted to ask you if you were at all, however slightly, uneasy about Mrs Foster's general health and spirits?'

Schramm started to make an instantly controlled gesture. 'I've stated repeatedly, to her solicitors, to the Coroner and to the police, that Mrs Foster was in improved health and in good spirits when I last saw her before I went up to London.'

'And when you returned she was dead.'

'Precisely.'

'You didn't know, did you, that she had Parkinson's disease?'

'That is by no means certain.'

'Dr Field-Innis thought so.'

'And is, of course, entitled to his opinion. In any case, it is not a positive diagnosis. As I understand it, Dr Field-Innis merely considers it a possibility.'

'So does Sir James Curtis.'

'Very possibly. As it happens I have no professional experience of Parkinson's disease and am perfectly ready to bow to their opinion. Of course, if Mrs Foster had been given any inkling – '

'Dr Field-Innis is emphatic that she had not – '

' – there would certainly have been cause for anxiety, depression – '

'Did she strike you as being anxious or depressed?'

'No.'

'On the contrary?'

'On the contrary. Quite. She was – '

'Yes?'

'In particularly good form,' said Dr Schramm.

'And yet you are persuaded it was suicide?'

An ornate little clock on Dr Schramm's desk ticked through some fifteen seconds before he spoke. He raised his clasped hands to his pursed lips and stared over them at Alleyn. Mr Fox, disregarded, coughed slightly.

With a definitive gesture – abrupt and incisive, Dr Schramm clapped his palms down on the desk and leant back in his chair.

'I had hoped,' he said, 'that it wouldn't come to this.'

Alleyn waited.

'I have already told you she was in particularly good form. That was an understatement. She gave me every reason to believe she was happier than she had been for many years.'

He got to his feet, looked fixedly at Alleyn and said loudly, 'She had become engaged to be married.'

The lines from nostril to mouth tightened into a smile of sorts.

'I had gone up to London,' he said, 'to buy the ring.'

IV

'I knew, of course, that it would probably have to come out,' said Dr Schramm, 'but I hoped to avoid that. She was so very anxious that we should keep our engagement secret for the time being. The thought of making a sort of – well, posthumous announcement at the inquest was indescribably distasteful. One knew how the Press would set about it and the people in this place – I loathed the whole thought of it.'

He took one or two steps about the room. He moved with short strides, holding his shoulders rigid like a soldier. 'I don't offer this as an excuse. The thing has been a – an unspeakable shock to me. I can't believe it was suicide. Not when I remember – not unless something that I can't even guess at happened between the time when I said goodbye to her and my return.'

'You checked with the staff, of course.'

'Of course. She had dinner in bed and watched television. She was perfectly well. No doubt you've seen the report of the inquest and know all this. The waiter collected her tray round about eight-thirty. She was in the bathroom and he heard her singing to herself. After that – nothing. Nothing, until I came back. And found her.'

'That must have been a terrible shock.'

Schramm made the brief sound that usually indicates a sort of contempt. 'You may say so,' he said. And then, suddenly: 'Why have you been called in? What's it mean? Look here, do you people suspect foul play?'

'Hasn't the idea occurred to you?' Alleyn asked.

'The *idea* has. Of course it has. Suicide being inconceivable, the *idea* occurred. But that's inconceivable, too. The circumstances. The evidence. Everything. She had no enemies. Who would want to do it? It's – ' He broke off. A look of – what? sulkiness? derision? – appeared. It was as if he sneered at himself.

'But she wouldn't,' he said. 'I'm sure she didn't – '

'Didn't – ?'

'It doesn't matter. It's silly.'

'Are you wondering if Mrs Foster did, after all, confide in somebody about your engagement?'

He stared at Alleyn. 'That's right,' he said. 'And then, there were visitors that afternoon, as of course you know.'

'Her daughter and the daughter's fiancé and Miss Preston.'

'And the gardener.'

'Didn't he leave his flowers with the receptionist and go away without seeing Mrs Foster?' Alleyn asked.

'That's what he says, certainly.'

'It's what your receptionist says, too, Dr Schramm.'

'Yes. Very well, then. Nothing in that line of thinking. In any case the whole idea is unbelievable. Or ought to be.'

Mr Fox, using a technique that Alleyn was in the habit of alluding to as his disappearing act, had contrived to make his large person unobservable. He had moved as far away from Alleyn as possible and to a chair behind Dr Schramm. Here he palmed a notebook and his palm was vast. He used a stub of pencil and kept his work on his knee and his eyes respectfully on nothing in particular. Alleyn and Fox made a point of not looking at each other but at this juncture he felt sure Fox contemplated him, probably with that air of bland approval that generally meant they were both thinking the same thing.

'When you say "or ought to be",' Alleyn said, 'are you thinking about motive?'

Schramm gave a short meaningless laugh. His manner, unexpected in a doctor, seemed to imply that nothing under discussion was of importance. Alleyn wondered if he treated his patients to this sort of display. 'I don't want to put ideas in your head,' Schramm said, 'but to be quite, quite frank that did occur to me. Motive.'

'I'm resistant to ideas,' said Alleyn. 'Could you explain?'

'It's probably a lot of bumph but it does seem to me that our engagement wouldn't have been madly popular in certain quarters. Her family, to make no bones about it.'

'Are you thinking of Mrs Foster's stepson?'

'You said it. I didn't.'

'Motive?'

'I know of no motive, but I do know he sponged on her and pestered her and has a pretty disgraceful record. She was very much upset at the thought of his turning up here and I gave orders that if he did he must not be allowed to see her. Or speak to her on the telephone. I tell you this,' Dr Schramm said, 'as a fact. I don't for a moment pretend that it has any particular significance.'

'But I think you have something more than this in mind, haven't you?'

'If I have, I wouldn't want too much weight to be given to it.'

'I shall not give too much weight to it, I hope.'

Dr Schramm thumbed up the ends of his moustache. 'It's just that it does occur to me that he might have expectations. I've no knowledge of any such thing. None.'

'You know, do you, that Carter was on the premises that afternoon?'

'I do not!' he said sharply. 'Where did you get that from?'

'From Miss Verity Preston,' said Alleyn.

Again the shadow of a smile, not quite a sneer, not entirely complacent.

'Verity Preston?' he said. 'Oh yes? She and Syb were old friends.'

'He arrived in the same bus as Bruce Gardener. I gather he was ordered off seeing Mrs Foster.'

'I should bloody well hope so,' said Dr Schramm. 'Who by?'

'By Prunella Foster.'

'Good for her.'

'Tell me,' said Alleyn, 'speaking as a medical man, and supposing, however preposterously, that there was foul play, how would you think it could be accomplished?'

'There you are again! Nothing to indicate it! Everything points to the suicide I can't believe in. Everything. Unless,' he said sharply, 'something else has been found.'

'Nothing as I understand it.'

'Well then – !' He made a dismissive, rather ineloquent gesture.

'Dr Schramm, there's one aspect of her death I wanted to ask you about. Knowing, now, the special relationship between you I am very sorry to have to put this to you – it can't be anything but distressing to go over the circumstances again.'

'Christ Almighty!' he burst out. 'Do you suppose I don't "go over" them day in, day out? What d'you think I'm made of?' He raised his hand. 'I'm sorry!' he said. 'You're doing your job. What is it you want to ask?'

'It's about the partly dissolved tablets found in the throat and on the tongue. Do you find any inconsistency there? I gather the tablets take some twenty minutes to dissolve in water but are readily soluble in alcohol. It was supposed, wasn't it, that the reason they were not swallowed was because she became unconscious after putting them in her mouth? But – I suspect this is muddled thinking – would the tablets she had already taken have had time to induce insensibility? And anyway she couldn't have been insensible when she put these last ones in her mouth. I don't seem able to sort it out.'

Dr Schramm put his hand to his forehead, frowned and moved his head slowly from side to side.

'I'm sorry,' he said. 'Touch of migraine. Yes. The tablets. She took them with whisky, you know. As you say, they dissolve readily in alcohol.'

'Then wouldn't you think these would have dissolved in her mouth?'

'I would think that she didn't take any more whisky with them. Obviously, or she would have swallowed them.'

'You mean that she was conscious enough to put these four in her mouth but not conscious enough to drink or to swallow them? Yes,' said Alleyn. 'I see.'

'Well,' Dr Schramm said loudly, 'what else? What do you suppose?'

'I? I don't go in for supposing – we're not allowed to. Oh, by the way, do you know if Mrs Foster had made a Will – recently, I mean?'

'Of that,' said Dr Schramm, 'I have no idea.' And after a brief pause, 'Is there anything else?'

'Do you know if there are members of the staff here called G. M. Johnson and Marleena Biggs?'

'I have not the faintest idea. I have nothing to do with the management of the hotel.'

'Of course you haven't. Stupid of me. I'll ask elsewhere. If it's convenient, could we look at the room?'

'I'll take you up.' He pressed a buzzer on his desk.

'Please don't bother. Tell me the number and we'll find our way.'

'No, no. Wouldn't dream of it.'

These protestations were interrupted by the entrance of the nurse. She stood inside the door, her important bosom, garnished with its professional badge, well to the fore. A handsome, slightly florid lady, specifically plentiful.

'Oh, Sister,' said Dr Schramm, 'would you be very kind and hold the fort? I'm just going to show our visitors upstairs. I'm expecting that call from New York.'

'Certainly,' she said woodenly.

Alleyn said, 'You must be Sister Jackson, mustn't you ? I'm very glad to see you. Would you be very kind and give us a moment or two?'

She looked fixedly at Dr Schramm, who said grudgingly, 'Chief Superintendent Alleyn.'

'And Inspector Fox,' said Alleyn. 'Perhaps, as Dr Schramm expects his long-distance call, it won't be troubling you too much to ask you to show us the way to Mrs Foster's room?'

She still looked at Dr Schramm who began, 'No, that's all right, I'll – ' when the telephone rang. Sister Jackson made a half move as if to answer it but he picked up the receiver.

'Yes. Yes. Speaking. Yes, I accept the call.'

Alleyn said, 'Shall we?' to Sister Jackson and opened the door.

Schramm nodded to her and with the suggestion of a bridle she led the way back to the hall.

'Do we take the lift?' Alleyn asked. 'I'd be very much obliged if you would come. There are one or two points about the room that I don't quite get from the reports. We've been asked by the local Force to take a look at the general picture. A formality, really, but the powers-that-be are always rather fussy in these sorts of cases.'

'Oh yes?' said Sister Jackson.

In the lift it became apparent that she used scent.

For all her handsome looks, she was a pretty tough lady, Alleyn thought. Black, sharp eyes and a small hard mouth, set at the corners. It wouldn't be long before she settled into the battleaxe form.

The room, No. 20, was on the second floor at the end of a passage and at a corner of the building. The Quintern police had put a regulation seal on the door and had handed the key over to Alleyn. They had also taken the precaution of slipping an inconspicuous morsel of wool between door and jamb. Sister Jackson looked on in silence while Mr Fox, who wore gloves, dealt with these obstructions.

The room was dark, the closed window curtains admitting only a sliver or two of daylight. It smelt thickly of material, carpet, stale scent, dust and of something indefinable and extremely unpleasant. Sister Jackson gave out a short hiss of distaste. Fox switched on the light. He and Alleyn moved into the centre of the room. Sister Jackson remained by the door.

The room had an air of suspended animation. The bed was unmade. Its occupant might have just left it to go into the bathroom. One of the pillows and the lower sheet were stained as if something had been spilt on them. Another pillow lay, face down, at the foot of the bed. The whisky bottle, glass and tablets were all missing and were no doubt still in the custody of the local police, but an unwrapped parcel, obviously a book, together with a vanity box and the half-empty box of marzipan confections lay on the table alongside a lamp. Alleyn peered down the top of a rose-coloured shade and saw the glass slipper in place over the bulb. He took it off and examined it. There was no oil left but it retained a faint reek of sweet almonds. He put it aside.

The dressing-table carried, together with an array of bottles and pots, three framed photographs all of which he had seen that morning on and in Sybil Foster's desk at Quintern: her pretty daughter, her second husband and the regimental group with her handsome young first husband prominent among the officers. This was a less faded print and Alleyn looked closely at it, marvelling that such an Adonis could have sired the undelicious Claude. He peered at an enormous corporal in the back row who squinted amicably back at him. Alleyn managed to make out the man's badge – antlers enclosed by something – what? – a heather wreath? Wasn't there some nickname? 'The Spikes'? That was it. 'The Duke of Montrose's' nicknamed 'The Spikes'. Alleyn wondered how soon after this photograph was taken Maurice Carter had died. Claude would have been a child of three or four, he supposed, and remembered Verity

Preston's story of the lost Black Alexander stamp. What the hell is it, he thought, still contemplating the large corporal, that's nagging on the edge of my memory?

He went into the bathroom. A large bunch of dead lilies lay in the hand-basin. A dirty greenish stain showed where water had drained away. A new and offensive smell rose from the basin. ' "Lilies that fester," ' he reminded himself, ' "smell far worse than weeds." '

He returned to the bedroom and found Fox, placid in attendance, and Sister Jackson looking resentful.

'And this,' Alleyn said, 'is how it was when you were called in?'

'The things on the table have been removed. And there's no body,' she pointed out sourly.

'No more there is.'

'It's disgusting,' said Sister Jackson. 'Being left like this.'

'Horrid, isn't it? Could you just give us a picture of how things were when you arrived on the scene?'

She did so, eyeing him closely and with a certain air of appraisal. It emerged that she had been in her room and thinking of retiring when Dr Schramm telephoned her asking her to come at once to No. 20. There she found him stooping over the bed on which lay Mrs Foster, dead and cooling. Dr Schramm had drawn her attention to the table and its contents and told her to go to the surgery and fetch the equipment needed to empty the stomach. She was to do this without saying anything to anyone she met.

'We knew it was far too late to be of any use,' she said, 'but we did it. Dr Schramm said the contents should be kept and they were. In a sealed jar. We had to move the table away from the bed but nothing else was disturbed. Dr Schramm was very particular about that. Very.'

'And then?'

'We informed Mr Delaware, the manager. He was upset, of course. They don't like that sort of thing. Then we got Dr Field-Innis to come over from Upper Quintern and he said the police should be informed. We couldn't see why but he said he thought they ought to be. So they were.'

Alleyn noticed the increased usage of the first person plural in this narrative and wondered if he only imagined that it sounded possessive.

He thanked Sister Jackson warmly and handed her a glossy photograph of Mr Fox's Aunt Elsie which was kept for this purpose. Auntie Elsie had become a kind of code-person between Alleyn and Fox and was sometimes used as a warning signal when one of them wished to alert the other without being seen to do so. Sister Jackson failed to identify Aunt Elsie and was predictably intrigued. He returned the photograph to its envelope and said they needn't trouble her any longer. Having dropped his handkerchief over his hand, he opened the door to her.

'Pay no attention,' he said. 'We do these things hoping they give us the right image. Goodbye, Sister.'

In passing between him and Fox her hand brushed his. She rustled off down the passage, one hundred and fifty pounds of active femininity if she was an ounce.

'Cripes,' said Fox thoughtfully.

'Did she establish contact?'

'*En passant,*' he confessed in his careful French. 'What about you, Mr Alleyn?'

'*En passant, moi aussi.*'

'Do you reckon,' Mr Fox mused, 'she knew about the engagement?'

'Do you?'

'If she did, I'd say she didn't much fancy it,' said Fox.

'We'd better push on. You might pack up that glass slipper, Fox. We'll get Sir James to look at it.'

'In case somebody put prussic acid in it?'

'Something like that. After all, there was and *is* a strong smell of almonds. Only "Oasis", you'll tell me and I'm afraid you'll be right.'

On their way out the receptionist said she had made enquiries as to the electrical repairs man. Nobody knew anything about him except the girl who had given him Mrs Foster's flowers. He told her he had been sent to repair a lamp in No. 20 and the lady had asked him to collect her flowers when he went down to his car to get a new bulb for the bedside lamp. She couldn't really describe him except that he was slight, short and well-spoken and didn't wear overalls but did wear spectacles.

'What d'you make of that?' said Alleyn when they got outside.

'Funny,' said Fox. 'Sussy. Whatever way you look at it, not convincing.'

'There wasn't a new bulb in the bedside lamp. Old bulb, murky on top. Ready to conk out.'

'Lilies in the basin, though.'

'True.'

'What now, then?'

Alleyn looked at his watch. 'I've got a date with the Coroner,' he said. 'In one hour. At Upper Quintern. In the meantime, Bailey and Thompson had better give these premises the full treatment. Every inch of them.'

'Looking for what?'

'All the usual stuff. Latent prints, including Sister J's on Aunt Elsie, of course. Schramm's will be on the book wrapping and Prunella Foster's and her mother's on the vanity box. We've got to remember the room was done over in the morning by the house-maids, so anything that crops up will have been established during the day. We haven't finished with that sickening little room, Br'er Fox. Not by a long bloody chalk.'

CHAPTER 5

Greengages (II) Room 20

' – In view of which circumstances, members of the jury,' said the Coroner, 'you may consider that the appropriate decision would be again to adjourn these proceedings *sine die.*'

Not surprisingly, the jury embraced this suggestion and out into the age-old quietude of Upper Quintern village walked the people who, in one way or another, were involved, or had been obliged to concern themselves in the death of Sybil Foster: her daughter, her solicitor, her oldest friend, her gardener, the doctor she had disregarded and the doctor who had become her fiancé. And her stepson who by her death inherited the life interest left by her first husband. Her last and preposterous Will and Testament could not upset this entailment nor, according to Mr Rattisbon, could this Will itself be upset. G. M. Johnson and Marleena Biggs, chambermaids on the second floor of the hotel, confessed with uneasy giggles that they had witnessed Mrs Foster's signature a week before she died.

This Will provided the only sensation of the inquest. Nobody seemed to be overwhelmingly surprised at Bruce Gardener's legacy of £25,000 but the Swingletree clause and the sumptuous inheritance of Dr Schramm caused a sort of stupefaction in court. Three reporters from the provincial press were seen to be stimulated. Verity Preston, who was there because her god-daughter seemed to expect it, had a horrid foreboding of growing publicity.

The inquest had again been held in the parish hall. The spire of St Crispin-in-Quintern cast its shadow over an open space at the foot of steps that led up to the church. The local people referred to this

area as the 'green' but it was little more than a rough lateral bulge
in the lane. Upper Quintern was really a village only by virtue of its
church and was the smallest of its kind; hamlet would have seemed
a more appropriate title.

Sunlight, diffused by autumnal haze, the absence of wind and,
until car engines started up, of other than countrified sounds, all
seemed to set at a remove any process other than the rooted habit of
the Kentish soil. Somehow or another, Verity thought, whatever the
encroachments, continuity survives. And then she thought that it
had taken this particular encroachment to put the idea into her head.

She wondered if Young Mr Rattisbon would expect a repetition of
their former conviviality and decided to wait until he emerged.
People came together in desultory groups and broke up again. They
had the air of having been involved in some social contretemps.

Prunella came out between the two Markos men. Clearly she was
shaken, Gideon held her hand and his father, with his elegant head
inclined, stooped over her. Again, Verity had the feeling that they
absorbed Prunella.

Prunella saw her godmother, said something to the men and
came to Verity.

'Godma V,' she said. 'Did you know? I meant to let you know. It's
the day after the day after tomorrow – Thursday – they're going to –
they say we can – '

'Well, darling,' said Verity, 'that's a good thing, isn't it? What
time?'

'Three o'clock. Here. I'm telling hardly anyone – just very old
friends like you. And bunches of flowers out of our garden, don't
you think?'

'I do indeed. Would you like me to bring you? Or – are you – ?'

Prunella seemed to hesitate and then said, 'That's sweet of you,
Godma V. Gideon and Papa M are – coming with me but – could we
sit together, please?'

'Of course, we could,' Verity said and kissed her.

The jury had come out. Some straggled away to the bus stop,
some to a car. The landlord of the Passcoigne Arms was accompanied
into the pub by three of his fellow jurors. The Coroner appeared
with Mr Rattisbon. They stood together in the porch, looking at their
feet and conversing. They were joined by two others.

Prunella, who still held Verity's hand, said, 'Who's that, I wonder? Do you know? The tall one?'

'It's the one who called on me. Superintendent Alleyn.'

'I can see what you mean about him,' said Prunella.

The three representatives of the provincial press slid up to Alleyn and began to speak to him. Alleyn looked over their heads towards Verity and Prunella and as if he had signalled to her Verity moved to hide Prunella from the men. At the same instant Bruce Gardener came out of the hall and at once the three men closed round him.

Alleyn came over to Verity and Prunella.

'Good morning, Miss Preston,' he said. 'I wondered if you'd be here.' And to Prunella, 'Miss Foster? I expect your splendid Mrs Jobbin told you I'd called. She was very kind and let me come into your house. *Did* she tell you?'

'Yes. I'm sorry I was out.'

'There wasn't any need, at that juncture, to bother you. *I'm* sorry you're having such a horrid time. Actually,' Alleyn said, 'I may have to ask you to see me one of these days but only if it's really necessary. I promise.'

'OK,' Prunella said. 'Whenever you like. OK.'

'My dear Alleyn!' said a voice behind Verity. 'How very nice to meet you again.'

Mr Markos had come up, with Gideon, unnoticed by the others. The temper of the little scene changed with their appearance. He put his arm round Prunella and told Alleyn how well Troy's picture looked. He said Alleyn really ought to come and see it. He appealed to Verity for support and by a certain change in his manner seemed to attach a special importance to her answer. Verity was reminded of poor Syb's encomium before she took against the Markoses. She had said that Nikolas Markos was 'ultra-sophisticated' and 'a complete man of the world'. He's a man of a world I don't belong to, Verity thought, but we have things in common, nevertheless.

'Miss Preston will support me,' Mr Markos said, 'won't you?'

Verity pulled herelf together and said the picture was a triumph.

Alleyn said, 'The painter will be delighted,' and to all of them, 'The gentlemen of the Press look like heading this way. I suggest it might be as well if Miss Foster escaped.'

'Yes, of course,' said Gideon quickly. 'Darling, let's go to the car. Quick.'

But a stillness had fallen on the people who remained at the scene. Verity turned and saw that Dr Schramm had come out into the sunshine. The reporters fastened on him.

A handsome car was parked nearby. Verity thought, that's got to be his car. He'll have to come past us to get to it. We can't break up and bolt.

He said something – 'No comment,' Verity supposed, to the Press and walked briskly towards the group. As he passed them he lifted his hat. 'Good morning, Verity,' he said. 'Hullo, Markos, how are you? 'Morning, Superintendent.' He paused, looked at Prunella, gave a little bow and continued on his way. It had been well done, Verity thought, if you had the nerve to do it, and she was filled with a kind of anger that he had included her in his performance.

Mr Markos said, 'We all of us make mistakes. Come along, children.'

Verity, left with Alleyn, supposed Mr Markos had referred to his dinner-party.

'I must be off,' she said. She thought, death creates social contretemps. One doesn't say, 'See you the day after tomorrow' when the meeting will be at a funeral.

Her car was next to Alleyn's and he walked beside her. Dr Schramm drove past them and lifted a gloved hand as he did so.

'That child's surviving all this pretty well, isn't she?' Alleyn asked. 'On the whole, wouldn't you say?'

'Yes. I think she is. She's sustained by her engagement.'

'To young Markos? Yes. And by her godmama, too, one suspects?'

'Me! Not at all. Or anyway, not as much as I'd like.'

He grunted companionably, opened her car door for her and stood by while she fastened her safety-belt. She was about to say goodbye but changed her mind. 'Mr Alleyn,' she said, 'I gather that probate has been granted or passed or whatever it is? On the second Will?'

'It's not a *fait accompli* but it will be. Unless, of course, she made yet another and later one, which doesn't seem likely. Would it be safe to tell you something in confidence?'

Verity, surprised, said, 'I don't break confidences but if it's anything that I would want to speak about to Prunella, you'd better not tell me.'

'I don't think you would want to but I'd make an exception of Prunella. Dr Schramm and Mrs Foster were engaged to be married.'

In the silence that she was unable to break Verity thought that it really was not so very surprising, this information. There was even a kind of logic about it. Given Syb and given Basil Schramm.

Alleyn said, 'Rather staggering news, perhaps?'

'No, no,' she heard herself saying. 'Not really. I'm just – trying to assimilate it. Why did you tell me?'

'Partly because I thought there was a chance that she might have confided it to you that afternoon but mostly because I had an idea it might be disagreeable for you to learn of it accidentally.'

'Will it be made known, then? Will *he* make it known?'

'Well,' said Alleyn, 'I'm not sure. If it's anything to go by, he did tell *me*.'

'I suppose it explains the Will?'

'That's the general idea, of course.'

Verity heard herself say, 'Poor Syb.' And then, 'I hope it doesn't come out. Because of Prue.'

'Would she mind so much?'

'Oh, I think so. Don't you? The young mind terribly if they believe their parents have made asses of themselves.'

'And would any woman engaging herself to Dr Schramm make an ass of herself?'

'Yes,' said Verity. 'She would. I did.'

II

When Alleyn had gone Verity sat inert in her car and wondered what had possessed her to tell him something that for twenty-odd years she had told nobody. A policeman! More than that, a policeman who must, in the way things had gone, take a keen professional interest in Basil Schramm, might even – no, almost certainly did – think of him as a 'suspect'. And she turned cold when she forced herself to complete the sequence – a suspect in what might turn out to be a case of foul play – of, very well then, use the terrible soft word, of murder.

He had not followed up her statement or pressed her with questions nor, indeed, did he seem to be greatly interested. He merely said, 'Did you? Sickening for you,' made one or two remarks of no particular significance and said goodbye. He drove off with a large companion who could not be anything that was not constabulary. Mr Rattisbon, too, looking gravely preoccupied, entered his own elderly car and quitted the scene.

Still Verity remained, miserably inert. One or two locals sauntered off. The vicar and Jim Jobbin, who was part-time sexton, came out of the church and surveyed the weathered company of headstones. The vicar pointed to the right and they made off in that direction, round the church. Verity knew, with a jolt, that they discussed the making of a grave. Sybil's remotest Passcoigne forebears lay in the vault but there was a family plot among the trees beyond the south transept.

Then she saw that Bruce Gardener, in his Harris tweed suit. had come out of the hall and was climbing up the steps to the church. He followed the vicar and Jim Jobbin and disappeared. Verity had noticed him at the inquest. He had sat at the back, taller than his neighbours, upright, with his gardener's hands on his thighs, very decorous and solemn. She thought that perhaps he wanted to ask about the funeral, about flowers from Quintern Place, it might be. If so, that was nice of Bruce. She herself, she thought, must offer to do something about flowers. She would wait a little longer and speak to the vicar.

'Good morning,' said Claude Carter, leaning on the passenger's door.

Her heart seemed to leap into her throat. She had been looking out of the driver's window and he must have come up from behind the car on her blind side.

'Sorry,' he said, and grinned. 'Made you jump, did I?'

'Yes.'

'My mistake. I just wondered if I might cadge a lift to the turn-off. If you're going home, that is.'

There was nothing she wanted less but she said yes, if he didn't mind waiting while she went up to the church. He said he wasn't in a hurry and got in. He had removed his vestigial beard, she noticed and had his hair cut to a conservative length. He was tidily dressed and looked less hang-dog than usual. There was even a hint of submerged jauntiness about him.

'Smoking allowed?' he asked.

She left him lighting his cigarette in a guarded manner as if he was afraid someone would snatch it out of his mouth.

At the head of the steps she met the vicar returning with Bruce and Jim. To her surprise Jim, a bald man with a loud voice, was now bent double. He was hovered over by the vicar.

'It's a fair bugger,' he shouted. 'Comes over you like a bloody thunderclap. Stooping down to pull up them bloody teazles and now look at me. Should of minded me own business.'

'Yes, well, jolly bad luck,' said the vicar. 'Oh, hullo, Miss Preston. We're in trouble, as you see. Jim's smitten with lumbago.'

'Will he be able to negotiate the descent?' Bruce speculated anxiously. 'That's what I ask myself. Awa' wi' ye, man, and let us handle you doon the steps.'

'No, you don't. I'll handle myself if left to myself, won't I?'

'Jim!' said Verity. '*What* a bore for you. I'll drive you home.'

'No, ta all the same, Miss Preston. It's happened before and it'll happen again. I'm best left to manage myself and if you'll excuse me that's what I'll do. I'll use the handrail. Only,' he added with a sudden shout of agony, 'I'd be obliged if I wasn't watched.'

'Perhaps,' said the vicar, 'we'd better – ?'

Jim, moving like a gaffer in a Victorian melodrama, achieved the handrail and clung to it. He shouted, 'I won't be able to do the job now, will I?'

There was an awkward silence broken by Bruce. 'Dinna fash yourself,' he said. 'No problem. With the Minister's kind permission I'll dig it mysel' and think it an honour. I will that.'

'The full six foot, mind.'

'Ou aye,' Bruce agreed. 'All of it. I'm a guid hand at digging,' he added.

'Fair enough,' said Jim and began to ease himself down the steps.

'This is a most fortunate solution, Bruce,' said the vicar. 'Shall we just leave Jim as he wishes?' and he ushered them into the church.

St Crispin-in-Quintern was one of the great company of parish churches that stand as milestones in rural history; obstinate resisters of the ravages of time. It had a magnificent peal of bells, now unsafe to ring, one or two brasses, a fine east window and a surprising north

window in which – strange conceit – a walrus-mustachioed
Passcoigne, looking startlingly like Sir Arthur Conan Doyle, was
depicted in full plate armour, an Edwardian St Michael without a
halo. The legend indicated that he had met his end on the African
veld. The familiar ecclesiastical odour of damp held at bay by
paraffin heaters greeted Verity and the two men.

Verity explained that she would like to do anything that would
help about the flowers. The vicar said that custody of all brass vases
was inexorably parcelled out among the Ladies Guild, five in
number. She gathered that any attempt to disrupt this procedure
would trigger off a latent pecking order.

'But they would be grateful for flowers,' he added.

Bruce said that there were late roses up at Quintern Place and he'd
thought it would be nice to have her ain favourites to see her off. He
muttered in an uneven voice that the name was appropriate – Peace.
'They endure better than most oot o' watter,' he added and blew his
nose. Verity and the vicar warmly supported this suggestion and Verity
left the two men to complete, she understood, the arrangements for
digging Sybil's grave.

When she returned to the top of the steps she found that Jim
Jobbin had reached the bottom on his hands and knees and was
being manipulated through the lych-gate by his wife. Verity joined
them. Mrs Jim explained that she was on her way to get dinner and
had found Jim crawling backwards down the last four steps. It was no
distance, they both reminded Verity, along the lane to their cottage.
Jim got to his feet by swarming up his wife as if she was a tree.

'It'll ease off once he straightens himself,' she said. 'It does him
good to walk.'

'That's what you think,' her husband groaned but he straightened up and let out an oath as he did so. They made off in slow
motion.

Verity returned to her car and to Claude, lounging in the
passenger's seat. He made a token shuffle with his feet and leant
over to open the door.

'That was as good as a play,' he said. 'Poor old Jobbin. Did you see
him beetling down the steps? Fantastic!' He gave a neighing laugh.

'Lumbago's no joke to the person who's got it,' Verity snapped.

'It's hysterical for the person who hasn't, though.'

She drove as far as the corner where the lane up to Quintern Place branched off to the left.

'Will this suit you?' she asked, 'or would you like me to run you up?'

He said he wouldn't take her out of her way but when she pulled up he didn't get out.

'What did you make of the inquest?' he asked. 'I must say I thought it pretty off.'

'Off?'

'Well, you know. I mean what does that extraordinary detective person think he's on about? And a further postponement. Obviously they suspect something.'

Verity was silent.

'Which isn't exactly welcome news,' he said. 'Is it? Not for this medico, Schramm. Or for Mr Folksy Gardener if it comes to that?'

'I don't think you should make suggestions, Claude.'

'Suggestions! I'm not suggesting anything, but people are sure to look sideways. I know I wouldn't feel comfortable if I were in those gentlemen's boots, that's all. Still they're getting their lovely legacies, aren't they, which'll be a great consolation. I could put up with plenty of funny looks for twenty-five thousand of the best. Even more for Schramm's little lot.'

'I must get home, Claude.'

'Nothing can touch my bit, anyway. God, can I use it! Only thing, that old relic Rattisbon says it won't be available until probate is allowed or passed or whatever. I suppose I can borrow on my prospects, wouldn't you think?'

'I'm running late.'

'Nobody seems to think it's a bit off colour her leaving twenty-five thousand of the best to a jobbing gardener she'd only hired a matter of months ago. It's pretty obvious he'd got round her in a big way. I could tell you one or two things about Mr gardener-Gardener.'

'I must go, Claude.'

'Yes. OK.'

He climbed out of the car and slammed the door. 'Thanks for the lift anyway,' he said. 'See you at the funeral. Ain't we got fun?'

Glad to be rid of him but possessed by a languor she could not understand, Verity watched him turn up the lane. Even seen from behind there was a kind of furtive jauntiness in his walk, an air of complacency that was out of character. He turned a corner and was gone.

I wonder, she thought, what he'll do with himself.

She drove on up her own lane into her own little avenue and got her own modest luncheon. She found she hadn't much appetite for it.

The day was gently sunny but Verity found it oppressive. The sky was clear but she felt as if it would almost be a relief if bastions of cloud shouldered each other up from beyond the horizon. It occurred to her that writers like Ibsen and Dickens – unallied in any other respect – were right to make storms, snow, fog and fire the companions of human disorders. Shakespeare too, she thought. We deprive ourselves aesthetically when we forgo the advantages of symbolism.

She had finished the overhaul of her play and had posted it off to her agent. It was not unusual when work in hand had been dealt with and she was cleaned out for her to experience a nervous impulse to start off at once on something new. As now, when she found herself wondering if she could give a fresh look to an old, old theme: that of an intelligent woman enthralled by a second-rate charmer, a 'bad lot' in Verity's dated jargon, for whom she had no respect but was drawn to by an obstinate attraction. If she could get such a play successfully off her chest, would she scotch the bogey that had returned to plague her?

When at that first Markos dinner-party she found that Basil Schramm's pinchbeck magnetism had evaporated, the discovery had been a satisfaction to Verity. Now, when a shadow crept towards him, how did she feel? And why, oh why, had she bleated out her confession to Alleyn? He won't let it rest, she thought, her imagination bolting with her. He'll want to know more about Basil. He may ask if Basil ever got into trouble and what'll I say to that?

And Alleyn, returning with Fox to Greengages via Maidstone, said, 'This case is getting nasty. She let it out without any pushing or probing and I think she amazed herself by doing so. I wouldn't mind betting there was more to it than the predatory male jilt and the humiliated woman, though there was all of that, too, I dare say.'

'If it throws any light on his past?'

'We may have to follow it up, of course. Do you know what I think she'll do about it?'

'Refuse to talk?'

'That's it. There's not much of the hell-knows-no-fury in Verity Preston's make-up.'

'Well,' said Fox reasonably, 'seeing how pretty he stands, we have to make it thorough. What comes first?'

'Get the background. Check up on the medical side. Qualified at Lausanne, or wherever it was. Find out the year and the degree. See if there was any regular practice in this country. Or in the USA. So much waste of time, it may be, but it'll have to be done, Br'er Fox. And, on a different lay – here comes Maidstone again. Call at stationers and bookshops and see if anyone's bought any Will forms lately. If not, do the same in villages and towns and in the neighbourhood of Greengages.'

'Hoping we don't have to extend to London?'

'Fervently. But courage, comrade, we may find that in addition to witnessing the Will, G. M. Johnson or Marleena Biggs or even that casket of carnal delights Sister Jackson, was detailed to pop into a stationer's shop on her day off.'

When they reached Greengages, this turned out to be the answer. Johnson and Biggs had their days off together and a week before Mrs Foster died they had made the purchase at a stationer's in Greenvale. Mrs Foster had given them a present and told them to treat themselves to the cinema and tea.

'That's fine,' said Alleyn. 'We just wanted to know. Was it a good film?'

They fell into an ecstasy of giggles.

'I see. One of those?'

'Aw!'

'Anybody else know about the shopping?'

'Aw, no,' said G. M. Johnson.

'Yes they did, you're mad,' said Marleena Biggs.

'They never.'

'They did, too. The doctor did. He come in while she told us.'

'Dr Schramm came in and heard all about it?' said Alleyn casually.

They agreed and were suddenly uninterested.

'There you are, both of you. Treat yourselves to another shocker and a blow-out of cream buns.'

This interview concluded, Alleyn was approached by the manager of the hotel, who evidently viewed their visit with minimal enthusiasm. He hustled them into his office, offered drinks and looked apprehensive when these were declined.

'It's just about the room,' he said. 'How much longer do you people want it? We're expecting a full house by next week and it's extremely inconvenient, you know.'

'I hope this will be positively our last appearance,' said Alleyn cheerfully.

'Without being uncivil, so do I. Do you want someone to take you up?'

'We'll take ourselves, thank you all the same. Come along, Br'er Fox,' said Alleyn. *'En avant.* You're having one of your dreamy spells.'

He led the way quickly to the lifts.

The second floor seemed to be deserted. They walked soundlessly down the carpeted passage to No. 20. The fingerprint and photography men had called and gone and their seal was still on the door. Fox was about to break it when Alleyn said, 'Half a jiffy. Look at this.'

Opposite the bedroom door was a curtained alcove. He had lifted the curtain and disclosed a vacuum-cleaner. 'Handy little hidey-hole, isn't it?' he said. 'Got your torch on you?'

'As it happens,' Fox said and gave it to him. He went into the alcove and closed the curtain.

The lift at the far end of the long passage whined to a stop. Sister Jackson and another lady emerged. Fox, with a movement surprisingly nippy for one of his bulk, joined his superior in the alcove.

'Herself,' he whispered. Alleyn switched off his torch.

'See you?'

'Not to recognize.'

'Impossible. Once seen.'

'She had somebody with her.'

'No need for you to hide, you fathead. Why should you?'

'She flusters me.'

'You're bulging the curtain.'

But it was too late. The curtain was suddenly withdrawn and Sister Jackson discovered. She screamed.

'Good morning, Sister,' Alleyn said and flashed his torchlight full in her face. 'Do forgive us for startling you.'

'What,' she panted, her hand on her spectacular bosom, 'are you doing in the broom-cupboard?'

'Routine procedure. Don't give it another thought.'

'And you, don't shine that thing in my face. Come out.' They emerged.

In a more conciliatory tone and with a sort of huffy come-to-ishness, she said, 'You gave me a shock.'

'So did you us,' said Mr Fox. 'A nice one,' he roguishly added.

'I dare say.'

She was between them. She flashed upward glances first at one, then the other. Her bosom slightly heaved. Alleyn was reminded of Mr Dick Emery and expected to be told he was awful.

'We really do apologize,' he said.

'I should hope so.' She laid her hand, which was plump, on his closed one. He was surprised to feel a marked tremor and to see that the colour had ebbed out of her face. She kept up the flirtatious note, however, though her voice was unsteady. 'I suppose I'll have to forgive you,' she said. 'But only if you tell me why you were there.'

'I caught sight of something.'

He turned his hand over, opened it and exposed the crumpled head of a pink lily. It was very dead and its brown pollen had stained his palm.

'I think,' he said, 'it will team up with the ones in Mrs Foster's last bouquet. I wondered what the electrician was doing in the broom-cupboard.'

She gaped at him. 'Electrician?' she said. 'What electrician?'

'Don't let it worry you. Excuse us, please. Come on, Fox. Goodbye, Sister.'

When she had starched and bosomed herself away he said, 'I'm going to take another look at that broom-hide. Don't spring any more confrontations this time. Stay here.'

He went into the alcove, drew the curtains on himself and was away for some minutes. When he rejoined Fox he said, 'They're not so fussy about housework in there. Quite a lot of dust on the floor. Plenty of prints – housemaids' no doubt, but at the far end, in the corner away from the vacuum-cleaner where nobody would go normally, there are prints, left and right, side by side, with the heels almost touching the wall. Men's crêpe-soled shoes, and beside them – guess.'

He opened his hand and disclosed another dead lily-head. 'Near the curtain I could just find the prints again but overlaid by the housemaids' and some regulation-type extras. Whose do you think?'

'All right, all right,' said Fox. 'Mine.'

'When we go down we'll look like sleuths and ask the desk lady if she noticed the electrician's feet.'

'That's a flight of fancy, if you like,' said Fox. 'And she won't have.'

'In any case Bailey and Thompson will have to do their stuff. Come on.'

When they were inside No. 20 he went to the bathroom where the fetid bouquet still mouldered in the basin. It was possible to see that the finds matched exactly and actually to distinguish the truss from which they had been lost.

'So I make a note – "Find the electrician"?' asked Fox.

'You anticipate my every need.'

'How do you fancy this gardener? Gardener?'

'Not much!' said Alleyn. 'Do you?'

'You wouldn't fancy him sneaking back with the flowers when Miss Foster and party had gone?'

'Not unless he's had himself stretched. The reception girl said slight, short and bespectacled. Bruce Gardener's six foot three and big with it. He doesn't wear spectacles.'

'He'd be that chap in the Harris tweed suit at the inquest?'

'He would. I meant to point him out to you.'

'I guessed,' said Fox heavily.

'Claude Carter, on the contrary, is short, slight, bespectacled and in common with the electrician and several million other males doesn't wear overalls.'

'Motive? No. Hang on. He gets Mrs Foster's bit from her first husband.

'Yes.'

'Ask if anyone knows about electricians? And nobody will,' Fox prophesied.

'Ask about what bus he caught back to Quintern and get a dusty answer.'

'Ask if anyone saw him any time, anywhere.'

'With or without lilies. In the meantime, Fox, I seem to remember there's an empty cardboard box and a paper shopping-bag in the wardrobe. Could you put those disgusting lilies in the box? Keep the ones from the broom-cupboard separate. I want another look at her pillows.'

They lay as they had lain before – three of them, luxuriant pillow-cases in fine lawn with broderie-anglaise threaded with ribbon. Brought them with her, Alleyn thought. Even Greengages wouldn't run to these lengths.

The smallest of them carried a hollow made by her dead or alive head. The largest lay at the foot of the bed and was smooth. Alleyn turned it over. The under surface was crumpled, particularly in the centre – crumpled and stained as if it had been wet and, in two places, faintly pink with small, more positive indentations, one of them so sharp that it actually had broken the delicate fabric. He bent down and caught a faint nauseating reek. He went to the dressing-table and found three lipsticks, all of them, as was the fashion at that time, very pale. He took one of them to the pillow. It matched.

III

During the remaining sixty hours before Sybil Foster's burial in the churchyard of St Crispin-in-Quintern the police investigations, largely carried out over the telephone, multiplied and accelerated. As is always the case, much of what was unearthed turned out to be of no relevance, much was of a doubtful or self-contradictory nature and only a scanty winnowing found to be of real significance. It was as if the components of several jigsaw puzzles had been thrown down on the table and before the one required picture could be assembled the rest would have to be discarded.

The winnowings, Alleyn thought, were for the most part suggestive rather than definitive. A call to St Luke's Hospital established that Basil Smythe, as he then was, had indeed been a first-year medical student at the appropriate time and had not completed the course. A contact of Alleyn's in Swiss police headquarters put through a call to a hospital in Lausanne confirming that Dr Basile Schramm had graduated from a teaching hospital in that city. Basile, Alleyn was prepared to accept, might well have been a Swiss shot at Basil. Schramm had accounted to Verity Preston for the change from Smythe. They would have to check if this was indeed his mother's maiden name.

So far nothing had been found in respect of his activities in the United States.

Mrs Jim Jobbin had, at Mrs Foster's request and a week before she died, handed a bottle of sleeping-pills over to Bruce Gardener. Mrs Foster had told Bruce where they would be found – in her writing-desk. They had been bought some time ago from a Maidstone chemist and were a proprietary brand of barbiturate. Mrs Jim and Bruce had both noticed that the bottle was almost full. He had duly delivered it that same afternoon.

Claude Carter had what Mr Fox called a sussy record. He had been mixed up, as a very minor figure, in the drug racket. In his youth he had served a short sentence for attempted blackmail. He was thought to have brought a small quantity of heroin ashore from *SS Poseidon*. If so, he had got rid of it before he was searched at the Customs.

Verity Preston had remembered the august name of Bruce Gardener's latest employer. Discreet enquiries had confirmed the authenticity of Bruce's references and his unblemished record. The head gardener, named McWhirter, was emphatic in his praise and very, very Scotch.

This, thought Alleyn, might tally with Verity Preston's theory about Bruce's dialectical vagaries.

Enquiries at appropriate quarters in the City elicited the opinion that Nikolas Markos was a millionaire with a great number of interests of which oil, predictably, was the chief. He was also the owner of a string of luxury hotels in Switzerland, the South Pacific, and the Costa Brava. His origin was Greek. Gideon had been educated at a celebrated public school and at the Sorbonne and was believed to be in training for a responsible part in his father's multiple business activities.

Nothing further could be discovered about the 'electrician' who had taken Bruce's flowers up to Sybil Foster's room. The desk lady had not noticed his feet.

'We'll be having a chat with Mr Claude Carter, then?' asked Fox, two nights before the funeral. He and Alleyn were at the Yard having been separated during the day on their several occasions, Fox in and about Upper Quintern and Alleyn mostly on the telephone and in the City.

'Well, yes,' he agreed. 'Yes. We'll have to, of course. But we'd better walk gingerly over that particular patch, Br'er Fox. If he's in deep, he'll be fidgety. If he thinks we're getting too interested he may take off and we'll have to waste time and men on running him down.'

'Or on keeping obbo to prevent it. Do you reckon he'll attend the funeral?'

'He may decide we'd think it odd if he didn't. After his being so assiduous about gracing the inquests. There you are! We'll need to go damn carefully. After all, what have we got? He's short, thin, wears spectacles and doesn't wear overalls.'

'If you put it like that.'

'How would you put it?'

'Well,' said Fox, scraping his chin, 'he'd been hanging about the premises for we don't know how long and, by the way, no joy from the bus scene. Nobody remembers him or Gardener. I talked to the conductors on every return trip that either of them might have taken but it was a Saturday and there was a motor rally in the district and they were crowded all the way. They laughed at me.'

'Cads.'

'There's the motive, of course,' Fox continued moodily. 'Not that you can do much with that on its own. How about the lilies in the broom-cupboard?'

'How about them falling off in the passage and failing to get themselves sucked up by the vacuum-cleaner?'

'You make everything so difficult,' Fox sighed.

'Take heart. We have yet to see his feet. And him, if it comes to that. Bailey and Thompson may have come up with something dynamic. Where are they?'

'Like they say in theatrical circles. Below and awaiting your pleasure.'

'Admit them.'

Bailey and Thompson came in with their customary air of being incapable of surprise. Using the minimum quota of words, they laid out for Alleyn's inspection an array of photographs: of the pillowcase *in toto*, of the stained area on the front in detail and of one particular indentation blown up to the limit which had actually left a cut in the material. Over this, Alleyn and Fox concentrated.

'Well, you two,' Alleyn said at last, 'what do you make of this lot?'

It was by virtue of such invitations that his relationship with his subordinates achieved its character. Bailey, slightly more communicative than his colleague, said, 'Teeth. Like you thought, Governor. Biting the pillow.'

'All right. How about it?'

Thompson laid another exhibit before him. It was a sort of macabre triptych: first a reproduction of the enlargement he had already shown and beside it, corresponding in scale, a photograph of all too unmistakably human teeth from which the lips had been retracted in a dead mouth.

'We dropped in at the morgue,' said Bailey. 'The bite could tally.'

The third photograph, one of Thompson's montages, showed the first superimposed upon the second. Over this, Thompson had ruled vertical and horizontal lines.

'Tallies,' Alleyn said.

'Can't fault it,' said Bailey dispassionately.

He produced a further exhibit: the vital section of the pillowcase itself mounted between two polythene sheets and set it beside Thompson's display of photographs.

'Right,' Alleyn said. 'We send this to the laboratory, of course, and in the meantime, Fox, we trust our reluctant noses. People who are trying to kill themselves with an overdose of sleeping-pills may vomit but they don't bite holes in the pillowcase.'

'It's nice to know we haven't been wasting our time,' said Fox.

'You are,' said Alleyn, staring at him, 'probably the most remorseless realist in the service.'

'It was only a passing thought. Do we take it she was smothered, then?'

'If Sir James concurs, we do. He'll be cross about the pillowcase.'

'You'd have expected the doctors to spot it. Well,' Fox amended, 'you'd have expected the Field-Innis one to, anyway.'

'At that stage their minds were set on suicide. Presumably the great busty Jackson had got rid of the stomach-pumping impedimenta after she and Schramm, as they tell us, had seen to the bottling of the results. Field-Innis says that by the time he got there, this had been done. It was he, don't forget, who said the room should be left untouched and the police informed. The pillow was face downwards at the foot of the bed but in any case only a very close examination reveals the mark of the tooth. The stains, which largely obscure it, could well have been the result of the overdose. What about dabs, Bailey?'

'What you'd expect. Dr Schramm's, the nurse Jackson's. Deceased's of course, all over the shop. The other doctor's – Field-Innis. I called at his surgery and asked for a take. He wasn't all that keen but he obliged. The girl Foster's on the vanity box and her mother's like you indicated.'

'The tumbler?'

'Yeah,' said Bailey, with his look of mulish satisfaction. 'That's right. That's the funny bit. Nothing. Clean. Same goes for the pill bottle and the whisky bottle.'

'Now we're getting somewhere,' said Fox.

'Where do we get to, Br'er Fox?'

'Gloves used but only after she lost consciousness.'

'What I reckoned,' said Bailey.

'Or after she'd passed away?' Fox speculated.

'No, Mr Fox. Not if smothering's the story.'

Alleyn said, 'No dabs on the reverse side of the pillow?'

'That's the story,' said Thompson.

Bailey produced, finally, a polythene bag containing the back panel of the pretty lawn pillowcase, threaded with ribbon. 'This,' he said, 'is kind of crushed on the part opposite to the tooth print and stains. Crumpled up, like. As if by hands. No dabs, but crumpled. What I reckon – hands.'

'Gloved. Like the Americans say, it figures. Anything else in the bedroom?'

'Not to signify.'

The telephone rang. It was a long-distance call from Berne. Alleyn's contact came through loud and clear.

'M. le Superintendant? I am calling immediately to make an amendment to our former conversations.'

'An amendment, *mon ami?*'

'An addition, perhaps more accurately. In reference to the Doctor Schramm at the Sacré-Coeur, you recollect?'

'Vividly.'

'M. le Superintendant, I regret. My contact at the bureau has made a further search. It is now evident that the Doctor Schramm in question is deceased. In effect, since 1952.'

During the pause of the kind often described as pregnant Alleyn made a face at Fox and said, 'Dead.' Fox looked affronted.

'At the risk,' Alleyn said into the telephone, 'of making the most intolerable nuisance of myself, dare I ask if your source would have the very great kindness to find out if, over the same period, there is any record of an Englishman called Basil Smythe having qualified at Sacré-Coeur. I should explain, my dear colleague, that there is now the possibility of a not unfamiliar form of false pretence.'

'But of course. You have but to ask. And the name again?'

Alleyn spelt it out, and was told he could expect a return call within the hour. It came through in twelve minutes. An Englishman called Basil Smythe had attended the courses at the time in question but had failed to complete them. Alleyn thanked his expeditious confrère profusely. There was a further interchange of compliments and he hung up.

IV

'It's not only in the story-books,' observed Fox on the following morning as they drove once more to Greengages, 'that you get a surplus of suspects but I'll say this for it – it's unusual. The dates tally, don't they?'

'According to the records at St Luke's, he was a medical student in London in 1950. It would seem he didn't qualify there.'

'And now we begin to wonder if he qualified anywhere at all?'

'Does the doctor practise to deceive, in fact?' Alleyn suggested.

'Perhaps if he was at the hospital and knew the real Schramm he might have got hold of his diploma when he died. Or am I being fanciful?' asked Fox.

'You are being fanciful. And yet I don't know. It's possible.'

'Funnier things have happened.'

'True,' said Alleyn and they fell silent for the rest of the drive.

They arrived at Greengages under the unenthusiastic scrutiny of the receptionist. They went directly to No. 20 and found it in an advanced stage of unloveliness.

'It's not the type of case I like,' Fox complained. 'Instead of knowing who the villain is and getting on quietly with routine until you've collected enough to make a charge, you have to go dodging about from one character to another like the chap in the corner of a band.'

'Bang, tinkle, crash?'

'Exactly. Motive,' Fox indignantly continued. 'Take motive. There's Bruce Gardener who gets twenty-five thousand out of it and the stepson who gets however much his father entailed on him after his mother's death and there's a sussy-looking quack who gets a fortune. Not to mention Mr Markos who fancied her house and Sister Jackson who fancies the quack. You can call them fringe characters. *I* don't know! Which of the lot can we wipe? Tell me that, Mr Alleyn.'

'I'm sorry too many suspects makes you so cross, Br'er Fox, but I can't oblige. Let's take a look at an old enemy, *modus operandi,* shall we? Now that Bailey and Thompson have done their stuff what do we take out of it? *You* tell *me* that, my Foxkin.'

'Ah!' said Fox. 'Well now, what? What happened, eh? I reckon – and you'll have to give me time, Mr Alleyn – I reckon something after this fashion. After deceased had been bedded down for the night by her daughter and taken her early dinner, a character we can call the electrician, though he was nothing of the kind, collected the lilies from the reception desk and came up to No. 20. While he was still in the passage he heard or saw someone approaching and stepped into the curtained alcove.'

'As you did, we don't exactly know why.'

'With me it was what is known as a reflex action,' said Fox modestly. 'While in the alcove two of the lilies got their heads knocked off. The electrician (*soi-disant*) came out and entered No. 20. He now – don't bustle me – '

'I wouldn't dream of it. He now?'

'Went into the bedroom and bathroom,' said Fox and himself suited the action to the word, raising his voice as he did so, 'and put the lilies in the basin. They don't half stink now. He returned to the bedroom and kidded to the deceased.'

'Kidded?'

'Chatted her up,' Fox explained. He leant over the bed in a beguiling manner. 'She tells him she's not feeling quite the thing and he says why not have a nice drink and a sleeping-pill. And, by the way, didn't the young lady say something about putting the pill bottle out for her mother? She did? Right! So this chap gets her the drink – scotch and water. Now comes the nitty-gritty bit.'

'It did, for her at any rate.'

'He returns to the bathroom, which I shan't bother to do. Ostensibly,' said Fox, looking this superior officer hard in the eye, 'ostensibly to mix the Scotch and water but he slips in a couple, maybe three, maybe four pills. Soluble in alcohol, remember.'

'There's a water jug on her table.'

'I thought you'd bring that up. He says it'll be stale. The water. Just picks up the whisky and takes it into the bathroom.'

'Casual-like?'

'That's it.'

'Yes. I'll swallow that, Br'er Fox. Just.'

'So does she. She swallows the drink knowing nothing of the tablets and he gives her one or maybe two more which she takes herself thinking they're the first, with the Scotch and water.'

'How about the taste, if they do taste?'

'It's a strong Scotch. And,' Fox said quickly, 'she attributes the taste, if noticed, to the one or maybe two tablets she's given herself. She has now taken, say, six tablets.'

'Go on. If you've got the nerve.'

'He waits. He may even persuade her to have another drink. With him. And puts more tablets in it.'

'What's he drink out of? The bottle?'

'Let that be as it may. He waits, I say, until she's dopey.'

'Well?'

'And he puts on his gloves and smothers her,' said Fox suddenly. 'With the pillow.'

'I see.'

'You don't buy it, Mr Alleyn?'

'On the contrary, I find it extremely plausible.'

'You do? I forgot to say,' Fox added, greatly cheered, 'that he put the extra tablets in her mouth after she was out. Gave them a push to the back of the tongue. That's where he overdid it. One of those fancy touches you're so often on about. Yerse. To make suicide look convincing he got rid of a lot more down the loo.'

'Was the television going all this time?'

'Yes. Because Dr Schramm found it going when he got there. Blast,' said Fox vexedly. 'Of course if *he's* our man – '

'He got home much earlier than he makes out. The girl at reception would hardly mistake him for an itinerant electrician. So someone else does that bit and hides with the vacuum-cleaners and puts the lilies in the basin and goes home as clean as a whistle.'

'Yerse,' said Fox.

'There's no call for you to be crestfallen. It's a damn good bit of barefaced conjecture and may well be right if Schramm's not our boy.'

'But if this Claude Carter is?'

'It would fit.'

'Ah! And Gardener ? Well,' said Fox, 'I know he's all wrong if the receptionist girl's right. I know that. Great hulking cross-eyed lump of a chap,' said Fox crossly.

There followed a discontented pause at the end of which Fox said, with a touch of diffidence, 'Of course, there is another fringe character, isn't there? Perhaps two. I mean to say, by all accounts the deceased *was* dead set against the engagement, wasn't she?'

Alleyn made no reply. He had wandered over to the dressing-table and was gazing at its array of Sybil Foster's aids to beauty and at the regimental photograph in a silver frame. Bailey had dealt delicately with them all and scarcely disturbed the dust that had settled on them or upon the looking-glass that reflected her altered face.

After another long silence Alleyn said, 'Do you know, Fox, you have, in the course of your homily, proved me, to my own face and full in my own silly teeth, to be a copybook example of the unobservant investigating officer.'

'You don't say!'

'But I do say. Grinding the said teeth and whipping my cat, I do say.'

'It would be nice,' said Fox mildly, 'to know why.'

'Let's pack up and get out of this and I'll tell you on the way.'

'On the way to where?' Fox reasonably enquired.

'To the scene where I was struck down with sand-blindness or whatever. To the source of all our troubles. To our patch. To the point marked bloody x.'

'Upper Quintern, would that be?'

'Upper Quintern it is. And I think, Fox, we'd better find ourselves rooms at a pub. Better to be there than here. Come on.'

CHAPTER 6

Point Marked X

Prunella was at home at Quintern Place. Her car was in the drive and she herself answered the door, explaining that she was staying at Mardling and had merely called in to pick up her mail. She took Alleyn and Fox into the drawing-room. It was a room of just proportions with appointments that had occurred quietly over many years rather than by any immediate process of collective assembly. The panelling and ceiling were graceful. It was a room that seemed to be full of gentle light.

Alleyn exclaimed with pleasure.

'Do you like it?' Prunella said. 'Most people seem to like it.'

'I'm sure you do, don't you?'

'I expect so. It always feels quite nice to come back to. It's not exactly riveting of course. Too predictable. I mean, it doesn't *send* one, does it? I don't know, though. It sends my father-in-law-to-be up like a rocket. Do sit down.'

She herself sat between them. She arranged her pretty face in a pout almost as if she parodied some Victorian girl. She was pale and, Alleyn thought, very tense.

'We won't be long about this,' he said. 'There are one or two bits and pieces we're supposed to tidy up. Nothing troublesome, I hope.'

'Oh,' said Prunella. 'I see. I thought that probably you'd come to tell me my mother was murdered. Officially tell me, I mean. I know, of course, that you thought so.'

Until now she had spoken in her customary whisper but this was brought out rapidly and loudly. She stared straight in front of her and her hands were clenched in her lap.

'No,' Alleyn said. 'That's not it.'

'But you think she was, don't you?'

'I'm afraid we do think it's possible. Do you?'

Prunella darted a look at him and waited a moment before she said. 'I don't know. The more I wonder the less I can make up my mind. But then, of course, there are all sorts of things the police dig up that other people know nothing about. Aren't there?'

'That's bound to happen,' he agreed. 'It's our job to dig, isn't it?'

'I suppose so.'

'My first reason for coming is to make sure you have been properly consulted about the arrangements for tomorrow and to ask if there is anything we can do to help. The service is at half past three, isn't it? The present suggestion is that your mother will be brought from Maidstone to the church, arriving about two o'clock, but it has occurred to me that you might like her to rest there tonight. If so, that can easily be arranged.'

Prunella, for the first time, looked directly at him. 'That's kind,' she said. 'I'd like that, I think. Please.'

'Good. I'll check with our chaps in Maidstone and have a word with your vicar. I expect he'll let you know.'

'Thank you.'

'All right then.'

'Super,' said Prunella with shaking lips. Tears trickled down her cheeks. 'I'm sorry,' she said. 'I thought I'd got over all this. I thought I was OK.' She knuckled her eyes and fished a handkerchief out of her pocket. Mr Fox rose and walked away to the furthest windows through which he contemplated the prospect.

'Never mind,' Alleyn said. 'That's the way delayed shock works. Catches you on the hop when you least expect it.'

'Sickening of it,' Prunella mumbled into her handkerchief. 'You'd better say what you wanted to ask.'

'It can wait a bit.'

'No!' said Prunella and stamped like an angry child. 'Now.'

'All right. I'd better say first what we always say. Don't jump to conclusions and read all sorts of sinister interpretations into routine questions. You must realize that in a case of this sort everyone who saw anything at all of your mother or had contact, however trivial, with her during the time she was at Greengages, and especially on the last day, has to be crossed off.'

'All except one.'

'Perhaps not excepting even one then we *do* look silly.' Prunella sniffed. 'Go ahead,' she said. 'Do you know a great deal about your mother's first husband?'

Prunella stared at him.

'*Know?* Me? Only what everyone knows. Do you mean about how he was killed and about the Black Alexander stamp?'

'Yes. We've heard about the stamp. And about the unfinished letter to your mother.'

'Well then. There's nothing else that I can think of.'

'Do you know if she kept that letter? And any other of his letters?'

Prunella began, 'If I did I wouldn't – ' and pulled herself up. 'Sorry,' she said, 'yes, she did. I found them at the back of a drawer in her dressing-table. It's a converted sofa-table and it's got a not terribly secret, secret drawer.'

'And you have them still?'

She waited for a second or two and then nodded. 'I've read them,' she said. 'They're fantastic, lovely letters. They can't possibly have anything at all to do with any of this. Not possibly.'

'I've seen the regimental group photograph.'

'Mrs Jim told me.'

'He was very good-looking, wasn't he?'

'Yes. They used to call him Beau Carter. It's hard to believe when you see Claude, isn't it? He was only twenty-one when his first wife died. Producing Claude. Such an awful waste, I've always thought. Much better if it'd been the other way round, though of course in that case I would have been – just not. Or would I? How muddling.'

She glanced down the long room to where Mr Fox, at its furthest extreme, having put on his spectacles, was bent over a glass-topped curio table. 'What's he doing?' she whispered.

'Being tactful.'

'Oh. I see.'

'About your mother – did she often speak of her first husband?'

'Not often. I think she got out of the way of it when my papa was alive. I think he must have been jealous, poor love. He wasn't exactly a heart-throb to look at himself. You know – pink and portly. So I think she kept things like pre-papa photographs and letters discreetly out of circulation. Sort of. But she did tell me about Maurice – that was his name.'

'About his soldiering days? During the war when I suppose that photograph was taken?'

'Yes. A bit about him. Why?'

'About his brother officers, for instance? Or the men under him?'

'*Why?*' Prunella insisted. 'Don't be like those awful pressmen who keep bawling out rude questions that haven't got anything to do with the case. Not,' she added hastily, 'that you'd really do that because you're not at all that kind. But, I mean what on *earth* can my Mum's first husband's brother officers and men have to do with his wife's murder when most of them are dead, I dare say, themselves?'

'His soldier-servant, for instance? Was there anything in the letters about *him?* The officer-batman relationship can be, in its way, quite a close one.'

'Now you mention it,' said Prunella on a note of impatience, 'there were jokey bits about somebody he called the Corp, who I suppose might have been his servant but they weren't anything out of the way. In the last letter, for instance. It was written here. He'd got an unexpected leave and come home but Mummy was with her WRNS in Scotland. It says he's trying to get a call through to her but will leave the letter in case he doesn't. It breaks off abrupdy saying he's been recalled urgently to London and has just time to get to the station. I expect you know about the train being bombed.'

'Yes. I know.'

'Well,' said Prunella shortly, 'it was a direct hit. On his carriage. So that's all.'

'And what about the Corp? In the letter?'

'What? Oh. There's a very effing bit about – sorry,' said Prunella. '"Effing" is family slang for "affecting" or kind of "terribly touching". This bit is about what she's to do if he's killed and how much – how he feels about her and she's not to worry and anyway the Corp looks after him like a nanny. He must have been rather a super chap, Maurice, I always think.'

'Anything about the Black Alexander?'

'Oh, that! Well – actually, yes, there is something. He says he supposes she'll think him a fusspot but, after all, his London bank's in the hottest blitz area and he's taken the stamp out and will store it elsewhere. There's something about its being in a waterproof case or something. It was at that point he got the urgent recall to London. So he breaks off – and – says goodbye. Sort of.'

'And the stamp was never to be found.'

'That's right, Not for want of looking. But obviously he had it on him.'

'Miss Foster, I wouldn't ask you this if it wasn't important and I hope you won't mind very much that I do ask. Will you let me see those letters?'

Prunella looked at her own hands. They were clenched tightly on her handkerchief and she hurriedly relaxed them. The handkerchief lay in a small damply crumpled heap in her lap. Alleyn saw where a fingernail had bitten into it.

'I simply can't imagine *why*,' she said, 'I mean, it's fantastic. Love letters, pure and simple, written almost forty years ago and concerning nothing and nobody but the writer. And Mummy, of course.'

'I know. It seems preposterous, doesn't it? But I can't tell you how "professional" and detached I shall be about it. Rather like a doctor. Please let me see them.'

She glanced at the distant Fox, still absorbed in the contents of the curio table. 'I don't want to make a fuss about nothing,' she said. 'I'll get them.'

'Are they still in the not-so-secret secret drawer of the converted sofa-table?'

'Yes.'

'I should like to see it.' They had both risen.

'Secret drawers,' said Alleyn lightly, 'are my speciality. At the Yard they called me Peeping Tom Alleyn.' Prunella compressed her lips. 'Fox,' Alleyn said loudly, 'may I tear you away?'

'I beg your pardon, Mr Alleyn,' Fox said, removing his spectacles but staying where he was. 'I beg *your* pardon, Miss Foster. My attention was caught by this – should I call it specimen table? My aunt, Miss Elsie Smith, has just such another in her shop in Brighton.'

'Really?' said Prunella and stared at him.

Alleyn strolled down to the other end of the room and leant over the table. It contained a heterogeneous collection of medals, a vinaigrette, two miniatures, several little boxes in silver or cloisonné and one musical box, all set out on a blue velvet base.

'I'm always drawn to these assemblies,' Alleyn said. 'They are family history in hieroglyphics. I see you've rearranged them lately.'

'No, I haven't. Why?' asked Prunella, suddenly alerted. She joined them. It was indeed clear from indentations in the velvet that a rearrangement had taken place. 'Damn!' she said. 'At it again! No, it's too much.'

'At it?' Alleyn ventured. 'Again? Who?'

'Claude Carter. I suppose you know he's staying here. He – does so fiddle and pry.'

'What does he pry into?'

'All over the place. He's always like that. The old plans of this house and garden. Drawers in tables. He turns over other people's letters when they come. I wouldn't put him past reading them. I'm not living here at the moment so I dare say he's having field days. I don't know why I'm talking about it.'

'Is he in the house at this moment?'

'I don't know. I've only just come in myself. Never mind. Forget it. Do you want to see the letters?'

She walked out of the room. Alleyn opened the door for her. He followed her into the hall and up the staircase.

'How happy Mr Markos will be,' he remarked, 'climbing up the golden stairs. They *are* almost golden, aren't they? Where the sun catches them?'

'I haven't noticed.'

'Oh, but you should. You mustn't allow ownership to dull the edge of appetite. One should always know how lucky one is.'

Prunella turned on the upper landing and stared at him. 'Is it your habit,' she asked, 'to go on like this ? When you're on duty?'

'Only if I dare hope for a sympathetic reception. What happens now? Turn right, proceed in a westerly direction and effect an entrance?'

Since this was in fact what had to be done, Prunella said nothing and led the way into her mother's bedroom.

A sumptuous room. There was a canopied bed and a silken counterpane with a lacy nightgown case topped up by an enormous artificial rose. A largesse of white bearskin rugs. But for all its luxury the room had a depleted air as if the heart had gone out of it. One of the wardrobe doors was open and disclosed complete emptiness.

Prunella said rapidly, 'I sent everything, all the clothes, away to the nearest professional theatre. They can sell the things they don't use – fur hats and coats and things.'

There were no photographs or feminine toys of any kind on the tables and chimney-piece and Sybil's sofa-cum-dressing-table with its cupid-encircled looking-glass, had been bereft of all the pots, bottles and jars that Alleyn supposed had adorned it.

Prunella said, following his look, 'I got rid of everything. Everything.' She was defiant.

'I expect it was the best thing to do.'

'We're going to change the room. Completely. My father-in-law-to-be's fantastic about houses – an expert. He'll advise us.'

'Ah, yes,' said Alleyn politely.

She almost shouted at him, 'I suppose you think I'm hard and modern and over-reacting to everything. Well, so I may be. But I'll thank you to remember that Will. How she tried to bribe me, because that's what it was, into marrying a monster, because that's what he is, and punish me if I didn't. I never thought she had it in her to be so mean and despicable and I'm not going to bloody cry again and I don't in the least know why I'm talking to you like this. The letters are in the dressing-table and I bet you can't find the hidden bit.'

She turned her back on Alleyn and blew her nose.

He went to the table, opened the central drawer, slid his finger round inside the frame and found a neat little knob that released a false wall at the back. It opened and there in the 'secret' recess was the classic bundle of letters tied with the inevitable faded ribbon.

There was also an open envelope with some half-dozen sepia snapshots inside.

'I think,' he said, 'the best way will be for me to look at once through the letters and if they are irrelevant return them to you. Perhaps there's somewhere downstairs where Fox and I could make ourselves scarce, and get it settled.'

Without saying anything further Prunella led the way downstairs to the 'boudoir' he had visited on his earlier call. They paused at the

drawing-room to collect Mr Fox, who was discovered in contempla-
tion of a portrait in pastel of Sybil as a young girl.

'If,' said Prunella, 'you don't take the letters away perhaps you'd
be kind enough to leave them in the desk.'

'Yes, of course,' Alleyn rejoined with equal formality. 'We
mustn't use up any more of your time. Thank you so much for being
helpful.'

He made her a little bow and was about to turn away when she
suddenly thrust out her hand.

'Sorry, I was idiotic. No bones broken?' Prunella asked.

'Not even a green fracture.'

'Goodbye then.'

They shook hands.

'That child,' said Alleyn when they were alone, 'turned on four
entirely separate moods, if that's what they should be called, in
scarcely more than as many minutes. Not counting the drawing-
room comedy which was not a comedy. You and your Aunt Elsie!'

'Perhaps the young lady's put about by recent experience,' Fox
hazarded.

'It's the obvious conclusion, I suppose.'

In the boudoir Alleyn divided the letters – there were eight –
between then. Fox put on his spectacles and read with the catarrhal
breathing that always afflicted him when engaged in that exercise.

Prunella had been right. They were indeed love letters, 'pure and
simple' within the literal meaning of the phrase, and most touching.
The young husband had been deeply in love and able to say so.

As his regiment moved from the Western Desert to Italy, the
reader became accustomed to the nicknames of brother officers and
regimental jokes. The Corp, who was indeed Captain Carter's
servant, featured more often as time went on. Some of the letters
were illustrated with lively little drawings. There was one of the
enormous Corp being harassed by bees in Tuscany. They were
represented as swarming inside his kilt and he was depicted with a
violent squint and his mouth wide open. A balloon issued from it
with a legend that said, 'It's no' saw much the ticklin', it's the
imperrtinence, ye ken.'

The last letter was as Prunella had described it. The final sentences
read: 'So my darling love, I shan't see you this time. If I don't stop

I'll miss the bloody train. About the stamp – sorry, no time left. Your totally besotted husband, Maurice.'

Alleyn assembled the letters, tied the ribbon and put the little packet in the desk. He emptied out the snapshots: a desolate faded company well on its slow way to oblivion. Maurice Carter appeared in all of them and in all of them looked like a near relation of Rupert Brooke. In one, he held by the hand a very small nondescript child: Claude, no doubt. In another he and a ravishingly pretty young Sybil appeared together. A third was yet another replica of the regimental group still in her desk drawer. The fourth and last showed Maurice kilted and a captain now, with his enormous 'Corp' stood to attention in the background.

Alleyn took it to the window, brought out his pocket lens and examined it. Fox folded his arms and watched him.

Presently he looked up and nodded.

'We'll borrow these four,' he said. 'I'll leave a receipt.'

He wrote it out, left it in the desk and put the snapshots in his pocket. 'Come on,' he said.

They met nobody on their way out. Prunella's car was gone. Fox followed Alleyn past the long windows of the library and the lower west flank of the house. They turned right and came at last to the stables.

'As likely as not, he'll still be growing mushrooms,' Alleyn said.

And so he was. Stripped to the waist, bronzed, golden-bearded and looking like a much younger man, Bruce was hard at work in the converted lean-to. When he saw Alleyn he grounded his shovel and arched his earthy hand over his eyes to shield them from the sun.

'Ou aye,' he said, 'so it's you again, Chief Superintendent. What can I do for you, the noo?'

'You can tell us, if you will, Corporal Gardener, the name of your regiment, and of its captain,' said Alleyn.

II

'I canna credit it,' Bruce muttered and gazed out of his non-aligned blue eyes at Alleyn. 'It doesna seem within the bounds of possibility. It's dealt me a wee shock, I'll say that for it.'

'You hadn't an inkling?'

'Don't be saw daft man,' Bruce said crossly. 'Sir, I should say. How would I have an inkling, will you tell me that? I doubt if her first husband was ever mentioned in my hearing and why would he be?'

'There was this stepson,' Fox said to nobody in particular. 'Name of Carter.'

'Be damned to that,' Bruce shouted. 'Carrrter! Carrrter! Why would he not be Carrrter? Would I be saw daft as to say my captain, dead nigh on forty years, was a man o' the name of Carrrter so you must be his son and he the bonniest lad you'd ever set eyes on and you, not to dra' it mild, a pure, sickly, ill-put-taegither apology for a man? Here, sir, can I have anither keek at them photies?'

Alleyn gave them to him.

'Ah,' he said, 'I mind it fine, the day that group was taken. I'd forgotten all about it but I mind it fine the noo.'

'But didn't you notice the replica of this one in her bedroom at the hotel?'

Bruce stared at him. His expression became prudish. He half-closed his eyes and pursed his enormous mouth. He said, in a scandalized voice, 'Sir, I never set fut in her bedroom. It would not been the thing at a'. Not at a'.'

'Indeed?'

'She received me in a wee private parlour upstairs or in the garden.'

'I see. I beg your pardon.'

'As for these ither ones: I never see them before.' He gazed at them in silence for some moments. 'My God,' he said quietly, 'look at the bairn, just. That'll be the bairn by the first wife. My God, it'll be this Claude. Who'd've thought it? And here's anither wi' me in the background. It's a strange coincidence, this, it is indeed.'

'You never came to Quintern or heard him speak of it?'

'If I did, the name didna stick in my mind. I never came here. What for would I? When we had leave and we only had but one before he was kilt, he let me gang awa' home. Aye, he was a considerate officer. *Christ!*'

'What's the matter?' Alleyn asked, Bruce had dealt his knees a devastating smack with his ginger-haired earthy hands.

'When I think of it,' he said. 'When I mind how me and her would have our bit crack of an evening when I came in for my dram. Making plans for the planting season and that. When I remember how she'd talk saw free and friendly and there, all unbeknownst, was my captain's wife that he'd let on to me was the sonsiest lass in the land. He had her picture in his wallet and liked fine to look at it. I took a wee keek mysel' one morning when I was brushing his tunic. She was bonny, aye, she was that. Fair as a flooer. She seems to have changed and why wouldn't she over the passage of years? Ou aye,' he said heavily. 'She changed.'

'We all do,' said Alleyn. 'You've changed yourself. I didn't recognize you at first, in the photographs.'

'That'd be the beard,' he said seriously and looked over his lightly sweating torso with the naïve self-approval of the physically fit male. 'I'm no' so bad in other respects,' he said.

'You got to know Captain Carter quite well, I suppose?'

'Not to say well, just. And yet you could put it like that. What's that spiel to the effect that no man's a hero to his valey? He can be so to his soldier-servant and the captain came near enough to it with me.'

'Did you get in touch with his wife after he was killed? Perhaps write to her?'

'Na, na. I wadna tak' the liberty. And forby I was back wi' the regiment that same night and awa' to the front. We didna get the news until after we landed.'

'When did you return to England?'

'After the war. I was taken at Cassino and spent the rest of the duration in a prison camp.'

'And Mrs Carter never got in touch? I mean, Captain Carter wrote quite a lot about you in his letters. He always referred to you as the Corp. I would have thought she would have liked to get in touch.'

'Did he? Did he, mention me, now?' said Bruce eagerly. 'To think o' that.'

'Look here, Gardener, you realize by this time, don't you, that we are considering the possibility of foul play in this business?'

Bruce arranged the photographs carefully like playing cards in his left fist and contemplated them as if they were all aces.

'I'm aware of that,' he said absently. 'It's a horrid conclusion but I'm aware of it. To think he made mention of me in his correspondence. Well, now!'

'Are you prepared to help us if you can? Do,' begged Alleyn, 'stop looking at those damn photographs. Here – give them to me and attend to what I say.'

Bruce, with every sign of reluctance, yielded up the photographs.

'I hear you,' he said. 'Ou aye, I am prepared.'

'Good. Now. First question. Did Captain Carter ever mention to you or in your hearing a valuable stamp in his possession?'

'He did not. Wait!' said Bruce dramatically. 'Aye. I mind it now. It was before he went on his last leave. He said it was in his bank in the City but he was no' just easy in his mind on account of the blitz and intended to uplift it.'

'Did he say what he meant to do with it?'

'Na, na. Not a wurrd to that effect.'

'Sure?'

'Aye, I'm sure,' said Bruce indifferently.

'Oh, well,' Alleyn said after a pause and looked at Fox.

'You can't win all the time,' said Fox.

Bruce shook himself like a wet dog. 'I'll not deny this has been a shock to me,' he said. 'It's given me an unco' awkward feeling. As if,' he added, opening his eyes very wide and producing a flight of fancy that seemed to surprise him, 'as if time, in a manner of speaking, had got itself mixed. That's a gey weird notion, to be sure.'

'Tell me, Gardener. Are you a Scot by birth?'

'Me? Na, na, I'm naething of the sort, sir. Naething of the sort. But I've worked since I was a laddie in Scotland and under Scots instruction. I enlisted in Scotland. I served in a Scots regiment and I dare say you've noticed I've picked up a trick or two of the speech.'

'Yes,' said Alleyn. 'I had noticed.'

'Aye,' said Bruce complacently. 'I dare say I'd pass for one in a crowd and proud to do it.' As if to put a signature to his affirmation he gave Alleyn a look that he would have undoubtedly described as 'canny'. 'I ken weel enough,' he said, 'that I must feature on your short list if it's with homicide that you're concerning yourself, Superintendent. For the simple reason the deceased left me twenty-five thousand pounds. That's correct, is it not?'

'Yes,' Alleyn said. 'That's correct.'

'I didna reckon to be contradicted and I can only hope it won't be long before you eliminate me from the file. In the meantime, I can do what any guiltless man can do under the circumstances: tell the truth and hope I'm believed. For I have told you the truth, Chief Superintendent. I have indeed.'

'By and large, Bruce,' said Alleyn, 'I believe you have.'

'There's no "by" and there's no "large" in it,' he said seriously, 'and I don't doubt you'll come to acknowledge the fact.' He looked at his wristwatch, a Big Ben of its species, glanced at the sun, and said he ought to be getting down to the churchyard.

'At St Crispin's?'

'Aye. Did ye no' hear? Jim Jobbin has the lumbago on him and I'm digging the grave. It's entirely appropriate that I should do so.'

'Yes?'

'Aye, 'tis. I've done her digging up here and she'd have been well content I'd do it down there in the finish. The difference being we canna have our bit crack over the matter. So if you've no further requirements of me, sir, I'll bid you good day and get on with it.'

'Can we give you a lift?'

'I'm much obliged, sir, but I have my ain auld car. Mrs Jim has left a piece and a bottle ready and I'll take them with me. If it's a long job, and it may be that, I'll get a bite of supper at my sister's. She's a wee piece up Stile Lane, overlooking the kirk. When would the deceased be brought for burying, can you tell me that?'

'This evening. After dark, very likely.'

'And rest in the kirk overnight?'

'Yes.'

'Ou aye,' said Bruce on an indrawn breath. 'That's a very decent arrangement. Aweel, I've a long job ahead of me.'

'Thank you for your help.'

Alleyn went to the yard door of the empty room. He opened it and looked in. Nothing had changed.

'Is this part of the flat that was to be built for you?' he called out.

'Aye, that was the idea,' said Bruce.

'Does Mr Carter take an interest in it?'

'Ach, he's always peering and prying. You'd think,' said Bruce distastefully, 'it was him that's the lawful heir.'

'Would you so,' said Alleyn absently. 'Come along, Fox.'

They left Bruce pulling his shirt over his head in an easy work-manlike manner. He threw his jacket across his shoulder, took up his shovel and marched off.

'In his way,' said Fox, 'a remarkable chap.'

III

Verity, to her surprise, was entertaining Nikolas Markos to luncheon. He had rung her up the day before and asked her to 'take pity' on him.

'If you would prefer it,' he had said, 'I will drive you somewhere else, all the way to the Ritz if you like, and you shall be my guest. But I did wonder, rather wistfully, if we might have an egg under your lime trees. Our enchanting Prue is staying with us and I suddenly discover myself to be elderly. Worse, she, dear child, is taking pains with me.'

'You mean?'

'She laughs a little too kindly at my dated jokes. She remembers not to forget I'm there. She includes me, with scarcely an effort, in their conversations. She's even taken to bestowing the odd butterfly kiss on the top of my head. I might as well be bald,' said Mr Markos bitterly.

'I'll undertake not to do that, at least. But I'm not much of a cook.'

'My dear, my adorable lady, I said Egg and I meant Egg. I am,' said Mr Markos, 'your slave for ever and if you will allow me will endorse the declaration with what used to be called a bottle of the Widow. Perhaps, at this juncture I should warn you that I shall also present you with a problem. *A demain* and a thousand thanks.'

He gets away with it, Verity thought, but only just. And if he says eggs, eggs he shall have. On creamed spinach. And my standby: iced sorrel soup first and the Stilton afterwards.

And as it was a lovely day they did have lunch under the limes. Mr Markos, good as his word, had brought a bottle of champagne in an ice bucket and the slightly elevated atmosphere that Verity associated with him was quickly established. She could believe that he enjoyed himself as fully as he professed to do, but he was as much of an exotic in her not very tidy English garden as frangipani. His hair luxuriant but disciplined, his richly curved, clever mouth and large black eyes, his clothes that, while they avoided extravagance, were inescapably very, very expensive – all these factors reminded Verity of Sybil Foster's strictures.

The difference is, she thought, that I don't mind him being like this. What's more I don't think Syb would have minded either if he'd taken a bit more notice of her.

When they had arrived at the coffee stage and he at his Turkish cigarette, he said, 'I would choose, of course, to hear you talk about your work and this house and lovely garden. I should like you to confide in me and perhaps a little to confide in you myself.' He spread his hands. 'What am I saying! How ridiculous! Of course I am about to confide in you – that is my whole intention, after all. I think you are accustomed to confidences – they are poured into your lap and you are discreet and never pass them on. Am I right?'

'Well,' said Verity, who was not much of a hand at talking about herself and didn't enjoy it. 'I don't know so much about that.' And she thought how Alleyn, though without any Markosian floridity, had also introduced confidences. Ratsy too, she remembered, and thought irrelevantly that she had become quite a one for gentlemen callers over the last fortnight.

Mr Markos fetched from his car two large sheets of cardboard tied together. 'Do you remember,' he asked, 'when we examined Prunella's original plans of Quintern Place there was a smaller plan of the grounds that you said you had not seen before?'

'Yes, of course.'

'This is it.'

He put the cardboards on the table and opened them out. There was the plan.

'I think it is later than the others,' he said, 'and by a different hand. It is drawn on the scale of a quarter of an inch to the foot and is very detailed. Now. Have a close, a *very* close look. Can you find a minute extra touch that doesn't explain itself? Take your time,' Mr Markos invited, with an air of extraordinary relish. He took her arm and led her close to the table.

Verity felt that he was making a great build-up and that the climax had better be good but she obediently pored over the map.

Since it was a scheme for laying out the grounds, the house was shown simply as an outline. The stable block was indicated in the same manner. Verity, not madly engaged, plodded conscientiously over elaborate indications of water-gardens, pavilions, fountains, terraces and spinneys but although they suggested a prospect that Evelyn himself would have treasured, she could find nothing untoward. She was about to say so when she noticed that within the empty outline of the stables there was an interior line suggesting a division into two rooms, a line that seemed to be drawn freehand in pencil rather than ruled in the brownish ink of the rest of the plan. She bent down to examine it more closely and found, in one corner of the indicated stable-room a tiny x, also, she was sure, pencilled.

Mr Markos, who had been watching her intently, gave a triumphant little crow. 'Aha!' he cried. 'You see! You've spotted it.'

'Well, yes,' said Verity. 'If you mean – ' and she pointed to the pencilled additions.

'Of course, of course. And what, my dear Miss Preston-Watson, do you deduce? You know my methods. Don't bustle.'

'Only, 'I'm afraid, that someone at some time has thought of making some alteration in the old stable buildings.'

'A strictly Watsonian conclusion. I must tell you that at the moment a workman is converting the outer half of the amended portion – now an open-fronted broken-down lean-to, into a mushroom bed.'

'That will be Bruce, the gardener. Perhaps he and Sybil, in talking over the project, got out this plan and marked the place where it was to go.'

'But why "the point marked x"? It does not indicate the mushroom bed. It is in a deserted room that opens off the mushroom shed.'

'They might have changed their minds.'

'It is crammed into a corner where there are the remains of an open fireplace. I must tell you that after making this discovery I strolled round the stable yard and examined the premises.'

'I can't think of anything else,' said Verity.

'I have cheated. I have withheld evidence. You must know, as Scheherazade would have said, meaning that you are to learn, that a few evenings after Prunella brought the plans to Mardling she found me poring over this one in the library. She remarked that it was strange that I should be so fascinated by it and then, with one of her nervous little spurts of confidence (she *is*, you will have noticed, unusually but Heaven knows, understandably, nervous just now) she told me that the egregious Claude Carter exhibited a similar interest in the plans and had been discovered examining this one through a magnifying glass. And I should like to know,' cried Mr Markos sparkling at Verity, 'what you make of all that!'

Verity did not make a great deal of it. She knew he expected her to enter into zestful speculation but, truth to tell, she found herself out of humour with the situation. There was something unbecoming in Nikolas Markos's glee over his discovery and if, as she suspected, he was going to link it in some way with Sybil Foster's death, she herself wanted no part in the proceedings. At the same time she felt apologetic – guilty even – about her withdrawal, particularly as she was sure he was very well aware of it. He really is, she thought, so remarkably sharp.

'To look at the situation quite cold-bloodedly,' he was saying, 'and of course that is the only sensible way to look at it, the police clearly are treating Mrs Foster's death as a case of homicide. This being so, anything untoward that has occurred at Quintern either before or after the event should be brought to their notice. You agree?'

Verity pulled herself together. 'I suppose so. I mean, yes of course. Unless they've already found it out for themselves. What's the matter?'

'If they have not, we have, little as I welcome the intrusion, an opportunity to inform them. Alas, you have a visitor, dear Verity,' said Mr Markos and quickly kissed her hand.

Alleyn, in fact, was walking up the drive.

IV

'I'm sorry,' he said, 'to come at such an unlikely time of day but I'm on my way back from Quintern Place and I thought perhaps you might like to know about the arrangements for this evening and tomorrow.'

He told them. 'I dare say the vicar will let you know,' he said, 'but in case he doesn't, that's what will happen.'

'Thank you,' Verity said. 'We were to do flowers first thing in the morning. It had better be this afternoon, hadn't it? Nice of you to think of it.'

She told herself she knew precisely why she was glad Alleyn had arrived. Idiotically it was because of Mr Markos's manner which had become inappropriately warm. Old hand though she was, this had flustered Verity. He had made assumptions. He had been too adroit. Quite a long time had gone by since assumptions had been made about Verity and still longer since she had been ruffled by them. Mr Markos made her feel clumsy and foolish.

Alleyn had spotted the plan. He said Prunella had mentioned the collection. He bent over it, made interested noises, looked closer and finally took out a pocket lens. Mr Markos crowed delightedly. 'At last!' he cried, 'we can believe you are the genuine article.' He put his arm round Verity and gave her a quick little squeeze. 'What is he going to look at?' he said. 'What do you think?'

And when Alleyn used his lens over the stable buildings, Mr Markos was enraptured.

'There's an extra bit pencilled in,' Alleyn said. 'Indicating the room next the mushroom bed.'

'So, my dear Alleyn, what do you make of *that?*'

'Nothing very much, do you?'

'Not of the "point marked x"? No buried treasure, for instance? Come!'

'Well,' said Alleyn, 'you can always dig for it, can't you? Actually it marks the position of a dilapidated fireplace. Perhaps there was some thought of renovating the rooms. A flat for the gardener, for instance.'

'Do you know,' Verity exclaimed, 'I believe I remember Sybil said something about doing just that. Setting him up on the premises because his room at his sister's house was tiny and he'd nowhere to put his things and they didn't hit it off anyway.'

'No doubt you are right, both of you,' admitted Mr Markos, 'but what a dreary solution. I am desolate.'

'Perhaps I can cheer you up with news of an unexpected development,' said Alleyn. 'It emerges that Bruce Gardener was Captain Maurice Carter's soldier-servant during the war.'

After a considerable interval Mr Markos said, 'The *gardener*. You mean the local man? Are you saying that this was known to Sybil Foster? And to Prunella? No. No, certainly not to Prunella.'

'Not, it seems, even to Gardener himself.'

Verity sat down abruptly. 'What *can* you mean?' she said.

Alleyn told her.

'I have always,' Mr Markos said, 'regarded stories of coincidence in a dubious light. My invariable instinct is to discredit them.'

'Is it?' said Verity. 'I always believe them and find them boring. I am prepared to acknowledge, since everyone tells me so, that life is littered with coincidences. I don't much mind. But this,' she said to Alleyn, 'is something else again. This takes a hell of a lot of acceptance.'

'Is that perhaps because of what has happened? If Mrs Foster hadn't died and if one day in the course of conversation it had emerged that her Maurice Carter had been Bruce Gardener's Captain Carter what would have been the reaction?'

'I can tell you what Syb's reaction would have been. She'd have made a big tra-la about it and said she'd always sensed there was "something".'

'And you?'

Verity thought it over. 'Yes,' she said. 'You're right. I'd have said, Fancy! Extraordinary coincidence, but wouldn't have thought much more about it.'

'If one may ask?' said Mr Markos, already asking. 'How did you find out? You or whoever it was?'

'I recognized him in an old photograph of the regiment. Not at first. I was shamefully slow. He hadn't got a beard in those days but he had got his squint.'

'Was he embarrassed?' Verity asked. 'When you mentioned it, I mean?'

'I wouldn't have said so. Flabbergasted is the word that springs to mind. From there he passed quickly to the "what a coincidence" bit and then into the realms of misty Scottish sentiment on "who would have thought it" and "had I but known" lines.'

'I can imagine.'

'Your Edinburgh Castle guide would have been brassy in comparison.'

'Castle?' asked Mr Markos. 'Edinburgh?' Verity explained.

'What's he doing now?' Mr Markos sharply demanded. 'Still cultivating mushrooms? Next door, by yet another coincidence – ' he tapped the plan – 'to the point marked x.'

'When we left him he was going to the church.'

'To the *church*! Why?'

Verity said, 'I know why.'

'You do?'

'Yes. Oh,' said Verity, 'this is all getting too much. Like a Jacobean play. He's digging Sybil's grave.'

'Why?' asked Mr Markos.

'Because Jim Jobbin has got lumbago.'

'Who is – no,' Mr Markos corrected himself, 'it doesn't matter. My dear Alleyn, forgive me if I'm tiresome, but doesn't all this throw a very dubious light upon the jobbing Gardener?'

'If it does, he's not the only one.'

'No? No, of course. I am forgetting the egregious Claude. By the way – I'm sorry, but you may slap me back if I'm insufferable – where does all this information come from?'

'In no small part,' said Alleyn, 'from Mrs Jim Jobbin.'

Mr Markos flung up his hands. 'These Jobbins!' he lamented and turned to Verity. 'Come to my rescue. Who *are* the Jobbins?'

'Mrs Jim helps you out once a week at Mardling. Her husband digs drains and graves and mows lawns. I dare say he mows yours if the truth were known.'

'Odd-job Jobbins, in fact,' said Alleyn and Verity giggled.

'Gideon would know,' his father said. 'He looks after that sort of thing. In any case, it doesn't matter. Unless – I suppose she's – to be perfectly cold-blooded about it – trustworthy?'

'She's a long-standing friend,' said Verity, 'and the salt of the earth. I'd sooner suspect the vicar's wife of hanky-panky than Mrs Jim.'

'Well, of course, my dear Verity' (Damn, thought Verity. I wish he wouldn't), 'that disposes of her, no doubt.' He turned to Alleyn. 'So the field is, after all, not extensive. Far too few suspects for a good read.'

'Oh, I don't know,' Alleyn rejoined. 'You may have overlooked a candidate.'

In the pause that followed a blackbird somewhere in Verity's garden made a brief statement and traffic on the London motorway, four miles distant, established itself as a vague rumour.

Mr Markos said, 'Ah, yes. Of course. But I hadn't overlooked him. You're talking about my acquaintance, Dr Basil Schramm.'

'Only because I was going to ring up and ask if I might have a word with you about him. I think you introduced him to the Upper Quintern scene, didn't you?'

'Well – fleetingly, I suppose I did.'

Verity said, 'Would you excuse me? I've got a telephone call I must make and I *must* see about the flowers.'

'Are you being diplomatic?' Mr Markos asked archly.

'I don't even know how,' she said and left them not, she hoped, too hurriedly. The two men sat down.

'I'll come straight to the point, shall I?' Alleyn said. 'Can you, and if so, will you, tell me anything of Dr Schramm's history? Where he qualified, for instance? Why he changed his name? Anything?'

'Are you checking his own account of himself? Or hasn't he given a satisfactory one? You won't answer that of course and very properly not.'

'I don't in the least mind answering. I haven't asked him.'

'As yet?'

'That's right. As yet.'

'Well,' said Mr Markos, airily waving his hand, 'I'm afraid I'm not much use to you. I know next to nothing of his background except that he took his degree somewhere in Switzerland. I had no idea he'd changed his name, still less why. We met when crossing the Atlantic in the QE2 and subsequently in New York at a cocktail-party given at the St Regis by fellow passengers. Later on that same evening at his suggestion we dined together and afterwards visited some remarkable clubs to which he had the entrée. The entertainment was curious. That was the last time I saw him until he rang me up at Mardling on his way to Greengages. On the spur of the moment I asked him to dinner. I have not seen him since then.'

'Did he ever talk about his professional activities – I mean whether he had a practice in New York or was attached to a hospital or clinic or what have you?'

'Not in any detail. In the ship going over he was the life and soul of a party that revolved round an acquaintance of mine – the Princess Palevsky. I rather gathered that he acquired her and two American ladies of considerable renown as – patients. I imagine,' said Mr Markos smoothly, 'that he is the happy possessor of a certain expertise in that direction. And, really, my dear Alleyn, that is the full extent of my acquaintance with Basil Schramm.'

'What do you think of him?' said Alleyn abruptly.

'*Think* of him? What can I say? And what exactly do you mean?'

'Did you form an opinion of his character, for instance? Nice chap? Lightweight? Man of integrity?'

'He is quite entertaining. A lightweight, certainly, but good value as a mixer and with considerable charm. I would trust him,' said Mr Markos, 'no further than I could toss a grand piano. A concert grand.'

'Where women are concerned?'

'Particularly where women are concerned.'

'I see,' said Alleyn cheerfully and got up. 'I must go,' he said, 'I'm running late. By the way, is Miss Foster at Quintern Place, do you happen to know?'

'Prunella? No. She and Gideon went up to London this morning. They'll be back for dinner. She's staying with us.'

'Ah yes. I must go. Would you apologize for me to Miss Preston?'

'I'll do that. Sorry not to have been more informative.'

'Oh,' Alleyn said, 'the visit has not been unproductive. Goodbye to you.'

Fox was in the car in the lane. When he saw Alleyn, he started up his engine.

'To the nearest telephone,' Alleyn said. 'We'll use the one at Quintern Place. We've got to lay on surveillance and be quick about it. The local branch'll have to spare a copper. Send him up to Quintern as a labourer. He's to dig up the fireplace and hearth and dig deep and anything he finds that's not rubble, keep it. And when he's finished tell him to board up the room and seal it. If anyone asks what he's up to he'll have to say he's under police orders. But I hope no one will ask.'

'What about Gardener?'

'Gardener's digging the grave.'

'Fair enough,' said Fox.

'Claude Carter may be there, though.'

'Oh,' said Fox. 'Aha. Him.'

But before they reached Quintern they met Mrs Jim on her way to do flowers in the church. She said Claude Carter had gone out that morning. 'To see a man about a car,' he had told her and he said he would be away all day.

'Mrs Jim,' Alleyn said. 'We want a telephone and we want to take a look inside the house. Miss Foster's out. Could you help us? Do you have a key?'

She looked fixedly at him. Her workaday hands moved uneasily. 'I don't know as I have the right,' she said. 'It's not my business.'

'I know. But it is, I promise you, very important. An urgent call. Look, come with us, let us in, follow us about if you like or we'll drive you back to the church at once. Will you do that? Please?'

There was another and a longer pause. 'All right,' said Mrs Jim and got into the car.

They arrived at Quintern and were admitted by Mrs Jim's key which she kept under a stone in the coal house.

While Fox rang the Upper Quintern police station from the staff sitting-room telephone, Alleyn went out to the stable yard. Bruce's mushroom beds were of course in the same shape as they had been earlier in the afternoon when he left them, taking his shovel with him. The ramshackle door into the deserted room was shut. Alleyn dragged it open and stood on the threshold. At first glance it looked and smelt as it had on his earlier visit. The westering sun shone through the dirty window and showed traces of his own and Carter's footprints on the dusty floorboards. Nobody else's, he thought, but more of Carter's than his own. The litter of rubbish lay undisturbed in the corner. With a dry-mouthed sensation of foreboding he turned to the fireplace.

Alleyn began to swear softly and prolifically, an exercise in which he did not often indulge.

He was squatting over the fireplace when Fox appeared at the window, saw him and looked in at the yard door.

'They're sending up a chap at once,' he said.

'Like hell they are,' said Alleyn. 'Look here.'

'Had I better walk in?'

'The point's academic.'

Fox took four giant strides on tiptoe and stopped over the hearth. 'Broken up, eh?' he said. 'Fancy that, eh?'

'As you say. But look at this.' He pointed a long finger. 'Do you see what I see?'

'Remains of a square hole. Something regular in shape like a box or tin's been dug out. Right?'

'I think so. And take a look here. And here. And in the rubble.'

'Crêpe soles, by gum.'

'So what do you say now to the point marked bloody x?'

'I'd say the name of the game is Carter. But why? What's he up to?'

'I'll tell you this, Br'er Fox. When I looked in here at about three o'clock this hearth was as it had been for Lord knows how long.'

'Gardener left when we left,' Fox mused.

'And is digging a grave and should continue to do so for some considerable time.'

'Anybody up here since then?'

'Not Mrs Jim, at all events.'

'So we're left,' Fox said –

'With the elusive Claude. We'll have to put Bailey and Thompson in but I bet you that's going to be the story.'

'Yes. And he's seeing a man about a car,' said Fox bitterly. 'It might as well be a dog.'

'And we might as well continue in our futile ways by seeing if there's a pick and shovel on the premises. After all, he couldn't have rootled up the hearth with his fingernails. Where's the gardener's shed?'

It was near at hand, hard by the asparagus beds. They stood in the doorway and if they had entered would have fallen over a pick that lay on the floor, an untidy note in an impeccably tidy interior. Bruce kept his tools as they should be kept, polished, sharpened and in racks. Beside the pick, leaning against a bench was a lightweight shovel and nearby a crowbar.

They all bore signs of recent and hard usage.

Alleyn stooped down and without touching, examined them.

'Scratches,' he said. 'Blunted. Chucked in here in a hurry. And take a look – crêpe-soled prints on the path.'

'Is Bob your Uncle, then?' said Fox.

'If you're asking whether Claude Carter came down to the stable yard as soon as Bruce Gardener and you and I left it, dug up the hearth and returned the tools to this shed, I suppose he *is*. But if you're asking whether this means that Claude Carter murdered his stepmother, I can't say it follows as the night the day.'

Alleyn reached inside the door and took a key from a nail. He shut and locked the door and put the key in his pocket.

'Bailey and Thompson can pick it up from the nick,' he said. 'They'd better get here as soon as possible.'

He led the way back to the car. Half way there he stopped. 'I tell you what, Br'er Fox,' he said. 'I've got a strong feeling of being just a couple of lengths behind and in danger of being beaten to the post.'

'What,' said Fox pursuing his own line of thought, 'would it be? What was it? That's what I ask myself.'

'And how do you answer?'

'I don't. I can't. Can you?'

'One can always make wild guesses, of course. Mr Markos was facetious about buried treasure. He might turn out to be right.'

'Buried treasure,' Fox echoed disgustedly. 'What sort of buried treasure?'

'How do you fancy a Black Alexander stamp?' said Alleyn.

CHAPTER 7

Graveyard (I)

Mr Markos had stayed at Keys for only a short time after Alleyn had gone. He had quietened down quite a lot and Verity wondered if she had turned into one of those dreadful spinsters of an all too certain age who imagine that any man who shows them the smallest civility is making a pass.

He had said goodbye with a preoccupied air. His black liquid gaze was turned upon her as if in speculation. He seemed to be on the edge of asking her something but, instead, thanked her for 'suffering' him to invite himself, took her hand, kissed his own thumb and left her.

Verity cut roses and stood them in scalding water for half an hour. Then she tidied herself up and drove down to St Crispin's.

It was quite late in the afternoon when she got there. Lengthening shadows stretched out towards gravestones lolling this way and that, in and out of the sunshine. A smell, humid yet earthy, hung on the air and so did the sound of bees.

As Verity, carrying roses, climbed the steps, she heard the rhythmic, purposeful squelch of a shovel at work. It came from beyond the church and of course she knew what it was: Bruce at his task. Suddenly she was filled with a liking for Bruce, for the direct way he thought about Sybil's death and his wish to perform the only service he could provide. It no longer seemed to matter that he so readily took to sentimental manifestations and she was sorry she had made mock of them. She thought that of all Sybil's associates, even including Prunella, he was probably the only one who honestly mourned her. I won't shy off, she thought. When I've done the flowers, little as I like graves, I'll go and talk to him.

The vicar's wife and Mrs Field-Innis and the Ladies Guild, including Mrs Jim, were in the church and well advanced with their flowers and brass vases. Verity joined Mrs Jim who was in charge of Bruce's lilies from Quintern and was being bossily advised by Mrs Field-Innis what to do with them.

An unoccupied black trestle stood in the transept – waiting for Sybil. The Ladies Guild, going to and fro with jugs of water, gave it a wide berth as if, thought Verity, they were cutting it dead. They greeted Verity and spoke in special voices.

'Come on, Mrs Jim,' said Verity cheerfully, 'let's do ours together.' So they put their lilies and red roses in two big jars on either side of the chancel steps, flanking the trestle. 'They'll be gay and hopeful there,' said Verity. Some of the ladies looked as if they thought she had chosen the wrong adjectives.

When Mrs Jim had fixed the final lily in its vase, she and Verity replaced the water-jugs in their cupboard.

'Police again,' Mrs Jim muttered with characteristic abruptness. 'Same two, twice today.'

'What time?' Verity asked, equally laconic.

'Two, about. And back again before three-thirty. Give me a lift up there. Got me to let them in, and the big one drove me back. I'll have to tell Miss Prunella, won't I?'

'Yes, I expect you must.'

They went out into the westering sunlight, golden now and shining full in their faces.

'I'm going round to have a word with Bruce,' said Verity. 'Are you coming?'

'I see him before. I'm not overly keen on graves. Give me the creeps,' said Mrs Jim. 'He's making a nice job of it, though. Jim'll be pleased. He's still doubled up and crabby with it. We don't reckon he'll make it to the funeral but you never know with lumbago. I'll be getting along, then.'

The Passcoigne plot was a sunny clearing in the trees. There was quite a company of headstones there, some so old that the inscriptions were hard to make out. They stood in grass that was kept scythed but were not formally tended. Verity preferred them like that. One day the last of them would crumble and fall. Earth to earth.

Bruce had got some way with Sybil's grave and now sat on the edge of it with his red handkerchief on his knee and his bread and cheese and bottle of beer beside him. To Verity he looked a timeless figure, and the gravedigger's half-forgotten doggerel came into her head.

> *In youth when I did love, did love,*
> *Methought 'twas very sweet –*

His shovel was stuck in the heap of earth he had built up and behind him was a neat pile of small sticky pine branches, sharpened at the ends. Their resinous scent hung on the air.

'You've been hard at work, Bruce.'

'I have so. There's a vein of clay runs through the soil here and that makes heavy going of it. I've broken off to eat my piece and wet my whistle and then I'll set to again. It'll tak' me all my time to get done before nightfall and there's the pine branches forby to line it.'

'That's a nice thing to do. How good they smell.'

'They do that. She'd be well enough pleased, I dare say.'

'I'm sure of it,' said Verity. She hesitated for a moment and then said, 'I've just heard about your link with Captain Carter. It must have been quite a shock for you – finding out after all these years.'

'You may weel ca' it that,' he said heavily. 'And to tell you the truth, it gets to be more of a shock, the more I think about it. Ou aye, it does so. It's unco' queer news for a body to absorb. I don't seem,' said Bruce, scratching his head, 'to be able to sort it out. He was a fine man and a fine officer, was the Captain.'

'I'm sure he was.'

'Aweel,' he said, 'I'd best get on for I've a long way to go.'

He stood up, spat on his hands and pulled his shovel out of the heap of soil.

She left him hard at work and drove herself home.

Bruce dug through sunset and twilight and when it grew dark lit an acetylene lamp. His wildly distorted shadow leapt and gesticulated among the trees. He had almost completed his task when above him, the east window, representing the Last Supper, came to life and glowed like a miraculous apparition, above his head. He heard the sound of a motor drawing up. The vicar came round the corner of the church using a torch.

'They've arrived, Gardener,' he said. 'I thought you would like to know.'

Bruce put on his coat. Together they walked round to the front of the church.

Sybil, in her coffin, was being carried up the steps. The doors were open and light from the interior flooded the entrances. Even outside, the scent of roses and lilies was heavily noticeable. The vicar in his cassock welcomed his guest for the night and walked before her into her hostelry. When he came away, locking the door behind him, he left the light on in the sanctuary. From outside the church glowed faintly.

Bruce went back to her grave.

A general police search for Claude Carter had been set up.

In his room up at Quintern, Alleyn and Fox had completed an extremely professional exploration. The room, slapped up twice a week by Mrs Jim, was drearily disordered and smelt of cigarette smoke and of an indefinable and more personal staleness. They had come at last upon a japanned tin box at the bottom of a rucksack shoved away at the top of the wardrobe. It was wrapped in a sweater and submerged in a shirt, three pairs of unwashed socks and a windjacket. The lock presented no difficulties to Mr Fox.

Inside the box was a notebook and several papers.

And among these a rough copy of the plan of the room in the stable yard, the mushroom shed and the point marked x.

II

'Earth to earth,' said the vicar, 'ashes to ashes. In sure and certain hope – '

To Alleyn, standing a little apart from them, the people round the grave composed themselves into a group that might well have been chosen by the Douanier Rousseau: simplified persons of whom the most prominent were clothed in black. Almost, they looked as if they had been cut out of cardboard, painted and then endowed with a precarious animation. One expected their movements, involving the lowering of the coffin and the ritual handful of earth, to be jerky.

There they all were and he wondered how many of them had
Sybil Foster in their thoughts. Her daughter, supported on either side
by the two men, now become her guardians-in-chief? Verity
Preston, who stood nearby and to whom Prunella had turned when
the committal began? Bruce Gardener, in Harris tweed suit, black
armband and tie, decently performing his job as stand-in sexton
with his gigantic wee laddie in support? Young Mr Rattisbon,
decorous and perhaps a little tired from standing for so long? Mrs
Jim, bright-eyed and wooden-faced? Sundry friends in the county.
And finally, taller than the rest, a little apart from them, impeccably
turned-out and so handsome that he looked as if he had been
type-cast for the role of distinguished medico – Dr Basil Schramm,
the presumably stricken but undisclosed fiancé of the deceased and
her principal heir.

Claude Carter, however, was missing.

Alleyn had looked for him in church. At both sittings of the
inquest Claude had contrived to get himself into an inconspicuous
place and might have been supposed to lurk behind a pillar or in a
sort of no-man's-land near the organ but out here in the sunny
graveyard he was nowhere to be seen. There was one large Victorian
angel, slightly lopsided on its massive base but pointing, like Agnes
in *David Copperfield,* upwards. Alleyn trifled with the notion that
Claude might be behind it and would come sidling out when all was
over, but no, there was no sign of him. This was not consistent. One
would have expected him to put in a token appearance. Alleyn
wondered if by any chance something further had cropped up about
Claude's suspected drug-smuggling activities and he was making
himself scarce, accordingly. But if anything of that sort had occurred
Alleyn would have been informed.

It was all over. Bruce Gardener began to fill in the grave. He was
assisted by the wee lad, the six-foot adolescent known to the village
as Daft Artie, he being, as was widely acknowledged, no more than
fifty p. in the pound.

Alleyn, who had kept in the background, withdrew still further
and waited.

People now came up to Prunella, said what they could find to say
and walked away, not too fast but with the sense of release and
buoyancy that follows the final disposal of (however deeply loved)

the dead. Prunella shook hands, kissed, thanked. The Markos pair stood behind her and Verity a little further off.

The last to come was Dr Schramm. Alleyn saw the fractional pause before Prunella touched his offered hand. He heard her say, 'Thank you for the beautiful flowers,' loudly and quickly and Schramm murmur something inaudible. It was to Verity that Prunella turned when he had gone.

Alleyn had moved further along the pathway from the grave to the church. It was flanked by flowers lying in rows on the grass, some in Cellophane wrappings, some picked in local gardens and one enormous professional bouquet of red roses and carnations. Alleyn read the card.

'From B.S. with love.'

'Mr Alleyn?' said Prunella, coming up behind him. He turned quickly. 'It was kind of you to come,' she said. 'Thank you.'

'What nice manners you have,' Alleyn said gently. 'Your mama must have brought you up beautifully.'

She gave him a surprised look and a smile.

'Did you hear that, Godma V?' she said and she and her three supporters went down the steps and drove away.

When the vicar had gone into the vestry to take his surplice off and there was nobody left in the churchyard, Alleyn went to the grave. Bruce said, 'She's laid to her rest, then, Superintendent, and whatever brought her to it, there's no disturbing her in the latter end.'

He spat on his hands. 'Come on, lad,' he said. 'What are you gawping at?'

Impossible to say how old Daft Artie was – somewhere between puberty and manhood – with an incipient beard and a feral look as if he would have little difficulty in melting into the landscape and was prepared to do so at a moment's alarm.

He set to, with excessive, almost frantic energy. With a slurp and a flump, shovelfuls of dark, friable soil fell rhythmically into Sybil Foster's grave.

'Do you happen,' Alleyn asked Bruce, 'to have seen Mr Claude Carter this morning?'

Bruce shot a brief glance at him. 'Na, na,' he said, plying his shovel, 'I have not, but there's nothing out of the ordinary in that

circumstance. Him and me don't hit it off. And forby I don't fancy
he's been just all that comfortable within himself. Nevertheless, it's
a disgrace on his head not to pay his last respects. Aye, I'll say that
for him: a black disgrace,' said Bruce, with relish.

'When *did* you last see him?'

'Ou now – when? I couldna say with any precision. My engagements take me round the district, ye ken. I'm sleeping up at
Quintern but I'm up and awa' before eight o'clock. I take my dinner
with my widowed sister, Mrs Black, pure soul, up in yon cottage on
the hill there and return to Quintern in time for supper and my bed,
which is in the chauffeur's old room above the garage. Not all that
far,' said Bruce pointedly, 'from where you unearthed him, so to
speak.'

'Ah yes, by the way,' said Alleyn, 'we're keeping observation on
those premises. For the time being.'

'You are! For what purpose? Och!' said Bruce irritably, 'the Lord
knows and you, no doubt, won't let on.'

'Oh,' said Alleyn airily, 'it's a formality really. Pure routine. I fancy
Miss Foster hasn't forgotten that her mother was thinking of turning
part of the buildings into a flat for you.'

'Has she not? I wouldna mind and that's a fact. I wouldna say no
for I'm crampit up like a hen in a wee coopie where I am and, God
forgive me, I'm sick and tired of listening to the praises of the recently
deceased.'

'The recently deceased!' Alleyn exclaimed. 'Do you mean Mrs
Foster?'

Bruce grounded his shovel and glared at him. 'I am shocked,' he
said at last, pursing up his mouth to show how shocked he was and
using his primmest tones, 'that you should entertain such a notion.
It comes little short of an insult. I referred to the fact that my sister
Mrs Black is recently widowed.'

'I beg your pardon.'

'Och, well. It was an excusable misunderstanding. So there's
some idea still of fixing the flat?' He paused and stared at Alleyn.
'That's not what you'd call a reason for having the premises policed,
however,' he said drily.

'Bruce,' Alleyn said. 'Do you know what Mr Carter was doing in
that room on the morning I first visited you?'

Bruce gave a ringing sniff. 'That's an easy one,' he said. 'I told you yesterday. Spying. Trying to catch what you were speiring. To me. Aye, aye, that's what *he* was up to. He'd been hanging about the premises, feckless-like, making oot he was interested in mushrooms and letting on the police were in the hoose. When he heard you coming he was through the door like a rabbit and dragging it to, behind him. You needna suppose I'm not acquainted with Mr Carter's ways, Superintendent. My lady telt me aboot him and Mrs Jim's no' been backward in coming forward on the subject. When persons of his class turn aside they make a terrible bad job of themsels. Aye, they're worse by a long march than the working-class chap with some call to slip from the paths of rectitude.'

'I agree with you.'

'You can depend on it.'

'And you can't think when you last saw him?'

Bruce dragged his hand over his beard. 'When would it have been now?' he mused. 'Not today. I left the premises before eight and I was hame for dinner and after that I washed myself and changed to a decent suit for the burying. I'll tell you when it was,' he said, brightening up. 'It was yesterday morning. I ran into him in the stable yard and he asked me if I knew how the trains run to Dover. He let on he has an acquaintance there and might pay him a visit some time.'

'Did he say anything about going to the funeral?'

'Did he now? Wait, now. I canna say for certain but I carry the impression he passed a remark that led me to suppose he'd be attending the obsequies. That,' said Bruce summing up, 'is the length and breadth of my total recollection.' He took up his shovel.

The wee laddie, who had not uttered nor ceased with frantic zeal to cast earth on earth, suddenly gave tongue.

'I seen 'im,' he said loudly.

Bruce contemplated him. 'You seen who, you pure daftie?' he asked kindly.

'Him. What you're talking about.'

Bruce slightly shook his head at Alleyn, indicating the dubious value of anything the gangling creature had to offer. 'Did ye noo?' he said tolerantly.

'In the village. It weren't 'alf dark, 'cept up here where you was digging the grave, Mr Gardener, and had your 'ceterlene lamp.'

'Where'd you been, then, young Artie, stravaging abroad in the night?'

'I dunno,' said Artie, showing the whites of his eyes.

'Never mind,' Alleyn intervened. 'Where were you when you saw Mr Carter?'

'Corner of Stile Lane, under the yedge, weren't I? And him coming down into Long Lane.' He began to laugh again: the age-old guffaw of the rustic oaf. 'I give him a proper scare, din' I?' He let out an eldritch screech. 'Like that. I was in the yedge and he never knew where it come from. Reckon he was dead scared.'

'What did he do, Artie?' Alleyn asked.

'I dunno,' Artie muttered, suddenly uninterested.

'Where did he go, then?'

'I dunno.'

'You must know,' Bruce roared out. 'Oot wi' it. Where did he go?'

'I never see. I was under the yedge, wasn' I? Up the steps then, he must of, because I yeard the gate squeak. When I come out 'e'd gone.'

Bruce cast his eyes up and shook his head hopelessly at Alleyn. 'What are you trying to tell us, Artie?' he asked patiently. 'Gone *wheer?* I never saw the man and there I was, was I no'? He never came my way. Would he enter the church and keep company wi' the dead?'

This produced a strange reaction. Artie seemed to shrink into himself. He made a movement with his right hand, almost as if to bless himself with the sign of the cross, an age-old self-defensive gesture.

'Did you know,' Alleyn asked quietly, 'that Mrs Foster lay in the church last night?'

Artie looked into the half-filled grave and nodded. 'I seen it. I seen them carry it up the steps,' he whispered.

'That was before you saw Mr Carter come down the lane?'

He nodded.

Bruce said, 'Come awa', laddie. Nobody's going to find fault with you. Where did Mr Carter go? Just tell us that now.'

Artie began to whimper. 'I dunno,' he whined. 'I looked out of the yedge, din' I? And I never saw 'im again.'

'Where *did* you go?' Alleyn asked.

'Nowhere.'

Bruce said, 'Yah!' and with an air of hardly controlled exasperation returned to his work.

'You must have gone somewhere,' Alleyn said. 'I bet you're quite a one for getting about the countryside on your own. A night bird, aren't you, Artie?'

A look of complacency appeared. 'I might be,' he said, and then with a sly glance at Bruce, 'I sleep out,' he said, 'of a night. Often.'

'Did you sleep out last night? It was a warm night, wasn't it?'

'Yeah,' Artie conceded off-handedly, 'it was warm. I slep' out.'

'Where? Under the hedge?'

'In the yedge. I got a place.'

'Where you stayed hid when you saw Mr Carter?'

'That's right.' Stimulated by the recollection he repeated his screech and raucous laugh.

Bruce seemed about to issue a scandalized reproof but Alleyn checked him. 'And after that,' he said, 'you settled down and went to sleep? Is that it?'

' 'Course,' said Artie haughtily and attacked his shovelling with renewed energy.

'When you caught sight of him,' Alleyn asked, 'did you happen to notice how he was dressed?'

'I never see nothing to notice.'

'Was he carrying anything? A bag or suitcase?' Alleyn persisted.

'I never see nothing,' Artie repeated morosely.

Alleyn jerked his head at Artie's back. 'Is he to be relied on?' he said quietly.

'Hard to say. Weak in the head but truthful as far as he goes and that's not far.' Bruce lowered his voice. 'There's a London train goes through at five past eleven: a slow train with a passenger carriage. Stops at Great Quintern. You can walk it in an hour,' said Bruce with a steady look at Alleyn.

'Is there indeed?' said Alleyn. 'Thank you, Bruce. I won't keep you any longer but I'm very much obliged to you.'

As he turned away Artie said in a sulky voice and to nobody in particular, 'He were carrying a pack. On his back.' Pleased with the rhyme he improvised, 'Pack on 'is back and down the track,' and, as an inspired addition, ''E'd got the sack.'

'Alas, alack,' Alleyn said and Artie giggled. 'Pack on 'is back and got the sack,' he shouted.

'Och, *havers!*' said Bruce disgustedly. 'You're nowt but a silly, wanting kind of crittur. Haud your whist and get on with your work.'

'Wait a moment,' said Alleyn, and to Artie, 'Did you sleep out all night? When did you wake up?'

'When 'e went 'ome,' said Artie, indicating the indignant Bruce. 'You woke me up, Mr Gardener, you passed that close. Whistling. I could of put the wind up you, proper, couldn't I? I could of frown a brick at you, Mr Gardener. But I never,' said Artie virtuously.

Bruce made a sound of extreme exasperation.

'When was this, Artie? You wouldn't know, would you?' said Alleyn.

'Yes, I would, then. Twelve. Church clock sounded twelve, din' it?'

'Is that right?' Alleyn asked Bruce.

'He can't count beyond ten. It was nine when I knocked off.'

'Long job you had of it.'

'I did that. There's a vein of solid clay runs through, three-foot depth of it. And after that the pine boughs to push in. It was an unco' weird experience. Everybody in the village asleep by then and an owl overhead and bats flying in and out of the lamplight. And inside the kirk, the leddy herself, cold in her coffin and me digging her grave. Aye, it was, you may say, an awfu', uneasy situation, yon. In literature,' said Bruce, lecturing them, 'it's an effect known as Gothic. I was pleased enough to have done with it.'

Alleyn lowered his voice. 'Do you think he's got it right?'

'That he slept under the hedge and woke as I passed? I dare say. It might well be, pure daftie.'

'And that he saw Carter, earlier?'

'I'd be inclined to credit it. I didna see anything of the man mysel' but then I wouldn't, where I was.'

'No, of course not. Well, thanks again,' Alleyn said. He returned to the front of the church, ran down the steps and found Fox waiting in the car.

'Back to Quintern,' he said. 'The quest for Charmless Claude sets in with a vengeance.'

'Skedaddled?'

'Too soon to say. Bruce indicates as much.'

'Ah, to hell with it,' said Fox in a disgusted voice. 'What's the story?'

Alleyn told him.

'There you are!' Fox complained when he had finished. 'Scared him off, I dare say, putting our chap in. Here's a pretty kettle of fish.'

'We'll have to take up the Dover possibility, of course, but I don't like it much. If he'd considered it as a getaway port he wouldn't have been silly enough to ask Bruce about trains. Still, we'll check. He's thought to have some link with a stationer's shop in Southampton.'

'Suppose we do run him down, what's the charge?'

'You may well ask. We've got nothing to warrant an arrest unless we can hold him for a day or two on the drug business and that seems to have petered out. We can't run him in for grubbing up an old fireplace in a disused room in his stepmother's stable yard. Our chap's found nothing to signify, I suppose?'

'Nothing, really. You've had a better haul, Mr Alleyn?'

'I don't know, Foxkin, I don't know. In one respect I think perhaps I have.'

III

When Verity drove home from the funeral it was with the expectation of what she called 'putting her boots up' and relaxing for an hour or so. She found herself to be suddenly used up and supposed that the events of the past days must have been more exhausting, emotionally, than she had realized. And after further consideration, an inborn honesty prompted her to conclude that the years were catching up on her.

'Selfishly considered,' she told herself, 'this condition has its advantages. Less is expected of one.' And then she pulled herself together. Anyone would think she was involved up to her ears in this wretched business, whereas, of course, apart from being on tap whenever her goddaughter seemed to want her, she was on the perimeter.

She had arrived at this reassuring conclusion when she turned in at her own gate and saw Basil Schramm's car drawn up in front of her house.

Schramm himself was sitting at the iron table under the lime trees.

His back was towards her but at the sound of her car, he swung round and saw her. The movement was familiar.

When she stopped he was there, opening the door for her.

'You didn't expect to see me,' he said.

'No.'

'I'm sorry to be a bore. I'd like a word or two if you'll let me.'

'I can't very well stop you,' said Verity lightly. She walked quickly to the nearest chair and was glad to sit on it. Her mouth was dry and there was a commotion going on under her ribs.

He took the other chair. She saw him through a kind of mental double focus: as he had been when, twenty-five years ago, she made a fool of herself, and as he was now, not so much changed or aged as exposed.

'I'm going to ask you to be terribly, terribly kind,' he said and waited.

'Are you?'

'Of course you'll think it bloody cool. It *is* bloody cool but you've always been a generous creature, Verity, haven't you?'

'I shouldn't depend on it, if I were you.'

'Well – I can but try.' He took out his cigarette case. It was silver with a sliding action. 'Remember?' he said. He slid it open and offered it to her. She had given it to him.

Verity said, 'No, thank you, I don't.'

'You used to. How strong-minded you are. I shouldn't, of course, but I do.' He gave his rather empty social laugh and lit a cigarette. His hands were unsteady.

Verity thought, I know the line I ought to take if he says what I think he's come here to say. But can I take it? Can I avoid saying things that will make him suppose I still mind? I know this situation. After it's all over you think of how dignified and quiet and unmoved you should have been and remember how you gave yourself away at every turn. As I did when he degraded me.

He was preparing his armoury. She had often, even when she had been most attracted, thought how transparent and silly and pre-dictable were his ploys.

'I'm afraid,' he was saying, 'I'm going to talk about old times. Will you mind very much?'

'I can't say I see much point in the exercise,' she said cheerfully. 'But I don't *mind*, really.'

'I hoped you wouldn't.'

He waited, thinking perhaps that she would invite him to go on. When she said nothing he began again.

'It's nothing, really. I didn't mean to give it a great buildup. It's just an invitation for you to preserve what they call "a masterly inactivity".' He laughed again.

'Yes?'

'About – well, Verity, I expect you've guessed what about, haven't you?'

'I haven't tried.'

'Well, to be quite honest and straightforward – ' He boggled for a moment.

'Quite honest and straightforward?' Verity couldn't help repeating but she managed to avoid a note of incredulity. She was reminded of another stock phrase-maker – Mr Markos and his 'quite cold-bloodedly'.

'It's about that silly business a thousand years ago at St Luke's,' Schramm was saying. 'I dare say you've forgotten all about it.'

'I could hardly do that.'

'I know it looked bad. I know I ought to have – well – asked to see you and explain. Instead of – all right, then – '

'Bolting?' Verity suggested.

'Yes. All right. But you know there were extenuating circumstances. I was in a bloody bad jam for money and I would have paid it back.'

'But you never got it. The bank questioned the signature on the cheque, didn't they? And my father didn't make a charge.'

'Very big of him! He only gave me the sack and shattered my career.'

Verity stood up. 'It would be ridiculous and embarrassing to discuss it. I think I know what you're going to ask. You want me to say I won't tell the police. Is that it?'

'To be perfectly honest – '

'Oh, *don't*,' Verity said, and closed her eyes.

'I'm sorry. Yes, that's it. It's just that they're making nuisances of themselves and one doesn't want to present them with ammunition.'

Verity was painfully careful and slow over her answer. She said, if you are asking me not to go to Mr Alleyn and tell him that when you were one of my father's students I had an affair with you and that you used this as a stepping-stone to forging my father's signature on a cheque – no, I don't propose to do that.'

She felt nothing more than a reflected embarrassment when she saw the red flood into his face, but she did turn away.

She heard him say, 'Thank you for that, at least. I don't deserve it and I didn't deserve you. God, what a fool I was!'

She thought, I mustn't say 'in more ways than one'. She made herself look at him and said, 'I think I should tell you that I know you were engaged to Sybil. It's obvious that the police believe there was foul play and I imagine that as a principal legatee under the Will – '

He shouted her down, 'You can't – Verity, you would never think I – I – ? Verity?'

'Killed her?'

'My God!'

'No. I don't think you did that. But I must tell you that if Mr Alleyn finds out about St Luke's and the cheque episode and asks me if it was all true, I shan't lie to him. I shan't elaborate or make any statements. On the contrary I shall probably say I prefer not to answer. But I shan't lie.'

'By God,' he repeated, staring at her. 'So you haven't forgiven me, have you?'

'Forgiven? It doesn't arise.' Verity looked squarely at him. 'That's true, Basil. It's the wrong sort of word. It upsets me to look back at what happened, of course it does. After all, one has one's pride. But otherwise the question's academic. Forgiven you? I suppose I must have but – no, it doesn't arise.'

'And if you "prefer not to answer",' he said, sneering it seemed at himself as much as at her, 'what's Alleyn going to think? Not much doubt about that one, is there? Look here, has he been at you already?'

'He came to see me.'

'What for? Why? Was it about – that other nonsense? On Capri?'

'In the long vacation? When you practised as a qualified doctor? No, he said nothing about that.'

'It was a joke. A ridiculous old hypochondriac, dripping with jewels and crying out for it. What did it matter?'

'It mattered when they found out at St Luke's.'

'Bloody pompous lot of stuffed shirts. I knew a damn sight more medics than most of their qualified teachers' pets.'

'Have you *ever* qualified? No, don't tell me,' said Verity quickly.

'Has Nick Markos talked about me? To you?'

'No.'

'Really?'

'Yes, Basil, really,' she said and tried to keep the patient sound out of her voice.

'I only wondered. Not that he'd have anything to say that mattered. It's just that you seemed to be rather thick with him, I thought.'

There was only one thing now that Verity wanted and she wanted it urgently. It was for him to go away. She had no respect left for him and had had none for many years but it was awful to have him there, pussy-footing about in the ashes of their past and making such a shabby job of it. She felt ashamed and painfully sorry for him too.

'Was that all you wanted to know?' she asked.

'I think so. No, there's one other thing. You won't believe this but it happens to be true. Ever since that dinner-party at Mardling, when we met again, I've had – I mean I've not been able to get you out of my head. You haven't changed all that much, Verry. Whatever you may say, it was very pleasant. Us. Well, wasn't it? What? Come on, be honest. Wasn't it quite fun?'

He actually put his hand over hers. She was aghast. Something of her incredulity and enormous distaste must have appeared in her face. He withdrew his hand as if it had been scalded.

'I'd better get on my tin tray and slide off,' he said. 'Thank you for seeing me.'

He got in his car. Verity went indoors and gave herself a strong drink. The room felt cold.

IV

Claude Carter had gone. His rucksack and its contents had disappeared and some of his undelicious garments. His room was in disorder. It had not been Mrs Jim's day at Quintern Place. She had shown Alleyn where her key was always hidden – under a stone in the coal house – and they had let themselves in with it.

There was a note scrawled on a shopping-pad in the kitchen. 'Away for an indefinite time. Will let you know if and when I return. C.C.' No date. No time.

And now, in his room, they searched again and found nothing of interest until Alleyn retrieved a copy of last week's local newspaper from the floor behind the unmade bed.

He looked through it. On the advertisement page under 'Cars for Sale' he found, half way down the column, a ring round an insertion that offered a 1964 Heron for £500 or nearest offer. The telephone number had been underlined.

'He gave it out,' Alleyn reminded Fox, 'that he was seeing a man about a car.'

'Will I ring them?'

'If you please, Br'er Fox.'

But before Fox could do so a distant telephone began to ring. Alleyn opened the door and listened. He motioned to Fox to follow him and walked down the passage towards the stairhead.

The telephone in the hall below could now be heard. He ran down the stairs and answered it, giving the Quintern number.

'Er yes,' said a very loud man's voice. 'Would this be the gentleman who undertook to buy a '64 Heron off of me and was to collect it yesterday evening? Name of Carter?'

'He's out at the moment, I'm afraid. Can I take a message?'

'Yes, you can. I'll be obliged if he'll ring up and inform me one way or the other. If he don't, I'll take it the sale's off and dispose of the vehicle elsewhere. He can collect his deposit when it bloody suits him. Thank *you*.'

The receiver was jammed back before Alleyn could reply.

'Hear that?' he asked Fox.

'Very put about, wasn't he? Funny that. Deposit paid down and all. Looks like something urgent cropped up to make him have it on the toes,' said Fox, meaning 'bolt'. 'Or it might be he couldn't raise the principal. What do you reckon, Mr Alleyn? He's only recently returned from abroad so his passport ought to be in order.'

'Presumably.'

'Or he may be tucked away somewhere handy or gone to try and raise the cash for the car. Have we got anything on his associates?'

'Nothing to write home about. His contact in the suspected drug business is thought to be this squalid little stationer's shop in Southampton: one of the sort that provides an accommodation address. It's called "The Good Read" and is in Port Lane.'

'Sussy on drugs,' Fox mused, 'and done for blackmail.'

'Attempted blackmail. The victim didn't play ball. He charged him and Claude did three months. Blackmail tends to be a chronic condition. He may have operated at other times with success.'

'What's our move, then?'

'Complete this search and then get down to the village again and see if we can find anything to bear out Artie's tale of Claude's nocturnal on-goings.'

When they arrived back at the village and inspected the hedgerow near the corner of Stile Lane and Long Lane they soon found what they sought, a hole in the tangle of saplings, blackthorn and weeds that could be crept into from the field beyond and was masked from the sunken lane below by grasses and wild parsnip. Footprints from a hurdle gate into the field led to the hole and a flattened depression within it where they found five cigarette butts and as many burnt matches. Clear of the hedge was an embryo fireplace constructed of a few old bricks and a crossbar of wood supported by two cleft sticks.

'Snug,' said Fox. 'And here's where sonny-boy plays Indian.'

'That's about the form.'

'And kips with the bunnies and tiggywinkles.'

'And down the lane comes Claude with his pack on his back.'

'All of a summer's night.'

'All right, all right. He must have passed more or less under Artie's nose.'

'Within spitting range,' Fox agreed. 'Come on.'

Alleyn led the way back into Long Lane and to the lych-gate at the foot of the church steps. He pushed it open and it squeaked.

'I wonder,' Alleyn said, 'how many people have walked up those steps since nine o'clock last night. The whole funeral procession.'

'That's right,' said Fox gloomily.

'Coffin bearers, mourners. Me. After that, tidying-uppers, and the vicar, one supposes.'

He stooped down, knelt, peered. 'Yes, I think so,' he said. 'On the damp earth the near side of the gate and well to the left in the shelter of the lych, if that's the way to put it. Very faint but I fancy they're our old friends the crêpe-soled shoes. Take a look.'

Fox did so. 'Yes,' he said. 'By gum, I think so.'

'More work for Bill Bailey and until he gets here the local copper can undisguise himself and take another turn at masterly inactivity. So far it's one up to Artie.'

'Not a chance of anything on the steps.'

'I'm afraid, not a chance. Still – up we go.'

They climbed the steps, slowly and searchingly. Inside the church the organ suddenly blared and infant voices shrilled.

Through the night of doubt and sorrow –

'Choir practice,' said Alleyn. 'Damn. Not an inappropriate choice, though, when you come to think of it.'

The steps into the porch showed signs of the afternoon's traffic. Alleyn took a look inside. The vicar's wife was seated at the organ with five little girls and two little boys clustered round her. When she saw Alleyn her jaw dropped in the middle of 'Onward'. He made a pacifying signal and withdrew. He and Fox walked round the church to Sybil Foster's grave.

Bruce and Artie had taken trouble over finishing their job. The flowers – Bruce would certainly call them 'floral tributes', no longer lined the path but had been laid in meticulous order on the mound which they completely covered, stalks down, blossoms pointing up, in receding size. The Cellophane covers on the professional offerings glistened in the sun and looked, Alleyn thought, awful. On the top, as a sort of baleful *bonne-bouche*, was the great sheaf of red roses and carnations: 'From B.S. with love'.

'It's quite hopeless,' Alleyn said. 'There must have been thirty or more people tramping round the place. If ever his prints were here they've been trodden out. We'd better take a look but we won't find.'

And nor they did.

'Not to be fanciful,' Fox said. 'As far as the footsteps go it's like coming to the end of a trail. Room with the point marked x, gardener's shed, broom recess, lych-gate and – nothing. It would have been appropriate, you might say, if they'd finished up for keeps at the graveside.'

Alleyn didn't answer for a second or two.

'You do,' he then said, 'get the oddest flights of fancy. It *would* in a macabre sort of way have been dramatically satisfactory.'

'If he did her, that is.'

'Ah. If.'

'Well,' said Fox, 'it looks pretty good to me. How else do you explain the ruddy prints? He lets on he's an electrician, he takes up the lilies, he hides in the recess and when the coast's clear he slips in and does her. Motive: the cash – a lot of it. You *can't* explain it any other way.'

'Can't you?'

'Well, can you?'

'We mentioned his record, didn't we? Blackmail. Shouldn't we perhaps bestow a passing thought on that?'

'Here! Wait a bit – wait a bit,' said Fox, startled. He became broody and remained so all the way to Great Quintern.

They drove to the police station where Alleyn had established his headquarters and been given a sort of mini-office next door to the charge room. It had a table, three chairs, writing material and a telephone which was all he expected to be given and suited him very well.

The sergeant behind the counter in the front office was on the telephone when they came in. When he saw Alleyn he raised his hand.

'Just a minute, madam,' he said. 'The Chief Superintendent has come in. Will you hold on, please?' He put his enormous hand over the receiver. 'It's a lady asking for you, sir. She seems to be upset. Shall I take the name?'

'Do.'

'What name was it, madam? Yes, madam, he *is here.* What name shall I say? Thank you. Hold the line, please,' said the sergeant, re-stopping the receiver. 'It's a Sister Jackson, sir. She says it's very urgent.'

Alleyn gave a long whistle, pulled a face at Fox and said he'd take the call in his room.

Sister Jackson's voice, when it came through, was an extraordinary mixture of refinement and what sounded like sheer terror. She whispered, and her whisper was of the piercing kind. She gasped, she faded out altogether and came back with a rush. She apologized for being silly and said she didn't know what he would think of her. Finally, she breathed heavily into the receiver, said she was 'in shock' and wanted to see him. She could not elaborate over the telephone.

Alleyn, thoughtfully contemplating Mr Fox, said he would come to Greengages, upon which she gave an instantly muffled shriek and said no, no that would never do and that she had the evening off and would meet him in the bar parlour of the Iron Duke on the outskirts of Maidstone. 'It's quite nice, really,' she quavered.

'Certainly,' Alleyn said. 'What time?'

'About nayne?'

'Nine let it be. Cheer up, Sister. You don't feel like giving me an inkling as to what it's all about?'

When she answered she had evidently put her mouth inside the receiver.

'Blackmail,' she articulated and his eardrum tingled.

Approaching voices were to be heard. Sister Jackson came through from a normal distance. 'OK,' she cried, 'that'll be fantastic, cheery-bye,' and hung up.

'Blackmail,' Alleyn said to Fox. 'We've only got to mention it and up it rises.'

'Well!' said Fox. 'Fancy that! Would it be going too far to mention Claude?'

'Who can tell? But at least it's suggestive. I'll leave you to get things laid on up in the village. Where are Bailey and Thompson, by the way?'

'Doing the fireplace and the tool shed. They're to ring back here before leaving.'

'Right. Get the local copper to keep an eye on the lych-gate until B and T arrive. Having dealt with that and just to show zealous they may then go over the churchyard area and see if they can find a trace we've missed. And having turned them on, Fox, check the progress if any of the search for Claude Carter. Oh, and see if you can get a check on the London train from Great Quintern at eleven-five last night. I think that's the lot.'

'You don't require me at the Iron Duke?'

'No. *La Belle Jackson* is clearly not in the mood. Sickening for you.'

'We'll meet at our pub, then?'

'Yes.'

'I shan't wait up,' said Fox. 'Don't dream of it.'

'In the meantime, I'll stroll down to the station hoping for better luck than I had with the Greengages bus.'

'Do. I'll bring my file up to date.'

'Were you thinking of taking dinner at the Iron Duke?'

'I was thinking of taking worm-coloured fish in pink sauce and athletic fowl at our own pub. Do join me.'

'Thanks. That's all settled then,' said Fox comfortably, and took himself off.

V

There were only seven customers in the bar parlour of the Iron Duke when Alleyn walked in at a quarter to nine: an amorous couple at a corner table and five city-dressed men playing poker.

Alleyn took a glass of a respectable port to a banquette at the furthest remove from the other tables and opened the evening paper. A distant roar of voices from the two bars bore witness to the Duke's popularity. At five to nine Sister Jackson walked in. He received the slight shock caused by an encounter with a nurse seen for the first time out of uniform. Sister Jackson was sheathed in clinging blue with a fairly reckless cleavage. She wore a velvet beret that rakishly shaded her face, and insistent gloves. He saw that her make-up was more emphatic than usual, especially about the eyes. She had been crying.

'How punctual we both are,' he said. He turned a chair to the table with its back to the room and facing the banquette. She sat in it without looking at him and with a movement of her shoulders that held a faint suggestion of what might have passed as provocation under happier circumstances. He asked her what she would have to drink and when she hesitated and bridled a little, proposed brandy.

'Well – thank you,' she said. He ordered a double one. When it came she took a sudden pull at it, shuddered and said she had been under a severe strain. It was the first remark of more than three words that she had offered.

'This seems quite a pleasant pub,' he said. 'Do you often come here?'

'No. Never. They – we – all use the Crown at Greenvale. That's why I suggested it. To be sure.'

'I'm glad,' Alleyn said, 'that whatever it's all about you decided to tell me.'

'It's very difficult to begin.'

'Never mind. Try. You said something about blackmail, didn't you? Shall we begin there?'

She stared at him for an awkwardly long time and then suddenly opened her handbag, pulled out a folded paper and thrust it across the table. She then took another pull at her brandy.

Alleyn unfolded the paper, using his pen and a fingernail to do so. 'Were you by any chance wearing gloves when you handled this?' he asked.

'As it happened. I was going out. I picked it up at the desk.'

'Where's the envelope?'

'I don't know. Yes, I do. I think. On the floor of my car. I opened it in the car.'

The paper was now spread out on the table. It was a kind as well known to the police as a hand-bill: a piece of off-white commercial paper, long and narrow, that might have been torn from a domestic *aide-mémoire*. The message was composed of words and letters that had been cut from newsprint and gummed in two irregular lines.

'Post £500 fives and singles to C. Morris, 11 Port Lane Southampton otherwise will inform police your visit to room 20 Genuine.'

Alleyn looked at Sister Jackson and Sister Jackson looked like a mesmerized rabbit at him.

'When did it come?'

'Yesterday morning.'

'To Greengages?'

'Yes.'

'Is the envelope addressed in this fashion?'

'Yes. My name's all in one. I recognized it – it's from an advertisement in the local rag for Jackson's Drapery and it's the same with Greengages Hotel. Cut out of an advertisement.'

'You didn't comply, of course?'

'No. I didn't know what to do. I – nothing like that's ever happened to me – I – I was dreadfully upset.'

'You didn't ask anyone to advise you?'

She shook her head.

'Dr Schramm, for instance?'

He could have sworn that her opulent flesh did a little hop and that for the briefest moment an extremely vindictive look clicked on and off. She wetted her mouth. 'Oh no,' she whispered. 'No, *thank* you!'

'This is the only message you've received?'

'There's been something else. Something much worse. Last evening. Soon after eight. They fetched me from the dining-room!'

'What was it? A telephone call?'

'You knew!'

'I guessed. Go on, please.'

'When the waiter told me, I knew. I don't know why but I did. I knew. I took it in one of the telephone boxes in the hall. I think he must have had something over his mouth. His voice was muffled and peculiar. It said, "You got the message." I couldn't speak and then it said, "You did or you'd answer. Have you followed instructions?" I – didn't know what to say so I said, "I will," and it said, "You better." It said something else, I don't remember exactly, something about the only warning, I think. That's all,' said Sister Jackson, and finished her cognac. She held the unsteady glass between her white-gloved paws and put it down awkwardly.

Alleyn said, 'Do you mind if I keep this? And would you be kind enough to refold it and put it in here for me?' He took an envelope from his pocket and laid it beside the paper.

She complied and made a shaky business of doing so. He put the envelope in his breast pocket.

'What will he do to me?' asked Sister Jackson.

'The odds are: nothing effective. The police may get something from him but you've anticipated that, haven't you? Or you will do so.'

'I don't understand.'

'Sister Jackson,' Alleyn said, 'don't you think you had better tell me about your visit to Room 20?'

She tried to speak. Her lips moved. She fingered them and then looked at the smudge of red on her glove.

'Come along,' he said.

'You won't understand.'

'Try me.'

'I can't.'

'Then why have you asked to see me? Surely it was to anticipate whatever the concoctor of this message might have to say to us. You've got in first.'

'I haven't done anything awful. I'm a fully qualified nurse.'

'Of course you are. Now then, when did you pay this visit?'

She focused her gaze on the couple in the far corner, stiffened her neck and rattled off her account in a series of disjointed phrases.

It had been at about nine o'clock on the night of Mrs Foster's death (Sister Jackson called it her 'passing'). She herself walked down the passage on her way to her own quarters. She heard the television bawling away in No. 20. Pop music. She knew Mrs Foster didn't appreciate pop and she thought she might have fallen asleep and the noise would disturb the occupants of neighbouring rooms. So she tapped and went in.

Here Sister Jackson paused. A movement of her chin and throat indicated a dry swallow. When she began again her voice was pitched higher but not by any means louder than before.

'The patient,' she said, 'Mrs Foster, I mean, was as I thought she would be. Asleep. I looked at her and made sure she was – asleep. So I came away. *I came away.* I wasn't there for more than three minutes. That's all. All there is to tell you.'

'How was she lying?'

'On her side, with her face to the wall.'

'When Dr Schramm found her she was on her back.'

'I know. That proves it. Doesn't it. *Doesn't it?*'

'Did you turn off the television?'

'No. Yes! I don't remember. I think I must have. I don't know.'

'It was still going when Dr Schramm found her.'

'Well, I didn't then, did I? I didn't turn it off.'

'Why, I wonder?'

'It's no good asking me things like that. I've been shocked. I don't remember details.'

She beat on the table. The amorous couple unclinched and one of the card players looked over his shoulder. Sister Jackson had split her glove.

Alleyn said, 'Should we continue this conversation somewhere else?'

'No. I'm sorry.'

With a most uncomfortable parody of coquettishness she leant across the table and actually smiled or seemed to smile at him.

'I'll be all right,' she said.

Their waiter came back and looked enquiringly at her empty glass.

'Would you like another?' Alleyn asked.

'I don't think so. No. Well, a small one, then.'

The waiter was quick bringing it.

'Right. Now – how was the room? The bedside table? Did you notice the bottle of barbiturates?'

'I didn't notice. I've said so. I just saw she was asleep and I went away.'

'Was the light on in the bathroom?'

This seemed to terrify her. She said, 'Do you mean – ? Was he *there*? Whoever it was? Hiding? Watching? No, the door was shut, I mean – I think it was shut.'

'Did you see anybody in the passage? Before you went into the room or when you left it?'

'No.'

'Sure?'

'Yes.'

'There's that alcove, isn't there? Where the brooms and vacuum-cleaner are kept?'

She nodded. The amorous couple were leaving. The man helped the girl into her coat. They both looked at Alleyn and Sister Jackson. She fumbled in her bag and produced a packet of cigarettes.

Alleyn said, 'I'm sorry. I've given up and forget to keep any on me. At least I can offer you a light.' He did so and she made a clumsy business of using it. The door swung to behind the couple. The card players had finished their game and decided, noisily, to move into the bar. When they had gone Alleyn said, 'You realize, don't you – well, of course you do – that the concoctor of this threat must have seen you?'

She stared at him. 'Naturally,' she said, attempting, he thought, a sneer.

'Yes,' he said. 'It's a glimpse of the obvious, isn't it? And you'll remember that I showed you a lily-head that Inspector Fox and I found in the alcove?'

'Of course.'

'And that there were similar lilies in the hand-basin in Mrs Foster's bathroom?'

'Naturally. I mean – yes, I saw them afterwards. When we used the stomach pump. We scrubbed up under the bath taps. It was quicker than clearing away the mess in the basin.'

'So it follows as the night the day that the person who dropped the lily-head in the alcove was the person who put the flowers in the hand-basin. Does it also follow that this same person was your blackmailer?'

'I – yes. I suppose it might.'

'And does it also follow, do you think, that the blackmailer was the murderer of Mrs Foster?'

'But you don't know. You don't know that she was – *that*.'

'We believe we do.'

She ought, he thought, to be romping about like a Rubens lady in an Arcadian setting – all sumptuous flesh, no brains and as happy as Larry, instead of quivering like an over-dressed jelly in a bar parlour.

'Sister Jackson,' he said, 'why didn't you tell the Coroner or the police or anyone at all, that you went into Room 20 at about nine o'clock that night and found Mrs Foster asleep in her bed?'

She opened and shut her smudged lips two or three times, gaping like a fish.

'Nobody asked me,' she said. 'Why should I?'

'Are you sure Mrs Foster was asleep?'

Her lips formed the words but she had no voice. 'Of course I am.'

'She wasn't asleep, was she? She was dead.'

The swing door opened and Basil Schramm walked in. 'I thought I'd find you,' he said. 'Good evening.'

CHAPTER 8

Graveyard (II)

'May I join you?' asked Dr Schramm. The folds from his nostrils to the corners of his mouth lifted and intensified. It was almost a mephistophelian grin.

'Do,' said Alleyn and turned to Sister Jackson. 'If Sister Jackson approves,' he said.

She looked at nothing, said nothing and compressed her mouth.

'Silence,' Dr Schramm joked, 'gives consent, I hope.' And he sat down.

'What are you drinking?' he invited.

'Not another for me, thank you,' said Alleyn.

'On duty?'

'That's my story.'

'Dot?'

Sister Jackson stood up. 'I'm afraid I must go,' she said to Alleyn and with tolerable success achieved a social manner. 'I hadn't realized it was so late.'

'It isn't late,' said Schramm, 'sit down.'

She sat down. First round to the doctor, thought Alleyn.

'The bell's by you, Alleyn,' said Schramm. 'Do you mind?'

Alleyn pressed the wall bell above his head. Schramm had leant forward. Alleyn caught a great wave of whisky and saw that his eyes were bloodshot and not quite in focus.

'I happened to be passing,' he chatted. He inclined his head towards Sister Jackson. 'I noticed your car. And yours, Superintendent.'

'Sister Jackson has been kind enough to clear up a detail for us.'

'That's what's known as "helping the police in their investigations", isn't it? With grim connotations as a rule.'

'You've been reading the popular press,' said Alleyn.

The waiter came in. Schramm ordered a large scotch. 'Sure?' he asked them and then, to the waiter, 'Correction. Make that two large scotches.'

Alleyn said, 'Not for me. Really.'

'Two large scotches,' Schramm repeated on a high note. The waiter glanced doubtfully at Alleyn.

'You heard what I said,' Schramm insisted. 'Two large scotches.'

Alleyn thought, This is the sort of situation where one could do with the odd drop of omnipotence. One wrong move from me and it'll be a balls-up.

Complete silence set in. The waiter came and went. Dr Schramm downed one of the two double whiskies very quickly. The bar parlour clock ticked. He continued to smile and began on the second whisky slowly, with concentration, absorbing it and cradling the glass. Sister Jackson remained perfectly still.

'What's she been telling you?' Schramm suddenly demanded. 'She's an inventive lady. You ought to realize that. To be quite, quite frank and honest, she's a liar of the first water. Aren't you, sweetie?'

'You followed me.'

'It's some considerable time since I left off doing that, darling.'

Alleyn had the passing thought that it would be nice to hit Dr Schramm.

'I really must insist,' Schramm said. 'I'm sorry, but you have seen for yourself how things are, here. I realize, perf'ly well, that you will think I had a motive for this crime, if crime it was. Because I am a legatee I'm a suspect. So of course it's no good my saying that I asked Sybil Foster to marry me. *Not,*' he said wagging his finger at Alleyn, '*not* because I'd got my sights set on her money but because I loved her. Which I did, and that,' he added, staring at Sister Jackson, 'is precisely where the trouble lies.' His speech was now all over the place like an actor's in a comic drunken scene. 'You wouldn't have minded if it had been like that. You wouldn't have minded all that much if you believed I'd come back earlier and killed her for her money. You really are a bitch, aren't you, Dotty? My God, you even threatened to take to her yourself. Didn't you? Well, didn't you? Where's the bloody waiter?'

He got to his feet, lurched across the table and fetched up with the palms of his hands on the wall, the left supporting him and the right clamped down over the bell-push which could be heard distantly to operate. His face was within three inches of Alleyn's. Sister Jackson shrank back in her chair.

'Disgusting!' she said.

Alleyn detached Dr Schramm from the wall and replaced him in his chair. He then moved over to the door, anticipating the return of the waiter. When the man arrived Alleyn showed his credentials.

'The gentleman's had as much as is good for him,' he said. 'Let me handle it. There's a side door, isn't there?'

'Well, yes,' said the waiter, looking dubious. 'Sir,' he added.

'He's going to order another scotch. Can you cook up a poor single to look like a double? Here – this'll settle the lot and forget the change. Right?'

'Well, thank you very much, sir,' said the waiter, suddenly avid with curiosity and gratification, 'I'll do what I can.'

'Waiter!' shouted Dr Schramm. 'Same 'gain.'

'There's your cue,' said Alleyn.

'What'll I say to him?'

' "Anon, anon, sir" would do.'

'Would that be Shakespeare?' hazarded the waiter.

'It would, indeed.'

'*Waiter!*'

'"Anon, anon, sir,"' said the waiter self-consciously. He collected the empty glasses and hurried away.

''Strordinary waiter,' said Dr Schramm. 'As I was saying. I insist on being informed for reasons that I shall make 'bundantly clear. What's she said? 'Bout me?'

'You didn't feature in our conversation,' said Alleyn.

'That's what you say.'

Sister Jackson, with a groggy and terrified return to something like her habitual manner, said, 'I wouldn't demean myself.' She turned on Alleyn. 'You're mad,' she said, exactly as if there had been no break in their exchange. 'You don't know what you're talking about. She was asleep.'

'Why didn't you report your visit, then?' Alleyn said.

'It didn't matter.'

'Oh, nonsense. It would have established, if true, that she was alive at that time.'

With one of those baffling returns to apparent sobriety by which drunken persons sometimes bewilder us, Dr Schramm said, 'Do I understand, Sister, that you visited her in her room?'

Sister Jackson ignored him. Alleyn said, 'At about nine o'clock.'

'And didn't report it? Why? *Why?*' he appealed to Alleyn.

'I don't know. Perhaps because she was afraid. Perhaps because – '

Sister Jackson gave a strangulated cry. 'No! No, for God's sake! He'll get it all wrong. He'll jump to conclusions. It wasn't like that. She was asleep. Natural sleep. There was nothing the matter with her.'

The waiter came back with a single glass, half full.

'Take that away,' Schramm ordered. 'I've got to have a clear head. Bring some ice. Bring me a lot of ice.'

The waiter looked at Alleyn, who nodded. He went out.

'I'm going,' said Sister Jackson.

'You'll stay where you are unless you want a clip over the ear.'

'And you,' said Alleyn, 'will stay where you are unless you want to be run in. Behave yourself.'

Schramm stared at him for a moment. He said something that sounded like, 'Look who's talking,' and took an immaculate hand-kerchief from his breast pocket, laid it on the table and began to fold it diagonally. The waiter reappeared with a jug full of ice.

'I really ought to mention this to the manager, sir,' he murmured. 'If he gets noisy again, I'll have to.'

'I'll answer for you. Tell the manager it's an urgent police matter. Give him my card. Here you are.'

'It – it wouldn't be about that business over at Greengages, would it?'

'Yes, it would. Give me the ice and vanish, there's a good chap.'

Alleyn put the jug on the table. Schramm, with shaking hands, began to lay ice on his folded handkerchief.

'Sister,' he said impatiently. 'Make a pack, if you please.'

To Alleyn's utter astonishment she did so in a very professional manner. Schramm loosened his tie and opened his shirt. It was as if they both responded like Pavlovian dogs to some behaviouristic prompting. He rested his forehead on the table and she placed the pack of ice on the back of his neck. He gasped. A trickle of water ran down his jawline. 'Keep it up,' he ordered and shivered.

Alleyn, watching this performance, thought how unpredictable the behaviour of drunken persons could be. Sister Jackson had been in the condition so inaccurately known as 'nicely, thank you'. Basil Schramm had been in an advanced stage of intoxication but able to assess his own condition and after a fashion deal with it. And there they were, both of them, behaving like automata and, he felt sure, frightened out of what wits they still, however precariously, commanded.

She continued to operate the ice packs. A pool of water enlarged itself on the table and began to drip to the carpet.

'That's enough,' Schramm said presently. Sister Jackson squeezed his handkerchief into the jug. Alleyn offered his own and Schramm mopped himself up with it. He fastened his shirt and reknotted his tie. As if by common consent he and Sister Jackson sat down simultaneously, facing each other across the table with Alleyn between them on the banquette – like a referee, he thought. This effect was enhanced when he took out his notebook. They paid not the smallest attention to him. They glared at each other. He with distaste and she with hatred. He produced a comb and used it.

'Now, then,' he said. 'What's the story? You went to her room at nine. You say she was asleep. And *you* – ' he jabbed a finger at Alleyn – 'say she was dead. Right?'

'I don't say so positively. I suggested it.'

'Why?'

'For several reasons. If Mrs Foster was sleeping, peacefully and naturally, it's difficult to see why Sister Jackson did not report her visit.'

'If there'd been anything wrong, I would have,' she said.

Schramm said, 'Did you think it was suicide?'

'She was asleep.'

'Did you see the tablets – spilled on the table?'

'No. *No.*'

'Did you think she'd been drugged?'

'She was asleep. Peacefully and naturally. Asleep.'

'You're lying, aren't you? Aren't you? Come on!'

She began to gabble at Alleyn. 'It was the shock you know. When he rang through and told me, I came and we did everything – such a shock – I couldn't remember anything about how the room had looked before. Naturally not.'

'It was no shock to you,' Dr Schramm said profoundly. 'You're an old hand. An experienced nurse. And you didn't regret her death, my dear. You gloated. You could hardly keep a straight face.'

'Don't listen to this,' Sister Jackson gabbled at Alleyn, 'it's all lies. Monstrous lies. Don't listen.'

'You'd better,' said Schramm. 'This is the hell-knows-no-fury bit, Superintendent, and you may as well recognize it. Oh, yes. She actually said when she heard about Sybil and me that she bloody well wished Syb was dead and she meant it. Fact, I assure you. And I don't mind telling you she felt the same about me. Still does. Look at her.'

Sister Jackson was hardly a classical figure of panic but she certainly presented a strange picture. The velvet beret had flopped forward over her left eye so that she was obliged to tilt her head back at an extravagant angle in order to see from under it. Oddly enough, and deeply unpleasant as the situation undoubtedly was, she reminded Alleyn momentarily of a grotesque lady on a comic postcard.

They began to exchange charge and countercharge, often speaking simultaneously. It was the kind of row that is welcome as manna from Heaven to an investigating officer. Alleyn noted it all down, almost under their noses, and was conscious, as often before, of a strong feeling of distaste for the job.

They repeated themselves *ad nauseam*. She used the stock phrases of the discarded mistress. He, as he became articulate, also grew reckless and made more specific his accusations about her having threatened to do harm to Sybil Foster and even hinted that on her visit to Room 20 she might well have abetted Sybil in taking an overdose.

At that point they stopped dead, stared aghast at each other and then, for the first time since the slanging match had set in, at Alleyn.

He finished his notes and shut the book.

'I could,' he said, 'and perhaps I should, ask you both to come to the police station and make statements. You would then refuse to utter or to write another word until you had seen your respective solicitors. A great deal of time would be wasted. Later on you would both state that you had been dead drunk and that I had brought about this pitiable condition and made false reports about your statements and taken them down in writing. All this would be very boring and unproductive. Instead, I propose that you go back to Greengages, think things over and then concoct your statements. You've been too preoccupied to notice, I fancy, but I've made pretty extensive notes and I shall make a report of the conversation and, in due course, invite you to sign it. And now, I expect you will like to go. If, that is, you are in a fit state to drive. If not, you'd better go to the lavatories and put your fingers down your throats. I'll be in touch. Good evening.'

He left them gaping and went out to his car where he waited about five minutes before they appeared severally, walking with unnatural precision. They entered their cars and drove, very slowly, away.

II

Fox had not gone to bed at their pub. He and Alleyn took a nightcap together in Alleyn's room.

'Well, now,' said Fox, rubbing his hands on his knees. 'That was a turn-up for the books, wasn't it? I'd've liked to be there. How do you read it, then, Mr Alleyn? As regards the lady, now? Dropped in on the deceased round about nine p.m. and was watched by crêpe-soles from the alcove and is being blackmailed by him. Which gives us one more reason, if we'd needed it, for saying crêpe-soles is Claude?'

'Go on.'

'But,' said Fox opening his eyes wide, 'but when the doctor (which is what he isn't, properly speaking, but never mind), when the doctor rings through an hour, or thereabouts, later and tells her to come to Room 20 and she does come and the lady's passed away, does she say – ' and here Mr Fox gave a sketchy impersonation of a female voice – '"Oh, Doctor, I looked in at nine and she was as right as Christmas"? No. She does not. She keeps her tongue behind her teeth and gets cracking with the stomach pump. Now why? Why not mention it?'

'Schramm seemed to suggest that at some earlier stage, in a fit of jealous rage, that Jackson had threatened she'd do some mischief to Mrs Foster. And was now afraid he'd think that on this unmentioned visit she'd taken a hand in overdosing her with barbiturates.'

'Ah,' said Fox. 'But the catch in that is, Mrs Foster, according to our reading of the evidence, was first drugged and then smothered. So it looks as if he didn't realize she was smothered, which, if true, puts him in the clear. Any good?'

'I think so, Br'er Fox. I think it's quite a lot of good.'

'Would you say, now, that Sister J would be capable of doing the job herself – pillow and all?'

'Ah, there you have me. I think she's a jealous, slighted woman with a ferocious temper. Jealous, slighted women have murdered their supplanters before now but generally speaking they're more inclined to take to the man. And by George, judging by the way she shaped up to Schramm tonight I wouldn't put it past her.'

'By and large, then, these two are a bit of nuisance. We'd got things more or less settled – well, *I* had,' said Mr Fox with a hard look at Alleyn, 'and it was just a matter of running Claude to earth. And now this silly lot crops up.'

'Very inconsiderate.'

'Yerse. And there's no joy from the Claude front, by the way. The Yard rang through. The search is what the Press likes to call nation-wide but not a squeak.'

'Southampton?'

'They sent a copper they don't reckon looks like it into "The Good Read", in Port Lane. It's an accommodation address-shop all right but there was nothing for "Morris". Very cagey the chap was – sussy for drugs but they've never collected enough to knock him off. The DI I talked to thinks it's possible Claude Carter off-loaded the stuff he brought ashore there. If he's thinking of slipping out by Southampton he could have fixed it to collect Sister J's blackmail delivery on the way.'

'Suppose she'd posted it today, first-class mail, it wouldn't arrive at the earliest until tomorrow,' said Alleyn.

'They've got the shop under the obbo non-stop. If he shows, they'll feel his collar, all right,' said Fox.

'If. It's an odd development, isn't it?' Alleyn said. 'There he is, large as life, mousing about up at Quintern Place and in and around the district until (according to Daft Artie) twelve o'clock or (according to Bruce) nine, last night. He comes down the lane with his pack on his back. He opens the squeaky lych-gate and leaves his prints there. And vanishes.'

'Now you see him, now you don't. Lost his nerve, d'you reckon?'

'We mustn't forget he left that note for Mrs Jim.'

'P'raps that's all there is to it. P'raps,' said Fox bitterly, 'he'll come waltzing back with a silly grin on his face having been to stay with his auntie. P'raps it was somebody else blackmailing Sister J, and we'll get egg all over our faces.'

'It's an occupational hazard,' Alleyn said vaguely and then to himself, '"into thin air" and but for the footprints at the lych-gate, leaving "not a wrack behind". *Why?* And then – where to, for pity's sake?'

'Not by the late train to London,' said Fox. 'They said at the station, nobody entered or left it at Great Quintern.'

'Hitched a lift?'

'Nice job for our boys, that'll be. Ads in the papers and what a hope.'

'You're in a despondent mood, my poor Foxkin.'

Mr Fox, who, although an occasional grumbler, was never known to succumb to the mildest hint of depression, placidly ignored this observation.

'I shall cheer you up,' Alleyn continued. 'You need a change of scene. What do you say to a moonlight picnic?'

'Now then!' said Fox guardedly.

'Well, not perhaps a picnic but a stroll in a graveyard? Bruce Gardener would call it a Gothic stroll, no doubt.'

'You don't mean this, I suppose, Mr Alleyn?'

'I do, though. I can *not* get Daft Artie's story out of my head, Fox. It isn't all moonshine, presumably, because there *are* those prints. Carter *has* disappeared and there *is* the layby in the hedge. I suggest we return to the scene and step it out. What's the time?'

'Eleven-ten.'

'The village ought to be asleep.'

'So ought we,' sighed Fox.

'We'd better give the "factory" a shout and ask if they can raise an acetylene lamp or its equivalent.'

'A reconstruction, then?'

'You find it a fanciful notion? A trifle *vieux-jeu*, perhaps?'

'I dare say it makes sense,' said Fox resignedly and went off to telephone.

Sergeant McGuiness on night duty at the station did produce an acetylene lamp, kept in reserve against power failures. He had it ready for them and handed it over rather wistfully, 'I'd've liked to be in on this,' he confided to Fox. 'It sounds interesting.'

Alleyn overheard him. 'Can you raise a copper to hold the desk for an hour?' he asked. 'We could do with a third man.'

Sergeant McGuiness brightened. He said, 'Our PC Dance was competing in the darts semi-finals at the local tonight. He'll be on his way home but if he's won he'll be looking in to tell me. I dare say if it's agreeable to you, sir – '

'I'll condone it,' said Alleyn.

A scraping sound and a bobbing light on the window-blind announced the arrival of a bicycle. The sergeant excused himself and hurried to the door. A voice outside shouted, 'Done it, Sarge.'

'You never!'

'Out on the double seven.'

'That's the stuff.'

'Very near thing, though. Wait till I tell you.'

'Hold on.' The sergeant's voice dropped to a mumble. There was a brief inaudible exchange. He returned followed by a ginger-headed simpering colossus.

'PC Dance, sir,' said Sergeant McGuiness.

Alleyn congratulated PC Dance on his prowess and said he would be obliged if they could 'borrow' him. 'Borrow' is a synonym for 'arrest' in the Force and the disreputable pun, if pun it was, had an undeserved success. They left Dance telephoning his triumph to his wife.

On their way to the village Alleyn outlined the object of the exercise for the gratified McGuiness. 'We're trying to make sense of an apparently senseless situation,' he said. 'Item: could a walker coming down Stile Lane into Long Lane see much or anything of the light from Bruce Gardener's lamp? Item: can someone hidden in the hedge see the walker? Item: can the walker, supposing he climbs the steps to the church and goes into the church – '

'Which,' said the sergeant, 'excuse me, he can't. The church is locked at night, sir. By our advice. Possibility of vandals.'

'See how right we were to bring you in. Who locks it? The vicar?'

'That's correct, Mr Alleyn. And once the deceased lady was brought in that's what he'd do. Lock up the premises for the night.'

'Leaving the church in darkness?' Fox asked.

'I think not, Fox. I think he'd leave the sanctuary light on. We can ask.'

'So it's after the arrival of the deceased that Artie's story begins?'

'And our performance too for what it's worth. Do they keep early hours in the village, Sergeant?'

'Half an hour after the local closes they're all in bed.'

'Good.'

'Suppose,' Fox said, on a note of consternation, 'Daft Artie's sleeping out?'

'It'll be a bloody nuisance,' Alleyn grunted. 'If he is we'll have to play it by ear. I don't know, though. We might pull him in to demonstrate.'

'Would he co-operate?'

'God knows. Here we are. We make as little noise as possible. Don't bang the doors. Keep your voices down.'

They turned a sharp corner through a stand of beech trees and entered the village; a double row of some dozen cottages on either side of Long Lane, all fast asleep: the church, high above, its towers silhouetted against the stars, the rest almost disappearing into its background of trees. The moon had not yet risen so that Long Lane and the bank and hedge above it and the hillside beyond were all in deep shadow.

Alleyn drove the car on to the green near the steps and they got out.

'Hullo,' he said. 'There's somebody still awake up Stile Lane.'

'That's the widow Black's cottage,' said the sergeant. 'There'll be someone looking after her – the brother, no doubt.'

'Looking after her? Why?'

'Did you not hear? She was knocked over by a truck on the way back from the funeral this afternoon. The blind corner up the lane.

I've been saying for years it'd happen. The chap was driving dead slow for the turning and she fell clear. He helped her in and reported it to us.'

'Would that be Bruce Gardener's sister?' asked Fox.

'That's right, Mr Fox. We're not likely to disturb them.'

'I don't know so much about that,' Alleyn murmured. 'If it's Bruce up there and he looks out of the window and sees light coming from where he dug the grave and had his own lamp last night, he may come down to investigate. Damn!' He thought for a moment. 'Oh, well,' he said, 'we tell him. Why not? Let's get moving. I'd like you, Sergeant, to act as the boy says he did. Get into the layby in the hedge when the time comes. Not yet. We'll set you up. I'll do the Carter bit. Mr Fox is Bruce. All you have to do is to keep your eyes and ears open and report exactly what you see. Got the lamp? And the shovel? Come on, and quietly does it.'

He opened the lych-gate very cautiously, checking it at the first sign of the squeak. They slid through, one by one and moved quietly up the steps.

'Don't use your torches unless you have to,' Alleyn said and as their eyes adjusted to the dark it thinned and gravestones stood about them. They reached the top. Alleyn led the way round the church: the nave, the north transept, the chancel, until they came to the Passcoigne plot and Sybil Foster's grave. The flowers on the mound smelt heavy in the night air and the plastic covers glinted in the starlight as if phosphorescent.

Fox and McGuiness crouched over the lamp. Presently it flared. The area became explicit in a white glare. The sergeant spent some time regulating the flame. Fox stood up and his gigantic shadow rose against the trees. The lamp hissed. Fox lifted it and put it by the grave. They waited to make sure it was in good order.

'Right,' said Alleyn at last. 'Give us eight minutes to get down, Fox, and then start. Don't look into the light, Sergeant, it'll blind you. Come on.'

The shadow of the church was intensified by the light beyond it and the steps took longer to descend than to climb. When they were back at the car Alleyn murmured, 'Now, I'll show you the layby. It's in the hedge across the lane and a little to our right. About four yards further on there's a gap at the top of the bank with a hurdle gate.

You can ease round the post, go through into the field and turn back to the layby. If by any chance somebody comes down the lane and gets nosey we're looking for a missing child thought to be asleep near the hedge. Here we are. Make sure you'll recognize it from the other side. There's that hazel plant sticking up above the level of the hedge.'

They moved along the hedge until they came to the gap.

'Through you go,' Alleyn whispered, 'turn left and then back six paces. You'll have to crawl in, helmet and all. Give one low whistle when you're set and I'll go on into Stile Lane. That's when your obbo begins.'

He watched the shadowy sergeant climb the bank and edge his bulk between the gate-post and the hedge. Then he turned about and looked up at the church. It was transformed. A nimbus of light rose behind it. Tree-tops beyond the Passcoigne plot started up, uncannily defined, like stage scenery, and as he watched, a gargantuan shadow rose, moved enormously over the trees, threw up arms, and the sweeping image of a shovel sank and rose again. Mr Fox had embarked on his pantomime.

The sergeant was taking his time. No whistle. The silence, which is never really silence, of a countryside, breathed out its nocturnal preoccupations: stirrings in the hedgerow, far-distant traffic, the movements of small creatures going about their business in the night.

'Ssst!'

It was the sergeant, back in the gap up the hill. His helmet showed against Mrs Black's lighted window in Stile Lane. Alleyn climbed the bank and leant over the hurdle.

'Artie *is* there,' breathed Sergeant McGuiness. 'In his hidey-hole. Curled up. My Gawd, I nearly crawled in on top of him.'

'Asleep?'

'Sound.'

'It doesn't matter. Come back into the lane and lean into the hollow in the bank below the layby. Your head will be pretty much on a level with his. I simply want to check that he could have seen what he said he saw and heard what he said he heard. Back you come.'

The sergeant had gone. Alleyn slipped into the lane and walked a little way up it. He was now quite close to Mrs Black's cottage. The light behind the window was out. He waited for a moment or two and then retraced his steps, walking, now, in the middle of the road. He wondered if Claude Carter had worn his crêpe-soled shoes last night. He wondered, supposing Daft Artie woke and saw him, if he would repeat his eldritch shriek.

Now he was almost opposite the layby. Not a hint of the sergeant, in blackest shadow under the hedge.

Alleyn paused.

It was as if an ironclad fist struck him on the jaw.

III

He lay in the lane and felt grit against his face and pain and he heard a confusion of sounds. Disembodied voices shouted angrily.

'Mr Fox! Come down here, Mr Fox.'

He had been lifted and rested against a massive thigh. 'I'm all right,' somebody said. He said it. 'Where's Fox? What happened?'

'The bloody kid. He chucked a brick at you. Over my head. Gawd, I thought he'd done you, Mr Alleyn,' said Sergeant McGuiness.

'Where's Fox?'

'Here,' said Fox. His large concerned face blotted out the stars. He was breathing hard. 'Here I am,' he said. 'You'll be all right.'

A furious voice was roaring somewhere out on the hillside beyond the hedge. 'Come back. You damned, bloody young murderer. Come back, till I have the hide off of you.' Footsteps thudded and retreated.

'That's Bruce,' said Alleyn, feeling his jaw. 'Where did he spring from? The cottage?'

'That's right,' somebody said.

Fox was saying, 'Get cracking, Sarge. Sort it out. I'll look after this!'

More retreating footsteps at the run.

'Here, get me up. What hit me?'

Take it easy, Mr Alleyn. Let me have a look. Caught you on the jaw. Might have broken it.'

'You're telling me. What did?' He struggled to his knees and then, with Fox's help to his feet. 'Damn and blast!' he said. 'Let me get to that bank while my head clears. What hit me?'

'Half a brick. The boy must have woken up. Bruce and the Sarge are chasing him.'

Fox had propped him against the bank and was playing a torch on his face and dabbing it very gently with his handkerchief. 'It's bleeding,' he said.

'Never mind that. Tell me what happened.'

'It seems that when you got as far as here – almost in touching distance of the Sarge – the boy must have woken up, seen you, dark and all though it is, picked up a half-brick from his fireplace and heaved it. It must have passed over the Sarge's head. Then he lit off.'

'But, Bruce?'

'Yes. Bruce. Bruce noticed the light in the graveyard and thought it might be vandals. There's been trouble with them lately. Anyway, he came roaring down the hill and saw the boy in the act. How's it feel now?'

'Damn sore but I don't think it's broken. And the sergeant's chasing Daft Artie?'

'Him and Bruce.'

'No good making a song and dance over it – the boy's not responsible.'

'It's my bet they won't catch him. For a start, they can't see where they're going.'

'I wonder where his home is,' said Alleyn.

'Bruce'll know. It must,' said Fox, still examining Alleyn's jaw, 'have caught you on the flat. There's a raw patch but no cut. We'll have to get you to a doctor.'

'No, we won't,' Alleyn mumbled. 'I'll do all right. Fox, how much could he see from the layby? Enough to recognize me? Go and stand where I was, will you?'

'Are you sure – ?'

'Yes. Go on.'

Fox moved away. The light still glowed beyond the church. It was refracted faintly into the centre of the lane. Fox was an identifiable figure. Just.

Alleyn said, 'So we know Artie could have recognized Carter and I suppose, me. Damnation, look at this.'

A window in the parsonage on the far side of the green shone out. Somebody opened it and was revealed as a silhouette. 'Hullo!' said a cultivated voice. 'Is anything the matter?'

The vicar.

'Nothing at all,' Alleyn managed. 'A bit of skylarking in the lane. Some young chaps. We've sorted it out.'

'Is that the police?' asked the vicar plaintively.

'That's us,' Fox shouted. 'Sorry you've been disturbed, sir.'

'Never mind. Is there something going on behind the church? What's that light?'

'We're just making sure there's been no vandalism,' Alleyn improvised. It hurt abominably to raise his voice. 'Everything's in order.'

By this time several more windows along the lane had been opened.

'It's quite all right, sir,' Fox said. 'No trouble. A bunch of young chaps with too much on board.'

'Get that bloody light out,' Alleyn muttered.

Fox, using his own torch, crossed the lane. The lych-gate shrieked. He hurried up the steps and round the church.

'You don't think perhaps I should just pop down?' the vicar asked doubtfully, after a considerable pause.

'Not the slightest need. It's all over,' Alleyn assured him. 'They've bolted.'

Windows began to close. The light behind the church went out.

'Are you sure? Was it those lads from Great Quintern? I didn't hear motorbikes.'

'They hadn't got bikes. Go back to bed, Vicar,' Alleyn urged him. 'You'll catch your death.'

'No matter. Good night, then.'

The window was closed. Alleyn watched Fox's torchlight come bobbing round the church and down the steps. Voices sounded in the field beyond the hedge. Bruce and the sergeant. They came through the hurdle and down the bank.

'I'm here,' Alleyn said. 'Don't walk into me.' The sergeant's torchlight found him.

'Are you all right, sir? 'E's got clean away I'm afraid. It was that bloody dark and there's all them trees.'

Bruce said, 'I'll have the hide off my fine laddie for this. What's possessd the fule? He's never showed violent before. By God, I'll teach him a lesson he won't forget.'

'I suppose it *was* Artie?'

'Nae doubt about it, sir.'

'Where did you come from, Bruce?'

It was as they had thought. Bruce had been keeping company with his shaken sister. She had gone to bed and he was about to return to Quintern Place. He looked out of the window and saw the glare of the lamp in the churchyard.

'It gied me a shock,' he said, and with one of his occasional vivid remarks, 'It was oncanny – as if I mysel' was in two places at once. And then I thought it might be they vandals and up to no good. And I saw the shadow on the trees like mine had been. Digging. Like me. It fair turned my stomach, that.'

'I can imagine.'

'So I came the short cut down the brae to the lane as fast as I could in the dark. I arrived at the hedge and his figure rose up clear against the glow behind the kirk. It was him all right. He stood there for a second and then he hurrled something and let out a bit screech as he did so. I shouted and he bolted along the hedge. The sergeant was in the lane, sir, with you in the light of his torch and flat on your back and him saying by God the bugger's got him and yelling for Mr Fox. So I went roaring after the lad and not a hope in hell of catching him. He's a wild crittur. You'd say he could see in the dark. Who's to tell where he's hiding?'

'In his bed, most likely,' said the sergeant. 'By this time.'

'Aye, you may say so. His mother's cottage is a wee piece further down the lane. Are you greatly injured, Superintendent? What was it he hurried at you?'

'Half a brick. No, I'm all right.'

Bruce clicked his tongue busily. 'He might have kilt you,' he said.

'Leave it alone, Bruce. Don't pitch into him when you see him. It wouldn't do any good. I mean that.'

'Well,' said Bruce dourly, 'if you say so.'

'I do say so.'

Fox joined them carrying his doused lamp and the shovel.

Bruce, who wasted no ceremony with Fox whom he seemed to regard as a sort of warrant-officer, asked him in scandalized tones what he thought he'd been doing up yon. 'If you've been tampering with the grave,' he said furiously, 'it's tantamount to sacrilege and there's no doubt in my mind there's a law to deal with it. Now then, what was it? What were you doing with yon shovel?'

'It was dumb show, Bruce,' Alleyn said wearily. 'We were testing the boy's story. Nothing's been disturbed.'

'I've a mind to look for mysel'.'

'Go ahead, by all means if you want to. Have you got a torch?'

'I'll leave it,' Bruce said morosely. 'I dinna like it but I'll leave it.'

'Good night to you then. I think, Br'er Fox,' said Alleyn, 'I'll get in the car.' His face throbbed enormously and the ground seemed to shift under his feet. Fox piloted him to the car. The sergeant hovered.

When they were underway Fox said he proposed to drive to the outpatients' department at the nearest hospital. Alleyn said he would see Dr Field-Innis in the morning, that he'd had routine tetanus injections and that if he couldn't cope with a chuck under the chin the sooner he put in for retirement the better. He then fainted.

He was out only for a short time, he thought, as they seemed not to have noticed. He said in as natural a manner as he could contrive that he felt sleepy, managed to fold his arms and lower his head, and did, in fact, drift into a sort of doze. He was vaguely aware of Fox giving what is known as 'a shout' over the blower.

Now they were at the station and so, surprisingly, was the district police surgeon.

'There's no concussion,' said the police surgeon, 'and no breakage and your teeth are OK. We'll just clean you up and make you comfortable and send you home to bed, um?'

'Too kind,' said Alleyn.

'You'll be reasonably comfortable tomorrow.'

'Thank you.'

'Don't push it too far, though. Go easy.'

'That,' said Mr Fox in the background, 'will be the day.'

Alleyn grinned, which hurt. So did the cleaning up and dressing.

'There we are!' said the police surgeon jollily. 'It'll be a bit colourful for a day or two and there's some swelling. You won't have a permanent scar.'

'Most reassuring. I'm sorry they knocked you up.'

'What I'm there for, isn't it? Quite an honour in this case. Good morning.'

When he had gone Alleyn said, 'Fox, you're to get on to the Home Secretary.'

'*Me!*' exclaimed the startled Fox. 'Him? Not *me!*'

'Not directly you, but get the Yard and the AC and ask for it to be laid on.'

'What for, though, Mr Alleyn? Lay on what?'

'What do you think? The usual permit.'

'You're *not* – ' said Fox, ' – you can't be – you're not thinking of digging her up?'

'Aren't I? Can't I? I am, do you know. Not,' said Alleyn, holding his pulsing jaw, 'in quite the sense you mean but – digging her up, Br'er Fox. Yes.'

CHAPTER 9

Graveyard (III)

When Alleyn looked in the glass the following morning his face did not appear as awful as it felt. No doubt the full panoply of bruises was yet to develop. He shaved painfully round the dressing, took a bath and decided he was in more or less reasonable form to face the day.

Fox came in to say their Assistant Commissioner was on the telephone. 'If you can speak, that is.'

Alleyn said, 'Of course I can speak,' and found that it was best to do so with the minimum demand upon his lower jaw. He stifled the explosive grunt of pain that the effort cost him.

The telephone was in the passage outside his room.

'Rory?' said the AC. 'Yes. I want a word with you. What's all this about an exhumation?'

'It's not precisely that, sir.'

'What? I can't catch what you say. You sound as if you were talking to your dentist.'

Alleyn thought, I dare say I shall be when there's time for it, but he merely replied that he was sorry and would try to do better.

'I suppose it's the clip on the jaw Fox talked about. Does it hurt?'

'Not much,' Alleyn lied angrily.

'Good. Who did it?'

'The general idea is a naughty boy with a brick.'

'About this exhumation that is not an exhumation. What am I to say to the HS? Confide in me, for Heaven's sake.'

Alleyn confided.

'Sounds devilish far-fetched to me,' grumbled the AC. 'I hope you know what you're about.'

'So do I.'

'You know what I think about hunches.'

'If I may say so, you don't mistrust them any more than I do, sir.'

'All right, all right. We'll go ahead, then. Tomorrow night, you suggest? Sorry you've had a knock. Take care of yourself.'

Alleyn hummed in great discomfort:

> 'There is none that can compare,
> With a tow, row bloody row to
> Our A. Commissionaire.'

'It's on, Br'er Fox.'

'This'll set the village by the ears. What time?'

'Late tomorrow night. We'll be turning into tombstones ourselves if we keep up these capers.'

'What's our line with the populace?'

'God knows. We hope they won't notice. But what a hope!'

'How about someone accidentally dropped a valuable in the open grave? Such as – er – '

'What?'

'*I* don't know,' said Fox crossly. 'A gold watch?'

'When?' Alleyn asked. 'And whose gold watch?'

'Er. Well. Bruce's? Any time before the interment. I appreciate,' Fox confessed, 'that it doesn't sound too hot.'

'Go on.'

'I'm trying to picture it,' said Fox, after a longish pause.

'And how are you getting on?'

'It'd be ludicrous.'

'Perhaps the best way will be to keep quiet and if they do notice tell them nothing. "The police declined to comment."'

'The usual tarpaulin, etcetera, I suppose. I'll lay it on, will I?'

'Do. My face, by the way, had better be the result of a turn-up with a gang outside the village. Where's the sergeant?'

'Down at the "factory". He's going to take a look at Daft Artie.'

Alleyn began to walk about the room, found this jolted his jaw and sat on his bed. 'Br'er Fox,' he said, 'there's that child, Prunella. We can't possibly risk her hearing of it by accident.'

'The whole story?'

'Upon my soul,' Alleyn said after a long pause, 'I'm not at all sure I won't have recourse to your preposterous golden watch, or its equivalent. Look, I'll drop you in the village and get you to call on the vicar and tell him.'

'Some tarradiddle? Or what?' Fox asked.

'The truth but not the whole truth about what we hope to find. *Hope!*' said Alleyn distastefully. 'What a word!'

'I see what you mean. Without wishing to pester – ' Fox began. To his surprise and gratification Alleyn gave him a smack on the shoulder.

'All right, fusspot,' he said, 'fat-faced but fit as a flea, that's me. Come on.'

So he drove Fox to the parsonage and continued up Long Lane, passing the gap in the hedge. He looked up at the church and saw three small boys and two women come round from behind the chancel end. There was something self-conscious about the manner of the women's gait and their unconvincing way of pointing out a slanting headstone to each other.

There they go, Alleyn thought. It's all round the village by now. Police up to something round the grave! We'll have a queue for early doors tomorrow night.

He drove past the turning into Stile Lane and on towards the road that led uphill to Mardling Manor on the left and Quintern Place on the right. Keys Lane, where Verity Preston lived, branched off to the left. Alleyn turned in at her gate and found her sitting under her lime trees doing *The Times* crossword.

'I came on an impulse,' he said. 'I want some advice and I think you're the one to give it to me. I don't apologize because after all, in its shabby way it's a compliment. You may not think so, of course.'

'I can't say until I've heard it, can I?' she said. 'Come and sit down.'

When they were settled she said, 'It's no good being heavily tactful and not noticing your face, is it? What's happened?'

'A boy and a brick is my story.'

'Not a local boy, I hope.'

'Your gardener's assistant.'

'Daft Artie!' Verity exclaimed. 'I can't believe it!'

'Why can't you?'

'He doesn't do things like that. He's not violent, only silly.'

'That's what Bruce said. This may have been mere silliness. I may have just happened to be in the path of the trajectory. But I didn't come for advice about Daft Artie. It's about your god-daughter. Is she still staying at Mardling?'

'She went back there after the funeral. Now I come to think of it, she said she was going up to London for a week from tomorrow.'

'Good.'

'Why good?'

'This is not going to be pleasant for you, I know. I think you must have felt – you'd be very unusual if you hadn't – relieved when it was all over, yesterday afternoon. Tidily put away and mercifully done with. There's always that sense of release, isn't there, however deep the grief? Prunella must have felt it, don't you think?'

'I expect she did, poor child. And then there's her youth and her engagement and her natural ebullience. She'll be happy again. If it's about her you want to ask, you're not going to – ' Verity exclaimed and stopped short.

'Bother her again? Perhaps. I would like to know what you think. But first of all,' Alleyn broke off. 'This is in confidence. Very strict confidence. I'm sure you'll have no objections at all to keeping it so for forty-eight hours.'

'Very well,' she said uneasily. 'If you say so.'

'It's this. It looks as if we shall be obliged to remove the coffin from Mrs Foster's grave for a very short time. It will be replaced within an hour at the most and no indignity will be done it. I can't tell you any more than that. The question is: should Prunella be told? If she's away in London there may be a fair chance she need never know, but villages being what they are and certain people, the vicar for one, having to be informed, there's always the possibility that it might come out. What do you think?'

Verity looked at him with a sort of incredulous dismay. 'I can't think,' she said. 'It's incomprehensible and grotesque and I wish you hadn't told me.'

'I'm sorry.'

'One keeps forgetting – or I do – that this is a matter of somebody killing somebody whom one had known all one's life. And that's a monstrous thought.'

'Yes, of course it's monstrous. But to us, I'm afraid, it's all in the day's work. But I am concerned about the young Prunella.'

'So of course am I. I am indeed,' said Verity, 'and I do take your point. Do you think perhaps that Gideon Markos should be consulted? Or Nikolas? Or both?'

'Do you?'

'They've – well, they've kind of taken over, you see. Naturally. She's been absorbed into their sort of life and will belong to it.'

'But she's still looking to you, isn't she? I noticed it yesterday at the funeral.'

'Is there anything,' Verity found herself saying, 'that you don't notice?' Alleyn did not answer.

'Look,' Verity said. 'Suppose you – or I, if you like – should tell Nikolas Markos and suggest that they take Prue away? He's bought a yacht, he informs me. Not the messing-about-in-boats sort but the jet-set, Riviera job. They could waft her away on an extended cruise.'

'Even plutocratic yachts are not necessarily steamed up and ready to sail at the drop of a hat.'

'This one is.'

'Really?'

'He happened to mention it,' said Verity, turning pink.

'He's planning a cruise in four weeks' time. He could put it forward.'

'Are you invited?'

'I can't go,' she said shortly. 'I've got a first night coming up.'

'You know, your suggestion has its points. Even if someone does talk about it, long after it's all over and done with, that's not going to be as bad as knowing it is going to be done *now* and that it's actually happening. Or is it?'

'Not nearly so bad.'

'And in any case,' Alleyn said, more to himself than to her, 'she's going to find out – ultimately. Unless I'm all to blazes.' He stood up. 'I'll leave it to you,' he said. 'The decision. Is that unfair?'

'No. It's good of you to concern yourself. So I talk to Nikolas. Is that it?'

To Verity's surprise he hesitated for a moment.

'Could you, perhaps, suggest he puts forward the cruise because Prunella's had about as much as she can take and would be all the better for a complete change of scene – now?'

'I suppose so. I don't much fancy asking a favour.'

'No? Because he'll be a little too delighted to oblige?'

'Something like that,' said Verity.

II

The next day dawned overcast with the promise of rain. By late afternoon it was coming down inexorably.

'Set in solid,' Fox said, staring out of the station window.

'In one way a hellish bore and in another an advantage.'

'You mean people will be kept indoors?'

'That's right.'

'It'll be heavy going, though,' sighed Fox. 'For our lot.'

'All of that.'

The telephone rang. Alleyn answered it quickly. It was the Yard. The duty squad with men and equipment was about to leave in a 'nondescript' vehicle and wanted to know if there were any final orders. The sergeant in charge checked over details.

'Just a moment,' Alleyn said. And to Fox, 'What time does the village take its evening meal, would you say?'

'I'll ask McGuiness.' He went into the front office and returned.

'Between five-thirty and six-thirty. And after that they'll be at their tellies.'

'Yes. Hullo,' Alleyn said into the receiver. 'I want you to time it so that you arrive at six o'clock with the least possible amount of fuss. Come to the vicarage. Make it all look like a repair job. No uniform copper. There's a downpour going on here, you'll need to dress for it. I'll be there. You'll go through the church and out by an exit on the far side, which is out of sight from the village. If by any unlikely chance somebody gets curious, you're looking for a leak in the roof. Got it? Good. Put me through to Missing Persons and stay where you are for ten minutes in case there's a change of procedure. Then leave.'

Alleyn waited. He felt the pulse in the bruise on his jaw and knew it beat a little faster. If they give a positive answer, he thought, it's all up. Call off the exercise and back we go to square one.

A voice on the line. 'Hullo? Superintendent Alleyn? You were calling us, sir?'

'Yes. Any reports come in?'

'Nothing, sir. No joy anywhere.'

'Southampton? The stationer's shop?'

'Nothing.'

'Thank God.'

'I beg pardon, Mr Alleyn?'

'Never mind. It's, to coin a phrase, a case of no news being good news. Keep going, though. Until you get orders to the contrary and if any sign or sniff of Carter comes up let me know at once. At once. This is of great importance. Understood?'

'Understood, Mr Alleyn.'

Alleyn hung up and looked at his watch. Four-thirty.

'We give it an hour and then go over,' he said.

The hour passed slowly. Rain streamed down the blinded windowpane. Small occupational noises could be heard in the front office and the intermittent sounds of passing vehicles.

At twenty past five the constable on duty brought in that panacea against anxiety that the Force has unfailingly on tap: strong tea in heavy cups and two recalcitrant biscuits.

Alleyn, with difficulty, swallowed the tea. He carried his cup into the front office where Sergeant McGuiness, with an affectation of nonchalance, said it wouldn't be long now, would it?

'No,' said Alleyn, 'you can gird up your loins such as they are,' and returned to his own room. He and Fox exchanged a nod and put on heavy mackintoshes, sou'westers and gum boots. He looked at his watch. Half past five.

'Give it three minutes,' he said. They waited.

The telephone rang in the front office but not for them. They went through. Sergeant McGuiness was attired in oilskin and sou'wester.

Alleyn said to PC Dance, 'If there's a call for me from Missing Persons, ring Upper Quintern rectory. Have the number under your nose.'

He and Fox and McGuiness went out into the rain and drove to Upper Quintern village. The interior of the car smelt of stale smoke, rubber and petrol. The windscreen wipers jerked to and fro, surface water fanned up from under their wheels and sloshed against the windows. The sky was so blackened with rainclouds that a premature dusk seemed to have fallen on the village. Not a soul was abroad in Long Lane. The red window curtains in the bar of the Passcoigne Arms glowed dimly.

'This is not going to let up,' said Fox.

Alleyn led the way up a steep and slippery path to the vicarage. They were expected and the door was opened before they reached it.

The vicar, white-faced and anxious, welcomed them and took them to his study which was like all parsonic studies with its framed photographs of ordinands and steel engravings of classic monuments, its high fender, its worn chairs and its rows of predictable literature.

'This is a shocking business,' said the vicar. 'I can't tell you how distressing I find it. Is it – I mean, I suppose it must be – absolutely necessary?'

'I'm afraid it is,' said Alleyn.

'Inspector Fox,' said the vicar, looking wistfully at him, 'was very discreet.'

Fox modestly contemplated the far wall of the study.

'He said he thought he should leave it to you to explain.'

'Indeed,' Alleyn rejoined with a long hard stare at his subordinate.

'And I do hope you will. I think I should know. You see, it is consecrated ground.'

'Yes.'

'So – may I, if you please, be told?' asked the vicar with what Alleyn thought rather touching simplicity.

'Of course,' he said. 'I'll tell you why we are doing it and what we think we may find. In honesty I should add that we may find nothing and the operation therefore may prove to have been quite fruitless. But this is the theory.'

The vicar listened.

'I think,' he said, when Alleyn had finished, 'that I've never heard anything more dreadful. And I have heard some very dreadful things. We do, you know.'

'I'm sure.'

'Even in quiet little parishes like this. You'd be surprised, wouldn't he, Sergeant McGuiness?' asked the vicar. He waited for a moment and then said, 'I must ask you to allow me to be present. I would rather not, of course, because I am a squeamish man. But – I don't want to sound pompous – I think it's my duty.'

Alleyn said, 'We'll be glad to have you there. As far as possible we'll try to avoid attracting notice. I've been wondering if by any chance there's a less public way of going to the church than up those steps.'

'There is *our* path. Through the shrubbery and thicket. It will be rather damp but it's short and inconspicuous. I would have to guide you.'

'If you will. I think,' Alleyn said, 'our men have arrived. They're coming here first, I hope you don't mind?'

He went to the window and the others followed. Down below on the 'green' a small delivery van had pulled up. Five men in mackintoshes and wet hats got out. They opened the rear door and took out a large carpenter's kitbag and a corded bundle of considerable size which required two men to carry it.

'In the eye of a beholder,' Alleyn grunted, 'this would look like sheer lunacy.'

'Not to the village,' said the vicar. 'If they notice, they'll only think it's the boiler again.'

'The boiler?'

'Yes. It has become unsafe and is always threatening to explode. Just look at those poor fellows,' said the vicar. 'Should I ask my wife to make tea? Or coffee?'

Alleyn declined this offer. 'Perhaps later,' he said.

The men climbed the path in single file, carrying their gear. Rain bounced off their shoulders and streamed from their hat brims. Alleyn opened the door to them.

'We're in no shape to come into the house, sir,' one of them said. He removed his hat and Bailey was revealed. Thompson stood behind him hung about with well-protected cameras.

'No, no, no. Not a bit of it,' bustled the vicar. 'We've people in and out all day. Haven't we, McGuiness? Come in. Come in.'

They waited, dripping, in the little hall. The vicar kilted up his cassock, found himself a waterproof cape and pulled on a pair of galoshes.

'I'll just get my brolly,' he said and sought it in the porch.

Alleyn asked the men, 'Is that a tent or an enclosure?' A framed tent, they said. It wouldn't take long to erect: there was no wind.

'We go out by the back,' said the vicar. 'Shall I lead the way?'

The passage reeked of wetness and of its own housesmell – something suggestive of economy and floor polish. From behind one door came the sound of children's voices and from the kitchen the whirr of an egg-beater. They arrived at a side door which opened on to the all-pervading sound and sight of rain.

'I'm afraid,' said the vicar, 'it will be rather heavy going. Especially with – ' he paused and glanced unhappily at their gear – 'your burden,' he said.

It was indeed heavy going. The shrubbery, a dense untended thicket, came to within a yard of the house and the path plunged directly into it. Water-laden branches slurred across their shoulders and slapped their faces, runnels of water gushed about their feet. They slithered, manoeuvred, fell about and shambled on again. The vicar's umbrella came in for a deal of punishment.

'Not far now,' he said at last and sure enough they were out of the wood and within a few yards of the church door.

The vicar went first. It was already twilight in the church and he switched on lights, one in the nave and one in the south transept which was furnished as a lady-chapel. The men followed him self-consciously down the aisle and Bailey only just fetched up in time to avoid falling over the vicar when he abruptly genuflected before turning right. The margin between tragedy and hysteria is a narrow one and Alleyn suppressed an impulse, as actors say, to 'corpse' – an only too apposite synonym in this context.

The vicar continued into the lady-chapel. 'There's a door here,' he said to Alleyn. 'Rather unusual. It opens directly on the Passcoigne plot. Perhaps – ?'

'It will suit admirably,' Alleyn said. 'May we open up our stuff in the church? It will make things a good deal easier.'

'Yes. Very well.'

So the men, helped by Sergeant McGuiness, unfolded their waterproof-covered bundle and soon two shovels, two hurricane lamps, three high-powered torches, a screwdriver and four coils of rope were set out neatly on the lady-chapel floor. A folded mass of heavy plastic and a jointed steel frame were laid across the pews.

Bailey and Thompson chose a separate site in the transept for the assembling of their gear.

Alleyn said, 'Right. We can go. Would you open the door, Vicar?'

It was down a flight of three steps in the corner of the lady-chapel by the south wall. The vicar produced a key that might have hung from the girdle of a Georgian jailer. 'We hardly ever use it,' he said. 'I've oiled the key and brought the lubricant with me.'

'Splendid.'

Presently, with a clicking sound and a formidable screech, the door opened on a downpour so dense that it looked like a multiple sequence of beaded curtains closely hung the one behind the other. The church filled with the insistent drumming of rain and with the smell of wet earth and trees.

Sybil Foster's grave was a dismal sight: the mound of earth, so carefully embellished by Bruce, looked as if it had been washed ashore with its panoply of dead flowers clinging to it – disordered and bespattered with mud.

They got the tent up with some trouble and great inconvenience. It was large enough to allow a wide margin round the grave. On one part of this they spread a groundsheet. This added to an impression of something disreputable that was about to be put on show. The effect was emphasized by the fairground smell of the tent itself. The rain sounded more insistent inside than out.

The men fetched their gear from the church.

Until now, the vicar, at Alleyn's suggestion, had remained in the church. Now, when they were assembled and ready – Fox, Bailey, Thompson, Sergeant McGuiness and the three Yard men, Alleyn went to fetch him.

He was at prayer. He had put off his mackintosh and he knelt there in his well-worn cassock with his hands folded before his lips. So, Alleyn thought, had centuries of parsons, for this reason and that, knelt in St Crispin's, Upper Quintern. He waited.

The vicar crossed himself, opened his eyes, saw Alleyn and got up.

'We're ready, sir,' Alleyn said.

He found the vicar's cape and held it out. 'No thanks,' said the vicar. 'But I'd better take my brolly.'

So with some ado he was brought into the tent where he shut his umbrella and stood quietly in the background, giving no trouble.

They made a pile of sodden flowers in a corner of the tent and then set about the earth mound, heaping it up into a wet repetition of itself. The tent fabric was green and this, in the premature twilight, gave the interior an underwater appearance.

The shovels crunched and slurped. The men, having cleared away the mound, dug deep and presently there was the hard sound of steel on wood. The vicar came nearer. Thompson brought the coils of rope.

The men were expeditious and skilful and what they had to do was soon accomplished. As if in a reverse playback the coffin rose from its bed and was lifted on to the wet earth beside it.

One of the men went to a corner of the tent and fetched the screwdriver.

'You won't need that,' Fox said quickly.

'No, sir?' The man looked at Alleyn.

'No,' Alleyn said. 'What you do now is dig deeper. But very cautiously. One man only. Bailey, will you do it? Clear away the green flooring and then explore with your hands. If the soil is easily moved, then go on – remove it. But with the greatest possible care. Stand as far to the side as you can manage.'

Bailey lowered himself into the grave. Alleyn knelt on the groundsheet looking down and the others in their glistening mackintoshes grouped round him. The vicar stood at the foot of the grave, removed from the rest. They might have been actors in a modern production of the churchyard scene in *Hamlet*.

Bailey's voice, muffled, said, 'It's dark down here, could I have a torch?' They shone their torches into the grave and the beams moved over pine branches. Bailey gathered together armfuls of them and handed them up. 'Did we bring a trowel?' he asked.

The vicar said there was one on the premises, kept for the churchyard guild. Sergeant McGuiness fetched it. While they waited

Bailey could be heard scuffling. He dumped handfuls of soil on the lip of the grave. Alleyn examined them. The earth was loamy, friable and quite dry. McGuiness returned with a trowel and the mound at the lip of the grave grew bigger.

'The soil's packed down, like,' Bailey said presently, 'but it's not hard to move. I – I reckon – ' his voice wavered, 'I reckon it's been dug over – or filled in – or – hold on.'

'Go steady, now,' Fox said.

'There's something.'

Bailey began to push earth aside with the edge of his hand and brush it away with his palms.

'A bit more light,' he said.

Alleyn shone his own torch in and the light found Bailey's hands, palms down and fingers spread, held in suspended motion over the earth they had disturbed.

'Go on,' Alleyn said. 'Go on.'

The hands came together, parted and swept aside the last of the earth.

Claude Carter's face had been turned into a gargoyle by the pressure of earth and earth lay in streaks across its eyeballs.

III

Before they moved it Thompson photographed the body where it lay. Then with great care and difficulty, it was lifted and stretched out on the groundsheet. Where it had lain they found Claude's ruck-sack, tightly packed.

'He'd meant to pick up his car,' Fox said, 'and drive to Southampton.'

'I think so.'

Sybil Foster was returned to her grave and covered.

The vicar said, 'I'll go now. May God rest their souls.'

Alleyn saw him into the church. He paused on the steps. 'It's stopped raining,' he said. 'I hadn't noticed. How strange.'

'Are you all right?' Alleyn asked him. 'Will you go back to the vicarage?'

'What? Oh. Oh no. Not just yet. I'm quite all right, thank you. I must pray now for the living, mustn't I?'

'The living?'

'Oh yes,' said the vicar shakily. 'Yes indeed. That's my job. I have to pray for my brother man. The murderer, you know.' He went into the church.

Alleyn returned to the tent.

'It's clearing,' he said. 'I think you'd better stand guard outside.' The Yard men went out.

Bailey and Thompson were at their accustomed tasks. The camera flashed for Claude as assiduously as a pressman's for a celebrity. When they turned him over and his awful face was hidden they disclosed a huge red grin at the nape of the neck.

'Bloody near decapitated,' Thompson whispered and photographed it in close-up.

'Don't exaggerate,' Fox automatically chided. He was searching the rucksack.

'It's not far wrong, Mr Fox,' said Bailey.

'If you've finished,' Alleyn said, 'search him.'

Bailey found a wallet containing twenty pounds, loose change, cigarettes, matches, his pocket-book, a passport and three dirty postcards.

And in the inside breast pocket, a tiny but extremely solid steel box such as a jeweller might use to house a ring. The key was in Claude's wallet.

Alleyn opened the box and disclosed a neatly folded miniature envelope wrapped in a waterproof silk and inside the envelope between two watch-glasses, a stamp: the Czar Alexander with a hole in his head.

'Look here, Fox,' he said.

Fox restrapped the rucksack and came over. He placed his great palms on his knees and regarded the stamp.

'That was a good bit of speculative thinking on your part,' he said. 'And the tin box we found in his room could have left the trace in the rubble, all right. Funny, you know, there it's lain all these years. I suppose Captain Carter stowed it there that evening. Before he was killed.'

'And may well have used some of the cement in the bag that's still rotting quietly away in the corner. And marked the place on the plan in which this poor scoundrel showed such an interest.'

'He wouldn't have tried to sell it in England, surely?'

'We've got to remember it was his by right. Being what he was, he might have settled for a devious approach to a fanatic millionaire collector somewhere abroad whose zeal would get the better of his integrity.'

'Funny,' Fox mused. 'A bit of paper not much bigger than your thumbnail. Not very pretty and flawed at that. And could be worth as much as its own size in a diamond. I don't get it.'

'Collector's passion? Nor I. But it comes high in the list as an incentive to crime.'

'Where'll we put it?'

'Lock the box and give it to me. If I'm knocked on the head again take charge of it yourself. I can't wait till I get it safely stowed at the Yard. In the meantime – '

'We go in for the kill?' said Fox.

'That's it. Unless it comes in of its own accord.'

'Now?'

'When we've cleared up here.' He turned to Bailey and Thompson. They had finished with what was left of Claude Carter and were folding the groundsheet neatly round him and tying him up with rope. They threaded the two shovels inside the rope to make hand-holds.

And everything else being ready they struck the tent, folded it and laid it with its frame across the body. Bailey, Thompson, McGuiness and the Yard men stood on either side. 'Looks a bit less like a corpse,' said Thompson.

'You'll have to go down the steps this time,' Alleyn told them. 'Mr Fox and I will bring the rest of the gear and light the way.'

They took their torches from their pockets. Twilight had closed in now. The after-smell of rain and the pleasant reek of a wood fire hung on the air. Somewhere down in the village a door banged and then the only sound was of water dripping from branches. Sybil's grave looked as if it had never been disturbed.

'Quiet,' said one of the men. 'Isn't it?'

'Shall we move off, then?' Fox said.

He stooped to pick up his load and the other four men groped for their hand-holds under the tent.

'Right?' said Bailey.

But Alleyn had lifted a hand. 'No,' he whispered. 'Not yet. Keep still. Listen.' Fox was beside him. 'Where?'

'Straight ahead. In the trees.'

He turned his light on the thicket. A cluster of autumnal leaves sprang up and quivered. One after another the torchbeams joined his. This time all the men heard the hidden sound.

They spread out to left and right of Alleyn and moved forward. The light on the thicket was intensified and details of foliage appeared in uncanny precision, as if they carried some significance and must never be forgotten. A twig snapped and the head of a sapling jerked.

'Bloody Daft Artie, by God!' said Sergeant McGuiness.

'Shall we go in?' asked Fox.

'No,' said Alleyn and then, loudly, 'Show yourself. Call it a day and come out.'

The leaves parted but the face that shone whitely between them, blinking in the torchlight, was not Daft Artie's.

'This is it, Bruce,' said Alleyn. 'Come out.'

IV

Bruce Gardener sat bolt upright at the table with his arms folded. He still bore the insecure persona of his chosen role: red-gold beard, fresh mouth, fine torso, loud voice, pawky turn of speech, the straightforward Scottish soldierman with a heart of gold. At first sight the pallor, the bloodshot eyes and the great earthy hands clenched hard on the upper arms were not conspicuous. To Alleyn, sitting opposite him, to Fox, impassive in the background and to the constable with a notebook in the corner, however, these were unmistakable signs.

Alleyn said, 'Shorn of all other matters: motive, opportunity and all the rest of it, what do you say about this one circumstance? Who but you could have dug Sybil Foster's grave four feet deeper than was necessary, killed Carter, buried his body there, covered it, trampled it down and placed the evergreen flooring? On your own statement and that of other witnesses you were there, digging the grave all that afternoon and well into the night. Why were you so long about it?'

Alleyn waited. Gardener stared at the opposite wall. Once or twice his beard twitched and the red mouth moved as if he was about to speak. But nothing came of it.

'Well?' Alleyn said at last and Bruce gave a parody of clearing his throat. 'Clay,' he said loudly.

The constable wrote, '*Arts. Clay,*' and waited.

'So you told me. But there was no sign of clay in that mound of earth. The soil is loamy and easy to shift. So that's no good,' Alleyn said. 'Is it?'

'I'll no' answer any questions till I have my solicitor present.'

'He's on his way. You might, however, like to consider this. On that night after the funeral when we had an acetylene lamp like yours up there by the grave, you, from your sister's window, saw the light and it worried you. You told us so. But you didn't tell us it wasn't Daft Artie who lay in the cubby-hole in the hedge, but you. It wasn't Daft Artie who heaved half a brick at me, it was you. You were so shaken by the thought of us opening the grave that you lost your head, came down the hill, hid in the hedge, chucked the brick and then set up a phoney hunt for an Artie who wasn't there. Right?'

'No comment.'

'You'll have to find some sort of comment, sooner or later, won't you? However, your solicitor will advise you. But suppose Artie was in bed with a cold that evening, how would you feel about that?'

'*Ans. No comment,*' wrote the constable.

'Well,' Alleyn said, 'there's no point in plugging away at it. The case against you hangs on this one point. If you didn't kill and bury Claude Carter, who did? I shall put it to you again when your solicitor comes and he no doubt will advise you to keep quiet. In the meantime I must tell you that not one piece of information about your actions can be raised to contradict the contention that you killed Mrs Foster; that Carter, a man with a record of blackmail, knew it and exercised his knowledge on you and that you, having arranged with him to pay the blackmail if he came to the churchyard that night, had the grave ready, killed him with the shovel you used to dig the grave and buried him there. Two victims in one grave. Is there still no comment?'

In the silence that followed, Alleyn saw, with extreme distaste, tears well up in Bruce's china-blue, slightly squinting eyes and trickle into his beard.

'We were close taegither, her and me,' he said and his voice trembled. 'From the worrrd go we understood each ither. She was more than an employer to me, she was a true friend. Aye. When I think of the plans we made for the beautifying of the property – ' His voice broke convincingly.

'Did you plan those superfluous asparagus beds together and were the excavations in the mushroom shed your idea or hers?'

Bruce half rose from his chair. Fox made a slight move and he sank back again.

'Or,' said Alleyn, 'did Captain Carter who, as you informed us, used to confide in you, tell you before he came down to Quintern on the last afternoon of his life that he proposed to bury the Black Alexander stamp somewhere on the premises? And forty years later when you found yourself there did you not think it a good idea to have a look round on your own accord?'

'You can't prove it on me,' he shouted, without a trace of Scots. 'And what about it if you could?'

'Nothing much, I confess. We've got more than enough without that. I merely wondered if you knew when you killed him that Claude Carter had the Black Alexander in his breast pocket. You gave it a second burial.'

Purple-red flooded up into Bruce's face. He clenched his fists and beat them on the table.

'The bastard!' he shouted. 'The bloody bastard. By Christ, he earned what he got!'

The station sergeant tapped on the door. Fox opened it.

'It's his solicitor,' he said.

'Show him in,' said Fox.

V

Verity Preston weeded her long border and wondered where to look for a gardener. She chided herself for taking so personal a view. She remembered that there had been times when she and Bruce had seemed to understand each other over garden matters. It was monstrous to contemplate what they said he had done but she did not think it was untrue.

A shadow fell across the long border. She swivelled round on her knees and there was Alleyn.

'I hope I'm not making a nuisance of myself,' he said, 'but I expect I am. There's something I wanted to ask you.'

He squatted down beside her. 'Have you got beastly couchgrass in your border?' he asked.

'That can hardly be what you wanted to ask but no, I haven't. Only fat-hen, dandelions and wandering-willy.'

He picked up her handfork and began to use it. 'I wanted to know whether the plan of Quintern Place with the spot marked x is still in Markos's care or whether it's been returned.'

'The former, I should imagine. Do you need it?'

'Counsel for the prosecution may.'

'Mrs Jim might know. She's here today, would you like to ask her?'

'In a minute or two, if I may,' he said, shaking the soil off a root of fat-hen and throwing it into the wheelbarrow.

'I suppose,' he said, 'you'll be looking for a replacement.'

'Just what I was thinking. Oh,' Verity exclaimed, 'it's all so flattening and awful. I suppose one will understand it when the trial's over but to me, at present, it's a muddle.'

'Which bits of it?'

'Well, first of all, I suppose what happened at Greengages.'

'After you left?'

'Good Heavens, not before, I do trust.'

'I'll tell you what we believe happened. Some of it we can prove, the rest follows from it. The prosecution will say it's pure conjecture. In a way that doesn't matter. Gardener will be charged with the murder of Claude Carter, not Sybil Foster. However, the one is consequent upon the other. We believe, then, that Gardener and Carter, severally, stayed behind at Greengages, each hoping to get access to Mrs Foster's room, Carter probably to sponge on her, Gardener, if the opportunity presented itself, to do away with her. It all begins from the time when young Markos went to Mrs Foster's room to retrieve his fiancée's bag.'

'I hope,' Verity said indignantly, 'you don't attach – '

'Don't jump the gun like that or we shall never finish. He reported Mrs Foster alive and, it would be improper but I gather, appropriate, to add, kicking.'

'Against the engagement. Yes.'

'At some time before nine o'clock Claude appeared at the reception desk and, representing himself to be an electrician come to mend Mrs Foster's lamp, collected the lilies left at the desk by Bruce and took them upstairs. When he was in the passage something moved him to hide in an alcove opposite her door leaving footprints and a lily-head behind him. We believe he had seen Bruce approaching and that when Bruce left the room after a considerable time, Carter tapped on the door and walked in. He found her dead.

'He dumped the lilies in the bathroom basin. While he was in there, probably with the door ajar, Sister Jackson paid a very brief visit to the room.'

'That large lady who gave evidence? But she didn't say – '

'She did, later on. We'll stick to the main line. Well. Claude took thought. It suited him very well that she was dead. He now collected a much bigger inheritance. He also had, ready made, an instrument for blackmail and Gardener would have the wherewithal to stump up. Luckily for us, he also decided by means of an anonymous letter and a telephone call to have a go at Sister Jackson who had enough sense to report it to us.'

'I suppose you know he went to prison for blackmail?'

'Yes. So much for Greengages. Now for Claude, the Black Alexander and the famous plan.'

Verity listened with her head between her hands, making no further interruptions and with the strangest sense of hearing an account of events that had taken place a very, very long time ago.

' – so Claude's plan matured,' Alleyn was saying. 'He decided to go abroad until things had settled down. Having come to this decision, we think he set about blackmailing Gardener. Gardener appeared to fall for it. No doubt he told Claude he needed time to raise the money and put him off until the day before the funeral. He then said he would have it by that evening and Claude could collect it in the churchyard. And I think,' said Alleyn, 'you can guess the rest.'

'As far as Claude is concerned, yes, I suppose I can. But – Bruce Gardener and Sybil – that's much the worst. That's so – disgusting. All those professions of attachment, all that slop and sorrow act – no, it's beyond everything.'

'You did have your reservations about him, didn't you?'

'They didn't run along homicidal lines,' Verity snapped.

'Not an unusual reaction. You'd be surprised how it crops up after quite appalling cases. Heath, for instance. Some of his acquaintances couldn't believe such a nice chap would behave like that.'

'With Bruce, though, it was simply for cash and comfort?'

'Just that. Twenty-five thousand and a very nice little house which he could let until he retired.'

'Oh, well!' said Verity and gave it up. And then, with great difficulty, she said, 'I would be glad to know – Basil Smythe wasn't in any way involved, was he? I mean – as her doctor he couldn't be held to have been irresponsible or anything?'

'Nothing like that.'

'But – there's something, isn't there?'

'Well, yes. It appears that the Dr Schramm who qualified at Lausanne was never Mr Smythe, and I'm afraid Schramm was *not* a family name of Mr Smythe's mama. But it appears he will inherit his fortune. He evidently suggested – no doubt with great tact – that as the change had not been confirmed by deed poll, Smythe was still his legal name. And Smythe, to Mr Rattisbon's extreme chagrin, it is in the Will.'

'That,' said Verity, 'is I'm afraid all too believable.'

Alleyn waited for a moment and then said, 'You'll see, won't you, why I was so anxious that Prunella should be taken away before we went to work in the churchyard.'

'What? Oh, that. Yes, of course I do.'

'If she was on the high seas she couldn't be asked as next-of-kin to identify.'

'That would have been – too horrible.'

Alleyn got to his feet. 'Whereas she is now, no doubt, contemplating the flesh-pots of the Côte d'Azure and running herself in as the future daughter-in-law of the Markos millions.'

'Yes,' Verity said, catching her breath in a half-sigh, 'I expect so.'

'You sound as if you regret it.'

'Not really. She's a level-headed child and it's the height of elderly arrogance to condemn the young for having different tastes from one's own. It's not my scene,' said Verity, 'but I think she'll be very happy in it.'

And at the moment, Prunella was very happy indeed. She was stretched out in a chaise-longue looking at the harbour of Antibes, drinking iced lemonade and half-listening to Nikolas and Gideon who were talking about the post from London that had just been brought aboard.

Mr Markos had opened up a newspaper. He gave an instantly stifled exclamation and made a quick movement to refold the paper.

But he was too late. Prunella and Gideon had both looked up as an errant breeze caught at the front page.

BLACK ALEXANDER
FAMOUS STAMP FOUND ON MURDERED MAN

'It's no good, darlings,' Prunella said after a pause, 'trying to hide it all up. I'm bound to hear, you know, sooner or later.'

Gideon kissed her. Mr Markos, after making a deeply sympathetic noise, said, 'Well – perhaps.'

'Go on,' said Prunella. 'You know you're dying to read it.'

So he read it and as he did so the circumspection of the man of affairs and the avid, dotty desire of the collector, were strangely combined in Mr Markos. He folded the paper.

'Darling child,' said Mr Markos. 'You now possess a fortune.'

'I suppose I must.'

He picked up her hands and beat them gently together. 'You will, of course, take advice. It will be a momentous decision. But *if*,' said Mr Markos, kissing first one hand and then the other, '*if* after due deliberation you decide to sell, may your father-in-law have the first refusal? Speaking quite cold-bloodedly, of course,' said Mr Markos.

The well-dressed, expensively gloved and strikingly handsome passenger settled into his seat and fastened his belt.

Heathrow had passed off quietly.

He wondered when it would be advisable to return. Not, he fancied, for some considerable time. As they moved off the label attached to an elegant suitcase in the luggage rack slipped down and dangled over his head.

Dr Basil Schramm
Passenger to New York
Concorde
Flight 123.

Evil Liver

Evil Liver was televised by Granada Television Ltd as part of a crime series entitled Crown Court where members of the audience were invited to act as the jury. It was recorded in 1975 at the Granada studios in Manchester. The cast included: William Mervyn as the Judge, Jonathan Elsom as the Prosecution Counsel, William Simons as the Defence Counsel and David Waller as Major Ecclestone. Miss Freebody was played by Joan Hickson who later became famous for her role as Agatha Christie's Miss Marple.

CAST OF CHARACTERS

MR JUSTICE CAMPBELL

THE PROSECUTION COUNSEL, MARCUS GOLDING, QC

THE DEFENCE COUNSEL, MARTIN O'CONNOR

MARY FREEBODY

MAJOR BASIL ECCLESTONE

DR STEPHEN SWALE

THOMAS TIDWELL

BARBARA ECCLESTONE

DR ERNEST SMITHSON

GWENDOLINE MIGGS

WARDRESS

CLERK OF COURT

COURT USHER

JURY FOREMAN

COURT REPORTER

Part One

COURT REPORTER: The case you are about to see is fictional. But the jury is made up of members of the public, who will assess the evidence and deliver their own verdict at the end of the programme.

(MAJOR ECCLESTONE *is called by the* PROSECUTION COUNSEL. *He takes the witness stand and takes the oath.*)

COURT REPORTER: On March 28th of this year, Miss Mary Freebody's cat was savaged and killed by Bang, an Alsatian dog belonging to her next-door neighbour, Major Basil Ecclestone. A week later, on the 4th April, meat ordered by the Ecclestones was delivered to the outside safe of their house. That evening Major Ecclestone took from the safe some liver for his dog. The dog ate a portion of the liver, was instantly thrown into violent convulsions, and died. The contents of its stomach were analysed and found to contain a massive amount of cyanide of potassium. A tin of wasp exterminator containing a high proportion of cyanide was found in Miss Freebody's shrubbery, half empty. The Major made to the police an accusation of attempted murder against Miss Freebody maintaining that she had had the intention of killing not only his dog but himself. A police investigation has led to her being charged, and she now stands trial at the Crown Court in Fulchester.

GOLDING: . . . Now Major, if you would just describe the events leading to the – the tragedy. You were away from your house, were you not, during the afternoon of April 4th?

MAJOR: Club. Bridge. Every Friday. *(He gestures at the accused)* As was well-known to my neighbour.

GOLDING: Quite so. Your wife was at home, I think?

MAJOR: Migraine. In her room.

GOLDING: Yes. And you returned – when?

MAJOR: Six-thirty.

GOLDING: May we have the order of events from then on?

MAJOR: I – ah – I had a drink. Listened to the wireless. Seven o'clock, I went to the safe and got the dog's food.

GOLDING: Yes. The safe: where is it?

MAJOR: In the outside wall by the back door. It's a two-doored safe; you can open it inside from the pantry. The butcher uses the outside door. So could anyone else. *(At the prisoner)* It's opposite her bathroom window and her side door. And her gate onto the right of way. And my gate onto the right of way. She could get to it in a matter of seconds.

GOLDING: Quite so. We shall come to that presently, Major. Did you use the inside door of the safe into the pantry when you got the dog's liver?

MAJOR: I did.

GOLDING: Major, can you describe the wrapping at all? Did you happen to notice it?

MAJOR: *(Pauses. Looks at prisoner)* Matter of fact I did. Two or three layers of the *Daily Telegraph*.

GOLDING: Good. So you removed the liver from the safe? And then?

MAJOR: I unwrapped the liver, put it in the dog's dish and took it out to the kennel.

GOLDING: The dog being tied up?

MAJOR: Certainly.

GOLDING: And then?

MAJOR: Put it in front of him

GOLDING: How many pieces?

MAJOR: Two. All there was. Only gave him liver on Fridays. Other nights 'Doggy Bits' or 'Yaps'. Sunday, a bone.

JUDGE: What are 'Doggy Bits' and 'Yaps'?

GOLDING: I understand they are proprietary canine food, my lord.

(The JUDGE *stares at the* MAJOR *and then nods to* PROSECUTION COUNSEL *to continue.)*

GOLDING: Yes, Major. So you put the dish before the dog. And?

MAJOR: He swallowed part of one piece.

GOLDING: Yes.

MAJOR: It happened at once. Frightful contortions. Convulsions. Agony. By Gad I've seen some terrible sights in my time, but never anything like that. And it was my dog, sir. It was Bang, my dog. My faithful old Bang. *(He breaks down, blows his nose and belches. The* JUDGE *contemplates him stonily.)*

GOLDING: A most painful experience and I am sorry to revive it. Mercifully it was soon over, was it not?

MAJOR: Nothing merciful about it. *(At the prisoner)* A fiendish, cold-blooded murder, deliberately brought about by a filthy-minded, vindictive old cat.

MISS FREEBODY: *(standing)* Cat! Cat! You dare to utter the word!

MAJOR: I do so advisedly, madam. Cat. Cat is what I said and cat is what I meant . . .

MISS FREEBODY: Poor defenceless little thing. It was . . .

JUDGE: Silence. Silence. If there is any repetition of this grossly improper behaviour I shall treat it as a contempt of court. *(Turning to the* MAJOR) You understand me?

MAJOR: *(mumbling)* Great provocation. Regret –

JUDGE: What? Speak up.

MAJOR: I apologize, my lord.

JUDGE: So I should hope. *(He nods to* PROSECUTION COUNSEL.*)*

GOLDING: My lord. Major Ecclestone, I want you to tell His Lordship and the jury what happened after the death of the dog.

MAJOR: My wife came down. At my suggestion, telephoned Dr Swale.

JUDGE: Why not a veterinary surgeon?

MAJOR: I've no opinion of the local vet.

JUDGE: I see.

MAJOR: Besides, there was my wife.

JUDGE: Your wife, Major Ecclestone?

MAJOR: She was upset, my lord. He gave her a pill. I had a drink.

JUDGE: I see. Yes, Mr Golding.

GOLDING: Go on please, Major.

MAJOR: Swale took away the remaining piece of liver to be analysed and he also removed the – the body.

GOLDING: Was there any other event before or at about this time that seemed to you to have any bearing on the matter?

MAJOR: Certainly.

GOLDING: Please tell the court what it was.

MAJOR: That woman's *(The* JUDGE *looks at him)* – The accused's bathroom window overlooks my premises. It's got a Venetian blind. She's in the habit of spying on us through the slats. I distinctly saw them – the slats, I mean – open in one place.

GOLDING: When did you see this?

MAJOR: Immediately after Swale left. She'd watched the whole performance. *And* gloated over it.

JUDGE: You are here to relate what you observed, Major, not what you may have conjectured.

GOLDING: Had anything occurred in the past to make bad blood between you and the defendant?

MAJOR: Yes.

GOLDING: What was it?

MAJOR: A cat.

JUDGE: What?

MAJOR: She had a cat, my lord. A mangy brute of a thing –

MISS FREEBODY: Lies! Lies! It was a beautiful little cat. *(The* WARDRESS *quells her.)*

GOLDING: *(coughs)* Never mind what sort of cat it was. Yes, Major?

MAJOR: About a week earlier it strayed into my garden at night. Not for the first time. Always doin' it. Yowlin' and diggin'. Drove my dog frantic. Naturally he broke his tether. Tore it away with a piece of the kennel.

GOLDING: And then?

MAJOR: Ask yourself.

GOLDING: But I'm asking you, you know.

MAJOR: Made short work of the poor pussy. *(He laughs shortly.)*

MISS FREEBODY: *Brute!*

JUDGE: Miss Freebody, you must be silent.

MISS FREEBODY: Pah!

JUDGE: Mr O'Connor, will you speak to your client? Explain.

O'CONNOR: Certainly, my lord. *(He turns and speaks to the accused who stares over his head, biting her lip.)*

GOLDING: What were the results of the cat's demise?

MAJOR: She kicked up a dust.

GOLDING: In what way?

MAJOR: Waylaid my wife. Went to the police. Wrote letters. Threatened to do me in.

GOLDING: Did you keep any of these letters?

MAJOR: Last one. Burnt the others. About five of them.

GOLDING: May he be shown Exhibit Two?

(The letter is produced, identified, circulated to the JUDGE, *to* COUNSEL *and to the jury.)*

GOLDING: Is that the letter which you retained?

MAJOR: Yes.

GOLDING: It reads, members of the jury: 'This is my final warning. Unless your brute is destroyed within the next three days, I shall take steps to insure that justice is done not only upon it but upon yourself. Neither you nor it is fit to live. Take warning. M E Freebody.' *(To* MAJOR*)* You received this letter – when?

MAJOR: First of April.

(Laughter)

USHER: Silence in court.

GOLDING: Did you answer it?

MAJOR: Good God, no. Nor any of the others.

JUDGE: Why did you keep it, Major?

MAJOR: Thought of showing it to my lawyer. Decided to ignore it.

GOLDING: *(quoting)* 'I shall take steps to see that justice is done not only upon it but upon yourself.' Can you describe the nature of the letters you had received before this one?

MAJOR: Certainly. Same thing. Threats.

GOLDING: To you personally?

MAJOR: Saying that my dog ought to die and if I didn't act smartly we both would.

GOLDING: And it was after the death of the dog and in consideration of all these circumstances, Major, that you decided to go to the police?

MAJOR: Precisely. Decided she meant business and that I was at risk personally. My wife urged me to act.

GOLDING: Thank you, Major Ecclestone.

(GOLDING *sits down.* DEFENCE COUNSEL *rises.*)

O'CONNOR: Major Ecclestone, would you describe yourself as a hot-tempered man?

MAJOR: I would not.

O'CONNOR: As an even-tempered man?

MAJOR: I consider myself to be a reasonable man, sir.

O'CONNOR: I said 'even-tempered', Major.

MAJOR: Yes.

O'CONNOR: You get on well with your neighbours and tradesmen, for instance? Do you?

MAJOR: Depends on the neighbours and tradesmen. Ha!

O'CONNOR: Major Ecclestone, during the five years you have lived in Peascale you have quarrelled violently with your landlord, your late doctor, the secretary of your club, your postman and your butcher, have you not?

MAJOR: I have not 'quarrelled violently' with anyone. Where I encounter stupidity, negligence and damned impertinence I made known my objections. That is all.

O'CONNOR: To the tune of threatening the postman with a horsewhip and the butcher's boy with your Alsatian dog?

MAJOR: I refuse to stand here and listen to all this nonsense. (He pulls himself up, looks at his watch, takes a small container from his overcoat pocket, extracts a capsule and puts it in his mouth.)

JUDGE: What is all this? Are you eating something, Major Ecclestone?

MAJOR: I suffer from duodenal ulcers, my lord. I have taken a capsule.

JUDGE: (after a pause) Very well. (He nods to DEFENCE COUNSEL.)

O'CONNOR: Major Ecclestone, was the liver the only thing in the safe that evening?

MAJOR: No, it wasn't. There was stuff for a mixed grill on Friday. Chops, kidneys, sausages. That sort of thing.

O'CONNOR: And these had been delivered with the dog's meat that afternoon?

MAJOR: Yes.

O'CONNOR: Did you have your mixed grill?

MAJOR: No fear! Chucked it out. Destroyed it. Great mistake, as I now realize. Poisoned like the other. Not a doubt of it. Intended for me.

O'CONNOR: And what about Mrs Ecclestone?

MAJOR: Vegetarian.

O'CONNOR: I see. Can I have a list of complaints, please? *(Solicitor gives him a paper.)* Major Ecclestone, is it true that, apart from my client, there have been five other complaints about the character and behaviour of your dog?

MAJOR: The dog was perfectly docile. Unless provoked. They baited him.

O'CONNOR: And is it not the case that you have received two warnings from the police to keep the dog under proper control?

MAJOR: Bah!

O'CONNOR: I beg your pardon.

MAJOR: Balderdash!

O'CONNOR: You are on oath, Major Ecclestone. Have you received two such warnings from the police?

MAJOR *(pause)* Yes. *(Nods.)*

O'CONNOR: Thank you. *(He sits down.)*

(DR SWALE is called to the stand. PROSECUTION COUNSEL rises.)

GOLDING: Dr Swale, you were called into The Elms on the evening of 4th April, were you not?

SWALE: Yes. Mrs Ecclestone rang me up and sounded so upset I went round.

GOLDING: What did you find when you got there?

SWALE: Major Ecclestone was in the yard near the dog kennel with the Alsatian's body lying at his feet.

GOLDING: And Mrs Ecclestone?

SWALE: She was standing nearby. She suffers from migraine and this business with the dog hadn't done anything to help her. I took her back to her room, looked at her and gave her one of the Sternetil tablets I'd prescribed.

GOLDING: And then?

SWALE: I went down to the Major.

GOLDING: Yes?

SWALE: He, of course, realized the dog had been poisoned and he asked me, as a personal favour, to get an analysis of what was left of the liver the dog had been eating and of the contents of the dog's stomach. I arranged this with the pathology department of the general hospital.

GOLDING: Ah yes. We've heard evidence of that. Massive quantities of potassium cyanide were found.

SWALE: Yes.

GOLDING: Did you, subsequently, discuss with Major Ecclestone the possible source of this cyanide?

SWALE: Yes.

GOLDING: Dr Swale, were you shown any letters by Major Ecclestone?

SWALE: Yes. From the defendant.

GOLDING: Are you sure they were from the defendant?

SWALE: Oh yes. She had in the past written to me complaining about the National Health. It was her writing and signature.

GOLDING: What was the nature of the letters to Major Ecclestone?

SWALE: Threatening. I remember in particular the one that said his dog ought to die and if he didn't act smartly they both would.

GOLDING: What view did you take of these letters?

SWALE: A very serious one. They threatened his life.

GOLDING: Yes. Thank you, Dr Swale. *(He sits.)*

(DEFENCE COUNSEL rises.)

O'CONNOR: Dr Swale, you have known the Ecclestones for some time, haven't you?

SWALE: Yes.

O'CONNOR: In fact you are close friends?

SWALE: *(after a slight hesitation)* I have known them for some years.

O'CONNOR: Would you consider Major Ecclestone a reliable sort of man where personal judgments are concerned?

SWALE: I don't follow you.

O'CONNOR: Really? Let me put it another way. If antagonism has developed between himself and another person, would you consider his view of the person likely to be a sober, fair and balanced one?

SWALE: There are very few people, I think, of whom under such circumstances, that could be said.

O'CONNOR: I suggest that at the time we are speaking of, a feud developed between Major Ecclestone and the defendant and that his attitude towards her was intemperate and wholly biased. *(Pause)* Well, Dr Swale?

SWALE: *(unhappily)* I think that's putting it a bit strong.

O'CONNOR: Do you indeed? Thank you, Dr Swale. *(DEFENCE COUNSEL sits.)*

JUDGE: You may leave the witness box, Dr Swale.

(THOMAS TIDWELL is called to the stand. PROSECUTION COUNSEL rises.)

GOLDING: You are Thomas Tidwell, butcher's assistant of the West End Butchery, 8 Park Street, Peascale, near Fulchester?

TIDWELL: Yar.

GOLDING: On Friday 4th April, did you deliver two parcels of meat at The Elms, No. 1 Sherwood Grove?

TIDWELL: Yar.

GOLDING: Would you describe them please?

TIDWELL: Aye?

GOLDING: How were they wrapped?

TIDWELL: In paper. *(JUDGE looks.)*

GOLDING: Yes, of course, but what sort of paper?

TIDWELL: Aye?

GOLDING: Were they wrapped in brown paper or in newspaper?

TIDWELL: One of each.

GOLDING: Thank you. Did you know, for instance, the contents of the newspaper parcel: what was in it?

TIDWELL: Liver.

GOLDING: How did you know that?

TIDWELL: *(to JUDGE)* It was bloody, wannit? Liver's bloody. Liver'll bleed froo anyfink, won't it? I seen it, din' I? It'd bled froo the comics.

(MAJOR half-rises. PROSECUTION COUNSEL checks him with a look. MAJOR signals to USHER, who goes to him.)

JUDGE: Are you chewing something, Mr Tidwell?

TIDWELL: Yar.

JUDGE: Remove it.

GOLDING: You're sure of this? The wrapping was a page from a comic publication, was it?

TIDWELL: That's what I said, din' I? I seen it, din' I?

GOLDING: If I tell you that Major Ecclestone says that the liver was wrapped in sheets from the *Daily Telegraph*, what would you say?

TIDWELL: 'E wants is 'ead read. Or else 'e was squiffy.

(The MAJOR *rises and is restrained by the* USHER.*)*

GOLDING: *(glaring at the* MAJOR, *turning to* TIDWELL*)* Yes. Yes. Very good. Now, will you tell the court how you put the parcels away?

TIDWELL: Like I always done. Opened the safe and bunged 'em in, din' I?

GOLDING: Anything at all unusual happen during this visit?

TIDWELL: Naow.

GOLDING: You left by the side gate into the right of way, didn't you?

TIDWELL: S'right.

GOLDING: This would bring you face to face with the side wall of Miss Freebody's house. Did you notice anything at all unusual about it?

TIDWELL: Nothin' unusual. What you might call a regular occurrence. She was snooping. Froo the blind. You know. Froo the slats – you know. Nosey. She's always at it.

GOLDING: Did you do anything about it?

TIDWELL: *(Turns to accused, gives a wolf whistle and a sardonic salute. She is furious.)* Just for giggles. *(Whistles.)*

GOLDING: Did Miss Freebody react in any way?

TIDWELL: Scarpered.

GOLDING: Why should she spy upon you, do you think?

TIDWELL: Me? Not me. I reckon she was waiting for the boyfriend.

MISS FREEBODY: How dare you say such things . . .

GOLDING: The boyfriend?

TIDWELL: S'right. *(He guffaws and wipes away the grin with his hand.)* Pardon me.

GOLDING: *(He has been taken aback by this development but keeps his composure)* Yes. Well. I don't think we need concern ourselves with any visitor the accused may or may not have been expecting.

TIDWELL: Her? Not *her. Her.*

JUDGE: What *is* all this, Mr Golding?

GOLDING: I'm afraid it's beyond me, my lord. Some sort of bucolic joke, I imagine.

*(*JUDGE *grunts.)*

GOLDING: That's all I have to ask this witness, my lord. *(He sits down.)*

*(*THOMAS TIDWELL *makes as if to leave the box.* DEFENCE COUNSEL *rises.)*

JUDGE: Stay where you are, Mr Tidwell. *(He has decided to push this unexpected development a little further.)* Mr Tidwell, when a moment ago you said, 'not *her'* – meaning the accused – but *'her',* to whom did you refer?

TIDWELL: It's well-known, innit? His missus.

JUDGE: Mrs Ecclestone?

MAJOR: What the devil are you talking about?

TIDWELL: S'right. Every Friday, like I said, reg'lar as clockwork.

JUDGE: What is as regular as clockwork?

TIDWELL: 'E is. Droppin' in. On 'er.

JUDGE: Who is?

TIDWELL: 'Im. It's well-known. The doctor.

MAJOR: God damn it, I demand an explanation. Death and damnation – *(*USHER *moves to restrain the* MAJOR.)*

MISS FREEBODY: *(laughing)* That's right. You tell them.

GOLDING: Major Ecclestone! Sit down.

USHER: Quiet!

(The commotion subsides.)

JUDGE: For the last time, Major Ecclestone, I warn you that unless you can behave yourself with propriety you will be held in contempt of court. Mr Golding.

GOLDING: My lord, I do apologize. Major, stand up and apologize to his Lordship. *(The MAJOR mutters.)* Stand up then, and do it. Go on.

MAJOR: *(He looks as if he will spontaneously combust. He rises, blows out his breath, comes to attention and bellows in court-martial tones)* Being under orders to do so, I tender my regrets for any apparently overzealous conduct of which I may appear to have been unwittingly guilty.

JUDGE: Very well. Sit down and – and – and imagine yourself to be gagged. *(The MAJOR sits. He is troubled with indigestion.)* Yes, Mr O'Connor . . .

O'CONNOR: Now, Mr Tidwell, you say, do you, that you know positively that Dr Swale visited Major Ecclestone's house after you left it?

TIDWELL: 'Course I do.

O'CONNOR: How do you know?

TIDWELL: I seen 'im, din' I?

O'CONNOR: What time was this?

TIDWELL: Free firty.

O'CONNOR: Describe where you were and precisely how you saw Dr Swale.

TIDWELL: I'm on me bike in the lane, arn' I, and I bike past 'is car and 'e's gettin' aht of it, inn'e? *(O'CONNOR signs for him to address the JUDGE. He does so.)* I turn the corner and I park me bike and come back and look froo the rear window of the car and see 'im turn into the right of way. *(He giggles.)*

O'CONNOR: Go on.

TIDWELL: *(still vaguely to the JUDGE)* Like I see 'im before. Other Fridays. 'Ullo, ullo, ullo!' I says. 'At it again?' So I nips back to the turning into the right of way, stroll up very natural and easy and see 'im go in at the garden gate. *And* let 'imself in by the back door, carryin' 'is little black bag. No excuse me's. *Very* much at 'ome. Oh dear!

O'CONNOR: And then?

TIDWELL: I return to bizzness, don' I? Back to the shop and first with the news.

O'CONNOR: Thank you.

(He sits. PROSECUTION COUNSEL *rises.)*

GOLDING: Did you notice the accused's bathroom window while you were engaged in this highly distasteful piece of espionage?

TIDWELL: 'Ow does the chorus go?

GOLDING: I beg your pardon?

TIDWELL: I don' get cher.

GOLDING: While you were spying on Dr Swale, could you and did you see the accused's bathroom window?

TIDWELL: Oh, ar! I get cher. Yar. I seen it. And 'er, snooping as per, froo the blind.

GOLDING: Dr Swale carried his professional bag, I think you said?

TIDWELL: S'right.

GOLDING: And he went straight into the house? Without pausing, for instance, by the safe?

TIDWELL: I couldn't see the safe, where I was, could I? But 'e went in.

GOLDING: Quite so. To his patient who was ill upstairs.

TIDWELL: Oh, yeah?

GOLDING: I have one more question. Do you deliver meat at the accused's house?

TIDWELL: Yar.

GOLDING: When was your last call there, previous to the 4th April?

TIDWELL: Free days before. She gets 'er order reg'lar on Wednesdays.

GOLDING: Do you remember what it was?

TIDWELL: Easy. Chops. Bangers. And – wait for it, *wait for it.*

GOLDING: Please answer directly. What else?

TIDWELL: Liver.

Part Two

GOLDING: I call Mrs Ecclestone.

USHER: Mrs Ecclestone.

(MRS ECCLESTONE *comes in with the* USHER. *Enters the box and takes the oath. While she is doing so we see* DR SWALE *and the* MAJOR *and then the accused, leaning forward and staring at her.* MRS ECCLESTONE *is a singularly attractive woman, beautifully dressed and aged about thirty-five. There is a slight stir throughout the court. At the end of the oath, she makes a big smile at the* JUDGE.)

GOLDING: You are Mrs Ecclestone? *(She assents.)* What are your first names, please?

MRS ECCLESTONE: Barbara Helen.

GOLDING: And you live at The Elms, No I Sherwood Grove, Fulchester?

MRS ECCLESTONE: Yes.

GOLDING: Thank you. Mrs Ecclestone, I want you to tell his Lordship and the jury something of the relationship between you and the accused. Going back, if you will, to the time when you first came to live in your present house.

MRS ECCLESTONE: We used to see her quite often in her garden and – and –

GOLDING: Yes?

MRS ECCLESTONE: And in her house.

GOLDING: You visited her there?

MRS ECCLESTONE: We could see her at the windows. Looking out.

GOLDING: Did you exchange visits?

MRS ECCLESTONE: Not social visits. She came in not long after we arrived to – to –

GOLDING: Yes?

MRS ECCLESTONE: Well, to complain about Bang.

GOLDING: The Alsatian?

MRS ECCLESTONE: Yes. He'd found some way of getting into her garden.

GOLDING: Was that the only time she complained?

MRS ECCLESTONE: No, it wasn't. She – well, really, she was always doing it. I mean – well, hardly a week went by. It was about then, I think, that she first complained to the police. They came to see us. After that we took every possible care. We put a muzzle on Bang when he wasn't tied up and made sure he never went near Miss Freebody's place. It made no difference to her behaviour.

GOLDING: Would you say that the complaints remained at much the same level or that they increased in intensity?

MRS ECCLESTONE: They became much more frequent. And vindictive. And threatening.

GOLDING: In what way threatening?

MRS ECCLESTONE: *(to JUDGE, a nervous smile)* Oh – notes in our letter box – waylaying us in the street – saying she would go to the police. That sort of thing. And when we were in the garden she would go close to her hedge and say things we could hear. Meaning us to hear them. Threats and abuse. *(The JUDGE is nodding.)*

GOLDING: What sort of threats?

MRS ECCLESTONE: Well – actually to do my husband an injury. She said he wasn't fit to live and she said in so many words she'd see to it that he didn't. It was very frightening. We thought she must be – well, not quite right in the head.

GOLDING: Coming to Friday 28th March *(She looks uncertain)* – was there any further incident?

(Miss Freebody sits forward.)

MRS ECCLESTONE: Oh – you mean the cat. I didn't remember the exact date.

GOLDING: But you remember the event?

MRS ECCLESTONE: Oh yes, I do. It was dreadful. I was horrified. *(She puts her head in her hands)* I was – I was so deeply sorry and terribly upset. I wanted to go in and tell her so.

GOLDING: And did you do so?

MRS ECCLESTONE: No. Basil – my husband – thought it better not.

GOLDING: And after this incident, what happened between you and the accused?

MRS ECCLESTONE: It was worse than ever, of course. She complained again; she telephoned several times a day and wrote threatening letters. My husband burnt them but I remember one said something like vengeance being done not only on the dog but on himself.

GOLDING: Yes. And now, Mrs Ecclestone, we come to the 4th April. The day when the dog was poisoned. *(Gestures to her.)*

MRS ECCLESTONE: I heard it happening – I was in my bedroom – and I got up and looked through the window. And saw. My husband shouted for me to come down. I went down and by then Bang was – dead. My husband told me to ring up Jim Swale – Dr Swale – and ask him to come at once. And he did.

GOLDING: What happened then?

MRS ECCLESTONE: They looked in the safe and Dr Swale said we should destroy the rest of the meat in case it was contaminated. So we did. In the incinerator.

GOLDING: How was the other meat wrapped? In what sort of paper?

MRS ECCLESTONE: Like the other – in newspaper.

GOLDING: You are sure? Not in brown paper?

MRS ECCLESTONE: No – I'm sure I remember noticing when we burnt it. It was the front page of the *Telegraph*.

GOLDING: Thank you. And then?

MRS ECCLESTONE: Dr Swale suggested getting the vet, but my husband wanted *him* to cope and he very kindly said he would. I was feeling pretty ghastly by then *(smiles at Judge)*, so he asked me to go back to my room and I did. And he had a look at me before he left and gave me one of my pills. I didn't go downstairs again that evening. *(She hesitates.)* I think perhaps I ought to say that there was never any doubt in our minds – any of us – about who had put the poisoned meat in the safe.

O'CONNOR: My lord, I must object.

MRS ECCLESTONE: After all, it was what had been threatened, wasn't it?

JUDGE: Yes, Mr O'Connor. *(To MRS ECCLESTONE)* You may not talk about what you think was in the minds of other persons, madam.

MRS ECCLESTONE: I'm sorry.

GOLDING: When do you think the meat was poisoned?

MRS ECCLESTONE: It must have been after the butcher delivered the order, of course.

GOLDING: Have you any idea of the time of the delivery?

MRS ECCLESTONE: As it happens, I have. The church clock struck three just as he left.

GOLDING: Did you hear any sounds of later arrivals?

MRS ECCLESTONE: *(hesitating)* I – no – no, I didn't. *(Rapidly)* But of course it would be perfectly easy for somebody to watch their chance, slip across the right of way. Nobody would see. My bedroom curtains were closed because I darken my room when I have a migraine.

(Grin from TIDWELL to SWALE.)

GOLDING: Yes. Had you seen anything of the accused during the day?

MRS ECCLESTONE: Yes, indeed I had. That morning the paper boy delivered her *Telegraph* with our *Times*. I didn't want to see her; I slipped out by *our* front gate and up to *her* front door. I was going to put her *Telegraph* through the flap when the door opened and there she was. Stock still and sort of glaring over my head.

GOLDING: That must have been disconcerting.

MRS ECCLESTONE: It was awful. It seemed to last for ages, and then I held out her paper and she snatched it.

GOLDING: Did she speak?

MRS ECCLESTONE: She whispered.

GOLDING: What did she whisper?

MRS ECCLESTONE: That I needn't imagine this would stop justice from taking its course. And then the door was slammed in my face.

MISS FREEBODY: Quite right.

GOLDING: And then?

MRS ECCLESTONE: I went back. And my migraine started.

GOLDING: Mrs Ecclestone, do you know what happened to the wrapping paper round the dog's liver?

MRS ECCLESTONE: Yes. My husband had dropped it on the ground and Jim – Dr Swale – said it shouldn't be left lying about and he put it into the incinerator.

GOLDING: Did you notice what paper it was?

MRS ECCLESTONE: It was the same as the other parcel – the *Daily Telegraph*.

GOLDING: Thank you.

(*He sits.* DEFENCE COUNSEL *rises.*)

O'CONNOR: Mrs Ecclestone, *anybody* could have come and gone through the right of way and through the garden gate and replaced one parcel of liver by another?

MRS ECCLESTONE: I suppose they could have.

O'CONNOR: Your husband has a lot of enemies in the neighbourhood apart from Miss Freebody, hasn't he?

MRS ECCLESTONE: *(deprecatingly)* Oh – enemies!

O'CONNOR: Let me put it another way. There had been a number of complaints about the dog from other neighbours, hadn't there?

MRS ECCLESTONE: None of them threatened to kill my husband. Hers did.

O'CONNOR: Did other persons, apart from Miss Freebody, write letters and complain to the police?

MRS ECCLESTONE: There were some, I think.

O'CONNOR: How many?

MRS ECCLESTONE: I don't know.

O'CONNOR: Two? Three? Four? Half a dozen? More?

MRS ECCLESTONE: No. No. I don't know. I don't remember.

O'CONNOR: How very odd. Had the dog ever attacked any of your friends? *(She is silent.)* Dr Swale, for instance?

MRS ECCLESTONE: Bang was rather jealous. Alsations can be.

O'CONNOR: Jealous, Mrs Ecclestone? Do you mean jealous of you? Did the dog resent anyone paying you particular attention, for example?

MRS ECCLESTONE: He was rather a one – I mean a two-person – dog.

*(*MRS ECCLESTONE *and* DR SWALE *exchange a brief look.)*

O'CONNOR: Had Bang, in fact, ever attacked Dr Swale?

MRS ECCLESTONE: I think – once. Before he got to know him.

O'CONNOR: Because Dr Swale was paying you 'particular attention', Mrs Ecclestone?

MRS ECCLESTONE: No. I don't remember about it. It was nothing.

O'CONNOR: The dog did get to know Dr Swale, didn't it?

MRS ECCLESTONE: Well, yes, naturally.

O'CONNOR: Naturally, Mrs Ecclestone?

MRS ECCLESTONE: Dr Swale is in our circle of friends.

O'CONNOR: Apart from being your doctor?

MRS ECCLESTONE: Yes.

(She has become increasingly uneasy. MAJOR ECCLESTONE *has been eyeing* DR SWALE *with mounting distaste.)*

O'CONNOR: On that Friday afternoon, Mrs Ecclestone – earlier in the afternoon, when you were lying on your bed in your darkened room, did Dr Swale come and see you?

MRS ECCLESTONE: I – don't know who you – I – I – *(She looks at* DR SWALE. *We see him very briefly close his eyes in assent.)* Why yes, as a matter of fact – I'd forgotten all about it, he did.

O'CONNOR: Thank you, Mrs Ecclestone.

*(*DEFENCE COUNSEL *sits.* PROSECUTION COUNSEL *rises.)*

GOLDING: As this earlier visit of Dr Swale's has been introduced, Mrs Ecclestone, I think that perhaps, don't you, that we'd better dispose of it? Dr Swale, you've told the court, is an old friend and a member of your social circle. Is that right?

MRS ECCLESTONE: *(she has pulled herself together)* Yes.

GOLDING: Was there anything at all out of the way about his dropping in?

MRS ECCLESTONE: No, of course not. He often looks in. He and my husband do crosswords and swop them over. I'd quite forgotten but I think that was what he'd come for – to collect the *Times* crossword and leave the *Telegraph* one. *(She catches her breath, realizing a possible implication.)*

GOLDING: Did you see him?

MRS ECCLESTONE: *(fractional hesitation)* I – think – yes, I remember I heard someone come in and I thought it was my husband, home early. So I called out. And Dr Swale came upstairs – and knocked and said who it was.

GOLDING: Exactly. Thank you so much, Mrs Ecclestone. *(He sits.)*

JUDGE: You may go and sit down, Mrs Ecclestone.

MRS ECCLESTONE: Thank you, my lord.

(She does so. As she goes to the witness seats, she and the accused look at each other. MRS ECCLESTONE *gets past the other witnesses, who leave room for her. She sits between* DR SWALE *and her husband, looking at neither of them.)*

GOLDING: That concludes the case for the prosecution, my lord.

*(*DEFENCE COUNSEL *rises.)*

O'CONNOR: I now call Mary Emmaline Freebody.

(The accused is escorted to the witness box and takes the oath. The CLERK *asks her to remove her glove.)*

O'CONNOR: You are Mary Emmaline Freebody of No 2 Sherwood Grove, Peascale near Fulchester?

MISS FREEBODY: I am.

O'CONNOR: Miss Freebody, did you attempt to poison Major Ecclestone?

MISS FREEBODY: I did not.

O'CONNOR: You are a practising Christian, are you not?

MISS FREEBODY: Certainly.

O'CONNOR: And you swear that you had no such intention?

MISS FREEBODY: I do.

O'CONNOR: Miss Freebody, I'm sorry to recall an extremely painful memory to you, but will you tell his Lordship and the jury how you first learnt of the death of your cat?

MISS FREEBODY: *(breaking out)* Learnt of it! *Learnt* of it! I heard the screams. The screams. I still hear them. *(To* JUDGE*)* Still. All the time. Asleep and awake. I am haunted by them.

(MAJOR snorts.)

O'CONNOR: Where were you at the time of the cat's death?

MISS FREEBODY: Indoors. In my house.

O'CONNOR: What did you do when you heard the screams?

MISS FREEBODY: I rushed out. Of course. I thought he was in my garden. I hunted everywhere. The screams stopped but I hunted. And then I heard that man – that monster – that fiend –

O'CONNOR: Major Ecclestone?

MISS FREEBODY: *(she gives a contemptuous assent)* Laughing. He was laughing. Devil! He was talking to it. To that *brute*. And do you know what he said?

GOLDING: *(rising)* My lord! Really –

MISS FREEBODY: *(shouting)* He said 'Good dog'. That's what he said: 'Good dog'. *(She bursts out crying.)*

JUDGE: If you would like to sit down, you may.

(The WARDRESS moves to lower the flap-seat in the box.)

MISS FREEBODY: I don't want to sit down. Go away. *(She blows her nose.)*

O'CONNOR: Miss Freebody, what happened after that? Please remember that you may tell the court if you heard people talking and you may say who they were and what you did but not what they said, unless they are going to give evidence or have done so.

MISS FREEBODY: Idiocy! Legal humbug! Balderdash!

JUDGE: *That will do.*

MISS FREEBODY: No, it won't. I won't be talked down. I won't be told what will do or won't do. I'll say what I've got to say and –

JUDGE: Be silent! Mr O'Connor, I'm afraid that I am bound to agree with Miss Freebody that your exposition of the hearsay rules was so inaccurate as to amount to legal humbug. If you must tell witnesses what the law is, do at least try to get it right.

O'CONNOR: I'm sorry, my lord.

JUDGE: Miss Freebody, you will answer counsel's question: what happened after that?

(She stares at him and he at her.)

MISS FREEBODY: *(suddenly and very rapidly)* 'What happened after that?' He asks me, 'What happened after that?' I'll tell you what happened after that. She talked and he talked and she talked and he talked and then – then – then – no, I can't. I can't.

O'CONNOR: Miss Freebody – however painful it is – please go on. Try to speak calmly.

MISS FREEBODY: Out of the air. At my feet. Wet. Bleeding. Torn to pieces. Dead.

O'CONNOR: You are telling the court, aren't you, that Major Ecclestone had thrown the body of the cat into your garden?

MISS FREEBODY: Cruel. *Cruel!* Horrible and wicked and cruel.

O'CONNOR: Please try to be calm. After that? Immediately after that and subsequently, what did you do?

MISS FREEBODY: I – I couldn't at first but then I did – I buried him. And then I – I went indoors and I felt desperately ill. I *was* ill and afterwards I lay on my bed.

O'CONNOR: Yes. You went to bed?

MISS FREEBODY: No. I lay there. As I was. All night. Sometimes I dozed off and then I had nightmares. I thought that brute was attacking *me* as it had my – my little cat. I thought it was coming at *me*. Here. *(She clasps her throat.)* And for night after night it was the same.

O'CONNOR: And during the daytime?

MISS FREEBODY: I kept thinking it was loose and outside my doors, snuffling at them. Scratching at them, trying to get at me. I telephoned the police. I was terrified.

O'CONNOR: Did you go out?

MISS FREEBODY: I was afraid to go out. I stayed indoors. Day after day.

O'CONNOR: But you sent letters, didn't you? To Major Ecclestone?

MISS FREEBODY: I gave them to my daily help to post. I was afraid to go out.

O'CONNOR: It has been suggested that you were spying upon Dr Swale and his visits to The Elms.

MISS FREEBODY: Those two! I didn't care about *them*. I used to think they were wicked but they were against *him*, weren't they? They were making a fool of him. They wanted to be rid of him.

JUDGE: Miss Freebody, you must confine yourself to facts. You must not put forward your notions as to anybody's wishes or intentions.

(Pause. She sniffs.)

JUDGE: Very well.

O'CONNOR: On the morning of the dog's death, Mrs Ecclestone called to give you your paper, didn't she?

MISS FREEBODY: I stood inside the door. I thought it was *him* with the dog. And then I heard her clear her throat. So I made myself open the door. And there she was! The adultress. Oh yes! She came.

O'CONNOR: Later in the day, did you see Dr Swale go into The Elms?

MISS FREEBODY: Oh yes. I saw him. In at the side door as usual. He always does that. And upstairs in her bedroom she had the curtains drawn. All ready for him. As she always does on Fridays. And of course *he (She indicates the* MAJOR) was out playing bridge at his club, poor fool.

O'CONNOR: Did you see Dr Swale enter the house?

MISS FREEBODY: *(indifferent)* I can't see their side door. There's a tree and bushes.

O'CONNOR: And the outside safe? Can you see that?

MISS FREEBODY: Not that, either.

O'CONNOR: So you wouldn't know if Dr Swale, for whatever purpose, paused by the safe before entering the house.

MISS FREEBODY: *(her fingers at her lips, staring at him with growing excitement)* Paused? By the safe? For whatever purpose? But you're right.

You're perfectly right. Fool that I am. Fool! Of course! That's how it was. He – the doctor –

(She points to DR SWALE, *who stands.)*

DR SWALE: My lord, I protest. This is outrageous.

JUDGE: You cannot address the court, sir. You must sit down.

DR SWALE: My lord, this amounts to slander.

JUDGE: Be quiet, Dr Swale. You must know very well that any such interruption is impermissible. Sit down, sir. *(*DR SWALE *sits.)* Very well, Mr O'Connor.

O'CONNOR: Miss Freebody, please answer the questions simply and without comment. I bring you to the death of the dog. Did you see anything or hear anything of that event?

MISS FREEBODY: I was upstairs. I heard a commotion – a howl and *his* voice shouting. So I went into the bathroom and looked. I saw the dog thrashing about and then I saw it was dead. And I was glad. *Glad.* I didn't know why it was dead. I thought at first that *he* – its owner – might have destroyed it at last but it was dead and I exulted and gave thanks and was joyful.

(She looks at the witnesses. Her gaze becomes riveted upon DR SWALE *and* MRS ECCLESTONE. *She leans forward, apparently in the grip of some kind of revelation. We see them. They exchange a quick look. He briefly closes his hand over* MRS ECCLESTONE's. MISS FREEBODY *licks her lips.)*

O'CONNOR: Did you see the arrival of Dr Swale? Miss Freebody!

*(*MISS FREEBODY *is still gazing at* DR SWALE *and* MRS ECCLESTONE.*)*

O'CONNOR: Miss Freebody, may I have your attention, please? *(She turns her head slowly and looks at him.)* Did you see the arrival of Dr Swale?

MISS FREEBODY: Oh yes! Yes, I watched that. I watched him – the doctor. I saw how surprised and put out he was when they showed him the dog. Just like he is now. I saw them look at each other.

O'CONNOR: What happened next?

MISS FREEBODY: *She* went indoors and *he* followed. And he came back after a time and they carried away the carcass.

O'CONNOR: The two men did? *(She nods.)* Afterwards, when you heard about the poisoned meat, what then?

MISS FREEBODY: Ah! *Then* I didn't realize. But *now! (With an extraordinary sly look towards the witnesses' seats)* It could have been an accident, couldn't it? The dog, I mean.

O'CONNOR: *(taken aback)* An *accident,* Miss Freebody?

MISS FREEBODY: *He* always has liver on Fridays. *She* is a vegetarian. They did it between them. They meant it for him. For him!

GOLDING: This is outrageous.

(GOLDING is on his feet and so are MAJOR ECCLESTONE and DR SWALE. They speak together.)

MAJOR: My God, what's the woman saying? By God, she means me. She means – *(He turns on SWALE.)* By God, she means *you* –

SWALE: This must stop. I demand that she's stopped. Major, for God's sake, you can't think –

USHER: Silence in court.

JUDGE: *(rapping)* Silence! *(ECCLESTONE and SWALE subside.)* This is insupportable. If there is any more of it, I shall clear the court. *(Pause)* Yes, Mr Golding.

GOLDING: Indeed, my lord. How much more of this *are* we to have? I protest most strongly, my lord.

JUDGE: Yes, Mr Golding. You may well do so. Well, Mr O'Connor?

O'CONNOR: My lord, I quite agree it is not for the witness to advance theories, but the point is not apparently without substance. I have no further questions.

JUDGE: Very well. In that case – Mr Golding?

(PROSECUTION COUNSEL rises.)

GOLDING: Thank you, my lord. Now, Miss Freebody, we have heard a great deal about emotions and all the rest of it. Suppose for a change we get down to a few hard facts. You admit to writing a number of threatening letters the last of which includes the phrase 'neither of you is fit to live, take warning'. Do you agree?

MISS FREEBODY: Yes.

GOLDING: You have heard the police evidence. A container half full of cyanide of potassium has been found in your shrubbery. You have heard the local chemist depose that he sold cyanide of potassium to the previous tenant of your house, who used it to exterminate wasps. The container, Exhibit One, is very clearly, even dramatically labelled. There it is. You see it there, don't you? On the clerk's desk?

MISS FREEBODY: For the first time.

GOLDING: What! You have never seen it before! Be careful, Miss Freebody. The chemist has identified the container and has told the court that he advised the purchaser to keep it in a conspicuous place. Had you never seen it in your garden shed?

MISS FREEBODY: My gardener saw that one.

GOLDING: Oh. The gardener saw it, did he? And reported it to you?

MISS FREEBODY: Yes. And I told him to get rid of it. So he did.

GOLDING: When was this?

MISS FREEBODY: Soon after I came. Five years ago.

GOLDING: Indeed. How did the gardener in fact 'get rid of it', as you claim?

MISS FREEBODY: I have no idea.

GOLDING: You have no idea! Is the gardener going to give evidence on your behalf?

MISS FREEBODY: Can't. He's dead.

(Somebody laughs. DEFENCE COUNSEL *grins.)*

USHER: Silence in court.

GOLDING: And how do you account for its being discovered in your shrubbery in a perfectly clean condition three days after the dog was poisoned?

MISS FREEBODY: I repeat, the one in the shed had been destroyed. This was another one. Thrown there, of course, over the hedge.

GOLDING: We are to suppose, are we, that an unknown poisoner brought a second jar of cyanide with him or her, although he or she had already prepared the liver and wrapped it. Why on earth should anyone do that?

MISS FREEBODY: To incriminate me. Obviously.

GOLDING: *(irritated)* Once more into the realms of fantasy! I put it to you that no shadow of a motive and no jot of evidence can be found to support such a theory.

MISS FREEBODY: Oh yes, it can. It can.

GOLDING: It can! Perhaps you will be good enough to explain –

JUDGE: Mr Golding, you have very properly attempted to confine the witness to statements of fact. Are you now inviting her to expound a theory?

GOLDING: My lord, the accused, so far as one can follow her, appears to be advancing in her own defence a counter-accusation.

JUDGE: Mr O'Connor, have you anything to say on this point.

O'CONNOR: *(rising)* Yes, my lord, I have. I must say again at once, my lord, that I have received no instructions as to the positive identity of the person my client apparently believes – most ardently believes – to have – may I say 'planted'? – the half-empty container of cyanide on her property. My instructions were simply that she herself is innocent and therefore the container *must* in fact have been planted. As a result of the way the evidence has developed, I'd be obliged for a short adjournment to see whether there are further enquiries that should be made.

(O'CONNOR sits. GOLDING rises.)

GOLDING: My lord, I submit that the antics, if I may so call them, of the accused in the witness box are completely irrelevant. If there were one jot of substance in this rigmarole, why on earth did she not advance it in the first instance?

MISS FREEBODY: And I can tell you why. It's because I've only now realized it – in this court. It's been borne in upon me. *(She points at* MRS ECCLESTONE *and* DR SWALE*)* Seeing those two together. Watching them. Hearing them! Knowing! Remembering! They're would-be murderers. That's what they are.

JUDGE: Be quiet, madam. I warn you that you do your own cause a great deal of harm by your extravagant and most improper behaviour. For the last time, I order you to confine yourself to answering directly questions put by learned counsel. You may not, as you constantly have done, interrupt the proceedings and you may not, without permission, address the court. If you persist in doing so you will be held in contempt. Do you understand me?

(She makes no response.)

JUDGE: Mr O'Connor, am I to understand that in view of the manner in which this case has developed and the introduction of elements – unanticipated, as you assure us, in your instructions – you would wish me to adjourn?

O'CONNOR: If your Lordship will.

JUDGE: Mr Golding?

GOLDING: I have no objection, my lord.

JUDGE: Does an adjournment until ten o'clock tomorrow morning seem appropriate?

O'CONNOR: Certainly, my lord.

JUDGE: Very well. *(Generally)* The court is adjourned until ten o'clock tomorrow morning. *(He rises.)*

(The JUDGE *goes out.* COUNSEL *gather up their papers and confer with their solicitor representatives. The accused in removed. The witnesses stand, and the* CLERK *issues instructions as to reassembly.* MAJOR ECCLESTONE *confronts his wife and* DR SWALE*. There is a momentary pause before she lifts her chin and goes out. The men remain face to face for a second or two, and then* DR SWALE *follows and overtakes her in the doorway.)*

(The court reassembles at 10:00 the next morning.)

(The JUDGE *enters and takes his seat.)*

JUDGE: Members of the jury, I am sure you apprehend the reasons for an adjournment in this, in many ways, somewhat eccentric case. I'm sorry if the delay has caused you inconvenience. Before we go on I would like to remind you that you are where you are for one purpose only: to decide whether accused, Mary Emmaline Freebody, is guilty of the attempted murder of Major Ecclestone. You are not concerned with anything that may have emerged outside the provenance of this charge unless it bears on the single question – the guilt or innocence of the accused.

(The accused is in the witness box. The ECCLESTONES *and* DR SWALE *now sit apart from each other, separated by* TIDWELL *and the local chemist. They are shaken and anxious. They look straight in front of them. The* MAJOR *keeps darting glances at them. He withdraws a small plastic case from his pocket. He extracts a capsule and swallows it.)*

JUDGE: Mr Golding, you may now wish to continue your cross-examination.

GOLDING: I have no further questions, my lord.

JUDGE: Very well. Mr O'Connor, do you wish to re-examine the defendant, and may I say, Mr O'Connor, that I trust there will be no repetition of yesterday's irregularities.

O'CONNOR: *(rising)* My lord, I sincerely hope not. I have no further questions to put to the defendant.

JUDGE: You may go back to the dock, Miss Freebody.

(The WARDRESS *puts an arm on* MISS FREEBODY *who glares at her.* MISS FREE-BODY *returns to the dock.* PROSECUTION COUNSEL *rises.)*

GOLDING: My lord, I must inform your Lordship that Major Ecclestone has waited upon me and has expressed a desire to amend some of his former evidence, and has asked me to put his request before your Lordship.

JUDGE: Did you anticipate anything of this sort, Mr Golding?

GOLDING: Not I, my lord.

JUDGE: *(after a long pause)* Very well.

GOLDING: I recall Major Basil Ecclestone.

(There is a general stir as the MAJOR goes back to the box. His manner is greatly changed. His animosity is now directed against DR SWALE.)

GOLDING: May I remind you that you are still on oath. *(MAJOR grunts.)* Major Ecclestone, is it true that because of certain developments you now wish to amend some of the former evidence that you gave earlier in these proceedings?

MAJOR: I do.

GOLDING: And that evidence concerns the identity of the person you believe to have been responsible for poisoning the meat?

MAJOR: It does, sir.

GOLDING: And will you tell the court who –

(A cry from the MAJOR. The CLERK stands sharply. The MAJOR is in a sudden agony of convulsion. He struggles, jerks violently, falls, suffers a final galvanic spasm and is still. The USHER goes to the box. The body slides half down the steps. DR SWALE hurries across and stoops over it.)

USHER: Quiet. Quiet! Silence in court. Silence.

(The JUDGE has risen. DR SWALE looks up at him and with a slight gesture of bewilderment shakes his head.)

JUDGE: Clear the court! Usher. Clear the court.

(The accused is standing triumphant in the dock and pointing at the body.)

MISS FREEBODY: Justice. Justice.

(Reporters scramble for the door.)

Part Three

O'CONNOR: . . . and I would submit, my lord, with respect that the evidence is admissible. My lord, may I very briefly review the somewhat macabre sequence of events?

JUDGE: *(smiling)* Briefly, Mr O'Connor? Very briefly?

O'CONNOR: My lord, I really am very much obliged. *Very* briefly then, my client is accused of putting cyanide of potassium into Major Ecclestone's meat. Major Ecclestone who laid the case against her has died and cyanide has been found in his body. There is a strong presumption – indeed an overwhelming probability – that cyanide was introduced into one of the capsules Major Ecclestone was in the habit of taking at stated intervals for a digestive disorder. He was seen to take one of these capsules immediately before his death. My lord, I shall, if permitted, call expert evidence to show that a capsule containing cyanide would only remain intact for an hour. After that, the poison would begin to seep through the container. Miss Freebody has not been left alone since the commencement of this trial. It is obvious, therefore, she cannot be held responsible for causing his death. Whoever murdered Major Ecclestone, it was certainly not Miss Freebody. So that if, as of course we most strenuously deny, she caused the death of the dog, we have to accept a grotesque coincidence of two persons independently attempting to kill Major Ecclestone. Thus, my lord, I submit that the circumstances leading to Major Ecclestone's death are admissible evidence.

(DEFENCE COUNSEL *sits down. A pause. The* JUDGE *has taken an occasional note during this submission. He now looks up and waits for a moment.*)

JUDGE: Yes. Thank you. *(He turns to* PROSECUTION COUNSEL.*)* Well, Mr Golding?

GOLDING: *(rising)* My lord, I shall oppose the introduction of any reference whatever to the death of Major Ecclestone. I submit that it would be grossly improper to confuse in the minds of the jury two entirely separate issues. The inquiry into Major Ecclestone's death is in the hands of the police. And if they make an arrest there will be a trial in another court under another jury. What will transpire on what accusations may be made is utterly irrelevant to these proceedings. I submit that it will be irregular in the highest degree to anticipate them. As far as this court is concerned, my lord, may I venture to remind my learned friend that 'the dog it was that died' and not its master?

JUDGE: And what do you say to that, Mr O'Connor?

O'CONNOR: *(good-humouredly) Touché* I suppose, my lord.

JUDGE: This is in more ways than one a most unusual case. The death in the witness box of the principal witness for the prosecution, the man who laid the accusation against the defendant, and the finding of cyanide in his body is an extraordinary circumstance. I may order the jury to dismiss all this from their minds, but gentlemen, I may do so until my wig turns black and falls off my head but they won't be able to do so. But to return to the argument. It would be remarkable if *two* people had independently desired to bring about the Major's death. Thus if the second, successful, attempt could not have been made by the accused, it seems to me to be relevant to the allegation that she made the first attempt. I therefore rule that evidence regarding the nature and characteristics of the poisoned capsule is admissible.

O'CONNOR: I am greatly obliged to your Lordship.

JUDGE: Very well. Here we go again, gentlemen. *(To the* USHER) The jury may come back.

(The court reassembles. The jury enters. MISS FREEBODY *returns to the dock.* DR SWALE *now sits by himself in the witnesses' seats.* MRS

ECCLESTONE, *in mourning, hesitates and takes a seat removed from his. A pause and then he rises and goes to her. He bends over her for a moment and then offers his hand. After hesitating, she takes it. He then takes a seat behind hers.)*

JUDGE: Members of the jury. Your attendance in this case was interrupted by an extraordinary and most distressing event which in the interval has received a great deal of publicity and has acquired a considerable amount of notoriety. You are of course not here to try anyone for Major Ecclestone's death. You are here to decide whether Mary Emmaline Freebody is guilty or not guilty of attempted murder and that is your sole duty. Having said this I add one important qualification. If, during the continuation of the hearing, evidence is tendered that arises out of the circumstances attending upon Major Ecclestone's death and that evidence has a bearing upon the question of the defendant's guilt or innocence, then I will admit it for your consideration. Very well, Mr O'Connor.

O'CONNOR: *(rising)* You are Dr Ernest Smithson, of 24 Central Square, Fulchester.

DR SMITHSON: Yes.

O'CONNOR: You, Dr Smithson, are consultant pathologist for the Fulchester Constabulary?

DR SMITHSON: I am.

O'CONNOR: Did you carry out a post mortem on Major Ecclestone?

DR SMITHSON: Yes. I found he had died of cyanide poisoning.

O'CONNOR: May he be shown Exhibit Six? Is that the bottle taken from the Major's body?

DR SMITHSON: Yes. I found it myself in his pocket. It was a bottle of Duogastacone which contained capsules of potassium cyanide.

O'CONNOR: Which suggests that cyanide had been introduced into a bottle containing capsules of Duogastacone?

DR SMITHSON: Yes.

O'CONNOR: Now will you please tell the court whether it would be possible to fill capsules of the sort commonly used in pharmaceutical dispensaries with cyanide of potassium?

DR SMITHSON: It would be possible, yes.

O'CONNOR: In what form would the cyanide be?

DR SMITHSON: In the form of powder.

O'CONNOR: And would the capsules be indistinguishable from those filled with a doctor's prescription?

DR SMITHSON: If the prescribed powder was the same colour, which it probably would be, yes. To begin with, that is.

JUDGE: To begin with, Dr Smithson? Can you explain a little farther?

DR SMITHSON: After about an hour, my lord, the cyanide would begin to seep through the capsule and this would become increasingly noticeable.

O'CONNOR: Let me get this quite clear. To escape detection, the whole operation, filling the capsules with the lethal powder and conveying them to the intended victim, would have to be executed within an hour before one of the capsules was taken?

DR SMITHSON: Before they had begun to disintegrate, I would prefer to say.

O'CONNOR: Dr Smithson, are you aware that from the day before the death of Major Ecclestone, my client has been under constant supervision?

DR SMITHSON: I have been so informed, yes.

O'CONNOR: And therefore could not, for instance, possibly have concocted lethal capsules of the sort we have been talking about and conveyed them to some person or place outside her own premises?

DR SMITHSON: Obviously not if she was under constant supervision.

O'CONNOR: Thank you.

(O'CONNOR sits. GOLDING rises.)

GOLDING: My lord.

JUDGE: *(with a slight smile and an air of knowing what's coming)* Yes, Mr Golding?

GOLDING: Well – yes, indeed, my lord. I merely beg to remind the jury of what your Lordship has already laid down. The defendant is not on trial for concocting lethal capsules and I submit that the evidence we have just heard is irrelevant. I have no questions to put to Dr Smithson.

JUDGE: *(to* SMITHSON*)* Thank you, Dr Smithson. You may go if you wish.

DR SMITHSON: Thank you, my lord. *(He leaves the witness box.)*

O'CONNOR: My lord, in view of the development of this trial since Dr Swale gave evidence and particularly in view of subsequent evidence, I ask for leave to reopen my cross-examination of him. I ask for him to be recalled.

JUDGE: What do you say to this, Mr Golding? Do you object?

GOLDING: My lord, I can find no conceivable reason for this procedure, but – I do not object.

JUDGE: *(after a moment's pause)* Very well, Mr Defence Counsel. Go back to the witness box, please, Dr Swale.

*(*DR SWALE *takes the stand.)*

O'CONNOR: Dr Swale, you realize that you are still on oath, do you not?

DR SWALE: I do.

O'CONNOR: You heard the evidence given by the previous witness?

DR SWALE: Yes.

O'CONNOR: Do you agree with it?

DR SWALE: I am not a pathologist, but I would expect it to be correct.

O'CONNOR: With respect to the deterioration within an hour of a capsule containing cyanide?

DR SWALE: I have had no experience of potassium cyanide, but yes, I would, of course, expect Dr Smithson to be right.

O'CONNOR: Yes. Dr Swale, I'm going to take you back if you please to April 4th, the evening when you were called in to the Ecclestones' and saw the dead Alsatian. You will remember that you removed what was left of the liver that had been fed to the dog and subsequently had it analysed and that cyanide of potassium was found in massive quantities.

DR SWALE: Yes.

O'CONNOR: There was also, in the same safe, the material for a mixed grill which was intended for the Major's dinner that night.

DR SWALE: So I understand.

O'CONNOR: Did you do anything about this meat?

DR SWALE: I have already deposed that I said it should be destroyed.

O'CONNOR: And was it destroyed?

DR SWALE: It was. I have already said so.

O'CONNOR: By whom?

DR SWALE: By Mrs Ecclestone and myself. In their incinerator.

O'CONNOR: As she subsequently deposed. After you had given your evidence.

DR SWALE: Quite.

O'CONNOR: Dr Swale, did it not occur to you that this meat which was destined for the Major's dinner should also be analysed?

DR SWALE: No. I was simply concerned to get rid of it.

O'CONNOR: Upon further consideration would you now say it would have been better to have sent it, or a portion of it, for analysis?

DR SWALE: Perhaps it might have been better. But the circumstances of the dog's death – their description of its symptoms and its appearance so strongly suggested a convulsive poison such as cyanide – I really didn't think.

O'CONNOR: I'm sorry, doctor, but you told us just now, you've had no experience with cyanide.

DR SWALE: No experience in practice but naturally during the course of training I did my poisons.

O'CONNOR: Is Mrs Ecclestone a vegetarian?

DR SWALE: *(a slight pause)* I believe so.

O'CONNOR: You believe so, Dr Swale? But as Mrs Ecclestone has told us, you are a member of their intimate circle. You are her doctor, are you not?

DR SWALE: *(less cool)* Yes, of course I am.

O'CONNOR: Surely, then, you know definitely whether or not she's a vegetarian?

DR SWALE: Yes. All right. I simply said, 'I believe so' as one does in voicing an ordinary agreement. I know so, if you prefer it. She is a vegetarian.

O'CONNOR: Are you in the habit of visiting her on Friday afternoons?

DR SWALE: Not 'in the habit' of doing so. I sometimes used to drop in on Fridays to swop crosswords with the Major.

O'CONNOR: But Major Ecclestone was always at his club on Fridays.

DR SWALE: He used to leave his crossword out for me. I visit The Hermitage private hospital on Fridays and it's close by. I did sometimes – quite often – drop in at The Elms.

O'CONNOR: *(blandly)* For a cup of tea, perhaps?

DR SWALE: Certainly. For a cup of tea.

O'CONNOR: You heard the evidence of Thomas Tidwell, didn't you?

DR SWALE: *(contemptuously)* If you can call it that.

O'CONNOR: What would you call it?

DR SWALE: An example of small town lying gossip dished out by a small town oaf.

O'CONNOR: To what part of his evidence do you refer?

DR SWALE: Clearly, since it concerns me, to the suggestion that I went to the house for any other purpose than the one I have given.

O'CONNOR: What do you say to Miss Freebody's views on the subject?

DR SWALE: I would have thought it was obvious that they are those of a mentally disturbed spinster of uncertain age.

MISS FREEBODY: *(sharply)* Libel! Cad! Murderer!

(The JUDGE turns and stares at her. The WARDRESS admonishes her. She subsides.)

O'CONNOR: You are not Miss Freebody's doctor, are you?

DR SWALE: No, thank God.

(Laughter)

USHER: Silence in court.

O'CONNOR: When you paid your earlier visit to The Elms on the afternoon in question, did you carry your professional bag with you?

DR SWALE: *(after a pause)* I expect so.

O'CONNOR: Why? It was not a professional call.

DR SWALE: I'm not in the habit of leaving it in the car.

O'CONNOR: What was in it?

DR SWALE: You don't want an inventory, do you? The bag contains the normal impedimenta of a doctor in general practice.

O'CONNOR: And nothing else?

DR SWALE: I'm not in the habit of using my case as a shopping bag.

O'CONNOR: Not for butcher's meat, for instance?

GOLDING: My lord, I do most strenuously object.

DR SWALE: This is intolerable. Have I no protection against this sort of treatment?

JUDGE: No. Answer.

DR SWALE: No. I do not and never have carried butcher's meat in my bag.

(DEFENCE COUNSEL *sits*.)

JUDGE: *(to* GOLDING*)* Mr Golding, do you wish to re–examine?

GOLDING: No, my lord.

JUDGE: *(to* SWALE*)* Thank you, doctor.

DR SWALE: My lord, may I speak to you?

JUDGE: No, Dr Swale.

DR SWALE: I demand to be heard.

JUDGE: You may do no such thing, you may –

DR SWALE: *(shouting him down)* My lord, it is perfectly obvious that counsel for the defence is trying to protect his client by throwing up a series of infamous suggestions intended to implicate a lady and myself in this miserable business.

JUDGE: *(through this)* Be quiet, sir. Leave the witness box.

DR SWALE: I refuse. I insist. We are not legally represented. I am a professional man who must be very gravely damaged by these baseless innuendoes.

JUDGE: For the last time I warn you –

DR SWALE: *(shouting him down)* I had nothing, I repeat, nothing whatever to do with the death of the Ecclestones' dog *(*JUDGE *gestures to* USHER*)*, nor did I tamper with any of the meat in the safe. I protest, my lord. I protest.

(The USHER *and a police constable close in on him and the scene ends in confusion.)*

*(*GWENDOLINE MIGGS *is sworn in on the stand. She is a large, determined-looking woman of about sixty.)*

O'CONNOR: Your name is Sarah Gwendoline Miggs?

MIGGS: Yes.

O'CONNOR: And where do you live, Miss Miggs?

MIGGS: Flat 3, Flask Walk, Fulchester.

O'CONNOR: You are a qualified medical nurse, now retired?

MIGGS: I am.

O'CONNOR: Will you give us briefly an account of your professional experience?

MIGGS: Fifteen years in general hospital and twenty years in ten hospitals for the mentally disturbed.

O'CONNOR: The last one being at Fulchester Grange Hospital where you nursed for some two years before retiring?

MIGGS: Correct.

O'CONNOR: And have you, since the sitting of this court, been looking after the defendant, Miss Mary Emmaline Freebody?

MIGGS: Right.

O'CONNOR: Miss Miggs, will you tell his Lordship and the jury how the days are spent since you took this job?

MIGGS: I relieve the night nurse at 8.00 a.m. and am with the case until I'm relieved in the evening.

JUDGE: With the 'case'?

O'CONNOR: Miss Freebody, my lord.

JUDGE: *(fretfully)* Why can't we say so, for pity's sake? Very well.

O'CONNOR: Do you remain with Miss Freebody throughout the day?

MIGGS: Yes.

O'CONNOR: Never leave her?

MIGGS: Those are my instructions and I carry them out.

(DR SWALE, *who has been looking fixedly at the witness, writes a note, signals to the* USHER *and gives him the note. The* USHER *takes it to*

MR GOLDING, *who reads it and shows it to his junior and the solicitor for the prosecution.)*

O'CONNOR: Do you find Miss Freebody at all difficult?

MIGGS: Not a bit.

O'CONNOR: She doesn't try to – to shake you off? She doesn't resent your presence?

MIGGS: Didn't like it at first. There was a slight resentment but we soon got over that. We're very good friends, now.

O'CONNOR: And you have never left her?

MIGGS: I said so, didn't I? Never.

O'CONNOR: Thank you, Miss Miggs.

(DEFENCE COUNSEL sits.)

GOLDING: *(rising)* Yes. Nurse Miggs, you have told the court, have you not, that since you qualified as a mental nurse, you have taken posts in ten hospitals over a period of twenty years, the last appointment being of two years' duration at Fulchester Grange?

MIGGS: Correct.

GOLDING: Have you, in addition to these engagements, taken private patients?

MIGGS: *(uneasily)* A few.

GOLDING: How many?

MIGGS: I don't remember offhand. Not many.

GOLDING: Nurse Miggs, have you ever been dismissed – summarily dismissed – from a post?

MIGGS: I didn't come here to be insulted.

JUDGE: Answer the question, nurse.

MIGGS: There's no satisfying some people. Anything goes wrong – blame the nurse.

GOLDING: Yes or no, Miss Miggs? *(He glances at the paper from DR SWALE.)* In July 1969, were you dismissed by the doctor in charge of a case under suspicion of illegally obtaining and administering a drug and accepting a bribe for doing so?

MIGGS: *(breaking in)* It wasn't true. It was a lie. I know where you got that from. *(She points to* DR SWALE.*)* From him! He had it in for me. He couldn't prove it. He couldn't prove anything.

GOLDING: Come, Miss Miggs, don't you think you would be well advised to admit it at once?

MIGGS: He couldn't prove it. *(She breaks down.)*

GOLDING: Why did you leave Fulchester Grange?

MIGGS: I won't answer. It's all lies. Once something's said about you, you're done for.

GOLDING: Were you dismissed?

MIGGS: I won't answer.

GOLDING: Were you dismissed for illegally obtaining drugs and accepting a bribe for so doing?

MIGGS: It wasn't proved. They couldn't prove it. It's lies!

GOLDING: I have no further questions, my lord.

JUDGE: Mr Defence Counsel? *(*O'CONNOR *shakes his head.)* Thank you, Miss Miggs. *(She leaves the witness box.)* Have you any further witnesses, Mr Defence Counsel?

O'CONNOR: No, my lord.

JUDGE: Members of the jury, just let me tell you something about our function – yours and mine. I am here to direct you as to the law and to remind you of the salient features of the evidence. You are here as judges of fact; you and you alone have to decide, on the evidence you have heard, whether the accused is guilty or not of the charge of attempted murder . . .

You may think it's plain that the liver which the dog ate was poisoned. The prosecution say that whoever poisoned that liver must have known that it might have been eaten by the late Major, and was only given to the dog by accident. The vital question, therefore, you may think, is who poisoned that liver. The prosecution say that

Miss Freebody did. They say she had the opportunity to take the meat from the safe, poison it and replace it, having for some reason or other changed the paper in which it was wrapped. They say she had a motive – her antagonism to the Major as evidenced by the threatening letters which she wrote. But, say the defence, and you may think it is a point of some weight, the fact that the Major actually died before *your* eyes of cyanide poisoning at a time when the accused would have had no opportunity to administer the poison is evidence that someone else wanted to and *did* kill the Major. So if someone other than the accused did kill the Major in the second attempt on his life, how can you believe that the accused rather than the culprit of the second attempt was guilty of the first attempt?

Remember that before you can bring a verdict of guilty you must be satisfied beyond all reasonable doubt that the accused did make this attempt on the life of the late Major. Will you now retire, elect a foreman to speak for you when you return, and consider your verdict.

CLERK: All stand.

(The jury leave the room. Time passes, and the jury return to their seats.)

CLERK: Members of the jury, will your foreman stand. (*The* FOREMAN *rises.*) Just answer this question yes or no. Have you reached a verdict upon which you are all agreed?

FOREMAN: Yes.

CLERK: Do you find the accused, Mary Emmaline Freebody, guilty or not guilty on the charge of attempted murder?

FOREMAN: *(answers either 'guilty' or 'not guilty'.)*:

CLERK: *(if guilty)* Is that the verdict of you all?

JUDGE: *(if not guilty)* Mary Emmaline Freebody, you are free to go.

COURT REPORTER: *(if guilty)* Mary Freebody was remanded in custody for psychiatric reports.

*

The Publishers gratefully acknowledge Granada Television Limited for its kind permission to print *Evil Liver*.